BLOODTOOTH

D.W. HITZ

www.FedowarPress.com

ISBN-13 (Digital): 978-1-956492-28-6
ISBN-13 (Paperback): 978-1-956492-29-3
ISBN-13 (Hardcover): 978-1-956492-30-9

Edited by Patrick C. Harrison III
Cover Design by Don Noble of Rooster Republic Press
Interior Design by D.W. Hitz

More from D.W. Hitz

Adult Fiction
Judith's Prophecy (Big Sky Terror Book 1)
Judith's Blood (Big Sky Terror Book 2)
Judith's Fall (Big Sky Terror Book 3)
Gods are Born
Brady: A Novella
Bloodtooth

Middle Grade Fiction
They Stole the Earth!
The Curse of Grohl

Contributions to Anthologies
Star Crossed
Bounties, Beasts, and Badlands
Remnants: Volume One
Fedowar Holiday Horrors: Volume One
Camp Slasher Lake: Volume One
Camp Slasher Lake: Volume Two
Fear Forge Anthology: Winter Quarter 2022

BLOODTOOTH

D.W. HITZ

Part One: Wake Up

1992

1

A ranger, somewhere out of sight, hit a switch, and the world inside the cave became the blackest place Wesley Henson had ever seen. Blacker than the Antarctic night where the Thing ran rampant. Blacker than the tunnels under New York where ninja turtles roamed. It was a darkness so intense, it seemed to drag on him, searching for any light that may cling after the switch, to crush it into oblivion.

Screams echoed through the immense cavern. Wes could pick out the voices of Jill Elden, Tommy Laskin, and Chris Conners from his right, left, and back. The rest of the cascading bellows were a sharp clash of alto and tenor tones, the remainder of his school's sixth and seventh-grade field trip attendees.

They were in the Bloodtooth Caverns, a yearly excursion for Custer Falls Elementary School's sixth and seventh graders. Most everyone had been there at some point, with it being right outside of town. But the lights going off got them every time. It was the type of thing one could never get used to. You could return to the surface and bathe in the sun's glow, and the everyday dimness of night would seem bright compared to this. So even if they'd seen it before, people screamed.

Wes did not scream. The unimaginable magnitude of gloom enveloped him in refreshment. His sensitive, blue eyes thanked the darkness, and his mind began constructing playthings from the phosphenes in his sight. Colors merged and twirled as electrical charges danced across his retinal surfaces. Wes tried to make out just a single thing nearby, and his eyes failed him. He imagined that the rest of existence may all be an illusion beyond the reach of the eternal nothingness around him. Even the sounds. There was no way to know if they existed beyond the borders of his own imagination. He was truly isolated in the absence of light. It was magnificent.

The screams died down, giving way to laughter and taunts. A soft, fifty-degree breeze brushed over Wes's arm. Humid air and the scent of earth filled his nose. A bat's chirp echoed from somewhere ahead. It occurred to Wes how strange it was that the creature could see him, but he could not see it. It could have been soaring at him that second, diving, mouth open, fangs spread, and he would remain unaware until he felt the sting of his blood being spilled.

He saw the bat in his mind. He saw it in the darkness ahead, and the animal became as real as the darkness itself. Chills ran over Wes's neck. They traveled down his shoulders and raised the hairs on his arms.

The image of the bat blossomed from a tiny, hairy bug-eater to a larger and larger specimen. It became a vampire bat from the jungles of South America, one he'd read about in *National Geographic*. He saw its long, hairy body, its pointed ears, its stubby nose... its fangs. It glided above the pack of students and circled, and Wes wondered what it was doing; was it...? Was it going to attack them? Was it searching the crowd for its next meal—their blood?

He fought with the idea as it came closer. It wasn't real—it couldn't be. But there it was. He saw it looming, despite seeing nothing else in the darkened space. The sounds of his peers were a wave of noise under the flap of its wings, and its focus narrowed on him alone.

It swooped down from above, and he covered his head, crouching. Why did it want him? Its hunger was obvious as its mouth spread, but why his blood? Its beady black stare hardened. Its jaws prepared to clamp down on his flesh. He could feel the wind curl around his neck from the flap of its wings as it hovered above him.

Now, Wes screamed.

Barton Smith, the ranger in back, flipped his switch, assuming he had gotten all the fright he could get out of this group of kids. Lights sputtered to life in sequence, one click at a time, until the expansive thirty-foot-high cavern was relit. He smirked, thinking about all the twelve and thirteen-year-olds that would be having nightmares tonight, the little girls among them clutching their sheets, wearing teeny tight pajamas.

Wes squinted, his eyes twitching from the bright light. He scanned the ceiling. Nothing. Of course, there was nothing. He was stupid for even looking. Stupid for screaming, letting the darkness scare him that way like a little child. After all, the darkness couldn't hurt you. What was in your mind couldn't hurt you.

Embarrassment formed a rock in his gut. It was worse than the first day of seventh grade when he mistakenly entered the girls' bathroom after trusting an eighth-grader's directions. He looked at his friends. Tommy and Chris grinned at something in the distance and rubbed their eyes.

Jill gazed curiously down at Wes. "Are you okay?"

He straightened himself upright. His mortification cast nearly as much shock across his skin as the fear of that bat had. *How stupid.* "Yeah. Of course."

"Okay..."

"So," Horace Maddoch, the ranger in front, began, "you really wouldn't want to get stuck down here without light, would you?"

A rumble of agreement passed through the visitors.

The ranger continued on about the trappers who had discovered the cave system in the early 1800s and the miners who later used it. He politely omitted the dozen-plus stories of those who had ventured into the caves over the years, never to be seen again.

Wes had heard those stories; most of the kids had. They were as common as nursery rhymes in Custer Falls. The one about the white woman and the Indian guide was the most common, but the tale of the outlaw gang that disappeared trying to hide their gold was Wes's favorite. He loved the idea of finding lost treasure, making himself and his friends into Montana's version of the Goonies.

After a few minutes, the ranger concluded, repeating his insistence on the need for light down there. Wes wholeheartedly agreed with that. He could only imagine the horror of not being able to get the lights back on. All those kids—they'd likely have trampled each other in fear or wandered off one of the dozens of cliffs inside the cave system.

"This way, now." Ranger Maddoch continued into the next chamber.

Middle graders followed in cliques of twos and threes. In the center of them were Mr. Jones and Ms. Sallow, or Jimbo Jones and Ms. Swallows, as Wes's classmates called them.

Jimbo carried an extra tire or two in his gut and spoke with a higher than usual voice. He'd earned a Purple Heart from the loss of his testicles to shrapnel in Vietnam, and this was rumored throughout the school as the cause of his abnormal voice.

Ms. Swallows was the object of every pubescent boy's (and some of the faculty's) lustful stares. Her collection of cleavage-exposing tops and her ever-red, smiling lips caused more daydreams in class and wet dreams at night than the blushing beauty could get tired of noticing or hearing about. When schoolboys ogled too long, she notoriously leaned into their desks to embarrass them back into the lecture; but never so severely as to permanently dissuade them from doing it again. She was accurately rumored to be dating Mr. Swann, the Gym/Health teacher. They'd been caught twice in his office by ninth graders enacting scenes from the Sex Education curriculum, though they skated past disciplinary action—it helped that Swann's dear uncle was the town's mayor.

Wes walked intentionally slow. The image of the diving bat replayed in his mind. While the silliness of that fear flooded Wes with shame, he couldn't help the feeling that the root of his sensation was somewhere up ahead. The bat noise had come from up front, but that alone wasn't it. There was a numbness crawling over Wes's feet, a trickle that rose within his legs, warning him of something. Something that he should be staying away from.

Jill walked beside him. Her mouth opened and closed twice, anticipating words but with no result. She studied him as she often studied things, with one eye squinted and the other perusing the visible clues. But she wasn't ready to level an assessment yet, either due to the unacceptable level of data or the possibility of showing some hint of her crush.

Jill had cried just this last weekend over the truth, that Wes was absolutely clueless of her existence beyond her being that chum he'd had since he was eight. But she kept trying, albeit subtly. She'd changed her hair. She'd started wearing earrings. She even wore perfume one day, hoping Wes would look at her the slightest bit different. All it did was bring teases from Tommy and Chris about her smelling like a rotting pile of flowers. Now, she simply studied him like a puzzle to be solved.

As the rest of the school group passed by, Tommy and Chris paused from chatting about Alison Steiner's breasts. It was a recurring conversation between the two, but today was extra poignant. Her nipples' exhibition beneath her shirt had proven that there was no bra. The cave's cold breeze, they figured, had conspired with them. It would later be argued whether that was a special event or, as Chris would say, "The girl always wants them to be free." They regarded Wes with interest.

"What goes with the slow motion, bro?" Chris said. His crossed arms rested on the AC/DC logo on his shirt.

Wes shook his head. He looked around the cavern. Ranger Smith fiddled with something back by the lighting controls. The stalactites dripped. The walls glimmered in seeping rock formations. There was no other way to go. He wanted another way to go. The ranger surely wouldn't let them exit backward. They'd have to continue on with the group. He'd have to keep moving toward whatever was giving him this sensation.

"I just feel like I need some space from the crowd." Wes stepped forward. Numbness rose from his feet to his knees.

As he reached the cavern's end and peeked around the corner, Wes saw a smaller cave, barely taller than a grownup. He heard the footfalls of his classmates ahead, beyond a winding turn to the right. Rusted iron railings were mounted in the ground and guided the way on both sides of the passage.

Jill followed Wes into the tunnel, trailed by Chris and Tommy.

"This place sucks." Chris clomped along. He pulled a Zippo from his pocket and began flipping it open and closed. It was black, with his favorite hero's logo painted in white, the Punisher's skull. Wes had wondered, but never actually asked, how Chris walked around with that. After his mother's diagnosis, Wes thought Chris would have gotten rid of anything signifying death. Of course, that would have meant half his wardrobe, with all of his Iron Maiden and Slayer shirts, and that was highly unlikely to happen. Still, though, it made Wes question every time he saw the thing. He answered in his head: *It's just Chris.*

Chris flicked his thumb, a flame rose from the lighter, and Wes caught a glimpse of something. It was in front of them, to the left, hiding beyond the cave's dim lighting. It was nestled in a crack in the rock, behind the iron railing, a hole in the cave wall, just shorter than Wes.

The numbness crawled over Wes's fingers. Blood inside his extremities cooled. Every inch of his body told him to turn away, but a whisper in the breeze seemed to say, *"Go."*

Wes stopped.

Chris pointed at the hole in the cave wall. "What's that? It's like they tried to block it up by putting the railing there." He walked ahead, around Wes and Jill. He leaned on the railing and held his lighter out inside the crevice. "Guys, it's a secret passage. It just keeps going and going in there."

Tommy joined Chris and peered inside. He looked at where the class had gone and back the way they'd come. Footsteps tapped against slick rock and echoed under the chatter of his peers, but the sound was diminishing. A determined smirk crossed his face, the same one that flowered every time he was told by his mom not to do something. "Go on." He stared at Chris and nodded into the pathway.

"Yeah?" Chris said. "I was going to." He actually hadn't made his mind up yet, but he was never one to back down from one of Tommy's dares.

"Well, do it." Tommy's grin widened. He loved getting Chris riled up. It was how they ended up racing through the mall last week with a giant sack of *free* candy from the Candy Shoppe. It was how detentions were earned and suspensions multiplied. It was how the real fun came to be with the pair.

"Fuck you. I'm going." Chris grabbed the rail and hoisted a leg over.

"Guys?" Wes said. "I don't think you want to do that." He didn't like those words coming out of his mouth. They felt oddly parental. It was like he wasn't himself; he definitely didn't feel like himself. But his gut was telling him that this was one place they shouldn't go.

Chris pulled his other leg over and squatted. He took a wobbling step into the tunnel. "This is so cool," he spoke into the passage, his attitude a complete U-turn from moments ago. His low voice echoed, and it gave Wes chills.

Tommy climbed over. He knelt as Chris moved deeper inside. "Come on." He waved at Wes and Jill. "Let's see where this bitch goes."

Jill crept to the railing and leaned over, gazing into the path. Light reflected and scattered from glistening walls. The surface inside was smooth yet bumpy, like polished lava rock. She looked at Wes, her smile eager and inviting. She wasn't sure if she really wanted to go in or just wanted to impress Wes, but she was committed now. "Come on."

Wes bit his lip. He didn't want to do this. He shed the unease from his mind with a shake of the head and replaced it with shame. Why was he allowing himself to be so frightened by a dumb feeling? He was probably just scaring himself for no reason. How bad could it be? It was just a cave. Maybe there were some stupid bats in there. The image of the vampire returned to his mind. *No, those aren't here. It's fine.* He moved forward. Jill climbed the bar and followed Tommy inside, and Wes took a deep breath before going in last.

Slick walls and a shiny ceiling reflected Chris's flame down the tunnel, but the three friends ahead of Wes blocked nearly all the direct light.

He leaned and moved on his hands and knees, feeling the floor as he went. The air grew colder, and the ground along with it. Wes imagined his breath was visible in front of his face, if only he had the light to see it. His arms and legs, the blood in his veins, all of it ran cold. He shivered and wished he had decided not to come.

"Cool," Chris's voice reverberated.

The shiny walls faded, and Wes was surrounded again by unforgiving blackness. *Fuck!* "Guys?" He hoped the tremble in his chest didn't make it to his voice.

"Oh," Chris said.

Firelight returned, and after several feet, Wes saw his friends standing again. The room had opened up into an expanse without a visible end. He heard water flowing somewhere in the distance. Rock formations grew down from an unseen ceiling and rose from the floor in spires as tall as a person.

"Wow." Jill wandered into the chamber. Stalagmites surrounded her like a forest. She turned back. "Wes, come see." It was her excited voice.

Wes joined her among the structures. Mist and droplets of water descended, sprinkling their heads. Jill looked up and giggled. Water smacked the tops of the rock formations and rained down again. Wes could feel her smiling through the darkness.

"Let's go this way," Chris said. He walked into the forest, taking the light with him.

"Hold on," Tommy said. His silhouette went after Chris.

"I guess we have to go," Jill said.

"Yeah, if we want light." Wes started walking.

All four moved as one, their eyes looking into the gloom and seeing nearly nothing. It was a mirror of when the rangers killed the lights for the world beyond the fiery dance of Chris's Zippo. Wes imagined what the cave must have been like before they were there, when the darkness reigned supreme, when any life that existed was imprisoned in the ultimate black. It gave him a feeling like ice on his skin. Like the world of light was warmth and happiness, and without it, well, was not where he wanted to be. He moved closer to Chris.

"Why do you think this place is blocked off?" Tommy said.

"Yeah," Jill said. "These pillars are the coolest things here."

"Probably lazy," Chris said. "They'd have to install all kinds of lights and rails for old people to come back here."

"Yeah," Tommy huffed.

Wes pondered, his mind roaming through the old stories. "Maybe it's where those outlaws buried their gold? Maybe they don't want anyone back here to find it."

"It's mine if *we* find it," Chris said. "My light, my claim."

"Fuck you," Tommy said. "We split that shit." He smacked the back of Chris's head, and Chris returned the gesture.

The stone structures around them fell away, and the cave kept going with no walls, no ceiling, no end within the small flame's glow. There was a sensation of enormity, that they had become ants, roaming through a world meant for giants.

"What's that?" Chris pointed. "There's something shiny over there."

Out in the middle of nothingness, there was a golden glimmer. It hung in the air, reflecting Chris's flame from an immeasurable distance like a hovering eye.

"What if it's the gold?" Chris said.

"Could be sapphires," Tommy said. "Didn't you hear the ranger-guy? They used to mine sapphires down here."

Chris moved faster. Tommy kept pace.

"Guys wait," Wes said. He was forced to walk faster as well to stay within the light.

"It's mine," Chris said. He broke into a run.

"No way, dude!" Tommy matched his speed. "Not if I get it first."

"Wait," Jill said. She brought up the rear. "Don't leave me alone."

Tommy then Chris, Chris then Tommy; they ran faster.

"Stop, guys!" Wes said.

Chris's light went out. The glimmer was gone. Everything was gone. Pure night set in, and Wes halted in his tracks as adrenaline surged and fear rose to cut it down.

He felt the return of that feeling, the one that had warned him away, but now it slammed into him with the force of a train, making sure he didn't miss its intentions. Fear grabbed him deep inside and jerked on his intestines. It clawed into his skin and trampled him like thousands of spider legs marching over every inch of his flesh. He stared into the utter black with both the disbelief that this could actually happen and the knowledge that this was the only realistic outcome after he refused to listen to the warning.

The air around Wes felt like a storm. It blew past him toward his missing friends. It was a hand from the unknown, urging him to follow them, demanding he finish the quest, wherever it led.

A scream echoed. Another. Dirt scraped against dirt. Screams muffled into the sounds of grunts and groans. Chris and Tommy howled.

"Chris!" Wes froze in place. "Tommy!" *Where did they go?*

This couldn't be happening. A thousand visions crossed Wes's mind at once. He saw them attacked by a hibernating bear they happened to stumble upon. He saw them bleeding, a pair of shredded bodies. He saw them broken and mangled at the bottom of a hole. He saw himself following them down and dying right beside them.

"Chris! Tommy!" Jill repeated. She crept forward, her shoes sliding across the ground. "I can't see, Wes. Where did they go?" Her voice was shaky. Wes could sense tears dripping down her cheeks.

"Stop," Wes commanded. Not her too. He imagined her falling, bloodied and broken, on top of their friends. He had to make sure she didn't disappear like the others. He couldn't be left alone. *God, no.* "Jill, don't move." He extended his arms, reaching toward her voice. "Give me your hand."

He wiggled his fingers to his left, where he thought she stood. He felt nothing. He swept his hands around toward his front. Nothing. "Jill? Where are you?"

"I'm here." Her voice was in front of him now.

Wes felt the ground ahead with his toes and inched forward. *Please, let her stay put.* His fingers reached. Again, he stretched and moved. Again. "Are you there?"

"Where are you?" Jill said. Now her voice was to the right.

"Don't move," Wes pleaded. He scooted right. His stomach tensed. His fingers shook.

"Wes?" Jill's voice was on the right again.

"Stop moving!" Wes's voice trembled. His reaching hand swayed under its own weight. His lungs pumped in and out, and a rhythm throbbed inside his head. Where was she? Why did she keep moving?

"I'm not moving," she cried.

Wes extended both hands in front. He stroked his shoe across the floor, feeling for a gap, a drop, anything that might explain what happened to Chris and Tommy, and hopefully avoid making it happen to himself.

A cold wind rose in front of his face. He imagined his short brown locks fluttering upward. A hand laid on his shoulder, and for a second, he was relieved that Jill had found him, then his right foot shot out from under him.

Wes felt the world spinning. His back slammed into something hard, then pointed, then tearing at the skin through his shirt. He felt a sting, a burn, and hot wetness. Stars shined in his eyes, then nothing.

2

Diana Henson's chin rested on her palm. She stared into the space between her desk and Ms. Legary's blackboard scribbles. Before drifting away, she had wondered how someone with such awful handwriting could become an English teacher. Her *I* looked like an *R*, her *R* looked like an *N*, and her words together seemed as meaningless as a two-year-old's scribbles. But still, the class was expected to read them and decipher what they meant, to summon homework the next day that happened to match her interpretation of the previous day's scrawl. Diana would worry about that later, after asking Joanne Higgins or Sarah Buckley what they had written down. Her friends would come together and do the assignment as they collectively agreed it should be interpreted, and together they would have a united front if, by some happenstance, it was incorrect. Ms. Legary would have to see it their way—they all read the assignment the same, after all.

A notebook slid across Di's desk, its steel spiral pressing against her elbow. The cold metal shocked her out of the nothingness of her thoughts and called her to the right, to Joanne.

Jo glanced down at the notebook, then back into Di's eyes. Her gesture became imperative as she repeated it twice.

Di yawned and lifted her head. She knew what this was about, Johnny DiMarco. Joanne had been drooling nonstop over the boy for a month now, since his family moved to Custer Falls during the summer, and he popped up at the city pool with his too old, but also delicious, older brother. They looked like they had walked into nowheresville, Montana, directly from the halls of Bayside High in Los Angeles. The girls expected Zack Morris and A.C. Slater to come strolling in right behind them. Their dark hair and tanned skin seemed to drive Jo nuts, and once school started back up and Johnny showed up in her homeroom, it had been her never-ending project to win his attention. But there were two problems: (1) Jo was incredibly shy, and (2) Shirley Minsk, who was already developed like a tiny swimsuit model. Shirley had Johnny's eye, and Jo's schemes to break her spell were now a daily conversation.

Di opened the notebook and flipped through the near-endless running conversation that had been documented in notes since the start of the school year. Three-quarters through the book, she found today's dilemma. Jo wrote, "S says that J is going to the mall with Lenny after school. I want to go!!! Maybe bump into them there?? But I know little miss look at my tits is going to be there. Grrr! What do we do???"

Di gazed at the blackboard and pondered. Did she even *want* to go to the mall? Of course, she did. Would she be able to go without having to convince Wes to go too? And, how to keep Shirley away? She wondered if Hannah Snider could convince her not to go. Hannah was Shirley's best friend and sat in the back of the room right now. Di turned and spied her. Hannah was scribbling something in her own notebook. Her curly red hair blocked half her page. Di returned her gaze to the front and saw that Jo had watched her look back. Jo nodded in agreement.

What they agreed on, Di wasn't sure, but Jo definitely was working on a plan to make it happen. If only Di understood what she had started, she might have been able to stop it.

The bell rang, signaling the end of third period. Diana stacked her English book and notebook on top of the conversation notebook and stood to leave. Jo was still looking back as Hannah packed her things and walked to the front. Di gave Jo a kick and a scowl, and they walked toward the hallway.

Diana had just stepped out of the classroom when she felt the strangest sensation. Her head buzzed. The walls seemed to spin around her, and her legs gave out. She sunk to the floor. Her back burned. Her feet numbed. And a feeling of dread swelled from her gut.

3

Wes opened his eyes to the flicker of Chris's flame. But Chris wasn't holding it. Instead, it sat on the ground, shining like a tiny lantern. Tommy laid beside it, his head in Chris's lap. Chris rocked forward and back. One of his hands rested on Tommy's head. The other was twisted backward with the ends of three bones jutting through his flesh. Blood, both dried and leaking from his wound, coated his arm and the ground below.

Tears ran down Chris's cheeks. They retraced the paths of those before them, clean lines on his dust-covered face.

"Chris?" Wes's voice was dry and broken. His head radiated pain from the front, back, and right cheek. He pushed himself up to sitting, and his back burned. His foot was numb at first, but once Wes was upright, it screamed at him with the sharpest pain he'd ever experienced. It was as if someone flipped a switch, and all he could do was howl.

He huffed and ground his teeth. "What the? What the shit is this?" He pulled his foot in closer, trying to decipher what the pain was all about. He screamed again. Nothing below his ankle followed his commands. The foot flopped right, and daggers shot into Wes's leg. "Goddammit!"

"You should be still," Chris whispered. "It hurts less."

Wes relaxed his leg and growled as thunderous pain shook his being. After a moment of heavy breathing, he sputtered, "What happened?"

Chris lifted a single finger, pointing up.

Behind Wes was the base of a cliff. It rose up into the nothing.

"No." Wes looked around. Glanced at Tommy. Fear struck his mind like lightning. His leg. What if it was broken forever? Chris's arm. What if they had to amputate it? Tommy—God, look at him. And— "Jill? Where's Jill?"

"She's gone for help—but, she can't see up there. It's been... like hours, I think."

"God. And Tommy? What—Is he okay?"

They looked Tommy over together.

"He's... I don't know. I think he's alive."

"Jesus, your arm." Wes's eyes fixated on the bones protruding from Chris's bicep and forearm. In the amber flicker, they looked like blood-stained, sharpened yellow sticks. The reality of what they were was hard to fathom. More than that, the layers of skin and shiny lacerated fat rocked Wes's stomach. If those parts of Chris could be on the outside, what other damage might there be on the inside? In his foot?

Chris refused to look. He shook his head. "We just have to wait." His voice trembled. "She'll get help."

"Jesus, Chris." Wes's back ached. He thought about leaning against the wall, but the pain was too much. The wetness of his shirt made him wonder just how bad his back was torn up. Were there scratches? Cuts? Was he bleeding at a critical pace back there?

The thoughts were a punch of reality. They made him want to puke.

Wes shifted his weight, trying to find a better way to sit. There was none. He laid on the ground, resting on his side. God, he hoped Jill would find her way back, and then could find help. She was their only shot.

He went over the events in his mind, repeating the question: How did this even happen? Why did they follow Chris, running into the dark? How stupid was that? Part of him wondered if he deserved this after being so dumb.

His eyes drifted from the flame to the darkness beyond. Deep in the endless night, Wes saw a flash and a sparkle. A light slid around, side to side, illuminating the cave floor.

His heart throbbed. Was this it? Was this their rescue? "I see them." Wes pointed at the light. "Over there!" He sat up.

Chris rotated and glanced where Wes pointed. He gasped, eyes wide, but saw nothing. Tears sped from his eyes as he whimpered. "Don't tease me. Fucking Christ, this isn't the time."

The light moved but didn't seem to be getting any closer.

"Tease you? You don't see that?"

"Shut up!" Chris cried. "I don't need that crap from you."

"From me?" Wes had to wonder what that meant. But more than that, why hadn't Chris seen it? It was right there, but Chris seriously wasn't seeing it. Was he hit on the head? Some sort of brain thing?

"Over here!" Wes shouted. "This way!"

Chris shook his head. His light voice held a soft growl.

Wes watched the light continue to circle without progression. What were they doing? Maybe they were lost? Maybe there was some obstacle in their way? He bit his lip, hoping they didn't run into trouble and turn around. That would be... he didn't want to think about how bad that could be. "I'm going to them."

"We stay here. They're coming." Chris resumed rocking in place.

"I know you don't see it over there, but I do. I'm going to go and look. Maybe they're having a hard time finding us."

"No, stay here," Chris begged with solemn eyes. "Please, don't leave." He froze in place, his jaw trembling. "Please."

"It's not far. I'm just going to check out that light. I have to." They didn't even know what had happened to Jill. Would she make it to help? Or would she get lost in the caves above? He shuddered at the thought of her needing rescue too. Maybe this light was from another cavern? From rangers? They couldn't risk not taking a chance on finding help. He needed to go look. As much as his leg hurt, he didn't think he had a choice.

Wes climbed to his hands and knees. Pain surged as he oriented his ankle. He restrained himself from screaming, lifting his injured foot and setting it atop his good one. With his hands, he felt the inches of ground in front of himself, and he moved. He crawled forward with his hands and slid his knees. Crawl, slide. Crawl, slide. Each movement, each inch of vibration on his legs seemed to scaped the broken bones in his ankle against each other. He wanted to howl, but instead, clamped his teeth together.

"Please don't leave," Chris repeated once more.

"Just chill." He panted through the pain. "I'll be back."

Chris didn't say another word.

The ground became bumpy below Wes's palms. His fingers sifted through rock and dirt. The light was closer. He was making progress. "Hello! Hello!"

Only his own echo returned the salutation.

He crawled on. As he moved further and further, Wes started to doubt that the light ahead was moving. It must have been some trick like how stars twinkled in the sky. The glimmer ahead faded from golden-yellow to a light blue, gradually growing darker as Wes reached a wall, then a crevice, and a glowing blue section within.

Wes's heart sank. There was no help here. He glanced at Chris and Tommy. The lighter flickered but felt like a mile away. He turned back to the glowing wall. "What is this?"

Wes's fingers caressed the rock. Why was it glowing? Maybe there was something inside—or behind it. Maybe something electrical that could help them?

His fingers searched. Their tips were raw, but he kept going. He now felt—no, *knew*—there was something inside that he needed. Something that would help them.

A layer of aged dirt crumbled away, revealing glowing stones encircling what felt like a shelf. On the shelf, he found a groove around a spherical bulge. It was slightly smaller than a baseball and halfway buried in its shelf. He lined his fingers along the bulge and pushed on it—nothing. He clenched and turned it—nothing. He pinched tightly around the edge and pulled. The bulging rock crackled and whispered a soft breath of air. That was it. It *would* open. He'd found it. A spark of hope flashed in his mind. He wondered if whatever was inside this stone could save them? It made no sense, but he knew this was somehow special.

He clamped his digits tighter around the stone's circumference. He twisted as he heaved. It was stiff, unwilling, then cracked and popped and exploded outward in a gust of dust and stale air.

4

Raymond Trent chomped on a hunk of Nestle Crunch as he pushed his Schwinn down 1st Avenue. The rusted chain hung from its gears, reminding him of when he walked in on his grandfather at the pool shower and saw his limp dick hanging under his old flabby gut.

When the chain broke, Ray had been jumping a curb to get out of traffic. He nearly rolled back into it and became a lesson for all the dumbass little kids around town learning to propel themselves without training wheels: "Don't ride your bike in the street, or you could end up like Ray Trent." Maybe. What Ray was sure of, though, was that if that piece of shit Honda hadn't swerved around him, his dad would have found the guy later and put him in the hospital. Dad was an asshole and didn't get much right, but he'd have gotten that one.

The whole thing was Dad's fault anyway. Ray had mentioned a dozen times that he needed to get a job to pay for things. The chain was a ticking timebomb. Dad wouldn't have it. He wanted Ray at the tire shop every day after school—he couldn't pay anyone else, so Ray would do. Someone had to greet customers, clean the bathrooms, and take out the trash. So, it may as well be his fifteen-year-old kid.

Ray ground his teeth as he turned left and crossed the street into the park. The bike rattled. The goddamn bike. Two bums sat on the bench to the left of the concrete amphitheater, and preschool kids screamed and yelled from the playground. Ray headed right up the middle path, wishing he could pull each bum and each screaming kid aside and slap their faces raw. He strode past the great green lawn and into the shady section by the tiny pond before 4th Avenue.

He stopped at the edge of the water and looked around. The chain between his wallet and pants jingled softly as it patted his leg. "Where is that fucker?" He clenched his fists.

Stony was nowhere to be seen. Of course, the seventeen-year-old dropout's name wasn't really Stony; it was Zach Ellis, but the guy was always high, and his profession was selling weed, so Stony became his moniker, whether he liked it or not—and he did. Unfortunately, today, his supply was on empty, so he was at home playing his Sega Genesis.

"Stony," Ray hissed into the bushes and toward the pond as if the guy was going to swim ashore and toss over a dime bag. Why not? He'd seen Stony do stupider stuff over the years. Like when he spent an entire week on the roof of the school. The cops and fire department eventually had to get him down. Once, Stony tried to walk from Main Street across town to the drive-in wearing only his girl's panties and a bag of weed taped to his left nipple. He was three-quarters of the way there before he got picked up, luckily having tossed the weed down a sewer grate before being grabbed. This time, however, he was not showing himself, dramatically or otherwise.

"Shit," Ray growled. After a day like today, he really needed something to smoke.

Footfalls shuffled through the grass behind Ray, and he spun around. An elderly face, gray-bearded and reeking of rot-gut whiskey, hovered inches in front of his own. The bum wore a ragged blue cap, crooked on the top of his skull, and as a breeze blew, Ray smelled shit from the old man's pants. Ray jolted back, shock and fear transforming into rage and disgust.

"What the fuck?" Ray shouted. "Get away from me." His face was hot, his blood boiling.

"Got any change, young fella?" the bum asked.

Ray tasted blood behind his teeth. A whisper in his ear said, *"Hit him."*

"Get lost, old man," Ray said.

"Just a couple dollars? I'm hungry. Help out a vet?"

"Fuck off!" Ray screamed.

The whisper repeated itself, *"Hit him."*

"I know you got money, you little punk." The old bum's face grew stern. "You're back here to buy drugs, aren't you?"

Ray took a step back, and the old man grabbed his shoulder.

"Give me some money, kid."

Three cop cars, sirens wailing, raced down 4th Avenue on the other side of the pond.

Ray swung at the bum. His fist crunched into the old guy's jaw. He felt something crack inside the man's face and didn't care what it was.

The old man stumbled along the ground, a trail of thick red ooze leaking from his lips. He splashed headfirst into the pond, and Ray Trent spun and ran off to look for Stony.

2022

1

Wes jerked and gasped. The sheets were wet with sweat. He exhaled and sat up, dropping his legs from the bed and setting them on the shaggy brown rug that bordered the bed's frame. He extended his toes and grasped the soft, warm nap between his digits as he blinked and let his eyes adjust to the bathroom's dim night light. He stood and stretched his arms backward. *Another night.*

"Nightmare?" Jill asked, her face unmoved against her pillow.

"Yeah."

"Going to write?"

"Yeah. Go back to sleep." Wes grabbed a shirt from the chair beside the nightstand and slipped it on. He glanced back at the bed and ran his gaze along the contours of the bedding. Jill had tossed the covers to her feet. Only a thin sheet draped over her curves. Wes smiled and thought back to high school, when those curves began to grab his attention. When for some odd reason, she was still his friend after all that had happened, and he realized her beauty. *You still got it, baby.*

Sam-I-Am, the cattle dog mix, hopped up and followed Wes as he walked into the hallway.

Wes limped for a step and a half as the tightness in his ankle reminded him that the joint was still a mess after all these years. He glanced into the girls' bedroom. Each was snug as a bug in their bed, dreaming away.

Samantha, who had been fascinated by *Green Eggs and Ham* a few years back and was tickled to death at another person called Sam, had named the dog. Now, her leg hung from the covers over the edge of the bed, beside the darkness, the void. Wes watched with some sense of pride. Himself, at nine, would have been paranoid to the state of panic to have an appendage hanging like that for fear of the creep under the bed. His kids had no such fears. They slept with the closet door open. They never looked under the bed except in search of an elusive toy. Their world was secure. For now.

Lisa snored away on the other side of the room, all of her covers kicked to her feet and Topsy, the gray cat, snuggled next to her head. Seven, and already taking after her mother more than she knew; she started every morning with an impetuous, "Hello, Father," and proceeded through the day with a sarcastic, yet sincere, air of confidence in everything she touched. A phrase reoccurred to Wes almost daily, *That one's going to leave a mark.* Whether physically, emotionally, or within the psyche, Lisa never failed to leave an impression on anyone she met.

Wes pulled the door to a two-inch crack and continued his nightly trek. He plodded down the stairs and into the kitchen, where he fetched a large mug from the cupboard, this one reading *Write Epic Shit*, and set it under the Keurig. He spun the K-cup carousel, examining his options: dark roast, French vanilla, caffe latte, hot chocolate.

"Feels like a dark roast night." He plucked his selection from its stainless steel seat and started his brew. The machine hissed and pumped, filling the kitchen with his third favorite smell in the world (number one being Jill in his arms, and tied for number two were Sam and Lisa—when they were clean).

Wes's gaze circled the room as he waited. He glanced at the artwork on the fridge, the *Homes and Land* magazine on the counter, and avoided eye contact with the picture on the far wall of himself, his mother, and Diana. His sister was not a subject he was in the mood to think about tonight.

Sugar in his coffee, Wes made his way across the house. *Clack, clack, clack* followed him into his office, where he closed the door behind Sam-I-Am. The dog spun in a circle twice and lay on the floral rug that extended under the desk.

Wes logged into his computer and stared at the music options in Tidal. He clicked *play,* starting a *Classical for Studying* playlist. His manuscript was already loaded and ready. The cursor blinked behind the last word: sister. He watched the vertical beam flash, and as much as he would have liked to, he couldn't avoid the memory that came next.

Diana, wide-eyed and amazed, walked right up to the white unicorn.

She held up her hand, palm out, expecting to pet the animal as easily as she had pet her friend Betsy's brown mare. She stepped with giddiness through the forest to the edge of the clearing, all as Wes repeated, "Leave it alone, sis. This isn't right."

She came within feet of the animal. It watched her with black eyes. They blinked as a breeze picked up through the meadow. Scents of honeysuckle and lilac drifted through the forest. It shifted its head, tilting just slightly.

"Good girl," Di whispered, moving closer still.

The unicorn lowered her head. Her knees crouched.

Wes shouted, "No!"

The beast leaped forward, running its two-foot-long horn through the center of Di's palm. The white spike burst through the back of her hand, dyed crimson.

Diana screamed. The animal shook its head as it raised its horn toward the sky. It lifted Di into the air, off her feet, dangling her from the beast's face. Blood streamed down her arm, over her shoulder, down her side.

"Di!" Wes sprinted through the brush. Why had he let her get so far ahead of him? Why did she have to do that? Try to touch it? Didn't she know?

The unicorn lowered its head then bucked straight up. Di's hand split, the flesh shredded apart between her index and ring finger. Blood bathed the animal's face as Di's hand drifted down.

Diana howled and dropped to the ground. She clutched her bisected hand as the beast hovered, reared up on two legs.

Blink. Blink. *Sister.* The scent of his coffee brought Wes back to his office. He sipped his mug and set it back down.

"The unicorn," Wes mumbled. It had been years since he had thought about that. Why would that memory return now? Probably the same reason he'd had the dream of Bloodtooth Caverns. That goddamn cave. Why did he go into that goddamn cave?

Wes pondered for a moment. "That was when it all started, wasn't it?"

His therapist's words echoed in his mind, "You can't overcome these dreams if you don't face them."

Wes regretted telling Jill about the dreams, about the nightmares. It wasn't like he could have hidden them from her, not when they were happening right next to her, but Jill might not have insisted he go to a shrink after they just kept coming, night after night, week after week.

But they weren't just dreams. They were memories. Things he had forgotten, but as the visions returned, his memory did too. And face them? What did that guy know? He'd never seen one of Wes's dreams. Wes tried to do it, though. Tried to face them as the man instructed. And they only seemed to get worse, just as they had before.

Blink. Blink. *Sister.*

"The blood." Wes shook his head. There had been so much blood in her bed. Mom didn't believe what had happened, but why should she have? Wes thought about Sam and Lisa. Would he believe them if they came to him with such a story? He hoped so. Yes, of course, he would.

Wes sipped his coffee and sighed. "Not a good night for writing." He rose from his desk, and Sam-I-Am followed him into the living room. He sat in the blue recliner and raised his feet. After clicking the television on and starting an old episode of *Survivor*, he was soon back asleep.

2

Diana Henson's eyes shot open. Her fingers flexed around her knife. Her gaze circled her shelter. Pine logs, her pistol, a red-coaled fire, Virb, who gazed back from his corner with a confident German Shepherd's stare. The wind howled in the forest outside; weather was coming.

Di sat up, unzipping her sleeping bag. The world seemed haunted by a red hue as her bloody dream slowly faded. She loosened her grip on the knife and looked down. The scar on her hand ached. All her scars ached.

Virb scooted closer and, with a whimper, laid in front of her. Di scratched his chest, then reached for a log and tossed it into the stone fireplace.

"Yeah, I like the dreams much better when you come along," she said.

It was true. The dreams where Virb was at her side were steady, worriless. Much like in the light of day, he watched out for the bears, the mountain lions, the stray hunter or hiker that might wander off the regular trails and find her camp. He was there like the knight she wished for, ready to die for her if the whim ever took her. But there were some dreams into which he wasn't allowed. The old ones. The ones that drove her to be what she was today.

The unicorn came to mind. She wished he could have been there.

Di looked again at the scar, squeezing her hand shut. It still screamed at her when she closed it more than three-quarters, the nerve damage never having properly healed.

Virb whined and met her gaze, and Di scratched for a few seconds longer. She reached behind her sleeping bag to a shelf above the bed and brought down a bag of Cheetos, and ripped them open. Virb spun to his belly and laid attentively. Di cracked a smile, popped one in her mouth, and one into his. His jaw hung in a smile that only Virb could offer, and in the hazy in between of the dream and the lucid, the wary and the secure, her eyes dampened.

A tendril of flame rose above the fire's fresh log, and then a second. Di watched the blaze grab hold of the wood like a fiery claw, and she wondered, *Why the unicorn?*

There had been years of mostly good dreams. She had all but forgotten the horrors of '92. It was in the rearview, suppressed as much as one can suppress a childhood trauma. The price had been committal, dangerous drugs, sex, and terrible choices in both men and women, some of the more recent scars would attest to that, but the dreams had gone. All until six months ago.

She flipped Virb another Cheeto.

Had it been six months? She remembered the day. She woke up at 3:16 am; she checked the time on her phone. She was drenched in sweat. The sheets were drenched in sweat. Her fingers shook, and all she could say was, *No air. No air.*

She was out of time. The old days were about to come crashing down on her, and all she could do was run. It might help, it might not, but it was something she could control.

Di slid on her panties, her pants, and a t-shirt. She grabbed her bra and her bag. Her fingers trembled. She was dripping with fear. She shouldn't have been this scared, but there she was. The dream was over; things were okay now. She was going to leave. Why did she still feel so frightened? Was it what had happened? Or what was to come?

That was when Carly woke up. "What the fuck are you doing? What time is it?" Her hair flared in three different directions. She squinted, and the edges of her nose were traced in blood.

"I got to go," Di said. "I'll see you later."

"What? Whatever." She rolled her eyes and buried her head in the pillow. She rocked and pulled the covers tighter around herself.

Di walked into the trailer's living room, scanning the coffee table. Beer cans, coke, but no keys. She went into the kitchen.

Her heartbeat picked up. Why was this taking so long? She needed to get out of here. A sense of urgency squeezed her gut and screamed. Where were the keys? There was something coming, and she needed to get out and get ready. She needed to pick up Virb and move on before... She didn't know precisely what, how it would come, but that part didn't matter just yet. What mattered was that she needed to get away from everyone, from anything that might hurt her—or who *she* may hurt.

The counter: more beer cans, empty bottles of whiskey, empty potato chip bags. On a whim, the fridge: a plate with a hunk of green-edged cheddar, a hot dog package with a single, lonely dog, a half-empty bottle of margarita mix from a month ago, and, right next to it, a key ring with a large diamond hotel room marker reading *217* and a dozen of Di's keys.

She snatched the keyring and headed out of the kitchen. She turned left to cross the living room and walked directly into Carly's bare chest. She stumbled backward.

"The fuck, Carly?" she snarled.

Di stared into her fling's eyes and realized: this wasn't Carly. It was Carly's body, Carly's tanned tits and narrow ass, but the thing behind the eyes wasn't her. At least not the girl she'd known over the past two coke-binge-filled weeks. It was... but it couldn't be. Inside, she thought she saw something she hadn't seen since Custer Falls... since *him*.

"Where do you think you're going, *Diana*," Carly hissed. "It's him, isn't it? Your fucking ex, *Kevin*?"

Di's brain seemed to be caught between gears. "What?"

"What's wrong? I don't fuck you good enough, so you need a real dick?" There it was in her eyes, an anger, a righteousness, as if its whispers were in her mind, urging her onward.

Chills ran through Di from her chest to her toes to the flesh of her scalp. The clenched feeling in her gut turned rock hard. She wanted to puke. She wanted to scream and run. She wanted to punch Carly in the eye just to get her out of her face.

"No," Di's voice cracked. She backed up. Her fingers shaking again.

"Oh, yes," Carly lurched forward. "You woke me up. Got me all *excited*." She gestured down and stroked her vagina with her middle finger. "I'll show you how I can fuck. Back in the bed, *now*."

Di backed up further and found herself in the kitchen once again.

"You're not leaving me!" Carly came, moving faster, reaching for Di like a starved dog, teased with hunks of raw meat.

"No!" Di shouted, her voice stronger but straining. Her eyes raced around the room, this time looking for a weapon, something to defend herself with. She'd been raped before and was damn sure not going to let it happen again.

Beer cans, no; trash, no. The knife block: empty. The sink: mold-coated plates and, yes, a rusting steak knife under brown, stagnant water.

She grabbed the knife and pointed the tip at Carly. "Leave me the fuck alone. I'm leaving now."

"The fuck you are!" Carly grabbed at Di's wrist, but Di pulled away. She grabbed at the other, missing, and seized Di's shoulders.

The knife dug up into Carly's abdomen, wedging itself between her stomach and her lungs. Blood streamed down her belly, and her eyes met Di's as if awakening from a dream into a nightmare.

Di gasped. She felt Carly's warm skin against her hand and her hot blood over her fingers. Regret instantly numbed every part of her that wasn't pressed against Carly's touch. She watched Carly's lips flare in pain and remembered her smile in the Lakeshore Bar where they met. That smile had kept her going all night long and lifted her up after Kevin, drunk, tried to force her into his truck in the parking lot less than an hour prior. But would she smile again after this?

Carly sank to the floor and crashed against the lower cabinets. "Di?" She studied the knife that now looked as much a part of her as her hand or foot. With shaking fingers, she gripped it, readying herself to rip the foreign object free.

"No!" Di shouted. Her gaze dropped to her bloody hands. What had she done? Carly's face was a portrait of fear, and Di flashed with self-doubt. Was that even real? Did she really see what she thought she saw in Carly's eyes? Her mind raced to a time when men and women in white coats ruled her life and told her everything she thought was real had only been a psychotic break. Had it happened again?

"What?" Carly groaned. "You stabbed me?" She was scared, breathing slow, shallow respirations.

Di sank to her knees. "Don't—Don't pull it out. I'll call 911."

She stood and worked the phone from her pocket. She dialed the number and tasted bitterness on her tongue. Her eyes went to the window over the sink, to a light beyond the trailer park, in the rear of a gas station. It was yellow, fading ever so softly, dimmer and brighter.

"911, what's the location of your emergency?" a man said from the other end of the line.

"Tell him," Carly hissed.

Di looked down. Carly's eyes were cold, not her own. Di stepped back, and the phone slipped from her hand. It drifted toward the floor with the speed of a feather falling on the moon.

"No!" She ran.

The phone cracked as it hit the linoleum. Carly reached with her sticky red hand, and the door slammed.

Di flipped another Cheeto through the air, and Virb caught it in his mouth. She scanned around her little place once again.

"It may be a hovel, but it's ours," she said.

Virb tilted his head. He got another snack.

"Hey, at least I haven't touched coke in six months." She flashed the dog a smile as if it had been by choice. She was just as much in hiding from the world as she was from the return of that thing, if that's what had really been inside Carly. Whether her need to isolate herself from the rest of the world was all an instinct, or if it was the return of a goddamn psychosis, she didn't know. But she felt safer in her tiny pine shelter than she did out there. She just wished she could talk to Wes.

3

The day had broken, though few in Custer Falls would have noticed, as the light from the dim sunrise was masked by dense drifting fog. It approached with an ominous warning, a hidden message: *something's up ahead, lookout, because you don't know what.*

Elias Keys had walked to work through the thick humidity. He locked the door on his dingy third-floor apartment, came outside, and felt a shiver from more than just the temperature and creeping moisture. Something else was in that fog; he couldn't put the thought into words or say what it was, but something was changing, and it was drifting into town just like that fog.

He'd walked down the sidewalk, his eyes on the road as he went. He carried an unease this morning, attentive to the noises of passing cars, with an undercurrent of fear in his observations. There was a nagging warning that one of them meant him harm. Sure, not knowingly—even with the cycles between meth, acid, cocaine, and shrooms, he'd never had a hallucination strong enough to make him believe an inanimate object could think and willingly want to hurt him—but still, he had an image in his head that at any second, one may burst through the fog, jump onto the curb, and run him down.

He held an anxious tension in his steps. He felt like he needed to be ready to jump out of the way at any second. Would he even have time to jump? It was a completely irrational fear, and he knew it. But still, it was there.

By the time he had crossed three streets, racing across the intersections like a frightened rabbit, he made it to the Huckleberry Café, and he found that he was five minutes early. The first time ever. The bell dinged as Elias opened the door, and there was Norris Cushing, the owner.

Norris's eyes fell on Elias, raising one disheveled, salted eyebrow. He stood paused, halfway through filling the coffee maker's basket. His gaze went to the clock in the center of the café, then back to Elias. The clock read 5:55.

"Everything all right?" Norris said with a smirk.

Elias hurried across the dining room and picked up an apron from behind the counter. "Yeah. Fine." They both knew it was a lie.

Norris nodded and resumed his work on the coffee. He started the brew and shuffled back toward the kitchen. Norris didn't take part in the same types of shenanigans that Elias got into, but neither was he a bible-thumper. His mistress was whiskey, and she paid him a visit damn near every break. Not too much at work, just a swig here and a sip there, enough to pass the day until they were done serving dinner and he could meet her at the Stage Coach or at home. No, as far as he was concerned, whatever his employees did on their off hours was their own business, as long as they showed up the next day ready to work, which Elias usually did.

Once Norris was out of sight, Elias leaned on the counter and took a long, deep breath. He felt his pulse still racing. Why was he so worked up?

He tried to brush away the embarrassment of running nearly all the way to work. He wished it away and found it replaced with a new feeling. It was one he'd had before, but he was confused by the flavor. It was the sensation he got when Officer Harrison pulled up to Elias as he walked home from work, the daily hassle and speech about how the officer better not catch him with drugs again, or it would be the last time. The thought made him scratch his arm where his Br/Ba tattoo lived, the logo of a show that was his inspiration for too many years.

Harrison never bothered to frisk him on that trip—or precisely, he didn't any longer. He used to, but never found anything, and assumed that these days Elias just didn't take anything to work with him. Harrison had been a friend of Elias's parents before they'd mysteriously driven off the dam and drowned in the lake. These days, he liked to tell himself he was looking after their kid. Maybe he was. Harrison would then drive off with a smug smile of satisfaction as if he'd jerked himself off just right, and as he did, Elias would ponder just what fluid he'd slip into the officer's coffee the next morning.

This was the feeling that now enveloped Elias. The one of delayed retribution. The difference from all those other times, though, was an understanding of finality. There was a knowing that after the next time, he wouldn't need to worry about Officer Bully or whoever the dumb schmuck was that wanted to hassle him. He was ready to say no to taking any more shit.

"*Yes,*" a whisper crept through his thoughts. It was a spec on the breeze between thought and action, pressing on that tiny synapse that flared whenever wrath was involved.

A smile crept across his face, and the door chimed. Officer Harrison stepped inside.

4

Officer Stuart Harrison of the Custer Falls Police Department sat in his city-issued SUV and set his large coffee in the cup holder between his radio and mobile data terminal. He'd just come on shift, and already the calls seemed like they were stacking up. Not just the normal morning commute fender benders or the person who'd discovered that their kindly elderly neighbor had passed in the night—there were four domestic calls listed on his MDT, and it wasn't even seven-thirty.

Harrison scanned the list and sipped his coffee. It tasted odd, and he wondered if it was extra strong today or if he still had the remnants of his breakfast orange juice on his taste buds. It was salty and bitter, more so than usual.

The second call on the list was around the corner. Dispatch hadn't sent it over the radio yet; they must have been getting the details down.

The house number was one Harrison had memorized, Debbie and Will Farmer. They usually didn't get into it until the afternoon, when Will was four or five Coors in and Debbie had been up to her ears in their two-year-old's shouting.

Harrison guzzled down several sips of his coffee and picked up the radio. "Dispatch, 735."

He waited for Dispatch to answer and took another drink.

The radio came back, "735, Dispatch, go ahead." It was Martinez. She had that kind of voice that cut through the radio like a knife. Each word was crisp and unmistakable, except when she came over after hours. On those nights, her words were sweet and syrupy in his ears.

It took Harrison a second to look past the image of her in her chair. "Yeah, I see the PFD around the corner on Butte. Put me on that call and mark me en route."

"Copy, 735." There was a spike in her voice, and he could see her smiling over the radio.

Harrison shook his head, guzzled twice more, and shut the door. He set the coffee, now half-empty, in his cup holder and put his vehicle in gear.

Waves of heat began to wash over Harrison as he drove. His temples bulged. Sweat cooled and tingled his scalp. His gut bubbled, and he became nauseous. He rounded the corner onto Butte Street and eyed the residence of Will and Debbie Farmer. Burning rose from his stomach, and his thoughts got lighter, cloudier. He wondered if he was going to pass out. He held onto his wheel with a tight, sweaty grip. He'd just entered their driveway when he lost consciousness.

Harrison's SUV smashed into the rear of Will Farmer's pickup, which smashed into the front of the Farmer's home. Officer Harrison's forehead came down on his deploying airbag, and vomit ejected from his mouth and nose, drenching the airbag and his entire face.

1992

1

Wes opened his eyes to a poster of Batman staring back at him. Next to it was Luke Skywalker, followed by Jack Burton and then Jill. She was deep into his copy of *Teenage Mutant Ninja Turtles Volume 1*.

Wes remembered how hard he had worked one day trying to convince her that the comic was so much better than the cartoon; a *more mature turtle*, he had put it. The conversation must have stuck. Here she was reading it without him even suggesting it.

He had left the book on his desk on the other side of the room at some point. Had she found it there while he was out? A nightmarish twinge ran through his thoughts as he wondered if she had opened any of his desk drawers while she was over there. Had she also found the copy of *Playboy* he had stolen from his dad's secret collection in the garage and added to his own a few weeks back?

The sheets rustled as he pushed himself up against his headboard. His broken ankle screamed. He looked up from wincing and saw Jill empathizing with a mirrored expression.

"Hey," Wes muttered.

"Hey. Still not used to that thing, huh?"

It had been a week since Wes's release from the hospital with a prescription of bed rest and quiet for his concussion and broken ankle. His lacerated back was treated with almost an entire tube of ointment and only about a dozen stitches scattered between his neck and his ass. The doctors thought it a miracle that he got off so lucky after a near thirty-foot fall. Luckier than his friends.

Tommy was still in the hospital. He'd woken up briefly during the ambulance ride from the caverns but hadn't opened his eyes since. The last Wes heard, the doctors didn't know how long this coma might last, but they were hopeful he'd snap out of it at any time. But that was a lie. Not a single MD in the building expected him to wake, let alone live through the week. With the intracranial bleeding and his brain swelling, they were amazed he hadn't died yet. Now, they figured he'd be nothing more than a vegetable for the rest of his life.

Chris had been sent to surgery and came out with twelve pins and two plates in his forearm. He stayed two nights and was sent home, only to return with repeated nose bleeds. They seemed to reappear every time he went to sleep for more than a half hour. The docs sent him home with directions for his mom to set up a humidifier and for him to keep his fingers out of his nose. Neither worked.

"I hate this thing," Wes said.

"Hey, you're alive." Jill gave him a *you-better-be-grateful* stare, one he'd see a thousand more times from her in the years to come.

"Yeah." He glanced over at his clock: 3:48 pm. She'd come over right after school. "How's Chrissy-boy doing? He still hasn't come by to say hi."

"He seems okay. Doesn't seem like he wants to talk to me. He practically runs when homeroom is over before I get a chance to get near him. I'm pretty sure he hates himself right now. I think he blames himself for everything."

"I tried calling him. His mom always says he's busy."

Jill nodded.

"Maybe he does feel bad. Any word on Tommy?"

"Nothing."

"Man..."

"Yeah. Good news is you guys are becoming legendary."

"Yeah? How so?"

"Someone started a rumor Chris's bone was replaced by titanium. People started calling him Robo-Boy. I can guess how that started; the cast he's wearing is huge."

"Ha, Robo-Boy. And me?"

"Oh, there's a rumor your entire leg's been amputated, and when you return, it'll be replaced with one from a dead guy."

"Like Frankenstein?"

"Yeah."

"No imagination—who's coming up with these?"

Without a word, Diana walked into the room and sat on the foot of Wes's bed. She leaned forward and clicked the television on, followed by the Super Nintendo.

"What're you doing?" Wes snapped.

The logo for Castlevania was drawn on the screen.

"What?" Di said.

"You just come in here and start playing?"

"They moved the Nintendo in here—what do you want me to do? I can't just stop playing because Mom and Dad think you're too precious to leave your room."

Wes rolled his eyes. "Well, turn it down at least."

"What? Then I'd have to listen to you and your girlfriend talk."

"Jill isn't my girlfriend." Wes looked at Jill, who quickly stood up. "What?"

"Nothing," Jill said. "I need to get home. Some of us have homework to get done before tomorrow." She didn't. Jill had finished it already, hoping to spend more time at Wes's. But now, after being reminded of his feelings—or lack thereof—she wasn't really encouraged to stick around.

"Oh. Okay."

Jill put the TMNT book down on the nightstand. "I'll see ya."

2

Jill stepped down from Wes's front porch, cursing herself for being so gullible. Just because she stopped by every day after school wasn't going to make him like her any more. It wasn't going to change the way he saw her. But, she knew that she would continue to do it. If nothing else, he was her friend, and she'd offer him that friendship.

She went left onto Spruce Street and walked for three blocks before turning right onto 4th Avenue. It was still the afternoon, but she could tell the days were shortening as they moved closer to Halloween. She hoped Wes's foot would be well by then.

Jill's thought's drifted to costumes, candy, and tricks. Last year she'd TPed Frank Roscoe's house with the help of Wes, Chris, and Tommy. The jerk had been bumping into her all week, pretending it was a mistake and putting his hands all over her ass and chest. After they left his house and

32

trees shrouded in white paper, he came back later that night and did the same to hers. But, he hadn't been a problem since summer, and now she wondered if there was a more deserving house to prank this year.

At the next street, Jill passed Trent Tires, and Ray Trent in the doorway. He leaned against the frame, one hand inside the shop, the other holding a cigarette. The chain hanging from his waist knocked against the frame as he shifted to see her better. His eyes went over Jill from top to bottom, his lip curling into a sneer.

Jill knew Ray by reputation alone. With him going to the high school and her to the elementary, they had no reason to interact. Still, though, in a small town like Custer Falls, the saying was true that everybody knew everybody. Whether it was from the city pool during the way too short summer, the mall, the movie theater, the church, or your mom's cousin's knitting circle, no one was unknown. As it happened, Jill heard about Ray through Mom's weekly beauty shop appointments more than anywhere else. Among the tidbits Mom brought home and conveyed to Dad was how Ray's mother ran off with a drifter, his father was a drunk, and Ray kept getting suspended for using his pocket knife to dig into school property. They caught him carving into a desk, and apparently thought he was to blame for the door to the principal's office, several seats in the bleachers, and the principal's car door. Jill had picked up most of this over dinners while her parents talked, and she was told to watch the television while they had "adult time."

As Ray stared at her now, she wondered what parts of the reports on Ray Trent were true and what had been exaggerated or even made up, knowing the type of gossip her mother's friends traded in.

A cold sensation traveled over Jill's body as if led by Ray's gaze. It was like the edge of an ice cube drawn across her flesh. She felt a shiver down her spine, and she walked faster.

Ray licked his lips and glanced inside the shop. His dad was balancing a tire, and he guessed that would keep Dad's attention for a while. He stepped away from the door, closing it softly behind him, and walked after Jill. He puffed on his cigarette and tossed it into the street for a silver Honda Civic to crush with a flowery puff of cinders.

Jill peeked back and saw him moving. Part of her wanted to paint a picture of coincidence. It said she should ignore him; he was just going for a walk too... She saw his eyes on her—no—she felt them. It was *not* a coincidence.

She walked faster and sensed Ray's steps behind her. There was an unseen radiation coming from him, a hazardous wave of something she couldn't name, but knew was bad. She sensed it as he got closer. It was like a dark essence creeping through the space between them, and it made no sense why she could feel it, but it pushed her forward. Why was he following her? What did he want?

That look he gave her, that stare—what was that about? She'd been stared at by boys, but this was different. It wasn't curiosity or that want she'd seen in Frank Roscoe's eyes when he was trying to touch her. It was... mean, somehow.

She searched ahead. Her street was still two blocks away; home, safety, it was too far. At the intersection, cars rushed by. She wanted to race through them, to dodge the cars like some madwoman and sprint home, but knew she didn't have the guts to do it. The second after imagining the feat, she saw herself getting bounced between vehicles like a ping pong ball and splattered across the roadway. She'd have to stop. And he'd catch up.

Jill reached the corner. Heat rushed through her veins. She clenched her fists and spun around to face him.

Ray stood inches from her, a grin across his face.

"Good afternoon, beautiful."

Jill's fists trembled. "What? What are you doing?"

"What do you mean, what am I doing? I'm taking a walk, same as you."

"You..."

"Can't someone take a walk?" Ray closed the gap between them. Inches squeezed down to nearly nothing.

Jill felt the wind as cars drove by behind her. She looked down at her feet. She stood on the edge of the pavement. Out of space. Nowhere to go. Another car, the engine noise, the wind. Her heart pounded.

"You know," Ray grabbed her arm, "you should really be more careful out here." He gripped it firmly. He drew her an inch forward and an inch back, using her arm to guide her like the strings of a puppet.

"Let—let go."

"I'm helping you. Don't you know how dangerous traffic can be?"

He pressed her toward the intersection. Her feet felt the edge of the sidewalk below them. A horn blew, and she grabbed his shirt.

His grin was without fault. He stared into her eyes. "What do you think would happen if I wasn't here and you walked off this curb, right into traffic."

Ray let her arm go and stepped back. Jill lost her balance. Her eyes shot wide. Her body fell backward into the road. She screamed. The world seemed to have lost its hold on time; she fell forever. She saw her mother looking over a body in the morgue, crying, the white body bag drenched in blood. She saw her father, a hand on Mom's shoulder, her aunt just beyond, shaking her head. The end was coming, a car's bumper to bash in her brains or a tire to squash her head. Her body stiffened into a rock.

Jill felt hard asphalt against her back. Her gaze spun to the oncoming cars. She didn't want to look, didn't want to see the thing that would take her life, but she had to. She saw a bumper, and it was still. She breathed and glanced up. The light was red. She climbed to her feet, shaking, and turned to yell at Ray Trent. He was a half block away, door closing as he stepped inside the tire shop.

3

Wes finished his dinner of pork chops and mac and cheese and picked up the SNES controller. He blasted away on Gradius for about an hour until Mom came in.

Betty Henson's brow sunk as she looked over her son. The pain of watching her boy injured and confined to bed made her stomach turn. She took his dinner plate downstairs and returned with Tylenol, his prescriptions, and a fresh glass of water.

Betty cleared her throat. "Take a break."

Wes looked up and saw his mom's serious face. He put down the controller. "Okay."

"Take this." She passed the pills and the water. "Di's going to bed now. I'll be back in fifteen minutes to tuck you in."

"Mom, I'm not five. You don't have to put me to bed." Wes's face wrinkled. He knew it was a pointless argument, but he had to put up a fight, or when this was all over, she might try to keep doing it. Ever since he came home from the hospital, she had been babying him. At bedtime, she'd sit with him and rub his back like she had done when he was little. He wouldn't admit that he liked it, no matter what court of law or game of truth or dare he would later be dragged into, but he did.

"I know, I know. But you're sick. Fifteen minutes."

"Okay." Wes had said his piece. He swallowed the pills and handed the glass back to his mother. Then he picked the controller back up.

Betty left the room and joined Diana in the bathroom. Di spat pink and blue toothpaste into the sink and smiled at her mother's reflection. She rinsed off her pink toothbrush and placed it upside-down in the Snoopy coffee cup on the back corner of the sink.

"All ready?" Betty asked.

"Yeah," Diana sighed. She flipped her dirty-blonde hair behind her shoulder and walked past Betty into her bedroom. She slid between her purple My Little Pony sheets, ones she already felt she had outgrown but loved too much to give away just yet. She laid her head on her pillow as the light went out, and Betty took a seat beside her.

"Ready?" Betty asked.

Diana rolled away from her mother, exposing her back to the delicate fingers of a back-rub professional.

Wes heard Mom through the walls. Not that she was being loud as she said the goodnight ritual, but the cadence and tone were the same every night. He didn't need to hear the words to know it was happening.

When Betty came back into Wes's room, he hit pause. She took the controller from Wes and turned off the television. She set the controller on his dresser between the TV and an object Wes didn't recognize.

"What's that?" Wes pointed to the rock. It was a little smaller than a baseball but gray and blue.

"You don't know?" Betty said. "It must have been in your jacket at the hospital. I was going through things and found it this morning."

"No, I don't know what it is. Can you hand it to me?"

"Under covers first." Betty stood and waited. Wes rolled his eyes and maneuvered his cast and then the rest of him between his sheets. She nodded and carried the rock to her son.

Wes extended his hand. "Okay?" His eyes followed as she placed the stone on his palm. A rush of lightheadedness filled Wes's brain. Tingles washed down his body. He looked at the stone, mesmerized by its color. The specs of blue seemed to have grown deeper since it was on the shelf. The layers of gray felt like an oversight, like they had been placed there by a fool, and if only Wes scraped them away, he'd see the full magnificence of this blue beauty. The stone, while he could not remember ever seeing it before, immediately felt personal, something of his and his alone. He needed to hold it close, to protect it.

"Okay, now give me that dirty thing," Betty said. She reached for it, and Wes moved his hand from hers. "Wes?"

Wes looked up at his mother, and after a second, he realized the expression on his face; he was caught in a sneer. He glanced around his room and felt like he had just returned from some other place. "What?"

"The rock," she said sternly.

"Oh, sorry." He held out the stone. She placed her hand underneath his, and his fingers were reluctant to release it. He shook his head, and the rock rolled into Betty's.

"Thank you." Betty placed the item back on his dresser and sat at the edge of the bed. She flipped the light off. "Okay?"

"Yeah." Wes faced away so Betty could reach his back.

She stroked his skin, avoiding the pink, tender areas of his wounds, and began the poem that she had repeated nearly every day to Wes or Diana or both since the day he was born:

> *It's been a long, wonderful day, and now it's time for sleep.*
> *Time to close our eyes and drift away and have sweet, sweet dreams*
> *Time to dream of dogs and cats and horses and cows*
> *Cars and trucks and bricks and blocks*
> *Princesses and faeries, rainbows and unicorns*
> *Dragons and dinosaurs, spaceships and astronauts*
> *And when you wake up, it'll be morning time*
> *Time to play, play, play all over again*
> *So close your eyes, drift away, and have sweet, sweet dreams*

Part Two: The Valley

Dogs and Cats, Horses and Cows

1

Wes walked through a field. It wasn't a field he had seen before, at least not one that he recognized, but an overwhelming sense of remembrance clung just out of reach, in the edges of his mind. The more he examined his surroundings, the more he was sure he had never been here, and the more he was sure he remembered it.

Tiny purple and red flower bunches tipped the foot-tall grasses. The green expanse stretched for a quarter-mile, and a forest lay beyond. Above the tops of far-away trees were the familiar peaks of mountains he couldn't place.

Wes gazed to his left and right. In the distance were the same trees and then mountains. He was at a low point in this place and envisioned himself at the bottom of a bowl.

"What a strange place." He knelt and examined the plants. Each floral bunch was smaller than his fingernail, containing a dozen blossoms; each individual flower held tight, like a pursing tulip, not quite ready to open.

"Where are we?" Di walked up behind Wes, her pajamas brushing their way through the grass.

"I don't know." Wes stood. "I've never been here before. You don't recognize it?"

Di frowned. "Duh—that's why I asked." But she *did* recognize it from a distant dream she wished she could remember.

Wes shook his head and looked at the sky. A dozen streaks of clouds converged in a single direction. "Look at that." He gestured up. "It's like the clouds are pointing that way."

"That's weird."

"I wonder what's over there."

Barking dogs echoed over the field from the direction the clouds pointed. There were deep, large dog bellows and high-pitched, small dog chirps. There were medium-pitched barks in the middle. Wes noted that even among the dozens, if not hundreds, of animal sounds, they felt to him like happy noises. While he didn't speak the language of dog, he concluded they weren't aggressive or angry. They sounded playful.

Wes and Di shared a glance, then focused into the woods.

"That's a lot of dogs," Di said.

Fifty feet away, a dark fissure formed in the sea of grasses. It made a line from the barking toward Wes and Di. Leaves spread apart. Flower bunches danced on their tips. The line moved closer.

"What is that?" Di took a half-step backward.

"I don't know."

Di's eyes narrowed. She thought of a shark racing through the water, and part of her expected a fin to surface above the vegetation.

It got closer, maybe thirty feet; twenty.

Wes stepped between Di and whatever was approaching. He felt his heart rate rise.

Ten feet. Footfalls overlaid one another, the sound climbing over the wind's whisper to that of a stampede.

"I'm sure it's fine," Wes said, not knowing if he was trying to calm Di or himself. Something was coming at them, and the feeling inside him was a strange clash between excitement and panic. The ground shook, and bass vibrated his legs. He braced his knees and held his hands in front of his chest, readying himself to respond to the oncoming mystery.

A flash of tan and gold burst through the grass. One, then another, then a third. They raced around Wes's legs, circling him and Di. They sniffed and bounced, tripped and rolled over each other. Floppy ears and wet black noses. Soft fur and swollen bellies.

"Aww," Di squeaked. "They're puppies!" She squatted and reached for the closest dog, one of three golden retriever pups, no more than nine weeks old.

The pup barked at its sister and jumped, missing its target and rolling onto its back. Di rubbed its little belly. It sniffed and licked her hand, rolled upright, and continued the chase. The three dogs circled around Wes and Di and scampered back into the grass, back toward the way they had come. Back toward the rest of the barking. Into the direction the clouds were pointing.

"Huh," Wes mumbled. "That was... interesting."

Di set off, following the pups.

Wes took another look around the lonely meadow. The trees, the grass, the mountains in every direction—other than that suggested by the clouds—seemed darker, uninviting. It was as if life in those other places was fading, and he was being pushed to follow his sister. He took a step after her, and the world brightened. He took another, and there was a gentile pressure on his back, urging him forward.

Okay. He followed Di, and with every subsequent pace, felt better. And so, he continued.

The ground beneath Wes's feet was soft, strangely soft, like walking on a bed. The sky beyond the clouds glimmered as his gaze moved from the mountain to the trees. A sense of gentle weight fell about his thoughts, and it occurred to him that this was a dream. That was why he was in this place he didn't recognize, why he felt no danger in a completely unknown location, and why every puppy in it could be silly and loving, and his sister... Di felt unusually real. Often in his dreams, she was either exceedingly harsh or overly compliant. This snarky person walking ahead of him was neither of those. That was a new thing, and he held the thought above the others to examine when he had a chance.

At the edge of the forest, Wes looked up into the trees. They resembled the spruces that lived on the hills behind his house, only these were a darker, deeper green. The closer he moved under their boughs, the higher their tops seemed to reach, climbing up and up toward the sky; and the more gloom seemed to envelop their branches.

Wes paused, watching the massive entities gently sway in time, in a slow dance, only Wes was ignorant of the beat. He got the sensation that someone was up there, someone with their gaze pointing back down upon him.

Wes stared harder, squinting, determined to spot the stranger, if there was such a being up there. The more he scanned, the more he was sure. Someone *was* up there. He could sense their glare on him. It was a cold, calculating glare, seeping into Wes's skin and gliding over his body, painting him with chills.

"Come on." Di grabbed Wes's shoulder and gave him a shake. "You have to see this." Her voice was all smiles.

Wes turned to his sister, his finger pointing upward. "There's—" He stopped as he saw her back. She was dragging him through the forest again.

"Come on!" Di shouted.

A crack echoed downward. Branches creaked.

"Wait." Wes glanced up one last time and hurried after his sister.

2

Diana ran along the trail, her pajamas brushing against the limbs of saplings. She heard them ahead, the big, the small, the puppies of all sizes.

A rare smile was glued to her face. As she stepped into the small clearing, a squeak of glee escaped her widening lips.

In a gap between trees, no wider than thirty or forty feet, there was a small cottage. Its whitewashed walls and thatched roof reminded Diana of a storybook she had read a thousand times, about a princess who had gotten lost in the woods, only to be found by forest creatures and given a place to live. The sight of the small cottage gave her almost as much joy as what was bounding in and out of its door: dozens of the cutest puppies she had ever seen.

There were breeds of all kinds, some she knew well, and some she had only *seen* before. Golden retrievers, yellow, black, and chocolate labs, poodles, shepherds, schnauzers, sheep dogs, cattle dogs, and mutts; they bounded over one another in every direction. They rushed in the door and out again. They circled the cottage, barking and chasing and playing.

To the right of the cottage was a small corral with a pair of horses. One was tall and black and majestic, his head aloof as he wandered from one side to the other. The second was a brown mare, who leaned over the fence and whinnied at Di to come closer.

To the right of the corral was a barn, and from within its closed half-door, a pair of moos issued.

Wes entered the clearing, a half-smile on his face. He eyed Di as she bent down between the cottage and corral to pet a German Shepherd. "Di, Wait."

Her hand was out in front. It sniffed her palm and licked it. She wasn't sure why, but she asked, "Virb?" It wasn't him—an image of a beloved pet was cemented yet distant—but in her mind, she saw a black and tan pup that would forever live in her heart.

The dog jumped forward and licked her face. She tumbled backward onto the soft grass, and the shepherd stood over her, licking and licking.

"Stop, stop," Di giggled. Dozens of others crowded around, licking and crawling over her chest, arms, and legs.

When Wes reached her, Di was climbing to her feet. "What was that?" he asked.

"Just puppies." She grinned and took a step toward the cabin. "Let's see inside." The mare whinnied again, and Di faced it. "I'm sorry, did I forget you?" She walked to the fence, and the mare sniffed the air as she approached. Di held out her hand, and the mare pressed her face against Di's palm, and Di scratched her chin. "That's a good girl. I wish I had—"

She reached into her pocket and found a pair of peppermint balls. She held one out, and the mare lipped it from her palm and chomped into it. The stallion trotted over and sniffed, and she fed one to him and stroked his neck.

Puppies tugged on Di's pajama pants, pulling her away from the horses. "Okay, okay." She turned and faced the cabin.

Dogs ran in and out, and through a crack in the door, she saw a warm glow and knew there was a gentle fire inside. She waded through the sea of dogs running inside and out with only a single one staying nearby, the one she had mistaken for Virb. When she reached the interior, she found a storybook home, just as she had pictured. A stone fireplace, a wood stove, soup or something in a pot on the top, and a hay-filled loft up above.

The loft was dim, the firelight barely reaching, and as she examined it, something seemed to move. "What is that?" Di wondered.

Wes joined her and followed her eyes up. He squinted, trying to make out the movement.

"I'm going to check it out," Di said. She grabbed the wooden ladder that led upward, and the puppy yipped. Di glanced at him. He was urging her toward the loft.

Di put one foot over the other and began her way up.

Wes crossed the cottage and held the sides of the ladder. "Careful, okay?"

"Yeah, yeah," she mocked. "Since when are you careful in *your* dreams?"

Wes thought to himself, *But this* is my *dream.*

Di reached the top of the ladder. She saw nothing but bales of hay and a hook for moving them around. She stepped off the ladder, and a flash of movement caught her eye. Something orange darted across the bales and under the one in front of her. She kneeled to look.

"Di?" Wes called from the bottom of the ladder.

"Yeah, yeah," Di repeated. She leaned closer toward a gap between two bales and spotted something shining from inside. "Who are you?"

The glimmer darted toward Diana. She jerked back, trying to get out of the way. She tripped and plopped down on her butt as a dozen kittens pounced on her chest.

Di squealed as soft fur rubbed against her, and tiny creatures purred. The puppy barked, and each little thing bore their claws and dug in. A thousand tiny needles shot into Di's hands, arms, and legs. Sharp, then burning, the pain tore from her wounds through her nerves. Her entire body shrieked. She swore she was on fire.

Di screamed and jumped to her feet. The kittens held on, yowling and whining. Blood ran down her arms, legs, and waist.

Wes raced up the ladder. "Di!" He reached the top as she grabbed for the rail and swung herself on.

Di's legs and Wes's arms fumbled over one another. The ladder wobbled and cracked. They both lost their grip and dropped to the cottage floor.

1992

1

The two streetlights in town threatened to quit for the day as golden rays crept over the top of the drugstore and Kelsy's Market.

Officer Dale Harrison parked along 4th Avenue beside the south entrance to the park. He glanced over at the pond and didn't see anything unusual. Then, there it was. A strange, oblong shape floated in the water near the other side. He couldn't believe the call that came in, that there was a body in the pond, but as he studied it now, it did look like something was bobbing over there.

Harrison got out of the cruiser, leaving the keys in the ignition and the engine running. This wasn't going to take long; it had to be a bag of trash that had blown into the pond from a strong wind. Or one of the bums left their sleeping bag unattended while they got drunk in the alley behind the market. As soon as he got over there and verified what it wasn't, Harrison would be back on his way.

The officer lifted his pants by his belt and let them settle below his belly's overhang. He checked his watch one more time, 6:55 am, and he headed into the park.

Dew hung delicately from the neatly-mowed grass. A light breeze carried the scent of lilac from the bushes near the amphitheater. Harrison thought of his wife as the smell registered; she had a perfume that smelled similar, and she even forced him to plant lilacs in the back garden a few springs ago. They had all died, something about over-fertilizing them. Carol decided that year that perfume was a much better use of her effort.

Harrison studied the floating shape as he moved closer. It was black and billowing but not quite as shiny as he'd expect a wet trash bag to be. He reached the edge of the water. The object was four feet inside, too far to grab from the bank.

The pond was only two feet deep; Harrison knew that from experience. A few summers back, he had to pull out a pair of hopped-up teenagers. The shrooms or mescaline, or whatever the hell they were on, made them think the tiny pond was the ocean, and it was MTV Spring Break 1989. A couple of good belts to the gut and several hours in a cell broke them of that delusion. But Harrison wasn't about to climb in there this time.

He went searching in the trees nearby and snapped off a near-dead pine branch. He carried it back to the bank and reached. Long enough. He poked at the object. It rocked in the water. It was slow and stiffer than he expected. Not plastic. Chills began to sink into Harrison's calm demeanor. He was not going to be happy with this outcome. He knew it.

He stretched a little further and hooked the object, pulled it closer to shore. As it came within reach, Harrison was washed with cold regret. Why did he take this call and come out here? He could have radioed it in as a hoax from the car. But now, there was no turning back.

The park brightened as the rising sun fully crested the market, and Harrison saw spindly legs attached to the floating thing.

"Shit."

The pond sloshed. Harrison held onto the slimmest of hopes that this was a mannequin in a suit, a blowup doll, some kind of early Halloween prank. He grabbed the side of the thing and flipped it over. Water splashed him in the face, and it stank of rotten meat. He wiped his eyes, his cheeks, and his nose and looked down.

A cavernous depression filled the face of what could only have been Sam the bum. The balding hairline, the slender frame, and the American flag pin on his collar were enough to identify him. No one knew his last name, not even the folks at the shelter he frequented during winter. People figured *he* didn't even remember. Now it didn't matter. His face sloped inward from his forehead to his lower jaw, from cheekbone to cheekbone. Bone shards poked through paper-thin skin and pulpy muscle. The eyes were unrecognizable. His lower jaw was unaltered; it hung like a ventriloquist dummy's, waiting for a hand to command it into action.

Harrison jerked his head to the side and puked two eggs and a slice of toast.

2

Chris awoke with sharp pains in his arm. It felt like the screws were turning inside his bones. His breathing was heavy, his head sweaty. He groaned and lifted the cast. There was nothing to see but plaster, only his arm bent at a semi-permanent right angle.

"Shit." He rested his cast and reached over his head with his good arm to the boom box on the shelf above him. He felt along the tape player's buttons, counting as his fingers passed the gaps between chunky plastic, and pressed *Play*, letting loose a blaring onslaught of Lee, Lifeson, and Peart. His heart jumped into his throat. Chris smacked at the radio until he found the volume knob and franticly cranked it down.

He exhaled and stared at his door for several seconds. No Mom. With her cancer only seeming to escalate despite the treatments, the last thing he wanted was to bug her. And thankfully, no Dad either, though he was probably passed out drunk.

Chris's arm-ache returned, and he wished he were still dreaming. At least in his dreams, his arm didn't hurt. It wasn't broken, and it worked just fine. But he didn't understand why Mr. Wimbley, the music teacher, was there.

He worked to summon the details of his dream as Rush played on in meticulous intricacy. He knew he'd been in detention, but instead of the lunchroom, it was being held in the band room. Wimbley circled the perimeter, a flute in his hands, and every few steps, he smacked a kid in the head.

It wasn't that the flute hurt—it did, but it wasn't that bad—the irritating part was that Wimbley flicked his wrist, and it snapped the end of the thing into Chris's skull like a whip. The pop of brass against his head rang from his dome to his jaw with a clang.

Wimbley circled. Whip, clang. Another kid, whip, clang. And on until he was behind Chris once again.

Chris felt the air parting, making way for the strike. His head was hot, sensing the torturous impact. His conscience told him to be still, that this was detention, after all. He was supposed to take his punishment. The rage building inside him said otherwise. It said he didn't have to put up with this shit. Corporal punishment was supposed to have ended in the seventies or something.

He spun, imagining himself as Frank Castle, The Punisher, ready to lay down some punishment of his own. This guy was breaking the rules, even if the kids had done so first. He snatched the flute mid-swing and yanked it away from the bald old geezer. He grabbed Wimbley by his silly blue vest and heard the weirdest whisper in his ear: *"Do it."*

Why the hell not?

Chris raised the brass instrument over his head and plunged it downward. There were wet crunches and gurgling gasps. He pushed and shoved and smashed the thing deeper and deeper into the old man's throat. There was warmth on his fingers. Wet, thick, slippery liquid. It had bubbled up from Wimbley, over his tongue, teeth, and lips as the teacher convulsed and shuffled backward. The geezer tripped over his own feet, slamming into the cinderblock wall. His head cracked, and a line of red followed him to the linoleum floor.

Then he awoke.

"Damn." Chris's fingers tapped at his sheets. "That was gnarly." The images of blood cycled through his mind.

His gaze searched the room, wishing Mom hadn't found his stash the other day. As sick as she was, she was still insistent on being there as an active parent, no matter how exhausted she might be. Chris respected that. It hurt; it twisted his guts every time he thought about how hard she was trying; there was pain in ways he didn't know were possible without being slugged. But he could really go for a hit of weed after a dream like that. Even just a cigarette to calm his nerves... The sock drawer only held socks now. Even his *special* sock had been emptied. Maybe tomorrow he'd get ahold of Stony and start a new stash out in the garage. She'd never find it there.

3

The rest of Wes's night had been without dreams. He'd closed his eyes and slept, but it was empty.

Di's had been the same. She rolled back and forth in her bed, waking and nodding off, but the rest was without a dream.

By the time dawn broke, Wes was back at work in Gradius, having forgotten about the strange scratches that he found on his legs. He heard Di using the bathroom ten minutes before her alarm buzzed and wondered if her night was as weird as his.

4

Gennie Lawrence, widow, once-mother, now grandmother-guardian of Edward Lawrence, dropped a pair of bread slices into the toaster, then poured a cup of orange juice. She went to the stove and scraped the pan of scrambled eggs onto a white plate and set the plate beside the toaster.

She glanced at the clock hanging over the kitchen table. Hands hovered over a proud black rooster, stating 7:10.

"That boy better bring his ass."

The toaster clicked, sprang, and clanked, and two slices jumped into the air. She snatched them and set them on the plate beside the eggs. After putting the plate and juice on the kitchen table, Gennie walked through the dining room and looked up the stairway. Neither the landing nor the stairs above held ten-year-old Edward Lawrence, and she ground her teeth together.

"Eddy!" Gennie scowled. "You better get down here if you want some of this breakfast before the bus comes."

"Coming, Gramma!" Eddy's muffled voice echoed from inside the upstairs bathroom.

Gennie shook her head. The boy was starting to take as long in the bathroom as a teenager, and she dreaded the mess that would be there when she went up later to clean.

She walked slowly back through the dining room, her eyes sweeping over the myriad pictures on the server and the walls above it. Pictures of her late husband, Herbert. Pictures of her wedding day, faded, the grimace of her father at Herbert's father. Pictures of Francine at thirteen—after her new and shapely body had started to get her noticed by the boys, but before she met that hooligan, Ty Porter, who would father Eddy and lead Francine into the gutter. Gennie sighed and touched her sweet baby's picture on the cheek.

She whispered, "Goddamn whore," and walked into the kitchen.

Less than a minute later, Eddy galloped down the stairs and plopped into his seat at the kitchen table. "Aw, eggs?" He pouted at his grandmother, making sure she could see the bright red T-shaped birthmark on his left cheek. She called it his mark of shame, claiming it was from his mother's drugs.

"You want to start picking what you get for breakfast, you can start getting downstairs at a reasonable time. It's been over thirty minutes since your alarm went off."

Eddy bit his lip. He knew he'd taken a long time to get downstairs, but he couldn't help it. The box called to him. From under the foot of his bed, it sang to him, the same sweet song he'd heard growing louder over the past week. The song in the alley behind school, in the neighbor's backyard, in the basement with Bobo, the Siamese. It had called to him, to come and study his treasures.

Eddy couldn't defend his tardiness with what he had actually been doing. Gramma might take away his box. Sure, he could make a new one, replace the contents, but he liked his treasures. He'd earned them through his own hard work and exploration. And each drop of blood was like a fingerprint—he couldn't possibly recreate those.

"I'm sorry, Gramma. I'll try to do better." He gave her the smile that usually lifted her sour lips. That was a show, a thing she did to placate him, as much as his smile was meant to satisfy her. She'd play the doting grandmother; he'd play the shy, respectful youth. It was nearly as much of a game as his experiments, but these were the roles they'd fallen into. It worked... most of the time.

Gennie closed her eyes and clicked her lips apart. "I'll make you something better tomorrow. Now, eat your eggs." She knew what the boy wanted: syrup-soaked waffles. She could have made them this morning, but the child needed to know that he did not control this house. As much as Gennie hated the boy and what he stood for, for being half that slime-sucking shitheel that poisoned her daughter, she also loved him. Tomorrow he'd get his syrup, and also a healthy dose of laxative for her trouble.

5

Chris climbed down his bus's stairs, careful not to slam his cast into the door. The line of kids behind him was quiet, as were the throngs ahead as they funneled into the school's brick entrance.

The lack of noise struck Chris as strange. Of course, there was talking, some goofing off, but what he heard was a muted landscape compared to any other day.

Chris stood on the sidewalk, watching the others. Their faces were drawn, tired, dazed. It occurred to him that he may look just as bad after his battle with sleep last night.

Classrooms filled, and Chris found himself in a homeroom of blank stares and kids with their heads on their desks. Holes in the usual seating assignments were broad, with quite a few empty desks.

Chris spotted Jill in the corner, who gave him her typical good morning smile. It was tired, but genuine—on the surface, at least. He looked away. She may have been smiling, but below it, he felt hate. He felt anger and blame. Sure, he deserved it, but, shit, he didn't have to look it in the face.

Mr. Jones entered the classroom, his half-tucked shirt hanging from his pants. He set his brown, scuffed-on-every-surface briefcase on his desk and waved at the class.

"Good morning, all," the teacher squeaked. He turned and waddled back toward the door. "I'll be right back. Keep your seats."

Chris's gaze passed over the room again, settling on Alison Steiner. It wasn't her breasts that caught his attention this morning, though; it was her eyes. Their almost glowing redness was stark against her pale face. And she wasn't wearing anything like her usual tight-fitting tops. Instead, she wore a sizable baggy hoodie. Its deep black beside her white skin made Chris wonder if she was thinking of going goth.

Todd Hertz leaned into view on the opposite side of Alison. His sneer was classic Todd, beaming from his high and tight haircut down to his Polo and khakis. His dad was a lawyer and a member of the only private country club in Custer Falls. While Todd's mantra used to be 'My dad will sue you,' after the start of sixth grade, he found other preppy kids to jerk off with, and the cult motto became group beatings of any non-prep they deemed worthy that day.

Chris flipped Todd the bird and turned back to the front.

The bell rang, and Mr. Jones returned, his shirt tail flapping in the same half-tucked laziness, but now he held a large mug of coffee. He took a seat at his desk and closed his eyes. After a long, deep breath, he opened them and guzzled from his mug.

"All right, everyone," old Jimbo said, "a few announcements for today."

The kids whose eyes were open glanced forward. Chris ran his fingers along his cast. The ache in his arm pulsed. Visions of blood flashed in his thoughts. *Do it...*

"It looks like Mr. Wimbley is out sick—if you're scheduled for music today, go instead to Study Hall. Also, there'll be an assembly during fifth period." The teacher paused and drank his coffee.

"What's the assembly about?" little Charlotte Baker asked from the front row. Her mousy eyes were bright behind her round glasses, not at all like the rest of the class.

"I don't know, Charlotte," Jimbo grumbled. He pulled the morning paper from his briefcase and unfolded it on his desk. "I guess we'll have to show up to find out."

As the teacher flipped through the newsprint, Chris caught a single headline: *Freak Explosion Seals Bloodtooth Caverns.*

6

Ranger Barton Smith leaned against a pale green F150 as he watched the Montana Fish, Wildlife & Parks investigators inspect the rubble around the cavern's main entrance. He'd been called at four in the morning and told about the explosions, though he took as long as he could to wash the dust and rubble from his hands and face before traveling down to the site.

He wanted to smirk, to enjoy the sight of them bumbling around, but he held his face in an expression of depressed awe. He may have gotten zero sleep last night, but he wasn't going to let it show.

Horace, his partner, ambled over and leaned on the pickup next to Bart. He shook his head. "Goddamn shame."

"Got that right." Pure bullshit. The only thing Bart was going to miss about those damn caves was watching the kids walk by in a line where he could lean back and enjoy the show. But he'd learned that the mall had become just as good for that. He'd even found a few of his favorites there, a few special young ladies that would soon make his acquaintance.

"It was a wonder of nature," Horace said. "They'll have to clear it out."

Bart nodded. "You think they will?"

"Shit. It may take a year and a million bucks, but yeah. They'll get it open again, eventually."

"I guess they will."

"Yeah."

Bart stared off into the surrounding woods. "Have they figured out what happened yet?"

"Nope. Someone said trapped methane, another said dynamite—but it had to be intentional; both the front and back entrances were caved in.

Who the hell would go through the trouble of dynamiting a cavern in the middle of the night?"

"That is a weird one." Bart smiled, thinking of the so-called experts. Both of their guesses were wrong. It was fertilizer. "I don't know."

"*Do it.*" The whispers from last night echoed in his ears. He would get all the little ass he wanted while on leave. They'd be ripe for the picking.

2022

1

Wes opened his eyes to the sight of the living room ceiling and the sounds of Samantha and Lisa giggling to Bugs Bunny's version of *The Barber of Seville*. It delighted Wes that they enjoyed this thing he had shared with them, especially with the flood of programming bombarding them from Hulu Kids, Netflix Kids, YouTube Kids, Disney+, and on and on. It may have been old-fashioned, but his old Loony Tunes DVD made them crack up every time. And the sound was music to his ears.

Wes lowered the recliner's footrest, and Jill came up from behind him, a cup of coffee in hand.

"One of those nights, huh?" She offered the cup. She was wearing her blue and black pinstriped suit. It meant she had showings today.

"Yeah." He took the offering and sniffed at the mug. "Early meeting?"

She spun around and grabbed her keys from the counter. Her bag was already on her shoulder. "The Thompsons. Hopefully, today they put their money where their finicky little mouths are and make the offer. That 6th Avenue house isn't going to stay on the market much longer." She leaned into Wes and kissed him on the lips. "See you later."

Sam and Lisa barely noticed as the door into the garage slammed shut. Sam-I-Am looked up at Wes expectantly. It was time for his breakfast.

Wes took his coffee into the kitchen and sipped. He glanced again at his daughters. Both were dressed and ready for school. They laughed and rocked in their seats, and he was struck with a bittersweet memory of himself and Di doing the same so many years ago. He shook it away and drank from his mug. The microwave said 7:35.

"Guys." Wes opened the pantry and grabbed a can of dog food. "Get shoes on. We leave in five minutes."

Ten minutes later, Wes, Sam, Lisa, and Sam-I-Am climbed into Wes's old Excursion. He started the engine and headed down the hill, hoping they had not missed the bus, but pretty sure they had. At the end of the street, the stop sign was abandoned. The neighbor kids, who he always forgot the names of, were nowhere to be seen. They'd missed it.

"Oh well," Wes said. "I guess you guys are walking today."

"Da-*ad*," Sam said.

"You have to drive us," Lisa said.

"Only if I get to stop for a donut," Wes said.

"Oo—oo, sprinkles," Sam said.

"Chocolate glazed for me!" Lisa said.

Wes headed north, around the state land that separated their street from Custer Falls proper and into the north side of town. He went through the drive-thru at Donut King, a Dunkin' Donuts clone that had popped up a year after the local franchise had shut its doors. Chain restaurants of any kind never lasted in Custer Falls. It was a mom-and-pop first kind of town. It made the place seem quaint, not having any of the familiar names a traveler may recognize, but it also meant more of their money stayed in town, or so they hoped.

With a sprinkled, a chocolate glazed, a regular glazed for Wes, and a plain cake for Sam-I-Am, the Hensons pulled into the school parking lot. Once nothing but crumbs were left, Wes collected kisses from the girls and sent them inside. He watched them walk through the front door of North Custer Elementary with a smile on his face. He glanced over at the drop-off lane, and a chill wiped it away. It was a feeling he'd only had a few times in his life, one that marked the end of one era and the start of another.

A pale green pickup pulled up to the curb, and Wes froze. He told himself it couldn't be the same one—the State had hundreds of those pickups in the nineties, and once they were done with them, they were auctioned off. Just as Barton Smith's had been. The odds of it being the same truck were astronomical. And Barton was dead. But just as Smith's vehicle had chilled Wes to the bone, this one did right now.

Wes leaned forward in his seat. He squinted, trying to get a better look at the driver. It was someone younger than himself, with short brown hair. If it was Barton, he had been reanimated and de-aged. But there was still something familiar with the man's movements.

The pickup's passenger door opened, and a girl got out. She must have been in Sam's grade; she looked nine—ten at the oldest. But Wes thought he knew every kid in her class.

The child closed the door, and the green vehicle sputtered down the row of parked cars to the exit. It pulled onto the street, and the girl vanished inside.

It definitely wasn't Barton Smith. But the chill refused to dissipate.

2

Joanne Higgins sat behind the North Custer Falls Elementary School's attendance desk. She sipped her coffee and nibbled a cheese danish as dozens of children walked past.

It was getting closer to winter, and Joanne was noticing the uptick in kids wearing coats as opposed to sweatshirts. In Montana, it was always getting close to winter unless it was June and winter had just ended. By July, everyone would start up again. Winter's coming.

The sight brought to mind a puffy purple jacket she had owned as a child and the trip to Georgetown Lake with her dad that she wished she hadn't taken. She could have said no when Dad asked her if she wanted to go ice fishing with him, but she was a daddy's girl. Any excuse to spend a few extra minutes with Dad was something she was going to take.

They had breakfast in Anaconda at some small café—she didn't remember the name, nor had she ever had the urge to go back. They chatted in Dad's pickup as he pregamed with half a six-pack between breakfast and the lake. They went out onto the ice, and it didn't even occur to Jo at the time that they were completely alone.

She hadn't been ice fishing too many times, but when she went, there were always people scattered across the lake. It was such a bizarre sight that each time the surreal nature of standing over water stuck in her mind. You weren't supposed to stand on water; you were supposed to sink. So when she walked above what must have been tens, maybe even hundreds of feet of lake water, it gave her heart a flutter.

He carried the auger and a small cooler, and she had a pole and tackle box. He picked the spot and set the auger on the ice. He popped open a beer and drank, and Jo set down the tackle and sat on it as she'd done in the past.

Wind blew across the lake, and snow swirled in the air. He put down his beer and readied the auger. The back of Jo's neck prickled with the blind knowing that something just wasn't right.

Dad had barely touched the steel tip to the ice when a series of cracks burst into a spiderweb beneath him. Jo had a brief thought of how pretty the pattern was before terror gripped her, and Dad dropped into the icy violet depths.

There had been no struggle after he fell. He didn't reach out and try to claw back to the surface. He was just gone. When the police recovered his body in the spring, most of his flesh having been eaten by the lake's fish (the same fish caught, taken home, and consumed by dozens of fisherman throughout the winter), they suggested he died instantly, the cold water stopping his heart, and the weight of the auger dragging him down, so that when he floated back up, he was no longer aligned with the hole he had fallen through. They said it was too early to be on the lake that year, that any ice fisherman should have known better.

Like the café in Anaconda, Joanne had never returned to Georgetown Lake. She never wanted to wear her puffy purple jacket again either, but once Dad was gone, they couldn't afford a new one that winter. So each time she stepped into the cold, the wind against the rippling fabric of her hated coat, she relived her screams and the hours of lonely fear as she prayed for Dad to resurface.

Joanne sighed and sipped her coffee. She shuffled the papers on her desk and forced a smile. Shoes squeaked against the polished floor, peaking over the dull roar of children's conversations.

A girl, later to be identified as Julie Redmond, came through the double-doored entrance. She wore a light red jacket, and her auburn hair was restrained with a braid that draped down her back. Instead of walking down the hall toward a classroom, Julie gleefully trotted up to the attendance counter.

Joanne swallowed her last bite of danish and quickly washed it down with a sip of coffee. "Hello, sweetie," she greeted the child. "Do you need help?"

Julie looked around the desk and pointed to a plaque that read, *Joanne Higgins, Office Manager.*

"What is it?" Joanne wondered if the girl could talk.

"Is that you?" Julie said. "Joanne?"

Joanne glanced at the plaque. "Yes. Though it's polite to call adults *mister* and *misses*."

Julie Redmond quietly slipped her hands into her jacket pockets, closed her eyes, and collapsed to the hard floor.

Joanne frowned, the image of her father sinking into the lake dangling in her mind. She mustered the strength to speak, "Sweetie?"

The girl didn't move. The flow of incoming kids slowed and then stopped, their eyes falling on Julie. The din of young voices quieted.

"Sweetie?" Joanne repeated.

Kids pointed. Little Billy Laramie's mouth gaped open. Daria Sparrow pointed and whispered to her bestie, Debbie Carlson.

"Shit," Joanne hissed. Just her luck to have a kid faint on the way in. She jumped up and ran to the office door. *The kid probably hit her head on that damned hard floor. Watch, I'll probably get blamed if she has a concussion.*

Joanne rushed around the corner and shooed away a wave of encroaching children.

"Back! Back!" Joanne demanded at the growing crowd. "Give her air." She waved her arms outward and sunk to her knees, leaning over the girl. "Sweetie?"

Julie's eyes were closed. Her breathing was steady.

Joanne touched her face. "Little girl?"

Julie's eyes shot open and found Joanne. Her hands backed out of her pockets, each holding something black. Her thumbs flipped at the objects in her grips, and five-inch black blades popped out of them both.

Joanne looked down, questioning what she was seeing. Surely, those weren't what they looked like. They had to be toys. Something made to resemble the real thing and look scary.

Julie Redmond swung her arms around Joanne's sides as if she were giving the woman a great big hug.

Joanne wanted to smile. She loved hugs from the school's children. It was like they were her own kids in many ways. But a burning sensation found its way onto her back. Two of them. The feeling moved toward her front, followed by wetness. It flowed under her ribs to her chest. She looked down from Julie's eyes and saw the child's small hands covered in blood.

Little Billy Laramie screamed. Daria Sparrow and Debbie Carlson howled. Half the gathered children joined, shrieking. The other half turned and ran.

Julie Redmond slid her blades free from Joanne's belly. She wore a curious smirk, and for a second, Joanne wondered what kind of joke she was missing out on.

As Joanne's expression rotated from shock to one of realization, Julie Redmond plunged one knife into each of the adult's eyes.

3

Edward Lawrence unconsciously stroked the birthmark on his cheek. He was alive. The years had gone by like a blur of tedium, only for him to wake up in what was now a crystal clear reality. He couldn't explain it if he tried—the closest he could come was that for a brief moment, his childhood world had evolved into a brightly lit utopia, and then, for some unknown reason, the lights went out. But now, they were back on and brighter than ever. The last six months had been like heaven. And the whispers told him it was only going to get better.

Why shouldn't it? Six months ago, he was bored day and night. Then they returned. The hunger returned. The blood, the hikers, knowing just where to find them. The whispers were always right. And then, last night's gift. All he had to do was open the door to the lost woman and her daughter, a gift from the whispers. He let them in to use the phone, and then the party started.

Ed was surprised at how much fun the little girl was. She jumped right in and got her hands dirty like an eager young apprentice. The blood, the screaming, she had giggled as much as he had as they sliced her mother and put her in a suitable place. The whispers said she would understand him. Again, they were always right.

Ed had dropped off the old green pickup and was now in his work van. The words *Walter P. Palmer & Son Extermination* were printed on all four sides of the vehicle. Ed didn't think there was a Walter and knew there wasn't a son. He was told it was supposed to be an old-fashioned name to inspire customer confidence. He had only been asked once if he had ever met Walter, to which he replied, "Yes, he's a great guy," as he had been trained to.

He didn't want to work; he wanted to bask in thoughts of what Julie was doing, seeing, feeling, but now, it was time to commit to the drudgery of the day job. So far, the whispers hadn't helped him pay the bills, other than the little bits of cash he was able to pull from their playmates' wallets. The job was a necessary evil, for now.

The radio was going, a classical station. The music wasn't his favorite, but it helped to settle his nerves as he prepared himself. The years that should have been nurturing and teaching him to deal with life and society had been exchanged for abusive foster homes and diddling guidance counselors. He'd learned to shut off what emotions he'd had other than the rage at his mother and father for being such garbage human beings. But the deactivation of his emotions later became a problem when he had to deal with customers—it was like they sensed his disconnectedness. The music helped him to prepare to act, to put on a smile that most people would believe and a charm that most of them fell for.

A second benefit of the classical station was the news. Every half-hour, there was a news report, and as soon as it became public, he'd get to hear how Julie's adventure went. He was sure he'd get each and every wet and sticky detail, later on, from the whispers or Julie herself, but he was eager for some crumb of it right now.

At 8:59 am, Ed pulled up in front of his first job. He could do it quickly, a spray around the home's exterior, then he'd be off to the real work of the day. He took a breath and listened, confident this news cycle would be the one. And it was.

"This just in," Clark Meyers, the station's anchor, announced, "tragedy has struck in North Custer Falls. Police report that a murder has taken place at the North Custer Falls Elementary School. We are being told no children were harmed, but the school has been put into lockdown, and a search is underway for the assailant."

Ed's face was swallowed by a grin. He slapped his hands together and jumped in his seat. "Good job, girl!"

4

Wes reached the top of the hill and turned down his driveway. A cold chill ran through him as he noticed a vehicle in front of his home. It was one he'd seen around town before, an exterminator. But why was there an exterminator here? He hadn't called one—couldn't remember Jill mentioning a need for one. Maybe they had the wrong house?

He parked in his usual spot between the garage and the front door. As he got out of the Excursion, Wes looked into the driver's seat of the foreign vehicle. It was empty. Beyond a pen sitting on the passenger seat, it was impeccably clean. Where was the exterminator?

"Hello?" he called to nowhere in particular. The other side of the van, the side of the house, the trees in the back, anywhere this ghost of an exterminator may be.

No answer.

Wes headed to the front door. His keys jingled in his hand as he stepped on the porch. He reached out for the knob and saw the door was cracked—not much, barely enough to see the strike plate's hollow. The hairs on Wes's neck stood up. The chills returned. Was the exterminator *inside* his house? A spike of anger ran through him.

Wes reached for his right side, his belt, where he often clipped a pocket knife. It wasn't there. He must have forgotten it this morning. *Shit*. For a second, he wished Sam-I-Am was with him. He'd dropped the dog off at the groomer before coming home, and while Sam was hardly the size to combat an intruder, having a little back up would have been nice.

The door swung inward. Edward Lawrence grinned from within a gray jumpsuit. A patch on his chest read *Ed*.

Wes took a half step backward, considering the man. He saw the name then the birthmark, and something about the T-shaped patch of skin felt darkly familiar. He spoke sharply, "What are you doing in my house— *Ed*?"

Ed took a step back as well. He swung his arm in a wide, sweeping welcome gesture. His grin only widened.

"Sorry about that," Ed said. He wasn't. "I'm just on such a tight schedule today, and I was told the call from your wife sounded urgent. I felt like I should just go ahead and get started." By getting started, he meant searching the home for the best site to lay in ambush, but unfortunately, Wes showed up too soon.

"My wife called?" Wes consciously eased his stance, but the hairs on his neck refused to lay down. "About what?"

"Mice. I was told your cat brought her a present, so she was concerned there were more around. I did a lap around the outside, looking for entrance points. Found a few and blocked them off. I was just getting started at looking for signs inside when I heard you pull up."

"Okay," Wes was slow in his response, still considering the man. Jill had said nothing about mice, at least recently. Wes lived in the country, so the little things were a constant nuisance as they tried to claw their way inside, especially once the thermometer dipped in the fall. "You shouldn't have gone inside."

Ed sighed and bowed his head. "I'm sorry about that. I should have thought about it. Like I said, I just have so many calls today, and I didn't want to have to leave without solving your problem. It could be a week before I make it back this way and..."

Wes didn't like it. But if Jill had called, he didn't want to get in the way. He ground his teeth.

"Okay," Wes said. "Go ahead." He stepped inside.

"Great." Ed pulled a large flashlight from his belt, one you would imagine a cop carrying and possibly beating you with if you were on the wrong end of a traffic stop. "I'll get started in the basement. There were a few holes I sealed up from the outside that looked like they led in there—I'll take you out and show them to you before I leave."

"That's fine." Wes closed the door.

"So... which way is the basement?"

Wes pointed across the house to a door on the other side of the kitchen. It looked like a closet, and Wes had even confused it with one when they first bought the home. "Over there."

"All right." Ed clicked on his flashlight and headed toward the door.

Wes followed into the kitchen and then strode to the counter and the Keurig. He regarded Ed as the man paused by the basement door.

"Let's see what we find," the exterminator sang as he opened the door. He left it ajar as he trotted down the steps.

"What a weirdo," Wes whispered as he plopped a dark roast K-Cup in the machine and set a mug under the spigot. He had just hit the *brew* button when a shout came from downstairs.

"You're going to want to see this!" Ed yelled up through the floorboards.

Wes watched his coffee begin to fill and turned toward the basement.

5

Jill opened the door to the 6th Avenue split level and stepped inside. The air was stale, and that wouldn't do. She set her prep bags on the kitchen counter and got to work.

She preheated the oven and pulled out a baking sheet, then unpacked fresh potpourri. She traversed the home, opening the windows and setting the air freshener in the bathrooms. She was grateful the house was empty and had been vacuumed last time, so at least she didn't have to do that. Jill was even more grateful they had replaced the carpet after all the blood stains.

The murders were the only drawback to the house. But it had been four months, and besides that stigma, the home had every item the Thompsons were looking for: good school district, four bedrooms, two full baths, attic space, and a giant yard. As well, the kitchen had been redone in the last ten years. It was a steal at the price.

Jill returned to the kitchen, placed the cookie dough from her bag onto the backing sheet, and slid it inside the oven. She set the timer for a minute early; nothing would ruin the effect she was going for like the smell of burnt cookies.

She leaned against the counter and waited. If her timing was right, she'd pull out the cookies, and while they cooled, she could close the windows back up. After the treats were plated, she would have about five minutes before the Thompsons showed. Enough time to take some deep breaths, center herself, and put on her persuasive face. She could do this. The Thompsons were going to buy this house today. She knew it.

Jill daydreamed as she waited. She thought of the girls' room and how she was way behind in repainting it. Sam had asked for wall decals she saw on television of stars and planets, so the idea was to paint one wall black and make it look like space—the child was in love with space. Then Lisa came up with the idea of unicorns and goblins. So, in order to maintain equal treatment under the law, they all agreed to paint a different wall with hills and forests, so her side of the room could have a unicorn decal and a painted goblin.

But the task was long overdue. It was an idea back in the spring, and life had gotten away from them. Hopefully, after this sale, there would be the extra money and the free time they needed to get the job done.

She hated the feeling of being behind, especially when it came to something she had promised the girls. She felt like she did a decent job as a mom overall—she knew every family had their faults and tried not to dwell too heavily on the ones she couldn't control—but messing up promises added to the ever-growing pile of deficiencies she already resented, and just made her see herself as a failure.

A sinking feeling set in. She shook her head. *No.* This wasn't the type of thought she should be having before a showing. She needed this to work for the family, the girls and Wes. An image of Wes entered her mind. She saw him at home after sending the girls off to school, in his office, working at his daily writing routine. But something was off. She wasn't sure why, but a grinding gnawed at her stomach.

6

Wes stepped onto the cool cement floor of the unfinished basement. It was darker than he expected. He could only see the five feet surrounding the bottom of the stairs—his eyes were used to the kitchen's brightness. Why was it so dark? Didn't the exterminator need light to find the mouse problem?

Wes reached for the light switch. Sharp pain raced through Wes's lower back. He lost the feeling in his legs, then his arms, then everything. He was dropping, and saw the room rise around him.

He managed to squeak out, "What?"

The world was uneven, and he was sure his legs were somehow bent behind his back. He stared up at shadowed ceiling rafters and the first-floor floorboards.

The exterminator's face seemed to hover as it emerged from the gloom. Ed grinned, though it wasn't quite like the one he had shown Wes upstairs. Wes could tell that this one was real—this was his real face. The other had been a disguise. Whatever the man had in store was his love, possibly his only love.

Ed carried a stun gun in one hand and large zip ties in the other.

The thought came to Wes, *I'm going to die.*

1992

1

Pain raced up Chris's arm as Heath Williams, an asshole and one of Todd Hertz's Khaki Klan friends, slammed into his cast. Chris had been walking past Ms. Swallows's classroom toward study hall and couldn't resist peering in. He was disappointed to find her covered in a button-up red sweater when his arm erupted in pain.

Chris raised his fist in time to see the clown ten feet away, walking in the other direction and chuckling.

"They're jerks," a small girl's voice said from behind him.

Chris spun around to see Charlotte Baker considering him with a raised eyebrow.

"They're not worth it, though," she said. She clutched her books against her petite frame and moved her stare to Ms. Swallows's room. She nodded and smirked. "Ms. Sallow isn't putting on a show today, it seems."

Chris blushed. "I don't know what you mean."

"Yeah, right." Charlotte narrowed her eyes at Chris. The hall traffic was thinning. "We better get going, or we'll be late."

Chris nodded and walked. Charlotte hustled up beside him.

Through the corner of his eye, Chris examined her. She pretended not to notice. She wasn't the shapely type he usually gawked at, but there was something cute below her rounded glasses, a sincere warmth that interested him, at least, if nothing better worked out—so he told himself. The truth, though, was that he could be pretty happy going out with Charlotte, but he was concerned with what Tommy and Wes would say. The boys drooled over swimsuit models as they talked about the girls in class who were growing into the shapes of their womanhood. He didn't know if he'd have to take shit for admitting he liked this tiny, but adorable, thing.

"What do you think is wrong with Mr. Wimbley?" Charlotte said. "I don't remember him ever being out sick."

An image of the teacher came into Chris's thoughts, blood rushing up his throat like a geyser around a silver flute.

"I don't know," Chris said, shaking away the gruesome thought. "Everybody gets sick."

"I guess. There must be something going around. It seems like a lot of people are out today."

"Must be." Chris shrugged.

Charlotte looked down at her feet. "So, how's your mom doing? Is the chemo working?"

Chris shook his head, seeing Mom's face at the dinner table, sullen and unable to eat. The bones in her cheeks peeking through the thinning skin. The paleness of her complexion. But her urging him to finish his meal and asking if he wanted seconds. His insides felt like they were slithering around under his skin at the thought. He really didn't want to talk about it. Not with anyone, and especially not at school. Still though, it brought an urge to smile back at her, the idea that Charlotte cared enough to ask.

"I don't know. She has, like, two more weeks, and then they'll do some tests or something."

"Oh." Charlotte struggled with what to say next. "Well, I hope it works. I'm sure it will."

"Yeah." He wasn't.

They turned at the end of the hall and climbed the stairs. Study Hall was on the corner, three rooms down from the now quiet music room. Mr. Wimbley's door was shut, a note taped to it with an arrow and instructions on where to go.

Chris thought the note would be up there for a while. It didn't make any logical sense, but he got the feeling that Mr. Wimbley wasn't ever coming back. Maybe his dream was some sort of premonition, or maybe the universe belched a tiny factoid at him that the teacher was gone. Or maybe he was just fooling himself with what was real and what wasn't. Whatever the idea came from, he was pretty sure they'd seen the last of the old man. And if that was the case, he felt kind of bad for dreaming such a mean dream about the guy.

A near deafening bell signaled the start of third period, and Chris followed Charlotte into Study Hall.

2

Wes set down his controller. His stomach was starting to grind against itself. It hadn't been that long since breakfast, but he wasn't incredibly hungry when Mom brought it up. Now he was paying the price for only nibbling on his sausage instead of finishing it and eating the Eggos too.

He swung his legs over the edge of the bed and gently lowered them. He gathered his crutches from beyond his nightstand and heaved himself up onto his good foot.

The directions on how to use the crutches replayed in his head from a few days prior, as did his catastrophic attempt at hopping without them. He'd been okay doing that from his bed to the bathroom (there were walls to lean on), but not so much downstairs. There, he had tried to get from the front door to the kitchen by jumping on one foot. That's when he discovered the pain of accidentally putting weight on his broken ankle once he was halfway across the room with nothing to rest against.

This time, once he was standing, he decided to go with one crutch. The house was small enough that it was worth a shot, and he wouldn't have to haul both around. He leaned the second crutch back where he'd gotten it and continued through the door.

The empty hallway gave Wes a sense of desertion. Not that he had never been left home alone, but right now, there was a larger sensation pressing down on him. He felt bound, and a creeping tingle of danger chilled his skin. There was a numbness he couldn't describe.

Di's door was shut. The bathroom door was shut, as was the guest room. Bob Barker echoed up the stairs, welcoming a new contestant onto *The Price is Right*.

Wes swung himself to the stairs and stood at the edge. There were only six steps to the landing, but it felt like a cliff, and he had no intention of falling down another cliff. Especially home—alone. The directions replayed in his head for how to go down steps with his crutches. They made logical sense. Mechanically they should work. But instead, he muttered, "Fuck that."

He leaned against the wall and let his body slide down until he was sitting. He held his broken foot in the air and slipped his arm through the crutch, dragging it forward as he moved. Wes scooted to the edge of the steps, then he proceeded down a stair at a time on his butt. At the landing, he dragged himself to the second set of six stairs and rested, gently letting his cast down.

Wes held his breath as the white plaster touched down on the carpet. An ache radiated as he let the muscles relax, but it wasn't bad.

From his spot on the landing, Wes could see the living room and the outer edge of the kitchen counter. Someone had left the light on in the kitchen and a plate with a half-eaten Eggo on the counter. On the television, Bob Barker stood next to a woman with Farrah Fawcett feathery locks and bright red bell bottoms. He explained that she would be pulling numbers out of a bag and had to put the digits in the appropriate places to win the 1982 Ford Escort with California emissions and a special coat of Bright Caramel orange paint.

The woman pulled a two out of the bag and looked to the crowd for help. They screamed, and she frowned, biting her lip. She decided the number should be last. A bell dinged, and she jumped, then dug for another number.

Wes slid the crutch down the next set of stairs and lifted his leg. He took a breath and went the rest of the way to the bottom. At the last step, he grabbed the crutch and pushed himself upward. The television dinged, the audience cheered. Wes pretended they were applauding him and began swinging himself toward the kitchen.

He paused at the counter. The plate sat next to a glass containing an inch of orange juice, Di's.

Wes flexed and extended his hands. He rubbed them together. The cold, numb sensation was still there and refused to relent. There was a tightness around his wrists as if they were tied to something, but they weren't—he rotated and examined them. He saw nothing strange. A lightness ran over him like he was being lifted, dragged.

"What the hell?" His thoughts fuzzed, his mind dizzied.

A scream howled from behind him. Wes spun, completely forgetting he only had one good foot. His broken ankle raged as it touched the floor. Wes lost his balance and dropped to the hardwood.

"Dammit!" A sharp pain shrieked from Wes's tailbone. But what was that scream? He saw no one. He crawled on his hands and knees into the living room.

On the television, Farrah leaped up and down in front of the orange Escort. She'd won. And behind the car was a man in a light gray jumpsuit dragging another man with bound arms across a concrete floor.

3

Diana flipped the notebook to a new page. Ms. Legary lowered herself to her desk after finishing her lecture on nouns and pronouns, expecting everyone to start working on their practice sheets. Di began her note to Joanne: "We have to go to the MALL today!! Wes is driving me crazy!! Lets go have some fun!"

Di glanced at the teacher, who was focused on paperwork. She slid the notebook in front of Jo.

Jo slid her handout aside and read Di's message. She brightened with a mischievous grin. Today was indeed a great day for the mall. She'd been waiting for Di to be able to go for what felt like ages, and she just knew that together they could figure out a way to get between Johnny DiMarco and that bitch Shirley Minsk. She wrote back: "Yes!! I know Johnny's going to be there too. Lets do it!!"

4

Officer Dale Harrison sat in his patrol car, wishing he had remembered to refill the supply of mouthwash he kept in the trunk for special occasions. As much as he tried to push away the image of tenderized facial tissue and cracked bones and teeth, what he'd seen in the park pond kept reappearing in his mind. He'd seen mutilated bodies from car wrecks and deer mashed six ways from Sunday, but those were accidents. This wasn't. This was malice and mania. It was an act of pure hatred and rage. The realization that one human could do that to another anywhere other than in fiction was something he'd known from a distance—from conventions and training—but he'd never had to accept it into his personal life. It was the worst thing he'd ever seen happen to a human with his own eyes, and fear now gripped his chest that something incredibly wrong was happening within his town.

"Dale?" the radio burped. It was Rhonda Higgins, the daytime dispatcher. At least that's what they called her position. More realistically, she was the office manager-slash-assistant. She did everything and anything that needed to be done between 5 am and 3 pm, including, but not limited to: coffee, trash removal, phones, lunch runs, paperwork, scheduling the town's four available officers' shifts, and occasionally using the radio. Her voice was tighter than usual today. Harrison assumed it was from hearing about the body in the park—she, of course, had to arrange the coroner, notify the state, and be privy to all the gory details to coordinate it all. But that alone wasn't it.

Harrison lifted the receiver. "Go ahead."

"We got a call from the school. Seems the music teacher, Mr. Wimbly, is no-call no-show today and isn't answering his phone. They asked if you could swing by and check on him."

Harrison glanced into the park, at the Emergency Medical Services techs who wheeled the lumpy black bag out on their stretcher. He was more than ready to go do something else.

"Copy that," Harrison said. "I'll head on over."

The 1988 Crown Vic came to life, attracting the paramedics' gazes. Harrison gave them a nod, checked his left mirror, and pulled out into the road.

Harrison knew Wimbley's house; no need to ask Rhonda for the address or directions. The Wimbleys had owned that house, and at one time, the entire street, for at least ninety years.

The family had moved to Custer Falls not long after congress had declared statehood, and they earned their place by setting up banks in the area. Their vaults were said to be a foot thick and made of solid steel, a big claim back then. Whether true or not, it became a trusted place for gold and gem storage, and earned the Wimbleys a high seat in the town's estimations. That lasted until the run on the banks in '29 when their vaults were cleared out, and the business went under. They sold much of their land to survive, and each generation since seemed to be getting poorer and meaner.

Some said the Wimbleys' bad luck was just that, but many well-known rumors said Old Mr. Wimbley used to own many of the mines he stored riches for, and one of the ways he stayed so rich was by caving in the mines when they ran dry, with the Chinese miners still inside. That way, he'd no longer have to support them or pay the cost to transport them back to California, as was in their contract. Those rumors suggested the

Wimbleys' situation was more of a curse than just bad luck.

Harrison drove into the South Hills, through the Mansion District, now more of a name than anything, as many of the mansions had been torn down. Most of those remaining had been converted into apartments, except for a precious few, including Mr. Wimbley's.

He turned onto the aptly named Banker's Street, and halfway up the block entered Wimbley's driveway. He parked beside a ten-year-old Volvo wagon in front of the dilapidated carriage house.

"Well, his car's here." Harrison got out and eyed the vehicle for damage or vandalism. All he found was rust around the panel edges behind the tires and a cracked windshield, both typical for Montanan vehicles.

He walked to the front door, wincing at the state of the siding. The once-white boards were cracked and gray. The windows appeared to be intact but were clouded and covered in filth, making it hard to see inside.

Harrison climbed the steps to the front porch. The stairs whined and creaked with exhaustion. He cupped his hands around his eyes to block the outside light and pressed against the entryway window.

The inside of the home was dark but calm. Harrison could make out an open hallway and the kitchen, which looked slightly better lit than the rest of the interior. Everything was motionless. The massive stairway was still. Nothing seemed out of place from where the music teacher would have left it when going to bed last night.

Harrison banged on the door. The siding shook and squeaked under the pressure. No one came. No noises. But a smell of dampness escaped under the door's jostling.

He cupped his hands again, this time around his mouth, and yelled, "Mr. Wimbley? Are you in there?"

Harrison strained his ears to listen. A meow caught his attention, followed by pressure against his leg. He looked down to see a fluffy, white Siamese mix rubbing against his left calf.

"Well, someone's home." He kneeled down and stroked the cat's back. It looked up at him. Its mouth, cheeks, and chin were all crusted with dried blood.

Harrison moved back a step. His heart jumped. The cat followed him, again rubbing its blood-stained face on his leg.

"What the hell?" Harrison lifted the cat's chin, wondering where it might be bleeding from. No cut, no wound. The next thought was, "What did you kill?"

A tag hung from the cat's neck. Harrison checked the name and address. The cat was home. Her name was Miss Kitty.

"Well, shit." Harrison stood and pressed the talk button on his radio. "Rhonda?"

Thirty seconds passed as Rhonda rushed from the coffee maker on the far side of the office to the radio.

"Go ahead." Rhonda was slightly out of breath.

"I'm at Wimbley's. He's not answering the door. I'm going to go ahead and check inside."

"Copy that, Dale." She sounded about normal again.

Harrison tried the knob. Locked. He looked down at the cat. "How did you get out here?"

Miss Kitty purred and rubbed, leaving a crimson stream on his calf.

"Okay, I'll check the back."

He smelled lilacs as he crossed into the backyard. He thought to himself how they'd all be asleep soon, gone until spring. He walked past a failed garden that did not smell as good, the year's unpicked and overripened tomatoes and peppers rotting. He found what looked like a door to a laundry room, once the old servants' entrance. Near the bottom of the door was a white cat door. Miss Kitty sprinted inside, the flap smacking against the frame after her.

"That's one question answered." He tried the knob. It opened with a long, low squeak. Harrison leaned inside and yelled, "Mr. Wimbley? This is the police. I'm coming inside to check on you."

Again, Wimbley said nothing.

Harrison stepped inside, leaving the door ajar. He walked through the laundry room and into the kitchen. Dirty dishes, cups, plates, and bowls with hardened food filled the sink. A thick scent of mold saturated the air. The wallpaper cracked and split in small patches and large swaths. Miss Kitty jumped onto the counter and sat next to a tiny dish decorated with a cartoon cat head, then meowed at Harrison.

"Maybe when I'm done, cat." The officer left the kitchen and walked down a hallway. He glanced into a dining room. Massive, built-in cabinets trimmed the walls. They were only half full of china, making Harrison wonder if the Wimbleys had pawned away their tableware through the generations. They had.

Further down the hall, Harrison found himself in the entryway. He unlocked the front door and kept searching.

"Mr. Wimbley?" He looked inside a study, a library.

No answer. Harrison began up the grand staircase. The steps alternated from feeling fragile to soft and squishy.

The upstairs halls held nearly a dozen rooms. As Harrison reached the last door of the corridor, he noticed the smell of something he likely didn't want to find.

He pressed his palm against the door's grimy yellow paneling. "Mr. Wimbley," he said out of a sense of obligation more than sincerity. He knew what he was about to find.

A heavy stench of fecal matter and urine soaked the air inside the bedroom. The scent of blood floated just above.

Wimbley was naked in his bed. His blankets were at his feet; only the shit-stained white sheets covered him. He faced away from Harrison, but the officer could clearly see the pillows were drenched in blood.

"God—damn." Harrison winced as he rounded the foot of the bed.

Wimbley's eyes were frozen in a shocked expression. His mouth was torn at the corners, and flaps of skin draped over his teeth. Blood was dried from his eyes, down his nose, over his mouth, and down his chin and neck. The mattress was so stained with blood, bile, shit, and piss that it looked to still be wet. Red kitty cat paw prints tracked from the pillows, across the floor, and out of the room.

Miss Kitty meowed and hopped up onto the foot of the bed.

5

The heartbeat monitor in Tommy Laskin's hospital room was silent yet steady. They may have had doubts about his brain after the fall down that cliff, but there were no concerns about his heart.

His mother was gone for now. After a week at his bedside away from work, they'd politely let her know that if she didn't come back, they'd find someone else to do her job. So he lay alone in his hospital room and dreamed.

Tommy found himself a fly on the wall, feeling like he was in a dream but not his own. He watched as events transpired, unable to communicate, unable to affect what was happening.

He was in a village. Homes were made of stone, mud, and grass. Fires scented the air with woodsmoke from the intersections of rows that may have become streets a thousand years later. Thick night drenched his view, and he couldn't make out the world more than a hundred feet beyond a specific man—a man he was bonded to in some way he couldn't understand.

He was tall and broad. His hair was long, strawberry-blonde, and dirty, matted with the same mud that spotted his grimy clothes. His muscles bulged under his shirt, and his appearance reminded Tommy of Conan the Barbarian.

Scenes urged themselves upon Tommy, images, sounds, and feelings from a life that was not his own. There was a boy, Conan, he assumed. He bled and watched as his mother was raped. He tasted blood and smelled fresh death in the air. Conan's sister was taken, and his mother left for dead in the snow.

But she wasn't dead. A shaman amputated her leg at the knee, burned the wound closed, and dosed her with mushrooms for weeks to alleviate the pain. The screaming. The stench of seared human flesh. The fluttering embers over the fire in the night. Conan ate the mushrooms as well, starving and not knowing what else to do, and by the time the wound was healed, she had gone mad.

Tommy saw years later, Conan standing over his mother's funeral pyre. Again the smoke, the stench of flaming flesh. He saw Conan with a woman, raping her behind a tree as others looked for them, bloody swords in hand. He felt adrenaline in his veins. He smelled the woman's scent, her sweaty body against his. There was a flash of Conan swimming, another of him strung up against boards and pelted with stones. He felt the sting of each impact, the crack as they shook his bones.

When the images ceased, Tommy was back with Conan, hovering as the man marched down the path between homes. His stride was swift and heaving. His breath was deep and quick. His fingers clenched around a stick. No, it wasn't a stick; it was a war hammer.

The head of Conan's hammer was blunt and etched with a symbol that resembled a skull. Opposite the head was a slightly curved maul. Its point was dull and jagged. Both sides dripped with blood. Both sides held tender bits of skin, fat, and hair that clung and trembled with each of the massive man's strides.

Tommy tried to look away but couldn't. He was tired of these dreams. He knew what was coming next and was ready for it all to be over. The same sequence of events seemed to be playing again and again, only with different characters and different places.

He'd tried to scream. He'd tried to move, to get away. But no one heard him. He could touch nothing. Affect nothing. He was a disembodied view of the worlds he was taken to, a prisoner, doomed to witness the events of these strangers of which he could glimpse very little other than the brief moments shown to him.

Conan approached a large building, framed in timber and walled in stone. It was lit more brightly than the rest of the village, and in front of its entrance, three men talked.

They turned to Conan as he neared, first with smiles, then confusion. This was where Tommy caught a glimpse of the thing.

He'd seen it a few times during these visions, these unclaimed memories. It hung from Conan's back like a kid on a piggyback ride, but this was no kid. Tommy never saw it clearly, as it faded from translucent to a shadow in wavering splotches, but what he did see turned him cold and numb and made him wish he could escape even harder.

It was skinny and small, like a child. It hung from its host with knees up to its chest, feet and hands clawed into its victim. Long, coarse hair hung from its head, and in the brief instances where it caught Tommy looking at it, it showed a mouth full of spiked teeth and eyes that shined amber through their translucence.

It was the one thing in these visions that interacted with Tommy, and he wished like hell it wouldn't.

Conan moved in toward the men, and the thing whispered into his ear. He held his hammer to the side and swung it around and upward. It glanced along the first man's head, leaving a gash across his cheek and ripping his nose from his face. Blood gushed. He covered himself and fell backward.

The middle man didn't move. His expression was frozen between wonder and horror.

Conan lifted his weapon and brought it down into the center of the middle man's ragged fur hat. Iron mashed the top of his skull into a pulp of bone, brain, and fur. Blood ran over his forehead, his nose, and flooded downward like a crimson waterfall.

Tommy wanted to look away. He wanted to puke. He could do neither.

The third man shouted in a language Tommy didn't know. He plunged his sword into Conan's gut. Conan turned his hammer and planted the maul deep inside the third man's ear. He ripped it back, jerking free the ear, a chunk of brain, and shards of bloody bone. The third man dropped.

The noseless one turned. He held his face and scrambled into the building in a half-run half-crawl. Conan followed.

Inside were a dozen men. They jumped to their feet, and Conan marched inside with his hammer poised.

6

Ray Trent didn't go to school. He'd heard his father get ready and head to the tire shop, and instead of waking up, Ray rolled over and went back to sleep. He deserved it, after all; it was a long, busy night.

When he finally stretched and pulled back the covers, his clock said 12:43 pm. He yawned and rubbed the back of his hand. It hurt. He examined the wound, a dotted half-moon where that bum had bitten him. He'd poured peroxide over it when he got home, but the thing still glowed red with infection.

"Dirty bum," Ray muttered, rising to his feet.

His boxers tented as he stood, so his first stop was the bathroom, where he jerked off while fantasizing about Misty Brolin's ass.

He'd had a thing for Misty for two years, since she started wearing those booty shorts, even after the weather turned cold. Fashion over function, he'd heard a girl say once. And man, did those shorts function to make his dick hard.

It was obvious to Ray, she wanted to be looked at, so he did. Every time she was in the room. He even asked her out a couple of times. The whore said no. Raymond's best guess why was that he was broke. He couldn't fix that, but he could give out a few black eyes to the guys she did go out with. But eventually, that got boring. Raymond still hadn't forgotten her, though—and one of these days, he'd let her know. One of these days, he'd get her alone and show her exactly what a broke guy could give her.

After his short but necessary stint in the bathroom, Ray dug through the pantry and refrigerator. Nothing but condiments, old-folk's cereal, and stale crap to cook with. There was nothing he could pick up and eat that was worth eating.

"Dad, you're such an asshole." He remembered what the pantry used to look like when he was little, before Mom left. He never felt spoiled as a child, but Mom always made sure the shopping was done and there was always food to eat. She was also always there to soothe him when he was mad. To tell him his anger was okay; everyone had it. Some people just had more of it than others. She was always on his side, unlike Dad, who couldn't even buy groceries right. He grabbed a box of stale Corn Flakes and a glass of water and headed for the couch.

Ray flipped through the channels, half looking for something to watch, half wondering if he would catch something on the news about his little night escapade. He saw nothing but soaps, crap talk shows, and *The People's Court* (also crap), and he started to wonder how it even happened.

He had woken from a dream and just knew he had to do it. He didn't understand why he had to but knew it would feel fucking good, and it did. It felt nearly as good as he imagined plunging his dick into Misty Brolin's sweet, perfect ass would.

He'd slipped on his shoes and pants and a black hoodie, and something told him to grab one of those shitty ponchos his Dad kept for fishing in the rain. He did. On the way out of the house, he picked up the small mallet they used for pounding stakes at the campsite. He could swing that pretty well.

The park was gloomily lit by two ball-shaped lamps, both near the amphitheater. The man-made light barely covered the stage area, likely the city's attempt to protect it from vandals. It worked sometimes. The moon lit the rest of the park, its crescent bathing the grass in pale dim ambiance. The air was crisp and sweet and smelled of fresh cut grass, maybe the last cut of the year.

That disgusting old bum was right where Ray expected, sleeping on the bench by the pond. Ray studied the man's angular face: his pointed nose, his skinny, bony cheekbones, his jutting chin. Ray tried to imagine what the skull would look like after he was done with it. An image of a bowl of pasta sauce came to mind. Could he do that? He'd try.

Ray raised the mallet. A streak of excitement bolted through him, and he knew this was what he was meant for. Not anything he'd been told at school that he'd need in life. Not working at the shop with the old man. It was *this*. This was his calling.

"Do it," a whisper crept through the back of Ray's mind. Its cold touch sent shivers over his flesh, then warmed him like sliding into a jacuzzi on a snowy winter's night. *"It'll feel good. The world doesn't need him. He's an asshole, and you'll love to be rid of him. Do it."*

Ray aimed at the dent in the man's top lip, just under the nose. That would be a good spot to start. And he swung.

He only remembered bits and pieces of the rest of the act, only flashes of blood and the sound of his own laughter. What he remembered clearly, though, was the rush. The adrenaline that filled his veins. The high made his entire body tingle, from his teeth to his toes.

His fingers twitched as he thought about it and skipped from station to station. As many channels as he flipped through, he couldn't find anything about it. Grunting, he settled for the Wapner rerun, dug into the cereal box for a handful, and shoved it into his mouth.

His mind drifted. He wondered if he should go out again tonight and just who he should visit.

2022

1

"Wes?" Jill said, opening the door with a beaming smile. She hurried to the kitchen, dropping her bags on the counter. Not seeing him there or in the living room, she rushed to his office. "Wes?" Not there either.

She thought about the exterminator van in the driveway. Maybe he was somewhere around the house with them. She wasn't sure why there was an exterminator, but whatever the reason, it couldn't have been as important as her news.

She'd sold the 6th Avenue split level. Her hard work and coddling of the Thompsons had finally paid off. The offer had been put in and accepted, and all that remained was to wait forty-five days for the closing.

"Hmm." She walked back to the kitchen, refusing to let the smile fade from her lips. She opened the bags she had set on the counter, removing a bottle of Pink Moscato. She looked at it fondly, remembering the first time she and Wes had opened a bottle of champagne. That was almost fifteen years ago. She'd stolen it from her mom's car after Mom had unloaded the groceries and missed it. The bottle had slipped free of its bag and rolled under the seat. When the couple took it to their special place by Bradley's Creek and popped the cork, they thought they were in for a treat. Instead, they each took a sip and spat it out. They didn't know what it meant at the time, but apparently, Mom was a fan of extra dry bubbly, and the taste was a shocker. Enough so that Jill didn't try any kind of champagne again for several years. Not until Joanne had given her a bottle of Moscato one birthday, and the sweet treat became her celebratory drink of choice.

She put the bottle in the freezer to chill. She would find Wes soon, and they'd celebrate together. She unpacked the other item in her bag, a container of sweet, crispy elephant ears. Nowhere near as good as the ones she'd found in the bakery of the Bellagio on their honeymoon, but they would do. She opened the box and took one out. She placed it between her lips and, as she saw a cold, abandoned cup of coffee resting under the Keurig, felt a numbness in her back. Her limbs fell limp, and she dropped.

Edward Lawrence reached over the incapacitated woman and lifted a palmier of his own from the box. He placed the edge of the pastry into his mouth and bit, nodding in approval.

2

Elias stepped out of the Huckleberry Café at 1:01 pm, earlier than he expected. The lunch rush had been slow, and Norris had told him to scram. Fine with him.

He began the walk back to his apartment. The fog was long gone, but clouds had moved in to block out the sun. He shivered and ran his fingers over his Br/Ba tattoo and then his arms to warm them up. As he crossed 5th Avenue, he scanned the street for cops out of habit, then remembered the bleach in Harrison's coffee and smiled. If he'd done it right, he might never have to look out for that asshole again.

A tan Subaru pulled out, skimming the curb inches from Elias's path. Its tires squealed, and Elias jumped.

"Fucking asshole!" Elias flipped the bird as the vehicle sped away. The driver never looked back. "Now that's a guy whose throat I'd love to pour bleach down."

Elias paused, surprised at himself. He really had done that. He'd spiked that cop's coffee and possibly killed him. That was something he wouldn't have had the guts to do on any other day. Sure, he'd spit in food, pissed in the soup; he'd even jerked off into a cup once, filled it with lemonade, and served it to a customer on a hot summer day. But that was expected from the wait staff. Everybody knows you don't fuck with the people who handle your food. But this was new. He'd never poisoned someone before—not with something that could actually harm them. He nodded and felt a jolt of confidence flow through his veins. Maybe he would do it again.

He resumed walking, for once in a long while, not thinking about whether he'd rather sniff some coke or smoke some crystal when he got home. Instead, he thought about what scumbag would be most deserving to get it next. There was a pretty good list of jerks who visited the restaurant, but it occurred to Elias that if too many people started dropping off after eating there, someone with a badge might get wise. He was somewhat surprised no one came looking this morning after Officer Douchebag left. No, he needed to be a little smarter than just bumping off customers if he wanted to do this again. And he did want it. He felt higher than he had in a while, and with his head feeling clearer at the same time.

There was his landlord—that guy had it coming for the smell of the building alone. But no, too close to home. There was the dude-bro that lived down the hall that was always banging on the walls and yelling, "Turn that fucking music down," and threatening to call the cops. No, still too close to home. But the thought of Dude-Bro reminded him of someone who wasn't. Chad-fucking-Parsons.

Chad was another dude-bro who, back in high school, seemed to make it his mission to find Elias at some point every day and punch him in the gut. It never mattered if Elias was talking to his friends, waiting in the lunch line, or headed to the bathroom to take a shit; Chad would show up with his posse of bros, slug Elias in the stomach, and laugh. He had done it once while Elias was in the middle of asking Maggie Leer out. Chad and his bros snuck up behind him, tapped on his shoulder, and thud, right in the middle of the hall, and hard enough that Elias dropped to his knees from lack of breath. He didn't have the nerve to ask Maggie out again after she turned and walked away that day.

That guy would work.

Good ol' Chad never had to get a job after high school; he'd gone off to the University of Montana—directly to Missoula after graduation. Six years later, he was back in Custer Falls with a BA and an MBA, and some other fancy words, and he started working in the big glass building just past downtown. The Mirror, they called it.

A grin crossed Elias's lips. He didn't know where the guy lived, but he knew where to find him, and that was enough to get started.

3

Diana had been feeling déjà vu all morning. She had told herself that after spending so many months in the same cozy hut, it was inevitable.

But there was more to it than that, and she knew it, even if she tried to convince herself otherwise.

The morning light creeping through the cracks in the insulation, the birds outside, singing their last songs before fleeing winter, the rustle of the trees as the wind blew through, these were all sounds she'd heard daily, yes—but the melody of today's composition was original. And still, she remembered it as if it had happened before.

She laid on her belly, on top of her sleeping bag. She held her well-worn copy of *NOS4A2* in her hands and tried to ignore her surroundings.

It stunned people who knew her past when they discovered she read horror novels. She would explain to them that the books were like a warm blanket. After the things she'd been through, experiences where she didn't know if she would make it out alive, she could read a story where other people faced their fears and survived. The process gave her hope. It gave her a cathartic release, knowing the end of the pain would come, and she could make it through. It was the truth within the fiction that helped, a therapy of sorts that got her through her shit more than any psychologist ever had. But today, her therapy was a dull tone below the discord that screamed all around.

Since early morning, her nagging wish to have Wes nearby had grown. She felt like he should be there. That she needed to set her hand on his shoulder, hug him like she did when they were little, when the lightning woke her from her dreams, and he was only a bedroom away to calm her. Ages ago, but not in her mind. And this morning, nothing seemed to be quelling the feeling that she needed to go to him.

Di found herself rereading the same passage for the third time. Each read seemed to end with her mind no longer following, and so she started again. Manx had thrown Vic's bike into the Shorter Way bridge for the third time when Di huffed and closed the paperback, rotated, and sat up.

Her hands trembled. Adrenaline pumped through her veins. It wasn't déjà vu she was feeling. Whatever was happening, it was more than a feeling. She couldn't deny it any longer. She snatched her pistol, her dead phone, and her keys.

"Come on." She burst from her shelter and set off through the woods, Virb right beside her.

4

Officer Stuart Harrison awoke for long enough to experience the lights and sounds he could only assume were from the inside of Custer Memorial Hospital. Beeping, the echoes of talking from another room, the smell of disinfectant; they bombarded his senses as much as the burning in his gut and the sharp pains in his head.

He remembered driving, about to crash. Is that what sent him here? If he was in the hospital, at least he was getting help.

He lifted his head and saw his uniform was cut open. There were bruises on his chest and smears of dried blood. How bad was it?

He heard machines on his right beep in alarm. His stomach clenched. His chest seized. The lights went out.

5

Samantha and Lisa Henson sat beside each other on the gym floor, surrounded by half the students of North Custer Falls Elementary School. They assumed the other half was at home or on lockdown in their classrooms after the girl attacked Ms. Higgins.

Sam had passed being fidgety an hour ago; now, she was getting angry. The kids who had packed their lunches were allowed to eat them, but the rest of the students were starving and tired of being locked in the gym with endless declarations from teachers that "It will only be *a few more minutes*"—*a few more minutes*—*a few more minutes*—maybe if *a few* meant a few hundred... She thought about the donut she had for breakfast and wished she had asked for two.

Lisa had gone through cycles of whining, reading, drawing, and chatting. She was on her third cycle of chatting now, this time with Tammy Brolin and Janet Steiner.

"What do you think happened?" Janet said. She flipped her hair from her face, something she seemed to do constantly. Sam thought it was to get noticed, to make everyone look at the stylish haircut she had to go all the way to Missoula every month to maintain. Janet would say the stylist there didn't compare to any of those she used to use when they lived in Chicago, but at least the Missoula girl was half-literate with a pair of scissors. The flip of the hair seemed as much a call to her old life as her high fashion backpack was, with its bold stripes and flourishes of gaudy gold trim. Janet turned from the group to look at the teachers by the door. There were two, Mrs. Gould and Ms. Bates, both with worried expressions.

Gould and Bates had either stood at the door or walked in laps around the children since the chaos at first bell started. Their faces were as intense and firm as soldiers on the front lines—to them, this was their front line, the battle they had been training for. And they did everything right, followed their training; if only they had instructions on what to do next.

"Jesus, Janet," Tammy scowled. "You've asked that like a hundred times. We don't know." She leaned away from the group of girls, accidentally exposing a burn from one of Valerie's cigarettes on her wrist. Her heart jumped, and she covered it back up with her sleeve. She scanned the others' expressions to see if anyone had noticed. Thankfully, Sam, Lisa, and Janet were all looking toward the teachers now. She was sure they knew something about her sister's outbursts and rages, but she didn't want to talk about it. Didn't want to get into how bad it really was or, God forbid, have anyone else hear and start rumors about it. Tammy followed the others' gazes.

Ms. Bates nodded as Mrs. Gould talked. Gould held a phone to her ear and placed her hand on the gym door.

"Look," Janet said. "I think she's going to open it." The door had only been opened twice since they went into the gym, once to let a police officer in, once to let the officer out.

Sam's eyes were wide. Her stomach growled.

"Open, open, open, open," Lisa chanted.

Mrs. Gould opened the door just enough to stick her head through. After a minute, she put her phone in her pocket and walked toward the assembled children.

"Ooo, ooo, ooo," Lisa said.

"Children," Gould spoke to the crowded gym floor in her authoritative principal's voice. "We are closing the school for the day due to an accident in the lobby. As you may be aware, Ms. Higgins was hurt very badly, and we think the best thing to do is to send you all home."

"What happened to Ms. Higgins?" a small voice asked from the far side of the crowd.

"That's not for you to worry about right now."

"Will she be okay?" another small voice asked.

Mrs. Gould shared a glance with Ms. Bates.

"We'll talk about that later," Gould said. "The point is, we are closing the school, and your parents are being notified to come pick you up."

Sam raised her hand. "What about lunch?"

Gould nodded. "We'll see what we can do."

1992

1

Wes opened his eyes and saw the living room. His head throbbed in waves from the back of his skull to his temples. He found himself sitting on the floor, his back to the peninsula between the kitchen and the living room.

He wondered in shallow thoughts how he'd gotten on the floor. He remembered walking with his crutch, thinking about food, and then Bob Barker. Why Bob Barker?

"Ow." Wes brushed his fingers over his head. He didn't feel any injury, no bumps, no blood, but just to touch his scalp was torturous.

He leaned forward and stood, not noticing until upright that his cast was gone and his leg was working—a dream.

Static burst from the television and consumed the entire audible spectrum. Wes spun toward the TV, his adrenalin pulsing as heavily as his head. The noise faded, and an image appeared.

On the screen was a basement and a man, the same one Wes had seen dragged across the set of *The Price is Right*. He lay on a wooden table next to a woman, and Wes couldn't help but feel he knew both of these people. As he looked closer, he saw what he expected: they were bound together and to the table, and their mouths were gagged.

Wes wanted to ask what kind of show this was, but he knew instantly; this wasn't a show. It was another place, and he was watching something unfold unlike he had ever seen, but also, much like something he vaguely remembered. It was a sense that what was on screen was happening now, in another place, but also had already happened.

He walked into the center of the living room and kneeled in front of the old Zenith's screen. He studied the man and woman's eyes—closed. They were sleeping, just like him. He looked at their faces and saw an eerie resemblance to his father and... Jill. The woman was like an older Jill—no, it *was* Jill. And the other one—was him.

"What the fuck," Wes muttered. Chills ran across his flesh. "How could that be me and Jill?"

The screen flickered. The scene shifted sideways and sped up. Whatever camera was filming this zoomed in to a darkened corner of the room, and an onslaught of dread flooded into Wes. There was something there. Something dark that he knew was unseeable until it decided to be seen. It was a being, or at least a consciousness that he knew was not human. It was a thing that drew in the energy, the life and emotion around it, and it fed. And as he stared through this television, across what he now realized was time and space, he knew this thing was staring back at him.

Wes pushed himself back from the television. He shuffled across the floor, his eyes glued to the TV. A terrifying sensation chilled his neck, and he knew that if he looked away from this thing, it would move. It was like staring down a lion. If he blinked, it would come for him.

His back touched the couch, and he leaped. He spun around to see what was behind him, and panic tore through his heart.

The television's image shot toward the darkened corner, and Wes searched his living room for the remote. He felt time slipping away. He only had seconds. The camera would surround itself in black, and that would be the end. The thing would come through. It would be here, in this room with him, and there would be no escape. It didn't make sense that he would know or be able to predict this other than the certainty that was the dream world. Thought, fear, expectation, these things were reality, and only the control of his own thoughts or swift actions could save him.

But the remote was missing. The end table was bare. He flipped away the couch's cushions. No remote. He searched his father's La-Z-Boy. Nothing. He remembered Di's unfinished breakfast on the counter and looked. There it was, long and gray, his savior from that thing.

He felt the darkness coming but wasn't about to risk another look at the television. The room dimmed, and Wes jumped onto the couch and hurdled over its back. He raced to the counter and grabbed the remote, spinning toward the TV, rotating the controller in his hand. He aimed and looked.

The screen was black. It wasn't the black of off or the black of a faded scene. There was no power failure or even reflection from the glassy surface of the device. The blackness was absence. It was nothing. A true nothing, a hole in reality that led to an abandonment of things material and real. And it was coming for Wes.

He slammed his finger into the power button, and he opened his eyes, staring at the ceiling of his living room—awake.

2

Children from eight to eleven years old flooded from Custer Elementary School's side exits as the afternoon recess bell rang. They latched onto swings, monkey bars, slides, and domes, securing their spaces before they were taken by others.

Near the rear of the exodus was Edward Lawrence. He wasn't in a hurry, though, he knew where he was going. If anything, he wanted to be slow, take his time, let his target acclimate to his surroundings. His plan would go more smoothly then, less likely to be noticed. He took a loop around the playground and spotted Ronny DiMarco on a bench near the soccer field.

That was Ronny's usual spot for afternoon recess. The boy hadn't had nearly as much luck fitting in as his older brother Johnny, now a preteen heartthrob. He wasn't quite at the age where girls would ogle over his Mediterranean skin and cheekbones, or skilled enough in athletics to impress his fellow boys, so he had pretty much given up on finding friends for the time being. Instead of playing ball on the soccer field or chasing other kids around the jungle gym, he'd developed the habit of claiming that bench every recess and reading a copy of *X-Men*, *Spider-Man*, or *The Incredible Hulk*. It was a habit of isolation that Edward had noticed.

After his second loop around the playground, Edward moved in. Ronny was six or seven pages into his book, having tuned out the screams, cheers, and jeers from the rest of the classes. That was just what Edward planned for.

The ten-year-old Edward Lawrence strolled over, his gaze on Ronny, and in his mind, he was a tiger creeping up on a gazelle. His heart pounded. He felt the breeze cross his face, the sun on his skin. His mouth watered, and his lips tightened. He took a breath as he stopped beside Ronny. Wolverine was on the page, his claws shining in front of his half-mouthed smirk.

"You ever read number one?" Edward watched Ronny, waiting to see if he would bite.

"What?" Ronny pivoted his whole body toward Edward.

Bingo. "Yeah, the first one of that series. You ever read it? Where they came back to the mansion, practiced in the Danger Room—man, it was the best."

"Of course." Ronny frowned. His focus darted from Edward's eyes to his birthmark and back. "I have it at home."

Edward expected this. The issue was only like a year old, and the kid's supply of comics seemed endless.

As Ronny's gaze swept back toward his book, Edward spoke again. "Ooo, what about the Uncanny X-Men? You read the one where the Reavers put Wolverine on the giant X cross?"

Ronny turned quickly back to Edward. His eyes glinted in the afternoon sunlight. "No. I've been looking for that one. Number 251, right? Can't find it anywhere. Do... What do you know about it?"

"Only that it's an awesome book!" He changed his voice from excitement to nonchalant with ease. "I have it at home. But I was thinking of selling it. I'm saving up for something special."

"What's that?"

"Ah, I don't want to say. It's bad luck to say what you want—you might not get it. But I've seen you out here reading and thought you might be interested. And I'd rather sell it to someone I know will enjoy it than to some comic shop in Missoula or Bozeman."

Ronny perked up. He closed his book, putting all his attention on Edward. "That—that would be incredible."

Edward smiled. This was going so perfectly. "You can come over and look at it later if you want. I have the whole run from '88 up until the X-Men number one split... if you're interested. They're in good condition, but you should see for yourself."

"Yeah." Ronny nodded. His eyes were practically glowing. Edward had to hold back his own excitement.

He pulled a corner of paper from his pocket. "This is my address. Come over after school, and I'll show you."

Ronny took the paper and looked at it. The address was written diagonally in pencil. "Okay. Great."

"Just—" Edward looked around. "Don't tell anyone, okay? I've told the other kids I don't have them anymore because I didn't want to sell them to them. I don't think they're as big of fans as you. Okay?"

"Yeah. I won't tell anyone." He shoved the paper in his pocket.

Edward turned back to the building. "All right. See ya." His heart felt like it was going to pound through his chest. He fought to control his breathing and not look like a weirdo. He'd done it. It was really going to happen.

Edward grinned from ear to ear.

3

By midmorning, Officer Dale Harrison had been called to check in on six other people.

He found Vanessa Lang dead in her bed, her stomach split open as if from a caesarean. All of her organs were strewn across the bed beside her. Her hands were free of blood, tucked gently under her pillow.

Jason Mertz was in a recliner, columns of Old Milwaukee stacked on the end table beside him, and his chest excavated in a fashion Harrison had only seen from a bear attack.

Doug Chambers was full of holes. His chest and abdomen had too many to count. Harrison could only imagine some sort of mob hit or action movie where a character was shot repeatedly by a machine gun. Only there were no bullets. No casings on the floor. No holes in the bed, wall, or furniture. There was no scent of gunpowder, which Harrison assumed the room would be soaked in after such a massacre.

Betty Peters, Shawn Billings, and Jesse Pool were all dead in their beds, wounds just as gruesome and circumstances just as mysterious.

Harrison had no idea what had befallen his town. A serial killer? Devil worshipers? A morbid homicidal gang of some kind? He wasn't capable of dealing with murder investigations like these. He called in the state. While he waited for them to arrive, requests came in from schools. Triple the usual number of absences, with no call or reason from their parents.

Harrison turned white. Could whoever murdered eight adults have killed children as well? He sat in his cruiser, his stomach still empty after losing his breakfast, still not settled from the park. It couldn't be that, it just couldn't, but he didn't want to find out. He didn't want to go knocking on homes with kids only to find dead and mutilated bodies of children, bodies like those he'd been deluged with so far this shift.

92

He took a breath. He thought of his daughter Gina. She was still asleep when he left home this morning—at least he thought she was. He imagined his son Stuart. He should have woken up and dressed for school soon after Harrison left, but did he? God, were his kids on the list of those students to check?

After digesting the schools' requests, Harrison picked the radio back up, a sour crawl in his gut. "Okay, Rhonda, give me the list." He hung the radio back on its hook, flipped open his pad, and readied his pen.

The radio crackled, and it sent a shiver down Harrison's spine.

"Here you go, Dale…" she read the list. Twenty-three names. Each one started with a jump in his heart and ended with a half-second of relief until the next began. At the very end, she said it, one of the names he'd been dreading to hear. It sent shivers across his chest and bile upward from his empty stomach. He scrawled the last one. The scratchy strings of blue ink on the page danced and taunted him.

Harrison barely made it to the window when thick, mucusy bile erupted between his lips. Most made it to the cement. One thin line dripped down the door of his cruiser.

Harrison panted. He gripped the wheel and flexed his fingers, his heart racing. He threw the vehicle into drive and sped toward home.

4

Under the cover of a hooded Denver Broncos sweatshirt, Ray Trent walked down Seeley Avenue. The chain on his wallet brushed against his side, its pace urging him forward. He'd tried to watch television and settle his mind, but it just hadn't worked. More and more, thoughts of Misty Brolin mixed with images of last night's meeting at the pond, and he became overcome with an irresistible urge. He needed to see her—today.

He crossed over Huckleberry and followed its sidewalk southeast. Every step seemed to steep his anticipation. He saw her face, her pouty lips, the curves of her waist. Every foot forward seemed to make his heart pump stronger. He imagined his hands on her skin, running down her back, her side, her ass. The pins and needles in his veins screamed at him to get there, get inside, and be ready when she got home from school.

He saw blood arching through the air, one of his misplaced memories from his night. He saw red-stained chips of bone scatter across the cold, dark ground. He felt the surge of adrenaline as if he were swinging that mallet once again. He felt its handle inside the large baggy pocket, sending tingles up his arm.

He cut through the playground that marked the corner of Misty's upscale neighborhood, Custer Estates, and paused. He could see her street from here. He could see her driveway. There was a minivan parked in front of her house, an ugly tan and brown abomination with nearly bald tires.

Ray paused in his tracks and tried to remember if Misty's mom or dad drove something like that. He didn't think so. So who could it be, and were they going to fuck up his rendezvous that was too long coming?

He gritted his teeth and considered the playground. He took a seat on the swings and watched.

5

Amanda Brolin, Misty's sister and owner of the brown minivan, sat on the living room couch with a romance novel in her hand, ignoring the episode of *Days of Our Lives* on the television. The book was about three-quarters through and just getting to the good part. The dastardly pirate captain had been hiding his broken heart, broken from a long-lost love. But now, he was about to discover that the prisoner in his brig was actually his paramour in disguise. She had concealed her identity after fleeing her wicked father under the threat of death, but she was about to reveal her secret. That was when the oven beeped.

"Shit," Amanda sat up, determined to finish the paragraph.

The oven beeped again.

Her nerves rose with the fear of burning her lunch, but she read on. Captain Vig ordered his first mate to have the prisoner brought to him, and the oven beeped again.

"Dammit!" She set her book face down on the coffee table and ran around the couch, dodging her yet-undone duffel bag of dirty clothes. She was dreading the smell of smoke as she rushed into the kitchen. Mom would kill her if she dirtied any part of the kitchen, even the inside of the oven. She flung the oven door open and studied her small pizza. Crisp on the top—not burned. She smacked the timer as it yelped one last time.

Amanda sliced and plated her food, anxious to get back to her book. She was sure Dominica would keep up her act for only moments longer, and the two star-crossed lovers would be in each other's arms for the rest of the chapter. They'd kiss—she knew it, maybe they'd even do more—she hoped. Her veins rushed with anticipation of their embrace. She'd been waiting for nearly two hundred pages, and she was ready for the release.

She carried the plate in one hand, a glass of pinkish Crystal Light in the other. She glanced at her laundry, thinking she should really start washing it; she only had three days before she needed to be back in Bozeman for classes. *Maybe tonight*, she decided. There were too many pages calling, and she wasn't going to prolong her wait; the captain was going to take Dominica. The warmth inside her grew as she thought about it, and she rushed back to the couch.

With a slice of pepperoni pizza in one hand and her book in the other, she dove back in. If her excitement had not been piqued, she might have noticed the pair of eyes watching her through the backyard window.

6

Harrison burst through the front door. "Gina!" his voice was hoarse but boomed. There was no waiting for a response. He rushed to the steps, climbing like a mad animal, leaving the front door to bang against the wall and swing back closed.

"Gina?" He bounded over the top step and into the hall.

Still no response.

He passed his bedroom, Dale's room, and the bathroom. He reached his daughter's door, his hand shaking as he touched the knob. For a second that felt like an eternity, he paused and took a breath.

She wasn't going to be in there. She wasn't going to be dead. She was at school, in her class; they had missed her, didn't count her present like they should have. It was all a mistake, and he was about to prove it. He was about to prove how dumb they were, inept at their jobs, unable to do the simplest part, counting children.

So why wouldn't his hand turn the knob?

He stared at the subtle white lines on the door, paint that traced the contours of the wood grain below. His face flushed, and he felt his heartbeat through his skin.

But what if they were right? If she wasn't at school? If she was dead like the others? He couldn't do it. He wouldn't survive if he walked into the next room to find that.

He clamped his fingers into the doorknob and braced for the end of his life, the end of his sanity, and he turned it.

The door swung inward, and a cloud of warm, humid air passed over Harrison's face. It smelled of salt, sweat.

"Gina?" Harrison stepped inside.

She didn't answer. A Gina-sized lump lay in the bed under a thick *Muppet Babies* comforter.

Harrison's mouth went dry. He stepped closer, his hand outreaching.

"Sweetie?" He grabbed the top of the comforter and drew it back hesitantly.

As the blanket slid, it revealed light brown hair, Gina's light brown hair. She was facing the other way. The blanket lowered; her shoulders, her back, covered in a hundred dancing Kermits, Fozzies, and Gonzos.

"God..." Harrison's voice trembled.

He pulled it lower, uncovering her entire top half. She didn't move, didn't respond, but he saw no blood.

"Gina?" He circled to the other side of the bed.

No blood. No wounds.

He kneeled next to the bed and saw her lip quiver. Her chest moved. She was breathing. She was alive.

"Jesus Christ!" A bolt of energy rushed through Harrison's body. She was alive. "Gina?" He grabbed her shoulder and shook her.

She didn't wake.

He shook her again. "Gina?"

She didn't wake.

Harrison put his hand on her cheek. She was warm, lightly perspiring. He rubbed the side of her head. Sweaty hair clung to his fingers.

"Gina, sweetie, wake up." The energy drained back out of his system. "Please? Wake up, sweetie."

He shook her again from the shoulder. "Wake up!"

He stood and stepped back. Fear raced through his heart as the truth set in. She wasn't going to wake up. Those other kids, all of them on his list, they weren't going to wake up. He didn't know who it was, but someone else had control here—and whoever it was, they were responsible for all the deaths he had seen this morning. And if he were going to save these kids, including Gina, he needed to find out how.

2022

1

Wes was restrained. His hands tied, his legs tied, a gag in his mouth and duct tape over it from ear to ear. He lay on a hard surface, looking up at the basement ceiling. He heard walking, creaking, someone was above him—the exterminator?

What was he doing up there? Why was the crazy bastard doing this to him? He thought of the kids—they'd come home on the bus eventually. God, what time was it? What would happen to Sam and Lisa if he were still like this—the crazy man up there to greet them? A jolt of fear shot through Wes, surpassing every other sense in his body.

He saw this maniac standing at the door as Sam and Lisa approached, the doubt in their eyes. Then they would think, *He must be okay. Mom or Dad let him in the house, so...* Wes clamped his hands into fists and shook his head no.

A dull, repeating throb pounded in time with his heartbeat. Pain deep in his head. Then he saw her. Jill lay next to him, her eyes closed. Another jolt of terror through his system—God, the lunatic was going to kill them both, wait for the girls, and... he couldn't imagine the rest. He could only see their small faces, eyes wide and weeping.

Jill was bound and gagged just as he was, but she was breathing; that was good.

Wes flapped his elbow out and poked her. After a few seconds, he did it again.

Jill grumbled and rocked her head side to side. Wes elbowed her again, and she moaned and opened her eyes. As she noticed her bonds, confusion turned her frustration into panic. She screamed into her gag, and her eyes fell on Wes. She screamed again at Wes, nodding down at her restraints, eyes bulging, face redder and redder.

Wes could only mumble back as fabric muffled his tones. Glue pulled at his cheeks and burned as he tried to spread his jaws with no luck. He hoped she could read his eyes. They said, "He's going to kill us! And the girls. We have to save the girls!"

Jill only saw his panic and reflected her own. She breathed deeply and looked around again. She tried rocking, jerking herself from the platform that held them. She found that she was anchored to Wes and could only move inches.

It clicked, and Wes understood what she was trying to do. He shimmied closer to her. She slithered toward the side of the platform. He followed. She grunted and inched to the edge. Her head hung over, her feet hooked on the side of the makeshift table.

Yes, Wes thought. They were going to do it. They'd get off the table, reach the floor, and then they'd conquer the next step. Wes tensed his legs, preparing to push her and follow her down.

Blue light flickered like lightning in the distant sky. Jill shook wildly and squealed, and she fell still.

Wes jerked wildly. He screamed into his gag. He only heard the deep consonance of his voice as it vibrated within his skull.

Jesus, what did they do to her? But he knew. In the back of his mind, he knew. The faint memory of his descent into the basement, the zap behind him; they replayed in an instant, and a feeling of true helplessness washed over him. Jill lay there beside him, and he could do nothing to help her. This crazy person zapped his toy, and all Wes could do was wiggle and scream hopelessly. The man could kill them both right this second, and there was absolutely nothing Wes could do about it.

Edward Lawrence walked from the darkness at the foot of the platform into view. His head was shaking *No*. A dry smirk was plastered to his face.

Wes screamed again, this time a muffled string of profanities. He felt none of the tears that ran from his eyes.

"You have to stay where I put you," Ed said. "That's a rule." He pushed against Jill's unconscious body, trying to slide them back to center. With Wes in the way, she was like a sack of meat, stubborn under his push. "Come on, now. Back up."

Wes stared, wishing his gaze could kill, wishing he had any power at all.

The monster. Wes saw evil behind the man's eyes, the type of evil he hadn't seen in years and had hoped he would never see again in his lifetime.

Ed raised his stun gun into view and tapped the button. Electricity hopped across its terminals, strobing the basement in blue flashes. "Back."

Wes couldn't hear it but knew words resonated inside his mouth, "Fuck you."

Ed's smirk grew as he leaned over, planted the terminals in Wes's side, and engaged the device.

2

Julie Redmond held the knives in her pockets as she walked past an old Excursion, a newer Subaru, and a van reading *Walter P. Palmer & Son Extermination*. She didn't expect to use them again soon, but she had grown to love the feeling. At the front door, she took a moment to admire the black bear chainsaw carving under the doorbell, then twisted the knob and went inside the home.

The house was much nicer than her own. She wondered what someone had to do to make enough money to live like this. The ceilings were tall; the rooms were large. A chandelier hung over the entryway with bulbs resembling flames, and the sight of it made her think of *Beauty and the Beast*. That was when it occurred to her that the people living here must be nothing like her. Were they like the beast, though? Could they be good, but buried inside the shell of an inhuman monster? Or were they just so alien that she and they could never understand each other? She saw Ed standing in the kitchen and realized it didn't matter. They would all bleed the same. And so would he.

She put on her happy smile and strutted into the kitchen, bobbing left and right in a stride that was merely hairs away from skipping.

Ed sat at the counter with two piles of books plus one in front of him. He closed the one he was reading and placed it on the pile to his right. He took one from his left and cracked it open.

As Julie stepped into the kitchen, Ed glanced at her. "I was starting to think you weren't going to make it." His eyes went back to the book.

"It was a longer trip than I thought. You'd think people would be more willing to help a child in need... But here I am."

"Here you are." His gaze followed words on the page. He raised a pastry to his mouth and took a bite.

Julie headed to the refrigerator and yanked on the door. It was tough. She had to pull three times before it opened. To her disappointment, there was only health food.

"I thought you said they had kids?" Julie whined.

"Two rug rats, just a little younger than you."

"Then what do they feed them? Nothing but carrots and spinach?"

Ed let out a fake chuckle. "Try the pantry." He pointed to the last door inside the kitchen, nearly to the basement steps.

Julie headed over. It had been a long day, and she'd had zero lunch—she was hungry. She wanted some Cheetos but, at this point, would settle for anything other than what her mom would have said okay to. That was the opposite of what was in that fridge.

As she passed the counter, Julie noticed that all the books Ed had stacked were written by the same guy. The spines read Wesley Henson. "Is that the guy that lives here?"

"What's that?"

"The books. Are those from the guy that lives here?"

"Yeah. I was checking them out."

"Oh. Well, how are they?"

"A bit long-winded for my taste. I found a page where he spent three paragraphs talking about how dark the night was. Like, yeah, the night's dark already..."

Julie opened the pantry, and her mouth dropped. At her house, the pantry was more like a double cabinet; this was like a little room. How did these people have an entire room for food? Even if it was a little one.

"So why do you keep reading?" She stepped inside the food room and began inventorying the shelves.

"I think it's good to know about the people you kill."

Canned veggies, boxes of gluten-free muffin mix. Gluten-free pasta. Gluten-free cereals.

"I think I know enough," Julie scowled. And then she spotted the back corner. "Where are they, anyway?"

"Downstairs. Waiting."

"Oh, how polite." The back lower corner of the pantry, Julie decided, must belong to the dad, or at least a single member of the family powerful enough to demand a space of their own. As well, it seemed to violently protest the rest of the food in the house. She grabbed a bag of Cheetos and a package of Oreos and spun back toward Ed. She took a seat two stools away from him.

"Why don't you ask him what you want to know?" Julie said.

"People never tell the truth."

"Even when they're tied up?"

"Especially then. They only say what they think you want to hear. This way, I get a glimpse into the mind without him being able to cloud what I see."

She slid a cookie into her mouth. She almost spoke, her face full of crumbs, and decided not to. After she swallowed, she said, "What do you see?"

"Someone very sad."

"Oh. Well, we can fix that."

"Yes, we can."

On the wall, the telephone rang.

Julie slid another Oreo into her mouth. "What's that?"

"The phone?"

She was staring at it curiously. "Why is it on a wall?"

Ed shook his head. "Can't believe some of you kids. It's a house phone. Someone's calling again. If I had to guess, I'd say it was the school."

The phone stopped, and buzzing sounded from Ed's pocket. He pulled Wes's phone out and set it on the counter. The screen read *N. Custer Falls Elementary*.

"Well." Ed stood and closed the book he was reading. "I guess our time here is running out."

"Oh?" She had opened the Cheetos and stuffed a handful in her mouth. Her mother would have shouted. She would have demanded Julie walk to the trash and spit it all out. She grinned as much as her full mouth would allow.

"Yeah." He walked to the basement door. "You coming?"

"Uh-huh." She nodded and shoved another handful in her face.

Ed opened the door. "Well, let's go."

3

Diana felt a rush of dread crawl over her spine. It was a feeling she hadn't had in thirty years, since a time she fought to forget.

Virb turned from the window and looked at her. He whined and stepped on the center console, leaning in to give her a sniff.

Di forced out a smile. "I'm okay, buddy."

He huffed on her cheek and stared doubtfully at her for a moment. Then he went back to his window.

Di sighed. She stared at the lonely road in front of her. It was at least another hour to Custer Falls, and something inside her worried whether Wes would make it that long.

4

Samantha watched Ms. Bates hang up her desk phone for what felt like the hundredth time. Everyone else had gone home; their parents or grandparents, even some older brothers and sisters, had come to pick up Sam and Lisa's classmates. Now it was only them, Mrs. Gould, and Ms. Bates left in the building, and Sam was getting the feeling that now she and her sister were unwelcome guests.

Bates sighed. She turned toward Mrs. Gould's office. "Hannah, they still aren't answering."

All three watched the principal's office, listening for direction. The lights in her office went out, and the principal emerged.

"Okay," Mrs. Gould said, glancing at her watch. It was 3:30 pm, past when the buses would have run, which meant the Henson kids would be late getting home. She could deal with watching the kids at the school as long as she needed to, but if their parents got home and Samantha and Lisa weren't there, it would cause worry and possibly a call to the police. Gould figured there'd been enough drama for the day and didn't want that added on top of it all.

"Shannon, you can head home," Gould said. "I'll give them a ride."

"Are you sure?" Bates's eyebrows raised. After the death and horror surrounding her school back in '92, her nerves rattled at any thought of breaking the rules in a school. Staff driving students anywhere in their own vehicle breached a few different policies.

Sam and Lisa traded glances. They liked Mrs. Gould enough, but the idea of being anywhere outside of school with her felt weird. Like the time they bumped into Mr. Jeffreys at the *Minions* movie. Sam was struck with the feeling she was in trouble, like she was out of class without a pass. And the weird look on Mr. Jeffreys's face was like he'd been caught by her—like *he* was doing something wrong. It stuck in her mind for days, and just, never sat right with her.

"Yeah," Gould reassured her assistant. "Please go ahead and lock up. I don't think we'll be open tomorrow, but I'll give you a call later tonight and let you know for sure once I hear back from the super."

"Okay." Bates started packing her things.

"Let's go, guys," Gould said and gestured Sam and Lisa toward the door.

5

Edward Lawrence went down into the Henson basement, Julie Redmond following closely behind. Ed had never had kids—never wanted them—but there was something in this little girl's eagerness to play with him that made him appreciate her, to a point.

They approached the Hensons, man and child grinning in eerie similarity at what was to come.

"Can I? Can I do it?" Julie said.

"You can start," Ed said. "I'll finish." He felt like a parent and stifled a genuine smile from coming out. But he was starting to appreciate that she had been sent to him. Last night had been fun, but now they were doing the real work.

"Ooo," Julie approached the platform, drawing one of her knives from her pocket and unfolding it. Her eyes were wide with wonder.

"Hold on." Ed dug into his pocket and produced a packet of smelling salts. "They both need to be awake for this." He pressed the center of the packet until it popped, shook it, and held it below Wes's nose. The basement filled with a violent wave of ammonia scent, and even at a distance, Ed felt his nose begin to run.

Wes scowled and jerked his head away. He blinked and searched for the startling odor.

Ed moved the salts under Jill's nose. After a second, her eyes shot open, and she pulled her head back, knocking into Wes's. Wes grunted. Jill whimpered. A second later, they were both focused on Ed.

"There we go," Ed chuckled as he spoke and shoved the salts into his pocket. The giddiness was returning. It always did as the time grew near.

"My turn? My turn?" Julie hopped. The blade jostled in her excited hand.

"Okay."

Julie stepped in front of Ed. She beamed. "Can I take off the gag?"

"Better not. Neighbors."

Jill tried desperately to inch away from the child, but Wes was in the way. She glared at Wes to move, but he was already trying, unsuccessfully. He squirmed, but his bonds were tighter. He was anchored to the table, and as much as he and Jill writhed within their bonds, they went nowhere.

Julie raised the knife. Its edge glinted in the dim basement light. The girl squealed as she watched the terror in Jill's eyes.

Jill shrieked into her gag, and Julie pushed the blade's tip through her sheer pants and into the woman's hip. Slowly, she pressed, her eyes darting from the wound to Jill's eyes, and stopping around an inch inside the woman's flesh.

Jill howled. Julie held still, entranced by the look in the woman's eyes. Wes strained and jerked. He wobbled and pulled, fighting to get free, fighting to even see over his wife at what the small child was doing. Ed retreated back into the shadows and watched.

Julie played in the wound. She twisted the knife a quarter turn, studying Jill's response. She pulled it free and watched blood leak from the cut, soak into her pants, and run onto the table. She touched the blade to her lips and tasted.

Muffled howls and muted screams filled the air. Wes shook violently against the table, tossing his body up and down on the wood.

Julie plunged the knife into Jill's leg, this time as deep as her tiny fingers. She pushed and dragged, and the blade tore through Jill's flesh toward her knee. Her pants split like tissue. Blood poured from the wound, a warm, red waterfall chasing after the blade.

Jill jerked, tried to roll away. It only made the blade shift in her flesh as if the child were sawing.

At the knee, Julie slid the blade out except for the tip. She sliced delicately until she reached the lower leg and thrust it back inside.

Jill screamed. By the time the wound reached her ankle, she was unconscious.

Julie soured at the faltered scream. "Ed." She pointed. "She fell asleep."

Wes thrashed at the table. His face was red. He howled into his gag, curses, demands, cries for help. As the blood pooled to the edge of the table, he finally caught a glimpse, and tears ran down his flushed skin.

Ed approached from the shadows, tugging the smelling salt from his pocket. "Oh, that's the pain. She's not asleep; she passed out from the pain. We'll wake her back up."

Wes argued and shrieked, only producing muffled tones that were ignored as if he weren't even there.

Finally, Ed chuckled and turned to Wes. "Oh, we'll get to you." He put the salt below Jill's nose, and after a few short seconds, she startled back to reality. "There you go," he told the child and backed away again.

Julie returned to Jill's side, a smile on her face and knife in hand. She raised it as high as her little arms would stretch, then aimed it down and slammed it into the top of Jill's thigh.

Jill jolted forward, slamming to a halt at the edge of her bonds. Again, she tried to sit up, tried to back up, tried to do anything to get away from the pain.

The child ripped her pants apart to see the wound better then dragged the blade down again, paralleling the first incision.

The leg gushed. Blood flowed onto the tabletop, drenching Jill's clothes and widening the pool below her. It ran under her other leg and soaked into Wes's jeans.

Wes felt the warm wetness spread across his lower half and convulsed with tears and moans. He couldn't resist the repeated questions in his mind: How was this happening? How had they gotten here? Why? Was this even real, or one of that *thing's* nightmares returning to punish him? His heart pounded in his ears, and his eyes burned from tears.

Julie removed the knife and walked up the side of the table, pausing by Jill's head. Blood dripped, leaving a trail of teardrop-shaped crimson on the floor. She looked into Jill's eyes and waved the knife in front of the woman's nose. Jill trembled and hitched and turned her head away. She breathed through short bursts as her nose sprayed mucus onto Wes and the table.

The girl lowered the blade against the side of Jill's neck and watched cords rise and fall as Jill cried and cowered away from the steel. Julie flexed the handle in her hand and pressed.

Ed seized the girl's arm. "Julie," he chided.

"Come on," Julie whined.

"Remember the rules."

She huffed and pulled the blade back. "Fine." She raised the knife again. "Is it time?"

Ed glanced at his watch and nodded.

She grinned and lowered the knife in a slow, deliberate charge. The tip, then blade, dug into Jill's belly, sinking an inch a second. Skin, muscle, intestine; it dove until Julie reached handle.

The child giggled.

6

Samantha and Lisa Henson rode in the back of Principal Gould's white Nissan Murano. Sam bit her lip as she watched the world go by through the window. Lisa stared at the back of Mrs. Gould's head.

The principal's GPS guided her through the neighborhood and into the driveway marked 511 Rodeo Drive. She chuckled to herself, thinking of cowboys on broncos in Beverly Hills and how they got the name all wrong.

"Girls, is this it?" Gould asked. She parked between Wes's Excursion and Jill's Subaru.

"Yes," Sam said. She picked up her backpack from the floor and opened her door. Lisa grabbed hers and mirrored her sister.

"Wait, wait." Gould turned off the car and got out as well. "I need to know your parents are here, especially after them not answering the phone." She hurried in front of the children and reached the front door first. She rang the bell and waited as only silence answered.

Sam grabbed the knob and turned. The door swung wide. "Mom? Dad?"

Lisa walked inside. Sam followed behind her—through the entry, through the kitchen. There was no one there.

"Mom?" Lisa called.

"Dad?" Sam yelled.

Lisa ran and looked inside her parents' room. Sam checked inside her own. They returned to Mrs. Gould in the kitchen.

"They aren't here?" Sam shrugged. "Their cars are here."

"What about there?" Lisa pointed to the cracked basement door. She rushed toward it, hand reaching.

"Wait," Sam said. She pointed at the brushed stainless knob. Its handle wore a layer of red blotches and lines. "What's that?"

"Back, children." Gould had been standing out of the way in the

106

kitchen as the sisters searched, but now she stepped in front. "I'll go first." She opened the door with the tips of her fingers, avoiding what she was sure was blood.

The steps, the basement, everything beyond the first few stairs were dark. Gould smelled the thick aroma of blood and thought she heard dripping. Chills ran over her flesh.

"Mr. Henson? Mrs. Henson?" Gould took a step down, peering into the darkness. "Hello?"

With a click from the wall beside the principal, the stairs lit up. Gould's gaze jerked from the sound to the lighted lower lever.

Lisa's hand was on the switch. "There you go."

Gould nodded and began down. "Wait here." She held up her hand to the children as she descended.

She smelled the faint scent of mildew, dust, and disinfectant. Someone was doing their best to keep the basement smell out of the basement with relative success.

The steps squeaked. She was almost to the bottom when she saw a dark pool of blood shimmering against the pale concrete floor.

She gasped and covered her mouth. She spun and checked the kids. Both at the top of the stairs, anxiously looking down.

"Do you see anything?" Sam said.

"Mom?" Lisa called.

"Just—stay there," Gould demanded.

She stepped on the basement floor cautiously, as if the ground may give below her feet or the blood may move in her direction. She hesitated, then looked right.

As much as Mrs. Gould may have learned to control her reactions for the kids' sake during school hours, she failed here. "Lord, Jesus!" She didn't hear the clomping of second and fourth-grader feet rushing down behind her.

"Mom!" Sam shouted.

Lisa shrieked.

Sam moved toward the blood pool and table, toward two still parents covered in dark, wet crimson. Gould held her back with one arm; she held the other arm in front of Lisa.

"Don't look." Mrs. Gould said. She spun Sam around, then Lisa.

Gould inhaled a ragged breath and jumped as Wes raised his head and screamed through his gag.

1992

1

As Chris watched buses pull out of the school parking lot, he locked onto the middle window of number eleven. He saw glimmering eyes with rounded glasses, and a smile—it was Charlotte. He smiled back and, for a second, said *fuck it*. He was going to ask her out, regardless of what Wes and Tommy had to say about it. Maybe they'd even like her enough not to give him any shit. And if they did, fuck 'em. If he'd only thought about it a few days earlier, it might have worked out.

That afternoon, Chris had decided to go see Tommy, which meant walking to Custer Memorial. He headed north along the outside of the school, passing the gym entrance. He heard the snide sounds of Todd Hertz and his Khaki Klan through the doors and sped up. He usually wouldn't try to avoid Todd or his goons, but something told him today wasn't a good day to push his luck, especially with only one arm.

He'd made it halfway to the street when the door squealed open, and the rumble of Todd's friends echoed through the parking lot—then silenced.

Shit, Chris thought to himself. *Just keep walking.*

"Hey, *Robo-Jerk!*" Heath Williams shouted. Heath was big for his age, a ginger, and Todd's friend since birth, it seemed. The two had been inseparable since kindergarten when they both showed up dressed by their mommies in the same Big Bird jumpers. Later, Todd would follow Heath into the khaki trend, as well as latent-homo-erotic fixations on each other when they tried on clothes at the Banana Republic and the Gap.

"Where you going?" Todd joined Heath.

Just ignore it. Not today, he told himself. He wanted to believe that but knew he was fooling himself. He could hear it in their voices. They weren't going to stop.

"Come back, Robo-Boy," Heath said.

Heath, Todd, Fred Louis, and Lane Freemont laughed and shook their heads. Fred and Lane were late arrivals to the Klan but shared the same taste in plain, pressed clothes and sharp-looking hair to hide their disdain for ninety-nine percent of the rest of the school for the crime of not being as wealthy and snobbish.

"Don't you know," Todd yelled, "he's got to rush to pick up condoms for his slut mom before she works the street corner tonight."

Chris's heart pounded. He saw his mother, dead-tired, on the couch after chemo treatment. He saw the worry on her face that she may not be around as he goes to college and starts his life, has kids. That he may be all alone if she dies and he gets stuck with his drunk father.

Rage curled his hands into fists. He dropped his backpack on the ground and stormed toward the Khaki Klan. He may have had only one arm, but he was going to beat the living shit out of Todd Hertz today.

Heath, Fred, and Lane laughed even harder as Chris came closer. Todd maintained a smile, but the corners were dropping. His eyes widened as Chris's fist soared at his face.

Chris howled, and his knuckles slammed into Todd's jaw. Blood gushed from Todd's cheek as his teeth ripped into the inside of his mouth. A spray of red fluttered from his lips as his head whipped back and dropped to the concrete.

Chris jumped on top of Todd's chest and whaled on the side of his head. "Mother fucker, your mom's the goddamn slut!"

Todd's eyes glazed over. His face glowed red.

Heath and Fred stared with jaws dropped.

Lane watched Chris's fist, then glanced at his buddies. "Guys!" He shoved Heath and seized Chris by the shoulder.

"Get off!" Chris slipped Lane's grasp and punched Todd again. Blood streamed from Todd's nostrils.

Heath, Fred, and Lane grabbed Chris and dragged him off Todd. Todd's eyes fluttered. Blood ran from his mouth down the side of his face, making a Y as it joined the stream from his nose.

Chris landed on his back, and the trio of klansmen kicked. His back, his gut, his head, and his cast. They pounded and yelled.

"Fucking asshole!" Lane shouted. He lifted his leg and stomped on Chris's cast.

It cracked, and Chris screamed. It was like he stabbed Chris in the arm and jolted the screws, grinding them against his bone.

Todd moaned. Heath kneeled beside him, and as the others glanced in that direction, Chris scrambled to his feet and ran.

2

Credits faded, and commercials blared from the television. Amanda Brolin jerked her head up from her book, her eyes searching, settling on the fireplace mantle. The clock there began its hourly chime. There would be four of them.

Amanda shook her head. Her sister would be home at any minute, and if Misty saw what her mother deemed *one of those smutty trash books*, she'd tell Mom. There'd be no end after that. Complaints would range from "This is the type of literature they have at that college" to "Do you want to come home pregnant? Because that's what reading those smutty books will make happen."

For most of her life, Amanda had wished she had been given a nice sister, one who was reasonable, liked the same stuff as her, and didn't run to Mom at any chance to gain leverage over her. Now, it was just a given, another shitty part of life that she had to deal with if she were going to survive in this misguided world. At least she had her books, though. In there, it all seemed to make sense—maybe not at first, when the lusty maiden was captured or being hunted or trying to make her way in a world not meant for a lonesome woman, but that was part of the fun.

She stood from the couch and headed to her room to hide the book. A curious feeling brushed over her neck, raising the hairs to attention. Was someone watching her?

She checked the windows and the room's corners. Tall brown curtains pulled to the windows' sides and tied back. A big, fake leafy plant. There was nothing strange there, but the feeling didn't abate.

Something was happening in this house. Through the corner of her eye, Amanda saw a blur in the kitchen. Something dark, slinking around the lower spaces of the cabinetry. She looked directly into the kitchen, crept inside, and checked the corners.

She walked with a timid reserve. "Hello?"

She didn't expect an answer. The house was empty except for her. She knew that was true, no matter what her eyes or her gut were telling her.

Her eyes traced the countertop tile. They passed a knife, and she briefly debated on picking it up.

Why would someone else be there? How could they even get inside? It was a stupid thought. But the feeling lingered.

Amanda shook her head and walked back into the living room. She went through the entryway to the stairs, swinging her book as she walked. Something said to keep looking, keep checking the corners. It was as if a voice were whispering to her, "Stay on the lookout. Something is coming."

She shook her head and huffed, and headed up the stairs.

The top floor of the Brolin home was for the girls and *only* the girls. Irene and Nick Brolin had a bedroom on the bottom floor next to the kitchen. It was nice when Amanda wanted her own silence and solitude in her room. Not so nice when she used to have friends over, and they were too loud making midnight snacks, bowls of ice cream, and grabbing chips in the kitchen.

At the top of the stairs, the landing joined a hallway. Misty's room was on the left, hers the right. She stepped onto the landing, preparing to turn, when another flash of shadow caught her eye.

"What the fuck? Who's there?" She glanced into Misty's room. "Misty? Are you home?"

Between Misty's dresser and open hamper stood a boy. Amanda had seen his face before but didn't know his name. She thought he worked in one of those grungy buildings over near Old Town. She opened her mouth to ask what he was doing and noticed what was in his hands. One of his fists was plump with a handful of Misty's panties. The other held a blood-stained mallet.

Amanda's veins went cold. Her eyes locked onto his. She stepped back. He stepped forward. Her stomach jumped into her chest, and her heart banged on her ribs. She stepped back again, turning. He ran, and she tore across the hall into her room.

Amanda slammed the door, and her fingers fumbled with the lock. The brass knob rattled in her hands. She squeezed it. It was hot under her fingers as it jerked from the other side, trying to spin, trying to open.

She bit her cheek as her jaw clenched, and she tasted blood. She focused on the small tab of brass in the center of the knob and prayed,

God, keep my fingers steady. She bit her lip as her fingertips found the lock and turned.

Grunting through the crack. The hunk of wood shifted and banged.

She pushed the brass tab to the end of its rotation, ensuring it couldn't turn any further. She tested the knob. It wouldn't twist. Her heart slowed ever so slightly, and as her chest eased its rise and fall, she realized how hard she was breathing, how loud.

The knob settled. The boy stopped trying. Amanda stepped back and breathed deeply. Was he done? Would he leave now that he couldn't get in? She listened over her breath for sounds beyond the door.

It was quiet. Had he gone? Hope raised inside her thoughts. She leaned right as if she could get a peek through the door crack. But that was stupid; she knew it was. She squatted. Maybe from below.

She bent down, getting closer to the carpet, staring at the threshold for any sign, any shadow.

Bang! The door rocked in its frame. The handle screeched with the sound of scraping, squealing metal.

Amanda fell backward as if the door had crashed into her. She screamed and scurried away like a wounded crab.

Bang! The knob jumped and popped out of the door, hanging limply from its hole. It rattled from the other side and wiggled around.

Amanda trembled. She pressed herself back against the wall. "Go away!" her words were as shaky as her hands. Tears streaked her face. "Leave me alone! I'm calling the police!" She squeezed her hands together to steady herself and wished Mom and Dad had given her the phone in her room that she'd asked for.

It was only a matter of time now. He was going to get in. She couldn't stop it. Amanda searched the room for anywhere to go, anywhere to hide. Under the bed? He'd look there. The closet? Just louvered doors. No. She spotted the window. She'd climbed through the window once to sneak out in high school. She was only a floor up. She'd had Henry Paige below her at the time to brace her and guide her down, but she could do it herself. Couldn't she?

She felt her pocket. She had her keys; she could get away.

Bang!

Amanda sprang at the window.

The knob crunched, and metal scraped wood.

She heard the door opening and refused to look back. She grabbed the latch, already unlocked. She seized the wood and lifted. Through the window, the neighbor's blue spruce shifted in the breeze as if calling her down. She wanted to answer, "I'm on my way." The window was going up. This was going to work.

Searing pain shot through Amanda's back. Cracks reverberated through her ribs, and she sunk to the floor. She turned as she drifted down. She saw him and remembered. His name was Ray. And he was staring down with a quizzical expression, the mallet hanging at his side.

Amber shifted her back leg and shoved it forward, aiming for Ray's nuts. Ray moved just enough for her to miss his testicles, and her heel planted in his leg. He stumbled backward, and she clawed her way back to the window.

She lifted it as little as she thought she could get away with. No time to raise it any higher. She dove into the opening, thinking only that this might kill her. It might be the last dumb mistake she ever got to make. If she landed on her head, she'd break it or at least knock herself out. If she landed on her neck, she could be paralyzed or dead. She could brace her fall with her hands, but was she strong enough? If she wasn't, she could just as easily break both hands. But there was no other choice.

Her arms went through, her head, breasts, belly. She felt her hips catch on the sill, and panic rocked her system. She hung half in and half out of the house. She reached back and pushed against the siding.

Pain rocked her right side. Her hip screamed and throbbed.

She swung her legs wildly and pushed harder.

Pain erupted in her right leg.

She slipped through the opening. She'd done it. But now, she was falling. All thought, all plans, all ideas about how not to die vanished from her mind as the ground came closer. Instinct was all she had, and it told her to hide her head.

She pulled her face into her chest and her arms over it. She felt gravity shifting around her as she rolled, until earth slammed into her side.

Amanda howled. Her back, her side, her leg, they all howled with her. She looked up. Ray had raised the window the rest of the way and was climbing out.

"No!" How could he? This was her win. She made it down. He wasn't supposed to climb too.

Amanda shoved against the ground, up, onto her good leg. She tried to walk and collapsed.

Ray was halfway out the window.

She got back up and moved. She limped, her weight on her good leg. She had to get to her van.

Ray hung from the window and dropped to the lawn.

Amanda dug the keys from her pocket. She came around the side of the house and saw the van. She forced herself to move faster, limping and grunting as she readied her keys.

Amanda grabbed the handle and pulled. The door squeaked and widened, and white light filled her vision. The pain came for only a second and drifted away with the world.

Ray took the keys from Amanda's hand. He looked up and down the vehicle and shoved her ragdoll of a body inside. He sat in the driver's seat and started the engine.

3

Barton Smith drove up Tower Road, his green pickup sputtering but keeping pace with the sparse traffic heading into town. His head pounded, and he was exhausted. But he was ready for the cherry on top of his day, and the thought brought him all the energy he needed.

The damn investigators had taken all day. He knew it was going to be a long, drawn-out thing, but he didn't think he'd have to be present at the edge of the rubble mound for all of it. Bloodtooth's entrances were blown up; he told his story, what had happened when he left last night. That should have been it. He had a phone at home; they could have called if they needed further info. But, no. Both he and Horace had to dick around, doing nothing for nearly eight hours before they'd let them leave.

But at least he didn't miss his scheduled appointment. He'd get to the mall just in time to watch all the little girls gather with their friends and walk in aimless circles around the place.

He passed the Avery Mill on the edge of town, then Custer Estates a few miles later. Bill Higgins, who he hadn't talked to since high school, turned into the estates. Barton shook his head, imagining Bill listening to classical music and counting his money once he got home. It was sickening. Bill had a cute kid, though. Barton imagined having her in his house every night, right down the hall, fruit ready to squeeze whenever he wanted. A few miles further, at the corner of Lake Street and 12th Avenue, he turned into Custer Valley Mall.

Barton had hated the idea of a mall when he heard the town council was talking to a developer about building it. The monstrous things are ugly and a blight on small businesses in the community. Both of his uncles had run shops—one a bakery and one a butcher shop—when he was a kid. Both were driven out of business later after chain grocery stores came to town. The last thing he wanted to see was more chain stores until someone mentioned that it would give the kids a "safe place" to gather.

That made him think. A place where all the kids gather? Before the mall, they were all over town. Hard to find, especially hard to find the ones that looked just how he liked. Now it was like a buffet. He could sit on a bench and watch as much as he liked. And now he had figured out just how to take the one he wanted.

So, in the end, he decided the mall was a good thing.

4

The afternoon air blew cold. It pressed into Diana Henson's face with hard and heavy gusts as if trying to drive her back. As if it were urging her to go home instead. She refused to listen. Today it wasn't just Joanne Higgins who wanted to go; she did as well. And she didn't care if Johnny DiMarco, Shirley Minsk, Hannah Snider, or Mahatma Gandhi were going to be there. She had done enough work, been her brother's nursemaid for long enough. She was going to do something for herself, something that she wanted to do.

Di and Jo crossed 7th Avenue and took the Holdover Bridge across the river. They skipped down Lake Street in near silence.

Jo played with introductions in her head, practicing and knocking down different ways to get Johnny's attention. She didn't know what she would do if Little Miss Look-at-My-Tits was there; she'd have to figure that out on the fly. But she knew one thing for sure—if Johnny was there, his eyes were going to be on her.

Di had absolutely no agenda. Her only desire was to stay out of the house for another few hours without being bothered by Wes or Mom. She hoped for a little bit of fun, wanting to see if Jo saw her crush and witness the chaos that might ensue—she loved Jo, but sometimes she just tried too hard. If the whole Johnny-Jo-Shirley triangle blew up in a cloud of

Orange Julius, giant cookie, and Cinnabon, Di was going to have a front row seat and a smile on her face.

At the corner of 12th Avenue and Lake, they walked into the parking lot for the Custer Valley Mall. It was overly big for the small town. The developers had convinced the town council that consumers would come from fifty miles in any direction to visit a Macy's, a Spencer's, and eat in a food court. While it did provide a curiosity in the area for about six months, followed by a rush during the 1991 Christmas season, since then, the place had been a ghost town. The largest contingent of visitors to the Custer Valley Mall today were Mall Walkers and kids, neither of which spent any money.

The Mall Walkers were the retired, fifty-five-plus crowd that came in as soon as the doors opened and walked laps. The constant sixty-eight degrees and perfect weather ensured no one tripped and broke a hip.

The kids that came ranged from tweens to teens, who walked nearly as much as the Walkers did. They did buy some junk food here and there, but they usually shared it. Their contribution to the mall's commerce wasn't nearly enough to run the lights for a few minutes in the cavernous enclosure.

The managers of shops talked during the slow opening and closing hours. Most were in agreement. This place wasn't going to last five years before it had to close down.

A dozen cars sat in the parking lot on the north side of the main entrance, ten of those belonging to employees. Di and Jo walked past Barton Smith's pickup, nestled between a Bronco that was the Macy's General Manager's and a Gremlin owned by a part-time kid at the Chinese buffet in the food court.

They were almost to the entrance, and Di could see the nervousness on Jo's face. She felt for her friend. Jo could be loud and obnoxious and drive Di up the wall. But she was also a raging pit bull when it came to standing up for her friends. When the salon had cut Di's bangs way too short in the spring, and Hannah was mid-sentence calling Di a five-head, Jo was nose to nose with her in a second. Di still came to school red-faced for a month as her hair grew back, but she didn't have to worry about Hannah's mouth.

Di stopped at the curb. "So, did you decide what you're going to say?"

Jo hemmed and hawed. "Hi Johnny, I was going to get a slice of pizza. You want to come along?"

Di wasn't impressed. "Pizza? You think that's going to drag him away from Shirley Tits?"

"No. I'm still working on that part. I think you'll have to distract her, and then I'll step in and lure him away."

"Not with pizza."

Jo frowned.

"Maybe a smoothie? I think I've seen him getting orange juice in the lunch line. I bet he likes those."

"You think?"

Di leaned in. "You'll have to do it all sexy-like."

"What does that mean?"

"I don't know. Haven't you seen any movies? Touch his hair and stroke it. Get all close and whisper it in his ear."

Jo stepped back and shooed the idea away.

"I know. Lean in and press your chest against him."

"What chest?" Jo gestured down. She'd guessed she'd have to wait another year based on what she saw. She was behind almost every girl in her class.

"Girl, it's all mental. You have to get in his head."

Jo nodded and shook herself loose. "Okay, let's go. But first, I have to pee."

Di chuckled and followed her friend inside.

Barton Smith took a deep, tingling breath and got out of his truck.

5

Di and Jo met at the bathroom sink, and Di scowled at Jo's chest. "I know you didn't just grow a cup size in there."

Jo straightened her tissue-filled bra. "Shut up."

"Okay. Just don't rub those on him, or he might hear them crinkle."

Together, they marched out of the bathroom and into the abyss of concrete commerce. Barton Smith followed fifty feet behind.

They passed Spencer's, scanning inside for any friends, went by Tower Records, and looked in there as well. They drifted along aimlessly by the shoe store, the candle shop, the perfume store, and a dozen others, all with no luck. Jo was starting to think they wouldn't find him when they wandered into the food court, and there he was.

Johnny's thick locks hung down past his collar, sweeping back and forth as he talked, and Jo felt chills. His olive skin was so smooth, Jo wanted to stroke it endlessly. His eyes sparkled, even in the drab light of the food court. The picture glowed inside her mind and halted her in her tracks. Then she saw who he was talking to.

That bitch, Shirley was hanging on his arm, chest out, flashing her helpless, save-me-from-the-world expression, which she always wore around him. It was beyond sickening. It was the type of crap that was going to get that bitch slapped and beat up.

Jo clenched her fists. Her chest was hot and bubbling with rage.

"There she is," Di said. She scrutinized them up and down. "How do we get them apart so you can have some *alone time?*"

It took Jo a minute to process the question. The rage fought to keep her logical thoughts out. It wanted her to go over there, grab Shirley's hair, and shove a fist down her throat. It wanted to gouge her eyeballs out, hold her by the ears and slam her face into the table.

Jo averted her gaze, shaking her head, and the question resonated. She saw workers on break at the food court's tables. They ate pizza, Chinese, burgers, and some had smoothies and Icees.

An idea crossed Jo's mind. She just needed a buck-fifty and Di's help.

"Come on," Jo said. "I got it."

She guided them to the burger place, where she bought a large fry, a small Coke, and a large cherry Icee. She remembered buying Icees that summer, the coolness when she and Di came to the mall on hot days. She remembered how Dad would never let her have one in the car because the red food coloring was like a permanent tattoo on any piece of fabric it touched—a permanent stain, just like Shirley.

She handed the Icee to Di and picked up the Coke and fries. She led them back into the seating area, her eyes fixed on her target.

"Okay," Di said, "we have food. So, now what?"

"So, we go say *hi.*" Jo demonstrated a half-bow. "I'll get Johnny to smile at me, and it'll totally piss Shirley off."

"Yeah. Then what?"

"While she's staring at me, pissed off, you fake-trip and pour the Icee all over her."

Di's eyes shot open. She covered her mouth with her hand. "No."

"Yes. She'll have to run off to the bathroom and clean up."

"Oh, my God."

"Yeah. Then I share some fries and Coke with Johnny and lure him away from the court so she can't find us when she comes out."

"I can't do that, Jo." Di shook her head. "I can't just... toss a drink on someone."

"You have to." Jo flashed her puppy-dog eyes so glassy that they seemed about to cry. "This is my shot. We're here and ready. We can do this."

"But it'll ruin her clothes. That's not cool." Di knew how mad her own mom would be if she came home in a red dress that should have been yellow. She would be grounded for weeks. And if Mom found out she'd done this, months. "I—"

"You have to, Di. Look." She pointed across the court. Shirley had scooted so close to Johnny, they could have been making out right there. "My time's running out. If I don't do something soon, they're going to be an item, and I won't ever get the chance again."

Di looked at the couple with a frustrated sigh. Jo had a point. She had to do it. Di nodded.

A smile crossed Jo's face from ear to ear. "I knew you would. I love you."

"Love you too. So when do we do it? Can we get this over now?"

"You bet. Now we walk by them, but pretend we don't see them. When we're really close, I'll be like, 'Oh, hey there, Johnny, didn't see you.'"

"Okay."

"Good." Jo led the way. As they got into a good stride, Jo started into a fake conversation, "And then Ms. Legary was looking at me—you know with that weird look she does?"

"I know," Di joined in. "So, what did you do?"

Jo glanced through the corner of her eye. They were within fifteen feet of Johnny and Shirley. "I told her I did the work like she said. And she was all-like, 'No, that's not what I wrote.' Can you believe that?"

"No, I copied the same thing—that *is* what she wrote."

"Thank you. And I told her other people did the assignment the same way." They were about to pass in front of Johnny. "So she'll ask you about it, I'm sure."

As they stepped right in front of their target, Johnny looked up, and Shirley scowled.

"Johnny?" Jo said. She stopped right in front of him. He looked up at her with his usual confident smile.

Di took another step and stopped in front of Shirley. She took in Johnny's smile and wondered if anyone had ever told him *No* before. A smile like that? He looked like he'd never heard it and never expected to.

Shirley glanced at Di, her face turning red. Her scowl deepened, and she huffed, turning back to Jo. She knew what they were up to, or half of it. She'd seen Jo staring at Johnny; it was one of the reasons she'd moved so fast. Not that she was scared of flat-chested Joanne, but if Jo was interested, other girls were too. And like Johnny's smile, she was used to getting what she wanted.

Jo flipped her hair and smiled at the boy. "We were just saying how Ms. Legary always writes so bad. We end up doing the wrong thing 'cause we can't read her chicken scratches."

Di felt the chill of the cup in her hand. It was extra big, seeming larger than it should be. It was extra cold, extra red. Her fingers shifted, felling the dimpling in the Styrofoam, the grooves, the roundness, the base, side, and rim. Her heart picked up. She didn't want to do this. But she saw Jo's face. She was so into this, loving every second, she had to talk to Johnny. Her smile was one Di had never seen. It was interest and adoration.

"Did you say you have the chicken scratch?" Shirley said. "Is that like herpes?"

"Gross," Jo laughed, hiding both her anger and irritation.

"I can never read what the board says." Johnny shook his head. "Always have to ask someone what she wrote. That's how I met Shirley here."

"I see." Jo smiled and glanced at Di. It was a look of, *get on with it*.

Di inched forward. She really didn't want to. But she had no choice. Her fingers readied themselves. She looked down at the cup and took a sip, then she saw a problem—the lid. It would ruin the whole thing. If she tried to spill it with a lid, it might block half the drink. She lifted the cup to her mouth, one hand on the lid and one on the Styrofoam. She took a sip and pried the two apart.

"Well, she's a good friend to have," Jo said.

Di could tell it hurt to say that one. She leaned a step forward again and, this time, felt the cup's spongy flex. She took a breath. This was going to be crazy. She jiggled her feet, putting one in front of the other, did a fake trip, and tossed the entire twenty ounces of Icee at Shirley.

A red wave of sweet, frozen ice-drink crossed the gap between them, trailed by the lid and straw. It collided with Shirley's sternum, splashing up against her chin, right and left over her shoulders. The majority of the red tsunami, though, went down. It soaked her shirt, her jeans, and anything else she was hiding in her pockets or beneath her clothes.

Shirley shrieked. She leaped to her feet, dripping, staring down in horror. "What did you do?"

"I, uh," Di looked at the same mess. "I mean, I didn't want to..." She indeed had done it correctly. The girl's look... it was horrifying. "Sorry..." Her face, her entire stance, shrunk with the word.

Shirley stared with rage as her clothes *pit-patted* ice-drink on the floor. She grabbed her small, cream-colored bag and strode off toward the bathroom, arms out, as if afraid to touch the redness.

Johnny DiMarco watched her walk away with an open mouth and questioning eyes.

"You want some fries?" Jo asked.

Johnny turned to her, spotted the open carton, and took one.

Barton Smith followed Shirley Minsk to the bathroom.

6

"We don't know," Dr. Gregory Johnson concluded.

The man had been talking for five minutes, but there was nothing in his words that helped. No voluntary movement. Unresponsive to stimuli, even pain-inducing. Alternate level of consciousness. It was all jargon that could describe their conditions from one doctor to another, but nothing that explained what had happened and, more importantly, how to fix it.

Officer Dale Harrison raised his hand in a *stop* gesture. "That's enough. When will we know? Either how to stop it from happening to any other kids—or how to wake them up?"

"We don't know. Just like with any coma, they could wake up in five minutes or in five years. But, the longer they're in it—the lower the chance that they'll wake." The doctor lifted the glasses from his face, opened his lab coat, and cleaned them with his shirt. "I wish I could help more. Maybe tomorrow, when the lab tests come back, we'll have more information."

Harrison fidgeted where he stood. He couldn't wrap his head around it. Doctors were supposed to be men of science, but he was saying science had no answer.

His daughter lay in a bed three rooms down with his wife and son. Sharing the room was another child in a bed, surrounded by his family. Ten other rooms were doubled up with families and children, and no answers were to be had. How could he walk back into that room with no answers?

"You have my card." Harrison pointed to the doctor's lab coat pocket where he'd stuffed the rectangular piece of cardstock. "Call me as soon as those tests come in."

"First call I make." Johnson slid the glasses back on his face and disappeared into the nursing area.

Harrison glanced at his daughter's room. He couldn't. Not yet. He headed toward the stairs, the morgue. The dead would be easier to deal with right now.

At the bottom of three flights of pale-green stairs, Harrison found the entrance to the basement and then the double doors leading to the hospital morgue, where the bodies he had been forced to discover this morning had been brought. Sgt. Padilla from the county and Cpl. Banks from the state were already there. Dr. Lillian Stephenson, the medical examiner, was in the middle, leaning over the table and spreading Jason Mertz's wounds for the law enforcement officers to see.

Harrison joined the circle. "Mind catching me up, fellas?"

Stephenson glanced up and gave Harrison a nod of recognition. She released Mertz and stood upright. "I was saying that each of these bodies is different. I don't see a single thing in their injuries to link them other than the fact that they all died last night."

"Nothing?" Harrison said. "I mean, I saw the wounds and causes of death were different—but how did the killer get them to be still? Most of their injuries would have been extremely painful. I would have expected anyone going through that to wake up and run for help—something."

"We've only tested three of the victims so far. The others' tests should be back soon. But I expect we'll find the same results. No drugs other than alcohol in this one." She motioned to Mertz. "And whatever else they regularly used. But nothing like I think you're implying. They weren't knocked out or given a mickey or anything like that. And there's no indication that they were bound or held down."

"So this guy?" Cpl. Banks pointed to Mertz, eyes squinting. "He laid still while a bear or something mauled him?"

"Yes and no." She leaned over the body again. "Yes, he was still—he made no effort to fight back. No, it wasn't a bear."

"But Doc," Sgt. Padilla said, giving her his patented *see-here-lady* expression, because she obviously knew less than him, "I've seen bear attacks several times. This is a bear attack."

"No, Sergeant, I'm sorry. It isn't. If you look closer, you'll see these cuts are smoother, sliced as if with a blade. The bear wounds that look like this are made with claws. Claws tear the flesh, not slice. The difference is obvious under the microscope if you'd like to see." She pointed to her optics in the far corner of the room.

The sergeant opened his mouth, then shook his head.

"Also," Stephenson pointed inside the wounds, "there is no evidence of debris. In animal attacks, we always have residual dirt, hair, rocks, things that cling to and shed from the animal's paws and fur. There are none of those here."

The sergeant pointed at Mertz. "You're saying someone sliced this bastard up to make it look like an animal attack, but it wasn't one."

"That's what the evidence suggests, Sgt. Padilla."

"Lilly," Harrison said, "what about the others?"

"I haven't had time to get to all of them." She looked sheepishly to the other side of the room as if she had the speed of five medical examiners but had been goofing off. "I've examined Mr. Wimbly. All I can say so far is that there were no drugs. He appears to have been killed by having an object scraped and battered around the inside of his esophagus repeatedly. It was..." She trailed off. "I'll keep working on it."

It was enough for now. Harrison knew she'd likely be down there until dawn to get through the stack of corpses they'd brought in this morning.

"I'll drop back by then," Harrison said. "I'm—going upstairs to check on Gina."

The other officers nodded.

"We'll catch up soon," Padilla said.

"Yeah." Banks nodded.

Harrison headed back to the stairs. He made it about halfway up when his knees gave out. Were it not for his grip on the handrail, he would have rolled down the flight. Instead, he twisted around and landed on his rear. Tears raced down his face. And all he could do was put his head in his hands and let them go.

7

Chris crept to the third floor of Custer Memorial Hospital, not knowing the visitation rules and procedures and scared to ask in case he was denied.

Through the fourth door on the right, he found Tommy Laskin's room.

He stopped in the doorway and took a breath. It had been two weeks since he was last here, and while Tommy was still alive and in the same bed, he looked smaller, thinner, and paler. He was hooked up to a heart monitor, IVs, and a few other machines Chris couldn't identify. He breathed softly. His eyes, though closed, were the only part of him that moved.

Chris had seen Tommy in a similar bed a year ago. Wes and Jill sat on the mattress's edges, grinning at him.

Only two hours before, they had been exploring the under-construction neighborhood east of Birch Street. The homes were in various stages of completion, and each of the four friends was taking turns riding Tommy's new skateboard through the houses' interiors.

As the sun set and it became too dark to see inside, they sat on a pile of plywood in front of the highest house on the block. At the end of the cul-de-sac, it was obliviously meant to be the pinnacle of the new neighborhood, looking down on all the rest. It had a driveway with a hump and a deep grade, and that spurred a glimmer in Tommy's eye.

"Watch this." Tommy grabbed the board and sprinted to the top of the challenge. He stood momentarily at the edge of the garage, where one day soon, a motorized door would be installed.

Chris looked on, a smile widening on his face; he wished he had thought of it first.

"Isn't that a bit high?" Jill said. "He did just get the thing."

Chris clapped. "Let's see it!"

Tommy gave his onlookers a thumbs up.

"Yeah." Wes nodded.

Jill winced and looked away.

As soon as Tommy placed both feet on the board, Chris saw the expression on his face. He was a daredevil at heart, sure, but this one may have been too much for a skateboarder with three days' experience.

Tommy kept his balance as he darted down the first half of the driveway. While steep, it was a straight shot. He picked up speed, the wind lifting his hair up over his ears. His face flushed. The sound of wheels on concrete reverberated through the neighborhood. And then there was the hump.

The driveway bulged from the earth. It wasn't huge, maybe six inches of change. But as it rose, the pavement turned left and down, and the look on Tommy's face was that of him realizing this was about to be out of his control.

He hit the hump and took flight. The board drifted away. By the time he came down, he was moving just as fast, but over a muddy yard with pallets of two-by-fours and drywall directly in front of him.

Tommy skid in the mud. It sucked his feet backward, throwing him into an uncontrolled roll. As he tumbled into the two-by-fours, his friends stood. He rolled up the side of the pallet, arms and legs flailing. Jill gasped. Tommy flew back into the air and face-planted on the drywall. His blood ruined the top sheet.

"Tommy!" Chris ran across the yard.

Wes and Jill followed.

When they made it to the hospital and sat in the room just like this, they got to look at the x-rays of Tommy's fractured tibia and joke about his broken nose.

But no one was there joking now. It was a room empty of cheer, empty of almost anything human. Just a boy in a bed and some machines.

Chris went in and sat in the chair at the end of the bed. An issue of *Martha Stewart Living* sat on a small table under the window; maybe Mrs. Laskin's? He stared at Tommy. He looked at the tube pressed into his nose, his flat hair, and his narrow cheeks. Chris had to shake his head and look away.

"I was really hoping you'd be looking better, man. It's time to wake up and get out of here." Chris leaned his head on the back of the chair. "Saw Todd and the Khaki Klan on the way over. Had to give them a tune-up. You should have seen it. They got in a few licks, but it was worth it. Yeah."

Chris sighed.

"So many people not in school today. And Mr. Wimbley—he was out too. It was so weird because I had this dream with him last night. He was pissing me off in music class, and I just took my instrument and rammed it down his throat. It was so crazy. I've never had a dream quite like it.

"Then... I spent some time with Charlotte. You know her—small, cute. I think if you guys spent more time with her—I think you'd like her.

"I was thinking about going by to see Wes. I know it's been a long time—shit—not sure I've seen him since the... Well, since the accident. I know I should go, but every time I think about it, I remember that cave. I remember us sitting there, hurt, and I was telling him not to leave us. And what did he do? He left.

"I think about it, and I get so angry. I feel like if I see him, I'm going to just punch him in the face.

"And then there's Jill. She's great, and she saved us, but... You know, she's like in love with him, even if she doesn't want to admit it. How can I talk to her, wanting to punch him in the face?

"Maybe you could just wake up? Then we would all get together and work it out?"

Chris glanced back at Tommy, then back at the ceiling. "Yeah. But keep trying, okay?"

He closed his eyes, and before he knew it, he was with Tommy in an entirely different way.

8

Chris looked around, confused. As the space became clear, fear raced through him. It was dark, but he could see. Voices echoed, bouncing off of rock walls, and all around were kids from his school. Somehow, he was back in the Bloodtooth Caverns.

This time it was different, though. A haze of dream drifted from thought to thought, illuminating the surrealism of this place. Something said it was the caverns, and at the same time, it wasn't.

The kids in the cave were not those from his field trip. The more he examined their faces, the more he realized that these were the students that didn't show up at school today. They sat and walked and explored, scattered around the massive cave in groups of twos, threes, and fours.

It settled into Chris's mind that this wasn't real, and the fear diminished to a tingling just below his threshold of thought. He was merely in a dream, and he didn't need to be so afraid of this place. He wasn't going to get stuck in it again. It was just a stupid, bad dream.

Across the massive space, he saw Phil Tailer, who he often sat with on the bus. Phil was one of the few kids alone in the cave.

Chris tried to walk toward Phil and realized he couldn't. When he tried to lift his leg and move, he had none. He looked down, seeing no body at all—no torso, no arms, no hands.

"Bad dream," he said to himself. "That's all it is."

"I wish that was the case," a voice spoke beside him.

Chris looked. He saw nothing, no one standing there. But he got a feeling, and the voice replayed in his head. It was familiar. "Tommy?"

"That's my name, Puddintane,"

Chris felt happiness swell inside him. It was a feeling he didn't think he'd had in weeks. If he had a face, he was sure he would be smiling.

"Ha! Glad to hear your voice," Chris said. "Even if it's just a shitty dream."

"This isn't a dream," Tommy's voice said.

"Sure feels like one. What—"

A boom rocked the inside of the cavern. The walls shook. Dust and rocks sprinkled down from the ceiling, and a wave of screams and murmurs reverberated around them.

"What the hell?" Chris shouted. He felt cold as he realized his voice had no echo.

White light flashed from the entrance ahead. The entire cave community watched the opening, waiting. After a few seconds, a girl entered, dark-hair in a ponytail. She scanned the space with focused eyes, fingers tapping at the sides of her legs. On her second pass, her face brightened, and she ran across the cave and joined a small group of girls.

"What is this?" Chris said.

"Purgatory," Tommy said.

"What does that mean?" He'd heard the word in a religious context, but that couldn't have been what Tommy meant. The question had barely left Chris's lips when blinding white light filled his eyes.

"Boy," a woman's voice scolded.

Chris shook. An arm was on each shoulder, and the luminous room dimmed just enough for him to see.

It was a nurse. She squinted, and her lips pursed. "It's time for you to go home, son."

"Okay, okay." Chris sat up straight in his seat.

The nurse stiffened as she looked Chris over. Her gaze settled on his arm. "Your cast is cracked, son." She looked closer at the bruises forming from red patches on his head and neck, and she sighed. "Come with me."

2022

1

It had been a slow day at Custer Memorial Hospital, slower than most this time of year. Though the morgue had been buzzing when Joanne Higgins's body came in with police from Custer Falls, the county, and the state, and briefly after that a few reporters, the main floors saw none of that ruckus. Beds on floors two through four were mostly empty, their ghosts long sleeping.

Jill's ambulance had woken the place up. Doctors, nurses, and administrative staff were all set in motion as Jill and Wes were rushed in. Principal Gould promised to follow along, and she did, escorting two wailing girls. Now, all but Jill sat in the hospital waiting room, Wes holding one girl under each arm, Gould uncomfortable leaving, a nurse hovering, insisting that she look at Wes's stun gun burns, and a member of the hospital board on the phone with the Custer Falls Police Department.

Wes held on tight. He heard his daughters' breaths, their whimpers. The rest of the world was as dull and insignificant as the buzzing of flies.

He tried to think the day through. He had been told about the murder in the school and how his daughters had spent most of their waking hours inside the gym. He wondered about the supposed murderer—a little girl. On any other day, he would have found the idea absurd, but after seeing what that child did to Jill. The way she cut her up—the thrill in her eyes. It had to be the same girl.

"She's going to be okay, right, Daddy?" Lisa said, muffled through her father's chest. It was the ninth time she had asked. On most other days, Wes would have scolded her at three. Not today.

"She's going to be okay, sweetheart." His stomach turned. *God, let her be alright. Let me not be a liar to my daughter right now.*

The hospital administrator gave Wes a worried stare. After the amount of blood Jill and Wes wore on their way in, she wasn't so optimistic. Red soaked the woman, her clothes, the EMTs, and the knife in the woman's gut. She was surprised Dr. Johnson hadn't joined them in the waiting room yet to say they'd lost her.

Wes firmed his grip and made sure both girls heard him. "She's going to be okay."

The automatic front doors slid open, and footfalls from outside approached. It was the sound of officialty, the clustered feet of government.

A uniformed officer and a detective in a light gray suit approached Wes. The administrator stepped back, breaking the circle and allowing the police in.

The one in uniform stood back and to the right of the detective. He waited.

Detective Mark Rand studied Wes, the girls, and their entourage and returned to Wes. "Mr. Henson." He waited for Wes to look up and meet his gaze.

Wes took a breath. He knew this was coming, but, God, he really didn't want to deal with it. Sure, he wanted them to catch Ed and the girl, but something in the back of his mind told him that wasn't going to happen. There was more to this situation than these cops could understand, more that Wes was yet to understand. He had no faith that this detective or anyone else in an official role would be able to help his family. Not with how he felt now.

It was an old sensation that crept into his flesh. It took the terrifying experience of the day to recognize the thing that had been growing inside him. A sensation he hadn't felt in thirty years, not since... an image of Ray Trent came to mind. Darkness, creeping things, blood, even more than today.

Wes locked eyes with the gray-suited man. Strands of hair the same color as his suit peppered his head. He was clean-shaven, dark-eyed, and firm-jawed. Wes imagined the man in fatigues with a general's stars on his shoulders, belting orders to his men. It didn't make sense; it was the curse of a writer's imagination, putting those around them in scenes and places that would never make sense to anyone else in the room. But still, something in his assessment of this man made Wes doubt the cop's inability to help for a second—just a second.

"Yes," Wes said. His voice was coarser than he expected.

"My name is Detective Rand. I know this isn't a good time, but I need to get your statement and ask you some questions while the event's still fresh in your mind." He waited, watching the gears turn in Wes's head. Making sure the words all sank in.

Wes glanced down at his daughters.

"Officer McKinney here can stay with your daughters—it would be best if we discussed things in private."

Sam leaned into her father. Lisa stared up at the detective.

Wes returned to Rand. "How about we wait? Just a little. Until we hear about Jill's surgery."

The lines on Rand's face deepened, and Wes knew what it meant. Rand was already assuming Jill would be a dead woman; it just hadn't been called yet. Wes wondered if Rand knew something he didn't. Had the doctors told him something or was it just the normal cop pessimism? Rand had to think that once the doc came out and told everyone the awful news, they would be devastated, and it would ruin his chance of getting a decent interview in the next few hours.

Wes refused to believe that. The thought that these others expected her death made his jaw clench. Jill was going to live. Yes, she'd lost a lot of blood—a lot. But the knife wound was in her gut; he'd heard stories of people getting shot or stabbed in the gut and living for days without treatment. This had just happened. She was going to make it. She had to... He thought of Jill snuggled in their bed with the girls watching movies. Her on their honeymoon in a too-tight snow bunny outfit at the top of the mountain. Her curves in their bed just a few hours earlier. Did he tell her how beautiful she was lately? Did he tell her he loved her?

"Sir, now would be better," Rand said.

Wes exhaled, sounding like a growl. He gave a shallow nod. She was going to be okay, but the longer this detective stood there, the more irritated Wes knew he'd become. He needed to get this over with.

"Girls, I need to go talk with the detective for a little bit."

Sam grabbed his arm. Lisa shook her head.

Principal Gould stood and took the seat beside Lisa. "I can wait with them."

"I'm not going far, guys. Just..." his eyes searched the room. Where were they going to go?

The hospital administrator pointed to a door marked *Private*. "You can use that counseling office if you like?"

Wes looked at Rand. Rand nodded.

"See, guys, I'll just be over there."

Sam held tighter. It took another moment of convincing before she relented and Lisa agreed. They watched with cautious stares as Wes and Detective Rand entered the tiny office.

2

Red and blue lights swirled in front of Wes Henson's home as Diana approached. Virb sat up in the passenger seat and watched the young policeman standing at the door.

A rush of panic raced through Di. What had happened here? Was Wes okay? God, the girls? She would have to make a decision: stop and ask what was happening or keep going. If they asked her for identification and ran her through the system, she'd end up in jail. She hadn't seen or heard from Carly in months. She thought Carly should have made it to the hospital and survived the stabbing, so they'd only have a warrant out for attempted murder, not murder, but now wasn't a good time to be locked up in a cell no matter the charge. Still, she had to know what happened. And it couldn't wait.

Di parked at the curb on the edge of the driveway. She rolled down Virb's window and told him to stay. He'd do it. He was a good dog. He'd sit and wait and watch, and if he saw any trouble, that was when he'd move.

The cop studied her as she shut the door and walked up the driveway. She wasn't dressed in anything tight or revealing, jeans and a t-shirt with a red and gray flannel, but still, the man's eyes moved up and down her body. Maybe that was good? Maybe it would keep him distracted from looking too deeply into her identity.

She started to swagger as she walked and gave her shirt a pull from behind, tightening it over her breasts. The officer straightened, hooking his thumbs under his belt and puffing his chest out.

"Can I help you?" the policeman said.

Di stopped, swinging her hips one way and tilting her head the other. She exposed a pair of puppy dog eyes and bit her lip. "Please, officer, I have to know. Is everyone okay? My cousin lives here."

"Oh." the cop sucked in a hiss. "I'm sorry. Who's your cousin?"

"Jill Henson. Is she okay?"

The cop looked away. "I'm afraid I'm not sure. There was an incident, and they took her to the hospital. The whole family's there, I think."

Di wanted to scream but held herself still. "Oh, God. What about her husband? The girls?"

The officer glanced inside and turned back. He spoke softly as if telling her a secret. "I *think* they're okay. I'm sorry about your cousin."

A brief second of relief passed over Diana. "What happened?"

"I can't really say." He puffed up his chest again. "It's an ongoing investigation."

Di nodded graciously. "I see."

"Yeah." He spoke low again, shaking his head. "It's bad in there."

Di's heart thumped. She needed to get to the hospital. Maybe the cop was right and Wes and the girls were fine, but maybe not. She flashed a small smile at the officer. "Thank you."

He firmed his hooked fingers in his belt. "Be safe, miss."

Di watched Virb's eyes as she walked back to the car. He stared down the cop but didn't budge. She'd gotten lucky.

3

Elias watched from a wooden bench a half block from a building called the Mirror. Six stories tall, it was the highest thing on this side of downtown by two floors.

The wait had been long, but Elias kept himself motivated. He had seen Chad Parsons return from lunch around 1:30 and expected to see him leave for the night at any time. The guy still walked exactly the same. He strutted with his entire body, head included. His face was tight with a pinched-lip expression that looked like he needed to take a shit. *Soon enough*, Elias thought, *he'll be flexing that face for a whole other reason.*

The Mirror's doors opened, and a bright reflection skated across the ground and up the street. Out came three suited men and two women in pantsuits. A few minutes later, a similar group came out. On and on, the building emptied. But none of those leaving were Chad.

Elias tapped his feet against the ground. He patted his fingers on his arms, rubbed his tattoos. Where was this fucking guy? It was hard for Elias to think Chad was actually a hard worker, a guy who stayed late to get shit done. But he wasn't coming out.

He looked up and down the avenue. The block of office buildings was dying as people retreated to their homes and their dinner plans.

Elias shook his head and stood from the seat. "Fuck." He gave the area one last scan and marched directly to the Mirror's front door.

He braced himself as he took hold of the brushed stainless-steel handle and pulled. Adrenaline flooded his veins, and he smelled the scents of floor cleaner, leather, and paper products on a climate-controlled breeze. He stepped inside the lobby onto a white and black swirled marble floor, and his heart pounded. He was doing this. He couldn't believe it was happening, but it was. He was going to find that asshole and make him pay for every punch, make him pay for ruining what could have been a fantastic thing with Maggie Leer. He wasn't sure how he'd do it just yet, but he knew it was time for some justice.

The lobby had an empty reception desk below a large printed directory. Elias scanned the names and floors, and there that son of a bitch was: *Sixth Floor - Parson's Consulting*.

That bastard had his own company? Probably a gift from his father, a man who everyone in town knew either from his immense list of DUIs or his charitable donations to excuse them.

Elias pressed the elevator button and waited patiently as every natural instinct in his body told him to do otherwise. One said *Run*. It said he should get the hell out of there before he did something stupid and got caught. Another said the elevator was too slow, and he should be running up the stairs; he could get there faster and start ripping this guy to pieces. He resisted both and kept waiting.

The hum of machinery paused, and the elevator dinged and opened. The interior walls shined, mirrors as well. Elias stepped inside and pressed 6.

The sound of the doors closing was like a song. Fireworks went off in his mind as Elias remembered his hate from school, remembered how much he wanted to take Chad's head and smash it in a door, to take a hammer and bash in his face, to get him on the ground and stomp until blood leaked from every orifice.

He thought about the sixth floor and what he would find, and a voice rose in his ears from a whisper to something louder. It was a familiar sound, one that had been rising for the past few weeks, nudging him toward choices, urging Elias to demand respect for himself. It helped him make the choice to rid that cop of his life. It was helping him now, reassuring him his life was about to get better. It tingled inside his sense of justice, teasing the exhilaration he would feel if he went through with it.

"It's almost time," it said, and the corners of Elias's mouth lifted.

The elevator dinged, the doors opened onto the sixth floor, and Elias swayed forward and back, his fists clenched and his feet poised to move.

No one was there. As in the lobby, the reception was empty. The elevator doors started to close, and Elias jumped off.

Gray carpet with darker gray stripes covered the floor. A shiny gray composite desk held the receptionist's phone, pencils, paper, and computer. Light gray walls lined the interior of the building; large, floor-to-ceiling panes of glass formed the exterior wall.

The *minimalist* corporate design made Elias want to puke. He stepped further inside, dying to scrape Chad's face across the rug and leave a red stripe—a pop of color. He hungered to slam Chad's head into the desks and shatter the gray plastic into blood-covered shards.

Past reception was a waiting area with more gray chairs. Beyond that was a cubical farm dressed in the same gray fabric, almost disappearing into the carpet in a sea of monochrome blandness. After the farm was a dozen offices against the exterior windows, and Elias was not surprised to find the corner office door closed and *Chad Parsons* printed on the darkly stained door.

This was it. Behind that door was the thing he came to do. Behind it was justice. Behind it was joy. Elias had started a new life this morning, and he was about to take the next step in making that life evolve into where he was meant to go.

He glanced down at his tightened fists. His knuckles were white. His arms were stiff and ready. The whisper said, *"Go."*

Elias took the knob and twisted. He was slow, deliberate. He wanted to surprise Chad, and he wanted to see that surprise. He wanted to see that face react in terror as he ran at the bully and tore into him with his fists.

The knob was smooth. It opened without a click. There was a television on; it sounded like a sports report, ESPN maybe. He pushed the door in slowly, and it swung in silence, revealing a slice of gray carpet and dark gray bookshelves filled with binders. He gently released the knob and pushed further.

Elias saw the room open up. More shelves, these with awards and plaques. He saw the desk, dark wood, the back of a computer screen. He saw the top of a head. A man was leaning forward, writing something with pen and paper.

Elias moved in. He crept left. He pictured himself getting as close as possible and then springing on Chad. He could feel the man's throat in his hands, the pressure of his flesh, the crack of his windpipe. His hands trembled.

Step by step, closer and closer. Elias knew something phenomenal was about to happen. His head warmed. His hair stood on end. His heart pounded. He neared the side of the desk. Chad was almost within reach.

As Elias moved past the final corner, he glanced at Chad's paper. He wasn't writing; he was drawing. Outlined in ink and shaded with hashed lines was the image of a man's face bursting from its skin. Bone, flesh, and blood soared. Elias got a chill and lunged at his quarry.

Chad spun in his chair, revealing his left hand in his lap, aiming a pistol up at Elias. His eyes were glossy. He grinned as Elias's hands encircled his neck and squeezed.

Pop. Pop. Pop. Elias felt heat in his belly, and his legs went limp. But his arms were fine, and he crushed as hard as he could. He saw insanity in Chad's eyes, and he was going to squeeze until it went dim.

Chad gagged. Elias went down, his grip firm. There was wetness soaking his lower half, and he ignored it. That didn't matter right now. He pulled Chad from the chair onto the floor with him.

Elias felt a crunch. He knew there was a bone in the throat, and he had found it, destroyed it.

Gurgles issued from Chad's lips. He fired again. He grabbed Elias's face with his free hand and dug his thumb into Elias's eye.

Elias screamed but did not let go. He could deal with only having one eye. Chad was dying. That was all that mattered. Blood streamed from his eye socket. Chad's thumb twisted and turned in there, pressing on the inside of his skull. The pain was immense, unimaginable, and it fueled his grip.

Chad fired again. He sucked air through a pin-sized opening in his trachea and knew it was shrinking by the second. His face was purple. His eyes bulged from their sockets, red-veined and plump.

Elias was growing pale. He was getting weak, but he knew he could finish this. He saw blood pooling below them. It reflected the clouds beyond the enormous window, and the thought occurred to him that the sunset would be beautiful from here.

Chad's hand raised, jerking, waving the gun. *Pop*. A shot went into the wall. *Pop*. The ceiling. *Pop*. The top of Elias's head exploded across the office window in an image resembling Chad's drawing.

Blood bubbled from Elias's head like a dying fountain. He collapsed onto Chad, his hands still firm. Chad fought for breath. He grabbed Elias's fingers and fought to peel them back. His vision faded to spots of black and gray as Elias's blood and brain dribbled down his face onto Chad's.

1992

1

Ronny DiMarco rode his bike up 3rd Avenue, then northeast on the slant street Laundale. His breath was heavy, and his legs burned. He didn't notice either. What he felt was his backpack on his back and the sensation that there was a missing thing in his life, and soon it would reside in that bag. He'd get it home, and tonight would be a marvel. He'd lay in his bed, and the world of heroes and villains would engulf his mind in a way the real world never could, with characters more solid and whole than those he was forced to interact with daily.

He could tell that other world was coming. It was inches away from him. Soon, he'd have another tool to step inside it, which made him pedal faster.

After three blocks, Ronny turned down Cooney Street, a winding road lined with ornamental spruces. Its homes were 50s-era bungalows with covered porches and stone brick sidewalks.

He squinted and read the address on each home carefully. 2035. 2037. 2039. Not yet. They rose, and he rode, his fingers tingling, wanting to touch, to hold those pulpy pages between them. 2061. 2063. 2065. His heart jumped, and he slammed his pedals backward to stop. He looked at 2067 from foundation to shingles.

Basement windows seemed to peek out over the side lawn. Neatly pruned rose bushes sat primly before the porch railing. The siding was light brown, accented by dark brown borders and molding. From both sides, a six-foot-tall wooden fence extended and enclosed the backyard.

Ronny gazed at the front door, where a brass knocker hung dead center.

He wasn't sure why, but it reminded him of his grandparents' neighbor in California. It didn't make sense because that house was beige stucco with pink tile roofing. But it wasn't the look that struck him; it was just a feeling. He remembered the half-bald man who came out and watched him play in the front yard with Grampa. It made him feel slimy, like he should go inside and get away. But Grampa always said to ignore it. He said the bald guy was just a nice man who liked to watch kids play. It was the same feeling that crawled across him now, that someone was like that man and wanted something from him. And like Grampa told him, he decided to ignore it.

Ronny pushed down his kickstand and started up the porch steps when he heard a voice from the right of the house.

"Over here." It was Edward Lawrence.

Ronny backed down the steps and saw Eddy leaning out from behind the fence gate.

"Come on," Eddy said. "Bring your bike." He looked across the street, up and down Cooney as far as his view would allow, then back to Ronny. "Hurry up, okay. I'm not supposed to have people over."

Ronny nodded and walked with his bike. Eddy held open the gate and shut and locked it as soon as Ronny was inside.

Eddy gestured at the bare spot of dirt in front of the door to the kitchen. "You can leave it there." He went to the door and waited while Ronny steadied his bike and followed along.

As they went inside, Ronny took in the thick smells of mothballs, medicines, and cleaners. The kitchen was decorated with tiny pieces of memorabilia from rodeos, which surprised Ronny. He pointed at the cowboy hats on the walls, figurines of rodeo clowns, spurs, and framed advertisements from newspapers and posters. He fought to keep his mouth from gaping too widely. "What is all this stuff?"

Eddy's gaze followed the wall-hanging photos and trinkets with a narrowed stare of distrust. "That's all my dead grampa's stuff. He was rodeo clown or something."

"Cool." Ronny gazed deeply into one of the black and white photos. A clown with a cowboy hat stood in a corral, leaning against the fence. He had a tilted gaze and a strange look. He was smiling, and his painted face was of an even larger smile, but while one side of his mouth seemed to hold the expression genuinely, the other half felt broken, as if the smile was a ruse, and something else lay deeper, waiting to get out.

Ronny took a step back and glanced at the door. The feeling of his grandfather's neighbor had returned. He should leave. He should forget about the comics and head back home. *But the comics...* he breathed, and the desire returned. He wanted them. He needed them.

"So, the books?" Ronny looked back at Eddy. "Um..."

Eddy smiled. It started as genuine, like one side of his grandfather's face, then seemed to shift into the other. "They're in the basement. Come on." Eddy left the kitchen and stopped at a door that opened under the stairs. He looked back at Ronny, the genuine smile returning. "This way."

Ronny glanced at the back door again, where his bike waited, then returned to Eddy. He took a breath and headed toward the basement door. His skin crawled. His fingers and toes lost their feeling. But he kept going.

Eddy opened the door. "This way."

The basement was dark. A faint orange glimmer flickered from the furnace and slivers of windowed daylight seemed to die by the distant walls.

"Oh." Eddy reached into the doorway and flipped the light switch. A single bulb stuttered on, casting an amber glow over a cement floor and dozens of shelves and boxes, cleaners, jars, and a hundred differently stored items. "After you." He swept his open palm toward the basement.

Ronny nodded and stepped forward. He slid his hand along the wooden railing and moved down. The stairs moaned with each step. Ronny's gut bubbled. An image formed in his mind of being trapped in this abhorrent place, of being stuck in the basement of this dreadful home with a weird, smiling boy and no light beyond a furnace's flicker and failing windows. He heard a creak from a step behind, and an ease gently brushed over him. Eddy was coming. That was good. He wasn't going to be alone.

His foot reached for the next step, and he felt it set down.

2

Wes Henson sat in bed trying to read a book his mother had brought home for him, *The Color of Magic*. It sounded interesting enough, but he reread the prologue three times, trying to make sense of it, and nothing sank in. He closed it and set it on the nightstand.

He dragged his dry hands down his face, a gust of breath escaping through his fingers. He looked around his room, wishing it felt more calming than it did. Why did his room not feel like it should? Why did this place feel strange and alien? His posters, his book, his desk, they all felt as though they didn't belong to him. It was like he was in a room that was more a replica of his space than his own. It didn't make sense.

His mother walked by the hallway door. He heard her go into Di's room. There was mumbling through the wall, then quiet, then the familiar cadence and tone of the nightly ritual.

Wes's thoughts went back to his day. He'd gone over the strangeness a dozen times, but it had yet to make any sense. Why did he see that stranger dragged across the floor in *The Price is Right*? Why did he have that crazy dream of the same stranger in the basement? Why did it feel like that stranger was him? Why was the dream even still with him? He'd had his share of weird and terrifying dreams throughout his short life, but they faded within an hour of being awake, usually in minutes. Why was this one sticking to him?

A darkness passed through his mind, and the memories of downstairs faded to the scenes from last night—his dream with Diana. The valley, the trees, the dogs, cats, and horses.

He focused on the horses in their corral, and he blinked. He opened his eyes to a whinny, and the brown mare was standing on the side of his bed. She huffed through her lips and leaned toward him.

"What the fuck?" His heart jumped, and he sat up. He moved so quickly that he wobbled at the mattress's edge, teetering off the bedside. He looked back at the horse, but she was gone.

Wes searched the room, but there was no sign of the animal. He would have sworn he still smelled her as he leaned back onto his pillow.

"It can't be." Of course, it couldn't. It was some kind of daydream that got away from him, that was all.

He found himself staring at that strange rock Mom had put on his shelf. The rock she had supposedly found in his things after the fall in the cave. And he couldn't shake the feeling that the rock was staring back at him.

What was this thing? As he watched it, he felt the room getting darker. Darker. And the blue splotches on the stone seemed to brighten, glowing in the dimming light. Something was there, inside that stone. It was, in fact, staring at him. It was doing something to him. It was the reason his room didn't feel quite like *his* room.

Wes inhaled and felt his heart tremble. Spots danced in his vision. A faint whisper spoke in the rear of his mind, but he couldn't make out the words.

"Okay," Mom said.

The room flashed into brightness. Wes spun to the door. Mom came in and sat on the bed beside him. Back to the rock. He looked at it curiously. There was no stare. No oddness. It was just an ordinary, round rock. Was he daydreaming again? Thinking that something was happening? He breathed and felt a flush of embarrassment at the silliness of it all.

"Let me see your back." Mom switched off the lamp.

He didn't want to complain or fight. At this point, he wanted *real* sleep. He wanted to forget about this ridiculous day and move on to more pleasant things. He pulled off his shirt and rolled away from her.

She sat and said the words.

Part Three: The Mountain

Cars and Trucks and Bricks and Blocks

1

Wes easily recognized the parking lot, though it was through the haze of unreality that could only happen in a dream. He gazed over the edge of the lot, across the tops of trees. He saw the valley below, the woods, and peeking back at him in the distance was the little cottage of dogs and cats and horses. He shook his head, happy to be away from that place, but as he turned and gazed at the entrance to Bloodtooth Caverns, he wasn't sure if he'd rather be here.

He wished Jill were here. He saw her lying in the hospital bed, in a coma from blood loss and shock. They said she'd wake up, that by morning she should be able to have visitors. The future prospect of seeing Mom in the morning didn't sit as well with the kids as Wes would have liked, but it had been enough to get them to agree to leave the hospital, even if home wasn't an option.

They'd gone instead to Maryville Manor and gotten two rooms: one for the girls and one for Wes. When Wes opened the doors, the girls refused to go into theirs. They only clung harder to him.

He put Samantha and Lisa into one queen bed and himself in the other, choosing to lay in the bed closest to the door, with each lock engaged and the room's table and chairs barricaded against it. It was overkill. He didn't care. It let the girls eventually sleep, and unbelievably, he soon followed.

He took a step toward the caverns' entrance. The rocks under his boots crackled and scraped. He wondered about his dream from earlier in the day. He wished he had been able to do something. Floating over his own body, floating over Jill, impotent to do anything; just the memory drove him crazy. He wasn't sure how he didn't recognize himself or what *The Price is Right* had to do with anything. Was it an out-of-body experience? He'd felt like a kid again, like the past thirty years hadn't happened. And the same sensation crept back in as he stared into the cave's entrance. At least Di would be there soon. He remembered she would.

In the early days, before Montana was a territory, when the cave was nothing but a natural phenomenon, it was a rocky open mouth. A mouth stained with jagged outcroppings, red from banded iron and hanging down over the entrance like fangs, which lead the native people to give it its ominous name. After it became a mine, a wall and a door were built to control entry. When it became a state park, the door was replaced, and the wall fortified for safety. As he approached it now, it had been restored to its natural state. Other than the parking lot beside it, there was no sign that a human had ever set foot inside the caves themselves.

Wes paused and put his hand against the upside-down U-shaped hole in the rock face. He gazed into the infinite darkness within and wondered if he'd remembered to bring his flashlight this time. He dug into his pockets. There it was, just like before.

He slid the switch on and a yellow-tinted beam shot inside.

"You going without me?" Di switched on her light and swept it across the cave's interior. Her pajamas were dirty, brown at the ankle hems. Her shoes were coated in mud, and she wore no socks. She wondered briefly how she was dressed like this. She hadn't seen those pajamas in years and wished she still had them. She hoped Virb was keeping quiet. She didn't want to get rushed out of the motel and forced to confront Wes before she was ready. If the dream went the same as last time, she...

Memories of before came back, and her heart raced. Fear, no—terror— sorrow and then blood overlapped in her mind, waves of rising anxiety. Images of gore and... It vanished from her view, lost to the whims of the wind.

"Wouldn't dream of it." Wes swept his arm toward the cave's innards. "After you."

She didn't have time to step inside before the whispers came. "*Come.*" "*Hurry.*" "*We're waiting.*"

Wes wanted to slap himself. Why was he going along with this again? He should turn around and run back down the mountain the other way. He was going to object and tell Di. But he'd go inside. That was what was supposed to happen.

"Wait." He put his hand on her shoulder. She was young. She was the kid. His kid sister. She was older. His long-lost friend. "Let's not do this. Let's go back."

"But this is the way." Di took a step inside. "It's waiting down there, big brother." Her words reverberated from every direction.

"Waiting for us." He took his own step inside.

They walked along a trail carved by the natives. There was no lighting, no stairs. Drawings stood from the walls. Not of hunting, like so many images of cave drawings he'd seen pictured. These were of killing. Men pierced others with spears. Arrows stabbed. Ropes hung. Bones were detailed dancing around fires. Infants burned in blazes.

The longer Wes stared at the images, the more he could see them happening, the more the firelight of the past danced in his mind. Blood from ancient times streamed across this land, across this rock. He felt its wetness. He tasted its salty copper on his tongue. In the distance, he heard the cries.

Hot pain flashed across his face—Di's hand.

Di to Wes: "Cut that shit out. We have too far to go."

Wes saw the dimples in her cheeks, the ones Mom used to poke and giggle at. "Yeah. I'm okay."

They went deeper.

The fog of dream thickened as their path shifted into a tunnel they hadn't chosen. They moved into the massive chamber where the rangers always killed the lights. Wes remembered the vampire bats and watched the ceiling. His flashlight fell short, so his eyes scanned the darkness above.

"It's this way," Di said. The conviction in her voice surprised Wes. Her small frame held her pointing arm and stiffened legs like a tiny adult. She aimed at the room's lower exit, the one with the hidden path to the strange rock that now sat on his dresser.

Fear rippled across Wes's flesh. "I don't want to go that way."

Di didn't either. Virb wasn't there. She had no weapons. The thing was probably there, and she didn't want to fight its creations again. But she had to. She had to go that way. It was the way the dream went now, the way it went last time. They didn't have a choice.

They both moved down the path in the center of the massive cavern. Their flashlights highlighted the hanging formations and the ones that grew from below, and in the passing amber light, the rock resembled the fangs of mountainous monsters. The gloom above issued sounds of flapping wings and the squeaks of a hundred creatures.

"Move faster." Wes took his sister's hand and guided her down the trail. He knew they were coming. They were going to swoop from the unseen and bite into his face and gorge themselves on his blood. He saw their wicked teeth in his thoughts. He saw their beady eyes and squat faces, angry, diving, hungry.

Di glanced back but moved as she was asked. They grew louder, closer, and she sped up. She could imagine them from their sounds, giant, ravenous beasts that looked much worse than the darkness portrayed. She ran in time with her brother and began to lead him.

Their feet seemed too slow. The ground moved by even slower. They pushed, the next tunnel in sight, but for each step, each grain of extra pressure they exerted, the world ground by in smaller and smaller increments. The air was quicksand, while the monsters behind were like the wind.

"This isn't right," Wes said. He was caught; he knew he was. The thing had snared him in its trap, and it was time to fight it. He remembered what it was now, if only for a fleeting second. He saw a Chinese finger-trap and knew he and Di were the fingers. "No." Wes stopped running. He turned and faced the blackness. He shined his light and shouted, "No!"

Di pulled on his arm. Then she watched him, and it came to her. They had to face it. "No!" Her light joined his.

Flapping soared at them, louder and closer. Wind brushed over them. Squeaks and squeals bleated in their faces. It washed through their hair. And it all faded.

Di squeezed Wes's hand. Their heartbeats lowered. They walked toward their exit, and came upon it as they should.

Through the lower tunnel, they found the cramped path. The floor was slippery with condensation and fungi. The roof was steep and slanted lower and lower as they walked.

The path they were supposed to take was on the left. They stopped and shined their lights, but it wasn't there. In its place was a brick wall.

"This isn't supposed to be here," Di said. She searched her memories. Wasn't this the way? She knew it was, but she realized it wasn't time yet.

"I—" The floor shook before Wes could say another word. He reached to brace himself against the wall, and the slippery, sloped floor dropped to the angle of a slide, and they plummeted down.

Wes screamed. Di screamed. The flashlight slipped from Wes's hand

and spun down the decline ahead of them. It highlighted brick walls at their sides, a brick ceiling above, and cut stone blocks for the slide below them. When it flashed ahead, there was no end in sight.

"Wes?" Di reached for her brother's hand. He reached for hers.

A ridge rose in the center of the slide. Wes was forced to its right, Di to its left. They tried to grab hands, grab at the floor, grab at the ridge. Nothing slowed their descent.

"We have to stay together!" Di shouted. Her fingers were an inch from his when the ridge shot to the ceiling, a wall between them.

Wes heard Di scream as she was shuffled off in her own direction.

2

Diana slid down what seemed like a never-ending slide, grabbing at the slippery brick floor, walls, and ceiling. She failed and felt her fingernails tear and rip. Her flashlight came loose from her grip and tumbled down the tube ahead. It flickered and went out, leaving her in a dark bottomless fall.

She screamed and called for help.

A voice answered her call; it was a whisper in her mind. *"Prove your worth."*

"What?" Di stared into the passing darkness, waiting for an explanation that didn't come.

The brick below Di vanished, and she went from sliding to falling. She screamed again, and the air around her brightened into the light of day. The sky was deep blue, and a body of water below her was crystal clear.

She'd been transported from a cold, claustrophobic tunnel to the sky around a Caribbean paradise. She saw an island nearby and a tropical rain forest across its surface. Hot air and the smell of the sea filled her. And as the ocean raced toward her, she wondered if she would survive the fall.

Di plunged into the warm, salty brine, her scream silenced by bubbles and waves. She sank four feet under the water before realizing that she needed to breathe back in. Her lungs screamed, and she swam upward. She fought to the surface and gulped down air, then took in her new location.

The mountain was nowhere in sight, and she definitely wasn't in Montana anymore. She floated in clear blue waters, and a hundred feet ahead, a half-moon beach encircled much of the sea around her. Behind that, a vast jungle. Rocks met the beach outside the moon, bordering the coast and blocking any passage.

Di swam toward the beach and studied the area ahead. Near-white sand, lush palm trees; it was beautiful, a place she'd love to go in the real world.

"Where am I?" she puffed and stroked. Her feet found soft sand, and she walked ashore. Her pajamas drained into the surf in streams of salt water, and she realized she was no longer wearing shoes. She didn't know if they were lost in the water, the air, or the cave, but she could feel the sand squish between her toes as she moved.

The sun warmed her, even through heavy, wet fabric. As she scanned the land around herself again, isolation invaded her senses. There was nothing around her, not a chair, a building, not even a cigarette butt in the sand. As the sun began to dim, and a dark cloud rolled across the sky to consume it, she wished Wes was there.

"Hello?" Di shouted. "Is anyone here?"

The only answer was the caw of native birds and then a low growl from the distant left.

Di's gaze shot toward the noise. She examined the shadowy depths of the forest floor. There was no movement, but the sound continued. She held her hands to her forehead to shade her eyes and stared harder. She saw only darkness until something crossed her view that froze her solid. A pair of eyes.

She could make out nothing more than the gleam of two floating dots, but she knew exactly what it was. She didn't have to see more. She would recognize those eyes in a second, no matter where she saw them, no matter the light, the place, the weather. It was the panther from her nightmares, Bagheera.

Most kids liked Bagheera. In *The Jungle Book*, he was a friend, a kind jungle beast. When Di was younger, though, she saw a documentary on panthers the same week as she first saw the beloved children's movie. The ideas conflated in her mind, and since then, regularly, she would find herself running through the jungle with Bagheera on her tail, trying his hardest to get a taste of her flesh.

And here he was, yellow-eyed, with the darkest black fur, sizing up his prey from down the beach.

This was going to be bad. She looked around again, this time not for others but for any kind of weapon. There was nothing. Not a stray stick on the beach, not a broken tree branch, not even a rotten piece of driftwood.

She saw his eyes move down, closer to the ground. That meant one thing. He was going to charge.

Di took off in a sprint to the right. She tossed sand in fans of glowing grains. Her feet struggled through soft mounds, and from behind, she heard the thump of panther paws on leaves and branches and jungle floor.

"Shit!" she shouted as she ran. She crossed the beach and reached the edge of the jungle. She stopped at the base of a massive palm. Should she really be going in there? She was out of room on the beach, with nowhere to go. But once in the jungle, the cat would have had the advantage. It could climb and jump and dodge the terrain much better than a human. Looking back at the beach, she asked herself: *What choice do I have?*

An idea struck her: the water. Maybe she could swim better than it? She glanced at the rolling waves, and as she imagined getting back in the sea and swimming away, the shore expanded. It stretched in front of her eyes, dozens of feet becoming hundreds. She'd never make it.

She dove into the shadows of the mighty palms and ran. There was barely a path to take. She ducked under fronds and jutted left and right around enormous spined bushes. The floor was a mix of sand and shed fronds and spikes, and every other step stabbed her feet with angry, dried vegetation.

The hungry cat's growl thundered through the jungle, drowning out the sound of crashing waves and frothy surf. Wood cracked, branches broke, and Di knew it was getting closer.

Hot blood and terror rushed through Di's veins. She ignored the pain in her feet, the warmth and wetness of bleeding soles, and just knew there had to be help ahead. Something had to be beyond the next clump of trees. That was how her dreams of Bagheera always worked; she ran and ran and found a hut to hide in or a boat to get away in. Something had to be ahead.

She clenched her fists and pounded her soles into the sand. She huffed and ran and felt hot breath behind her neck.

No, no, no, no.

She darted around the next tree and spotted a hollow log on the ground. It was slightly larger than her pre-teen body and definitely smaller than Bagheera.

Di leaped into the hollow space and crawled on her hands and knees.

The log smelled of rotten wood, dirt, and cat urine. She shuffled her arms and legs, wiggled her back, and quickly inched deeper into the tree.

Bagheera roared. Sharp pain seized Di's leg. She howled and fought through it.

"It's just a scratch. Just a scratch," She repeated over and over again. The great cat had never caught her before; she always woke up if it was about to. She knew this could be bad. The pain was hot and stinging. But she'd deny it. She would refuse to believe it had caught her in any meaningful way. Instead, she'd crawl onward. She'd go where it couldn't reach, and she'd make it.

After several more feet, Di saw that the log was more than a hiding place. It went farther than a fallen tree would. The bright day's light faded as she moved deeper. Bagheera roared and clawed back at the log's opening, but he couldn't get inside, and his roar was getting softer.

After a few minutes, Di saw light ahead. It was dim and made her think of the inside of a building. She kept crawling. When she reached the end, she looked around before climbing out. The path opened into a parking garage with a dozen different cars, trucks, and sports utility vehicles. It was familiar.

3

Tommy hovered over a tropical beach, viewing as he had been for what felt like ages. It was a scene he'd never expected to be in. The sand, the heat, the salt; all of it was the stuff of annoyance to him.

When Tommy was five, his mom and dad took him on a trip to the Washington coast. He never learned the name of the place but later filed it away in his head as the same beach where the Goonies found a pirate ship. It wasn't really, but it made sense in his head.

That was the first time he'd ever seen the ocean. As soon as they arrived, Mom and Dad walked him straight from their rented house a block down the road to the beach. They paused where the sidewalk met the sand and took off their shoes; Mom carried Tommy's.

From the moment Tommy's foot touched the grit, his hair stood up. He wondered if the whole thing was a joke of some kind. The air smelled like salty rotting fish. The sand was scratchy and stuck to his feet. As he walked, it was kicked into the air and stuck higher on his legs.

"Come on," Mom said, and she began down to the water.

He protested. Said he didn't like it.

She ignored him and repeated, "Come on."

Tommy looked back at the sidewalk, down the beach at a half-dozen people on towels or standing in the water. He didn't want to do this. Why did Mom want to go out there?

"Go on," Dad said. He wore a smile that would have ruined Tommy's trust had he lived through the night.

Tommy walked slowly, lifting his feet high with every step, trying to scatter as little sand onto himself as he could. He made it past the dry mounds and onto the flat, wet swath of beach where land met sea. It was cold under his feet. Goosebumps rose up his legs.

"Come on." Mom smiled from ear to ear. Her feet were under the water. Waves barreled toward her, and Tommy gasped. They looked like they were feet above him, at least as high as Mom's chest, and they flowed over the sea right at her. The entire coast felt like it was rushing to crash into his mother.

"No!" Tommy ran at his mother. "Move, Mommy!"

The ocean collided with Mom, first splitting at her back and causing an expression of shock and fear across her face, then pushing her toward the beach while sucking her feet backward and out from under her. The wave lifted her up and carried her as Tommy tried to get closer.

Sea foam, water, and pressure slammed into Tommy. He screamed and reached for his mother. The wave crested up over his head and knocked him back.

He saw the sky through a veil of light green liquid. Water rushed into his mouth and down his throat. The salty wetness made him gag, and as he tried to breathe back in, it burned his lungs, and he coughed. He reached for the ground to push himself up, but it didn't seem to be there. Up was down, and down was up, and more water raced into his lungs. The green sky faded. He coughed and gagged. He wondered if he would die now and what that would feel like. His eyes burned under the salty ocean, but part of him was happy because probably no one would see his tears.

"Tommy!" Dad seized him from under the arms and lifted him high. Tommy puked his lunch of McNuggets and seawater down his father's back.

The waves drew back into the great Pacific, and Mom was climbing to her feet. Her hair wrapped around her head, her entire being coated in wet sand. She coughed as she staggered up the beach, then let herself collapse onto her rump on the dry sand.

Tommy coughed and fought to get down from his father's hands. He ran and hugged his retching mother, freezing seawater and rough grit between them. That was the last time they went to the beach that trip. The last time ever for Tommy.

They returned to the rental house, changed their clothes, and went out for dinner. On the way back, rain came down like a monsoon, and a car skidded through a red light in front of them. The crash killed Dad instantly.

As Tommy scanned the crescent-shaped tropical beach from many feet above, he couldn't shake the sense of shame he felt for that long-ago summer day. He wished he had it to do over again. As much as he hated the sand and water, he would have tried to act like he enjoyed it. He would have gone back in, maybe even drowned for real if... He would have tried to keep Mom and Dad there at any cost instead of going out to dinner. It could have changed everything.

Tommy's gaze crossed the crashing waves and saw Wes's little sister. Why was Di in his dream? She was running into the forest. Then Tommy heard the panther.

He flew across the sky and hovered above Di. He watched her fight the jungle. He saw her fear and saw the jungle split as the giant panther hunted. He had to help her. He was no good against a panther, but he had become good at something else.

Tommy watched Di's gate and guessed her next turn. That was where he imagined the log.

4

Wes watched his flashlight get further and further away as it slid down the tube ahead of him. He grasped at the side of the tunnel. He thought about Di and what she must be going through, and his stomach turned.

He screamed. He rolled onto his belly and tried to grip the slide with his fingers, his nails—nothing took hold.

"That won't work," a whisper slinked into his thoughts. *"If you want to survive, you'll have to prove yourself."* The whisper sunk into his bones with a low, creepy resonance.

"Who said that?" Wes shouted. He pivoted onto his back. "Who's there?"

There was no answer, but at the far end of the tunnel, he saw his flashlight drop out of sight. It fell out of the cave as if it had vanished over the edge of the world.

Wes strained to see. A faint light, dull with the night's gentle hue, outlined the tunnel ahead. As Wes flew toward it, he could see a building and the tops of some trees. It was the end of the slide, but where was he sliding to?

He tensed. He had no idea what was about to happen. His flashlight had disappeared with a drop; he would likely do the same. But drop to where? And how far? Was it a few inches or a mile?

Wes planted his feet into the tunnel, trying to slow himself. He pushed his palms flat. He slid just the same.

The end came closer. Within a breath, it was in front of him. He held his lungs full as he was tossed out into...

It was a night. He saw stars and the fullest of moon as he fell. It was a glorious night. The craters of the moon presented themselves in crisp, clean clarity. He saw Orion, the Big Dipper, and Sagittarius standing from the sky so clearly that they could have had lines connecting their points. The breadth of the Milky Way radiated with brightness and color that shamed the poultry sight that usually filled his night's sky. He found his eyes glued to the heavens, and his back thumped to grass.

The world was a spinning collection of colored dots and darkness. He held himself steady and began to get a picture of his surroundings.

He sat on neatly mowed grass. Etched stone markers of similar size surrounded him in rows. He was in a graveyard.

Wes stood. The enormous moon's light showed acres of graves. They went on in every direction. He saw no fence or border where the graveyard ended, only mausoleums of various sizes in a row a quarter mile away.

"Where the hell am I? Hello?"

Crickets chirped. A light breeze ran through Wes's hair. By his right foot, a rotting hand burst through the soil.

"Shit!" Wes jumped back. This couldn't be real. He already knew he was dreaming. It was a bad dream. He had watched *The Return of the Living Dead* last week and had gone without nightmares since then. It was just catching up to him, is all.

Another hand burst through the ground. This one's fingers were tipped with bone. Its skin was ripped at the knuckles exposing slimy ligaments as the hands worked together to grip the land and hoist itself upward.

"No, no, no." Wes backed away further. The glistening rot on the creature's hands, the gathering dew on the grass, the humidity that blew across his neck from the wind: it was all too real. He had been dreaming, he knew that; but this, this didn't feel like a dream. The terror that rose through his spine didn't feel like a dream's terror. It felt like the waking fear of real and impending death. He had to get away from this. The question of dream versus reality had to wait. No matter which, he needed to be gone when this creature escaped the earth.

Wes forced his brain to work overtime. Where to go? He had seen no fence or wall, but he saw those buildings, the houses for the dead. That was a good start. He could have walls around him while he figured the rest out.

The monster in the ground strained, and Wes spun to run. He slammed chest to chest into something. A gnarled face greeted his own. Its nose was gone. One of its eyes was split open, maggots escaping over its eyelids. The other was grayed and clouded but fixed on Wes. Its decaying hands grabbed Wes's shirt. Crumbs of dirt ran down Wes's clothes as it leaned in and spread its yellowed teeth.

Wes screamed. His brain was frozen, but his fight or flight system chose fight. He shoved the monster in the chest with both hands, and it stumbled backward.

"Gotta go," he mumbled. But his legs weren't moving.

A whiff of rotten meat clawed inside his nose and hung on. He felt pressure on his ankle and looked down. The one crawling from its grave was pawing at his foot.

"Fuck!"

Wes sprinted past the undead thing and around a gravestone. He saw the hole it had come from and leaped over it. Around the next stone, more hands grabbed for a hold.

"Fucking zombies?" Wes's heart pounded through his chest, through his breaths. The movie returned to him in drips and drabs. Hungering corpses with no way to kill them—they were already dead—unless they were burned.

He rounded the next grave. A woman crawled across the grass. She must have been in her twenties and recently buried. Her skin was pale, her white dress stained with dirt, her lower leg dragged behind her, held on by black thread that ripped from her rotting skin. Her eyes found Wes, and she crawled after him, groaning.

Wes's stare fixed on the row of mausoleums a hundred and fifty yards ahead. Zombies had dug themselves up in every direction, and as they rose, each turned and headed toward him. He ran through grave after grave, getting closer, but the path ahead was growing denser by the second.

He slid past a tree and around another grave. A decaying older man with gray hair and a disco-era blue suit grabbed at Wes, who shoved him and jumped back. An elderly woman clawed into Wes's forearm. Red scratches lined his skin. He punched her in the side of the head and slipped free, then leaped around the next gravestone. Two enormous zombies came from the left. Their bulbous fat pulled their shirts untucked as they shuffled forward. On the right, a monster of more bone than meat stumbled at him. Its skinless mouth moved up and down as if it were already chewing, and its empty eye sockets stared down Wes as if it could see clearly into his soul.

Wes braced himself, planning to slip right through them. But as his foot stiffened, he found not stable ground but the exit hole of some beast.

"Fuck!"

He sank into the earth. The giants, the bag of bones, those behind him, all moved closer. Wes grabbed at the grass and dirt around him. Panic ripped his mind to shreds. They were inching closer—they were slow, but every inch counted, and second by second, he was losing his escape window. He'd seen enough zombie movies to know what would happen once the mob got a grip; it would be all over. His intestines and brains would be stripped free and passed around like hors d'oeuvres.

Each handful of earth Wes grabbed seemed to come loose in his grip. Each time he shifted his body to grab again, he sank deeper into the hole. He grabbed again, lower. Again, lower. He was down to his chest. The mob closing in kneeled. Their hands were out, reaching.

Wes screamed. A zombie laid its crumbling hand on his arm. He pulled it away and grabbed again; the soil around him pulsed. Inside the hole, something seized his feet. Wes screamed again. Was another one in there? He thought the hole meant one had escaped, but was that not true? He kicked and thrashed. Whatever had his feet pulled.

Wes sunk to his shoulders. Only his arms and head were above ground. Mouths spread as they moved in on his flesh. He pulled in his arms and covered his face.

The ground pulsed again. Around his chest, down to his hips, he felt a wave of pressure—and again. It felt like the earth was trying to swallow him.

A howl of terror escaped Wes's lips, and his entire body shot down into the depths of the grave.

5

Diana recognized the garage. It was the one downtown that most people used for the movie theater. She was on one of the middle floors and could see the front of the theater through the gaps in the concrete.

She walked to the closest exit, an elevator and staircase. She was ready to be home. She was ready for this dream to be over. She wanted to see Virb. She wanted to be back in her bed and know that Mom and Dad were downstairs in their bedroom.

Di pressed on the push bar; the exit didn't open.

"Shit!" She heaved the bar in again. "Open!"

A car door slammed somewhere across the lot. Di spun to see where it was. The garage was about a third full, dotted with pickups, minivans, and various sedans and hatchbacks. They all seemed to stare at her. Not that they had eyes, but their essence seemed to be watching her, the way a resting tiger may look the other way while being well aware that prey is in its den.

She shook her head, hoping the strange thoughts would drift away. But they didn't; the more her gaze drifted from vehicle to vehicle, the more she was sure. She was surrounded by things that meant her harm. She was surrounded by a memory of terror and sorrow.

A scream echoed against the concrete walls. It was muffled at first. Di searched for the sound. Across the garage, on the next row, where the road inclined to the next level up, feet dangled from the ceiling. Then legs came down, then a torso. Lastly, the entire body dropped through. It was Wes.

He thumped against the roadway, and Di ran to him, watching each vehicle suspiciously as she passed them.

Wes sat in the middle of the path as Di reached him. His clothes were covered in dirt. His face was blank, his eyes wide and unfocused. Somewhere across the lot, an engine started.

"Wes," Di grabbed him and hugged him.

He pushed her back and scooted away across the ground. His eyes met hers, and she could see panic. His teeth were clenched. He pressed his back against the rear bumper of a small Honda and looked her up and down.

"Wes..." She reached into the empty space between them. "It's me: Di. What's wrong."

His breath was heavy. He looked her over again and seemed to ease, then examined the world around them. "Di?"

She went closer. Another engine started. Now, she looked around the garage again. "Wes, we need to go. I don't think it's safe here."

Wes's breathing calmed. He stood up. He bit his lip.

Diana joined him on her feet.

Tires squealed above them. From the top of the incline, a maroon Ford Ranger flew down the concrete toward them.

Di saw the pickup. She didn't know why it was coming, but she knew it was coming for her and her brother. She grabbed Wes. He scowled as she pulled him around the Honda, past its front, and pushed them both against the concrete wall.

The Ranger shot by, scraping the Honda's rear bumper and showering the garage in sparks.

"What the hell?" Wes shouted, finally looking like he was awake.

The Ranger turned the corner and kept going. A few seconds later, tires squealed, and an engine revved.

Di grabbed Wes's hand. "We need to get out of here."

Wes looked for an exit. He saw where they were and focused on the door across the lot. He didn't understand why some places in his dreams tonight seemed so familiar while everything happening to him was a surprise.

"Over there." Wes pointed at the door.

"It's locked. I tried it," Di said. "I think we need to go to the top or the bottom floor."

The Ranger sped around the corner, followed by a Bronco. Their engines harmonized in acceleration. The Honda beside them started and reversed from the space. No one was in the driver's seat.

"Shit, shit, shit," Di pulled at Wes's shirt.

The Honda's wheels turned, aiming the car at Wes and Di.

Wes grabbed Di and yanked them both in front of the neighboring Ramcharger. The Honda smashed into the passenger side of the sports utility vehicle, crunching into its door and scraping forward into the engine compartment. It ground against the Dodge's metal, screeching until it collided with the garage wall.

The SUV shuddered forward under the Honda's pressure, and Wes pushed Di further away from the import. They almost reached the corner of the Ramcharger's hood when the Ranger crashed into the wall on the driver's side. Concrete chips and sparks rained over Wes and Di. Black smoke billowed from the Ranger's hood, and exhaust and gas fumes flooded the air.

Di saw the Bronco coming and knew what it was about to do. "Up!" she yelled at her brother. She grabbed onto the hood of the SUV and climbed. "Up!"

Wes stared for a second, and it sunk in. He jumped onto the hood and pulled himself toward the roof.

Under the swelling noise of Honda, Ranger, and Bronco engines, the Bronco crashed into the rear of the Ramcharger. The vehicle skidded forward below Wes and Di, its front bumper and then its grill smashing into the garage wall. The brother and sister slid on the SUV's roof and steadied themselves. And then its engine started.

"Shit, shit, shit!" Wes shouted. "Come on!"

He leaped from the Dodge onto the hood of the Honda, then down to the floor. Di watched, feeling the roar of the Ramcharger's engine, unable to escape the thought that it was growling angrily. It lunged forward into the wall, and Di jumped to the Honda. She took a step and hopped down.

Wes grabbed his sister's hand and pulled. They ran up the incline toward the top floor, and the Bronco reversed back into the roadway.

Tires squealed, and all Wes could think of was, *I wish Dad was here.*

He glanced back and saw the Dodge reverse until it was beside the Bronco. The Honda reversed, and the three stood as a wall, blocking any downward escape.

"How—" Di muttered.

Wes saw his dad standing twenty feet in front of them. Was that possible? It must have been because he wanted it; he made a dream-Dad show up in this crazy place.

"Dad!" Wes put his free hand out to grab his father's.

They crossed under the ledge of the top floor, where the path led them onto the roof. Wes took Dad's hand and pulled, but Dad didn't move.

"What's going on here?" Dad pointed at the line of unmanned, revving vehicles.

"No time, Dad, come on!" Wes shouted.

"What—" was all Dad could say before the Honda, Bronco, and Ramcharger shifted into gear and raced up the incline. They crunched into each other as they accelerated. The noise of scraping steel and the smell of burning gas filled the garage.

"Come on!" Di shouted. Her voice was shrill. She didn't know if she had ever been this scared, but as her heart throbbed in her chest, she knew she never wanted to be again.

Dad clicked into motion, and they ran together onto the top floor. They turned right, following the road toward the rooftop exit that let off onto 8th Avenue. Tires screeched behind them and then in front. A red Jeep Cherokee swerved into their path and raced toward them.

"That way!" Wes pointed to a line of parked cars on their left: a van, a backed-in sedan, and a station wagon.

Di hopped up onto a sedan's hood. Wes hopped up after her. Dad ran and stood between the sedan and station wagon.

"Dad!" Di screamed. But she was drowned out by the roaring engines and squealing tires.

Something glinted across the garage and caught Wes's eye. Through the noise and the madness, it held his attention for a fraction of a second that felt like much, much longer. The flash faded into shadow, but against the far wall, Wes was sure there was a man. He wore a wide-brimmed hat and a yellowish shirt. His eyes shined in the gloom like a predator, and the darkness of the shadow seemed to sway with him as he leaned to the side.

Tires screeched. The Jeep slammed into the station wagon. It slid and pinned Dad between the two vehicles. He screamed a blood-curdling howl.

The other three cars rounded the corner and raced in a line, Honda, Bronco, Ramcharger.

The Jeep reversed and then rammed the wagon again. Dad folded forward onto the sedan's hood. The sedan started, and then the wagon.

"Dad!" Di cried. She reached out but may as well have been a thousand feet away.

Wes pulled his sister over the sedan's roof and onto its trunk. The car darted into the road, scraping flesh from Dad's legs and yanking him forward. Di and Wes fell against the garage wall, tumbling to the ground.

Dad dropped to the cement clutching his knees and thighs. Blood gushed from his wounds. Shredded flesh poked through holes in his jeans.

Di moved toward Dad. Tears ran down her face like a river. Wes stopped her and dragged her in front of the neighboring van.

The sedan backed up. It thumped over Dad's chest. It rolled forward again. He coughed blood and spat a glob of chunky red flesh onto the parking space. He gurgled and reached toward Di and Wes. He tried to say something, but they couldn't tell what it was.

The Honda squealed, turned, and crashed into the space. It rammed into the wagon, its tire crushing Dad's face.

Di screamed.

The man was motionless.

Wes froze, not a part of him knowing what to do.

The Bronco slammed into the rear of the Honda, crunching the Honda and the wagon into one. The Ramcharger barreled into the Bronco. The front end of the Bronco lifted, and it climbed onto the Honda like a monster truck. It drove over the passenger compartment and slammed down on the Honda's hood.

Wes was deafened by his own screams as the Honda's tire crunched down, and his father's head exploded across the parking space.

2022

1

Frayed brown curtains swayed against the motel window as air from the wall-mounted HVAC unit blew past. Virb ignored the curtains, the noises that fell through the paper-thin walls from the ladies of the night in adjacent rooms, and the shouts of arguments over sex or drugs that drifted in through the window's thin glass panes. He laid on the edge of the bed, his gaze focused on Diana, his paws pressed into the bedding, and his body tense and ready to pounce.

No one had seen Virb guard Diana this way. Before six months ago, he never had to do it. But when the nightmares started back up, he watched, wishing he could help. If only he was allowed in.

Di whimpered through sleeping lips, "Dad." She sucked in a gasp and grabbed her sheets. Her eyes opened. She lifted her head and searched her room. Where was she? How did she get here? Where were the cars? Dad?

The year sunk in. It was 2022, not 1992. It had been thirty years. It had been seconds. Tears burst from the corners of her eyes. She slammed her head back onto the stiff foam pillow, and Virb crawled up the bed on his belly. He sniffed her face and licked her cheek.

"Yeah, yeah." She gazed through the gloom into his deep brown eyes, and he brought her to smile. It was small, but it helped. She stroked his neck, and he rolled into her. He pressed his back into her side and nuzzled against her arm. She scratched his chest. "I wish you could have been there too."

She forced herself to sit up. Sleep wouldn't be possible for the foreseeable future. She scooted back against the headboard and dug through the sheets for the television remote. She switched it on and continued to scratch Virb's chest.

Reruns and infomercials ruled the lineup. She passed CNN and Fox News without pause. There was enough bad in this town without worrying about the rest of the world's horrors.

Her eyes focused on the screen, but her mind was elsewhere. She thought about the dream. Why did she dream it again? She'd had recurring dreams in the past, but not like this one. Not like the cottage of cats and dogs. These weren't recurring; they were the same. Exactly the same, down to every detail. But they felt live, like she was making the decisions all along, even though she'd been through it all before—was that even possible? To have the exact same dream, the exact same experience, make the exact same choices? Watch your father—

She shuddered, and tears returned.

It really was back. She had been leaning against a hope that what was happening to her was a returning psychosis, that it never really happened back then. But it did. And it was happening again.

"Wes." She threw back the sheets and grabbed her clothes.

2

Sweat dripped from Wes's chin, his neck, and his back. He lay on his side, staring across the room at his sweet little girls.

Sam and Lisa huddled together in the middle of the queen bed, their heads nearly touching, their shoulders pressed against one another. No limbs or appendages extended from under their bedding. No parts hung over the side. Not tonight. The world was no longer the innocent place it once was for Wes's little girls, and that pained him in an unexpected way.

Unlike some parents who wanted their children to remain small and dependent on them, Wes and Jill always agreed to praise their growth. Not rush it, but encourage it. They wanted to be excited for Sam and Lisa as they crossed each stage into greater childhood and eventually into adulthood. Wes wanted to see them go off to college and thrive. Get married and experience the joys of kids of their own. But the lesson they got today, the thrust of his babies into the vicious world of adult reality, was one that tore at his heart.

As soon as he'd opened his eyes, he turned and found them. He watched their chests rise and fall and knew that, at least for the moment, they were okay. The visions of his father's exploding skull resurfaced and hung behind his thoughts like nesting insects inside a wall, but Sam and Lisa's faces soothed so much of the memory away.

Wes pushed himself up. He felt a chill over his damp chest and back. He brushed his hand over the sheets, testing the wetness. They were soaked. A small grace of having the bed to himself, he could lay on the other side, Jill's side. That would be dry.

He stood and tiptoed to his bag on the dresser and dug out a clean pair of pajama pants and sneaked into the bathroom. After shutting the door with the smallest of clicks, he started the shower.

As water rushed over Wes's face, yesterday, the day he tried to forget, returned to him. It had been one of the worst days of his life, barely behind those of thirty years ago, when it all happened the first time.

In the back of his mind, Wes always knew this was coming. Not exactly what had happened to Jill, but he knew the thing would return. He felt it then, and as the weeks and days got closer, he should have felt the change coming.

He shook his head. Tears swelled in his eyes, and he thought of the child, one that could have been his own, plunging that knife into Jill's leg. And then her waist. The slices in Jill's flesh. They'd looked more like something that should be lying on a butcher's table than part of a human. The image as they waited for the ambulance—lacerated muscle and the bone beneath, him trying to slow the bleeding—they'd be with him forever.

And he did nothing. He screamed, sure, but he was incompetent. He couldn't get free; he couldn't save her. The only reason he saw that he and Jill lived was that that madman and child wanted them to. But why?

He saw Jill in her hospital bed, her legs covered. He only got a glance before they were kicked out of the hospital. He wanted to hold her and hug her. But he only got a glimpse. Her leg wrapped in bandages floated in his thoughts.

He hung his head under the water for as long as he felt he could get away with before shame gripped him for allowing thoughts of self-loathing. He stopped the water and dried himself off, and he heard a knock at the door to the room.

A glance at his phone showed 3:15 am, no time for visitors. He slid on his pajama pants and draped a towel across his shoulders. Out of the bathroom, he checked on the kids: still snoring away.

The light on the opposite side of the peephole flickered. Another knock, this one softer.

Wes brought his eye to the lens, placing his hand on the door's lock. What he saw sent shivers down his back.

Blink, blink, blink... sister.

He saw the reception area of Elnore Jones Recovery. He saw the group therapy circle on Family Visit Day at the RiverSong Institute. He saw an empty chair at Mom's funeral that should have been filled with his goddamn sister. And then he heard the screaming.

It didn't matter what age she was, it was all the same. At least in the beginning. In the beginning, she actually wanted help; she actually thought she was going insane. No matter what Wes said, "keep quiet," "it really happened," "don't tell anyone or they'll lock you up"—none of it sunk in. She had to tell everyone who would listen. Maybe Wes should have understood her need, but even now, he just didn't.

Then there was her committal. Then release and the drugs. Then committal, and round and round it went, each time like a screw that unwound Wes's ability to deal with her.

He wanted to. He wanted to help her. But she would never listen. Instead, there was only a rampage of accusations and torrents of blame at everyone in her life while no acceptance of what she had done to herself. Mom's funeral was the last straw.

And now, there she stood, fidgeting in front of his door. Now? After what had happened to Jill? This is when she shows up for another of her *visits*?

Wes clenched his fists and decoupled his barricade.

3

Edward Lawrence cracked the door open and peered into what was once his grandmother's bedroom. He swallowed and closed off his nose from inhaling the room's stench any further.

Julie Redmond lay on the coverlet, her dead mother's arm draped over her back and midsection. Ed had offered the child the couch, but she had said she wanted to sleep with Mommy. Who was he to argue? She'd done her job. As far as he was concerned, she could have ice cream for dinner and cake for breakfast. He figured it would only be a matter of time anyway before the voice would ask for her blood. So, might as well let her have what she wanted.

Ed looked over the corpse. In that bed, her thin limbs and long hair reminded him of his grandmother. He remembered sneaking into her bedroom when he first moved in with her, scared, after nightmares of his mom and dad's murders. All he had wanted was to crawl under the covers with her and feel a warm body beside him. All he wanted was to know that he wasn't alone in the world. He only did that once.

"Your whore of a mother and drug addict father are burning in Hell," she said through cracked eyelids. She used as little energy to disparage them as she felt they were worth. "I will not let you soil my bed with their filth, Eddy. Go back to your room."

"But, Gramma?" was all he could eke out through the tears.

"Come in my room again, and I will stain your bottom red. Now go." Her eyes never widened. Her tone grew no louder. But Eddy Lawrence knew then that he was the darkness left behind by his mother and father. And he wasn't going to be welcome, not in her bed or anywhere.

Blood had soaked the wood, the sheets, and the floor below, by the time his grandmother's banishment was repealed. Now they were wet again. Sticky. The putrefaction was underway with little more than twenty-four hours of decay, but in some ways, it was a welcoming scent. It was a scent that reminded Ed that with the voice's help, he would make the things he wanted his own. He just had to do a few simple jobs along the way.

4

Wes opened the hotel room door and examined his sister. She was cleaner than he expected. The color in her cheeks, her eyes, they actually looked normal. He doubted the image. When was the last time she appeared sober in front of him? He couldn't remember.

He took a breath, and before he could utter a word, she said, "Can we talk?" Her voice was steady. The hesitance of begging and underlying accusations he would have expected were missing.

Wes saw his sister standing on his home's doorstep eighteen months ago. He was wedged between the door and the frame, blocking her from seeing in and any wandering children's prying eyes from seeing out.

"Just a little—like a few hundred," she said back then. Black bags hung from her eyes but didn't compare to the dark purple bruise that covered the left half of her face. If he had seen something like her in a movie, he would have thought the makeup had been overdone, unrealistic, and exaggerated. But there she was, trembling, barely able to hold her hand steady as she reached out to him with an open palm. "Three hundred? You can spare it."

"I'm not giving you any money. I told you that last time."

She leaned right, peering through the tall windows that framed the front door. "What about Samantha? Can I see her? Little Lisa?"

"No." He shook his head, more confident in this decision than most things in his life. "You're strung out. I can see it. You want to see them? Come back clean."

He could see the rage building, her tightening fists, her clenching jaw. Then the shame. She didn't want to be there. She didn't want to be asking for money. She *did* want to see her nieces. She had only seen them from afar. Only said words to them as babes in someone else's arms. Tears welled in the corners of her eyes as she thought about the aunt she could have been and wished she was. She spun and slinked away.

He had seen the sickness in her flesh through and through that day. In the hallway of the Maryville Manor, he saw none of it.

He gestured to the right. "Got to the room next door. Give me a sec."

He shut the door and locked it, threw on a shirt, and went into the adjoining room, closing the door with a brief glance at his girls. He didn't know what was about to happen, but they didn't need to be involved in any part of it.

When Wes opened the door, Di was staring down at the worn and dusty hiking boots on her feet. Her jeans were spattered with drops of dried mud, but even so, it was a *clean* look—one of being dirtied through work, not junk. She looked up and met his gaze. Her eyes were sincere and clear.

He held up his hand.

"I don't want any money."

"Five minutes. And be quiet. The girls are sleeping."

Di nodded. Wes stood aside and gestured her in. After she sat on the edge of the closest bed, he shut the door but held onto the handle.

"How's Jill?" She fidgeted with the folds of her jeans. She didn't realize how nervous she would be after being apart for so long. She remembered that day on his doorstep as well, the crawling need inside her, the spikes running through her blood and crawling under her skin, and the humiliation of having to go there, beg, and be turned away. There were years she wished she could take back. That was one of them. "They wouldn't tell me anything other than she was in Memorial."

Wes sighed. His fingers relented, and he took a seat on the bed's other corner. He stared at the television's blank screen, glanced at the cracked door into his adjoining room, and back at the TV.

"She's in critical condition. They say she has a good chance of making it, but she's lost so much blood..."

"My God." Her jaw dropped. "What happened?"

Wes went through the previous day's events, from the kids' drop-off at school all the way to leaving Jill at the hospital. He didn't mention the nightmares. Thirty years ago, they had been part of what sent her to the nut house and started her downward spiral—that piece could stay with him.

"And the dreams?" Di said as if reading his mind. "Are you having them again too?"

Wes's face went blank. She couldn't be serious. He hoped to God she wasn't also having them.

"Last night—before all this happened—it was cats and dogs. Were you there?"

He turned and faced her, still unable to hold an expression on his face.

"Tonight, it was..." Tears ran down her face.

"Dad..." His lips trembled.

"Dad."

Every hair on Wes's body stood on end. They were the same dreams. He had tried to believe they were recurring memories that refused to fade. But they weren't. It was like they and their past selves were somehow experiencing the same dreams together. Old Wes and Young Wes. Old Di and Young Di. And that meant they still had a long way to go.

He squeezed his grip on his knee. This wasn't fair. They had found the way to end it. They *had* ended it.

"It can't be." He shook his head, refusing to accept what he knew was true.

"He's back," she said, nodding.

1992

1

Ray Trent crept around his father's hunting cabin; his eyes squinted in anticipation, his tongue hanging from his mouth like a drooling dog. He was eager to see what she had been up to in his absence. Had anything happened?

He peeked through a dust-layered window. There she was. The candle had gone out. The lights were all out. Amanda Brolin lay on the floor, asleep, having knocked over the chair she had been bound to. The gag was on her chin. The blindfold was still in place. It was an interesting sight but not what he was hoping to see. Her struggling, red-faced, angry, maybe her clothes disheveled in her attempts to escape—there was none of that.

He wished he had been there to see her fall. He wished Dad would have gone to sleep sooner so he could have snuck out to her minivan and gotten here earlier. Either way, he'd make sure he had some fun.

2

Amanda Brolin sat in the dirt in a backyard. She'd never seen this place before. Large oak boughs spread into a canopy above the far half of the fenced-in space. By the house were toys arranged in a neat half-circle around a storage container. Sitting on top of the storage container was a boy.

Amanda didn't know the child but immediately found his name on her tongue. "Eddy?"

Eddy Lawrence nodded. He was playing with something reddish and black that Amanda didn't recognize.

"Where are we?" She examined the house. The windows were all blocked, black shades drawn inside. It seemed to tower over the boy, and as his head leaned left or right, turning the item in his hand, the building creaked and bent with him.

Amanda clenched the dirt below her fingers. There was something wrong with this situation. Not just the child, not just the house, there was something else there, laying below the surface, watching them all. She felt its eyes through the house's closed windows. She felt its breath as a warm breeze blew through the oak's branches.

She scooted back in the dirt, testing to see what the boy would do, what the house would do. They didn't seem to notice.

She jumped to her feet and ran to the rear of the yard. At the back fence, she glanced at them again. They hadn't changed, although the toys on the ground looked different. She hadn't paid much attention to them before, but now she saw red dots and stains across their plastic. She was too far to see for sure, but she already knew—it was blood.

Beyond the fence, she saw a row of backyards, meticulously manicured and tidy. She grabbed the tips of the wood planks and put her feet on the crossbeams. She heaved herself up, scraping her hands, arms, and chest against the splintery wood. Her heart pounded as she climbed. She felt it in her fingertips as they strained to pull.

Amanda threw a leg over the top. She leaned toward the other side and readied her hands to take the weight of her shifting body. She glanced again at the neighboring yards as her foot crossed the fence's peak.

Each of the other homes was now darkened. Their windows blocked with black curtains. The unseen eyes of whatever was watching her peered through each neighboring home.

Dread washed over Amanda as she dropped from the fence. It chilled her heart and branched down her limbs. It was a feeling that this was the end. This was the last jump she would take.

Her feet touched down on the dirt, and the world around her darkened to the inside of another place. The dirt was no longer just dirt; it was a layer over concrete, and surrounding her was a dimly lit basement. In front of her was Eddy Lawrence.

He flipped the object back and forth in his hands. He didn't look up.

Amanda could see it now. She still wasn't sure what it was but saw it was hairy. A toupee?

He flipped it over into his other hand. Its inside was blood red. His hands were blood red. It wasn't a toupee; it was a scalp. A white line of skin traced its jagged outside edge, and dark lines formed patterns from where it had laid over the muscle of its owner's head.

She screamed and jumped backward. She spotted the stairs on the other side of the child and ran for them.

Eddy let his left hand fall to his side, the scalp brushing the folds in his jeans. He slid the straight razor from his pocket that he had used to remove Ronny DiMarco's skin and flipped it open. As Amanda's right foot touched the bottom step, Eddy swung his blade.

Amanda felt the strength release from her leg, and she sank. Her ass hit the floor, and a sharp pain radiated from her tail bone, then the back of her ankle. She howled and looked down. Blood streamed from an open gash in her Achilles tendon.

3

Ray cut the ropes holding Amanda's sleeping body. He dragged her beside the table and tied her wrists to its legs. He expected her to wake at any moment, to fight, scream, struggle. She didn't do any of those, and his eagerness became anger.

He thought to himself about speeding up the process and unbuttoned her pants. He spread them at the waist and lifted her ass to slide them over her panties and off her hips. He didn't want to remove the underwear yet. He'd wait for that. For her to watch.

She still didn't wake up.

Ray saw her eyes shift back and forth under their lids. She was really under. He took off her shoes and finished sliding the jeans from her legs. As he turned to toss the pants across the room, he noticed they were wet. Red. Bloody.

"What the fuck?" Ray lifted her legs, one, then the other. He saw the laceration on her left. It oozed red onto the cabin floor. "How the fuck…"

He looked over the rest of her body and saw blood seeping through from under her shirt.

4

Amanda looked up and saw Eddy Lawrence in her way. He stood on the bottom step, his hands swinging as if part of a game. One with the scalp, one with a blade.

"Let me go," she whimpered. "Please, Eddy."

Eddy flipped his blade toward her and then pointed with it to the back, to the left, to a single spot on the basement floor that was dirt instead of concrete. "Over there."

"Please?"

He raised the blade over his head.

"Okay, okay." She scooted herself back. She used both feet at first, then screamed as she put pressure on the left.

He flicked the blade, slashing a line across her belly. "Keep going." His voice was low and clear. There was excitement below his tone, but he hid it well.

Tears poured down her cheeks. She used her right foot.

Eddy slashed at the air and giggled, following just beyond her.

When Amanda reached the corner, it wasn't dirt but mud. It stuck to her skin and oozed as she put weight on it.

Eddy pointed to the sides of the mud where chains lay on the ground. "Put them on."

"No." She shook her head. She felt only darkness coming. It felt inches away, but she couldn't do what he asked. She couldn't give in. Her thoughts went to her book, to that dashing scoundrel pirate. If only he was here to save her.

"Wake up," a voice shouted. She felt stings on the sides of her face. Her hands felt bound, but she looked, and the chains weren't on her.

"Put them on!" Eddy shouted. He pointed the tip of the razor at her.

"Unhand her," another voice called from the other side of the basement. It was him, the bare-chested pirate captain. His open shirt hung loose, and his sword pointed at Eddy.

He glanced at the pirate and smirked. He walked to Amanda as the captain moved across the room. "You don't know how it works here." He jumped on the ground beside Amanda, his blade descending on her neck. She screamed. The pirate screamed. Eddy's cold steel dug into the flesh of her throat and slid from one side to the other. Amanda felt warmth as her scream turned to gurgles.

5

Betty Henson's scream tore through the house. Wes had only just awakened, trying to catch his breath, his eyes wide. Her torment vibrated inside his ears, and he knew it would have woken him up if he had been asleep.

"Mom?" Diana ran past Wes's door. He heard her thump down the stairs in machine-gun succession.

Wes tore back his covers and swung his cast over the edge of his bed. He reached for his crutches and then muttered, "Fuck it."

He rose up on one foot as Di screeched.

"What's happening?" He hopped on one leg through his door and to the stairs. He sat down and slid step by step as fast as he could manage while suspending his foot. "Di? Mom? What is it?"

"My God, oh, God, my God," Di blubbered in repetition. Mom wailed.

At the bottom of the steps, Wes returned to one foot and hopped into the living room. The screaming was on his right, in his parent's bedroom.

Betty Henson knelt between the door and the bed. She covered her mouth with her hands. Di stood beside her, mirroring her facial expression.

"What's going—" Wes hopped closer. His mother took her left hand from her face and held it in front of her view of the bed, and Wes noticed two things simultaneously: her left hand, arm, and the entire left side of her body were coated in red liquid and pink and red crumbs, and in the place where his father's head should have lain was a mashed pile of bloody meat. Bone shards, teeth, and skin were compressed into a bowl above the mangled opening of what had once been Dad's neck. "God—"

Blood, brain, and bone dripped from the headboard as if Dad's skull had exploded—and Wes remembered the dream, Dad's head under the tire. It had exploded across the pavement.

Wes's leg gave out, and he tumbled backward to the living room floor. "Dad..." words shook as they left his mouth. "No..." Tears welled in his burning eyes.

This couldn't be real. It couldn't be actually happening. It was a continuation of the nightmare he had been in; it had to be. Somehow, he thought he had woken up, but it was really the same dream. He ripped his eyes away from his bloody mother, down to the carpet.

"Wake up," he told himself. He saw marks on his arm, ones from the graveyard, ones from that old zombie that scratched him. "Still a dream." It had to be. He wore the same wound from that dream. Wounds don't follow you from dreams to reality.

He looked up at Di. Her pajama pants were soaking wet, coated with sand, just as they were in the parking garage.

"Wake up, wake up," he said.

Di turned and looked at him. Her face was glowing red from crying. Her eyes said, "*Help*."

He shook inside. He had to help. It may just be a dream, but they needed him.

"Just a dream," he muttered and raised himself back up on one foot. He hopped over to Di and pulled her, hugged her, and gently pushed her out of the room. He hopped over to Mom and grasped her shoulder. "Mom."

She turned and looked at him. She was trembling. Tears left lines on her bloody left cheek.

His gaze skated over the bed, the carnage, onto her face—bits of brain dangled from her cheekbone. *Just a dream.*

"Come on, Mom," he said softly, just above the deluge of her sobs. He tightened his grasp and pulled her. She rose, and he led her out.

With Mom and Di on the couch, Wes shut the bedroom door. His hand rattled the knob, and the last image of the headboard hovered in his mind—the thought of what had happened in that garage raced through him, every scene, every memory. He saw blood, sprayed up and then dripped down in lines over white painted oak, and he realized that he had brought Dad into that dream. But this was still just a dream, too—wasn't it?

6

Officer Dale Harrison sat at Custer Memorial Hospital, gazing down the hallway at door after door of horror. Each room with two or more kids, each kid in some unexplained coma. There was something behind this that he needed to get his finger on—something that no one was seeing yet.

He'd heard rumors through the night, guesses by parents and nursing staff—all bullshit.

"It's a toxin. All the water in this town is poisoned after the runoff from the old mines."

"It's a madman. Someone's getting their kicks by attacking children."

"It's a curse. White men took this land from the Indians, and now the land wants us gone."

Three more kids had been brought in during the eight hours since he carried Gina through the emergency room doors. There were too many. No madman could do this by themselves. No toxin would affect just these kids. No curse—the idea of that was just asinine.

A nurse came out of the room marked *Private* next to his chair, their break room. She gave him only the most cursory of glances as she passed. The staff was used to him now, barely moving other than wandering into room 204 every now and then to check on Gina and Carol.

He'd sat in a chair on Gina's half of her room for part of the night, even slept for close to an hour sitting up. Beyond that, his brain wouldn't let him rest. It kept circling through the previous day's events.

Dead people with horrific wounds, inexplicable wounds—all while in their own homes or, at least, places where they should have been safe. Then these kids—sleeping—stuck in comas with no clue as to why— inexplicable as well. What was missing? What was the same?

It dawned on Harrison the way one finds that their missing sunglasses were sitting on their head all along. They were all asleep when whatever caused this happened. The dead were in their beds, with the exception of Jason Mertz, who must have fallen asleep in his recliner. The kids were all in their beds.

But who would have known each was asleep and been able to use that time to attack them? Who could go from home to home, to so many homes, broken in, done whatever to them, and leave no trace, most times without other family members in the home realizing someone had been there? Was this some kind of cat-burglar/serial killer, the likes of which had never been recorded?

It made sense as much as it didn't. That was when the phone behind the nurses' desk rang.

The sweet young woman who had introduced herself as Marian around midnight and offered Harrison a cup of coffee answered. Her eyes shot to the officer as soon as the voice on the other end started. She stood from her post and leaned over the counter.

"Officer?" She held the phone toward him.

Harrison had left his radio in his cruiser, hoping not to bother the rest of the town's distraught parents with its chirp. Rhonda had volunteered to pull an over-nighter at the station after the extent of the murders and comatose children had been revealed, and she had the number for the nurses' desk handy. It looked like she finally needed him.

He stood and took the phone from Marian, and she quietly removed herself to the break room.

"Harrison," he said into the receiver.

"Jesus, Dale, you sound like shit," Rhonda said from the other side. Her voice was low and dry. "You gotten *any* sleep over there?"

"You don't sound so hot yourself, Missy. What's up?"

"I hate to pull you away from the hospital with Gina there and all…"

"Go on."

"We got another weird one—and you said you wanted to know if we got another weird one."

"Yeah."

Ronda rattled off the Henson address along with the peculiarity of the Henson boy's story. An ambiguous tale about the mom just waking up to find a mutilated dad beside her. Another inexplicable death if taken at face value.

"Okay, I'll head over. Gimmie five, and you can catch me on the radio if you need me."

"Ten-four."

He reached over the counter and hung up the receiver. He turned toward 204 and found Marian standing in front of him with a Styrofoam cup, steaming with coffee.

"Thought you may need this." She flashed him a smile that quickly disappeared. "Sounded like you needed to head out."

Harrison nodded politely and took the cup.

Inside 204, he crept past the comatose child in the first bed and his parents. He paused by Gina's bed and held back a tear that wanted to burst from his watering eyes. He leaned over and kissed her forehead, and Carol startled awake in the bedside chair.

"You have to go, don't you?" Carol stared with a down yet understanding expression. She'd seen enough family moments ruined from calls on his phone or radio. It had gotten to where she expected it. If they actually got through a birthday or Christmas, or celebration of any kind without being interrupted, she would have called it a miracle.

His absences had gotten so bad during the summer that she even went to a town council meeting and demanded they hire more officers. Three full-time officers was not enough, in her opinion. It may have been fine ten or twenty years ago, but this was the nineties. Crime was up, and the town was only getting bigger. They'd said no, a decision they'd likely grow to regret in the upcoming days, but Carol had felt better doing it. She would say someone had to.

"Got a call," Harrison said. He reached over the bed and touched Carol's hand. "I'll stop in and check on Stuart while I'm out."

"Will you be back?"

Harrison glanced at the window and the rise of false dawn behind it. "When I can." He bit his cheek and held back the same tear.

7

Barton Smith gazed at the seven-inch monitor he'd set up on his kitchen counter nearly a year ago. The unit, the wiring, the camera in his basement, all together, had taken almost a month's salary to purchase. The installation of the mounting bracket and running the wiring only took a day after reading the pamphlet that came with the camera. It was proving to be worth every penny and each bead of sweat he'd shed. And he wondered why he didn't take advantage of his work sooner. He had to thank the voice.

His heart rate was slowing. He hadn't been into the room since he put Shirley Minsk in there. He didn't trust himself yet. He wanted to wait. He wanted to cherish the moment to come, and he knew if he went in there unprepared and overly excited, he'd ruin it. So instead, he'd use the monitor and his hand, for now.

2022

1

Officer Stuart Harrison watched the sunrise through his window at Custer Memorial. Each part of him hurt. His gut, his muscles, his lungs, his heart. It reminded him of the talk he had with his father the day he had started at the Custer Falls Police Department so many years ago.

They sat on the back deck, dad and son off-shift for the day, a beer in both of their hands. The grill was warming, but for now, there was nothing to do but sit and enjoy the break.

Stuart had only seen a few traffic stops that day. Rhonda, not yet retired, had routed all the harder calls to the more experienced officers. He had written some tickets, covered a few accidents, and before he knew it, the day was done. It was a good first day.

Dale had dealt with domestic abusers, a teenager shoplifter, a dead elderly woman who had passed in her sleep, and a lost dog, whose owner swore her across-the-street neighbor had either abducted or killed and disposed of. He had spent the entire day with Stuart in the back of his mind, looking forward to this moment.

"So, how was it?" Dad said. He sipped from his can.

"Good." Stuart kept his response cheerful. It wasn't the most exciting day, but he was happy to finally be on the job after years of waiting. He'd done as Dad asked and gotten a Criminal Justice degree before applying. What Dad said had made sense; he could get farther with it, and on the off chance he didn't like the job, he would have more options afterward. It meant he had to hold off an extra three years before he could apply, but he waited patiently, and he got through it. Now that the first day was over, and the cold beer was in his hand, he couldn't have been told that this was anything other than paradise.

"Anyone give you a hard time? You're the only one out there with a baby face right now." Dad reached out and pinched Stuart's cheek between his thumb and knuckle.

"That's assault, buddy," Stuart grinned and sipped his can and tried to hide his embarrassment. He had to change the subject because he did have an issue during one stop, and just for that reason. The elderly Mrs. Mertz, who lived west of town, had been one of his stops. She was driving too slow, failed to use her blinker, and just looked otherwise drunk. When he pulled her over, all she could do was go on about how he was too young to be an officer, and if her boy Jason were still alive, he would have been head of the Fire Department by now and given him what-for after stopping an old woman for no reason. Stuart saw the whole thing as a learning experience, tried to laugh about it when he got back into his cruiser, but he really didn't want to talk about it. So, he changed the subject.

"You know, Dad," Stuart tipped his head, "you told me that once I was on the job, we could talk about a few things."

"I don't remember that."

Stuart knew that was a lie. The saying was almost a mantra when Stuart asked questions that he didn't want to answer. "You know what I mean."

Dad shook his head. "What do you want to know?"

"I know you only got banged up a few times on the job, but I was thinking today as I walked up on some of these unknown cars—what was the worst one? The worst you've ever been injured out there."

Dad didn't speak. He sipped his beer and glanced at the grill. It was ready, had been for a few minutes; they had just ignored it in favor of their seats and their beers. "You really want to know?"

Stuart nodded.

"Really?" He glanced at the sliding glass door. They were still alone. If Mom needed them for anything, she was likely holding off to let them have a little time to themselves.

"Yeah."

"Barton Smith."

"The—uh—pedophile, right?"

"Yeah." He sighed and sipped his can. "It was in '92. That was a horrible year."

"I remember."

"I doubt you remember as much as you think you do."

Stuart frowned. "That was when Gina—"

"We're not going to talk about Gina."

Stuart froze. He had been surprised his father was going to tell him anything at all. He half-expected Dad to put him off or straight out refuse. But today was not a regular day, and he wanted Dad to keep talking. "Okay. It was the year that all those murders happened."

"Yeah. The *murders*." He drank. "Well, there was also the disappearances—a few young girls—and as much as some wanted to ball it all together as one perp, some of us figured on it being someone else.

"By the time we narrowed it down to a shortlist and started checking on possible suspects, folks were pretty on-edge. Smith was too.

"When I got to his house that day, he was already agitated. Said I should come back later, like that ever worked.

"Anyway, by the time the interview was over, and I was going to bring him down to the station to keep an eye on him, he somehow caught me looking away. I don't know if I heard something or saw something or exactly what happened—my memory's a little fuzzy from that point. But the next thing I knew, I was on the ground, and he was kicking the ever-loving shit out of me."

"Jesus."

"Yeah. He broke three ribs, gave me a concussion, bruised about every square inch of me."

Stuart grew cold trying to picture this. Since he was a boy, he always saw his dad as some unbreakable monolith. Mom made jokes about Dad's Superman strength whenever she needed something done. He expected this was a typical vision every boy had about their father, their first hero, and of course, it faded as he progressed through high school and college. But now, the idea of Superman on the ground getting the shit kicked out of him was mind-blowing.

He tried not to look bothered and took a sip. "So, how did you get out of it?"

"He took a break from kicking me and went for my piece. I don't know how I was quick enough, but I got my hand on it first. While he was fighting to peel back my fingers—sprained two of them—I used my other hand to pull my knife."

Dad slid the little hooked knife from his belt sheath and held it up.

"That's the one?" Stuart patted his own on his waist. His father had given it to him years ago and insisted he take it with him always, along with the mantra, *You never want to need a knife and not have it.*

"Same one." He turned it in his hand. Fine lines marked the finish, but it looked otherwise perfect. He held it sideways and drew it across his other hand—an inch above, just to demonstrate. "I ran it over the back of his hand so deep, his fingers went limp, and he jerked away.

"Like I said, it was a bit fuzzy after that. I don't know exactly what happened, only that he got away and I ended up in the hospital."

Images came back to Stuart. Days when he visited Gina on one floor of Memorial and Dad on another.

Dad slid the knife back into its sheath. "Yeah. That had to be the worst one. I think every muscle and bone in my body hurt after that one."

Stuart ran his hand over the hospital bed's rail and wished Dad was there now. Wished he could ask him if he'd ever been poisoned by some nitwit at a coffee shop. Dad would probably give that a chuckle.

2

Jill Henson felt a rumble below her feet and a crack that hurt her ears. The air around her was heavy and humid. She walked from the darkness toward a light somewhere ahead. A wall curved between her and it, twisting the way only carved or worn things could, rounding left and then wavering. Her breath echoed. Her feet reverberated around her. She was in a familiar place, though couldn't yet name it.

She neared the curved wall and saw what was around it. It was the caves, Bloodtooth Caverns. It was the same shape, but it looked different. She hadn't been here since she was twelve, since the entrance was demolished, but she remembered the many times she had come before then.

She stood in the large open room where the rangers liked to kill the lights and make everyone scream. The lamps were here, though some flickered, and some were burned out. Everything was coated with what Jill guessed was thirty years of dust, and while the last time she was here, she was surrounded by kids from her school, this time she was alone.

"Hello?" Her voice echoed without answer. The already-cold room seemed colder as she realized how alone she may be. If the entrances were still caved in, she wouldn't be able to get out.

"How did I even get here?" She traced the handrails to the far side of the cave, which should have been the way out if it were open, and she walked. "Hello?"

Again, only her own voice made a sound.

The lamps dimmed as she reached the far side of the cavern. From the entrance, she saw a tunnel darker than she could imagine, even after knowing what this place looked like once the lights had been killed.

"Hello?"

She stared into the gloom. Chills raced over her. Should she do it? Risk going into that? It may have been the way out, but it may have been blocked too. She tried to remember the path from thirty years prior. She could recall bits and pieces, and that was okay—what wasn't was the memory that, along the way, were drop-offs. There were cliffs along the path. Thirty years ago, those cliffs were guarded by railings, but were they now? If she wandered that way in the dark—the utterly unimaginable dark—she would have no way of knowing if she walked right up to one of those cliffs, and no way of testing if a railing was there before she plummeted off of one.

Visions of her and her friends' secret cave popped into mind. The shock of Wes falling, and only the sound of his body banging against rock, his meaty flesh against solid stone. And then her trek for help.

She had crept with one foot constantly tapping the floor. She held her hands in front of her head, blocking any potentially hidden stalactite from gouging into her face. She saw death in her mind. Wes, Tommy, Chris down inside whatever pit had grabbed them, and herself up here, failing to find her way back and being forever lost in gloom.

Wetness was on her cheeks. She was crying. She tried to stop it, but it just kept coming. She bumped into rock pillars and eventually found the wall. She searched for what felt like hours for the tunnel home, tortured by the distant echoes of her class.

She had screamed, and no one responded. Even when she reached the lit tunnel and howled for help, it seemed to take an hour for them to find her.

And now, she was here again, on the edge of a darkened labyrinth through which she had no idea the way. It didn't matter. She had no choice. She had to get back to Wes, to Sam, to Lisa. She had to brave the path.

Jill went into the darkness, tapping her toe before each step to make sure the ground existed. She felt a wall to her side and skated her finger over it as she walked. She heard the squeal of bats overhead. She heard dripping water. She heard her own breath heaving in and out of her mouth.

She didn't call out at first. She wanted to hear the world around her in case there was an echo from anything: a person, a rock tumbling down a cliff, a lion, anything. She paused and decided to risk it.

"Hello?"

Her voice was a stranger in the wind, calling her from a thousand directions. And something changed.

"Over here," a low, husky voice called.

The tone raised every alarm Jill held inside. The primordial mind in the back of her brain screamed at her, *Run!*

She couldn't run. She would slam into a wall, fall off a cliff; a thousand other means of blind death raced through her thoughts. Her chest trembled. It traveled down her arms and legs.

"It's okay," the voice said from behind her.

How did it get behind her? She knew the darkness and the walls could play tricks with sound, but this was different. She felt breath on the back of her neck. Was it real, or her mind misinterpreting the wind?

"Fuck!" Jill shouted through gritted teeth.

She moved forward at a hurried pace. Tap, move, tap, move.

"It's all right," the voice said, still behind her.

She moved faster. Up a rocky hill. Down a narrow cave. Cold breath blew through her hair—until a light appeared ahead.

That's it, she thought.

Adrenaline pulsed through her; it urged her on. "*Run*," it said. "*You can make it now.*"

She did. Her feet pounded against the stone floor. She raced at the light. It was her savior. It was her way out. She only had to go a little further, and she'd be closer to Wes and her babies.

Jill snagged her foot in a crevice. She saw the ground coming at her. It was something she could see. It didn't matter now if she fell; she had light, she had escape.

Her hands caught her fall on the jagged rocks below. She saved her face, but blood ran from each palm.

Jill laughed and lifted her gaze, wondering what salvation looked like. She saw the lighted expanse of the same room she had started in.

1992

1

Jill Elden's alarm buzzed, dragging her away from a dream of her grandmother's birthday at the lake the previous summer. She had been on the dock with her older cousin Yolanda, and the two of them were judging the boys on a scale from one to ten as they passed by on boats. She smacked her alarm and thought that there had been many more nines and tens in her dream than were at the actual event.

She wondered if Yolanda ever dreamed about that day. She guessed probably not—her cousin was a "looker," as Chris and Tommy would have said. She expected that if her friends ever met Yolanda, the conversations about Alison Steiner's breasts would probably stop in favor of ones about her cousin's. She wondered if hers would ever rival Yolanda's and if that was what it would take to finally grab Wes's attention.

She blew air through her lips, raspberrying the day ahead. If only she could skip school today. She had a strange feeling about today and a feeling about Wes. She wanted to fast forward and get over to his house and see how he was doing.

"Honey?" Mom knocked at the door.

"I'm up." Jill threw back her covers.

"Okay, I'll start your shower."

Jill went to her dresser and opened the top drawer. Her gaze ran across overlapping socks, and she got a chill.

2

When Officer Dale Harrison pulled up to the Henson home, the boy who had called it in sat on the porch's front steps. The bright white cast on his leg almost glowed in the early morning light.

Harrison parked in the driveway and stood, all the while followed by the boy's eyes. The closer he got, the more he wondered about those eyes, the more he could see their strain and exhaustion, and something else he couldn't pinpoint—it wasn't fear, and it wasn't quite trauma. It was a cold knowing, as if the world were going to end, and he knew the horrible truth but couldn't say a word.

Harrison stopped in front of the boy. "Officer Harrison." He nodded.

"Wes," the boy said. There was a quavering in his voice.

"You called about your father?"

Wes pointed at the door and looked away.

Harrison caught a flash of Stuart where the kid sat, and he was glad to not have to look him in the eye. He imagined Stuart losing him, a thought not unfamiliar for any officer, though less frequent, he assumed, for small-town cops like himself. But still, it hung there, a pain he could only imagine and would never wish on his son or this kid.

He stepped past Wes, patting him on the back. He paused at the front door and raised his fist to knock, then saw it was open an inch. He pressed the center of the door, and it swung open with a quiet squeak.

The mother was on the couch, her arm firm around her daughter. Blood was smeared across her face, her hair, and her entire left side. They rocked in a rhythmic sway until the mother saw Harrison. She cried harder, shaking her frame and her daughter with it.

Harrison stepped inside. The air was thick with grief. His palm brushed the handle of his service weapon, and he forced himself to hook his hands on his belt instead. If it were any other time in his life, his first response would have been to get the wife in cuffs, control her in case she was the perpetrator. He knew it wasn't the case here. Some other horror had taken place.

"Ma'am?"

Like her son, the woman only pointed to a door. The daughter grabbed hold of the woman and squeezed. Their sobs grew louder as Harrison took the knob in hand.

He swung the door open and felt his insides clench. Where the man's head should have been, blood and bile oozed from the neck onto the pillow. His chest was compressed in the center like a narrow canyon. A red line coated the sheets up the center of the body from his crotch to his splattered head; the headboard and wall... he could barely glance there before having to turn away. Harrison's gut seized, and he pulled the door shut while covering his mouth.

He firmed his throat as stiff as possible, trying to keep himself together. "Ma'am, I'll need to use my radio. I'll be right back. Please keep this door shut."

The mother and daughter didn't even look at him.

Harrison retreated to the cruiser and had Rhonda call the county. Then he returned to the house and got the exact statements he expected from the Hensons.

3

Ray Trent drove the back streets of Road 12 and Moose Creek Road as he edged around town, trying to avoid getting pulled over in Amanda Brolin's vehicle. He parked it behind Wesker Pump, which hadn't held a drop of gas since Carter was in the White House.

He huffed and shook his head. Amanda was supposed to be his plaything, and something took her from him. The voice may have told him to *relax*, that it was all part of *the plan*, but relaxing was the furthest thing from where he sat. Maybe after he got Misty. Maybe then he could relax.

Amanda's purse sat on the passenger seat where he had left it. He picked it up and dumped it out: change, cherry lip gloss, balled-up receipts, hair pins, two tampons, a pink zip-up wallet, and a dozen makeup implements that were beyond Ray's comprehension. He picked up the wallet, hoping for some piece of luck to go his way.

He unzipped the faux leather billfold to find an inner accordion with membership cards, cardboard punch cards for buy-ten-get-one-free programs, and a thin sheaf of folded currency. All counted, it added up to thirty-one dollars. Not a huge score, but enough to make his day a little brighter if he could put it to good use.

Ray gathered his hoodie and shoved the money into his pocket. He did a quick look around to make sure he hadn't left anything in the car that could identify him, in case the cops found it before he came back. Satisfied, he got out and locked it up, jingled the keys and shoved them under a rusty oil drum beside the old service station. Maybe he'd get lucky, and it would still be there if he needed it again later.

It took Ray about ten minutes to go up West Raven Street, turn on Milwaukee Road, and then find Stony's house on the corner of Milwaukee and the east spur of the incoming railroad tracks. He saw Stony's faded blue Schwinn leaning against the garage and got the idea his luck may be about to change.

Stony's mom's car was in the driveway. As Ray passed it, he saw her door had been left cracked. All he could think was that the stupid bitch was going to have a hell of a time when she tried to go to work with a dead battery. Then he remembered who he was thinking about. Stony's mom was a notorious deadbeat and lush. Who knew if she even had a job right then.

He stepped up to the door and knocked, hoping Stony and not his mom would answer. It wasn't that he worried about her asking questions, like why he wasn't in school, or why he was there (was it for drugs?), or any of the usual bullshit that moms would be annoying about; it was that she was a drunk, and drunks always made him sick. Whether it was the bums in the park, the losers in the casinos, spending their entire paychecks on slots and tables, or even his dad when Monday Night Football was on— the whole package of sloppiness that booze brought on was disgusting.

She didn't answer the door, though. It creaked open under his knock, and a putrid smell of something rotten hit Ray in the face.

"Jesus." Ray spun away and covered his nose. What was going on in there? Did the dumb bitch leave food out all week? He would have expected Stony to do something about it, but maybe he'd just grown used to it by now.

"Stony?" Ray shouted through the opening. After a few seconds, he pushed the door the rest of the way and stepped inside.

The living room was a rat's nest of junk: boxes, mail, unidentifiable mounds of crap piled everywhere. The dining room may have had a table, but Ray couldn't see it. Stacks of garbage circled the room and overflowed in a heap in the middle.

"Stony?" Ray slid through a narrow path between piles of takeout wrappers and plastic shopping bags of who-knows-what to the hallway, trying not to touch any of the columns of trash along the way. "Jesus, no wonder he never meets anyone here."

The hallway was half the width it should have been. Stacks of urine-soaked magazines and newspapers reached from the floor to eye level and only broke for the doors to two bedrooms and a bathroom.

Ray opened the first door a crack. "Stony?"

The floor inside was scattered with trash a foot deep. He pushed the door open enough to see the end of a bed and two feminine feet. He was hit in the face with a heavier dose of the same putrid smell he'd encountered at the door. Pinching his nose, he pulled it shut.

The next door wore a yellow diamond road sign, saying, *Keep OUT.*

Ray rapped the back of his knuckles on the sign. "Stony?" It banged against the door in an annoying clatter that made Ray smirk.

There was no answer. No music? No sound at all.

Ray turned the knob. As the door opened, he saw the cleanest room in the house so far. Not a thing on the floor. There was a desk covered in the usual teenager crap—deodorant, hairbrush, skin mags—but compared to the rest of the house, the room was sterile, except for the bed.

On top of the covers laid Stony. He wore headphones connected to his Walkman, which had run dead. Beside him on the bed was a half-smoked pipe with charred weed in the bowl. He also had a three-inch-wide chasm in the right side of his head, as if a large ice cream scooper had dug in and scooped away his skull and brain.

The wound was completely dried. Blood had run down to the pillow and soaked into the bed, but it was all stained and crusted. Not runny, not sticky—the scene had to have been several days old.

"Jesus Christ, Stony." Ray thought about the mom in the other bed. Was she going to wake up from whatever beer or drug-induced coma she was in and walk in here and catch him? He did not want to deal with that.

He grabbed the pipe and searched quickly around the room. On top of the dresser was a small bag of weed, which he shoved into his pocket. But something told him that wasn't all there was. He went through the dresser drawers. He saw stained underwear and jeans, balled-up shirts, and socks that used to be white. In one drawer, he found three bags of pills: red, tan, and white, a different color in each bag.

Ray didn't take pills. Like beer and other drugs, he thought they'd cause a lack of control. But as he looked at these, the whisper came into his ear, *"Take them... you can use them."*

2022

1

Julie Redmond did not like that her mommy was making the bed a bit sticky in places or that the room was getting dense with a smell she thought was more at home in a trash can than as a mommy's perfume. So, when she walked out of Ed's grandmother's room, she was sure to take all her things with her and shut the door tightly. While she did want to go back in there again, tonight, she would find a better place to sleep.

She walked through the wood-trimmed hallway staring at the antique photos of long-dead people on the walls. She saw an old clock on the hallway table beside a shiny sculpture of a child and a dog. She assumed all of these things belonged to Ed's grandmother. Maybe he had gone out and hunted them all down? Maybe he was an antiquer, but she didn't think so. She saw Ed as a homebody who, as much as he disliked people and crowds and public places, also hated the idea of redecorating the old house if he were to throw away all of his grandmother's things. It wouldn't be much effort to put it all in bags and leave it by the street, but picking out new pictures, knickknacks, and accents would require him to go to stores— deal with people. Or, maybe, he was just a creature of habit who hadn't ever given the house's accessories a second thought in all these years.

A few feet from the kitchen, Julie smelled coffee and toast. When she went inside, she found just that sitting in front of Ed at the kitchen table. He held the mug in one hand and a tablet in the other.

"Is there any more toast?" Julie said with a smile. It was the "pretty-girl" one her mother had taught her to use when she wanted something from a man.

He glanced up at her and pointed to the counter where a still-open half-loaf of buttermilk and honey bread sat beside the toaster. "I'm not your mother. You can do it yourself."

"Of course, I can." Julie trotted to the counter's edge, never dropping her smile. "What do you see?" She sang the question to him.

"Everything. It's perfect."

"Like the whispers said?"

"Maybe better." He tapped at the screen. "One paper says they think you may be a rumor or a mass hallucination since they can't find you. Another says the school's lockdown was from a botched active shooter attack."

"Oh." She didn't know what a *mass hallucination* was but didn't want to look dumb in front of her new friend, so she just kept the conversation going. "That's funny."

"Yeah. There was also a cop that got poisoned with bleach yesterday and some businessman who was attacked in his office—no survivors."

"And our afternoon play date?"

He clicked the tablet again and spoke in a stiff news anchor's voice, *"Jill Henson, local realtor, remains hospitalized in intensive care after a home invasion gone bad."*

She loaded bread into the toaster and pressed the lever down. "Goodie, she's still alive."

"Yes, ma'am."

"So, we did good?"

"Right on schedule."

Julie walked to the refrigerator and peered inside. "No Jelly?"

"Check inside the door. And none of them have figured out it's the anniversary yet."

"Oh, I found it." She closed the door and walked back to the toaster. "Do you think they will?"

"Maybe. But either way, it doesn't matter. I'm sure we have the Hensons right where they need to be, so—"

"So we just keep doing *our* thing?"

"That's right." He smiled.

Julie glanced at the boxes of envelopess and sealed bags of white powder at the end of the counter and began humming.

1992

1

The rooster in Gennie Lawrence's kitchen stared past the clock arms on his chest. It was about to be seven am, and he watched Gennie lift two four-inch laxative-laced pancakes from the iron skillet on the stove and set them on a white plate for the boy.

She'd called him down, and she'd heard him moving around up there, but she had yet to see him. She expected he was looking through that shoebox she had found under his bed while cleaning his room yesterday. Gruesome things, and she knew that someday his intentions would turn. After his whore mother and the nastiness of that man, the boy was destined to turn dirty one way or the other. Besides, when it came to dead things, boys would be boys. If she took it away, she was sure he'd just make another box and hide it somewhere where she might not find it. At least she knew where it was, and it was under control, for now.

"Eddy!" She put the plate on the dining table and set a fork beside it. She placed the bottle of sugary syrup next to the food and stared at the pancakes. Did she add enough? She wished she could be there at school when it hit him. If he lasted all the way to school. If she used too much, it might hit him on the bus. Either way there'd be a lesson in it.

Eddy heard his gramma call, but he couldn't pull himself away. Not yet. He laid Ronny DiMarco's scalp on his knee and stroked it as if it were a pet. In some ways, it was. Each item in his box had taken on its own life, had its own meaning; they were memories that he could return to and relive, and this idea made his heart jump. As his fingers slid through the light-brown clump of hair, he felt a tingle in his veins. He smelled blood in the air and tried to taste it. He swore he could. He felt the excitement that had warmed his insides in that cool basement yesterday afternoon. It was as though he were there all over again.

He still had to go back down and clean up. He'd hidden Ronny under a blanket, behind a box of Gramma's sewing fabrics that she never seemed to use. Hopefully, this afternoon he could finish when he got home from school. That would be best.

"Eddy," her voice was muffled through the floor. "Do I need to come up there? It's seven-o-five."

He bobbed left and right and sighed. "I'm coming!"

Sure he was. Gennie went back into the kitchen and warmed up her coffee. That, at least, was one thing she could always count on. Her coffee was strong and sweet, and it would never let her down, not unless she let Eddy make it.

2

Chris got off the bus with sleep still in his eyes. More than that, though, his dreams still rattled around in his head.

He'd been out at some strange restaurant with the mousy Charlotte Baker, and as the meal progressed, he'd become more and more attracted to her. Her eyes radiated, even through those rounded glasses. Her small smile and its gentle upturned corners raised his own in reflection. They'd talked as they ate, actually talked, not just a dreamworld feeling of conversation. He'd opened up about his mother's treatment, and she'd shared how sad she was that her sister was her mother's favorite and she could do nothing right at home.

When dinner was over, they ended up taking a walk along a lake and making out on its beach. It was hot and heavy and one of the most vivid dreams about a girl he could remember having. Now, he couldn't seem to think of anything but her. Memories of the dream, memories from real life, they blended together as if the experiences were real.

As he walked toward the school's entrance, he thought about the adoring look she gave him as they talked about Rush and Zeppelin, the dimples in her cheeks when she went bashful at his compliments, and he realized that he was looking for her.

It was silly. Just a dream. It wasn't really her, and though he always felt she had a crush on him, it wasn't serious. It wasn't like the *her* in his dream would be anything like the real her. He knew enough about dreams to know that they were like fantasies, and what happened was only what he wanted to happen subconsciously. But if his subconscious wanted it, maybe there was something to it.

She wasn't anywhere he could see. Buses unloaded, and he looked at the numbers. She rode bus 63, and it wasn't in the line. That was fine. It would give him a little longer to get his head straight before he saw her in homeroom.

He cut to the left, diverting from the stream of kids heading to the entrance. He went to the side and down the steps, taking the outside path to the cafeteria. He had been dragging ass on his way out the door and didn't have time to snag so much as a piece of fruit. He thought that if he hurried, he could grab a box of cereal and a carton of milk before the bell rang. His plans changed, though, when he rounded the corner and saw Todd Hertz—all alone and without the rest of his Khaki Klan.

In that moment, every bruise and ache from the day before rose in his mind. What had been below the surface became a beacon of anger. He glanced at the new cast the nurses had forced him to get and found his gut tightening along with his fists.

Todd's words echoed in Chris's mind—*for his slut mom before she works the street corner tonight*—and before he knew it, he was moving toward the Khaki leader. Before he knew it, he was standing next to Todd, his fist back and ready to swing, the tail of a whisper leaving his thoughts, "*Do it.*"

Todd's eyes went wide. His hands raised in front of his head. Dark red covered most of Todd's face, bruises from the afternoon before. Tears welled in his eyes. His lips trembled.

Chris faltered and stepped backward. What was he doing? A shock wave resonated over his limbs. The fear in Todd's eyes may have been the most revolting thing he had ever seen—and he had done that. He had put that fear in Todd, and he felt sick inside from seeing it.

Todd stepped back as well. He watched Chris, waiting for an imminent blow.

As Chris lowered his hand, he noticed there were more wounds on Todd than those he had inflicted yesterday. There were deep scratches on the other side of his face and a bandage on his forearm.

"What happened to you?" The words left Chris's lips, and he was unsure of where they had come from.

"Nothing." Todd backed up further, inching toward the closest door.

Todd was in trouble, and it felt strange to see. While Chris wanted to say that the Khaki asshole deserved it, he couldn't. He felt bad for him, especially after approaching with a raised fist.

"Really, Todd? What's going on?"

Todd turned and darted through the door. It clunked shut, and the sound filled Chris with dread—not for himself, but for something he knew was coming for Todd.

"Fuck this." Chris turned his back on school and headed toward the street.

3

The police had come and gone except for the crime scene unit and a single officer that stood at the door to Mom and Dad's bedroom and occasionally checked in on Wes and Diana. There wasn't a single officer that thought Mom could have killed Dad—she simply didn't have the strength to crush a man's head the way it looked. But policy (and the necessity to cover their own asses) dictated that the county detectives take Mom down to the CFPD station for extended questioning. The only thing that seemed to keep her from breaking down in front of the entire house of law enforcement was the benevolence of Dale Harrison, who went into the master bathroom and retrieved her Valium. After taking two with a mug of hot tea, she floated out the door with them.

Wes and Diana sat on Wes's bed, neither wanting to talk about the tragedy in Mom and Dad's bed and neither wanting to discuss that Dad had died in their dream. They took turns playing Castlevania and dying, unable to concentrate on the controls or the screen.

"This is stupid." Di dropped the controller on the bed. She pushed herself back against the headboard and closed her red eyes.

Wes didn't pick it up. "Yeah." He laid back on his pillow.

They sat in silence. The officer thudded up the stairs, looked into Wes's room, and returned down. The television played Castlevania's music, waiting for another player.

Wes turned to his sister. She was crying again, and he felt anger and hatred for himself. He didn't want to say it, but he had to. He had to tell someone. "It's my fault."

"What's your fault?" She wiped her eyes.

"Dad. I don't know how it happened, but I had a dream. He was in it, and he died, and then he died here. I killed him."

Di's eyes firmed on her brother. She looked down at the fresh wounds that hadn't been there when she went to bed and the scrapes on her brother's arm. "I saw it—in my dream. It wasn't you. It was—a truck."

Their eyes, examining, wondering.

"You saw a truck?" Wes asked. "In a garage?"

"We were both there."

"Yeah, but—it just can't..."

Di frowned. "We were both in the same dream? I did this there." She pointed to her cuts, then to Wes's. "I'll bet you got those there too."

Wes fought for words. "Yeah. But how? It's like some bad *Nightmare on Elm Street* ripoff. How could we share a dream?"

"And how did Dad get there?"

The events replayed in Wes's mind. "I think I called him. It was my fault."

"What—what do you mean, you *called* him?"

"I remember, we were being chased by cars."

"Trying not to get run over."

"Yeah. And, I remember thinking, *I wish Dad was here*—because he would know what to do, he could help us."

"He just showed up."

"After I wished for him."

Di shook her head and scooted half a foot down the bed. To Wes, it felt like a mile.

"I didn't mean to. I didn't know it was real, or that it would..."

"Kill him."

Tears ran from Wes's eyes. "I killed him. I called him there, and I killed him."

Di swallowed hard. She crawled out of the bed and headed to the door, her gaze on the ground. She paused before leaving, glancing back at Wes. She opened her mouth to say something, then shook her head and left.

Wes heard her bedroom door shut.

4

Jill walked among kids at the bus drop-off lane. Through a window between wannabe cheerleaders and the newly goth, she saw something weird: Chris crossing the street, walking away. Was he ditching?

She had to go too. She didn't usually skip; she could count the number of times she had done it on one hand. But she felt compelled. She missed Chris and had been trying to connect with him since Bloodtooth Caverns. She wanted to know how he was doing and why he was avoiding her. This seemed like the perfect time to do both of those.

She wiggled her way through the crowd and double-checked—no teachers in sight. She followed him.

One, then the other, made it a block up 5th Avenue. By the time Chris had reached the next intersection, Jill was right behind him. She tiptoed up and tapped his shoulder.

Chris raised his fist and spun around.

"Whoa!" Jill stepped back. "Easy, bud!"

Chris at once looked embarrassed and relieved. He lowered his fist and raised his palm, gesturing *what*. "Jill?"

She saw worry inside him. What had he been going through? She leaned forward and hugged him.

"Ow," he pulled away. "Not so hard."

"Sorry."

A smile broke through. "What are you doing here?"

"I saw you skipping—I thought, '*I hadn't done that in a while*' and thought you could use some company."

He sighed and shrugged toward the next block. "Come on."

2022

1

Wes drove the Excursion, Di beside him, Sam and Lisa in the back. His hands sweated under his grip, his mouth clamped tight.

Jill's nurse had called Wes's room at the Maryville Manor. Wes pried, but all the woman would say was, *You need to come down here*, and, *The doctor will tell you everything he can when you get here*. What else could Wes do but agree to come? He had already planned to go within the next hour, but now the urgency hung around his neck like a bundle of bricks.

Rain patted against the windshield, and the smell of damp asphalt crept into the vehicle. It made Wes think of the cold autumn nights that had already started, how Jill hadn't opened her closet of hoodies yet this year, and terror gripped his spine at the thought that she may not get to.

Was she dying? Last night they said to stay cautious, that she wasn't in a safe zone yet, but she was relatively stable. What could have happened? The nurse had refused to talk, and Wes couldn't think of any good news they'd refuse to give over the phone—it had to be the other kind.

Sam stared from the window, ignoring reality and chewing the tips of her fingers, a habit her mother had scolded her for dozens of times. She blocked out the world around her with thoughts of her dragon books. She wondered if the green one, whose magic was the forest, could use the same portals to travel the continent as the blues, whose power was ice. Would the prophecy allow a low-born red to marry a high-born gold, or would they have to escape into the wilderness to live their lives together? It was all she could do to ignore the horrible idea that her mother was on Death's door.

Lisa had grabbed her sister's hand almost immediately as they got into the vehicle. Sam acted like she hadn't noticed, but Lisa felt her snug grip. Lisa was not lost in her own world; she was dead-center of the SUV's world and was determined not to miss a beat if the adults said a word about Mom, no matter how scary the conversation could become.

Di watched her brother drive and waited. If the demon-thing was back, that meant they had to deal with it. They both knew that, even if Wes was preoccupied at the moment. She understood his dilemmas; she loved Jill and the girls, too, no matter the limited amount of time she had been allowed to see them over the past few years—shit, all of the girls' lives. But this thing would eat them all from the inside if they didn't deal with it. And just like last time, Wes would have to be in the center of everything.

The hospital was less than a mile from Maryville Manor, less than a three-minute drive. In Wes's mind, it felt like an hour. The wondering. The waiting. Had her body rejected the new blood? Was there an infection in her legs? In her gut? Had the scar tissue from the C-section she had with Lisa somehow got in the way and—he had no idea, but every medical procedure Jill had gone through over the past twenty-five years cycled through his mind as he tried to pinpoint the complication before he got there.

He parked the vehicle, and all four of them hurried into the building at a pace that, in Wes's mind, was rhythmic, slow, hypnotic, and other-worldly. He felt each step below his feet, each crack in the pavement, the grooves of the building's metal threshold, the gaps between the tiles. Each sound resonated in his ear, from the whoosh of traffic to the automatic doors. The sounds of the elevator, like each and every other noise, made Wes wonder, *Will this be a noise I remember forever as the path to her death? Will Sam and Lisa forever be reminded of the day they lost their mother when it rains in autumn?*

Dr. Gregory Johnson was already in Jill's room when they arrived. He spoke softly to a nurse who immediately fled the room. He studied Jill's monitors as the four Henson's entered the room and shut the door.

"Doctor?" Wes's heart thumped as he looked down at Jill. He felt himself breathing fast, tingling inside to know what was happening. She looked the same as yesterday. Asleep. Her chest rose and fell. Her IV dripped. Her heart monitor showed seventy beats per minute, her blood ninety-eight percent oxygen. "What's going on? Why were we rushed here?"

Dr. Johnson stepped aside, showing a laptop beside the monitors with colorful readouts and graphs. "Mr. Henson," he looked and then gestured at

Sam and Lisa, "I wonder if maybe they should step outside for us to talk?"

Wes glanced at his children. Their eyes were glued to the doctor—why shouldn't they be? Their mother was on the edge between life and death. Shouldn't they get to hear what the doctor says? A vision of Sam crying crossed Wes's mind; Lisa wailing and grabbing her sister. And it occurred to Wes that without knowing the news Johnson had to tell... Whatever it was, Wes wanted them there. He'd have to trust the man's discretion not to bludgeon the kids with information too blunt for them to handle. No, that didn't make sense; it was selfish. He needed to hear the entire truth of the situation, and they needed to be protected, to get it from him later as he wished to tell it. And then he thought of them alone in the hall. An image of Ed and his little partner stealing or slicing his children shook his core. He couldn't leave them alone either.

Wes looked at Di, his lost druggie sister, and, with hope in his heart, asked, "Di, can you please..."

She put her hand on Sam's shoulder, then Lisa's. "Yeah, yeah. Girls, let's wait in the hallway."

They looked at Jill, then Wes for approval.

"Go on, girls." Wes nodded.

The three stepped out, and the click of the closing door made Wes shudder. Whatever it was, the doctor was going to say it now. It would be uttered into existence in front of Wes, and after that point, it would become reality. The worry and unknowing would become a manifest thing inside whatever this man had to say. He shook inside, half wanting to hear, wanting to know, half furious and preferring to remain ignorant. He looked up, and Dr. Johnson and nodded.

Johnson took a breath. "Your wife has fallen into a coma that we don't seem to be able to wake her from."

It was like lightning struck. The words shook his frame and sent shivers through his being. *Coma*—like too many kids back then. *God, no. Not her.* His gaze went to Jill. He felt wetness on his cheeks watching her shallow breaths, her eyes darting back and forth below their lids. And then he felt rage. How could this happen? They said she'd wake up. How could they lie to him? Why didn't they make her wake up before it got her?

"You guys said she would wake up this morning—after her blood pressure normalized. Her brain was supposed to kick back into gear."

"I know. Something has gotten in the way of that. Her vitals were improving all night, her pressure building back up. She reached the threshold where we would expect to start seeing a change, and something did change—but we aren't sure what."

The doctor's words sank deeper and deeper into Wes's reality, forming concrete pillars and walls of daggers. They were sharpening this moment into something deadly, and the eerie feeling seized him. He'd been through this before. He should have known it was coming. And even as he asked the next question, he already knew the answer. "What does that mean?"

The doctor pointed to his laptop, to the wavy blue lines and colored image of a brain. "When we realized there could be a problem, we rushed her to get an MRI, to get a better picture." He paused as if to compose himself. "Her brain looks fine; normal, in fact."

"If she's normal—"

"Looks normal, but not for a coma." He pointed closer at the waves. "These brain waves are what we expect from a sleeping patient, not a coma victim. These are signs she's dreaming."

"Coma patients don't dream?" Wes knew some did. Maybe it was, and maybe it wasn't medically relevant, but he knew one coma patient that had.

"Some say they do, but not in the same way—not with brain patterns like this." He pointed to a colorful image of Di's brain. "These areas that are lit up are what we expect from a dreaming brain, not..."

"Not from a coma." Wes felt his stomach sink through the floor. "What does this mean?"

"Frankly, we aren't sure. I haven't seen something like this in... thirty years."

Wes's blood ran cold. He asked, hoping the doctor would prove him wrong. "What do you mean *thirty years?*"

"We had a rush of kids come in here, same symptoms."

It was back, and it had Jill. He knew he'd have to deal with it, but, Jesus, it had her already. And he knew the doctor was right; there was nothing this man could do.

2

Norris Cushing scanned the three customers still seated in the Huckleberry Café, ready for his breakfast service to be over. Ready to take a long break and a longer drink.

His thoughts this morning we on Elias and how each customer he waited on should have been the kid's. He was filling in for a ghost, and the feeling filled him with agitation and sadness.

Two of the diners looked like late-season tourists who must have been looking for more *local color* for their trip. Norris had refilled their coffees twice since they'd finished eating, and they still seemed to be in no rush to move on. The other customer was Earnest Billings, a World War II vet that came in twice a week and always ordered two pancakes and two pieces of bacon. He nibbled on his last strip, and within the next two minutes, he would stand, tip his hat to Norris, and leave ten seventy-five on the table: enough to cover his check and a dollar-fifty tip.

Norris checked the coffee pots. Each of the two regular pots had a little less than a cup left. He had an irritable feeling that the tourists would ask for more, but he had no intention of making a whole new pot just for them. He grabbed the half-full decaf pot and poured its contents into one of the regulars. Problem solved.

He turned around and saw Mr. Billings' hat tip. He nodded, and Billings headed out. As he bussed the old man's dishes, the tourists waved him over.

Norris issued a gentle smile and left the dishes where they were. The couple gave him aloof stares as he joined them at the end of their table.

"Folks?" Norris said.

The man spoke, "Hi, so we were wondering if you could tell us if there's anything worth seeing in this town?"

Norris hid his irritation. The idea that his whole town may be a piece of shit with nothing worthwhile was fine for him to have—he lived there. But having tourists suggest it? That gave him the urge to smack the smile off the customer's face.

"Oh, well, that depends," Norris said. "What are you looking for?"

The woman looked at the man, cocked her head, and glanced up at Norris. "Well, I know there's nothing cultural here. We've just dropped off our son at the university in Bozeman, and the most significant thing we saw was a museum filled with dinosaurs. That's great for kids, but..."

The man interjected, "You know, anything historical, like—what was it? Where all those Indians were massacred, or one of those missions that took them in and brainwashed them to be like white people?"

Norris wanted to slap him again. He settled for playing dumb. They didn't want to know the real history of this place. That didn't suit most visitors. Besides, that was local business.

"Tell you what," Norris said. "I'm not a good historian-type. Why don't you folks put a town called Philipsburg in your GPS. They have some locally-mined sapphires and jewelry. And a real nice candy shop too. Everyone who visits says they love it."

The woman brightened at the mention of jewelry. It was unlikely that anything in a backwater Montana town would meet her standards, but the novelty of it would likely provide her with a topic of condescending gossip once she returned back east or west, or whatever *civilized* place she had come from.

The man nodded. "We'll give that a look. Oh, maybe one more refill, please, too?"

"Happy to." Norris fetched the pot and filled their cups. He counted down the seconds until they finally got up and left, leaving him a generous tip of two dollars on the table. But that didn't matter. He was just happy to have them gone and becoming Philipsburg's problem instead of his.

Norris locked the front door and threw the dishes in the back sink. He gazed at the massive stack and sipped his hip flask. "Goddammit, Elias. Why'd you have to be an idiot and leave me alone with all this shit?" He took another gulp. "Could have given me some notice. Let me know to hire some other asshole to help out." He turned and headed to his tiny office.

It wasn't much of a room. There was enough space for a three-foot desk with a laptop and printer, and behind him, a three-drawer filing cabinet that held the last three years of receipts and vendor invoices. Anything older was in the trash, part of Norris's tax season spring cleaning efforts. He figured it would be his luck that if he ever got audited, they'd find some old *I* he forgot to dot or *T* he forgot to cross on some irrelevant piece of paper, and that would be the end for the Huckleberry Café. Better to get rid of that stuff and let the past rot away. Much like the town.

"Let it rot," he muttered, taking a seat and another swig.

He dug into the filing cabinet and pulled out Elias's application from a year ago. Christ, had it only been that long? Maybe he liked the kid more than he realized because it seemed like Elias had been there much longer.

It listed zero references and a last work experience from five years prior at a grocery store. He had asked Elias about it. "You only list the jobs you didn't get fired from, right?"

Elias had chuckled nervously.

But Norris knew the kid, not personally, but had known of him, what had happened to his parents. He had cut the kid a break and given him the job. Now, he wanted to strangle the guy that took him away. No matter what the cause, why Elias went over, who was at fault, Norris was pissed. He'd grown to like Elias, and now he had a burning feeling inside that someone needed to pay. The guy who did it was dead, but there had to be someone around that could pay the check.

"Do it," a whisper said. *"Someone needs to pay."*

3

Officer Stuart Harrison forced a bite of Jell-O down his scratchy throat. He hated Jell-O, but he was so goddamn hungry. They would only let him eat mushy white foods and Jell-O for now. They said they needed to see how his body would react. This diet was giving him the shits, and he was dying for a cheeseburger.

He dropped the spoon on the galley tray, and in walked Detective Mark Rand. Mark and Stuart had been in a few of the same criminology classes in Bozeman, but Mark graduated first, which meant he got hired on first, and later, he had seniority when a detective position opened up. Mark was also in charge of the case of the bleach-poisoned patrol officer.

"Mark," Harrison reached out to shake.

"Stuart, buddy. How're you feeling?" Rand shook the hand.

"Like every inch of my flesh has been through a tenderizer. How are you doing? Any luck tracking down that Elias kid?"

Rand shook his head, then told Harrison about the brawl between Elias Keys and Chad Parsons. "I stopped by to tell you yesterday, but you were passed out when I came by. Snoring and all. Figured I'd come back."

"Holy shit."

"Serves him right, huh?"

Harrison shook his head. "I knew Chad."

"Friends?"

"No, just knew him. Kind of an asshole."

Rand chuckled. "Yeah, well, every asshole's got a father, it seems, and this one wants someone to pay."

"You said Elias was dead. Who else does he want to pay?"

"Anyone. Everyone. He's threatening to sue the city if we don't find any accomplices and lock them up."

"Accomplices? Don't tell me the boss is taking that seriously?"

"In the long run, he has no grounds. But if he takes the city to court, it could be a whole lot of wasted money and time, and no one wants that."

"So, what then?"

"Orders are to crack down on all the meth dealers we know of and make a show of cleaning up the town."

"Ah, someone let it slip Elias used?"

"Too many people. It's going to be a nightmare of paperwork. You're lucky you're here—shoot, they may even bring you some forms and a pen to get through this."

Harrison chuckled, causing ripples of pain through his abdomen. His face tightened and then relaxed. "Hey, what was up with that school lockdown?"

Rand's mouth pursed. "Short story: a woman dead and a little girl—the murderer—on the loose."

"Jesus. How little?"

"No one seems to know who she is, but they guess eight or nine."

"An eight or nine-year-old?" Something struck Harrison, and he got chills. It was a vague memory, something from his childhood. It rang against thoughts of his father, those old cases he never liked to talk about. The thought eluded him. "And she got away?"

"Walked right out the door. Kids were so traumatized, they got out of her way, and there were no adults around."

"Your only witnesses are kids? Jesus."

"Tell me about it. It's almost as bad as the case down the hall. A woman and her husband were attacked in their home by a guy and a little girl. Sliced her up pretty good."

"Another little girl?" The thought fluttered behind his eyes, above his lips, just out of reach. "Could it be the same one?"

"It could be, but I don't think so. They were practically on opposite sides of town. How would a child travel that far? Besides, this one had an accomplice. Here's the funny thing—he drives an exterminator van, but the info the company had on file for him is 100% bullshit. The name, the address, all fake. The Social Security number checked out, but the person it was assigned to, dead for ten years."

As if out of nowhere, a memory came to Harrison. "This reminds me of the 90s."

"What do you mean? The 1990s?"

"That's right, you're not from here."

"I've been here since high school," Rand snapped.

"Trust me, it's better that way. Check my dad's files from the 90s. He never really liked to talk about those cases, but this really rings a bell."

"Why would a case from back then have anything to do with this? That girl isn't a serial killer. I mean, even if she is, she wasn't alive decades ago."

A headache was forming around Harrison's temples. "I just..." He rubbed his head, and Rand put a hand on the bed rail.

"Listen, I don't know what they have you on, but it sounds like good stuff. Just take it easy for now and let us professionals handle this. Okay?"

"Yeah." Harrison's voice was tired. "You got this."

Rand tapped on the railing. "Get some rest. I'll check back in tomorrow." He watched Harrison for a response, but when none came, he left.

Inside Harrison's head, bells rang. They rocked his skull and flamed his ears. He clutched his head with tense fingers. And the more it hurt, the more he felt sure he needed to get home and look at Dad's old notebooks.

1992

1

Jill refrained from saying anything more than small talk at first. She still wasn't sure why Chris had been avoiding her but thought this may be the day she would get the answer if she didn't press it.

She asked about his mom and tried to let him know she cared. She asked about his new scratches and scrapes and wasn't surprised to hear they were from Todd and his Klan—except the way Chris fought back. She never really saw Chris as a fighter—not a runner, but not a fighter either. He always seemed to have a way about him, a calmness that let the harsh realities of their surroundings tumble away. But this week, things seemed a bit different for them all.

Before Jill knew it, they were walking down Milwaukee Road, a street she didn't recognize. "Where are we?"

"I need to drop by a friend's place." Chris looked away and shrugged.

It was a mannerism Jill recognized. He didn't want to talk about it, but he needed to. "Okay. Who's the friend?"

"Stony. I think you've met him before."

"That weirdo with the bright orange backpack who sells weed?" She paused for a moment. "Are we going to buy weed?"

Chris took a deep breath. "Well..."

Jill squinted and looked him over. She knew he smoked it sometimes but didn't really want to be a part of it. But she didn't want to abandon him right now, either. He seemed like he needed the company.

"I'm not smoking anything," she said.

"You don't have to. Shit, I didn't offer you any." He chuckled with tightness in his tone.

She elbowed him symbolically in the ribs. He did the same back, and she felt the air lighten.

"Does it help?" she wondered. "I mean, with what's going on with your mom and stuff."

"I don't know. I guess, maybe. She doesn't like it, though. She says it'll rot my brain."

"You have something in there to rot?"

"Ha-ha." He rolled his eyes. "I guess it helps. Some days, she's just so out of it. Or she spends the whole day in bed. I try to talk to her, and she won't—like she thinks if she talks to me about it, it'll make it worse, or make me sad, or whatever. The fact is, it makes me sad—like she doesn't want to let me in. So, yeah, if I sneak outside and take a few puffs, I feel better. At least for a while."

"I guess I get it. I don't know what I'd do if my mom was sick."

They reached the railroad tracks, and Chris stopped. He studied the open door of a home on the other side of the rails.

"What is it?" Jill followed his gaze. The home seemed dark, even in the daylight. The front door was open. A cat walked out of the house and sat just beyond the threshold. It raised a paw to its face and licked. "That's..."

"That's his house." Chris pointed.

"It gives me the creeps."

A breeze blew at them from the house's direction carrying a putrid stench.

"Yeah," Chris said, "me too." He took a step forward, crossing the first rail.

"You sure we should go over there?"

"He's not going to come to me. You can wait outside if you want."

Jill took the next step with him. "I think I will."

The smell only got worse as they approached. By the time they reached the door, Jill thought she might puke.

"Stony!" Chris knocked on the door frame. "You in there?"

The cat stared at the two guests, not giving up his seat.

"Stony!" Chris repeated. After a moment, he set a foot inside.

"You're going in?"

"Just to take a peek and see if he's here. He probably has headphones on or something."

Jill took a step back. "Okay." She tried to breathe facing away, but it didn't help the smell or the sour taste in the air. She walked down the driveway and leaned on the back of the car, Stony's mom's, she guessed by the beads and feathers hanging from the mirror.

A moment later, Chris ran from the house, gagging, his hand over his mouth. His face was white, eyes wide and glassy. He fell to his knees in the grass and threw up. Jill held back her own puke, thankful that she couldn't smell Chris's. As she questioned why he was puking, her stomach turned tighter from the house's odor.

Chris retched a second time, then wiped his mouth with his hand before rubbing the vomit-laced drool on the grass. He shot back to his feet and glared at Jill.

"We got to go." He was out of breath and clutching his stomach with his clean hand. He started running back the way they'd come. "Come on."

Jill glanced at the open door, the cat, the vomit patch on the lawn. What had just happened? She felt as though the house's darkness may be a tangible thing. The breeze picked up, blowing the home's scent across her. She envisioned it rubbing into her skin and she felt ill—not just nauseated, but weak, light-headed.

"Let's go!" Chris had made it to the tracks and waited, waving her over.

Jill forced her feet to move. She made them walk and get her the hell out of there. With each step she took, she felt clearer and better.

They were three blocks away before Chris would stop running. He leaned on the back of a rusted-out delivery truck that was sinking into some stranger's yard.

"Jesus, that was gross." He panted and kneeled, then rocked back onto his butt.

Jill took a knee beside him. "What did you see back there?" Her words were breathy but calm. She was curious, but at the same time, not sure if she really wanted to know. The look on his face when he came out of that place still hung in her mind. Thinking back, he looked ill, or even undead.

Chris checked around. The yard was clear, as was the rest of the street. Only the cars of retirees were on the road, and all of those were parked in front of homes. "They're dead. Stony and his mom. They—they were— *God*, it was disgusting."

Jill scanned the neighborhood herself, not sure if his investigation was good enough. Her lips tightened as she worked on what to say next. Part of her didn't want to believe him. She didn't want to think she had just been so close to death or so close to a crime scene. Part of her knew he was right. The smell, the dark aura of the house.

"Are you sure?" Jill asked. "I mean—how do you know they were really dead?" She could see Chris's face go white again as he thought about what he had seen.

"They are dead. Fucking holes in their bodies, maggots, all the way around. Dead." He covered his mouth and turned away. The look on his face said he was going to puke again, but none came.

"Well, what do we do?"

"What do you mean?"

"Aren't we supposed to call the cops? I know we're skipping, but—"

"No. We're skipping and at a drug dealer's house... no way."

"Then what?"

"We walk away. Pretend we never saw it."

Jill spotted a little old lady across the street. She stepped outside and lifted the flap on the mailbox that hung from the wall beside her door. She turned and went back inside empty-handed. Jill wondered what it was like to be that old. To live alone in an old house—all alone. Would that be her one day? Chris tapped at the soles of his shoes, bringing her back around, and she asked herself what she thought was the next logical question: Who had done this?

"But what about the killer?" she said. "Don't the cops need to know so they can catch the killer?"

"The cops have their hands full with all the kids in the hospital right now."

"What are you talking about?"

"I heard about it yesterday at Memorial. Kids are in comas, and they think someone's behind it."

"Wait... What were you doing there?"

Chris hemmed and hawed and then admitted, "I went to visit Tommy."

Jill's face went red. "You're going by to see our brain-dead friend who may never wake up, all the while ignoring the others who are still alive. Is that right? You're ignoring Wes and me, and..." She felt so hurt she couldn't continue. It wasn't that he was visiting Tommy. She would actually be happy knowing that Tommy wasn't forgotten, but... "Wes thinks you don't like him anymore. I've frankly thought the same, the way you've been brushing me off in class. But you have time to sit with Tommy?"

"I just..." Chris swayed in the grass. "I'm afraid to be around you two." He pointed at his arm, his face wrinkling with worry. "This is all my fault."

"Your arm?"

"My arm, Wes's leg, Tommy laying there like a vegetable. It's all my fault, and... I just figured I'd save you the trouble of deciding not to hang around me anymore."

"What? You think we don't want you around?"

"It would make sense."

She reached out and rested her hand on his leg. "For Chrissake, Chris, we've been friends practically since diapers. I don't think you could get rid of us if you tried."

He breathed softer. "Yeah?"

"I mean, you may owe us some tokens and pizza the next time we go to the arcade, but... yeah... we love you, Chris." She leaned in and hugged him. He rested his head on her shoulder, and she felt wetness from his eyes. That was okay. "Now, what was that about missing kids in the hospital?"

2

A corner of the old Custer Falls City-County building had been designated in the sixties for the police department. It was a four-room section, allowing for three officer desks, an area for reception, where Rhonda usually sat, an office for the chief, and a lockup for evidence and weapons. While the department still used it, they had outgrown the space in the mid-seventies and now had four full-time officers. They also took up several rooms in the basement for storage, interrogation, and a two-cell holding area.

Officer Dale Harrison took a seat at the desk under the east window. While the other two desks were shared by one officer from morning and one from late shift, he had his own, partly due to seniority, being the longest on the job other than the chief, partly because he didn't actually have a shift.

They joked around the office—that is, when the chief wasn't there— about the chief's position being, for all intents and purposes, honorary. The man only showed up in the office when he was expected for a meeting with the mayor or town council and had a hair up his ass about looking like he was doing his job; on other occasions, it was because he wanted time away from his wife to sit and work on his fly fishing lures. So, in practice, Harrison was the acting chief.

211

Harrison sat with his feet on the desk, staring out the window at an overcast sky. It looked like rain, cold rain. He had just finished getting a rehash of Betty Henson's story and left her in the interrogation room as he took a moment to think it through.

The story made about as much sense as the others from yesterday, only this one had something of a witness—a sleeping witness, but a witness. Add to that the fact that she physically didn't have the strength to commit the murder and that no physical evidence in the room suggested a third party—the kids didn't have the ability to do it either, nor did the evidence bare out their involvement—he'd send her back home to her kids. They should be together after losing their father anyway. But what had happened?

A single smaller cloud drifted along with the sky's blanket of gray cumulonimbus cover. It reminded him of the old saying, something about staring at the clouds to fall asleep. And the idea of sleep came back to mind. Why sleep? The kids in the hospital, comas, but still sleep as he saw it; the deaths of those in their beds, all sleeping victims. But what was the connection? How did it all fit together?

He knew he was brushing away the old bum in the park and the missing kids, but those had to be outliers, unrelated. Didn't they?

The door opened, and Harrison heard Officer Barry Johnson come in. He lowered his feet and looked the officer over. "How'd it go?"

Johnson was given the job of searching for the missing minors. The Brolin girl, with her vehicle gone too, wasn't so much of a concern yet. College-age kids often got wild hairs up their asses and ran off to do things with their friends. Johnson had told the mom yesterday to file a report if she hadn't shown up in forty-eight hours. The Minsk girl and the DiMarco boy, though, they were a more sensitive subject. While technically still not missing person cases, they were minors, which meant the department would look into the cases even though they weren't required to. Perks of living in a small town, if you'd call it a perk, Harrison would say.

"Nothing," Johnson dropped into the seat at his shared desk. "The Minsk mom said she had mentioned going to the mall after school, but I can't find any proof that she went there. The DiMarco boy was home by himself. When the mother came home from work, she couldn't find him. I was thinking about going by the school and asking some of their classmates, but wanted to get your take on that, being this isn't *official* yet."

Harrison shook his head. "No, you're right. Not official yet, and I'm sure the moms will contact the close friends. It's better not to stir too much up just yet. Drop by the kids' houses one more time before your shift's over and see if they've come home. And if either aren't home by morning, we can discuss school interviews. And, shit..." Harrison leaned where he could see reception. "Hey, Ronda?"

She raised her head from a copy of *Guns & Ammo* and looked back. "Yeah, boss?"

"Better get a hold of the Chief. With all that's going on right now, he's going to want to advise the council on a curfew, or at least a statement to parents."

"Okay." She closed her magazine and picked up the phone.

Harrison glanced back out the window, imagining how much of a pain in the ass it was going to be if he had to report to the council.

"Gotcha. Any news on Gina?" Johnson asked.

Harrison sighed. "Those docs don't know nothing. I guess it's true; sometimes medicine's more art than science, because science don't seem to be doing shit over there."

"I'm sorry."

"Yeah. Me too."

3

Eddy Lawrence had made it to school without shitting his pants, but only by squeezing his butt cheeks together as hard as he could. He ran immediately to the bathroom and reached the toilet for most of the show, but his underwear was a loss and ended up in the bathroom trash.

By the time Eddy finished and was ready for class, the bell had rung. He walked to the front office and, under his breath, repeated every curse word he knew and aimed them at his grandmother. He didn't know why or how she was to blame, but he was sure she was, just like when his favorite rabbit stuffy had ripped and lost all its fluffiness in the dryer. It wasn't an accident. Gramma had been trying to make him get rid of it for months. Then there was the time he accidentally broke Grandaddy's urn. The next day his penis stung like it was on fire. Even after a bath and new clothes, it stung for a week, and Gramma wouldn't take him to the doctor or do anything to help. No, this had to be her. He didn't know what he did to make her mad, but she had done this.

In the school office, the receptionist, Ms. Nash, frowned at Eddy. "Why are you late?"

"Um. I was sick," he said. He wasn't going to say what actually happened.

"Do you have a note from your mom?"

"No. I was in the bathroom."

She rolled her eyes behind her horned-rimmed 1960s-inspired glasses. There was a picture of Eddy's grandmother wearing what looked like the exact same pair on the server in the dining room at home. It brought bile up in Eddy's throat, and he wished Ms. Nash would come and visit him in his basement.

Ms. Nash filled in the tardy slip and handed it to Eddy. His fingers touched it, and she said, "One more of these, and it'll be detention, mister."

"I was sick," Eddy said. He snatched the paper and looked at it. A big red X filled in the square next to *Unexcused*.

"No note." She shook her head.

Eddy ground his teeth and headed toward class. He pondered: he may not be able to get Ms. Nash in his basement, but he could get Gramma down there.

2022

1

Wes, Di, Sam, and Lisa climbed back into the Excursion. Their faces were tender from tears, and Wes couldn't shake the surreal feeling that had enveloped him. He gazed over the parked cars to the signs for *Emergency Entrance*, and the morning of his father's death rushed back into his mind. He may have just taken part in the dream for the second time, but he hadn't thought about it in years. He wouldn't fault himself if he had blocked it out, and he wondered if he had.

He remembered that morning, thinking he was walking through a dream. His mind felt similar now.

Each door clunked shut, and Wes started the SUV.

How were they going to stop the thing this time? Last time, they had tricked it, and deep inside, he always knew it would figure it out. This time, they'd have to do something different—but what?

All the breath in his lungs seemed to fall away, and he worked to refill them. He glanced at the girls in the rearview mirror. They were looking back at him, hoping for direction.

"We're going to get some food, guys. I know you may not be hungry now, but you need it."

He put the vehicle in reverse, and the girls looked at each other and whispered. He'd figure this out. He had to. Jill was relying on him to do it. He didn't know exactly what would happen to her if he didn't wake her up, but he was pretty sure she would end up dead.

He backed up and drove toward the Country Kitchen on 7th.

Di put her hand on his shoulder. "We're going to save her."

"I don't know how."

1992

1

Ray Trent walked along Academy Street, a once prosperous section of town. In the twenties, Treasure State College, a Mining and Gemology school, resided at the intersection of Academy and Main. It was dedicated to new techniques of finding anything in the ground, from gems like sapphires to precious metals like gold and silver to other metals such as copper and cobalt. The school spawned the mansion district around it for the Custer Falls elite, most of whom moved away during the great depression. By the time Ray was born, the area was falling apart, one majestic pillar at a time. Most of the residents were either elderly children of long-ago elites or renters of one of the several mansions that had been converted to low-income apartments.

There was an itch crawling around Ray's insides. He'd felt it growing since the night before when he was looking through that cabin window and thinking about the things he would do to Amanda Brolin. And then that was taken from him. But the itch wasn't.

He looked at the stained and peeling paint of the buildings as he passed, and he felt there was something nearby that could help. He knew this neighborhood well, his house was only a few blocks away, but as he examined the homes, he couldn't figure out where the feeling was pointing him.

There was a six-unit apartment with a woman on the porch beating a carpet. He saw an old home with a dumpster in front and a large sign stating, *New Units Soon*. There was a greenish monstrosity that looked as if it hadn't been cleaned since the seventies. And then there was Mrs.

Kappe's place.

Mrs. Kappe was an original Academy Street inhabitant, the daughter of a tenured professor. He taught at both Treasure State College and a junior college in Butte, where the primary subject matter was copper. When Kappe's parents were struck down by polio in the 1930s, everything passed to her. Determined to make her parents' death a blessing rather than a tragedy, she quickly sold much of her inherited possessions and bought land with the returns. Over the next few decades, she became first a celebrated apartment landlord, later a dreaded slumlord.

Ray didn't know much about the old woman other than the rumors that she had a safe in her bedroom with thousands of dollars locked away. As he walked down Academy Street and looked her place over, an urge rose inside him: he wanted that money. As far as he knew, he had no immediate need for it, but as he got closer to her home, a voice inside whispered, "*You deserve it. You need it. Go get it.*"

He paused on the crack between her dry and barren front yard and the crumbling sidewalk. He looked inside the windows and saw nothing. That was good. He could go inside and find the safe. She was an old hag who probably couldn't remember the combination—she may even have it written where he could see it.

Ray walked into the Kappe yard, along the side of the decrepit mansion. He didn't run or slink. He just walked. There was a confidence in his movement. He'd already decided he was in the right; he was just going to get something that was his. So he walked.

Behind the house, like in the front, he saw no one. He went up the back porch to a six-paned window door and tried the knob. It was locked, and he was shocked, flabbergasted. How dare someone lock him out from *his* money. He looked around at the rocking chairs and small tables that decorated the rear porch and grabbed a pair of scissors that sat atop a newspaper. Holding them by the folded blades, he slammed the handles into the glass pane nearest the doorknob.

Glass shattered and tumbled inward, and Ray was hit in the face with the smells of ammonia, moth balls, and mold. It was something like his grandmother before she died, but even more sickly.

He reached through and unlocked the door. Glass tinked and scraped along the floor as the door moved. This was good. Now, he just needed to find the old woman's bedroom.

Room by room, Ray searched the bottom floor. She was old, after all;

she had to have a bedroom on the first floor. He found three of them, all dusty and unused.

In the front of the home, he found the entryway, a two-story cavern accentuated by a five-foot-tall crystal chandelier. Even under years of undusted grime, it was the shiniest thing Ray had ever seen. He wished it were nighttime, so he could turn it on and watch it glow. And the voice whispered, *"Keep going, and you'll find enough loot to buy your own."*

The stairs were dark oak, trimmed with decorative carpet runners. They followed the treads in a curved upward arc to a second-floor balcony that overlooked the front door.

Ray peered over the edge, and a desire raced through him. He wanted to see—needed to see—someone hit the dingy white marble entrance tiles. He needed to throw them over and watch as they hit and red waves rolled over the floor below. It was like a tingling in his fingers—they needed to grab, needed to pull, needed to throw.

He blew a hard breath and started through the upstairs rooms. Closed door after closed door, dusty beds, specs and dirt suspended in dark and gloomy unused spaces. Air was stale and still. Ray wondered if anyone actually lived there until he found it.

A large room, trimmed from head to toe in woodwork, fancy antique furniture, and actually clean, lay at the end of the long hallway. Two lamps lit the extremities of the luxuriously large space, one near the door and one beside the bed. The bed itself was dented in the shape of a thin body as if someone had recently been on the ancient mattress.

Ray examined the room. Could she be here? Maybe the old bat had been in bed taking a nap while he was searching? Maybe. But if so, he didn't see her.

2

Zelda Kappe stood in the closet, peering at the boy in her bedroom. She watched him cross the room through a crack between the hinged side of the door and the frame. Her fingers trembled around the two-shot .22 pistol in her arthritic right hand, but her gaze was steady on him.

She had been awakened from her mid-morning nap by noises downstairs, then hid as they got closer to her bedroom. She dreaded her decision years ago to not run a phone line up to the second floor. It had seemed so horrendous to put more wires in the house. She had worried about the plaster, the moldings, having to pay contractors and having them in her home, and then never getting it to look right again. But maybe it would have been worth it.

But she had dealt with intruders in her house before. Granted, she had been at least twenty years younger then, with a much stronger body. She never looked away from the sight of blood. She just wished her hand would stop shaking and that she were strong enough to wield the double-barreled shotgun by her feet. At this age, she worried the thing might break both her hand and her shoulder from the recoil. But if it saved her life, it may be worth it.

She looked the boy up and down. His clothes screamed *poor*, his walk screamed *poor*. Everything about him screamed a greedy beggar boy who thought he could come into her home and get a free ride off her well-earned wealth. Maybe one day after she was dead—she knew she couldn't control what happened to her things after the blood-sucking lawyers got their fingers on her money—but not while she was alive. Her fear slipped away, and anger stiffened her grip on the weapon.

The boy looked under the bed. Then he searched inside her bathroom. He must have been looking for something specific, as he didn't open any drawers or touch her jewelry box on the bathroom vanity or her large dressers. It then occurred to Zelda what he was doing. He was after the legend, the story that popped up in the seventies, and every few years after that, someone would ask her about it. She could deal with this.

As the boy reached for the closet door, she stuffed the small pistol into the pocket of her dress.

The door swung open, and Zelda stepped into the boy's face, screaming as loudly as she could muster, "What are you doing in my house?"

The boy stumbled backward. His eyes sprang open, and his mouth dropped.

"Well? Why are you in my house?" she shouted again. She bore her teeth. She knew how to deal with riffraff kids. You put them in their place, and they cower back under the rock they came from. She was sure the only reason he'd come this far was because he thought no one was home.

The boy lunged forward and shoved Zelda in the chest. She felt a snap in her ribcage, and searing pain rippled across her front. The boy was following, moving in on her as she drifted backward. She was falling, and he was closing in.

Zelda's hand moved toward her dress pocket when a sharp pain and white light flashed across her vision.

3

Ray loomed over the old bat as her head cracked against the closet door. She left a line of blood as she slid down the old oak and thudded on the floor. Her eyes fluttered, and Ray scoffed as he stepped around her to investigate the closet.

He pushed aside clothes, silk dresses, designer outfits from twenty years prior, and surprisingly, a few plain, gray jumpsuits, like those a gas station attendant might wear. He scanned the rear of the closet and found a cedar-lined interior from floor to ceiling and left to right. No sign of a safe. No sign of any money.

The whisper spoke, "*Find it,*" and Ray's anger heated.

He looked down at the old woman. She knew where it was; he needed to make her say. He grabbed her arms and yanked on her, leaning her against the closet door.

"Wake up!"

She didn't move.

"Wake up, you old bitch!"

She didn't move.

Ray placed his hand on his chest as if he were about to say the pledge, then swung it outward, crashing his backhand across the old woman's face. He felt something give below, and as his hand returned to his side, her nose fountained blood down her wrinkled face, and she shuffled around where she sat.

"Wake up, bitch!"

Her eyes found him, and her hands went to her nose. "You little shit!"

Ray cracked a smile. He walked backward and sat on the bed. "Where's the safe?"

"There is no safe." She pinched her nose shut. Her voice sounded thin and frazzled as if her lungs barely had the strength to force words from her mouth.

"I know there's a safe, and I want what's in it."

"That's just a rumor my old tenants started because I wouldn't let them squat in my buildings for free. I don't have a safe. My money's in the bank

220

like any other sane person." She continued holding her nose with her left hand. Her right lowered and braced her ribs. "I have a few dollars in my purse in the kitchen. Please, take that and go."

"No, no, no." He shook his head.

"*She's lying*," he heard inside.

"You think I'm a dumb kid, and you can fool me. I know it's here."

"It isn't." Her voice was on the edge as if she were about to break down and cry. "Please, I'm an old woman, and I think you broke my ribs."

Ray ground his teeth and stood. He stepped toward the old bat and felt hot wind rush past his face. Then, he realized there was a loud pop. He touched his cheek. It was wet; a three-inch scrape was drawn just below his cheekbone. He looked at the woman. The fucking woman held the tiniest gun he had ever seen in her shaking hand. Her aim swung wild from right to left, up and down, and cold shock ran down Ray's back.

Blood streamed from her face as she released her nose. Drops fell from her fingers until she used her left hand to brace her right. The gun steadied, and Ray spun and sprinted toward the bedroom door.

Pop. A hole dug into the doorframe as Ray ran through, splinters brushing across his face. "Fuck!"

"You better run!" the old woman shouted. "Get the fuck out of my house!"

But Ray didn't run to the stairs. He didn't intend to leave without what he came for. He turned and ducked into one of the other bedrooms. She would have to come out, and when she came looking for him, he'd knock that stupid little thing from her hand—maybe he'd break her fingers, crush her entire hand in the process. Then, he'd make her talk. Oh, that bitch would talk.

He rubbed a finger over his cheek. The cut was deeper than he'd thought. Blood ran down his jawline and dripped from his chin. *It's okay*, he told himself. *I'll be fine once this is all over.*

"Where are you, you son of a bitch?" Her raspy old voice filled the hallway. She was closer.

He forced himself to breathe slowly. He needed to surprise her. He couldn't let her hear him coming.

The room to the right let out a bang. She must have flung the door open and slammed it into the wall.

"Get out here," she yelled.

Ray heard staggered footsteps in the hallway. They moved closer. She was about to push his door in. This was the moment. His cheek stung, and he didn't want another shot from whatever that little gun was. He braced his legs and held his palms open and ready to grab her—he didn't know what he'd do next, but once she was in his hands, he'd have her.

The door swung in. Ray rocketed at the opening.

She saw him coming, and her eyes went wide. She pivoted left, and at her waist, she held a double-barreled shotgun, zeroing in on Ray.

"Fu—" Ray couldn't finish his word. He stiffened his legs to stop and turn, but instead, they came out from under him.

Boom, the shotgun went off.

Ray flopped to the floor under a shower of dust and chipped plaster. Kappe fell backward and screamed. The shotgun skated across the floor, resting against the balcony railing.

Zelda Kappe moaned and looked through the door for Ray. Ray sat up and looked at the old woman. She clutched her wrist, and he saw the gun was gone.

"Bitch!" he crawled toward her.

"No," she hoisted herself up and crawled toward the balcony.

"No way." He pushed himself to his feet. He didn't see the gun, didn't know where she was going, but he'd had enough of this. He was going to get his fingers around that old woman and ring the life out of her. Damn the safe. She was going to die.

He closed in on her, but she kept moving. She was remarkably fast for an injured old hag.

"*Get her*," the whisper insisted.

She reached the railing before him and dropped onto her chest. She lay still as he closed in and grabbed her shoulder.

"That's enough, you crazy bat!" he rolled her over and saw the shotgun in her hands. She swung its barrels toward him, and he saw his death inside those tubes. He growled and grabbed the blue steel.

She pushed toward him; he twisted it toward her, clamping hard into its steel, and pressing the muzzle beneath her narrow chin.

"Dammit!" he screamed but didn't hear the words. The gun boomed and singed his hand. Zelda Kappe's nose, lips, and chin disintegrated in a flash of white flame.

Blood pulsed from the old woman. It streamed from the red chasm of what had been the lower half of her face and spattered over her cheeks and neck.

"Jesus fucking Christ!" Ray stumbled back. His entire body tingled.

Zelda grabbed the railing and steadied herself. Blood ran like a river down her front, down her dress, pooling on the floor. She set her sights on Ray and moved toward him, hands forward. Her eyes were cold, bloodshot, and determined, regardless of the carnage that her face had become.

Ray saw hate in her eyes. He saw the deepest determination he'd ever witnessed in a human and the pure rage driving it. He took one step and shoved. Zelda flew back, over the railing, down and down to that white marble floor. He heard nothing over the ringing in his ears. But he beamed as red waves of blood soaked the grandest entryway he'd ever get to see.

2022

1

The building was quiet in a way that gave Principal Hannah Gould chills. Sure, it was quiet on teacher work days, planning days, even nights after all the students had left and only a handful of faculty remained, but right now, there was a stillness in the air that grated on her skin like sandpaper.

She looked down at Joanne Higgins's dried blood on the entryway floor. It stretched for yards, much larger than she remembered. But she wasn't trying to see it before; she had been trying *not* to see it.

Around where her arms had been, it spread in swooping arcs as if someone was trying to make a blood angel. It traced the outline of her chest and dried in thick contours as if it were still flowing in rolling waves. It ran into the grout, making her wonder if it would ever come up. Would there always be a horrid reminder of that day etched into the floor for each staff member and student?

The superintendent had given the teachers the day off, along with the students and administrative staff. Today it would just be her and Heath Williams, the custodian. He was supposed to be in sometime in the next half hour or so, and as she measured the outline of Joanne Higgins's blood, she hoped he was up to the job.

Hannah walked back to her office feeling somewhat shameful. A woman was dead, children were traumatized, and here she was worrying about the floor. But she had to. Her job was keeping the school running as a safe and healthy environment. That meant doing certain jobs unemotionally and making sure they got done. At least, that was the way she wanted to think about it. Somewhere under the surface, she knew it was because she just couldn't deal with what was coming that night.

She hadn't let herself feel anything yet. Not for Joanne, not for Mrs. Henson, not for the Henson kids (beyond what she had to do to comfort them at the moment). She had finished helping them at the hospital, went home, ate, practically blew off her husband and his attempts to console her after the school's tragedy, and then she slept. She had ignored the strangeness of her dreams, knowing they were only due to the horror at school, and now she had to make sure the job was finished. The school would be ready by the end of the day whether the superintendent wanted kids back tomorrow or was going to keep them home until Monday. And when she got home tonight, she would cry. Her job would be done, and she would be able to let it all flow, ball her eyes out on Dawson's shoulder. But not yet.

She sat at her desk, and a sense of déjà vu washed over her. Her papers, the positions of the chairs opposite her, the light coming in the window from the gray, overcast sky beyond; they struck a memory, and she struggled to place it.

She shook her head. It was just a random feeling, she told herself, an instance of being in that office so much more than she was at home. It didn't mean anything. Until she remembered her dream.

She had been at this desk but on the other side. Her clothes were tattered and torn. Her hands were against the hard oak, her legs spread, and Heath Williams behind her—inside her. She hadn't wanted it, but she did. She found him repulsive, but something beneath his bulging uniform and mop of red hair, something on the other side of his facial scar, it stirred a heat within her.

She found her hands gripping her legs tightly, her mouth watering. A clank echoed from the front of the building. He was there, and a whisper in the back of her mind told her to stand up and go greet him.

2

Officer Stuart Harrison shut the door to his hospital room and dug into the closet for his clothes. Someone had been nice enough to bring his duffel from the PD, so he had it when needed. He needed it now; even if he had wanted to wear the torn, puke-covered uniform he was wearing when he came in, the hospital had already disposed of it.

His body ached as he stretched his jeans over his legs. His joints and gut burned as he pulled on his shirt. He sat and tied his shoes and groaned.

It took another moment for Harrison to center himself. He stood and headed downstairs to the main entrance, where an Uber was waiting for him.

He was halfway home when his phone rang, the hospital calling him to come back. He sent it to voicemail. He couldn't go back now. He needed to get home. Whether Mark wanted to listen or not, he knew there was something in his dad's old notes that was relevant.

It had been a few years since Dad died, and he was forced to go through all his things. But he remembered those notes being special, and not just because the man would never talk about that period of time—after Gina, he didn't blame him.

He paid the driver and went inside. Jester, his black lab mix, ran up and welcomed him.

"Hey, buddy." He scratched Jester's chest as his thick, black tail thumped against the wall. "Glad to see you too."

Harrison made his way into the kitchen, Jester at his heels. He picked up Jester's food bowl, and Jester planted his butt on the floor and licked his lips. In the pantry, Harrison filled the bowl the usual amount with dry food and grabbed one of the cans that he kept around for special occasions from the shelf. He put them both on the counter, and as the top popped on the can, Jester's tail thumped the side of the cabinet. Drool dripped from his lips.

"I know. It's coming." He scooped out the thick mixture of meat and gravy, wincing at the pungent smell, then stirred the wet and dry foods together. It was an ungodly concoction, but Jester loved it.

Harrison set the bowl on the floor. Jester watched, still, saliva dripping and gently patting against the kitchen floor.

"Get it." He leaned his head to the right as he spoke, and his muscles whined. Jester tore the three feet across the kitchen and dove into his bowl. At the sound of tongue smacking and crunch, Harrison headed to his office.

The room was designed to be a bedroom and maybe would have been if he had ever managed to make one of his relationships stick. Harrison had the recurring tendency of ruining every chance at long-term happiness once a woman said those dangerous words: *I love you*. In his brain, it was a timer's switch. *Tick, tick, tick*. From that point on, there would be ignored calls, canceled dates, and picking up extra shifts so as not to be available. What was close would become distant until either he or she—usually she—decided enough was enough and broke it off. He imagined a shrink would have told him it was because of his sister, or his mother, some form of abandonment fear. Maybe he was right. Maybe he just didn't want to get too attached. Maybe he had seen his own death in a dream at the age of twelve and didn't want anyone else to suffer like he had at the loss of his loved ones. It wasn't a concern he focused on, and not one he'd ask anyone about. He was just who he was, an acceptance that his adult life had settled into. And though he could have seen this office being a nursery or some other type of kids' room for some other owner when he bought the place, it never occurred to him after that.

He rounded his desk and opened the closet. He kneeled down and lifted moving boxes from the middle to the right as he groaned. From the left, he grabbed a banker's box marked *Harrison* and set it on the floor just outside the closet.

Chills ran across his sore muscles. He hadn't so much as glanced into that corner of the closet in years. Part of him knew that he actively avoided it. With a thick sigh, he flipped open the top and set it aside.

He saw dozens of notepads, a gallon Ziploc of pens, pencils, staples, and other various office supplies—he wondered why he had left those in here the last time he sorted through this box and decided that, just like now, he had wanted to get the job done and over as quickly as possible, and he ignored them. There were three downward-facing picture frames, and they gave Harrison pause. He didn't know which one was which, but he was pretty sure he didn't want to flip them over.

He picked one of the notebooks up and read the writing on the cover, *Feb-May, 1991*—not it. He lifted the next one, *Dec-March, 1992*—not it. He kept digging. Summer '92, early '93, late '91, mid-1994, none of which he was looking for. He dug deeper, setting aside the ones he had checked. The notebooks changed from dark blue to black to light blue, all with the same date designation and covering three to four months. None seemed to be the one he needed of Fall 1992.

"Shit," He mumbled. His knees ached, his back, his arms, and all with nothing to show. He was about to give up when a sharp pain flashed against the back of his head, and he saw nothing but white.

3

Norris Cushing stood over Officer Stuart Harrison's unconscious body, a half baseball bat in his hand. It was the bat he kept under the counter in the café. He called it a half-bat, but really he had sawed only a quarter of it off to make it more maneuverable if someone ever made it behind the counter. They never had, but he still held onto it, just in case.

Harrison breathed the sweet slow breaths of deep sleep, and Norris rolled him over. He was a big guy, and Norris was glad he had been able to take him from behind. Not that Norris was small, but at his age, he didn't heal as fast as he used to.

Norris picked up the books Harrison had set to the side and put them back in the box. Curiosity struck as he saw the picture frames. He flipped them right side up, one at a time. The pictures were old, from the 90s, he guessed. Their color was fading, and a light sepia seemed to be fading in. There was a teenage boy, a younger girl, and a rather attractive woman in her thirties. He watched her for a moment, and the unmistakable, cold sensation set in that he was looking at a dead woman. He flipped the photos back over, looked around, found the lid, and placed it on top.

"There we go," he whispered.

The clack of claws against the hardwood floor came down the hallway. Norris picked up the banker's box and set it on the desk. He reached into his back pocket as a black canine face peered around the corner.

Jester sniffed and then huffed as he walked through the door frame.

"I see you, fella."

Jester locked eyes with Norris, and Norris pulled an object from his back pocket. He snapped it in half as Jester sniffed at the air. He tossed, and Jester snatched the half hotdog mid-flight, just like he had earlier when Norris came in the back.

"Good boy."

Jester finished chewing and panted, his eyes stuck on Norris.

"Here you go." He tossed the other half. Snapped in mid-air. Norris lifted the banker's box and walked out of the office, out of the home. As he set the box in his trunk, he muttered, "Okay, I did it. Now, who pays for Elias?"

1992

1

Jill and Chris kept walking, neither wanting to stop, neither wanting to continue their conversation. The death and gore at Stony's, the kids in the hospital, they were thoughts that needed wrangling.

Before they realized how far they'd walked, they found themselves on Academy Street. Jill didn't intend to go there. She was just wandering.

"Did you bring us here?" She looked Chris in the eye for the first time in thirty minutes.

He examined the street as if everything he was seeing was new. "No. I never come down here."

Jill felt as if a hand were on her back, gently nudging her forward, quietly urging her on. "I don't understand." She felt cold all of a sudden and shivered.

She looked up at the row of mansions and got the feeling that maybe she shouldn't have come this far. She stopped, and Chris stopped beside her. Whatever this was, it wasn't right. There was a tingling sensation like a spider walking down her spine.

"What?" Chris asked. "Want to go another way?"

"I don't know." She felt like there was a reason she was there. She fought to understand it, but the answer hung just out of reach. Building by building, she studied the doors. Was she supposed to go to one?

That was when Ray Trent stepped out of the third house down.

"Look at that," Jill said.

"Ray? What about him? He's not your friend, is he? He's a bit of a dick."

"*No.* Not at all."

"Good, because I was being kind—he's a total dick."

Ray came down the porch steps and crossed the large dead lawn before stepping onto the sidewalk. As his foot touched concrete, Jill thought she saw blood on his hands.

Jill pursed her lips to speak when Ray turned and locked eyes with her. She felt a sheet of ice wrap around her. He stopped in his tracks and looked her up and down, then did the same to Chris.

"What is going on?" Chris whispered.

"I don't know. But I don't like it."

Ray turned and headed down the block.

"Go back," Jill said.

"What?"

"Back the way we came. I don't want to run into him."

"Jesus, Jill." He pointed at Ray as he rounded the next corner. "He's going away."

"I don't care. I talked to him the other day, and I think if he could have, he would have tossed me into traffic. I'm not going the same direction as that guy."

"Okay, okay. We can go the other way. But where to?"

"I think we should go by Wes's house."

Chris inhaled deeply.

"We're going."

2

Barton Smith closed the door. He felt relieved, calm. He'd waited years for just that moment, and as he crossed the house and entered the kitchen, he wondered how he had lasted as long as he had. He thanked the whispers. He didn't know where they came from, but they had given him the courage to do what he had always wanted.

He poured a glass of milk and sat at his kitchen table. He sipped and thought about the girl. She was fantastic, but not perfect. He wondered if he could find the perfect one. Could it have been the girl he was following yesterday before this one distracted him? Or maybe he had yet to meet her. He thought about the hundreds of young asses he had daydreamed about in his job at the caves and his trips to the mall. One of them had to be it.

Before he knew it, he'd finished his milk. His sense of satisfaction seemed to fade with it. He clunked the glass down, his blood warming. He needed to do it again. The girl in the other room was going cold, and he needed a new one. He'd have to go back to the mall.

"*She'll be there,*" the whisper said.

3

As rain started to drizzle, Jill led Chris down Laundale and into Custer Estates. They walked a block and turned right, freezing at the corner. A Custer Falls Police Department cruiser was parked in front of Wes's house.

Jill's mind went to Stony's place, to her and Chris being out of school, to Ray Trent and whatever chaos that kid was up to.

"What's that about?" Chris said.

"I don't know. Do you think..."

He looked at her. "It can't be about us."

"Stony?"

"No way. Wes doesn't even smoke."

They watched Wes's house in silence for half a minute. Nothing changed except the road getting darker as the rain made it wetter and wetter. The street was calm. But even in the stillness, a cold crept into Jill's mind. Something was off. Yet another thing was wrong, and now whatever it was had been to Wes's house.

"I think we should go." Chris shook his head. A drop of rain ran down his nose. "We can come back later."

Jill saw fear in the cold squint of his eyes. He was biting his lip. He felt it too.

"No." Jill put a hand on his shoulder. "If something's happened here— whatever it is—we need to go see if he needs our help."

Chris took a step back. "I—I get the feeling something bad's in there. I don't think it's a good idea."

Jill shook her head. It wasn't just that something bad had happened. Something bad was still happening. "That's even more of a reason to get to Wes and help him."

Chris's gaze returned to the cop car, the house, its windows and doors. Raindrops splashed and exploded against the cruiser's body. Nothing moved, neither to scare him away nor to prove its safety.

"I'll go first," Jill said. "You wait here. I'll wave you over if everything's okay."

He hung his head but said, "Okay."

Jill trotted her way across the street. She slowed as she passed the cop car, taking in its official presence and thinking that maybe this was a bad idea. It shined, even as rain patted against its hood. Bad idea or not, she needed to check on Wes.

She stood under the front door's overhang and glanced from the doorbell to the knocker. She usually used the knocker; it felt funny and abnormal, a way to get people's attention and keep them on their toes. Today, that didn't seem like a good idea. She pressed the bell.

It chimed, and she felt adrenaline seizing her. She wanted to turn and run but planted her feet. She heard steps, low and heavy. The door creaked open.

A young officer from Custer Fall's finest looked down at her. He studied her clothes and her backpack. "Can I help you?" His voice was cold and accusatory.

"Uh." She didn't know what to say. His gaze hardened, and words fled even further from her lips. He had to have known she was skipping. He had to know about Stony's place—the death. She was caught and should run right there.

"Who is it?" A familiar voice from far inside, Wes.

The officer looked back, and the door widened just slightly. She saw Wes at the top of the stairs, leaning against the wall.

"That's my friend," Wes said. "Let her in."

The cop shook his head. "Kid, I'd like to, but this is a crime scene—until it's released..."

"She'll come up here," Wes argued. He was firm. How was he talking to a cop like this? Her heart thumped harder. "She'll be out of the way, just like us."

The cop ground his teeth. He was about to open his mouth, and Jill called to Chris, "Come on!"

He was across the street, and they were up the stairs before the cop got a word out.

"Just... stay up there," the cop demanded.

They went into Wes' room, where Di was sitting on the bed. The brother and sister both had bags under their eyes and long pale faces.

"What's going on here?" Chris said.

4

"It's... hard to explain," Wes said. He gestured for Jill and Chris to have a seat. Jill took a corner of the bed near Wes. Chris sat at Wes's desk.

He wondered if there was a proper way to get through what had happened. Dad, the dreams, the sense within his dreams that he knew more than he should, was older than he should be, the consequences of it all. Where to begin? He thought: *Go with the easiest to believe.* But what was that?

"Just try." Jill put a hand on Wes's shoulder.

He nodded. "Dad died this morning."

Both Jill and Chris's mouths dropped.

Wes watched the horror travel across Chris's expression. He saw Chris imagine what may be coming for his mother if her treatments didn't work, or as he expected, *when* her treatments didn't work.

Jill's hand tightened on Wes. "My God. What happened?"

Again Wes struggled. "In his sleep. Because... because of the dreams."

Wes went through the past two nights' dreams, explaining the injuries in dreams and their real world results. He talked about how he and Di shared them, how Dad joined, and how his wounds—his death—were exactly replicated in both places.

The room was silent. Wes saw blood, his father's headless corpse in the bed, then the garage. He saw the graveyard and realized just what could have happened to him if he hadn't run so fast.

The gears turned in Chris's head. He didn't believe it, couldn't believe it. He remembered Charlotte in his dream last night. Would that mean it was actually her? Shame and embarrassment flushed his face. *No.* Then his dream from two nights ago, Mr. Wimbley's bloody throat. That couldn't have been real. Wimbley hadn't been to school since then, but it had to be because he was sick, because if what Wes was saying was true... he couldn't imagine what that meant.

Jill rubbed her fingers together. She could feel the sand from the lake in last night's dreams between her fingertips. Wes was telling the truth. She knew it.

"I'm so sorry, Wes." Jill leaned in to hug him. He didn't move, and she hugged him anyway. "I'm so sorry."

Chris's eyes sharpened. His lip raised in a half snarl. "I can't believe that. You're hallucinating or something. Too much meds... There's too much trauma from what you saw and—"

"It's real," Di spoke up. "All of it."

Chris shook his head. "You too. You're full of trauma. That's what it is."

"You want to see trauma?" Di said. "Why don't you spend the night, and we'll show you how *not-real* it is tonight."

"What?" Chris lost his breath. His chest was cold from the idea. If they *were* telling the truth, it might be someone in his family who got hurt next. But that was all nonsense. "Bullshit."

Chris was shaking. He got up and tore across the room. He stopped at the door and glanced back at Wes, whose gaze was fixed on the bed. "I'm sorry, Wes." He vanished through the door, down the stairs, and out the front.

Jill watched Wes. He was deep inside himself, closed off to the room beyond more than a surface-level acknowledgment of its existence. She wanted to know what was going on in there. It was painful, she could see that, but she also knew the pain wasn't over. She wanted to help. "I think we should do it," Jill said.

"Do what?" Di asked.

"Spend the night. I think we can help each other through this."

2022

1

Stuart Harrison felt wetness on his face and something soft flicking against his cheek. He saw Jester's big brown eyes and felt his head throbbing. He reached to pull up the covers—they seemed to have completely slipped away—but all he felt was carpet. He was on the floor.

"Ah," he covered his face. "Jester, no." He sat up in his office in front of the open closet and remembered what he had been doing. The box was gone. His father's box. Rage took over where pain left off. "What the fuck, Jester? Where were you?"

Jester hung his head and backed away.

"Fuck."

But why did someone want his father's box? Did it mean he was right about the child murderer being related to his father's case? He forced himself to his feet and then into his desk chair.

"Fuck," he repeated. If only he had found the notebook first, put it away before… But he hadn't found it. He had seen dozens of books with dates, none matching the date he was looking for. But he knew he had seen the notebook when he had first brought that box home and went through it. He remembered seeing the date and thinking about Gina in that hospital bed—of Dad working day and night to figure it out. And a shock rippled through his system. The book wasn't in that box anymore.

He remembered picking it up and flipping through the pages. He remembered thinking he should keep it separate because he wanted to read it to better understand what had happened that year. He had never had the time to get back to the book, but it meant that the thing was still there, somewhere. If only he could remember.

Harrison went to his bookshelf. He passed over books on serial killers, crime scene techniques, and the minds of modern criminals. He had almost no fiction. He hated how they always got it wrong, and he had stopped trying to find fiction he enjoyed.

He was about to stop and move on and try searching his bedroom when he spotted a black gap at the end of the shelf. At first, he thought it was a shadow. Just a black mark on the inside of the case where the last book cast darkness. But then he saw a faint gray line running down. No, that was a black-spined notebook.

He seized the book and read the cover. His heart pounded as he saw the words *Aug-Oct, 1992.* This was it. He cracked it open to a page in the middle.

—

and they said it was a demon. I checked if they were on drugs—eyes, temp, breathing—everything was normal.

A demon? Maybe they weren't high at that moment, but they surely weren't in their right mind. Maybe they came down from the stuff, but they still thought it was real.

There was only so much I wanted to argue. Two of them had a dead father, and they'd just been through Hell. But a chaos demon? A magical dream thing to make you hear voices? It was like they'd gotten their heads stuck in a comic book. At least they were alive, which is more than I could say for the Minsk girl. God help her.

2

Hannah Gould walked through the offices, past the front entrance, past the blood. She didn't see Heath. She continued into the main hallway that divided the school between kindergarten through second grade on the north and third through fifth to the south. Halfway down the corridor, she found him.

Heath Williams stood inside the small custodian's room which held his supplies, kept his tools, and housed a large utility sink. He leaned forward against a shelf of cleaners, hand over head and eyes shut.

Hannah stopped in the doorway and examined him. His overalls hung from his body; their ragged appearance and his dense messy hair repulsed her. But the bagginess of his clothes draped over a thick muscular build, and she had to stop and touch the doorframe to keep her balance.

Her heart pounded against her chest. She felt the wedding ring around her finger, and she wished she had never said yes. She and Dawson had been so young when she put it on, too young to know how long a lifetime really was. It was like a chain holding her back, an ever-tightening hunk of metal that anchored her to some distant fairy tale.

Heath turned around, his eyes falling on her. He was unsurprised. It was as though he knew she would come, and she felt his stare move over her body like a hunter examining his prey. And she liked it.

All Hannah could think of was her dream—Heath behind her, pounding away, his tight grip on her hips, demanding her obedience in a way Dawson never had.

He watched her grow warmer, her face flushing, her grip on the door frame tightening. He grabbed her wrist, and she trembled from her thighs to her fingertips. He pulled her inside the room and pushed her to face the shelf. She made no fight, said no words. She didn't want this, but she did. He was repulsive. He was a beast. She wanted him now.

He took her hands and placed them on the edge of a chest-high shelf. His fingers followed her arms back to her chest, and she gripped the metal structure hard. She felt him pressing against her rear, and she found herself back inside her dream. This wasn't real; it had to be some extension of that dream. She had fallen asleep at her desk, and here she was again doing something she knew she would never do, loving what she would never love.

His hands slid to her waist, met in front, and unbuttoned her jeans. He spread them. He pulled them down to her knees, dragging her panties along with them.

She was ready for him, grabbing the shelf firmly, pushing her rear back, presenting herself. She knew it was coming and didn't care if it was a dream or not, real or not. She wanted it more than she had ever wanted Dawson or any other man.

Hannah's gaze passed over the myriad objects on the shelf in front of her: cleaners, solvents, screws, a screwdriver. She felt her heart throbbing as she focused on the screwdriver. It was large, nearly a foot long, and her hand began to sweat; she wanted to hold it.

The sound of Heath's jumpsuit unzipping ratcheted in her ears. He was coming, and she was ready for him. She could feel his heat moving closer, and her hand wrapped around the screwdriver.

His hot breath touched Hannah's neck, and she could no longer contain herself. She spun, her hands like blurs. She brought them to his bare chest, steal plunging deep, and thick hot blood poured from his ribs.

It ran down his chest, across his stomach, and she swung the screwdriver again. It dove to the right of his sternum, and he dropped down onto the grimy closet floor. She pulled it out as he convulsed. Blood fountained from his chest, and she tossed away the tool. Her fingers ran over his wounds, smearing red across his body.

Hannah's mind was a blur of exhilaration. She forced a finger from each hand into Heath's chest wounds to feel his insides. Color, warmth, depth. She writhed and squeezed.

His heart stopped. His blood seeped instead of sprayed. She felt her mind slow, her body ease. She exhaled and saw where she was. A sinking realization washed over Hannah. She was not in a dream. The blurred line was gone.

She gazed at the red on her hands. She trembled as she looked down at Heath Williams, his wounds, his crimson chest, the floor, now pooling with his blood.

A wave of shock washed every sensation free. Hannah jumped to her feet and ran. She slipped on the blood. Her legs were bound by the pants around her thighs. She saw herself falling, and then saw nothing as the side of her head collided with the tile floor.

1992

1

Tommy Laskin had accepted that he may never return to his own world. Moment after moment, drifting from one dreamland to another, he'd seen things that may have once filled him with exhilaration, others that made him want to puke, and others that filled him with dread.

He hovered above the amassing residents of Bloodtooth Caverns and watched as his thoughts drifted. Jamie Madison, Cherry French, and Shelly Sullivan seemed to chat endlessly about Lonny More, Jeff Ramos, and Billy Caldwell while longingly staring at them across the cave. Lonny More, Jeff Ramos, and Billy Caldwell talked about Jamie Madison, Cherry French, and Shelly Sullivan, glancing back again and again. None of them noticed that their conversations never ended. None seemed to remember what they had said thirty seconds earlier.

Tommy thought of the barbarians. He thought of the man in the streets of New York trying to gun down the mob and instead being gunned down himself. He thought about watching Chris shove a flute down Mr. Wibley's throat and an SUV crush Mr. Henson's head in that garage.

Randy Benson screamed on the far side of the cave. No one noticed. He ran out and popped back in on the far side a few moments later. "Let me out!" he howled, and ran through the exit, then emerged on the far side of the cave once again. Again he howled. Again he tried to escape and returned.

Hugo Langeland clawed at the stone wall. His fingertips bled. Margaret Shiner sat behind a ring of boys who pushed and prodded a smaller boy in the middle, chanting, "Fag," repeatedly. She pulled her hair out, strand by strand. Kathy Wake sat in a puddle in almost the exact center of the room and rocked herself forward and back. She muttered something about eggs and watermelon, but Tommy couldn't hear exactly what it was.

He knew what was in front of him was some sort of prison. What else could it have been? He could sense that each kid was a real entity; none were made up as the product of another's dream. What he didn't know was why he could see it but wasn't bound there. Why he was more of a ghost-traveler who could fade in and out from there to the dreams of others in town. Why they were being held there at all.

There was something behind it, behind the scenes and pulling the strings. He imagined the man behind the curtain in the *Wizard of Oz*. Who was behind this curtain? Who was making this all happen? There had to be clues.

Tommy moved in over Kathy Wake. Her hair shifted and slid over her shoulders as she rocked forward and back. Her words rose and fell with her sway. Tommy leaned closer but couldn't make it all out: "Eggs are hard, but small... cracks and leaks... Watermelons are big... juice and meat... Blood and bone... juice and meat."

He watched her move, trying to make sense of the words. He focused. The rantings of a crazy girl, that's all it was, that was all he could understand. He was about to move when he noticed a small fine line coming from her hair. It was nearly invisible other than a slight shimmer.

A faint glittering light walked up the line, and then it vanished. Tommy reached to touch it, but it was gone.

"juice and meat... Blood and bone..." It glittered again.

Tommy grabbed the line. It was like silk, soft and sleek and slippery. He tried to hold it, but it vanished right out of his hand. He watched it go up, up, and into the cave wall.

"What the hell?" Tommy muttered to himself. For the first time, someone heard him.

Kathy looked up into his eyes. "Blood and bone..."

Tommy shot backward. That look. Her eyes into his. For a fraction of a second, he saw inside her. He saw her dream within a dream. It was like being inside another living thing, a worm, or some other parasite. Blood ran, muscles flexed and relaxed. Bone shone, holding it all up. Everything was wet, sticky, and slimy. And he was trapped there, pressed between a layer of skin and something's inner tissues.

Tommy had seen for an instant, then he was back in the cave.

Kathy faded away, back into her own darkness. "Eggs are hard, but small..."

"What the hell?" Tommy repeated.

"Fag." One of the boys in the ring fell backward. He collapsed on the ground, and the ring shrunk, filling the hole and paying him no mind.

Tommy went over to the fallen one. The boy sat up, staring into the darkness and froze. His lips moved, mouthing something but saying nothing. A glittering strand flowed from his head to the cave wall. It vanished, and after a few seconds, returned.

"There it is again." Tommy reached for it and stopped. He didn't want to be back inside something, another parasite. He didn't know what this kid was seeing or saying, but he didn't want to take the chance. He decided to follow the string instead.

He hovered through the air as the line came and went. He floated to the cave wall, where the shimmer ended and rock began. The wall was hard stone, but the string seemed to go right through it. As soon as a strand faded into the facade, he touched a glowing dot where it had vanished. It was warm and softer than the rest of the wall. What had he found?

Another strand appeared, and Tommy jerked his hand out of the way. The glowing string faded into the wall, and Tommy pressed hard into the stone. It mushed inward as if it wasn't a wall but some kind of rubber valve.

The next strand came, and Tommy moved aside. As soon as it was gone, he thrust his whole body forward, diving into the wall like some dreamworld Superman.

Light flashed and went out. Flashed again, and Tommy's eyes hurt. He closed them and opened them to see the guy called Stony. He stood in a Baskin-Robbins behind the counter. He was scooping brains from his head and piling them into a waffle cone. Hungry children waited on the other side of the counter for their treat.

Tommy jerked away as blood and brain dripped down the side of the cone and splattered against the counter. He saw a man on the ground in a forest. He was watching a bear dig into his body, rip out his organs, and eat them.

"No." Tommy flew backward. A wave of heat slammed into his back. He felt the gaze of someone watching him this time, and he spun around.

It wasn't just a feeling. Someone *was* watching him. Its image shifted like a face made of liquid. It looked white, then black, then Indian, then

Asian. Its arms were large, then skinny, then long and black, like the tentacles of a squid. Then furry with paws and the claws of a lion. It came from a cave that looked much like the Bloodtooth Caverns and closed in on Tommy.

Tommy wished he were in a normal dream, in a normal sleep, but he wasn't. He wanted to be startled awake and have it all be over, but he knew it wasn't that simple. The thing inched ever closer, and Tommy felt its wants draining him. It wanted his fear. It was getting it. It wanted his confusion, his inner panic and chaos.

The thing opened its mouth, but Tommy heard its words in his mind. *"I've been watching you."*

Tommy saw a glittering line stretch from his face toward the creature. He snatched at it, and his fingers passed right through.

"You haven't proven yourself yet," the creature hissed. The line flowed to the thing's mouth and dissipated inside it. *"Keep trying, though."*

"No!" Tommy shouted. The world around him flew by like a video stuck in fast rewind. He was jerked from that place, back through the wall, back into the cavern of prisoners.

"No, no, no. Not here." He closed his eyes hard and focused. When he opened them again, he was sitting in his room. Not his actual room but in a better place, for now.

2

Charlotte Baker had no idea what she was doing. She had left school. Not seeing Chris once all day long, she was now looking for him. Looking for a boy.

She told herself it was dumb. It was just a stupid dream, and it didn't mean anything. He didn't really like her like that. If he did, he would have said something, did something to show it.

But the other half of her was a romantic. She cried during *The Princess Bride* and knew her true love was somewhere out there. She may have been small and boyish-looking to some, but inside, she was a woman, she knew it, and she wanted her own Dread Pirate Roberts. And to this side of her, the dream was a sign.

They had talked and eaten, held hands and walked. They had looked into each other's eyes, and what she saw there was real. Something like that couldn't have just been the product of a dream. It meant something. So, she was looking for him.

As she walked through the rain, she realized she knew his friends but nothing that they did. Since none of his friends were in school today, he must have been hanging out with them. But where did they go? She shook her wet head and figured one obvious option to check out was the mall.

By the time she reached the doors of the Custer Valley Mall, rain had crept through the ends of her jacket sleeves and down her back, so even under her jacket, she felt wet and sticky. She took off the jacket and hooked it on her backpack, then noticed the smell of fresh salty pretzels and headed in that direction. If Chris was there, after all, he might be in the food court. She did not notice the thirty-nine-year-old man on the bench that took a long interested look as she passed by.

Her steps squeaked as she walked past clothing stores, shoe stores, the perfume store, the record store. She laughed at the sound, but as it continued, she began to feel self-conscious. She didn't want to be the annoying kid that caused everyone to look her way. She slowed down and tried to stop the sound, minimizing the twist of her feet as she stepped. Even as she quieted, she felt eyes upon her.

She looked back, sides, ahead. She saw a trickle of shoppers, mostly kids from her school. She had no idea how they got there so quickly before her, but none of them paid her a glance. Just like in school, she was invisible.

The smells of Asian food, pizza, cookies, and burgers drew her onward. The normally white shine of the food court floor was a pale gray as it reflected the overcast hue from the skylights above. Rain tinked and tinged against the ceiling, filling the gaps in echo between the rowdy teens and preteens that populated the seating area.

Charlotte didn't see Chris or any of his friends. She sighed, and hoping she might be wrong, she decided to take a lap around the court to verify.

There were a dozen high school kids grouped into four different cliques. She only knew one of them, Billy Jenkins, who lived on her street. He sat with three other almost goth kids wearing nearly all black.

Four other kids from her school were there that she wished weren't, and when she saw them, she was glad Chris was somewhere else. Todd Hertz, Heath Williams, Fred Louis, and Lane Freemont sat at the table nearest the Burger King. Todd and Fred had fries. They all had sodas and sour pusses on their faces.

Charlotte turned around as nonchalantly as possible, lifting her chin and miming that she had forgotten something in the other direction. She listened as she walked, hoping not to hear that she had been recognized, and praying not to hear her name. As she rounded the last set of tables, she passed the same man she had failed to notice earlier. She failed again.

Just outside the food court proper, she took a breath and glanced back to see if the Khaki Klan, as Chris called them, were coming. With no one in sight, she stepped to the counter for a cinnamon pretzel. The man got in line behind her.

3

Officer Barry Johnson was past the end of his shift. He'd met with the Minsk mother, the DiMarco father, and dropped into the Brolin house. None had seen their missing kid, and with each visit, the knot in his stomach had grown larger. He could have called Harrison, radioed in, or even waited until morning, but the knot wouldn't let him. Something was wrong that he couldn't shake, and he needed to talk to someone about it.

The rest of the City-County building staff had left the place a ghost town. Even the small corner for the PD was empty beyond Rhonda, who'd practically been living there this week while coordinating calls between county and state agencies. When Johnson saw Harrison's desk vacant, he shook his head. He should have checked in first to see if he was here. Then he noticed the chief in his office.

The balding boss sat behind his desk, reading reports. He wore his meet-with-the-council suit and mouthed the words as he read. Johnson stepped over to the door and leaned on the frame.

The chief mouthed a few more words and glanced up at Johnson. "What's up, Barry?" His voice was rough and condescending.

"Oh, just was curious what was going on. I didn't know there was a council meeting tonight."

The chief ruffled the paper in his hands. "Emergency meeting. Keep your mouth shut about it, though."

"Yes, sir." Johnson's gaze switched to Rhonda, who shook her head at him, pursing her lips and squinting.

"You know," the chief said, "we may need you later, so stay by the phone."

"Sir?"

"I may request a curfew. So be ready to come back if Rhonda calls."

Johnson wished he hadn't stopped in. He was ready to go home and get drunk after the day he'd had. Now a curfew? Could they even do that? "Yes, sir."

The chief went back to his papers. "Keep your lips sealed for now."

Johnson strolled over to Rhonda and had a seat beside her. She was the busiest person he knew, and he watched her in motion, waiting. Her paper shuffling blew a soft breeze his way. It carried a light scent of perfume that reminded him of baby powder and roses.

She stopped and looked at him. It was a subtle smile mixed with an expression of, *you dumb-ass, you should have known better*. He nodded back and rolled his eyes.

"What are you doing here?" Rhonda said. "You're off."

"Looking for Dale."

Her smile sank. "Oh, dear, he's back at the hospital."

"I should have figured."

"Is it important?"

"He wanted me to check back on those missing kids and let him know." He tapped on the desk. "I guess I can swing by there."

"Let me call him, save you some time."

Johnson had wanted to speak in person, but now he was imagining himself back on duty and patrolling for curfew violators. A call would do. Then he could get home and relax for a bit before they called him back in. Maybe he could even fit in a beer or two—no more than two.

"Yeah," Johnson said. "Let's get him on the phone."

Rhonda secured her papers and noted her place, then grabbed the phone and got a nurse on the line. A few seconds later, she was handing the receiver over to Johnson.

"Hey, boss," Jonson said. "How's Gina?"

"Ah. No change. What's going on?"

Johnson explained that the kids were still missing, their families were still worried, and he was heading home for the evening. He could feel Harrison's disappointment through the line. If they at least knew where the kids went missing from, they could form a search party and look from there, but he had no idea where to even start.

"So, school tomorrow?" Johnson asked.

"Yeah, I guess so. I'll meet you there at eight-thirty."

"I'll see you there."

Harrison breathed into the phone. "By the way, is the chief there?"

"Yeah."

"He in his council duds?"

"Yup."

"We may see each other before morning, then."

"That's what I heard." Johnson tapped the desk.

"I know, but it may help."

"Yeah, I guess so."

Johnson heard beeping through the phone. Several noises at once, alarming sounds of medical equipment. The line went dead.

4

Ray Trent sat on the couch with the television on. It was playing *Wheel of Fortune*, but despite his eyes pointing that way, he wasn't watching. He was thinking about Misty Brolin. He was thinking about his missed opportunity with her sister.

He'd smoked the little bit of weed he had found at Stony's, and that had gotten him through the afternoon, but once he came down, the need to do something was returning. It felt like a tingling in his veins. He flexed his hands and ran his fingers over his crotch. They passed over the lump in his pocket and reminded him of the pills.

Why did he have pills? He pulled them out and looked them over. Three colors, so three different kinds—but what did they do? He knew there were uppers and downers, and he'd heard there were some that made you horny. If one of these did that, he really had plans for Misty. But how could he find out which was which?

There was a thump at the door, and he heard his father's keys rattling inside the lock. He shoved the baggies back into his pocket and sat up on the couch.

Larry Trent walked into the house and glared at his son, ignoring the cut on his cheek. "You go to school today?" He shut the door and dropped his keys on the table.

"Yeah, Dad." Ray lied. "I went."

Larry tonged at his teeth as if shifting free a stuck morsel from lunch. He pulled a pack of Marlboro reds from his jeans and gestured with his head for Ray to get up. "Go get me a beer."

Ray rose, and Larry took his seat, lighting a cigarette as he sat. He picked up the television remote and started flipping through the channels.

In the kitchen, Ray walked to the refrigerator, his previous question still in mind. How was he going to figure out what these pills did? He opened the door and knew the answer.

He grabbed a bottle of Budweiser and set it on the counter. He grabbed a plate and spoon and decided to try the tan pills first. They seemed like a good place to start.

He dropped two tan pills on the plate and crushed them with the spoon. They broke into dust easier than he thought they would. It occurred to him that two pills may not be enough. If he wanted to make sure he could see the effects, he should probably double that. He put two more on the plate and crushed them.

"Where's my beer?" Larry shouted over the television.

"Coming!" Ray opened the bottle of Bud and dropped the powder inside, one pinch at a time. He swirled the bottle around and carried it to his dad.

Dad had found a rerun of *M.A.S.H.* and snatched the bottle from Ray's hand. He blew out a cloud of smoke and guzzled his beer.

Ray sat on the end of the couch and watched his father puff, laugh, and drink. In less than ten minutes, he set the bottle on the coffee table.

"Ray, get me another beer." He didn't seem any different.

Ray wondered if the pills were even real. The man didn't seem more tired, energetic, anything. Maybe he needed more?

"Yeah." Ray headed to the kitchen and smashed up two more pills. He dissolved them in another Bud and came back into the living room. "Here." He extended the bottle.

Dad sat still in his seat. A new cigarette burned between his fingers, and his eyes were fixed on Hawkeye Pierce.

"Dad?" Ray stepped between his father and the TV, something he would usually never do. The man was frozen, except for shallow breathing and an occasional blink. Ray chuckled. He set the beer on the coffee table and took the cigarette from his father's fingers. He took a puff and put it out in the ashtray.

"So that's what the tan ones do."

5

The nurse jumped from her seat as heart monitors raged. Her hand, and then her watch, snagged the line and ripped it from the back of the telephone. She shouted and ran toward a patient's room, leaving Officer Dale Harrison holding a dead receiver.

He watched her run down the hall, the only thought inside his head being, *Not Gina.*

She passed Gina's room and darted into the next one. Harrison set the phone on the counter and wandered down after her. Another nurse joined the first, followed by a doctor. When Harrison reached the room, he saw nearly ten people watching a child the same age as Gina get CPR. Her face was pale, lips blue. They rolled a defibrillator past him and readied it.

"She's gone," Harrison whispered to himself. "Jesus."

He was right. It only took another few minutes before the doctor would agree and call the time of death.

6

Eddy Lawrence sat across from his grandmother, eating his last few bites of mashed potatoes. He'd eaten his pork chop and peas. The potatoes were all he had left.

Gramma had finished a few minutes ago. Her plates always held two-thirds of Eddy's. She had told him years ago that old people don't need as much food as younger ones—something about how he was still growing and needed the calories. He wasn't sure if he believed her then and definitely didn't now, but he was hungry enough, so he ate. She sipped her coffee and watched him.

He finished his potatoes and grabbed flatware in both hands. He was about to climb to his feet when Gramma said, "Eddy, how was your day today."

At first, his experience from that morning didn't even register. Then, there it was: his shitty underwear. The tardy slip. Being late for class. It was all her. She sat in her chair with a smirk on half of her face, and Eddy could tell she wanted to laugh at him. She wanted to laugh loud and point. He saw it in her eyes. And he wanted to cut those thin, wrinkled fingers from her bony hands and put them in his box.

His face reddened. *Soon*, he thought. He picked up his dishes and took a breath. "It was good. I got a new assignment, and it should be fun."

He turned to take his dishes to the sink.

"Oh," Gramma said. "What's the new project?"

"I can do it, don't worry. I'll let you know if I need your help."

2022

1

Norris Cushing watched the sun disappear over the ridge that marked the edge of Alec Parsons' property. The two-hundred acre estate rested east of Custer Falls, bordering state lands on one side and cattle ranches on the other. Alec often boasted that his private lake had the best fishing in northern Montana, and when they showed themselves, his views of the northern lights put even those near the glaciers to shame. As Norris took in the red and orange streaks that backlit ridge after ridge of spruce forest, he imagined that the asshole might be right. And for no reason other than stoking his own anger, he thought Parsons should hurt for it.

Norris stepped out of the car, his shotgun in hand. He crossed the road and walked through the open gate that marked the front of the Parsons' property. The gravel driveway crunched under his feet, and he saw Alec Parsons' small mansion over the trees and the winding path ahead.

The image of Elias serving customers every morning drifted through Norris's thoughts. It was strange how much he missed him. Before the kid died, he barely spoke to him. Now, Elias felt like a lost friend he had known his whole life. He wondered how it had taken Elias's death to realize how much the friendship meant to him.

Norris paused in his tracks. The front of the home looked too open. He didn't want to be spotted by Alec or anyone else until he was ready. He changed his path, moving into the trees that lined the right side of the driveway. He could follow them to the house, and no one would notice him.

Pine needles crunched under his feet, and their scent filled his nose. He listened as he walked. No cars, no talking, no noise other than the tweets and caws of passing birds. He gripped his shotgun and heard the boom it made in his mind. It was going to end Alec Parsons, and that sound would be the sweetest thing he had ever heard. A smile crossed Norris's face, and a loud whack crunched from below.

He replayed it in his mind as he looked down to see what the sound was. It had started with a nearly inaudible *tink*, followed by rushing air, and finally, the clunk of iron into flesh and bone. Fiery pain soared up Norris's leg as his eyes met his feet. The jaws of a sixteen-inch bear trap were tight on his calf and shin, its teeth inside his flesh.

Norris's legs gave, and he felt the bone inside shift through a lightning storm of pain. He tumbled backward, slamming into the earth. The Neanderthal inside his brain demanded him back away from the trap, the thing causing his pain. Burning agony ripped through his leg.

His teeth clenched. He looked at the wound and saw fractured bone piercing through skin on both sides of the trap's teeth. His foot was hanging on by only the meat in his lower leg, completely detached from his skeleton. His hands shook, wanting to touch it and not wanting to simultaneously. Through his clamped teeth, he tasted blood. He'd clipped the tip of his tongue nearly off, and the ridiculous similarity came to mind that his own trap had closed on his tongue. It made him grin through the pain.

Norris looked around. Had anyone heard him? How could they have not? The shotgun's stock creaked under the stress of Norris's grip. He heard the drip of his blood as it patted against the forest floor.

That bastard Parsons had done this to him. He'd set out traps, knowing that Norris would come. But he wouldn't let Parsons win. *No fucking way.* Parsons was going to die today. Like his son. Like Elias. That man would be dead.

Norris examined the trap. It was an old one and obviously strong. It wouldn't come off his leg without tools, which he didn't have. But he did have a knife.

He flipped up the right side of his shirt and drew his hunting knife from his belt. He propped himself forward and scooted closer to the trap.

"No," he muttered. Blood ran down his chin. "Gotta be smart about this." He undid his belt and rocked left and right as he slid it from his pants. He wrapped the belt around his calf, just under the knee. That would do.

Norris placed the blade of his knife along the top of the trap and pressed it into his flesh. Blood streamed down red rusted iron. His teeth clenched once again, and he swallowed a mouthful of blood.

He was amazed that it didn't hurt more. His leg was already in such torture that as his blade moved inch after inch through his flesh, it didn't hurt much more.

He sliced through the shin skin, its muscles, and moved deeper. He heard the slurp of blood and meat suction against his blade and forced it from his mind. He sliced under his fractured bone and swallowed another gulp of blood. He imagined slicing through Alec Parsons' throat this way—only slower. A blazing sensation shot up his leg as his blade cut through tendon and skin.

And just like that, he was free. He scooted back and felt a tingle in his toes. He looked down at his dismembered foot and thought how funny that was. He grinned again, and blood dripped from his chin.

Norris wished he had a shot of whiskey right about now. He gazed up at the huge house. There had to be some in there. But first, he had to get inside.

He picked up a dead branch, broke it into something resembling a Y, and put it under his armpit as a crutch. He wasn't sure it would hold his weight, but he'd try. If it worked, it would be easier than hopping to his enemy.

Norris moved across the Parsons' yard, crutch in one hand, shotgun in the other. He panted, then seethed. The branch under his arm creaked each time he leaned on it, but it held.

He headed straight for the front door. He was done with hide and seek. He was going to go right for that asshole and take him down, and get a drink along the way.

A dark red line followed Norris across the grass and up the steps, all the way to the door. He raised the shotgun to his shoulder and tried the knob. It squeaked and opened.

The entry was decorated in carved wood, hanging furs, and mounted heads of moose, elk, and bear. To the right was an immaculate parlor, appointed in fine furniture and paintings, the likes of which Norris could never afford, let alone name. On the left was a library as intricately finished as the entrance and filled with thousands of books he imagined Parsons had never read—and never would. He headed into the parlor for a taste of the amber liquid he spotted in a crystal decanter. He was trailed by a line of red dots.

He glanced momentarily at the crystal tumblers beside the decanter and muttered, "Fuck it." He took his hand from the stick and removed the stopper, dropping it on the table with a clank. He raised the decanter to his lips and gulped what may have been the smoothest whiskey he had ever tasted. He took a rushed breath and gulped again. And again. His leg bled a little more and became a little numb, or at least he cared a little less, and a shot sounded from behind him.

The whiskey slipped from Norris's hand, crashing onto the table and shattering into a sea of brown waves and crystal chunks. He dropped behind a chair as another shot rang. Blood sprayed from his side.

"Took you long enough!" Parsons shouted from the parlor entrance. His voice was gruff and low. His long gray eyebrows and mustache seemed to dance as he talked. He aimed a pistol at the chair and fired repeatedly into it. "He told me you'd come!"

A boom shook the parlor, and Parsons fell back. He thumped on the dark wood entry floor. Buckshot holes bled from his cracked hip and upped leg. He screamed as he fired into the parlor furniture.

Norris crawled along the floor behind the couch. He followed it to the end, where he saw Parsons' feet through the doorway. He aimed and waited.

Parsons stopped shooting and grunted, "Fuck!" He gritted his teeth and crawled toward the parlor entrance.

Norris saw a hand come into view, gun gripped, and he couldn't resist any longer. He squeezed the trigger and watched fingers explode into shredded meat across the entryway. The gun sparked and tumbled, strips of skin stuck to the steel. Tendrils of flayed flesh dripped blood from Parsons' peppered palm.

Parsons howled.

Norris's laughter boomed across the parlor.

They both crawled forward toward each other.

Alec Parsons' head came into view, and the butt of Norris's shotgun swung from the heavens, thumping into his temple.

Parsons took a rattling breath while rolling back. Norris raised the shotgun for another blow, and Parsons' other hand came from his belt with a compact pistol.

Norris swung as a white flame burst from the small gun. Burning pain ripped through his cheek and then his arm. He felt the shotgun slip away without having told it to, and rage flooded his being. Damn this man! First, he took away Elias, then took his leg, and now he dared to try to stop his revenge.

The gun popped, this time with stabbing pain in his jaw. It was the screech of a rotten tooth.

Norris charged on one leg and one hand.

Another shot. His shoulder burned. He didn't care.

He was above Parsons. He slid his knife free. A new pain in his gut. He stabbed down into Parsons' wrist. As he flicked up, his blade split the man's hand, and the small pistol slid across the floor, chased by a trail of bright red.

"I'll kill you!" Parsons shouted.

"I'll kill *you*!" Norris repeated.

Parsons jerked himself upright and dove at Norris. His face plunged into Norris's chest, his limp and broken hand smearing blood on Norris's shoulders as he pounded.

Norris tried to pull back and pain crisscrossed his chest. Parsons ripped away a mouthful of shirt, skin, and strands of Norris's pectoral muscle.

Norris's scream became the loudest thing in the house. He drove his blade into Parsons' neck and tore through the man's spine.

Blood gushed, and Parsons fell limp. He thumped against the floor and the blood drained from the gap in his neck.

Norris let himself drop onto his back, sighing. He'd done it. "*Thank you,*" he whispered to the voice. But something told him he wasn't done. Then, he heard footsteps from upstairs.

2

Hannah Gould looked down at the shiny, clean spot that had once held Heath Williams' blood and corpse. Now, it was a shallow layer of mop water that would soon be dry.

It had been tough, but thanks to Heath's utility sink and tools, she'd been able to prepare his body nicely into a bundle of garbage bags. The trash men would come and empty the dumpster tomorrow, take away the body and her bloody clothes, and that would be the end of it. She'd even moved his car into an abandoned parking lot down the street and walked back. She would just say that he had never shown up for work, and she figured he was being lazy, as usual.

She shut the door and grabbed her bag from her office. As she drove home, she wondered about dinner. Would Dawson have something ready? She hadn't even thought to check her phone in hours.

The Weekend played on the radio. She turned it down, imagining she'd have to call Dawson.

She had four text messages: "When will you be home?" "What do you want for dinner?" "Is everything ok?" "I'm starting to worry about you."

It wasn't what she wanted to hear. He could ruin everything.

"*Kill him,*" the voice said. "*He'll get you caught. You'll never see your job again. Never see those wonderful kids.*"

"He'll ruin it all," she whispered back.

She texted: "On my way. Bringing dinner"

Dots pulsed in the chat, and then, "Great! :)"

She pulled into the driveway. "Find us a movie"

"Ok"

Hannah went into the house and slipped into the kitchen. She could hear Dawson in the living room clicking through Amazon Prime, doing what she'd asked.

She looked at the block of knives on the counter. She pulled the big one, looked it over, and slid it back. She looked at the next. Put it back. She looked at the paring knife, picked it up, and smiled.

"Where's the food?" Dawson said from the doorway.

3

Edward Lawrence dropped the last of his envelopes into the blue box at the corner of Lake Street and 4th Avenue. They wouldn't get picked up until tomorrow after most of the rest had been delivered, but that was the plan, after all. Once the state troopers looked into the US Mail and found these, it would shut down mail all over the state and send their investigators after the right-wing militia nuts in the western part of the state, leaving his eastward escape plan wide open.

The girl watched from inside the car. She really was a gift from *Him.* She'd grown on him, and his expectation that he'd have to eventually get rid of her had faded from inevitability to possibility. He imagined all the fun they would have together once this was done and this town was behind them. So many places to explore and so many people to share the magic with. He never would have pictured himself the father type, but here he was—at least until she fucked up too bad.

He climbed back into the driver's seat. She looked down and up and out the window. She obviously wanted something but was afraid to ask.

"What is it, Julie?"

She looked him in the eyes, then out the window. "I was getting a bit hungry..."

It was getting late. There were still things to do back at home, things to do at the Maryville Manor to tie this all up. But, he was a little hungry himself.

"I think we can do something about that." He started the car and headed north.

4

Norris Cushing left lines of blood, red handprints, and smears across the Parsons' floor and up the stairs. He dragged himself left, around the balcony that overlooked the parlor, and into a hallway with a much gentler, female touch than the downstairs. White walls, gold decorative moldings, hallway tables with knickknacks and crystal—it all screamed *Mrs.* Parsons—and those noises had to have been her.

Thump, drag, thump, he moved down the hall. The floor squeaked from blood and hard, heaving steps. Tapping noises came from ahead.

Every door in this hallway was sealed except for one. Each room Norris passed seemed a hollow space of waste and emptiness. Unused beds. Wasted furniture. Wasted air, wasted light, wasted life. The Parsons, they were wastes of existence from head to toe. He didn't know why he had never seen it, never knew it before now. He should have been ridding the world of this garbage long ago.

"*Yes,*" the whisper said. "*A waste. Rid us of her.*"

"Waste..." he said under his breath.

The door at the end of the hall opened an inch, exposing a blue eye, a sliver of pale face, and blonde hair. A gasp escaped the room, and the door slammed.

"Waste!" Norris was ten feet from the door. He leaned against the wall and raised the shotgun to his shoulder. The boom shook the home, and the center of the door evaporated.

Mrs. Parsons stood in the gap. Eight holes poured blood from her neck and chest. One exploded blue eye hung from her face in gobs of flesh. One nostril was a gap into the interior of her skull. Her jaw hung limp, broken-toothed and bleeding. From her arms boomed a shotgun of her own.

5

Inside their Maryville Manor room, Sam and Lisa watched reruns of *Sponge Bob* on the television. Wes kissed each of them on their foreheads and pulled up their covers. He replayed having to explain their mother's coma in his head and hoped to God they would be able to fall asleep. It was enough having to think about what may be coming by himself—he wasn't ready to have his girls pulled into it just yet.

"Goodnight," Wes said as he stood.

Both the girls' eyes went to him. They were serious, more so than any seven or nine-year-old should have to be.

"I'll just be in the next room with Aunt Di. Door open."

Lisa looked at Sam. Sam nodded, and they went back to their show.

In the adjoining room, Wes found Di on the Bed, Virb beside her with his head in her lap. Virb didn't move, but his eyes tracked Wes as he crossed the room. The dog hadn't quite warmed up to Wes yet, and that was okay, as long as he was good with the kids, which he had been so far. He had let Sam and Lisa scratch him, but he was no Sam-I-Am.

Wes thought about his dog at the groomer. He was lucky they had a vet attached that did boarding; it was one less thing to worry about. Though, thinking about scratches and licking, comforting the kids, he wondered if he should have brought Sam-I-Am along too.

No, he thought, *probably better off alone. Everyone is.* It was a recurring thought today. He'd done no good helping Jill. He'd failed at escaping from those maniacs and let her get taken and tortured. Christ, if those psychos didn't leave on their own, Sam and Lisa could have ended up on the tables beside them. He had to figure out the rest, how to stop the demon again. And this time without Jill. He couldn't do it alone; he knew that. How was he supposed to do it without her?

Wes sat on the bed. He saw dogs on the television; it was some competition where dogs had to run and jump and sniff things out. Sam-I-Am would have been a failure at it. He glanced at Virb—that dog may have been able to.

"Girls okay?" Di said, her eyes still on the screen.

"As well as can be expected."

"Yeah, I guess." Her voice was dry and hesitant. She stroked Virb's back.

Wes shook his head. How was he going to fix things this time? His mind was clouded with a thousand tiny things, tired just from existing. He tried anyway.

Wes recounted as much as he could remember from that week in 1992, then recapped each year since. He knew what started it in the first place, but—no.

"Do you think someone disturbed the rock?"

Di turned from the television. Her face was alert as if a light had just come on inside. "Has to be. It all started when you brought that stupid thing home. Maybe someone found it and woke it up."

"God, I hope not." But what else could it be?

She spun to get off the bed. Virb's head raised, and he sat up to watch what she'd do next. "I'll go check it out."

"You can't get in there until tomorrow."

"Oh, I can get in."

"Di..." He had no right to ask her for anything. Not after so many years with the drugs, ignoring her, and despising her. But he decided he didn't have a choice. "Please. If you get caught and arrested..."

"Then we all could lose."

"Yeah."

1992

1

Ray Trent watched his father. All the movement had stopped. No more convulsing and shaking. No more foam frothing from the mouth. No more vomit spilling over his lips and getting sucked back into his lungs. He leaned to his side, over the armrest. Then he pissed himself.

It was more than Ray thought would happen. In all the movies, when people took pills, they just went to sleep. This was much more entertaining. So far.

The voice had told him a few times to get ready, but he was enjoying this too much to move. On the fourth whisper, he finally gave in. He knew he should have been listening. The whisper had done so much for him, but it seemed like he had been waiting to see his father suffer for so long, and it was finally there. He had to savor it.

He went to his room and shed his clothes. They stank like his old man's puke and beer. He didn't know what his plan was just yet, but he didn't want the smell to give him away. He slid on new jeans and a faded Metallica T, a hoodie over that, and he dug into Dad's nightstand for his .45. Its reflective steel shined and caught Ray staring for a moment.

He thought about how Misty's face would look when she saw the gun. The fear in her eyes, those tight little lips of hers. It was going to be priceless. He slid the piece into his hoodie pocket and got his shoes on.

2

Charlotte woke to the dark and a sense of weightlessness. The ground was below her somewhere, but she couldn't touch it. She couldn't see it. Was something on her head? Pressure pushed up from under her waist: an arm. She was being carried.

For a moment, she thought she was at home and had fallen asleep on the couch. Dad had picked her up more awkwardly than usual and was carrying her to bed. She was overcome with a warm thanks. She was always warm in Dad's embrace, always felt like everything would be okay.

Charlotte moved her arms. They wouldn't go far, her hands were stuck together—tied. Why were they tied? Dad never did this at bedtime. What was happening? She tried to speak. Her lips wouldn't part. Were they taped shut? Her heart jumped. A bolt of shock ripped through Charlotte's tiny body. This wasn't right. This had to stop.

She screamed. Nothing but muffled words came from her mouth. She wiggled and squirmed, and something punched her in the gut. It was like concrete squeezing her insides, and pain rippled through her intestines, stomach, and liver.

No, no, no, her mind raced.

She coughed and fought for breath but could only get sips of air through her tiny nostrils. And as tears welled, they began filling with snot.

Her stomach clenched. *God*, she wanted to puke. She held it back and swung her arms as much as her binds allowed. She flailed like a beached fish. *Stop this*, she screamed inside. *Let me go!* Her heart pounded. Her whole body flexed.

Another thump in the gut.

Vomit poured up her throat and into her mouth, but it had nowhere to go. She fought to open her jaw and spread her lips, but they were stuck. It rushed up into her sinuses and through her nose. It burned like acid inside her head and sprayed from her nostrils. She saw a gray world and realized there was a bag on her head. Tiny pinpricks of light came through, and vomit spattered against the inner cloth, dimming the graying world even more.

It was only a second later when she felt her lungs starting again. Her diaphragm dropped, and her chest rose. Panic ripped through her as she realized her throat and nose couldn't pass air. They were full of puke. She clenched and fought not to inhale. She didn't want to die. She didn't want to drown in the burning sick that filled her passages.

The angry fist must have thought she was fighting it. It thumped her in the gut once again. "Knock it off!" It sounded pissed.

The blow clenched it. Her lungs were stronger than her will. She remembered Dad telling her to stay close to the shore at Seeley Lake. She remembered a kid had drowned there last year. Was this what they felt? Were their lungs stronger than their will? When the vileness came, she wondered if it would hurt. The burning in her head said it would.

Vomit shot down her throat into her chest. Her sinuses clogged and stopped everything from moving. Drops of bile hit the inner lining of her lungs, and she coughed. Everything rushed out again, pounding through her windpipe, sinuses, nose. Pain and pressure slammed her skull. But there wasn't enough air inside her to move it all.

Her chest sucked back in, caught the vomit, and pushed back out. Agony rippled through her head and every muscle in her clenched little frame.

Suck back in, clogged the works, cough out. Out of air. Suck back in.

The dim light inside the bag grew darker. The world was drifting away. She felt her body shaking, fighting for life. She couldn't help it. She couldn't make air. She couldn't clear the way. All she could do was shake and ride the rhythm of this roller coaster, knowing that at the end of the track was going to be death.

Dad returned to mind. Why did Dad let this happen? Why wasn't he here to fix this? Mom smiled at her. She wondered if it would be the last one. She wanted to hug Mom. Maybe tomorrow after this was over.

She stopped feeling her body fight. She sensed it was still happening, that she was still flopping around, but she was unconcerned about it now. The fear had faded. Sleep lay ahead, and she was looking forward to it now. Sleep was nice. It was freedom from the scary things of the real world. Maybe she would even see Chris there.

Her gray world became a blinding light, and her eyes screamed. Burning ripped across her face, and her mouth opened. Puke fell out. A hard object was against her chest, and something was pounding on her back. Wetness heaved over her tongue and lips. Air rushed inside. Coughing scraped her throat. Air rushed in. Her belly flexed. Coughing, coughing, coughing. Her entire body hurt. She felt the floor against her face and side.

The coughing lessened. The burning and pain didn't, but she still felt sleep on the horizon. She thought she saw the face of Shirley Minsk ahead.

Why was Shirley lying on the floor too? Why wasn't she blinking?

3

By the time Ray Trent stepped outside, the night had become chilly. The sidewalk and road glistened with wetness. Tiny ripples moved in the gutters as raindrops demanded that they weren't done yet.

He walked toward Academy Street with the shapes that made up Misty Brolin on his mind. Her legs, her ass, her waist, her chest. Tonight, he was going to get her. Tonight, he wouldn't be taking no for an answer.

He walked past old lady Kappe's house and smirked. He'd been so dumb. That whole thing was dumb. He could have done so much better, maybe even gotten the money, if he'd grabbed Dad's .45 first. Still, though, Maybe he'd go back and try again later—hopefully before the house started to stink.

He made it past the mansions, down half of Madison Street, and was about to walk into the Wesker Pump parking lot, when he noticed taillights ahead. Someone was in the old gas station lot. Someone was looking at Amanda Brolin's vehicle.

Ray put his hand on the .45's grip and slowed his pace. He stepped carefully. He didn't want to scrape pebbles underfoot or drag his shoes.

He kneeled at the corner of the station's rusted-out dumpster and watched. The intruder raised a flashlight and shined it inside the minivan. As slices of light reflected back, Ray saw it was a cop. He wasn't sure why, but he didn't care. Right now, it didn't matter to Ray that it was a cop. What mattered was that some asshole was messing with his vehicle. He may have left it to rot earlier, but since then, he'd decided it was his. And you don't mess with a man's vehicle.

Inside his pocket, Ray pulled back the pistol's hammer. He slid it out and aimed it forward. The cop was a blob of a man's back. He didn't want to shoot him in the back. The back could mean anything—a shot in the lungs, a shot in the heart, a shot in the stomach. Which of those would even do the job? He wanted a headshot. That would make sure the guy dropped. There'd be no questions after a headshot. But the guy was crouched over.

Ray stood and stepped closer. He was silent. He was like Batman, moving in on a criminal. He kept the gun up, ready for the instant this guy's head came into view. Then, a goddamn pebble.

It was just a small stone against concrete. It was stuck between the treads of Ray's shoe, and as it scraped against the crumbling ground, the cop spun.

Shit, was all Ray could think.

The cop seemed to move like liquid. He swooped down and to the left. Ray tried to track where his head went, but it was so fast. The officer's hand went to his belt, seized his pistol, and raised it.

Ray saw a glint from the cop's barrel. He saw the shine in the cop's eye as he lined up the shot. Ray pulled the trigger.

Blood sprayed up. The cop's gun fired, and he went down.

Ray's heart pounded. He felt his chest and head. He was fine. There was no way of knowing where the cop's shot went, but it didn't hit him.

"Fuck." He stared at the cop. The man lay on the ground like a slug. "Fuck." Ray ran to Amanda Brolin's minivan. His body was shaking. He looked for the keys and couldn't find them. He punched the door, and then he remembered—under the barrel.

He raced to the barrel, watching the cop from the corner of his eye, and as he tipped it, there they were. "Shit, thank you." He ran back to the minivan, careful of the blood pooling on the ground, and he hopped insde the thing.

A flash of light caught Ray's eye, and he spun to his left. It was the cop—it had to be. He was bleeding, sure, but he was also up and going to shoot him.

A car drove past and went down the road.

"Fuck." Ray found the cop on the ground, right where he'd left him. He turned the key, threw the transmission in *Reverse*, and sped toward Misty's house.

4

Diana Henson unrolled a sleeping bag on her bedroom floor. She heard Jill brushing her teeth in the bathroom and wondered if there was any way this would work or if they were all just going crazy. Dad was dead. It was perfectly reasonable to think they were going crazy. Only crazy people would think they could share dreams. And losing a dad could make you crazy.

Di sat on the bed, having figured out nothing, when Jill came in. She wore a T-shirt and shorts borrowed from Wes—nothing of Di's fit her. She could have gone home and gotten clothes, but they all worried that if she left, the parents might change their minds. It felt like a tenuous situation as it was, convincing all the parents to let her stay over and console Wes and Di. The condition was she slept in Di's room. The parents were compassionate, however Wes and Jill were still preteens hovering over the edge of puberty, and that fact wasn't lost on Jill's mom and dad.

Jill sat beside Di. Neither of them said anything for a while. Di finally scooted back in her bed and slid her feet under her covers.

"This is crazy," Di said. "I don't know what we're doing."

"Yeah," Jill said. "I don't know. Maybe it'll work. Maybe I can help you guys. But if it doesn't—hey, at least you have some company here if you need to talk or something."

Di thought about the parking garage. What could another person have done? If they weren't crazy, if there was something after them, what could she have done to help? She probably would have ended up getting killed, just like Dad. Tears welled in her eyes. Dad didn't deserve that. He was kind. He was always there to hold her when she needed a cry and a hug. She remembered all the silly things she had gone to him for over the years: a hole on her Pokemon stuffed animal, fights with Wes, arguments with Mom over chores, housework, even the stupid things, like when she really wanted a milkshake with dinner and Mom said no. It was all kid stuff, nonsense, and he always treated her like it mattered. He hugged her and wouldn't let go until she did. She felt heavy. The weight of the day seemed to lay on top of her, making it tough to move and breathe. There was no more time for kid stuff now. He was gone, and they'd need to grow up fast if they were going to make sure no one else died because of them.

"What can I do?" Jill said. She raised her hand and offered it.

Di turned away. "Just pray it doesn't work. I don't want anything to happen to anyone else."

Jill sighed and slid to the floor, snaking herself into the sleeping bag. She stared at the ceiling, thinking how this wasn't going to work. They'd wake in the morning and realize how silly it all was—that would be the hardest part, when they all found there was no one to blame, no one to fight over this, and the grieving would really take over.

Wes leaned into the doorway and scanned the room. Jill watched his bangs drape over his face, and she bit on her lip.

"Hey," Wes said. He hopped closer and leaned on the door frame. "So, I guess this is about it."

"Yeah," Jill said.

"I'll get in bed too."

"Okay."

He didn't move right away. "Be careful in there. Okay?"

"Yeah." She flashed a halfhearted smile, trying her best to look confident.

Wes hopped away, thumping on the floor.

"You really like him, huh?" Di asked.

Jill turned. Di was facing the other way. Jill checked the door as if Wes could still be standing there. "What—what do you mean?"

"It's pretty obvious. Well, maybe not to him."

Jill clenched her fists. Was her secret out?

"I won't say anything. I think you're okay."

"He doesn't seem to know I exist, other than to pal around with and read comics or whatever."

"He's dumb like that. He'll come around."

"You think so?"

"Yeah."

Jill wanted to talk more. She wanted to ask what Di would suggest to get Wes's attention. She had no one else to talk to about this except Mom, and Mom was no good. All she had to say was *Be yourself*, and *It'll happen if it's meant to be*. But Di knew her brother. She might have had something real and helpful. Jill held her tongue. It wasn't the time to pester this poor girl. She rolled to her side and closed her eyes.

Part Four: The Caves

Princesses and Faeries, Rainbows and Unicorns

1

Wes Henson saw the final cave, the end of the Bloodtooth Caverns tour. It was lit in rainbow colors, highlighting the pools of ever-dripping water and mounds of rising mineral deposits. Behind him were the rest of the caverns. Ahead was a large wooden door, the start of the double-doored airlock that kept high-speed winds from rushing from one end of the cavern to the other.

The room was not exactly as he remembered it, though. There were no throngs of students with echoing voices. There was only the drip of water into water and its pat against growing formations. There were no rangers watching his every move. The place was empty. And beyond the rainbow pools, beyond the ripples of eternal drip, there was no solid cave wall. There was the opening of a new cave.

"That's not the way," Di said. "That's the way to him."

He gazed into the tunnel. Wasn't that where he wanted to go? To see him—the whisperer? Wasn't that what this entire thing was about?

"What do you mean that isn't the way?" Wes asked. "We had a plan, didn't we?"

"Not that." She was tall today, more like the woman she would become than the one he'd said goodnight to just a few minutes ago.

Had he just said goodnight? It seemed like weeks ago. It unfolded to him like a haze that blew away and then rolled back in. They had come to this dream to find the thing that was doing this. And—Jill, she was supposed to be here too.

"That *is* that way. The thing—it killed Dad. It's down there." Knowing that didn't make sense. It was knowledge that came from somewhere else, from a place with Sam and Lisa. "Who are Sam and Lisa?"

"What?" Di climbed over a handrail and stood beside the first pool."

"I don't know." It was a mythical cloud of believing and doubting and wondering which truth was the real one. But he knew where he wanted to go.

Di stared at herself in the water. She saw a woman's face, one that reminded her that Virb was absent. She wanted him there but knew he couldn't be.

She took a step around the puddle. "Is Jill coming?" Di asked. "How does she get here?"

Wes wondered. He had called Dad just by wishing for him, not even on purpose. Would that work for Jill? "Let me try."

He closed his eyes and thought of her. He thought of Chris. He imagined them standing right beside him.

2

Jill Elden watched over the lake's gentle waves. They lapped against the shore and made a soft popping sound that reminded her of Pop Rocks. The more she stared and the sound invaded her thoughts, the more like the dissolving candy it became. She heard a whooshing sound like a cheering crowd. A boat raced by, towing a skier, and she imagined the crowd was cheering for them. The points of evergreens surrounding the water were the tall arms of thousands of waving onlookers, and when the boat was gone, Jill was overcome with the feeling that those onlookers were watching her now.

That was when she saw the man. He was across the lake. He wore a light-colored shirt and a wide-brimmed hat, and though she could not see his eyes, Jill was positive he was staring at her.

A shiver of worry raised the hairs on her arms. She took a step away from the water's edge, her eyes studying the man and the spying trees.

It was just a silly thought, she told herself. He's way over there. And trees don't watch you. And they don't cheer.

The forest echoed with the sounds of creaking limbs and shuffling dirt. She took another step from the water, pretending that fear wasn't driving her. She was on the shore of her grandmother's house, and now seemed like a good time to go back inside.

A loud crack issued from her left. She jerked to see. Branches swayed in the summer breeze, nothing more. Something moved in the dirt behind her. She spun around. Swaying spruce boughs, nothing more. But a warning lit inside her mind. Were those trees in the same place they were before? The dirt below was rippled, piled in lines and swirls as if...

"Its roots moved," she whispered.

She looked back for the man. He was gone.

Jill turned toward her grandmother's home and ran. She heard cracking and crunching behind her, sweeping sounds of rushing wind and the scuffing scratch of bark against dirt. It was faster and louder, closer and moving. It was chasing her.

The tiny three-bedroom cottage sat a hundred feet away but felt like a thousand. The forest on either side closed in. The trees beyond the home moved as if their roots floated under their soil.

Jill froze. She was surrounded. Why was this happening? What did they want from her?

3

Chris Conners looked down at the weed on the tin Coca-Cola Christmas tray in his lap. He rolled the buds between his fingers, letting the seeds fall and ting against the tin Santa's face. He loved that sound, it was like a tiny metal drummer gearing up for a show. The peppery smell of the Mexican junk weed fluttered by his nose as he piled it onto a rolling paper and began twisting. He wondered why it had taken so long to get the stuff from Stony—and he froze.

Stony's bloody bed. The spatters on his walls. The gaping hollow in his head. They all rushed into Chris's thoughts and seized his insides like a clenching fist. Stony's mouth moved. It fell open with a whisper of, *"Smoke it."*

Chris jumped from the edge of his bed, the tray crashing to the floor. Weed floated in the air like exploding confetti, and Santa seemed to glare at him disappointedly. He spun and pressed his back to the wall.

"What the fuck?" He scanned the room as if Stony's corpse had been transported there, as if it wasn't just a thought. The voice *had* been there— hadn't it?

There was no Stony, no source of the voice. But on the far side of the room, there was a curious view from his window. It was Charlotte. It wasn't her round glasses or petite physique that he recognized (he saw neither), it was something like her aura.

She sat in a dim room. The view was clouded, but it was her. She was on the floor, rubbing her hands together. Her black hair was all over the place, not neat and well brushed as usual. Her face was drawn, her eyes low, sad like he'd never seen them.

Every image of Stony and his gruesome death scene faded from Chris's thoughts. The window seemed to call Chris over. Why was she acting that way? On the floor? So sad? It dragged a sorrow from Chris's gut and pulled him to the sill.

Charlotte held her face, her nose. She rubbed her throat and then her temples. She glanced into the far corner of her room and forced her eyes away.

Chris pressed his face against the glass. What was going on in there? "Charlotte?"

She couldn't hear him.

He pushed on the window. It was stiff. He checked the lock and unlocked it, and tried again. The window refused to open.

"Charlotte!" He jerked and yanked on the window frame. Nothing. She glanced into the corner of her room again, covered her face with her hands, and wept.

"What?" He flexed his fingers into a tight fist, then cupped his hands around his eyes. He looked into the same corner, barely able to see into her room's gloom. He saw a pair of feet and felt a cold sensation pass over him. They were tiny, a pair of unsocked girl's feet. He fought through the gloom to follow her bare legs, wondering, what the hell was going on over there. He saw her hips, covered in white frilled panties. He saw her top half propped up against the corner, her bare belly, and then her face.

Chris had seen this girl before. He didn't know her, but he'd seen her. Her eyes stared blankly into the room, unmoving, unblinking. Her jaw hung open and uneven, the right side dipping, her tongue resting on her lower lip.

She was dead.

Chris jumped back from his window. What the fuck had he seen? He banged on it again. "Charlotte!"

"She can't hear you this time," a whisper said.

Chris shot around. On his bed, on his pillow, rested Stony's head. The rest of the body was missing, but Stony stared into Chris's eyes. His mouth opened, blackened blood seeping from between his teeth and cheek over his lips. "*No more of that for you,*" Stony whispered, only his mouth didn't speak; it spread wider, its blood escaping, flooding over Stony's jaw onto Chris's sheets.

"Fuck!"

4

Wes opened his eyes and found Jill on his right. Chris was on his left. He wondered, had it worked? Were these his real friends? Or were they figments of his imagination, created by his subconscious and placed beside him?

"What the shit?" Chris jumped backward. His gaze shot left, right, up, and down. "Where the hell am I?"

Jill nodded at Wes and approached Chris, her hands raised. "It's okay, Chris. We're with you."

He backed away from her. "No. Why am I here?" His heel caught on a rise in the stone floor, and he fell ass-first into the ground. His head practically spun in circles as he looked for anyone to blame. "What is going on?"

Jill kneeled beside him. "It's okay, Chris. It's just us."

He regarded her with narrow eyes.

Di came over to Wes. "You did it? You brought them here."

"I think so." Wes had surprised himself. On some level, he knew he could, but the last time was an accident. To do it on purpose and have it work seemed like a strange feat that he wasn't sure he should take credit for.

Jill put a hand on Chris's leg. "You're with friends."

Chris took a breath and calmed. He stood and hesitantly joined Wes and Di. "What's going on?"

"It's a dream," Jill said.

Chris finally seemed to recognize the cave. He glanced at his cast-free arm and Wes's cast-free leg, and Wes could see the wheels turning and the upcoming question, "Why are you all in my dream?"

"We think it's a shared dream," Wes said.

Jill spoke softly, "Remember their dad?"

"That's not a thing," Chris argued. "You can't share a dream." And Chris remembered the dream with Tommy. Was that a shared dream? That was in these caves—those kids, the coma kids.

Wes shook his head. "There's no way to prove it is or isn't, I guess, until we talk tomorrow. For today, just be safe, because if you get hurt..."

"You'll feel it when you wake up," Di said. "*If* you wake up."

Chris's jaw hung open, Mr. Wimbley rising in his mind, Wes and Di's dad quickly following. He didn't want to believe this was happening. It would be so much easier to ignore them and decide they were all characters in his own head. But—Stony's blood—inside, he knew—walking with Charlotte—that wasn't right. He looked around the cave once more. What choice did he have at this point? He'd have to just wait and see what happened and test their knowledge tomorrow. Maybe he'd get lucky. "So, what are we doing?"

"The thing responsible for all this is in here," Wes said. "I can feel it. Each dream we've had lately seems to center around this place. It's like— on one side it's calling us here—on another, it's keeping us away."

"Do you have a plan?" Jill said

"Uh, we look for it? I think we'll feel it as we get closer. Then—I don't know, but that has to be the first step—to identify it."

"Then we kick its ass," Di said.

Wes nodded. "Yeah."

"I wish Tommy was here," Chris said.

Wes looked at him, wondering if it were going to happen. A few seconds passed, enough time for Chris to raise his hands, gesturing *what?*

As if from thin air, Tommy faded into view on Chris's right.

Chris jumped away. Wes smiled. Jill ran over and hugged the new arrival.

"Tommy!" Jill said. "I didn't know..."

"If you'd see me again?" Tommy said.

She hugged him again.

"I'm in a coma. Not dead."

Chris stared at his friend with unbelieving eyes. "It's a dream."

"It is, and it isn't," Tommy said. He told each of them how he had seen them in their dreams and helped where he could. "It's one way I think this coma is a good thing."

"You think the coma's a good thing?" Jill said.

"It's like it's given me a superpower to see you in your dreams—and others."

"You mean like that cave," Chris said. "Where the kids are trapped."

"Yeah. Like that."

"What kids?" Wes said.

"There are kids in the hospital," Chris said. "In comas. Like, not regular comas, more like, they just can't wake up."

"They're trapped in some kind of dream-cave," Tommy said. "I've seen them."

Wes frowned. "They're in... is it like your coma?"

"I don't think it's the same. I seem to be able to move around. They're stuck."

"Because of the accident," Jill said.

"What?" Wes said, then Chris.

"This all started after the accident when you guys fell." Jill pointed to the walls around her. "Here, that's why we're here." In her mind, she saw the man across the lake, just before the tress came after her. "He must live here. Jesus—we must have done something that day to piss him off."

Shivers ran over Wes's flesh. He remembered the fall, the pain, Chris, bloody, holding Tommy's body, the glow in the distance. "That glow," he mumbled.

"What?" Jill said.

"After the fall. There was this glowing light in the cave—it was calling me. It made me come to it."

"You were in shock, dude," Chris said. The anger returned. He heard his pleas for Wes to stay. He had been injured, Tommy dying, but instead, Wes had crawled away chasing after nothing.

"No. It called me. I felt it even before we fell. In that stupid room where they cut off all the lights. It..." He remembered the rock on his shelf, the one a little smaller than a baseball that Mom said was in his things when he came home. And somehow, the rock became the man—the guy in the garage with the wide-brimmed hat. "Holy shit."

"There is a being behind it," Tommy said. "I've—I don't know how to describe it—I brushed past it in people's dreams. It whispers in their minds and makes them do things. I think it gets off on bad shit happening."

"This is nuts," Chris said. "You're all fucking nuts."

Jill frowned. "If this is all nuts, Chrissy, then you're *all nuts*, because you think we're in *your* mind."

He shook his head. "Shut up."

Wes raised his hand in front of his chest. "Whatever this thing is, it started, so there has to be a way to stop it. I've got a rock in my room. I brought it home with me that day. I think that's why Di and I started dreaming together. Maybe that's the key?"

Di walked into the center of the group with a scowl. "Whatever the answer is, we're not going to solve it by standing around. Let's go kick its ass."

"Di..." Wes reached for her, but she spun and headed into the tunnel that didn't exist in the real Bloodtooth Cavern.

"Let's go!" Di shouted.

Her voice echoed and Wes wasn't sure he'd ever heard her speak so confidently. He gestured for them to move.

Tommy chuckled to Chris.

Chris gritted his teeth and followed. "I don't like this."

The new cave was darker than the Forest Service sections, though it was lit with a flicker from some unseen flame. Its walls were slick, and its ceiling hung thick with bats. A smell of putrid death grew heavy as they ventured deeper, and a cold wind from somewhere ahead shoved the smell into their faces.

Wes walked behind Di, followed by Jill, Tommy, and Chris. They said nothing other than groans about the smell and huffs as they climbed over boulders and squeezed through narrow passages. But they didn't resist. It was as if each had accepted that this was the way they needed to go, regardless of their objections. They all needed to see where this went and what was at the end.

Soon, they found themselves standing at a precipice. At their backs were columns of merging stalactites and stalagmites, the forest of rock.

Ahead was the drop and Wes knew exactly where they were. "This is where we fell." It was as cold as winter. Numbness ran through his digits. He remembered the weightlessness after slipping away into the darkness. Then the impact, the scraping, the sliding, his skin ripping open, and the crack of bones in his foot. He may have lost consciousness at the time, but in this dream, he remembered it all, every last pain. It urged him away, screamed at him to keep his distance. But he knew that was impossible. As much as fear pushed him, a rising dread told him that cliff was inevitable.

Chris shook his head and backed away. "No."

All their eyes went to the bottom of the cliff. Thoughts ran rampant as if shared by telepathy: Wes, Chris, and Tommy, waiting for who knows how long for help, unrelenting pain, fear that no one was coming, tears knowing that the light would only last so long while the darkness was eternal.

Wes's gaze followed the floor, searching for that glowing place—where he must have gotten the rock—but he couldn't see it. He could picture it vaguely in his head. Light blue in the deepest pitch, there was a depression where the thing sat; and some kind of markings said—no, warned, he knew that now—there were warnings to keep away.

"You've found your way home," a deep voice carried from the stone forest. It boomed through the walls, the floor, and the rock formations.

They all jerked back toward the monuments of rock.

"Who's there?" Di shouted. Her voice was strong and only pitched with worry at the very end, where only Wes was familiar with the sound.

"I am that whom you seek," the voice said, still shrouded in the unknown darkness. His voice dripped in sarcastic tease.

"Come out!" Wes yelled.

"Show yourself," Di demanded. "You can whisper, but you don't want to show us who you are."

"I am many," the voice said. "Marenor, Salizar, Jam'a'qi, Harmor-di-al. But I doubt *you* know me. I can show you, but that may ruin the game. If you ruin the game, then you lose."

"Guys," Tommy said, "Don't tempt it."

"We're not here to play," Di said.

Jill reached out to Di, Tommy's words sinking in.

"You're here to kill me," the voice said. "For revenge for your daddy."

Di stepped forward. "Don't you talk about him!"

"I didn't kill him," the thing said.

Wes flinched. He knew what was coming.

"You killed him," echoed from the blackness into their minds. Images of tire through skull and flesh broadcast into their heads. "You brought him into this world."

Wes felt a punch in his gut. So, it really was his fault.

"But enough," the voice said. "I only need one of you. The strongest. That one will get the prize. The rest of you will be meat, just like the others in your town."

"What is it saying?" Chris whispered.

"Show yourself!" Di shook her clenched fists in front of her chest. Her face was tight, the cords in her neck at attention.

A deep thump shook the cave. Another. Another. The sounds came together in the distance into one object, growing closer, growing louder. They were footfalls. Heavy, charging, footfalls.

"Something's coming," Wes said.

Booms shook the cave. Rocks crunched and shattered in the columns ahead. Dust rained from above and pebbles bounced from their heads.

"What is it?" Jill asked. She grabbed Wes.

"I don't—"

The nearest column exploded before them. In its place was a charging beast like none of them had ever seen. It was as tall as the cave with thick, matted brown hair. It walked on six monstrous legs like a mutant mastodon. Throngs of horns and tusks protruded from its face and brown-haired tentacles waved from its spine.

Wes moved away without thinking. He felt pressure on his back, something was stopping him—Jill. *The cliff.*

The creature roared and Wes's ears ached from the loudness. It ran toward the group, its head swinging left and right, its horns thrashing, its tentacles whipping through the air, blocking the possibility of escape.

"Where do we go?" Jill said.

"There's no room," Chris said. "We're going to fall!"

A rush of scents slammed Wes in the face, smells from their trek here but stronger now: rot, decay, rancid meat. A tentacle smacked him in the chest like a sack of bricks. He crashed into Di, into Jill. They landed on the edge of the cliff. Chris and Tommy balanced inches from falling.

"He's going to knock us over," Tommy shouted.

"Wes!" Di screamed.

A barrage of stinking brown limbs collided, one after another, after another: Wes into Di, Di into Jill, Jill into Chris, Chris into Tommy, each swept over the edge.

5

Chris howled. He knew he wasn't the only one, but his voice was all he heard. He twisted as he fell, trying to see the ground he knew was rushing at him. He caught a glimpse of Wes, then Wes faded into blackness. To his right was Tommy, who was overtaken by a black fog. When he finally looked down, the ground was gone.

His heart raced even faster. How did the ground disappear? Where had his friends gone?

He stopped screaming and found the air silent. Even the wind that raced by his ears made no noise. He closed his eyes and screamed again.

A thud rocked Chris's chest and forehead, followed by his arms and legs. He'd slammed into something hard. His head aching, he opened his eyes.

He was in a room, not a cave. It was gray stone brick, lit by lantern and torch. He saw a huge fireplace, and as he turned, he spotted a row of thrones.

It was as if the room only existed as his eyes met it, like it revealed itself around him. A woman sat on one of the four thrones. The rest were empty. She stared at him with a disgusted gaze, her sour sneer curling her upper lip. Men in medieval dress stood on her left and right. They watched him, hands on the hilts of their undrawn swords.

Chris groaned as he rocked himself upright. His entire body hurt. His thoughts pivoted between pain and wondering where he was. He climbed to his feet, and five men drew their swords and pointed them in his direction.

"What the hell?" Chris backed away.

Each swordsman stared him down with cold eyes, practiced and trained. Chris could feel their eagerness to slice him to pieces. The only thing that held them back was the woman. Their queen?

She wore no crown. Her thick, dark clothes looked nothing like what he would consider royalty, but maybe he'd just seen too many Disney depictions of royals.

"Hold." She spoke without looking at her men. She eyed every bit of Chris, from his black leather boots to his Rush shirt. She held herself with the confidence that if she only uttered a syllable, her men would cut him into meat for their dogs' dinners. Her lips pursed. "You are here for the princess?"

"What?" He had barely uttered the word when a massive gothic door flew open on the right, ushering in the scents of campfire and blood. The screams of a girl filled the room, and two men stomped in. Each held an arm of a screaming maiden. She lifted her head, and Chris saw... it was Charlotte.

He took a step toward her, and every armed man in the room took a step toward him. "No." Fear jolted through him, for himself and for her. He backed away. "Let her go."

They threw Charlotte on the floor in front of the woman. She whimpered and glanced at the throned lady, then locked eyes with Chris.

Chris was awed by her. Her eyes seemed to glow. Her hair was long, almost touching the floor. Her face was flushed, beautiful in a way he had never seen. She wore a dress the same shade as the woman, but even as she lay on the floor, it made her look stunning. The image latched onto his heart. He had to save her, to have her.

"Charlotte." Chris extended a hand. She raised one toward him, and even with the ten feet they stood apart, he could feel the warmth of her grip.

"That's what I thought," the queen said. "Take her."

The two thugs that had dragged her in grabbed her wrists once again.

"No!" Chris shouted. Five swords took another step closer, and he held still.

Charlotte howled. They dragged her back through the door. She shouted, "Chris!" as the slab of wood slammed shut.

"You want her?" the queen asked.

"Yes."

"Good."

Another massive door on the other side of the queen opened. It slammed against the wall, shaking the room. The vibration ran up Chris's legs and rattled his chest. No one seemed shocked except Chris. He jerked away from the queen, away from the door, and saw a man in a full suit of medieval armor. Dark bloodstains encircled the metal suit like the calligraphy of the damned. His face was familiar, but Chris couldn't place him, and he smiled with an eerie jaw that protruded from his mouth more like a row of barbs than teeth. Hanging from his hand was a long stick, and at the end of that stick was an iron ball, radiating spikes.

"Jesus Christ." Chris unconsciously raised his hands in defense. Not a word had been said of what was to happen, but inside he knew. He was going to have to fight this guy—this beast in armor. "Don't I get a weapon?"

"Of course," the queen laughed. She gestured to the wall behind Chris, which held a rack of swords, axes, clubs, and morning stars like his opponent's. Chris heard iron clanking. It was a crashing sound, an incoming train wreck that demanded the destruction of his flesh. He glanced over and saw the man-beast charging him, his weapon high above his head.

The queen's guards cheered and shouted, and her cackle lifted above every other sound.

This isn't real, repeated in Chris's head. But real or not, his attacker's spiked weapon flew at his head, and Chris jumped.

He fell to his right. Steel spikes pounded on the stone floor, sending chips of sharp rock flying at his face. Three shards sliced his left cheek, and three warm streams flowed down.

"Fuck!" He scrambled to his feet and ran toward the rack of weapons.

The air split in a whistle as metal shredded and wood swung. Steel spikes sliced Chris's trailing foot as it hovered in the air, about to take his next step.

It felt like a bee sting, sharp and immediate, and he jerked his foot forward. His shoe held back, throwing him off-balance, then ripped free from his ankle. Chris dared a glance at the monster of a knight as he plummeted face-first toward the stone floor. He saw his shoe clinging to the man's weapon and a fountain of blood spraying from his foot.

He raised his arms and crashed. The knight rampaged toward him, ripping the shoe free and tossing it aside.

Fear gripped every inch of Chris's flesh. What was he supposed to do? He was no knight. Even if he reached the weapons, this guy was three times his size. He had no chance of winning this. Thoughts came to him of the other day, of the Khaki Klan as they kicked him on every side. He was pinned in place with nowhere to go—again.

Charlotte's face rose in his mind. They had her. Who knew what they would do to her if he failed. But how could he help if he couldn't even get to a weapon, let alone wield it?

The knight's morning star whistled, and Chris rolled to his right. It was the opposite direction from the weapons but also away from planting his wounded foot. He remembered running from the Klan as they looked away, and he only hoped he could make some distance.

He sprinted toward the door where the knight had entered. Bloody tracks traced his path. He was ten feet away, and the door slammed shut. The queen's guards stepped in front and aimed their swords at Chris.

"Ah!" Chris threw himself against the wall and froze. He heard the slam of metal against stone, footfall after footfall, heaving breaths from lungs twice the size of his chest. The knight was closing in.

"This is not the way to save your princess," the queen mocked. She rested her head in her hand and leaned on her right armrest. Her face was low, bored. "I'm afraid if you cannot slay him, she will be his."

His? The word struck him as hard as the stone wall behind him. If *he* took her—Chris shuddered. The giant monster of a knight, he'd kill her, maybe rape her first. But what was Chris supposed to do? They had to know he couldn't beat the man physically. It finally occurred to him that this was not a physical confrontation. They were not in the middle ages. This was not the inside of a castle or some deranged queen's court. This was a dream. He didn't have to beat the man as himself, a small twelve-year-old boy. He could be anything.

His first thought was a mirror of the knight in front of him. His arms bulged; his legs thickened and lengthened. Armor faded into existence, and a morning star of his own appeared in his hand.

The knight halted, his arm raising to strike. He looked Chris up and down, and his weapon soared at Chris's head.

Chris ducked and lifted his own weapon to block. A clang echoed through the room. The queen shifted in her seat, resting on her other side.

Chris barely held the weapon in place. He felt cold as the steel hung inches from his nose.

The knight's knee came up, slamming into Chris's gut. Metal armor clanged, and he stumbled backward. The knight swung again, the spikes of his star slicing into steel and then Chris's leg.

Chris screeched. A rainbow of blood arced away from his limb as the knight hauled his weapon back.

This isn't going to work, Chris thought. *I don't know how to fight. I know other things.*

He steadied himself and forced a change. His skin grew dark and thick and burst with hair. His fingers extended, dropping the weapon. His nails sprouted into claws. His legs grew. His face warped into a snout with fangs as long as fingers, and his ears rose to points and stood above his head.

The knight's eyes widened. Chris towered over everyone in the room, and for the first time, Chris saw fear in the man's stare. And he smelled it through his long canine snout.

He took a step forward. The knight swung, and Chris grabbed the weapon's wooden handle as it flew. He stripped it from the man's grip and snapped it with one hand. Slivers of wood rained to the floor.

The knight backed away. He turned, eying the rack of weapons.

Chris seized the man by the shoulders and lifted him. His claws pierced armor, and streams of blood ran along the metal's crimson markings. "You can't have her." His voice was a growl, low and rumbling. He squeezed and felt blood flow over his fingertips, warm and wet, and he was overwhelmed by the strange urge to feed. Was this monstrous shape affecting his mind?

His jaws spread. Saliva dripped from his tongue. It overflowed from his mouth and onto the knight's chest.

The knight screamed, and just as Chris's arm had faded into existence, the knight dissolved into nothingness in Chris's arms.

Chris searched around the room as if his prey had fled. He saw only the queen and her men. She sat up straight now, facing him.

Chris felt his strength swell inside and walked to her. "The princess," he growled.

She shook her head. "You did not win."

"He's gone!" His rage boiled over. Was it the monster he'd become?

"He awoke. You were too slow. She is still his."

"What?" A wave of sadness and anger ripped through him. He lunged at the queen, claws first.

She waved a hand, and Chris fell to the floor on hands and knees. His skin was his own, the monster gone.

"You can still save her," she said.

Chris looked up.

"Your mother, too."

6

Tommy landed in a meadow, surrounded by knee-high grass and flowers that seemed to sing with the passing wind. It was someone's dreamland, but not quite his.

On three sides of the meadow was a forest. On the third was a river, and more forest lay beyond that. Surrounding it all were mountains higher than he could imagine, with snowy peaks that reached up into the clouds.

"Where am I?" he muttered to himself. He knew he was dreaming. The coma had been nothing but dreams. They no longer fooled him into believing he was in some situation that was real—the haze of the *unreal* was like the air of another planet he had learned to breathe.

He walked toward the river. Maybe if he kept walking, he would see something more worthwhile than grass and trees. Maybe a village? Maybe he would try to create one? Somewhere in the back of his mind, Tommy had accepted the fact that this coma may be the only place he would call home for a very long time, if not ever, and he needed to get used to it, learn to live in it.

The songs of the flowers grew louder as he went. They were five-petaled things, about as wide as his hand. They were pink and purple and yellow, and he wondered what the sound was all about.

He paused a few dozen feet from the river and kneeled, looking closer at a swaying purple beauty. Black lines ran through its petals, a white one in between. The white line pulsed with the song, growing brighter and fading with the volume, which rose and fell with the wind's gusts.

He concluded it must be a trick of this strange place and braced himself to rise, when he saw something hovering over the center of the plant. It was nearly invisible at first, but once he saw it, it seemed to fade into view: a three-inch-tall naked flying girl, a fairy.

It sent him reeling onto his rear. Of all the crazy things he'd seen lately, this, in his face right now, was the most mind-blowing.

He watched her buzz around the flower. The melody of her wings shifted as she settled on a petal. He studied her from head to toe and thought she must be the most beautiful thing he had ever seen. Her skin was smooth and glowed with a gentle light like a sunrise over a sleeping valley. Her face was just a little plump with a smile, dimples, and a slightly upturned nose. Her hips and chest were full and round. It was not a girl fairy; it was a woman.

She floated uninterrupted as if he wasn't even there, and Tommy had to wonder for a second if she was right. Was he, in fact, in this dream? Was it someone else's, and he was again just an observer? He saw his hands and feet and legs; his body was indeed there.

He tilted his head and watched her. He wished he could have wings and float up to her and say hello. He leaned forward, and it felt as though he were floating. Looking down, he saw his feet dangling and bare. He was naked as well, his skin glowing; he was flying like her, he was one of them.

He felt the hum of his wings behind his back. It was like a soft massage. His gaze went to her, and he drifted forward again. A brief second passed, where he was embarrassed about his nudity, but as he saw her, he realized it didn't matter. He was in a natural place, as she was, as the entire forest around them was. This was how he was supposed to be, how she would expect to see him. Some fairy underwear or loincloth would have been an oddity.

He buzzed over the flower and waited. He watched her work, knowing there would be a moment soon where she would see him, and then it would happen. He wasn't sure yet how it would go, but he was excited.

It was then that he was finally able to see what she was doing. As her existence had been revealed from a plane of invisibility, the veil over her work lifted.

The petals of the flower were tipped with hundreds of extended arms. Each took turns reaching into the center of the petal and ripping away a tiny strip of the plant, then holding it up into the air. She would swoop by and take the plant's flesh and shove it into a pouch that hung from her right hip. Then, she would fly to the next petal, do the same, and continue around and around.

Tommy watched the waving hands. They were eager. Even the empty ones waved in the air, ecstatic to have the fairy around. He watched them rip and tear into their petal, and a chill rolled over him. Each shred of torn flower dripped with the plant's inner juices. Each eager hand was as vicious as a starving beast after its payload had been taken. He saw anxious children wanting to impress their parents and jealous schoolmates wanting to outshine the others.

The inner petal looked tender and raw, and as Tommy looked back upon the entrancing face of the hovering woman, his heart jumped. He wanted to please her as well. His skin flushed. He felt his glow brighten, and she turned and saw him.

His insides froze. Panic took over, and for a moment, he thought even his wings might stop, and he might fall from the air.

She was staring at him with a smile that grew as wide as her cheeks. It was inviting, loving, calling to him in a way a girl never had. He felt his insides swell and knew for a concrete fact that he loved this fairy like nothing he had ever loved in his life.

The softest of giggles escaped through her lips. It was a light, airy sound, hidden from every other being in the universe. It was meant solely for him, and it made his body vibrate and tingle. She saw his smile rise, and like a bolt of lightning, she tore across the grass toward the river.

What happened next to Tommy was without thought or feeling or will. He simply watched as his body reacted. His wings moved, his being shifted gears, and wind ripped by his face as he soared in pursuit.

"Wait!" Tommy shouted, but his speech came out in another language: *laoomd...* It was a fairy word for wait. He knew it.

She heard him, he was sure she did, but she refused to stop. She shot across the river bank and over the water. He followed, keeping pace but not gaining, and she glanced back. He couldn't see to know for sure, but he thought she smirked at him. It was half her mouth, followed by a wink, and his heart skipped a beat.

He felt his wings pumping now. He pushed them harder and made himself go faster.

She flew over the other bank, and he rocketed over the water. She paused, hovering just above another flower. It widened its petals. Its arms outstretched toward her.

"No!" Tommy pleaded with the air. The petals had no right. They reached and grabbed for her, but she was his.

He pushed himself faster. He crossed the river and spread his arms. He was almost there, and he was going to have her. He would take her in his embrace, and she would love him the way he loved her.

He flew over the river bank, above the grass, and slammed into his love. His hands wrapped around her body and caressed every inch of it. He moved his mouth toward hers. He saw her eyes; they were twinkling. Her lips, inviting. She spread them apart to welcome him, but as her mouth widened, her teeth didn't seem to end. She opened wider, and when her mouth was fully agape, he saw each and every tooth was tipped with needle-like points. He didn't care. They were the most beautiful fangs he had ever set his eyes upon.

Tommy pressed his lips into hers. She tasted like strawberries. His eyes rolled back, and he saw the sky. It wasn't still, though. He saw clouds in the deep blue. They spun—no, he was spinning. Together, they kissed and held each other; and they were spinning and falling.

The ground thumped against his wings. They cracked and snapped. It was like lightning through his body, a crunch like fracturing bone. The pain electrified him, made him want to scream, then faded into the ecstasy of her lips. His hands glided over her glowing skin. He could deal with double the pain, triple, quadruple—a hundred times this pain if he had to—if it was for her.

She floated up above him, and his fingers slipped from her glorious flesh. She hummed as she floated. He stretched but couldn't touch. He tried to get up, but his legs wouldn't work, and his waist wouldn't move. Had he done something to himself in the crash? More than just his wings?

She smirked, and his heart pounded inside him like a raging drum. He needed her. She was his, and she could never go. He had to keep her here. But how?

He thought of the flowers. She stayed for the flowers.

He reached behind his head and grabbed his wing. He yanked on the slick layers of flesh that encased his slim, hollow bones. He felt burning as he tore. It was a hot and ripping pain, and his hand came away with a few inches of his wing's flesh.

Tommy held the bloody thing into the air. She hovered above him and took it. She sucked it into her mouth. It slid over her lips and danced and flitted over her needles. She gulped it down and hissed with a forked tongue as she winked at him, her wings humming a high-pitched song.

It was wonderful, and his face widened with glee. She'd taken him inside her. He would be a part of her. It was more than he could have hoped for. He reached back again, ripping more of himself away. He held it out and tingled as she slurped it down. He ripped again. He could feel his face, so wonderfully smiling. If he wasn't so happy, his cheeks would be aching. It was just so perfect.

But before Tommy knew it, he was out of wings. Panic stormed through him. What would she do? He had more flesh to offer, but he realized that eventually, he would run out of that too. If she didn't leave now, she surely would then.

He reached down and dug into his belly, peeling back his skin. Exquisite pain tore across his flesh with a long strip of glowing dermis. He held it up and watched her hover closer. She reached out, and as her fingers brushed across his own, he seized her wrist with his other hand.

She screeched. It was high and loud. His ears felt so pained they instantly grew numb.

She jerked her hand, and he gripped tighter. He dropped the strip of his belly flesh and seized her with his other hand. He would not lose her again.

She shook him up and down, his head banging into the dirt. Without thinking about it, his skull seemed to grow thicker. He dug his fingers into her—she would not get away.

His legs, which had been without feeling, now burned with his will. They lifted from the ground and circled around her leg. She jerked, and he writhed. He threw one leg up and around her other thigh and hooked his ankles and feet around hers. She squealed. Her fangs snapped.

The fairy clawed at Tommy's face with her free hand. She broke the skin below his eye and ripped into his cheek. He seemed to grab it with a third hand. She lunged with her teeth, snapping at his neck. He sprouted a fourth hand that took her by the throat.

"Yes!" He twitched at his waist and flipped her around. Her wings slammed into the dirt, and he sat on top of her. "You're mine now!" His eyes bulged. His jaw spread in the smile of a madman.

She grunted and squirmed, and a sound drifted across the grass. It was something like the snap of someone's fingers.

Tommy looked up for a second and saw nothing. He looked back down, and she was gone. "No!" a sinking hooked inside his gut. He screamed. It was like every good feeling inside him had been stripped away, and his heart was being scrapped across fiery coals.

Thumping shook the ground. Tommy looked up and saw a man.

7

Waves lapped against the shore. Out in the lake, a boat with a skier rode in and out of Jill's view. She tugged at her striped, one-piece bathing suit, pulling it into alignment around her hips and chest. It just didn't seem to fit right, tight in all the places she wanted it loose and loose in the places she wanted it tight. She gave up and leaned back onto her towel to watch the clouds.

One looked like a rubber duck. One looked like a cruise ship. One looked like a crane about to take off. Set in front of the sky's dark blue, they all reminded her of the lake water and the immense depths she had heard were below.

The first time she'd come to visit grandmother here, she must have been four and forced to wear donut-shaped floaters on her arms, even to sit in the water. She didn't understand why, just to rest her butt in the shallow breaking waves and sift through the pebbles below the surface? When she was eight, Dad told her a story.

She had been cross-legged on an old blanket, much like today. Dad sat beside her, the scent of Aqua Velva still thick from his shave, coconut oils from the bottle in his hand.

"Be careful out there today." He leaned back, tenting his arms behind him.

"I had lessons," Jill argued. "I'm probably the best swimmer here." She was, in fact, that. Dad hadn't swum more than ten feet in ten years. Mom avoided the water like it would melt her. Grandmother didn't even come to the shoreline—she liked to watch it from her bench under the shade of the back deck.

"Maybe so, maybe so. But you don't know how dangerous this lake is."

"What do you mean?" She tried to wrap her head around how one body of water could be more dangerous than another.

Dad pointed to the middle of the lake. "You see how dark it is out there?" Sun glinted from the tips of small crests like floating crystals.

"Yeah."

"That's because of the depth. This is one of the deepest lakes in this hemisphere."

Her brain searched for the meaning of *hemisphere*. She thought it must have to do with a ball of some sort, but how it related to lakes, she wasn't sure.

Seeing the question in her eyes, Dad said, "This side of the Earth... It's so deep, some of the people that've drowned here still haven't been recovered. Divers go down to look, and it gets so dark, they can't see to find them."

Jill imagined dead people, the corpses of poor swimmers floating beneath the surface. Pale-skinned bodies, gaping eyes, skeletal chests and limbs. She saw other eight-year-olds, their mothers and fathers. Gooseflesh rose on her sunlit arms as she envisioned them trying to swim up, clawing at the water to get back to the surface.

"It's okay." Dad rested a hand on her shoulder. "You don't have to be afraid. But you have to respect it. Because that's not all."

His face came into focus. He was waiting for her gaze.

"There's also a current. I know it looks like a lake, but two miles east, water fills it from the dam; and seven miles west, another damn lets the water out. The whole thing is actually a really fat section of the river. And underneath the calm surface, you see, there's a strong current that can take you a mile before you could blink."

Suddenly the skinny dead were racing downstream, struggling to get out. They scratched and grabbed at each other as they fought. Dead strips of skin and hunks of hair floated to the surface and drifted toward her beach.

"So." Dad patted her shoulder again. "Just, be safe out there. Stay near the shore. Okay?"

Jill nodded. Her gaze darted along the water's edge as if she would spot a clump of hair, or worse, the decayed clutching hand of a lost swimmer, a swept-away soul that finally found its way back to land.

Dad stood and wandered back toward the house, and Jill wondered what she was even doing there. Humans were air-breathers. Why did they go into the water at all? Down there may as well have been another planet or the blackness or space. It seemed just as inhospitable to human life. Her toes were the only part of her to touch the lake that day.

A cloud floated by that resembled a face. The more Jill watched it, it seemed to change into one that reminded her of Wes. A smile lifted her cheeks, and someone sat down beside her.

Jill felt cold as she glanced over, expecting her dad or her cousin, maybe even Mom, if she was able to drag herself from the deck and her pitcher of margaritas. Instead, it was a man. A long-brimmed hat sat on his head, shading his face and hiding all but his dark stubbled chin. He wore a linen shirt, yellowed and tattered on its seams.

Jill shot up and stumbled to the side on hands and feet like a panicked crab. She felt the ground below change from her soft, cotton towel to mostly-rounded river rock as she refused to release the man from her gaze.

He watched her but lazily from the black shadow that covered his eyes as he faced the water. She got a sense that he knew each action she took, even with his focus on that dark center stretch where the cold depths lay. She felt that he was admiring it, adoring it in some way.

He opened his mouth, his gaze immobile. "They each had fun, you know. Each was enjoying one of their best days." His voice was low and smooth, and while it may have even been a handsome tone in another circumstance, the frequencies chilled her flesh.

Jill blinked, the words stuck in her mind. They clunked and rolled and knocked around in there, seemingly unable to lock into place like language should. *Each-who? They?*

"They laughed and played, swam; some skied... If you were to die today, wouldn't you prefer it be on a day you enjoyed?"

"Wh—who?" Jill squeaked.

"You know who." The stranger's words rang like a song.

Jill saw half-flesh half-bone hands swimming through the shiny crests in the distance. She staggered back from the water. She wanted to stand and run, but she knew she couldn't escape. Somehow she knew if she turned, the stranger would be on her. She knew his grip would be as cold and icy, as sharp and bony, as those things in the water.

"Don't worry, Jill." His voice still sang, but it was calm, endearing, as one would speak to a toddler to win them over. "No one's here for you today. It isn't one of your best—though I guess they don't all get that pleasure. Today, I'm just here to talk."

Jill wanted to be eased by this. She wasn't. The same sense that told her that she couldn't run, told her this man lied as expertly as he breathed. "Talk?"

"Just talk." He turned, and she could sense his eyes under the blackness of his hat, but she saw no shine. Not a glimmer. "If you help me, I can help you."

She wanted to ask, *Help me how? Help you?* His blackened face held her tongue idle.

"You see, I know what's in your heart. I see it in your dreams. And what you want is Wes."

A shiver rode down her spine.

"I can give him to you. All you have to do is open the door for me. Let me in. Not much, just so I can share a few... *whispers*. And I can give you what you want."

8

Wes walked through a forest he knew more than he wanted to. He was rushed with the same feeling, not *déjà vu*, but stronger. He remembered this place: the tall, thick trees, the lush floor, the bushes, the sounds of exotic birds, and the smells of alien flowers. He had never been here, but he had. When he was young? But he *was* young. It made as much sense as the fact he knew, not felt, but knew inside his bones, that something bad was coming for them.

Di heard her brother walking toward her. She paused, examining the blue flowers that hung from the vines. She always loved how they looked, how they smelled. She caressed the petals as Wes stepped behind her.

"We lost everyone else," Wes said.

"Only for a while." Di took a deep inhalation of the flower in front of her.

"I guess so."

"Is this where we finally meet him?"

Wes thought about it. The forest was right. If what he remembered was correct, the river was ahead, and beyond that, they would find a tall man in a wide-brimmed hat. "I think it is."

"Good." Di looked Wes in the eyes with a hard determination. She curled one fist and struck the palm of her other hand. "Let's do it."

They hiked over a worn game trail through the woods, stopping at the edge of a river. The water was crystal clear beyond the ripples and waves of its lazy current.

"I'll go first." Wes stepped down onto the muddy bank. He waded in, warm water rising up to his knees. Before he knew it, he had crossed and was on the other side. He waved Diana over. "Come on!"

She stepped in, the water at her mid-thigh. She had just crossed when they heard the clop of hooves against dirt, then stone, then the crunchy leaves of the forest floor.

"Come on," Wes said, waving her into the nearby trees. His stomach turned. Something bad was on its way, and he wanted a tree to hide behind. He knew he couldn't avoid it. It was coming whether he wanted it to or not, but the urge inside his gut said they needed to hide and get out of the way.

Di scaled the river bank and rushed alongside Wes. They hurried until two rows of trees were behind, and they stopped and listened.

The noise moved toward the water. Wes and Di held their breaths and peered through the woods. On the river bank stood an animal that both amazed and intrigued Wes. Head down, drinking from the river, was a tall white horse; and on its head was a two-foot-long, white horn.

It lifted its head, and Wes was mesmerized by its onyx eyes and long, flowing mane. He wasn't one to be interested in horses, or even unicorns, but being face to face with the majestic beast struck a chord inside him. It was like seeing a once-in-a-lifetime event, a comet, or an eclipse—it was both real and ethereal, accompanied by a nagging itch inside his mind that this was not a good thing.

He turned to Di. She had to be freaking out. If the sight was affecting him in this way, someone who liked unicorns, he figured, had to be dying. He thought of her room, with unicorn art on the walls, a half-dozen posters, and drawings hanging in frames. Then there were her notebooks, sheets, and pajamas, though some she no longer wore, feeling that they were too childish—but the bulk of it would stay where it was for years to come until she moved away. But as Wes looked for his sister, she was not standing beside him.

"Di?" he whispered.

The sound of hooves moved into the woods, and behind it, the sound of someone trampling over underbrush. Wes strained his eyes to see through the vegetation and spotted the back of her head. She was following the beast.

"Di, no," he whispered.

She kept moving. It was as if she were in a trance. The unicorn moved, and she matched it.

Wes cursed under his breath and hurried after her. He slipped between trees, around bushes, and was blocked by a three-foot-tall patch of brambles. He had to turn back and find another way. He questioned how Di had gotten through, thinking he had followed the same path. He rounded a stand of immense trees and found himself back at the river.

"What the?" He stepped onto the bank, trying to get around the trees, and he felt his foot sink into silty mud. He pushed with his second foot, trying to lift the first, and was shocked—his foot didn't want to move. It was stuck. He pulled, and it held on with a suction that reminded him of some Acme glue he'd seen on *Loony Tunes*.

He groaned and pulled, and his shoe slipped from his foot, but his foot was free. He swung it back to the shore and planted it on dry land. He pressed it into the soil and heaved against his other foot. The mud slurped, and Wes's mind went to Di. He was goddamn stuck, and Di was getting further and further away.

He heaved again, and again his foot released minus a shoe. "Shit!" He tumbled backward through weeds and thumped into a tree.

Rage boiled inside him as he stared at the stupid mud. He jumped to his feet and darted back into the forest. He went past the brambles, around another dozen stands of monstrous jungle trees. He rushed over dead leaves and broken limbs, his bare feet stinging with every step.

He didn't look down. He knew his feet could be bleeding, and if he saw it, he might stop, and if he stopped, Di would get further away. No. He had to catch up. He had to run faster. The sensation that she was in danger mounted by the second. He needed to find her, or else... he wasn't sure, but the dread inside him swelled.

Step after step, he felt himself closing in on Di. His feet were going numb from the pain. He didn't know if that was good or not, but he kept running.

That was when he heard it. The crunches of a quadruped on leaves and undergrowth. It wasn't far. He saw light through a break in the trees and green from an open meadow. And a rush of cold washed over Wes. The bad thing was coming. It was something he knew and should remember, but the idea wouldn't show itself. It nagged behind his brain, hiding, like a word that he knew the definition of, and was sure started with *sh*, but he couldn't grasp the rest.

Through the trees, he saw Di. She walked forward slowly, her hands up, palms facing something. Wes couldn't see what she was approaching, but he was sure what it was: the unicorn. She'd found it. She muttered soothing words which he couldn't hear. They both reached the edge of the trees and stopped.

"Leave it alone, sis," Wes shouted. "This isn't right."

She stepped from the trees into the meadow's knee-high grass. "Good girl," she whispered as she closed the gap between them.

A rush of fright gripped Wes inside his chest. It wasn't for himself, but for Di. Why was she doing this? Didn't she know that something terrible would come from it? He saw it through a hazy mist inside his mind. But she kept moving forward.

Her eyes were bright, the eyes of someone intoxicated by wonder. Her smile was glorious, and it scared Wes as much as the same smile would have delighted him at any other time.

"This isn't right!" He repeated.

His words didn't faze her.

The beast's black eyes studied her. Its head tilted as if thinking, deciding what to do about this human girl.

A breeze blew across the meadow, and it sank into Wes that what was coming was inevitable. It was already written. It was a moment carved in time that he had no way of affecting, no matter how much he called or how loud he yelled. He gritted his teeth and drove his feet faster.

"Good girl," Di whispered. She moved closer still.

The great white beast lowered her head, moving in toward Di. She bent her knees as Di reached to pet her long white muzzle.

Wes shouted, "No!"

The words traveled across the meadow as the unicorn jerked its head upward. The tip of its horn shot through the middle of Di's palm and ripped through her flesh with quiet precision.

Di's eyes shone, widening from wonder to fear. Her blood sprinkled on her cheeks as two feet of unicorn horn ripped up through her hand, a red spike of pain.

Di howled.

The beast's head continued upward. It lifted Di from the ground, tossing her back and forth, swinging Di like a pinned piece of meat. Blood gushed down her arm, drenching her chest, covering the unicorn's face in a grotesque mask of crimson war paint.

"Di!" Wes was almost there. He didn't know what he would do when he got there or how to stop this madness, but dammit, he was going to help her. Why did he let her slip away and get into this mess? Why did she have to touch it? How could she have not had the same feeling that this was trouble waiting to happen?

The beast leaned down, and for a moment, Wes thought it might let her go. Then, it yanked itself upward. The flesh in Di's hand split, spraying blood like a fountain. She drifted down, two sides of the same hand flapping around like hunks of raw meat.

Di slammed to the ground, clutching one hand with the other. She screamed as the beast reared back on two legs.

Rage swept over Wes. It raced through his breath. That thing had destroyed her hand with two lunges, and what was it going to do now? He sprinted faster. He grew taller. His muscles felt strong, bulging to match his temper, and he reeled his fist back.

The beast was coming down, bringing its massive weight toward Di through two black hooves.

"No!" Wes's fist flew. It crashed into the unicorn's head and crushed its skull inward. The thing's head seemed to pop like an over-ripened tomato, and its body went limp. Unicorn blood sprayed over Wes, Di, and the forest floor as its massive carcass flopped down and shuddered. Piss sprayed from beneath its tail, and bloody bile heaved from the open wound where its jaw once was.

Wes remembered something he had read once about unicorn blood. It was supposed to be magic, and it could heal. It was a silly thought; magic wasn't real—but neither were unicorns. Maybe...

Out of the grassy ground where they stood, Wes watched flowers grow and bloom in fractions of a second. They sprung up around the quaking body of the dying beast.

Di's screams diminished, and she spoke, "What?"

Wes turned. She was covered with blood, hers and the beast's, and her hand seemed to be knitting itself back together.

Di's eyes went to Wes. "It's…"

"Healing," he finished and realized he was towering over her. He had become something of a giant. His hands, his arms, his legs, they were all massive. He had done this to himself. He had wanted to be stronger to face that thing, and he had done it. Why had it not occurred to him before that these were dreams, and he could affect them—he could control them, just as he had controlled bringing the others to him? The thing had separated them, but he could change that.

Wes looked down at Di and let himself deflate. He kneeled and looked her over; beyond an ugly pink scar, her hand looked good. It was soaked in blood but in one piece. "Are you okay?"

Her eyes were glued to her hand. She rotated it in front of her face. "I—I think so."

A wave of relief washed over Wes. He had done this. He'd killed the unicorn, and his thoughts had made its blood heal her. They really could kill whoever was behind this—the thing in the rock, the man in the long-brimmed hat—but first, they needed to be a team.

Wes straightened himself and closed his eyes. He demanded Jill, Chris, and Tommy come to him. He heard steps in the grass and opened his eyes. His friends were there.

"Wes?" Jill said. She was wearing a bathing suit.

"Yes."

Chris was examining the dead unicorn. "What the fuck, dude?"

Tommy surveyed the meadow, seeming wary of the flowers.

"We're going to kill this thing," Wes said.

Di stood. They all looked at Wes.

"I'm going to call it. I'm going to make it come."

Jill, Di, Tommy, and Chris all watched him with concerned gazes. Wes could see they weren't ready, but he was, and if he had to do this all himself, he would.

Wes closed his eyes and clenched his fists. He screamed into the dreamscape, "Show yourself!"

9

Dark clouds swarmed in and crowded the sky. Daylight grew dim, and a cold wind rushed across the meadow.

"Wes?" Di scanned the trees, the sky, and the grass.

The distant sound of the river became louder, its once-subtle waves crashing and colliding, roaring like rapids over the wind.

"What's happening?" Chris asked.

Wes held the command tightly within his mind. This thing would show itself no matter how hard he had to call it. Blood streamed down his face, and he felt pressure pushing back; it was fighting against him. It didn't want to come. Was it afraid? It had manipulated his dreams so easily over the past few days; was it really scared to show itself now? Or was it up to something else?

Wes squeezed his fists. He felt the air around them thickening. He pushed against this thing. His thoughts were daggers, aiming at the boundaries of this forest world.

"Jesus, Wes!" Jill ran to him. She lifted his shirt from his chest and pressed it against his face. "The blood."

The wind roared around them, and Wes yelled, "Call it! Everyone! Make it come!"

Di stood next to Wes and grabbed his wrist. "Get out here!"

Chris watched what was looking more and more like the onset of a hurricane. Jill put her hand on Wes's shoulder and prayed his bleeding would stop. Tommy spread his arms, and as the wind raged against him, he looked like he may float away.

Lightning crashed, shaking the ground with rolling vibrations. It cracked again, flooding across the sky in webs of glowing white filament. It boomed again, and a stalk of light as thick as a tree slammed into the meadow's center. When it faded, everything was still.

The wind stopped. The clouds froze. The roar of the rapids vanished, and where lightning had crashed into the earth stood a man.

"It's him," Jill said. "He was at the lake."

And the garage.

He stood as tall as any ordinary man, but his presence towered over the group from twenty feet away. His hat made Wes think of an evil version of the the Man with No Name from *The Good, the Bad and the Ugly*, and while his face seemed to be hidden in the shadows, Wes was sure there was a grin across his wide five o'clock shadow.

"What the hell?" Chris took a step back.

"It's him," Tommy said. "That's not his real face, but I'm sure that's him."

"No, it's a mask," Wes mumbled. The linens the man wore looked old, but Wes knew this thing was much older. He felt it through the stare, through nothing but his presence, as though something from the man was traveling from his limbs into the ground and radiating across the meadow's material plane.

"What do you want?" Di shouted. Her voice was massive in the now-silent world.

The man tipped his head forward. He spoke with soft words that echoed inside each of their minds. *Just to have a little fun, my sweet.*

"You call this fun?" Tommy said.

A shrill laugh erupted from the man, painful inside Wes's head.

"Why?" Wes shouted. "Why are you trying to kill us? Why'd you kill my dad?"

"You cheated, my boy. It was a test for you, and you brought him into the challenge."

"Cheated?" Di screeched back. "You ran over his face!"

"There's always a risk when you play games, isn't there? Well, any of the good ones."

"You bastard!" Wes felt himself growing larger again. His arms bulged. His legs lengthened. His fists swelled. Jill moved away, her jaw dropping.

Di, from nowhere, was now holding a sword. Chris stepped forward, scales forming over his clothes and claws bursting from his fingers.

"You'll pay!" Wes charged at the man in the wide-brimmed hat. His skin was hot, his fists hard and steaming.

A wall of wind pounded into Wes's front, lifting him from his feet and tossing him backward. He watched the stars above streak as he flew and wondered, *What happened to the sky?* Jill, Di, Chris, Tommy all rose from the ground. The forest on every side went dark. The sky disappeared. Only they and he remained.

The stranger soared at them, chasing the wind. He exploded from the size of a man to that of a building, tearing from his clothes and revealing dark green skin with golden tattoos in shapes and strange languages. His arms and legs split, doubling themselves as lines bulged like veins and sprouted spikes, trails of massive porcupine-like spines. Three tales emerged from his rear, snapping like whips, and his face extended into a fanged snout. Claws sprang from each finger, and they were faster than him, slicing at the air and closing in.

Wes felt terror run through him, the kind he thought only existed in books and movies. His heart beat so fast, it was a numb humming in his chest. His body was cold, and not a single molecule of his existence listened to his command. He wanted to scream. He wanted to wave his arms and make his falling body get out of that thing's way. He wanted to run, even if his feet couldn't reach the ground. God, he prayed for anything, any control over any part of this. But there was nothing. Only freezing cold fear, like the setting sun over a snow-drenched day. In his mind, it was fifty below outside, and his feet were cemented under three feet of snow. A blizzard was smothering the sky, and all he could do was wait for death.

A roar shook the fabric of the dream universe. Wes vibrated in mid-air. He saw the sharpened edges of claws descending on him, and he finally forced out a scream.

1992

1

Light flickered in the living room window of the Brolin house. It was the pale blue flash of a room with nothing on but the television. The rest of the downstairs was dim, save a light over the stove. The upstairs was dark, and Ray Trent had to wonder who the lone sole was who couldn't sleep.

He guessed it was the mom. Misty was dumb but smart enough not to lose sleep over someone as worthless as her sister. The father would have to work the next day; that was his job, right? Fathers had to go to work regardless of how many mistakes their stupid kids made. For a second, Ray hoped it was the father in the living room, so he could meet the man before this whole thing got too crazy. But he didn't think it was the man; it was going to be the mom.

Ray watched from the other side of Canyon Street. He'd parked the minivan three houses down and done nothing but sit in the grass and watch for close to an hour. Well, not nothing—he did have to lean behind a bush once as a neighbor drove by and then turned left on Franklin Street, but other than that, it had been a peaceful sit so far.

The voice hadn't told him to sit. It had stopped whispering for a while as if it had been tied up somewhere else, but that was okay. Ray was good where he was.

He played the game *Who's Awake* and visualized what it was going to be like once he got Misty to the cabin. He wondered what color panties he would find her in and realized it had better be one he liked since she wouldn't be able to change into any others at the cabin. Then, he retracted that thought. If he didn't like them, he'd throw them out, and she could be completely bottomless. That wouldn't be bad. He could watch her walk around with her little peach poking out and enjoy the sight. No covering up for her. The more he thought about it, the more he thought that may just be his rule once they got there, even if she was wearing something he liked.

He wondered how much trouble Mom and Dad were going to be. This time, he was taking Misty with him; there was no doubt in his mind about that. So, were Mom and Dad going to put up a fight? Sleep through it all? Maybe he could just convince them he was just there to take her on a date. He had chuckled when he thought about that. It was going to be a roll of the dice, but a game he was ready for and determined to win.

"*Enough thinking*," the whisper finally said. "*Go get what's yours.*"

Ray nodded. "Damn straight it's mine."

He was calm as he stood. It was a strange sensation after dealing with the cop earlier. He wondered if maybe it was because the cop was a surprise. There could be a surprise inside, but, no, he thought, he knew what was coming—and he was calmly ready to accomplish his goal.

Ray crossed the street, his hands inside his hoodie pocket. The .45's steel had cooled while he waited, and now it felt refreshing in his grip. He walked over the curb and then up the front steps. The porch light was on—again, an expectation of weak minds that Amanda may come home. And with that weakness, Ray expected the door to be ready and waiting for her to walk right in.

He grasped the knob with soft, controlled pressure. He turned it slowly, listening for clicks, ticks, springs, and locks. It glided under his touch, smooth mechanics, and again, he thought he might like to meet the father; while weak-minded, he must be a man who takes care of his home.

Not a squeak, not a whine, the door spread like a well-greased wheel. The television blared from the living room, and Ray realized that he might as well have banged the door around because no one would have heard. Still, he had already decided he would do this properly, so he closed the door with the same silent exactness he had used to open it.

Chanting repeated from the living room: "This is my rifle. This is my gun. This is for fighting. This is for fun." Ray recognized it but couldn't place it—not until he stood at the entrance to the darkened room. He looked over the couch, where the balding head of a man lay on the armrest, and saw Gunnery Sergeant Hartman marching his maggots through the barracks in T-shirts and boxers. Ray watched for a moment and wished he had time to watch the rest. Then he saw the VCR, with the word *PLAY* on its display—maybe he could see the rest?

He slid the .45 from his pocket and pointed it down over the bald man's head. It dangled like a frozen pendulum, its barrel eager. Private Pyle's mouth closed, and before he could begin the next refrain, Ray squeezed the trigger.

There was some smoke, a flash, and a bang, but the television kept going. Ray walked over to the VCR and tapped eject. The machine clunked and twittered, and the tape popped out of its mouth. Ray took the cassette and slid it into his hoodie packet, then headed for the stairs.

2

Wes Henson woke in his darkened room. For just a moment, he thought he saw a pale blue glow on the shelf, but as his eyes adjusted, it seemed to fade. Then he heard crying from the other side of the wall—Diana's room.

"Shit." He scooted to the edge of the bed, and he felt a tiredness that reminded him of the days after the accident when the anesthetic was still in his veins, and he felt more asleep than awake. He threw his legs over, hoisted himself onto his good leg, and hopped through the door.

Wes gazed into Di's room with a burning mix of sadness and rage. She held the hand the unicorn had ripped open. Jill sat beside her, hugging his sister as she wept.

The hand wasn't bleeding or flayed apart as Wes had expected when he hopped down the hall furiously. It was together, but with a thick red scar from the center of her palm to the webbing between her ring and middle finger, where the wound had occurred. Blood soaked her pajamas and half the bed. It took a few seconds, and then Wes understood. She had been wounded in the dream, but then she had been healed—the same must have happened to her sleeping body.

He shuddered as he thought about what could have happened if he didn't kill the unicorn. Di could have woken with a giant split in her hand. He saw his mother screaming, once again waking to blood and gore. Or, the unicorn could have stomped Di into a pulp. He saw his mother again, now in black, standing between two graves: his father's and his sister's.

302

Wes hopped to the bed and sat with the girls, placing his hand on Di's knee. She jumped toward him and wrapped her arms around him. She trembled and squeezed.

"Does... Does it hurt?" Wes hugged his sister back.

"Shit, yeah." Her words trembled with her body as they broke through the tears. She held her hand forward where they could all see it. The mounds of scar tissue made Wes think of a flesh-colored mountain range that traversed some alien world. She tried to close her hand and reached a quarter of the way before bursting with another wave of tears and burying her face in Wes's arm.

"Jesus," Wes said.

"Let me get something," Jill asked. She rose and paused at the door. "Aspirin?"

"Yeah," Wes said. "Kitchen cabinet, above the microwave. For some reason, Mom thinks we still can't get up there."

"Okay." Jill vanished from the doorway.

Several seconds passed, Wes holding, Di crying.

"Can we do this?" Di finally said. "Can we really kill that thing?"

"I'll do it." Wes glanced at the blood on the sheets and saw the thing charging at his sister. He felt the immeasurable weight of helplessness. "You should stay away from it."

Di pulled herself back from him. "Screw you."

"What?"

"I'm not some damsel you can tell to wait on the sideline. It killed my dad too."

"I just meant," he gestured at her hand, "it could have been a lot worse."

Tears welled in her eyes once again. Her face hardened. She held her hand in front of him, clenched her jaw, and started closing her fingers. The hand shook wildly. Her face flushed.

"Okay, okay, stop."

She reached two-thirds of a fist before she exhaled a gust and let her hand relax. "It can try to take all of me. It can try to kill me again. You aren't going to stop me from doing this."

"I'm sorry."

She hugged him again.

"We'll do it together. And, yes, we're going to kill that fucker."

Wes looked up and saw Jill in the doorway. Her eyes were down, her lips pressed together to hold in her words. In one hand, she had a cup of water. In the other was a box of Advil and a cold, wet rag.

3

Todd Hertz heard the crowd chanting. It was the same as last time. He wanted out, but there was no way. The walls were solid stone brick. The door behind him was thick wood, riveted with iron and hiding an army of guards. The door in front of him was where he would have to exit, and he dreaded what was out there.

He checked his armor, his gauntlets, his boots, all tight. They were dinged and scratched and stained with blood, but they would do. He heard the pounding from above, tens of thousands of feet slamming into the seats and aisles. Dust rained down on his head, and he picked up his helmet and slid it on.

A slice of daylight crashed into his face. The door was opening. He picked up his gladius and tightened his fingers around it.

"*Win, and be rewarded*," the whisper said.

"Like I have a choice," Todd mumbled to himself.

He was afraid, but just as the night before, he was filled with energy, a rush that pushed him forward from his tiny cell and out into the arena.

His feet crunched against the sand, and his gaze swept over the crowd. Thousands looked down on him, cheering, chanting, booing, screaming. He was on display, exposed and trapped, and though he would not have chosen it, he was freed. Freed from the constraints of what others thought. He had been freed of having to make any other choices—there was only one path and one choice: fight or die.

He was thirty feet into the arena when the other doors opened. Three on his right, three on his left, one behind him, a lion coming through each, collared and chained and swiping at the air, wishing they could reach him. Wishing they could taste his flesh. But they couldn't. The center was the only safe place on the battleground until the last door opened.

Through the door opposite his own, Todd watched the other gladiator emerge. Tall, strong, armored, it was Heath Williams. He wore an eagle crest on his chest plate. A small ax hung from each hand.

From somewhere in the crowd, the drums slowly began to beat. The sound was low, primal; it vibrated through Todd's chest like the throb of his own heart. It grew louder, deeper, faster, and the crowd of savage onlookers cheered, raised their arms, and shook their fists. He could taste the excitement in the air like a salty mist. It hung in front of him and called to him, tickled his insides, and sent tingles through his veins. It was time.

Todd began across the sandy floor. His sword hung low, his body swaying, his pace methodical.

Heath moved inward, his axes at his sides. He trotted, matching Todd's speed. The crowd on his side chanted his name; the opposite side repeated Todd's.

The hundred feet between them drew down to fifty, and their pace increased. It became a jog, a run, a sprint.

At twenty feet, Todd felt the ground vibrate with the voices of thousands. His hand tightened around his sword, and it became an extension of his arm. At ten feet, he held it back. At five, he rotated his chest, bringing it back further and preparing to swing.

Todd leaped. His sword was a blurred arc until it crashed against the blade of Heath's ax. Heath swung his other hand. Todd stepped back, the ax slicing the air an inch from his helmet. He pulled back his sword and lunged toward Heath's broad chest.

Heath slammed an ax down against the blade. The tip caught on a fold in Heath's armor, and the gladius snapped in half.

The crowd hushed.

Todd was breathless as half his blade tumbled to the ground. He took a step back, and one of Heath's axes collided with his arm. There was a crunch as blade met armor and a sting as his bicep tore. His entire arm went warm from blood and cold from shock simultaneously.

The crowd cheered.

Todd screamed and slammed the edge of his broken blade into Heath's helmet. It knocked Heath to the side and jerked the ax from his arm, and Todd swung again. He hit Heath's shoulder, and leather and blood sprinkled on the ground below.

The crowd shouted even louder.

Heath's axes swung from both of his sides. They met in Todd's chest, hacking into his ribs.

Blinding pain tore through Todd's insides. His sword fell from his hand, and his knees buckled under his weight. As he sunk, he felt the axes rip from his flesh.

Blood poured down Todd's sides. It bubbled up his throat and sprayed as he coughed.

Heath raised his axes, stared down, and prepared to take Todd's head. The crowd was deafening. Blood streamed along the dirt, and lions roared and snapped and stretched to reach it.

Todd swayed on his knees, gurgling blood and coughing with half-breaths. He looked into Heath's eyes and saw only savage anger. He saw a glint of midday sun on the blades poised to remove his skull and thought how short his life had been. He remembered his plans to rule the halls of Custer Falls High. He saw himself at the University of Montana, partying with his fraternity and banging drunken chicks from every sorority on campus. He was going to move to a bigger city, a bigger state, and rule the business world one day. But now, all of that was about to be taken away by his dumbass friend's axes. Maybe so, but he wasn't going to get away with it.

Todd pulled together every bit of strength and will and pushed it into his legs, into his arms. They ached—all of him ached—all of him wanted to lay down and rest. But not yet.

He thrust himself upward at Heath. He raised his arms wide.

Heath brought his axes down, missing Todd's neck but colliding with his back.

Todd felt white heat in his ribs, back, and sides and forced himself forward. He threw his arms around Heath's waist and locked his hands behind his friend in a bear hug.

Heath grunted as Todd lifted. Todd screamed. The crowd booed and cheered and shouted profanity in a language Todd didn't understand.

"Get off," Heath yelled.

Todd turned and marched to his left.

"What are you doing?" Heath shouted. He raised his axes and slammed them into Todd's back again.

Bone cracked, and meat tore. Blood painted Todd's rear red. It flowed down his armor, down his legs, across the sand, clumping it together in paths of crimson. He grunted and screamed through his teeth; he marched both gladiators toward snapping jaws.

Roars shook the crowd as they saw what Todd was doing, roars from the lions as food approached; Todd now heard none of it. The world beyond himself and his friend was nothing but white noise and echoes.

"Let me down!" Health buried his axes into Todd's arms. Blood sprayed in a ring around them. He saw a swipe from lion paws only a few feet away, and he raised and brought them down again.

Todd's grip waned, and he dropped to his knees. His right arm went limp and hung from his shoulder by a thread of stringy flesh. His left dangled with deep gashes, not bleeding so much, as Todd's blood was nearly gone.

Heath stumbled and fell. Todd fell on top of him.

Heath scrambled to get from under his opponent as a claw dug into his shoulder.

"No!" Heath was ripped from where he lay and felt a crunch on his helmet. His leg was a gleaming beacon of pain as another pair of teeth sunk into him. His helmet was ripped from his head, and Heath felt the humid air of the arena brush over his scalp. There was a breeze over his sweaty hair and cheeks before hot breath that smelled like decay closed in.

From the corner of his eye, Heath saw his helmet tumbling, and then he felt an enormous pinch of piercing heat on his neck. He saw a clawed paw grab Todd's shoulder and drag him away, then felt nothing at all.

4

"Help!" Nurse Emily Schroeder stared at the scratches on the boy's face. His sheets were coated in blood as she ripped them away. "Help in here!"

The senior nurse on duty rushed into Tommy Laskin's room and gasped, "How did this happen?" She ran to the drawers, grabbing gauze and bandages.

"I don't know—I was just checking in..." She stopped talking as she lifted Tommy's gown and looked over his chest and belly. It was red with blood, but there was no wound there. There were layers of thick scaring, strips where she could tell massive lacerations had been but were now healed in the most grotesque way. It made her dinner roll around in her belly and claw to come up.

"My God," the other nurse said.

2022

1

Officer Stuart Harrison's eyes were dry and tired. He'd reread *Aug-Oct, 1992* four times, and each time it all made a little more... and a little less sense.

They never found a reason for the cluster of comas. Each kid who woke said nearly the same thing: they were all trapped in a cave together, and it felt something like a nightmare recess. All in all, fifteen kids had died in the hospital with no apparent cause.

The bodies found in beds, supposedly sleeping, all over town were never explained adequately enough for his father. The county detectives on the case filed it all away as a traveling serial killer once it stopped, but that didn't sit with Dale. Stuart could understand why the more he read. The timing didn't make sense—too many of the deaths overlapped. The killer would have to have sprinted from house to house all over town. And for it to all have just started and stopped over the course of a week? With no continuation, no other bodies in other parts of the country to show the killer had relocated?

But the pages about Barton Smith chilled him the most. The ending of that case was one part of the book he wished he had been there to witness.

He flipped through once again, this time with focused eyes. He'd gotten so caught up in his father's words and living through them, he'd lost the point of his initial search: child killers.

As much as he thought there should be more—it seemed like this should have been a big deal—he only found one entry. The script was scratchier than the rest as if written hastily to get the idea down and be done with it. Had it affected his father that badly?

2

Oct. 3, 1992

We found the DiMarco boy's remains on the bottom of the pile. A pile containing four other children and three adults. Skin had been removed from DiMarco's skull, and although putrefaction had been the worst in his case—especially since lye had been poured heavily over the bodies—the medical examiner still believes it matches the scalp found in the Lawrence boy's shoebox.

The smell—and I don't know why I'm writing this, but it has to be said—the smell was like Hell. I know people talk about Hell being fire and brimstone and sulfur, but this rot... this scene of liquefying organs and skin dripping and muddling together from one corpse to another— the children included—it may have been the single worst thing I've ever encountered. If there is a Hell—and I have to believe that if Lawrence did this, he's going there—Hell has to be something like that basement.

The boy isn't very strong. He's small, in fact. Most have posited that he lured each of his victims into the basement and attacked them from behind, possibly above them on the steps. Blood stains on the concrete at the bottom of the stairs support this. Imagining it and seeing the pile, I have to think it was getting harder and harder for him to convince others to go down, unless he had some story about needing their help with the smell?

I put myself in their shoes, descending the old oak, the creaking, the stench, just trying to help a small boy—and then, the end. He's smaller than Stuart, for Christ's sake. I shouldn't say this here, but I know I'll have nightmares from this one.

Last I saw him, he was in a cell with coloring books. Rhonda, bless her—she thought he was sad, and the books may cheer him up. I don't have the heart to explain to her what we found here and what must be inside that kid.

3

After crossing the near-majestic acreage of the estate, Edward Lawrence pressed on the Parsons' front door. The smell of gunsmoke was faint. The smell of blood weighed more heavily. He flicked on the light, its plastic switch sliding smoothly along the silicone of his gloves.

The room was a masterpiece: beautiful furniture and beautiful death and destruction. He could trace the shots with his gaze, see the movements over time through the blood trails, and... it led upstairs.

"Come along." He gestured for Julie to follow and swung his bag as he walked.

She carried a large cup with only swallows of a chocolate shake remaining. She slurped through her straw as she trailed behind. As Ed climbed the stairs, she studied the corpse on the hardwood floor. The blood no longer ran, the pool now stagnant and sticky, and she felt a burning inside that, if she were older, she could have identified as jealousy. She examined the bloodied clothes and then the dark holes within them. It was still shiny in there. It was like a mysterious other world under those clothes, inside that skin—she wanted to see it, to know it.

The urge drew her empty hand to her pocket and around the base of her knife. She stepped closer to the late Mr. Parsons, mindful not to get the nasty stickiness of the floor on her pretty pink shoes, and she kneeled.

She checked his hazy eyes. They gazed across the room, and she wondered if that was where the lucky one who got to shoot him stood. She wanted to see what he saw. She wished she had been there.

She drew the knife from her pocket and pressed the tip of its blade into the white of Mr. Parsons' right eye. She pushed sideways. It didn't eject as she hoped. The steel only dug in and ripped, spilling slimy yellow goo with red streaks. She saw the inside of his eye and sighed. If she wanted an eye, she'd need to take a fresher one. This one was stuck.

"Julie." Ed was waiting patiently, halfway up the stairs. The whispers had said to hurry, and while he mostly listened, he thought the girl deserved a brief bit of exploratory time. He would have appreciated that at her age. But they needed to get to it. "This way." When she rose to follow, he continued up.

More fun waited on the second level. It was all over the dead woman's face at the end of the hall, an exquisite maw of agony. She clutched her weapon with a grip that appeared even death couldn't break, and Ed felt a twinge of admiration for her.

On the hallway floor, Ed squatted beside Norris Cushing. If the whispers hadn't told him, he would have assumed Norris was dead. He leaned in and listened to Norris's mouth. There was a low hiss of air moving in and out. He was alive; the whisper was right again. Now they had to move.

From the hallway, Ed could see a gas fireplace in the master bedroom behind the dead woman. He pointed to it and told the child, "Go in there and look for a button or switch by that fireplace."

Julie slurped her shake and danced through the door, around the dead Mrs. Parsons, and searched the area around the large brick hearth.

Ed put his bag on the floor and hooked his hands under Norris's armpits, then dragged him into the bedroom.

"Aha!" Julie sang as she found what looked like a light switch beside the mantle and flipped it up. Flames roared to life behind the glass window.

Ed dropped Norris beside the fire.

"Now what?" Julie asked.

"Now we need to plug up his holes."

"You mean like stitches?"

"No time for that." He glanced at Norris's oozing stump, then to the set of brass decorative fireside tools hanging beside the hearth. He lifted the shiny, never-been-used ash shovel. "This should work."

Ed looked around the room, and his eyes landed on the dead woman. He leaned over and grabbed her shotgun. He pulled, and for a good fifteen seconds, she refused to let it go. His admiration bloomed once again. *Death grip.*

He set the shovel beside Norris and glanced at the girl. "You may want to cover your ears." Once she did so, he pumped the shotgun and pointed it into the fire.

A boom shook the room. Glass erupted from the window that blocked the flames, and a hole led through the wall behind the bright tendrils' glow. They danced and intertwined, uncaring and unaffected by the passing of pellets above.

"Wow!" Julie shouted and sipped her drink. It was empty now, but she still got a drip here and there and that wonderful noise that her mother would always yell at her to stop.

Ed set the shovel inside the blaze and began looking Norris over. He sliced open the old man's shirt and found buckshot holes around his gut and another wound in his side. He couldn't stop the man from dying eventually, but he could stop this bleeding, he was pretty sure. At least, that was what he had been told to do.

He fetched his bag from the hallway and removed two syringes: a painkiller and an antibiotic. Both were meant for horses, but a begging slob of a dying old man couldn't be a chooser.

He plunged the needles one at a time into Norris's thigh, and as he finished, he saw the shovel glowing orange inside the flames.

"Come here." He pointed to Norri's stump. "Hold up his leg."

Julie set her drink down beside Mrs. Parsons and trotted over. "Like this?" She grabbed the sides of his calf and lifted. The gnarled and bloody thing was suspended a foot into the air.

"Just like that." He grabbed the shovel and swung it toward Norris. A trail of smoke and wavering air followed. He pressed the flat, orange underside of the tool against the bottom of Norris's stump.

It crackled and smoked. First, there was an aroma that reminded Ed of breakfast, sizzling bacon and sausage on his grandmother's stove, and for an instant, he missed her. Not her cruel pranks, which he had later in life decided were meant to teach him to be stronger, but the rare occasions when he saw in her eyes a love for him. He knew that love was never actually for him. She never loved him, being half his dad precluded that. The love, he decided, was for some long-lost memory she had of his mother, probably the only thing in the universe she ever actually loved. But on those few and far between times when he saw that glimmer in her eyes, he could pretend it was for him. And even though it was a lie, he missed it a little.

A few seconds passed, and the smell changed. It turned sour. Unlike cooked meat, it smelled like charred fat.

Ed pulled away the shovel. It stuck at first, clinging to fried bits of Norris. The wound was black, crispy, and wet looking, but it wasn't bleeding. He put the shovel back into the flames and reexamined Norris's belly. "Which one to do next?"

4

Wes and Di both jerked from their sleep with gasps, Wes in the bed by the door, Di in the one by the window. Virb stood on all fours beside Di, examining her, questioning her.

"It's okay." She scratched his cheek and then hissed.

"What?" Wes rolled to his side where he could see her. She was staring at her hand. The unicorn scar was bright red as if it had just happened.

"I forgot how bad that hurt." She traced the bumpy ridges of her palm with her fingertips. Virb licked the back of her hand.

Wes rose from the bed and peeked into the adjoining room. Sam and Lisa were fast asleep. He sat on the corner of his bed. "It happened again. Just like before. I'm not sure I get it. Why are we having that dream again? Why is it attacking us the same way?"

Diana pushed herself up against the headboard, and Virb rested his head on her lap. "I don't think we're having it again. I think there's more to it than that."

"What do you mean?"

"I mean... People still don't know what dreams are. I've done so much reading since getting out of the loony bin, and everyone has different ideas. Some scientists say they're just random neurons firing while you sleep, and your brain is trying to make sense of them. Some psychologists say they're your subconscious mind trying to sort through the events of the day and solve problems. Spiritualists say they're a peek into another plane."

"Wow. So no one knows shit. That's helpful."

"I think it is. I think it's a mix of all those things. Our brains, our thoughts, our spirits—but I think there's more. I think something happens in our dreams that's also outside the bounds of time."

"Time?" Wes sighed. "Where'd you get these books from?"

"Maybe not all dreams, but the ones we're having about this asshole. Think about it. This dream—my hand is hurt in the exact same place." She held up her scar. "It's not a new scar on top of the old one. It's the same one. Last night, the dream of Dad. It wasn't a memory of Dad, it was the same dream. The night before? The cats and dogs, and all that shit. It wasn't a copy; it was the same dream. I think... I think the dreams we're experiencing are like... somehow on a plane where past and future are the same place. When we enter that dream, I think we rejoin our old selves and go through it with them."

"That—it doesn't make any sense." He shook his head. "Like time travel?"

"Inside those dreams, don't you feel like you're young—the old you?

But you also feel like you've done it before?"

"Yeah. It's a recurring dream. That's how those work."

"But recurring dreams—falling from the sky, running from some unseen thing, whatever—those feel similar, but aren't always the same. Not like these. These are exactly the same."

Wes had to look away. Chills rolled over his flesh as her words sank in. Were these dreams *exactly* the same? He knew he didn't have to think about it, didn't have to evaluate the thought—he knew the answer was yes. But dreaming outside of time? Joining his younger self? That sounded like science fiction. It sounded like some hippy-dippy New Age crap he'd put in one of his books as a red herring and then twist the plot away from it at the last minute.

"So you think..." He had to pause and fully wrap his mind around the thought. "Tonight, we'll see..."

"Dinosaurs."

"And, Chris..."

"Yeah."

"Jesus Christ."

"Yeah."

"I don't know if I should be happy or cry." He lifted his leg and rubbed on his aching ankle.

"We got to see him tonight, though, right?"

"And Tommy." He smiled. "That was good."

Di stroked Virb's back and scooted back under her covers. "At least we know it won't be back tonight."

"You sure about that?"

"Last time we were safe until—"

"Until Bloodtooth."

5

Samantha and Lisa Henson floated. It was a strange sensation, not quite like one would float in space or float while hanging from a parachute and waiting to land—not that Sam or Lisa would recognize either of those feelings. But this floating reminded Sam of what she thought being a ghost must be like, only she could see herself and Lisa right beside her. She reached and took her sister's hand, and the room around them came into view.

The walls were curved, leading up to the ceiling, also curved, and around behind them, curved again, and down to a, yes, curved floor. It made Sam think that maybe they were inside some kind of giant egg.

The inside of the egg wasn't white, though; it was made of a glowing collage of images. As she scanned from image to image, she watched them move. They were like videos, windows into other places.

"Where are we?" Lisa said.

"I don't know." Sam squeezed her hand just slightly, verifying her grip on her sister.

"What are all these videos?"

"I don't know that either," Sam said. She tried to hold her eyes still on a single image. She saw her mother in it. "Mom?" She pointed.

Lisa followed Sam's gesture and found the same scene. Their mother was inside a dark cave, wandering around. She shouted at the picture, "Mom!"

Mom didn't hear and didn't respond. She just kept exploring her cave.

"Why is she doing that?" Lisa said. "What—I mean, *is* that her? No, I'm dreaming, right?"

"You? I'm dreaming. You're in my dream."

The sisters stared at each other, analyzing at first, and then pulled each other closer.

"If this is a dream, Mom could be doing anything," Sam said. "It doesn't matter because it isn't *really* her."

Lisa focused on her mother's face. It was dirty but determined, hard with a concentration she had never seen there. But it was a face she knew and loved in an unmistakable way. "That's Mom. I don't know what's happening to either of us, but that's her."

In another of what both girls had decided were video windows, Lisa watched a man in an army uniform hike through the jungle.

Sam watched two men fight in a Roman arena. When blood gushed from both sides of one's ribs, she turned away. Her eyes landed on a scene much like her mother's, though this cave held dozens of children.

Lisa watched a boy cram a flute down an old man's throat and covered her eyes. She turned to her sister. "I don't like this, Sam."

"Yeah. Me neither."

"How do we get out of here?"

"I don't know." Sam saw a video of a small boy playing in his backyard.

It was nicer than so many others, without fighting or blood or gore. She reached out to feel the screen—maybe there was a wall behind it, a way out somehow.

She floated toward the boy in his backyard, and Lisa drifted with her. She touched the image, and where she expected to feel a glass or plastic surface, she felt liquid. It was cool and thin, lighter than water. Her finger caused a ripple over the boy and a swing he sat on. As she watched the ripples flow, she expected them to stop at the edge of the scene. They didn't. They continued from one scene to another, warping the images from window to window to window.

"What is that?" Lisa said.

Sam said nothing. Her thoughts consumed her. If it was all water, did that mean they were in some kind of bubble? Were they surrounded by a pool, a tank, or a sea? If they floated up, could they swim through it and get to the surface? How far might the surface be, and could they hold their breaths that long if there was no air beyond the wall of images?

"If we want out, we have to go through there," Sam said. "But I don't know if it's safe."

"Then, maybe we try, and if it gets scary, we come back?"

Sam smirked. She hadn't even thought of coming back. Maybe that would work? "Okay. But I'll go through first to see what it's like. And if I squeeze your hand really hard, you pull me back. Deal?"

"Deal." Lisa shook the hand that joined them.

"Okay." She looked at the video of the boy. She was already at the edge of his video; it was as good a place as any to go through, and they could swim up from there. "Don't let go of me."

Lisa nodded forcefully, dropping her chin all the way to her chest and back up.

Sam reached for the wall again and watched the waves ripple as her fingertips breached the surface of the image. She willed herself further into the wall, and a strange thing happened: her fingers went through a plane of liquid and out into what felt like air. The wall was a bubble, after all, but not a bubble under water; it was more like a bubble floating in air, in between the video worlds. She pressed onward, her hand, her arm, her shoulder breaching the barrier. The air was warm on the other side. She felt the rays of the sun on her skin, and the boy in the video turned and looked at her.

She wasn't sure what struck her the most, whether it was the dullness of his eyes, the flatness of his expression, or the eagerness in the smile that enveloped his face, but Sam was overcome with repulsion. She began pulling herself back from the video wall, and he jumped after her.

"No!" She jerked her hand away, but her floating would only back up so fast.

The boy grabbed her hand with both of his and pulled.

"No, no, no," She pulled back. But she didn't seem to be moving, either in or out. She was frozen between the two worlds.

"What?" Then Lisa looked at the video. She saw Sam's hand inside and the boy... he was dragging her in.

"Pull me back," Sam cried.

Lisa took her sister in both hands. She willed herself backward and felt it work. It was slow, but she and Sam moved toward the center of the rounded room.

"It's working!" Sam shouted, stretched between both worlds.

She studied the boy. She wondered: *Why does he want me?* She watched the anger on his face as she was dragged out of his world. His mouth spread, baring teeth that ground into each other.

"No!" the boy shouted. "You're mine!"

"Keep pulling!" Sam screamed.

Lisa did. Sam did. The boy did. He jumped and yanked.

Sam felt the warm rays fade from her skin. They retreated past her elbow, down her forearm. Hope bloomed in Sam's mind, even while she watched the boy get madder and madder, his face glowing red. She was going to do it. She was going to get her hand back and...

Sam watched in terror as the boy opened his mouth. Her hand was just a palm and fingers in his world, and as his lips spread, a mouth full of shark-like fangs emerged.

He lunged upward, releasing her hand, and his teeth clamping down on Sam's fingers.

Sam howled. Blood coated the boy's grinning face, and she and Lisa flew backward. She looked down at her hand and found herself screaming in her Maryville Manor bed.

Lisa jerked awake beside her, and they screamed together, staring at Sam's bloody hand. Her first three fingers were thoroughly gnawed away above the first knuckle, and cracked bone and jagged flesh dripped red.

1992

1

By three in the morning, Officer Dale Harrison had watched a pair of nurses, a doctor, and a defibrillator cart race in and out of four different rooms. Six kids had been pronounced dead, and each time he saw that cart move, his heart jumped and pounded like a drum until he saw they weren't setting up shop in front of Gina's bed.

It was the worst thing he'd ever have to admit. He was glad another kid died instead of his own. Because at this point, he thought they would eventually come for her. It was only a matter of time. And he had never felt so helpless in his entire life.

What was he supposed to do about this? It was like when she was three and choked at the table at Country Kitchen. He knew she needed help. He pulled her from her chair, and Carol pressed on her belly, and goddamn, all he could do was pray it would work. He'd had the training, but his goddamn hands were too big to reach inside her tiny throat and pull out whatever minuscule thing was standing between her life and her death. So he walked through the steps, a raging maniac inside, the calm demeanor he'd learned to show the public during a crisis on the outside. And *POP*, out it came. A pea. A vegetable smaller than his tiniest toenail—that was the pendulum that swung between her life and death and chose her fate. But that had only lasted thirty seconds. It may have felt like a lifetime, but it was only thirty seconds. This had been going on for hours.

Harrison clenched his trembling fists. There was absolutely nothing he could do here, and he wanted to run. He wanted to go ahead and get to work, a place where he could control things. He might not have solved the cases at his feet yet, but it was something he could do. There were steps he could take. But Gina was here. Carol was here. And even if there was nothing he could do here, Carol wouldn't understand if he left. He'd have to wait another hour. He'd have to wait until he could reasonably lie and say his shift was starting.

The nurse's phone rang, and Emily Schroeder called in a soft voice. She must have been trying not to wake patients, or more realistically, the fifty-plus parents asleep in their rooms. "Officer?"

Harrison watched her sweet smile. It was fake; he knew it. She'd probably helped pronounce more kids dead tonight than she had in her previous years on this job combined. But she tried. He wasn't sure if it was for his sake or hers, but she tried.

"It's your station."

Harrison took the phone and nodded. "Yeah..."

"Dale," it was Rhonda, "Barry's dead."

2

Charlotte Baker opened her eyes to the gloom-filled room she'd been tossed into. As she lay, she brought her arms and knees to her chest. It wasn't just a dream, after all. She was really here, really trapped, trapped with a dead girl that told her just by existing that sooner or later, Charlotte would be next.

The lock rattled, and the doorknob creaked. He was coming. Fucking Jesus Christ, he was coming. Charlotte closed her eyes and froze. She felt blood rushing through her veins, her heart working overtime, her lungs demanding more air. It was time. Time to fight.

She heard Mom's voice inside her head, complete with the faint southern drawl she'd brought up from Georgia fifteen years ago and worked to lose ever since: "If you're ever taken, you need to be ready to fight, girl—you need to scratch and poke and claw—you need to use every ounce of strength to kill, or you might never make it home to me again."

Charlotte knew her mom was right. She could practically feel the death in the corner, the direction she had refused to look since she first saw it over there. That girl would be her if she didn't fight. It still might be her if she did fight, but at least she'd have a better chance—right?

The door whined as it opened slowly.

Why was it so slow? The man thought she was asleep. That's why. He was planning to come in here and kill her as she slept—or worse. God, what did he want from her?

She knew. She knew too well, as much as she wanted to deny it. She'd seen men glancing at her in ways that gave her chills since she was nine. She may not have gotten her boobs yet, but she knew men wanted more than that, and as much as she wished to ignore it, her mother's words again rang: "Always listen to your gut, not their words." Had she not listened in the mall? Had she avoided looking at that other poor girl's body just because she knew what she'd find over there?

Now the floor was squeaking. He was inside the room. He was getting closer. Her chest pounded. Her lungs demanded more air, and she denied them. She breathed slow, kept still.

"If you're ever taken, you need to be ready to fight, girl," the words repeated, "ready to fight…"

She clenched her fists and flexed her knees. He'd come and touch her, and she'd be ready. She'd swing and hit him where it counts. If he was close to her legs, she'd shoot them out and cause him the real pain of being a man. Inside her mind, she saw her fingernails ripping his skin. She saw herself blowing up like a nuclear warhead and punching, scratching, screaming, tearing. Just wait. As soon as he touched her…

The squeak was on the other side of her now. It was moving away. It was moving toward that other girl.

Charlotte's hands shook. What was happening? He was going to attack her, she knew it, but when? She let her eyes open a crack and saw the door. It was wide open. There was light in the hall, soft light that showed wood framing against a cinderblock wall. That was the way out. That was her way out. Maybe this was her chance to get away. She should jump up and go, sprint to the door, swing it shut, lock it. She could run.

Fear cascaded over her arms, her fingers loosening their fists.

What if she failed?

What if she got up and ran, and he grabbed her? She wouldn't have been ready to punch and kick. What if he was watching her right now? Maybe he didn't plan to hurt her, but if she ran, she could provoke him.

The floor squeak returned. It was coming back toward her now.

She clamped her eyes shut. She held every muscle still.

What was he doing? What did he want? Was he going to grab her and kill her now?

You need to be ready to fight, girl. But she wasn't. She wanted to be. But now he was coming back. He was going to grab her, and knowing it was coming, she fell limp. She was unable to move as much as her fingers. What was Mom going to say after she heard her daughter did nothing—didn't fight like she was supposed to. She saw her mother's crying face. She wore a billowing black dress on the side of a grave and mouthed the word: *Why.*

The floor creaked between Charlotte and the door, and again, closer to the door. He was going. He was going! Her entire body filled with elation. He was leaving, and she was okay—better, she didn't have to fight. The door clicked shut, and a wave of relief washed over her.

She jerked around to the other side of the room. The body was gone. He was there to get the body, not to kill her.

The door clicked again, the lock, and a wave of sadness followed. The cold grip of shame shook her insides. She had wasted her chance. She could have gotten up and run while he was on the other side of her. She could have escaped. And she didn't. And now, her death would be her own fault.

3

Red and blue strobes raced in circles around the Madison Street Wesker Pump. Sgt. Padilla from Custer Falls County and Rolland Morrow, the usual CFPD graveyard shift officer, gazed down on Barry Johnson as Officer Dale Harrison arrived.

Rain patted against his face as he shut his door and approached. The usual stupid questions ran amuck in his brain, the same ones that always came when unanswerable things happened in the world. Why did Mom have a heart attack? Why did Dad get into his pickup drunk and drive off the cliff into the quarry? Why did an earthquake happen? Why anything—it was just life. And other than the precious moments he spent with Stuart, Gina, and Carol, none of it made any sense.

Puddles circled Johnson, and under the rain, the black asphalt and the dark of night, Harrison was unable to tell how much of their contents was water and how much was blood. He faced up, drop after drop smacking his eyes and running down his temples and into his hair. Harrison knew the man wasn't crying, something he could never do again, but each drop that streamed down Johnson's face felt like another twist in his stomach after a night of gut-wrenching deaths.

"Jesus, can we cover him up?" Harrison asked Padilla.

"Not yet. Waiting on the crime scene guys."

"Yeah, yeah." Of course, the CSI guys would bitch. "Any idea what happened?"

Rhonda had told him that Johnson had stopped to investigate a vehicle, but he never radioed back after that. Padilla's resume had him working on murders all over the county and in Denver before that, so Harrison expected the guy to see more in this scene than himself. It turned out he was wrong. The county cop pointed out where he thought the car was that Johnson was investigating and that the shooter had to have had his own piece, but he couldn't tell much more. Too wet, too dark, too isolated for witnesses.

Harrison shook his head. It was getting worse. Kids in comas dying, another kid missing. It was like death itself had come to town. It made him think of the Pied Piper, only this musician was calling people to their deaths.

"When will it end?" Harrison muttered.

"When we catch the son of a bitch," Padilla said.

Harrison wasn't so sure they could. The way it spread seemed to affect so many different people and ages in town. There was no common factor, no link. It seemed to spread more like a virus than a flesh and blood killer. But how do you say that to another cop? How do you tell someone whose job it is to examine evidence that you think something other than a human was murdering people in your town?

The thought occurred to him with a jolt. Was he actually thinking something other than a maniac was at work in his town? Something that could steal kids, put others in comas, kill men, women, and kids in their sleep? He wasn't a religious man in the slightest, but the things he'd seen in the past ninety-six hours or so had gotten him wondering if something spiritual may be behind this—something evil.

He looked Padilla in the eye. "What about the others? Turn up any leads on those yet?"

Padilla's bottom lip firmed against his top. He squinted angrily as if Harrison had insulted his wife. "No. Half of their homes were sealed shut. The other half, we're told, practically lived with unlocked doors. We're looking into family and friends of the victims, but the most we've been able to link together is that three-quarters of them shopped at *Dan-O's* for their groceries."

"Like three-quarters of the town."

"Yeah. So, not much. I heard you have a few missing kids—any luck with those?" Padilla knew how to stick it right back. He already knew the answer.

"Johnson was working on those. We were going to do some interviews at the school today. I guess I'll be handling those solo."

"Good luck."

"You too." Harrison turned toward his cruiser. "I guess I'm off to let his brother know."

Padilla just nodded, and Harrison headed back to Memorial to catch Dr. Johnson before he started on his rounds.

4

Ray Trent pulled Amanda Brolin's minivan up to the cabin. There was barely a peep from the back seat up until he killed the engine. Then he could hear each heaving breath from Misty's nose. Why was she so loud? It wasn't attractive at all.

He glanced into the backseat and studied her. The duct tape on her mouth was still firm. The layers around her wrists, hands, and ankles were bunched up over her joints but still tight. Pride enveloped him. He'd done it. He'd brought her here.

Ray got out and walked to the side door. It swung open with a squeal, and he silently cursed Amanda for not taking better care of the vehicle.

Misty stared at Ray with wide eyes. She said something, though all he heard were muffled consonants.

He raised the .45 from his pocket and showed it to her. "I'm going to undo your feet because I don't want to carry you. I'm trusting you to control yourself."

Her eyes froze on the gun. She made a muffled noise and then nodded.

"Okay." He slid the piece back into his hoodie pocket and took the knife from his belt. He locked eyes with Misty as he leaned in and placed the blade between her ankles, underneath the tape. He flicked it upward. She flinched to her right and gulped, then squealed as Ray ripped the tape from her feet.

The skin on her ankles was red but smooth. He ran his fingers over one foot and calf, then the other. She slowly pulled her feet toward herself, and he stopped. Not because he cared if she liked it or not, but because it would be easier if she walked inside on her own than if he had to fight with her. He'd get all the touching he wanted once he had her inside.

"Come on." He stood and pointed to the cabin with the knife.

She glanced through the windshield but didn't move.

Ray watched and smirked. He wondered if she knew she probably wouldn't leave the cabin alive—not unless she cooperated.

"Let's go," he insisted.

Misty planted her feet on the vehicle floor and scooted toward the door. She reached the edge and stared at the cabin.

Ray could see the thoughts inside her head. *She knows this is where I brought her sister. She thinks I killed her in there.* "You need to move." He flicked the knife upward.

She said something. Muffled and soft.

"I won't tell you again." He pointed the blade at her. "You need to follow directions."

Misty stretched a bare foot from the vehicle and placed it on the pine needle-covered ground. She stood, and her face twinged as needles stabbed into her soft soles.

"Now, in." He gestured at the cabin.

Misty took a step toward the log building, then sprinted to the right. Her bare feet pounded on raw earth, broken twigs, and blankets of pine needles.

"Mother-fuck," Ray shook his head and ran after her.

Misty screamed through her gag. She reached for the tape on her mouth and scraped at it through tape-bound fingers, finding no grip. She howled into the black forest, desperate to be heard.

Ray followed, anger building inside his chest. His grip on the knife tightened. "You can't get away! There's nowhere to go, sweetheart!"

She kept running, dodging under branches, yipping at the pain in her feet every few steps. Shots echoed in her mind. First, the one that woke her, the one that made her sit up in bed, wondering if someone was doing old Fourth of July fireworks out in the street. She didn't put together what that sound had been until Ray left her bound by the front door while he went for the minivan, and she was forced to stare at the blood on the couch and the top of Dad's head peeking from behind the cushion. Forced to watch the blood pool under the sofa as tears streamed from her eyes.

Then there was the second shot. She'd just opened her bedroom door on her way for a sip of water after the noise. She jerked toward it, toward Mom and Dad's room, when she saw the flash from the third shot through the crack in their bedroom door. It lit up his face, lit up his maniacal smile, and she ran.

"This is the forest, Misty! No one for miles!" he screamed. Then, to prove his point, he howled at the sky like some rabid wolf.

Misty's heart pounded. Air raced through her nose, and her nostrils felt smaller and smaller the more air she forced through them. Her head was getting heavy, and her lungs burned.

She couldn't believe a word he said. He had to be trying to trick her. If she stopped, she was dead. She knew that as much as she knew her feet were bleeding.

Misty made it two more paces and felt a blinding pain in the back of her head. One foot caught on another, and she saw the ground flying at her. She covered her face with her hands and crashed into the forest floor.

A stick jabbed into Misty's gut as something heavy thumped down onto her back and smashed her into the ground. A muffled grunt escaped her gag, and tears ran from her eyes like rivers.

This was it. She was caught. She felt pressure on her sides: Ray's legs. The creepy bastard that had been stalking her for years had finally gotten her. He'd taken her sister—how else could he have gotten her van—and now he was going to rape and kill her just like he must have done to Amanda. Poor Amanda. The tears hit the ground and muddied the earth. Snot filled her nose and blocked her breath. She tried grabbing at the tape on her mouth again. Another sharp pain rocked her skull.

5

Tommy Laskin floated in the void between dreams. It swayed from black to white to any color of the spectrum as his thoughts shifted and changed direction. He wondered about the thing, the monster, the fairy, and tried to understand what it had said. While he did that, he felt the sensation of something moving along his stomach.

The thing had promised to help him. That was the strange part. It said he could wake up and live a life—not even a normal one, a magnificent one. It was the strange type of promise that seemed too good to be true but so convincing it had to be.

Why would it send the fairy, attack his friends, attack him again, scare the ever-loving shit out of him?

Did he answer it? He couldn't remember. He couldn't imagine he had said yes, but the idea of waking seemed so wonderful while as distant as the surface of the moon to a drifting astronaut.

He wanted to hold things again with his real hands. He wanted to feel the real touch of another person. He wanted to taste food in his mouth. He wanted to see his mother with his actual eyes.

The ether around his presence illuminated with a dark blue light, and he was overwhelmed with a pressure that told him it was time to move. It was something that had been happening whenever a dream was near, like a pat on the back pushing you toward something, only here, it was more like a swelling of the universe that pressed you forward. He thought of it like being swallowed and shot into the next phase of his existence.

The blue fog of one reality faded, and the endless night of another snapped into place.

It was the stars. Tommy floated past planets and imagined himself not flying in a ship but being one. He saw glowing worlds with rings and nebulae with rainbows of colors and spinning black holes that belched cosmic rays, and the more he drifted, the more the question pressed on his mind: had he answered the man—the thing?

The universe around Tommy slowed, and he wondered about the thing. It was a demon, he was fairly sure of that. It was preying on the souls that slept, the ones locked in that cave—that *it* must have locked in that cave. But what was it really? Where had it come from?

He thought back to the first dream where he felt it. The barbarian that killed mercilessly in his village. His vision shifted from the beautiful stars and exoplanets back to Earth, to what felt like a thousand years ago.

There was Conan. He raged. He swung an ax, a hammer, a sword, one after the other, whatever he could get his hands on, and he ripped each man and woman inside that building to bloody shreds of flesh and bone. His eyes were inhuman. His hunger for flesh was unrelenting and unaffected by the cuts and punches and kicks, the stabs and loss of blood; nothing seemed to slow his rage.

When he was done, a roaring fire in the center of the village hall reflected on his bloody skin. But the hunger was still in his eyes. Bones stabbed through flesh and dripped to the floor. Eyes hung from skulls. Teeth littered the floor as if spilled from a bowl. And Conan panted as he gazed around the room, unfulfilled.

Tommy stared into those eyes, and he knew the thing was in there somewhere. Had it been in Conan's dreams? Could dreams push a man to this type of madness? There had to be more. There had to be something else to this demon.

It was almost without thought. A movement on a whim. Tommy found himself diving inside the barbarian, into the man's mind.

It was a bleak world. It was a place where starvation and sickness kept the weak powerless and made the strong brutal. He saw that Conan was actually named Snarre. He was loved by his mother until she died when he was nine. He was loved by his wife until she died delivering his child. He was a hunter for the village and a valued warrior when his home was attacked by the kingdom to the south or the bandits from the east. His life had been hard, but he had managed until a few days ago.

For Snarre, it had started in a dream. He was on a hunt in the wilderness to the west. It was a day with a dusting of snow which led to bore tracks and ruts in the tall grasses by a stream. But the trail ended there. As night threatened, he had decided to camp inside the bush, far enough from the trail to hear but not be seen or smelled by any roaming bears or packs of wolves who may be following the bores.

His fire was down to embers, and as his dream began, the embers remained. He looked up at Loki's Torch in the sky as it shone for the Hellewagen and brightened the path for the Eagle and Dain. And then they faded as his ash turned from red to black.

The brush crunched with hooves and horns. He heard the snort of breath through snouts. He heard a growl and claws digging into the earth, and his heart raced.

Snarre jumped to his feet and held his back against a wide oak. Steps neared, the forest darkened, and he realized his blades and spear were on the other side of the fire.

Snarre knew this was the end. He thought of his wife, her closed eyes and the curl of her lips when he was inside her. If this was his death, he would meet her in Hel and be grateful for their embrace.

All light faded from the camp, and Snarre felt himself jerked forward. Something wrapped its giant hands around his head and dangled him above the ground.

A single torch lit in front of him. He felt the hard, sharp claws of his captor pressed against his head. Hot breath scented like rot blew into his face, and then it showed itself.

A face of oozing gray flesh, half man but with a beak and dragon spires on the sides of its head, thrust itself inches from Snarre's. A black tongue darted from inside the beak and tasted Snarre from his face to his chest. The appendage split and slid around his legs. The tongue recoiled into its face, and he was left dripping with slime that smelled of fish rot and vomit.

"End it, demon!" Snarre shouted. "Kill me and be done!"

Its claws pinched harder around his head. Blood dribbled down his neck, and his ears screamed. Only a bit more pressure, and his head would pop like a tiny berry in the fingers of a giant.

"Not yet," it whispered inside a growl. Its other hand shot from the darkness. It was closed, other than a single extended claw that tapped on Snarre's chest and split his skin apart.

He could see his ribs and the meat around them, and a line of worms crawled along the giant's claw and dug their way into his chest. They burned as if they were flames. They wriggled and dove deeper, and he flexed and writhed but could do nothing as he felt them squirm inside him.

Snarre howled, and Tommy knew, this was when it found its way inside him. And just as before, this was when Tommy moved without thinking, diving into the head of the giant monstrosity.

Tommy found himself outside of Snarre's dream, hovering over another who sat on the barbarian's chest with his claws in the sides of Snarre's head. The black tips of the monster's fingers twisted and swayed inside the man's flesh as if they were playing a harp. Its gray face hovered over Snarre's, wrinkled and deformed, like an old man who had melted and been stretched by the hands of gods, or demons.

Tommy saw its thoughts. He didn't understand the words, but images came in waves. It was a sleep demon. It had been doing its job for a thousand years on Earth, longer before that, but now it had decided it wanted more. It had sat on thousands of men and women as they slept and seen their fears—and fulfilled them—but it was no longer enough. It wanted to drive them in the waking world. It wanted to feel the power of not just the unconscious but their waking fears, their waking nightmare as well.

Tommy felt himself move. He was shaking, trembling. It wasn't just inside the dream either—he felt through the veil of the dreamworld that someone was moving his body. Chills ran over his flesh. Fear wrapped him from his fingers and toes to his chest and his heart. He watched the demon; here, its name was Marenor, and it turned to him and smiled. Its fingers continued to play inside Snarre, but its black drooling fangs opened for Tommy.

2022

1

Wes Henson carried Sam in his arms through the Emergency Room door. They dripped with rain, and her face ran with tears. Her shirt, as well as her father's, was blotted in blood. Her hand was wrapped in a once-white towel monogrammed *MM* for the Maryville Manor.

"Help!" Wes shouted as he approached the vacant reception desk. "Please, help!"

A gray-haired woman peeked through thick glasses from a room behind the desk. Her eyes widened, and she rushed out.

"Yes, yes. What happened?" She plopped down into her chair and banged on the keyboard, trying to log in quickly. Her digits stumbled, and she tried again.

"Her fingers—she needs help."

The old woman called into the back room, "Suzy, get out here." Her fingers slowed down and tapped at the keys, and the system allowed her entry. "Sir, has she ever been here before? I need her name and date of birth."

Wes was dumbfounded. His daughter was bleeding in his arms, and this woman wanted a name and birthday? He knew this would be the case, that they wouldn't see her without checking in, but at this moment, his weeping daughter in hand, it felt like the most asinine thing he could imagine. He held his rage, restrained his urges to jitters of the foot and fingers, and provided the receptionist the info she asked for.

They were almost through when a nurse burst from the door to the left with a wheelchair. She looked Sam over, her face tensing. "Let me have her. I can get started while you finish checking in."

2

Diana Henson sat with her back against the headboard and Lisa's head resting in her lap. She ran her fingers through the girl's hair and wondered if she had fallen asleep. Di wouldn't blame her if she didn't sleep again for the rest of this week after what had happened to her sister. If it weren't for the fact that she had never seen Marenor come more than once in a night, she would have fought to keep the child awake.

"Where did that come from?" she whispered to herself. She hadn't thought of its name in ages—she had actively tried to keep it away from her thoughts—and then she remembered the creatures that would come tonight.

Virb whimpered softly from the edge of the bed. He had been facing away, but his eyes fell on Di, then darted forward.

He feels it, she thought. She gazed at him with loving admiration. He would join them if he could, and give his life to save them. But she couldn't call him in like they could the others. And as much as she knew she would want his companionship, she didn't want him to be there. Because she knew he *would* give his life.

He was too good for her.

Her fingers brushed through Lisa's hair, and a cold wash of sorrow rushed over her. This poor kid. This poor family. Dad (his blood on that bed), and years later, Mom. They may have called it cancer, but it was the demon. Jill in a coma, Sam and her fingers, and it could be Lisa's name on the list soon. Was it the demon's intent to wipe out her entire family? If Lisa had shared the dream with Sam, it was after her as well. Di had no doubt.

"So many," she whispered. Tears escaped the corners of her eyes, but as they ran down her face, her gaze met Virb, and her thoughts shifted.

He had turned and was looking straight back into her. His stare was firm, the way he watched when she challenged him, when they trained in the woods. He wanted to please her, to protect her; it was his job. The look rocked Di's insides, the confidence, the love.

What did he know? What was he ready for? She realized then, if he was ready, she had to be as well. And maybe they could end this first, before anyone else died.

Her blood boiled with an anxious want. She needed to go and get the stone. She needed to have the damn sphere in her hands. If they could solve this today, maybe she wouldn't see the creatures tonight. Maybe they could put Marenor back in his place before it could hurt anyone else—hopefully this time for more than thirty years.

Di looked at her niece and shook her head. She had to wait for now. But she would get that stone today.

3

By the time Wes had finished Sam's paperwork, she had been rushed into surgery. Instead of sleeping in her bed at home, she had been in a hotel room because of a madman and a psycho child. Instead of resting easily with her sister, she was now getting the ends of her dismembered fingers sewn up in an operating room because of an insane demon. And at this moment—blood soaked through his T-shirt, with only himself in the waiting room, no Jill, no Di, no friends—his insides were so filled with hate that he wanted to scream.

His thoughts went to his basement. The name Ed rang in his mind. That asshole. That sadistic piece of shit. By the time this was over, he was going to find him. And that lie of a little girl? Little girls were sweet and kind, thoughtful and caring—he knew this, he had two of them. But this one was a profane abomination. If the police didn't find her, he would, and he'd hand-deliver her right onto the cops' doorstep.

The cops? he thought. *A goddamn joke.* Where were they? What had they done to help find Ed and the girl, the people who started this all?

A cold streak walked down Wes's back. "Had those two started this all?" he muttered to himself. His mind went back to the dreams, to thirty years ago, to Ray Trent and Barton Smith. Those were real people affected by the demon. They had been its puppets. Not that they weren't pieces of shit before the demon came along, but... was the demon pulling Ed's strings? That little girl's?

It struck Wes that he had been dropped into a chess game where all the pieces were already in play, and he was shivering with shame for having missed it.

They were. Ed and the girl, they were sent by that monster. It had sent them to attack him and Jill. It had put her in a coma like those kids thirty years ago. It had somehow invited Sam into that fucking dream. But why?

Why did it attack them and not him?

Wes looked around the room with a distinct feeling that someone was watching him. The demon wanted him to do something, was trying to get something from him.

Wes's jaw dropped, and he felt himself turn white. This was about the stone.

1992

1

The sun rose, and Wes, Di, and Jill sat on his bed, watching streaks of daylight break through shades and creep across the wall. They crossed the abnormal stone that his mother had placed on his shelf, and it cast a blinding glare back into Wes's eyes.

He blinked and blocked the light, then shifted in his seat. "What the hell is that?" He pointed.

Jill looked.

Di looked.

"Mom said it was in my stuff after I came home. I don't remember picking it up."

Jill's head cocked to the left. She leaned forward and crawled across the bed, then grabbed the stone. "It's cold." She crawled back and showed it to Wes.

At first, it just looked like any other stone, only odd because it was nearly perfectly round. But the longer she held it, the longer they stared, the more it seemed to reveal itself. Small lines threw shadows across its surface, detailing marks that may have been some strange language. Faint drawings circled the rock, but without enough depth of definition to make out what they were.

"Huh," Jill said. She rolled it from one hand to the other. "It makes my hand feel funny. You know—They said you were out of it when they pulled you from that cave. Maybe you put it in your pocket without realizing it?" She slid it back into the other hand, numbness rising and hope sinking.

Wes took the rock from her and instantly lost some feeling in his hand.

A faint blue light flashed around the room, and he blinked repeatedly, trying to shoo it away.

"What are you doing?" Di asked.

"That light."

"What light?" Jill said.

"You didn't see that light?"

The girls shook their heads, no.

"It was—" the memory slammed him like a thump in the gut. "There was a blue light in the cave, after I fell and Chris was trying to help Tommy. I thought it was someone trying to rescue us, and I went after it. The flash just now—it was the same as that light." He looked at the stone. "It was this."

A freezing sensation crawled up his body. It felt like a thousand frozen centipedes with a million frozen legs, walking up his skin, crawling toward his head. It drove a monument of dread into his flesh, a beacon of bad that was unrelenting and on the way, ready to put to shame all the horrors he had known so far.

Wes turned his hand and let the stone ball drop into his lap.

"What happened?" Di said. "You're white."

He was. All the color had drained from his face.

"Wes?" Jill touched his leg. "Are you okay?"

Di reached to pick up the stone.

"Don't." Wes seized her wrist.

She shot him an angry gaze, then stopped and looked at the rock.

"That's it," Wes said. "That's the cause of all of this."

"How do you know?" Di said.

"I—I just do. Everything that's wrong with us, with our dreams... It's coming from that thing."

They stared at the rock together. Di looked at the scar on her hand, Jill at Wes's leg.

"We should get rid of it," Di said. "If that's where this thing is coming from."

"I don't think that's enough," Jill said. Her thoughts went to what Chris had said about Stony. "This whole town's being turned upside down. The rest of the people dying, those kids in comas—they're nowhere near that rock. I mean, how far would we need to take it to get rid of it?"

Wes took a deep breath. "I think it has to go back."

"Back to the caverns?" Di asked.

Jill shook her head. "It can't. It was in the newspaper. The caverns' entrance collapsed. You can't get in there."

Wes leaned back on his pillow. The walls of his room felt too close, like they were closing in on him. "Then it's only a matter of time before it gets us."

2

Chris Conners looked through his cabinets until settling on the box of Honeycomb cereal and taking it to the table. He sat and put the box in his lap, reached in, and unrolled the inner bag. Then, he grabbed a handful and shoved it into his mouth.

"Hey," it was Mom, coming into the kitchen from the rear mudroom/laundry room. "How about a bowl and some milk?" Her face was thinner, more so than it seemed even yesterday. The bones on her cheeks stood out like stone forms guarding her sunken eyes. She was wearing the blue scarf over her bald head today. It was the one she thought brought out her eyes. It was the one that bothered Chris the most because when her eyes shone, the rest of her face looked even more like death.

Chris held up his cast and pushed the food to one side of his mouth. "It's easier this way."

Mom frowned. The expression made her look more foreign to Chris than he'd admit. She paused at the kitchen counter and regarded the dozen-plus bottles of beer Dad had left behind, and she opened the cabinet. She brought Chris a bowl, a spoon, and the half-gallon jug of milk from the fridge.

He managed a smile and started making his cereal, and Mom cleared off the counter, trying to set the bottles in the trash gently enough to not wake the dead (or the Dad). Chris watched her, his heart sinking deeper into his gut by the second, and the queen returned to his thoughts.

She had said she could make Mom well. But that was just a dream. It was as silly as thinking that she could give him Charlotte.

He was overcome with the urge to find Charlotte when he got to school today. He had wanted to yesterday, and it didn't work out; and after two dreams where she was in danger, the thought sharpened. He needed to prove it wrong. He'd go to school and find her, and she would be just fine. That would prove that it was all his dumb imagination—seeing her through the mirror, the fight with that knight, the queen. She couldn't really help his mom—that was him wishing—it was the part of his brain that already accepted that Mom was dead, and it was looking for a way out.

A flash of hate raced through Chris's thoughts, first for Mom for letting this disease catch her, then for Dad for treating her this way, then for Wes and Jill for putting those dreams to work in his head.

"Everything okay?" Mom asked. Her sunken face was concerned.

He forced himself to meet her eyes and imagined what she used to look like. It made it more bearable. "Yeah, just thinking about a book report I have today that I'm not ready for."

She crossed the kitchen and stroked the side of his head. "It's okay, baby. Just do your best."

Chris's eyes burned. He wanted to cry. This shit was the worst. She would have yelled at him for saying that nine months ago. She would have reamed him for not doing his work. Now, she soothed him instead. More than anything, this drove the dagger into his heart. It screamed that she had given up. Her days were running out, and she didn't want to be remembered for shouting and raging about his grades. She didn't want to spend her last days angry at him. She wanted to spend that time loving him, and that's how she wanted him to remember her. What it did to Chris was reassure him that she knew her time was almost up.

"Yeah, Mom." Chris forced himself up and made himself move before the tears broke. He grabbed his backpack and headed toward the door. Facing away, he said, "Love you, Mom," and grabbed the knob. Dad's hangover snores sounded from down the hall, and as soon as Mom said, "Love you," he bounded outside.

He couldn't deny that Mom had tears in her voice as she spoke, so he filled his mind with other things as he stomped toward the bus stop. He awkwardly pulled his headphones over one ear and then the other, and blasted his worn-out copy of *Fly by Night*.

He pictured the queen again. What would she have wanted from him? It was stupid, he knew, but what would someone want from him to fix Mom?

Four other kids waited at the bus stop. They were a pantomime of *By-Tor and the Snow Dog*. One tried to talk to him, and he turned the other way. He remembered the tentacles on the beast's back. He remembered his fight with that knight. He wished he had some pot. He was about to say *fuck it* and take a walk when the yellow behemoth screeched to a halt in front of him. Its door opened, and he remembered Charlotte.

Chris closed his eyes and shut out the world as the bus rolled. He didn't watch the road, the stops, or the kids. It would be eight pickups and a transfer, almost forty-five minutes before he got to school.

The blackness under his eyelids faded to Charlotte in a sparse room. Was it the same one? It gave him a feeling of desperation—that whatever happened in that room was horrible in a way that he had never known. She was on a small, bare mattress, curled up. She stared across the room at a locked door. Her face was clenched, and he didn't know if it was fear or anger, or sorrow. Fury gripped his fingers. He felt himself overcome with fear for what was on the other side of that door, and more than anything, he wanted her out of there.

3

Eddy Lawrence was downstairs early this morning. Gennie wondered what could have the boy so worked up. He was almost chipper, a giddy change from the usual dread the boy seemed to have on schooldays.

He plopped himself down at the kitchen table and watched Gennie.

She cracked an egg into the frying pan. "What's got your bees buzzing this morning, boy?" The child must want something. Her mind spun a mental Rolodex of the boy's interests: those two-legged turtle things, the superhero dolls, matchbox cars, bugs. He probably wanted a new one of those.

"Oh." He grinned. "It's show and tell today."

This was an odd turn. Did he want to wreck some other child's presentation? "And why is that making you grin like the cat that ate the canary?"

"We were talking about the war the other day—the one Grampa was in. I wanted to show his helmet if you let me. The big green one with all the scratches and dents that he wore to fight the Nazis..."

Gennie took a step back from the stove. She remembered Roy coming home in 1946 and flushed as the images of their wedding day a month later flashed in front of her eyes: His suit, her dress, their kiss.

"Do you think I can?" Eddy swung his feet from the chair.

She remembered how he smelled as they danced in the Blue Moose for their fifth anniversary. It made her legs tremble on that dancefloor and again in this kitchen.

"Gramma?"

The helmet was in her closet, in the trunk. She squinted. She could get it, but should she? Could the little shit take care of it? It was a steel helmet that had been through a war—what could he do to it?

"I'd really like to show how cool Grandpa was."

She felt a warm urge to say yes. It would be good to have him mind for the day.

"Okay." She pointed dead center of his chest. "But I will skin your hide if you lose it or don't bring it back in just the same shape as I hand it to you."

"Yes, Gramma." He nodded like his head was on a spring.

Gennie slid the eggs onto a cold burner and turned off the stove. She walked to the bedroom door, and the boy followed.

"You finish getting ready." She shooed at him. "I'll get the helmet."

She passed the basement door and grimaced as a smell came up from the cracks around the frame. It was a sour odor, and she wondered if the black water pipe had come loose again from the city drain in the far wall. She'd have to call someone to check it.

She walked into her room and opened the closet. The smell of mothballs caught her nose as she kneeled in front of the trunk.

There was a sound like a gong that registered in Gennie's ears. She decided it wasn't; it was one of her iron skillets. The closet, her room, her bed, all rotated in front of her eyes as a hot crackling pain radiated through her skull. She was falling. She had been hit. She remembered that sound and where she had heard it before. It was the same sound as when she used the skillet on Roy—when he was chiding her over what he called *burned* meatloaf. Maybe it was a hair dry but burned? No. That son of a bitch; it was the last time he would complain about her cooking. The last time he'd dare to complain in the kitchen and then drag her to the bedroom to perform her wifely *duty*.

As the memory cleared, she wondered where the sound had come from this time. She saw Eddy standing over her, the skillet in his hand, and she decided she would feed him to the furnace. She raised a trembling hand toward him, and it fell back onto her chest. She would slice his hands off first as punishment for touching her cookware, then—there was a crunch as the black skillet slammed onto Gennie Lawrence's nose. When Eddy raised it, blood raced from her flattened nostrils.

Her eyes searched the room but couldn't find him. It was a blur. The room shook.

Eddy watched for a moment, imagining what was going on inside the old woman. Her brain, her heart, her guts. He wished he could see what they did from the inside as all this happened.

Her lips fluttered. She blinked wildly. A gurgling sound passed her lips as he took a seat beside her.

"Silly Gramma," he raised the skillet and brought it down on her forehead.

4

Jim Jones parked his small Datsun pickup in the teacher's parking lot. He reached for his briefcase and realized his hand was trembling. It was the dream. It was hanging around in his mind like a song you couldn't shake.

But it wasn't real. He'd never do anything like that in real life, he knew.

Scenes came back: Kathy Sallow chained to the bed, leather straps outlining her breasts and hips, a red gag in her mouth, and that prick, Gordan Swann, cuffed on the other side of the room, watching.

He couldn't believe he had a dream like that. He'd barely had a hard-on in fifteen years, but it was rock hard when he awoke.

He shook his head. The thoughts had to go. He was only doing what the voice in his dream told him to. Yes, he had enjoyed it—up until the end—but the whips, the cutting, the tears he had left her in... those, he didn't enjoy. Not at first anyway. At first, he was just following what it said. He had to. He was told to. And damn, it felt good to feel his balls once again, even if it was only in a dream.

He seized his case and stood from the car.

"Hi, Mr. Jones." It was Mary Keys, a sixth-grader, walking through the teachers' lot toward the front of the building.

He waved and realized his pants were tight around his crotch, then covered himself with his briefcase. He thumped back into his seat. The pickup rocked. He trembled. He wanted to be back in that dream. He did what the whisper said and brought his pistol inside his briefcase—but he wanted to be back in that dream.

2022

1

Julie Redmond had wondered if anyone would notice that all the handwriting looked the same on the envelopes. It was a question that Ed Lawrence found remarkable for a child to ask. She would have a future, not getting caught like so many others of their kind that he'd read about.

He had assured her that it would be okay. They would deposit them in different mailboxes, and while the FBI may match it up later, the tools at the local post office wouldn't. If anything, they'd think it was someone having a party and sending lots of invitations or something—it wasn't anything that would stop the plan from happening.

She seemed satisfied with that—as much as a child needed to be. It had shut her up anyway.

When the sorting machine shuffled letters from one slot to the next, and they were loaded into delivery vehicles, Ed would be proven right. When Emmit Peterson started his route, he had packed over a dozen of the envelopes without a second thought.

Emmit drove his 1994 Jeep YJ through the drive-thru at the Beens and Rounds kiosk. The little shack looked like a remnant from a war zone in the parking lot of the shuttered Custer Valley Mall. He gave the girl inside a nod and then ordered his usual: a triple-shot latte with extra milk.

She rolled her eyes at the order but was all smiles when it was time to hand him the cup and take her payment and tip.

He sipped as he drove to the edge of town. His thoughts were already on quitting time. He was going to meet Benny and Juan for cards and beers, and he could already feel their cash in his wallet.

He passed Maxine in one of the city vehicles, a new, shiny white and blue model. He waved and hoped she'd get pregnant and quit like so many of the city workers did, and then maybe he'd get a shot at one of those white and blues.

He sipped again.

In the bin to his right, Ed and Julie's letters waited.

2

Wes Henson tapped his fingers against his legs. His phone was long dead after he'd tried to distract himself for what felt like hours with Snake and some game that had him rearranging colored pipes.

He'd thought about visiting Jill but didn't want to miss the doctor once Sam's surgery was done. Besides, he knew visiting her wouldn't matter anyway. He'd accepted that her coma was from the dream demon. If he wanted to do anything to help her, it would have to be ending this. If he wanted to help anyone, his daughters especially, he needed to end this. And that meant recovering the stone.

The waiting room door opened with a gentle breeze, followed by a middle-aged doctor in green surgical scrubs. A salt-and-pepper five o'clock shadow covered his square jaw. "Mr. Henson?"

Wes stood. "How is she?"

The doctor examined Wes, his radar up. A kid with this type of injury was strange enough, even stranger without it being caused by an adult.

"Doc?"

"She's going to be okay. We had to remove the broken bone fragments from each finger and seal the wounds."

"Jesus."

"Even if you had the tips, we couldn't have fixed it. The damage was too severe."

Tears welled in Wes's eyes. "Will she—how bad is the recovery?"

"It'll take a few weeks. She should expect phantom pains and itches. But after that, what's left of the digits should recover well."

Wes slumped back into his seat. He saw her at prom with deformed hands. Writing, reading, working on models, her favorite, with slow care and failing, crying. She held a baby sometime in the future with only two full fingers.

"You said she was caught in a bed?"

Wes snapped back into the moment. This had to be correct. He was sure whatever he said with this type of injury would get repeated to the police if he didn't make it believable, and he'd need his freedom if he was going to stop the demon.

"Yeah, a foldaway at the hotel. The girls were up—you know how kids are in hotels, it's like a playground and vacation mixed in one. They were fooling around with the sofabed in the room, and it closed and folded and pulled her all the way inside."

The doc's face loosened, the idea in his head making more and more sense as he visualized the metal frame and hinges inside a sleeper sofa. He wrung his hands together. "I'm sorry. We did our best, and I think given the timing—it was good you got her here so fast."

"When can I see her?"

"She's in recovery. Someone should come and get you in a few minutes."

"Thanks."

The doctor left, and Wes leaned his head against the wall. He saw Sam's hands, perfect little hands, playing with Legos, building her models, twirling her hair in her fingers. How could he have let this happen? How could he have not ended this thing years ago? Sure they had stopped it, but only for it to come back again. They had to do better this time. *He* had to do better this time.

3

Diana Henson scribbled on the Maryville Manor stationery she had found in the nightstand.

> *Wes,*
> *Headed to get the stone and some supplies. Taking Lisa for the ride. Back soon.*
> *—Di*

"Okay, girl, your dad knows where we're going."

Lisa didn't say anything. Her eyes drifted from her estranged aunt to the bloody bed to the dog. She didn't want to go anywhere except home, and she wanted Sam to be there with her. The dream, the blood, what happened to Mom, it all weighed on her like someone standing on her chest.

She didn't know what was right to do now. Dad wasn't here, but he had left her with Aunt Di—that meant he trusted her, right? But now she wanted them to go. It was all Lisa could do to frown and wonder, "Are you sure we should go without Dad?"

She wanted to hear *No.* She wanted to hear that they would wait for Sam and Dad.

"Yeah. I'm sure." The woman kneeled beside Lisa. She sighed, realizing what was happening and what she had to do: comfort and persuade a child. "The dream you had last night was bad, right? It hurt your sister, right?"

Lisa nodded.

"We have to go get something. So it can't happen again."

"Like a weapon?"

"Something like that."

Lisa thought of the little boy in her dream, the wall of videos. She found it hard to imagine how a gun or a sword could stop all of that. It all seemed like a bunch of magic.

"Is it a magic weapon?" Lisa said.

Di nodded. "I guess so." She watched the loose expression of a confused child firm into a determined face she had seen on Mom when she was little. The hard-set gaze from Lisa was a tiny clone of the look she got when she and her friends knocked over the altar of candles for the dead at church when she was seven. Of course, that was back before Dad died, when they went to church. But even then, the look struck fear in her heart without Mom having to raise a finger.

"Okay," Lisa said. The urge to move rose within her. They'd go get this weapon, and they'd stop Sam, or anyone else, from getting hurt by their dreams. She walked to the door as Di stood and called Virb.

4

Hannah Gould opened her eyes from what may have been her best sleep in twenty years. She slid her fingers along the empty sheets around her and stretched. She rolled from her side to her back, relishing the feeling of the smooth, cool cotton on her naked skin, and thought back to her dream.

There had been Heath and her husband, then Dawson and four nameless men who only served when she asked or needed them to. It was a marathon of lust that only strayed when she needed a dose of pain to remind her how good the rest of it felt. And once she had her fill or, as she thought of it, chuckling to herself within the sheets, once her cup runneth over, she awoke with the idea in her head of what she was to do next.

She hung her feet from the bed and stretched once more. From her closet, she flipped through the stuffy principal's clothes she'd gathered over her career and opted for a bright orange sundress she had wanted to wear every time her gaze had fallen on it for the past three years. She'd always found a reason why it was too silly to wear—but not today. In the kitchen, she tiptoed over Dawson's body, minding the blood, and made a bagel with chive and onion cream cheese. She filled a travel mug with coffee, grabbed a large knife from the block on the counter, and headed out the door.

She didn't know when she was supposed to be there but figured it would all happen just as it was supposed to. And that was such a relief. She started her car thinking how nervous and worried she had been only twenty-four hours ago; how restraining her desires and stuffing herself into those confining clothes and working with those horrid children had made her into—she wasn't quite sure what, but the stiff thought of those memories made her feel like someone imprisoned in concrete. She felt the smooth fabric of her dress—this was going to be her now. No worries, no constraints, just listen and go, and it would all work out. Today, it would all work out at Mount Custer—the whispers would be sure of it.

1992

1

Chris Conners stepped off his bus and looked up and down the drop-off lane. Five other buses lined up against the yellow curb, and as students walked from vehicle to door, a notion ground against Chris's thoughts and pushed his heart to beat a little faster: there were even fewer kids here today.

He spotted number 36 (Charlotte's bus) and regarded each kid that exited. He didn't see her.

He ran and placed a hand on its accordion door as it began to close. "Did Charlotte ride today?"

Mrs. Tanger, the sixty-one-year-old whose drinking made her look closer to ninety-one, snapped at him from the driver's seat, "What?"

"Charlotte? Was she on the bus today?"

The woman looked dumbfounded. "Who?"

"Girl. Short. Short, curly hair. Glasses. Was she on today?"

She glanced up at the long mirror above the windshield, then back to Chris. "If she was, she's off now. Now, get out of the way. I'm closing the door."

Chris's heart dropped even lower. Maybe she'd been on the bus, and Mrs. Tanger was too drunk to notice, but he knew it was worse than that. He stepped back and thought of her in that room, on that mattress, hauled away by that knight. *You were too slow. She's still his.*

"Fuck." The door clanked shut in front of his face. "Maybe it's still okay. Maybe she's in homeroom already."

His feet shuffled below, and before he knew it, he was running. He remembered the cave of kids lost in comas at the hospital, and, for the first time, he really believed.

He rushed past kids, darted through the double doors and down the hallway. He took a right and ran past his locker, then hers. He took a left and slammed into the doorjamb of Mr. Jimbo Jones's classroom.

Jones looked up from inside his briefcase and locked eyes with Chris.

"Sorry." Chris scanned the room. Six kids sat in desks. One squeezed past him through the door and found a seat in the third row. There was no Charlotte in sight.

"Have a seat, Chris." Mr. Jones said, his eyes back in his briefcase. His hand reached inside and gripped something.

The bell rang, and Chris crept to his desk.

2

Officer Dale Harrison sat in the teacher's lounge as the bell for first period rang. He tapped on his notepad, waiting for Elenore Nash, the school's receptionist, to bring him friends of Ronny DiMarco, Shirley Minsk, and Charlotte Baker. He wondered if any of them were still alive and hated himself for thinking that.

He'd heard it was a part of the curse of being a cop before he started, always expecting the worst from people. He'd fought it, and for a large part, he'd been able to avoid the assumptions his big city counterparts may have been consumed by. It helped living in a town this small, where people knew each other. It didn't mean people were nicer to each other—in some ways, they were worse. If you've had a grudge against the same neighbor your whole life, you're less likely to cut them any slack the fiftieth time they cut you off after church. But it also meant Harrison had a good idea of what people's intentions were before even starting a conversation.

But the past week weighed more on his shoulders than anything he'd seen yet in his career. More death, more horror, more missing people than all his years combined. The fact that he hadn't just quit and resigned himself to sitting in the hospital next to Gina amazed him. But he also had Stuart to think about—all the kids—the rest of the town. After Johnson's death and Sgt. Padilla's unimpressive theories, Harrison was convinced the guy was in over his head. Shit, weren't they all. The least he could do was try to find a few missing kids—and keep a rational hope that they might be okay.

Ms. Nash returned with four kids: Mazy Louis, Sean Nollan, Sarah Buckley, and Sasha Stevens. She mentioned in passing that with so many kids out and the craziness in town, he was lucky that she dug up this many. Some parents were keeping their kids at home until it all settled down, and there was talk that the school may be shut down later today.

Mazy and Sean were in Ronny DiMarco's class. Sarah was from Shirley's class, and Sasha was from Charlotte's. Harrison asked that they all wait in the hall except for Mazy, and he'd call them in one at a time.

It didn't take long for Harrison to realize Mazy knew nothing about Ronny's disappearance. She wasn't friends with him; it seemed no one in his class was. The way she told it, he sat by himself every lunch and recess and read comics. The teachers had asked other kids in the class to befriend him, but it hadn't helped.

Sean said nearly the same thing as Mazy, except in his telling, he had tried to make friends with Ronny, but Ronny yelled at him and chased him away when he accidentally tore a page in one of the kid's comics. Harrison wasn't sure if the whole ripped-page thing was true. The kid refused to meet his eyes. Maybe Sean knew more—maybe he was trying to hide from blame since he was talking to a cop. Neither kid was helpful in figuring out where Ronny was or where he might have gone after school the other day.

Sarah had an interesting tale, that Shirley Minsk had gone to the mall the day she disappeared with Ronny's brother, Johnny. Maybe just a coincidence, maybe not, but it further piqued Harrison's interest when Sasha indicated that Charlotte had also gone to the mall the day she went missing. Harrison wondered if perhaps little Ronny had taken a trip to the mall as well and hadn't told anyone. He hadn't spent much time in Custer Falls Mall but guessed there may be a store that sold comic books there.

The bell rang, ending first period, and Harrison sent the last of the kids back to class. He was torn between asking Ms. Nash to gather more children and heading right over to the mall. He knew he should do more interviews, get more information before proceeding—but the mall... Something in that idea gnawed at him. Something about that lead felt real. And maybe he'd get lucky, and they'd have a security camera or two. Something had to go right for him in this investigation sooner or later.

He stood and felt the compounding days of sleep deprivation pulling at him. It wanted him to sit back down, close his eyes for a few minutes, and rest. His muscles were sore, and it was starting to encase his head in threads of subtle headaches.

He forced himself out of the school and into his vehicle.

3

Ray Trent looked down at his prize. This one was his, for sure. The whispers said so.

He was still pissed about Amanda; he had really wanted her, but if this worked out, he could let that go. It sucked, he was still stuck with having to do something with her body—eventually, the thing was going to stink, and he'd have to bury it or something. But for now, it was out back, and he couldn't smell it from inside. So, he had time.

He'd held a towel to Misty's head until the bleeding stopped. He really didn't mean to hit her so hard, but dammit, why'd she have to run? When she finally stopped leaking, he took her into the cabin bedroom, which consisted of one queen bed and a set of bunk beds. He stripped her bloody clothes off, laid her in the queen bed, and duct taped her hands to the rails so she couldn't escape if she woke up. She hadn't yet.

His gaze walked up and down her naked flesh, his prick getting harder as he did. His heart raced. He was going to have her after all. She had given him eat-shit looks for so long, but she was going to get it now...

"*No,*" the whisper said. "*Not yet.*"

"What the fuck?"

"*Go to the mall,*" the whisper said. "*She's yours when you return.*"

Ray clenched his fists. He clutched one of her breasts in his hand, then pulled the covers over her.

2022

1

Margery Adams set her three-month-old son, Timothy, down in his crib for his morning nap. Her nose brushed past her shoulder as she stood, and the scent of spoiled milk and vomit made her want to retch.

In her bedroom, she tossed her shirt in the hamper and debated taking the thing to the basement and dumping it in the washer. George's blue boxers peeked from under her shirt, and she remembered he hadn't washed a damn thing this week. He could do it when he got home. Shit, maybe he could make dinner too; because if she was as tired then as she was right now, dinner would end up being frozen pizza or orange chicken or anything else that would require no more steps than tossing it in and pulling it out.

She flopped onto the bed and closed her eyes. Guilt opened them back up and forced her to look at the nightstand and make sure the baby monitor was on. There he was on the screen, his little mouth pursing and releasing; he stretched, his eyes still closed, and blew out a gentle breath.

Her phone buzzed beside the monitor. She knew who it was. There was no doubt in her mind. It was Mom.

Day or night, no matter the depth of Maggy's exhaustion, it was always Mom. She had one more thing to recommend for the baby, one more method that would make the baby's life perfect, one more worry that would kill the child if Maggy didn't do something immediately. Right now, though, she was sure it was about the package.

Mom had sent a package of baby clothes and toys. Maggy knew this because the moment it was sent, Mom texted with the tracking number.

The next day, she texted with the location where it had stopped overnight. The next day she made sure Maggy knew it was out for delivery. Today, Mom hadn't yet received a call or text with pictures of every opened item together with the child, a note about how much little Timmy loved it, and an itemized thank you. And Maggy's phone would keep buzzing ceaselessly for the rest of the day if she didn't go down to her mailbox and get the package and sort through it all.

"Fuck." And she thought she had it bad in high school.

Maggy rolled out of the bed and accepted that she would be doing this instead of the forty-five-minute nap she really needed. She reached into her closet and grabbed the first shirt her hand touched. She dragged it down over her body and saw a giant Budweiser logo stretched across her breasts. *That's a perfect image, isn't it?* She chuckled. *Nothing says wholesome mom like the idea of drunken breastfeeding.*

She slid her feet into a pair of giant black slippers resembling bear paws, headed into the living room, grabbed her keys from the table, and walked out the front door. The rain had stopped, but the sky was still thick with overcast gray. She glanced at the mud between herself and her pickup and wondered for a moment how dirty this may make her slippers. She landed on, *Fuck it—I have a washer*, and crossed the path to her vehicle.

The inside of the pickup was cool, the cracked leather sticking to her pajama pants as she slid into her seat. She paused for a second before shutting the door, hearing a distant sound that made her think of Timmy's cry. She concentrated, and it didn't return, so she closed the door and turned the ignition.

Mud sprayed, and brown water splashed from the potholes and ruts on Maggy's street. Her oversized mailbox was a half mile plus a hundred feet down the private road, enough that letter carriers weren't obligated to bring packages to her door. Instead, they stuffed them inside her one-foot by two-foot box where her street intersected with State Highway 9.

The puddles were deep beside the row of five boxes for her and her neighbors, so Maggy decided she'd pull up to it. She usually parked and walked for fear of snagging one of the steel boxes with her mirror and ripping it off—either the mirror or the box. Her slippers pushed her to chance it today.

The inside was stuffed. Mom's box was there, as was a week's worth of bills and advertisements crammed in on either side. She tugged at the letters on the sides and then the top, expecting them to all tumble down into the mud if she were to remove her mother's package first. She laid them on the seat, then the brown cardboard box on the floor. Lastly, she put a white envelope on the stack of mail, and this one caught her eye.

The white envelope was addressed in rounded letters that varied in size, reminding her of how she used to write when she was a child. The name on the letter was Timmy Adams.

It made her smile. There was something in the thought of another child writing to her child that caused her joy—it was as if her boy had made his first friend.

There was no return address. She flipped it over and looked at the back—sometimes she'd seen addresses placed on the envelope's closing flap—nothing. She felt the weight of it—a piece of paper inside. A letter? Not a card. Not a stack of things, just a single piece of paper.

Maggy wedged her fingertip under the edge of the flap and ripped the envelope's top. She nearly giggled as she grabbed the letter by the folded edge and pulled it free. She unfolded the paper, and white powder sprinkled onto her lap and her shirt. As she held up the letter and sneezed, she saw the page was blank. There was nothing there. Her joy hung in the air like a lost balloon, just out of reach and drifting away.

"What the hell?" She flipped it over and looked at the back. White powder flicked onto her lips and nose.

Was this a joke of some kind? A joke on a mom and her new kid?

"Assholes."

She crumpled the letter and envelope into a ball and tossed it on the floor, spraying a cloud of white into the cab.

The smell of talc and lilac filled her nose and made her sneeze. Why did they pack it in baby powder? Another weird joke? She remembered something about powder in the mail she'd heard as a kid, a faint recollection from her days in elementary school, but it didn't quite click.

She carefully pulled away from the line of mailboxes and drove home.

2

Wes Henson stared at his little girl's hand. Three fingers were bandaged from their tips—two bones shorter than they should have been—down to her palm and around her thumb as an anchor. He took Sam's other hand in his and gently held it.

Chills of grief and shame soured his insides. This was his fault. He may not have cut her fingers off, but he had failed to protect her. He was supposed to get rid of this thing thirty years ago, and he didn't. Now it was back, and every life taken, every person injured, they were all his fault.

He looked down at her closed eyes, and tears ran from his.

Jill, now her. They were both his fault. Sure, a deranged child did the work on his wife, but Wes knew, deep inside, he was sure now, this was the work of that damned demon. Just like Ray Trent. Just like Barton Smith. Just like that kid that—it was like lightning struck Wes's spine. The shock pulled him vertical with a gasp.

Memories of the days after his dad's death were fuzzy things. He had been so focused on saving himself and Di, and then forgetting when it was all over—but there was a story there. There was that kid who killed his grandmother—Wes remembered that—he had been taken away to a mental institution afterward. His name—Wes reached through the fog of years of memory, but it was just out of reach. The exterminator's badge came into view: *Ed.* It was Ed. Wes didn't have a shred of proof behind it, but he knew in his gut, that was Ed. At his house was Ed. And behind Ed was the demon.

"Dad?" a small voice rose from the bed. Her eyes were open, and tears streamed more heavily down Wes's face. She lifted her crippled hand toward him. "Dad?"

"Don't move it." His voice was quavering. "You don't want to damage the stitches."

Her face wrinkled. Her lips receded into her mouth.

"It's going to be okay, baby." He stroked her head with one hand and held her tightly with the other. "We're going to get through this.

She looked up at her father. He watched her empathy for him eclipse the fear for herself. Her face loosened. A tear ran from each eye. "We'll be okay, Daddy."

Wes couldn't help himself from smiling. It was pride in her. It was love for her. It was a ray of hope that they might get through this, if only through her strength, not his own. But to do that, they couldn't stay in the hospital.

He needed to go, and she needed to come with him. He needed to make sure she was safe. And if he failed, he would need to make sure she didn't sleep.

3

Diana Henson had said little to Lisa on the drive from Maryville Manor to Mount Custer. She'd gone over it in her mind again and again: the path they'd taken thirty years prior, the tears they'd shed, the darkness. When she had decided to come and find Wes three days ago, she didn't expect to have to go through this, to relive some of the hardest moments of her life, but as she glanced at her young niece, she knew she had no choice. She may have tried to forget it all, with shock therapy, with drugs and alcohol, with men, and sometimes women. There was never any use. No matter how much she put herself through or how dirty she felt for everything she used to forget, this was always going to happen. Because they didn't do it right the first time, and there was more at stake this time than just herself and her brother. So, she'd better remember the way.

She parked in the lot for the Skyline Trailhead, which would take hikers up the gentle side of the mountain to a viewing area near the peak. There, they could snap photos and take selfies with the entire town in the picture behind them. Virb whined as soon as the vehicle stopped, which he never did.

Di looked in the back, where the dog was sitting pretty in the middle of the bench seat. She could see the anxiety on his face. He was worried about something.

She looked around the vehicle in all directions. No one was there. A Toyota SUV was twenty feet to the east, empty. A Honda to the west, also empty. Both, she assumed, belonged to hikers that were already on the trails.

"It's okay," Di reached back and let Virb lick her hand.

Lisa turned around in her seat and caressed the top of Virb's head. "Good boy. You're a good boy."

"Come on," Di got out, grabbing Virb's leash and looping it over her shoulder. She made a clicking sound with her tongue pressed against the roof of her mouth, and Virb bounded over the driver's seat and stood by her side. She patted her hip and felt a shock as she realized she didn't bring her pistol. It was back at the hotel inside her bag. She took another look around the lot—nothing of interest, no danger. She'd have to chance it.

Lisa got out and waited by the hood, between the vehicle and the entrance to the trail. "Are we going to the top?"

Di looked at the trail and felt broken that she could no longer see the joy in it. "You've been up there?"

"Yeah. Lots of times."

"With your dad?" She couldn't believe Wes would come here.

"No. Dad hates hiking. We came with Mom, and once for school."

Di nodded, remembering what had happened to Jill the previous night—thirty years ago tonight. "Ah. Well, we're not going that way. We're headed over here." She pointed west to the game trail that ran toward the south side of the mountain's base. She started walking with Virb at her side, along the line of dirt that led toward tree cover and eventually darkness, and Lisa followed.

"I haven't been this way," Lisa said.

"Let's hope you don't have to again."

Neither noticed the white Nissan Murano pulling in and parking on the far side of the lot.

4

Stuart Harrison had debated most of the morning. As much as he knew what he had found meant something, he didn't quite know what. And the idea of looking like a fool held his fingers from the phone while he tried to figure it out.

There was the cold psychotic nature that Edward Lawrence had shown when killing and an unemotional confession when Dad found the bodies—but after it was over, he acted like a switch had been flipped. Doctors found it hard to believe that the boy they were brought could have committed those acts, even though he admitted to doing them. He said he couldn't control himself, that it was like another voice was inside his head. But after testing, he wasn't found to be suffering from schizophrenia or any other psychosis.

Harrison had to wonder if the same thing could be happening to that little girl—some sort of temporary mental break, a transient schizophrenic episode? Was that even a thing?

The more he replayed the brutality of the school murder in his mind, the more he became convinced there was more to this than what he could see on the surface. If there was something that could have caused Edward Lawrence's behavior, and possibly this girl's, maybe someone needed to check in with Lawrence for some insight?

It was flimsy. The cases weren't related by anything other than a child's brutality. The victims were unrelated. The assailants were unrelated. They didn't even happen in the same century.

But still. He couldn't shake the feeling that there was something there. He glanced at his phone. The sense of foolishness came back. He'd call Rand, but maybe he'd go by and talk to Lawrence first. Maybe then he'd have a better idea of what to say when he called.

1992

1

Jim Jones walked into the teacher's lounge, his empty coffee cup in hand. The smell of a fresh pot pulled him in further. He shut the door behind him and lunged forward before realizing Kathy Sallow was pouring herself a cup.

She wore jeans today, not one of her usual tight skirts. It made Jim focus on her hips to see what he wanted, and, in part, the concealment of the goods made him want her even more.

Ms. Swallows, crossed his mind. She may have had a gag in her mouth last night, but the name still drew him in. Maybe in his dream tonight, he'd pull off the gag.

Kathy turned, blowing on her mug. Her eyes met Jim's and shot wide open.

"Morning, Kathy," Jim stepped toward the coffee machine, and her.

She pressed herself back against the counter and slid sideways. "Jim." Her voice was shaking, her lips trembling. Her eyes were glued to him as he moved. Her fingers tensed on her cup.

He set his mug on the counter. "Everything okay?"

She slid further away, backing toward the door. "Y—yeah." She nodded stiffly. "Gotta go." She grabbed the knob and raced from sight.

Jim smirked. "I'll catch up."

2

Tommy Laskin ran, fangs snapping at his back. There was black all around and a forest floor's debris below. He heard the crunch of claws and the howl of a beast behind him. Was it the mare? Was it the same thing that had sent him reeling away or one of its minions? He wasn't sure, but his legs pumped all the same.

He couldn't remember how long he'd been running. Step after step, breath after breath, he realized he was going nowhere. He'd seen the thing for what it really was—but was this a ploy to make him comply, or did it really want him dead? Or was it toying with him to keep him occupied? Either way, this couldn't last forever—he couldn't last forever. He needed to wake up.

Tommy pushed with every part of him and launched himself into the air. He grabbed hold of the world around him and pulled himself up. He sunk his grip into the emptiness of black around him and heaved as if it were solid ground.

He felt claws swipe at the air behind him as he climbed. It was still following him.

Tommy moved faster, grabbing, yanking himself upward. He pushed the world apart, thrust himself on, and flew.

The sounds of the beast faded, and the sky lightened ahead. From black to purple to blue, he saw the horizon of a world he liked much more, but it wasn't where he wanted to be. He climbed ever higher, imagining that the world of the waking was ahead. It had to be. He couldn't spend the rest of his life in this dream, and he couldn't count on that monster to keep its word if he took the deal. He needed to wake himself.

Tommy saw a world of white in the distance. If he could get to it, he knew the real world was beyond.

The sky faded to lighter shades of blue as he climbed, and beyond the haze of his thoughts, he felt a bed below his body. He rushed even higher and felt sheets on top of him. He barreled into the white wall of the unknown and felt air, real air, flow into his lungs. His eyes opened.

3

"What if we break it?" Diana Henson pondered. "Dad has all kinds of hammers and stuff in the garage."

The room seemed to freeze around the three of them at the mention of their father.

"Had," Di muttered.

Jill examined the stone, careful not to touch it again. Each of them had held it now, each feeling the strange numbness followed by rising dread the longer they had contact with it. "It has writing on it. What do you think it says?"

"Something evil, I'm sure." Wes looked the other way. He was drained. It was only morning, but with every minute that passed since he'd woken up, he felt less and less energized.

"I bet it's a spell," Jill said.

"I'm going to get a hammer." Di left the room.

Jill followed the writing with her finger as if it might reveal itself if only she stared harder. "I think I've seen these types of letters before. They're like Celtic runes or something."

"Where've you seen Celtic runes?" Wes turned to her.

"My aunt—you know my family's from Scandinavia—she, like, lives for all things of the old world."

"Scandinavia? What does that even mean?"

"I don't know. My mom says our people came from Sweden, but my aunt says Norway. I don't know how that works. But, I swear, I've seen things like this. I wonder..."

"What?"

"Maybe my aunt could read it?"

"Got it." Di carried a large carpenter's hammer into the room. "It's the biggest one I could find."

She showed the first smile she'd worn in what felt like an eternity. Wes noticed. It was small, but it was there.

He looked at the stone. They'd set it back onto his shelf. He imagined it broken into a hundred pieces, and a chill set into his gut. He wondered if it was a warning not to do it or a trick to discourage him.

"I don't know." He shook his head. It ached as he did. "I think it might be a bad idea to break it."

Di frowned. "What do you mean? If that's what's causing this, how could it be bad to break it?"

"It's just a feeling."

Di walked toward the stone, raising the hammer.

"Wait!" Wes shouted.

Di froze in her tracks. "The thing killed Dad," she snapped.

"Just wait. We don't know what it is. What if you broke it, and it made two of them? Like cutting off the head of a hydra?" He turned to Jill. "Do you think your aunt could read it?"

"I don't know. Maybe?"

"Can you try?"

"Yeah. She works on 7th; I can take it to her." She reached toward the shelf.

"No!" Wes shook his head. "Don't touch it. Copy the writing down and take that. I—I don't want it to hurt you."

Jill flushed and tried to hide it by looking back at the stone.

"Jill thinks her aunt can read the writing," Wes said. "Let's wait to see what it says first, before we smash it and possibly make things worse."

4

Officer Dale Harrison spotted at least four security cameras on his way to the Custer Falls Mall office. One was outside, one pointed at the exit, one pointed down an interior hall, and one watched him as he entered what looked like any other drop-ceilinged last-decade office space.

Harrison's gaze met Becky Adams at the reception desk. She flashed him a wink and a smile as if they were still in high school together. The next stop would have been the closet outside the gym to escape the pep rally. He pushed the memory aside before it encouraged him to smile the same way.

"Dale?" She leaned back in her chair and crossed her legs. She brushed her blond bangs from her face and crossed her hands over her lap. "What are you doing here?"

Harrison nodded. "Good to see you too, Becky. How are you doing?" Her eyes sparkled, even under the fluorescent lights, and he had to force himself not to stare.

"Oh, I'm good. Best job I've had in years." She waved at the empty mall beyond the office door. "Almost nothing to do all day."

"How's your mom?" Harrison grimaced, knowing the Adams matriarch had undergone triple-bypass heart surgery a few weeks back after a lifetime of smoking and diabetes.

She sighed. "Doc says if she doesn't stop smoking, she won't last another year."

"Think she'll quit?"

"Momma? They've been telling her that for years. Said she was going to lose her feet if she didn't lay off the sweets too—she's still the first in line for a glazed donut and a coffee with two sugars every morning at the Bakers Dozen."

"That so?"

"She won't change. She'd rather die than listen."

"Well, she's a strong one."

There was a long enough pause for Becky to get a better look at Harrison's face. Her smile faded as it sunk in that he was there for something a little more important than catching up with a high school fling. "What's going on, Dale?"

He straightened his back. "I need to see your security camera footage. Would that be possible?"

She glanced at the door behind her, the boss's office. "I imagine so. Ernie's not in, though. What's going on?"

Harrison told her as little as he thought he could get away with about the missing kids. He saw the worry on her face as she glanced back at Ernie's office again.

"I'm not sure when Ernie's going to be back." She shook her head. "The tapes are in his office."

"Can you call him?"

"Yeah." She tried. No answer.

"When was the last time you saw him?"

"Wow." She looked up. "I don't think I've seen him in a few days. It's been rather nice." She grinned at the idea of his absence.

Harrison saw a bloody bed in his future. He'd have to stop by Ernie's house and check in on him later, though. "How about you let me in there to look. If he happens to come by while I'm in there, you can blame me."

Her lips pursed, and she nodded. "Okay." Her voice had gone dry.

Ernie's office had enough room for the desk, Ernie's chair, and a large bookshelf behind it which held the monitor, recording deck, and stacks of VHS tapes. The monitor showed four images from the mall, one in each corner. They rotated to new images from other cameras every few seconds. As Harrison looked closer, he saw they weren't moving. This particular system didn't actually record video; it recorded still images looping from camera to camera.

"Do you know how this system works?" Harrison asked.

Becky shook her head. "I can't make my VCR at home work."

"I'll figure it out then. Thanks." He took a seat at Ernie's desk, getting a sensation that Ernie wouldn't be coming back to sit there ever again. He looked at the controls on the deck, then glanced at the tapes. Each one seemed to span a period of two days. The deck itself was stopped, the tape at its end. "I guess he should have changed the tape."

Harrison hit *Rewind* and waited and hoped it had stopped after Charlotte Baker had been there and not before. It had gone about a quarter back, and Harrison hit *Play*.

The feed on the monitor mostly looked the same, but the timestamp at the bottom of the screen changed. It was last night. *Good*. He rewound further and hit *Play* again. Four o'clock, still too late. He shuffled the machine between *Play* and *Rewind* a few times until landing at 3:15 pm, a few minutes after Charlotte's school would have let out.

He sat and waited.

The next few minutes felt like the slowest he'd experienced in years. Worry crept into his thoughts as he watched. It had likely already been there, but he was the type to keep moving, and when you're moving, you don't have time for worry. But right now, he did. This girl had been missing almost twenty hours, and if she was in danger, that was a long time to be missing.

The images trickled by. No Charlotte. He wondered about Shirley Minsk. It had been much longer for her now. The blood he'd seen this week moved through his thoughts. How had he not been here before now? Sure, Johnson had been looking into it, but he should have helped. But he was so consumed at the hospital, with Gina, with all the other kids, but especially with Gina. He covered his face as if his hands could conceal him from the shame he felt. The Minsk girl was likely dead. He knew that now, especially with another one being abducted. He peeked at the screen.

Charlotte Barker walked through the mall entrance, and his heart jumped. She was such a small thing, smaller than he expected, but he recognized her face from the pictures he'd been given. God, she was so small. If only he worked fast, maybe he could find her.

She walked across the mall, reappearing in different corners of the monitor.

Harrison moved with her image, and Becky had to ask, "Is that her? The missing girl?"

"One of them." Harrison's eyes were glued open. He wasn't going to miss a frame.

She left the food court, and Harrison noticed a man walking a few feet behind her. He was a monster compared to this little thing. He held a bag in one hand and what looked like a white rag in the other.

"Who the hell is that?" Harrison pointed. He didn't expect an answer, and Becky didn't offer one.

The pictures shifted, and Charlotte was now in the opposite corner. The man was right behind her. The bathrooms were to their left, and between them, a door marked, *Authorized Personnel*.

Harrison felt a rock in his gut. He wanted to reach in and grab that girl, pull her to safety. He wanted to scream at her: "Look behind you! Watch out!" All he could do was clench his fist and watch.

The images shifted again—Charlotte was nowhere to be seen.

Harrison moved up and down, left and right, searching every pixel. "Where'd she go?"

The images rotated again. Still no Charlotte.

"Where the hell did they go?" Harrison tapped *Rewind*, then *Play*. Charlotte stood in front of the bathrooms again, and he hit *Pause*. "What is that?" He pointed to the screen.

Becky said nothing.

Harrison turned to her, his eyes on fire. "What is that? That door marked *Authorized Personnel?*"

"That? Oh, that's a maintenance hallway. It runs behind all the stores in that wing for merchants to come and go, accept deliveries and stuff."

"Where does it let out?"

"Um... that's the west side... so, by the north and south entrances."

"Are those on camera?"

"I don't know?" Her face was tense. She held her arms tightly crossed below her breasts.

"Shit." He hit *Play* and waited. He'd seen a few shots of the parking lot rotating through the slideshow. Now, he had to hope they'd exit through one of those.

Images flashed. They rotated. Teen boys laughed at a table in the food court. A girl bought a cookie at the cookie store. Most wings of the mall looked as empty as they would be at closing time. Images rotated again. A janitor emptied a trash can beside a bench. They rotated again.

There they were. The large man carried her. Charlotte Baker laid across this man's arms as he stepped from the mall's surrounding sidewalk into the parking lot.

"There." Harrison pointed. His finger itched. All of them did. They wanted to reach into the screen and snatch the girl from his arms. The inability to do just that sent a cold shiver of shame and impotence down his spine. He should have come sooner. He should have seen this sooner. He should have been helping her sooner.

"Oh, my God," Becky covered her face with her hands.

Harrison clenched his fists. He waited for the image to rotate and show the next moment. It felt like time had stopped as he watched this man mid-stride, a helpless girl in his arms. Harrison's hands felt hot and uncomfortable as if they weren't his at all.

The images rotated. Boys laughing at the table. Harrison was overcome with rage. How could they do that? How could they sit there enjoying themselves while this girl was being stolen? What kind of scum were the kids in his town? The frame hovered in his way, blocking what he needed to see, and with each heartbeat, his anger grew. The girl at the cookie store had turned and was walking away. The treat was frozen in front of her face, and more than anything, Harrison wanted her to drop it, run outside, and save Charlotte before it was too late.

Rotate. The janitor had moved from one trashcan to another on the opposite side of the hall. He held the lid in his hand, preparing to remove it and access the inside. He looked slow. He looked like the kind of man that had never rushed and went about his life at one speed. Harrison realized he was clamping his jaws together, but it made no difference, the goddamn thing was about to shift. One more time, and he could know. One more rotation, and maybe he could be on his way.

The tiny white phosphors faded from the small monitor as if toying with Harrison. He held his breath as squares lit up. There they were. The man was setting Charlotte down in the passenger seat of an old pickup. The screen may have been black and white, but he knew the color instantly. It was light green with a faded circle on the door. He'd seen the same trucks all over Montana. It was a retired Forest Service truck, auctioned off at the end of its duty to the public. He could find it. This was huge. There may be hundreds of them around the state, but maybe only one or two in town.

"That's it!" he shouted.

Becky's hands still blocked her chest. Her eyes were glossy.

He hit eject on the deck and grabbed the tape. He grabbed the previous one from the shelf, thinking it likely had similar footage of Shirley Minsk, but he didn't have time to watch that now. He could verify Shirley on the tape later—right now, he needed to track down that vehicle.

Harrison spun, and the monitor switched back to a live feed. He stormed from the tiny office as his vehicle came into view, a boy standing beside it.

5

Ray Trent kneeled beside the Custer Falls Police Department cruiser. He scanned the parking lot again. All he could see was the side of the neighboring Honda and the front of a Ford, nose to nose with the cop car.

He drew his father's hunting knife from his hoodie.

"*Do it now*," the whisper said.

Ray pressed the blade's tip into the car's rear passenger tire. It was stiff at first, but once it penetrated the rubber, it slid in smoothly. Air hissed across his knuckles, reminding him of how Mom used to blow on his cuts and scratches after dabbing them with hydrogen peroxide. Dad never did that. The most he got from Dad was, "Walk it off." He was glad to never have to hear that again.

He pulled the knife free and watched the car slowly sink.

"*Go*," the whisper commanded.

He slid the blade back into its sheath and sneaked to the rear bumper. Left, right, there was no one. He stood and sprinted three rows to Amanda Brolin's van and hopped inside.

He looked around again. No one watching. A smile crossed his face. He'd gotten away with it. Slashing a cop's tires. People were so dumb. A wave of confidence made him straighten himself. He could get away with anything.

With a twist of the key, the van started, and he drove to the exit. His mind went to Misty. It was time for her now. He'd waited so long, it seemed. He'd earned her. He'd be back to her soon and show her how much he wanted her. Maybe then she'd even see it—then she wouldn't have to be tied down. She'd understand him and want to stay with him. There was still the sister's body to deal with, the blood on the cabin floor— but Misty would understand that—she'd forgive him once she saw how much he needed her. He glanced left and right and had to freeze. A block ahead, he saw Jill Elden.

It wasn't that Jill in any way measured up to Misty, fuck no, couldn't happen. There was something else about seeing her that made the other kind of desire rise, remembering the other day, dangling her into traffic. He wanted to feel that again. Misty was good where she was; she could wait a little longer.

2022

1

Diana Henson guided Lisa along the shaded trail. Ponderosa pines monopolized the landscape at this altitude, but the scent of the trees and creeping juniper made her think more about her shelter than where they were.

She missed her tiny log shelter. It was a hiding place, a temporary retreat, barely fit for a scavenger, but it had become a sanctuary for a very short while. It was a place that only she and Virb knew, their place, and she really wished she could be there instead of here. And instead of going where she really didn't want to go.

Di glanced at Virb. He caught her stare and passed in front of her legs, rubbing his side against her.

"Good boy." She touched his back. This would be over soon. It had to be.

Virb's head jerked left, back the way they had come. He circled around Di and growled low and long.

Lisa stopped, staring at the dog. "What's he doing?"

Di looked into the woods and ushered Lisa behind her. "I don't know."

Twigs snapped, and from behind the trunk of a massive pine stepped Hannah Gould.

"Mrs. Gould!" Lisa smiled and scurried from behind Di.

Virb growled louder, and Di grabbed Lisa's shoulder.

"Oh, there you are." Gould smiled and held a hand out to Lisa. "I didn't see you at your house—I came by the hospital. And here you are."

"And how did you find us here?" Di squinted. Her hand rested on the knife on her belt.

"I just happened to be driving by and saw you pull in."

Virb crept toward Gould, his growl growing louder.

Gould held a hand toward Lisa, the other behind her back. "Come here, sweetie. Give me a hug."

Lisa nudged forward, but Di held on. She didn't know what this lady was up to, but it wasn't right, and Virb's reaction proved it.

"Let me go," Lisa said. She squirmed under Di's grip.

"Lisa, just wait," Di said.

Virb crept closer to Gould. Gould's eyes darted back and forth from the dog to the child. Her hidden hand moved closer to view.

"What's behind your back, Mrs. Gould?" Di asked.

"Nothing." Her voice was shrill. She leaned toward Lisa. Virb barked. "Hey, control your dog!"

"What's behind your back!" Di said. She pulled her knife from her belt, her grip tight.

"Fine!" Gould swung her hidden hand forward. She held a package. It was one of those chocolate eggs that hid a toy inside. "It was supposed to be a surprise, but here you go."

"Oo, surprise egg!" Lisa jerked free. She ran to Mrs. Gould and wrapped her arms around the principal.

"Here, sweetie. I know it isn't much, but hopefully, it'll brighten your day just a little." She handed Lisa the treat, and the girl immediately unwrapped it.

Di took a breath. She didn't know what this was, but it wasn't what she had thought. Could she have been overreacting? Maybe Virb was too? He could have heard a strange noise in the woods and just switched on. Logic suggested they were mistaken, but something inside her still doubted. Something was still off about this.

"Where's your sister, Lisa?" Gould said.

Lisa cracked the chocolate. "She had to go to the doctor. She hurt her hand." Her expression dropped but picked up as chocolate hit her tongue.

"Oh, I'm sorry to hear that. Hopefully, it's not too bad." Gould glanced at Di, a smile now across her face.

"Virb." Di tried to relax. She tried to breathe and lower the tension. Whatever this woman wanted might be easier to figure out if she did. Virb looked back and stifled his growl. He sat and returned his stare to Gould. "She's going to be okay."

"And you all went out for a hike?" Gould asked Lisa.

"We're looking for something," Lisa said, working very hard on her egg, focusing on every broken shard of chocolate and refusing to let a single crumb fall from her grip.

"We're looking to relax a little," Di said. "I thought a short walk in the woods might relieve some stress."

"Right," Gould said. "And who are you exactly? I don't think I've ever seen you at our school." It was a tone of superiority, nearing indignation.

Diana held back her frustration. This was the same tone, the same doubt she heard when anyone discovered her time in committal or her past with drugs and alcohol. "I am her aunt."

"Ah. On her mother's side or father's?"

"She's Dad's sister."

Gould's expression turned instantly. "You're Diana Henson." And there it was. The smug gaze had reached full bloom. She had heard the name, known the town history, maybe even remembered her from elementary school—this was the *crazy* Henson.

"We need to go, Lisa." Di nodded toward the trail.

Gould glanced down at the child, still engrossed in the last bit of chocolate eggshell. "I'll see you later, sweetie. Try to enjoy your hike."

"Okay, Mrs. Gould." She wandered back toward Di, not lifting her view in the slightest.

"Goodbye, Mrs. Gould," Di said.

The principal flashed a superficial smile and headed toward the parking lot. As she moved away, Di felt her heart slowing. She didn't even know it was beating so fast. She watched the woman disappear into the woods and knew this wasn't the last time she would see her.

2

Wes Henson handed Sam her clothes and turned the other way as she dressed. They had been transferred to a room of her own, checked in so they could monitor her. He watched the door, wondering what he would say if someone came in. They wanted Sam to stay for observation, at least until tomorrow. They couldn't do that.

He heard her groan as she dressed, and his heart pained. "Try to do it one-handed, Sam."

"Yeah." Her voice was low, tired. "I'm trying."

The door seemed to tease him, mocking, saying any second a doctor was going to enter or a nurse with a security guard who would force them to stay. He didn't know if that was possible or not. He thought he could take her whenever he wanted, that it was his right as a parent, but he'd seen shows where they called the police, and judges let doctors overrule parents. He didn't want to ask either. If he was wrong, it would clue them in on what they were doing.

"Okay," Sam said. She stepped beside him. "But can we see Mom before we go?"

It was a bad idea. He wanted to get out of there. But he also wanted the same thing. *God, Jill*, he thought. "Okay." He spotted a magazine on the table and handed it to Sam. "Hold this in front of your hand so no one sees and just follow me. Okay?"

"Okay."

He opened the door and peeked down the hall. A nurse entered a room two doors down. Another pushed a cart of medical supplies toward them, paused, and entered a room.

"Let's go," he whispered. She came out behind him, and he shut the door.

They walked toward the nurse's desk, and Wes thanked God it was empty. They turned, and he pressed the elevator button. It dinged before the button had time to light up, and a stern-looking nurse stared him in the face.

He was frozen. What was she going to say? She had to know what they were doing. Was she going to scream for security?

"Sir?" she said.

"Yes?"

"Excuse me, sir?"

"Yes?"

"Can you move, please, sir?"

Wes blinked and realized he was blocking the elevator door. He stepped to his right, and the nurse walked right by him. He got into the elevator and pressed 3. Sam got behind him.

A heartbeat later, the elevator dinged and opened. The third floor was busier than the second, with visitors, patients, and nurses moving around.

"Come on," Wes said softly, leading Sam to the right and down the hall.

Every noise, every footstep echoed in Wes's ears. Each voice had to be analyzed—were they talking about him? About Sam? Did they know?

The door was closed to Jill's room, and the tiny window was blocked by a curtain inside. Wes turned the knob and pushed. He went in slowly. He looked for nurses, doctors, anyone. He saw no one.

Sam closed the door behind them as Wes reached for the curtain that blocked the view of his wife. He slid it back, and tears welled in his eyes. She had been there two days, and she already looked thin. Her cheeks were bonier, her skin paler, her lips dry.

He took her hand, minding the IV. He watched her chest slowly raise and lower and heard a whimper behind him.

"She's…" Sam's words failed her. Tears streamed down her face.

"Come on," Wes waved her to the side of the bed. "She's… just sleeping right now."

Sam stood next to her father. She rested a hand on her mother's leg. "Will she wake up?"

"Yes." Wes placed a hand on Sam and pulled her close. "We are going to wake her up." He felt a tear crawl down his cheek. He took a deep breath and told Jill inside his head, *We're going to beat that bastard. We'll be back.*

More tears ran down his cheeks. They made his skin cool in the dry hospital air.

"Come on." He let go of Jill's hand and stepped back.

"I love you, Mom," Sam whispered. She followed her dad from the room.

3

Diana Henson led Lisa along the side of the mountain, through dips and rises in the land until the game trail ran west and into the forest. They crossed a dry creek bed, where Di took a moment to think, then went north, following the creek.

Virb ran into the woods, exploring deer and ground squirrel scents, came back to check in, then went off again.

Lisa played with the tiny yellow hat-wearing bear that came from inside her egg. She barely raised her gaze unless Di told her to look out or watch her step. She said almost nothing until the dry bed headed up onto the next mountain, and Di led them out and further west.

"What are we looking for?" Lisa finally said. Her arms rested at her sides, the toy dangling from her fingers.

"Someplace I really wish we didn't have to go."

That answer held Lisa for around twenty seconds as she took in the green and brown and cracks of blue above. "That doesn't really answer my question. Am I not allowed to know? Is it a grownup thing?" She thought of all the things Mom and Dad always told her *we'll explain when you're older*, and older never seemed to come. Like when Sam explained to her how babies come from her lady parts and not from her belly button like Janet Steiner said. When Lisa asked Mom if that was true, Mom, with a shocked face, refused to answer at first, and that alone was enough to tell her it was.

"No. It's not a *grownup* thing. It's just a thing I don't want to think about." Yet, Di was forced to.

It was 1992, weeks after they thought it had all ended, and each death was proving a few inches farther from the now and slightly less sharp in their minds. They had debated the best place to put it, one where it wouldn't be found by human hands within their lifetime.

Di suggested throwing it in the river, but Wes was concerned it may wash up on some riverbank. Jill thought the lake may be a good place, in the deepest, darkest spots of the damned up Missouri or Flathead. That could have worked but would have required an adult to drive them there, or they'd have to wait until next summer, which they really didn't want to do. It was Wes's idea to explore the abandoned mines outside of town. They were all boarded up with *Keep Out* signs and *Danger* warnings. People thought they may cave in at some point because of century-old supports and rot. So he figured no one would go in there. It wasn't the safest idea, but they agreed that would make it even better. Now, as she neared the entrance of the mine they had decided on, Di wished she had waited for Wes and not brought the little one along.

The cliff face, in its timeless stone, was identical to that day almost thirty years ago. Bands of light-gray, brown, and tan granite ran horizontally from the base to a hundred feet up, where the mountain inclined more gradually and the higher elevation spruces and firs co-mingled with pines.

The entrance itself had aged only from the defacement of man, or more probably, teenagers. There was a new *Keep Out* sign since last time, this one metal instead of wood and bearing the phone number and logo of the Bureau of Land Management. There were dozens of graffiti images, some expletives and body parts, some names, and some designs of animals and landscapes. Di put on an archeologist's hat for a second and wondered if, after a thousand years, these images could become as highly regarded as indigenous cave drawings after our downfall and the rise of the next society had been completed. *Fuck no*, is what she came up with.

They stopped at the mine entrance, and Di withdrew a flashlight from her pocket. She shined it past the wooden boards and a pair of chains that blocked the way. The inside was littered with broken beer and liquor bottles, beer cans, and fast food wrappers. She shined the light back as far as it would reach and only saw black, nothing to block her path.

Di kneeled next to Lisa and unlooped Virb's leash from her shoulder. She stretched it out, and Virb came to sit beside her and licked her face. An uneasy smile broke through; Virb always made that happen. She clipped the leash onto Virb's collar and held the leash out to Lisa.

Lisa cocked her head left. "You want me to hold him?"

"Yes. It's dangerous in there for kids and dogs, and I want you both to wait here."

"Is it dangerous for adults too?"

Di chuckled. "Yes. But even more so for little ones."

Lisa contemplated this, looking into the cave and back over the forest they had hiked through. "I'd rather go inside."

"I bet so. You're very brave." She rested a hand on Lisa's back. "But I need you to wait out here. If you got hurt in here, help would be very far away. And, your dad and mom would kill me."

Lisa huffed and took the leash by the handle. "I'll keep him safe. There could be bears or lions in the woods."

"Thank you." Di leaned in and hugged the girl. "I'll try to be quick."

4

Janet Steiner sat on the couch, bored with her Nintendo, bored with her phone, and bored with her toy Maltese, Bridget. She didn't like school, but with it being closed and her being home with no friends to talk to and tease, she was finding herself wishing it was open again. It wasn't her fault that the old lady had died. Why should she suffer?

She heard a car outside and glanced through the window. There was a mail car, and the lady inside was shutting her mailbox. Janet wasn't expecting anything to come in the mail but decided she would go check it out anyway. It would be better than playing Roblox for the hundredth time today.

"Come on," she told the tiny dog as she got up from the couch. Bridget yipped and jumped to the floor.

They went through the front door and past the note from Mom asking Janet to stay inside, practice her flute, feed the animals, and clean her room. She had fed Bridget—well, she had given Bridget the Frosted Flakes that she didn't eat—the rest could wait. As for her room and the flute... the day had just been too stressful, and she needed a mental health break—at least that was what she planned on saying when Mom got home from work.

With the rain gone and the sun shining, Janet wished even harder to be out doing something. She groaned at the stupidity of that woman who let herself get killed.

The neighborhood was quiet, beyond the songs of birds hidden in the trees. The rows of 1960s bungalows were neat and tidy, and as a shout and then a laugh came over a neighboring fence, Janet wondered why there weren't more cool kids on her street. She ignored the idiot, home-schooled neighbor kids and moved on.

At the curb, she opened the box. There was only one thing inside: a white letter with her address and Mom's name. She pulled it out and examined it. It was light and probably only had a single page inside. She wondered what it was and clamped her jaw shut. There were no markings or logos or symbols.

She shut the box and held the letter up to the sky, blocking the sun with it. Nope, there was nothing more to see from that angle either. Definitely no money in there.

Bridget yipped.

"What? You can't have it."

The dog looked at her and panted, tongue hanging. She yipped again.

"Okay, treat for you, candy for me." She walked back toward the front door and it occurred to her that Mom wouldn't mind if she opened the letter for her.

5

Diana Henson stepped past what seemed like an imaginary demarcation, a line on the stone floor that signified the end of the beer bottle dump and the beginning of a place too putrescent for even the petulant youth of the past thirty years to dare to venture. There was a change in the air, a chill that didn't seem to come from temperature but from the mine's heart.

Di gauged the timber supports as she moved. The hundred-year-old wood was permeated with dust, cracks, and chips. She didn't want to think about them or about what could happen if just one of them gave way from the years of rot and stress, but her mind played it out regardless. She saw crashing rock and clouds of dust. She saw never-ending night as she was trapped there forever. She saw herself not moving fast enough to evade the fall of thousands of tons of earth and her bones crushing under their weight.

She was glad she left Lisa and Virb behind. Her life was enough to risk, not a major loss to anyone else if something bad happened. She thought of Carly in her kitchen with a hole she put there. She was an asshole but didn't deserve that. Maybe the world would be better off if she didn't make it out of there? Maybe having that rock buried permanently in this cave was what should happen? If it didn't make it out... and she recognized what was happening.

The whispers wanted in. They wanted her to give up and let them push her around the way they did Ray Trent. The way she was sure they did Barton Smith.

"Get out of my head, you son of a bitch." She pushed herself onward. She filled her head with rage instead of doubt. Rage about her mother, her father, the lost friends this asshole had cost her.

She found the first fork. Old narrow gauge tracks went right; the left was a step down to a ladder a few feet in. She could hear the miners in her mind. The tracks were the second phase of the mine. The downward shaft was the third. She saw young Wes climb down, Jill gazing into the shaft as he went, her fingers balled into fists. Di had to go down.

She took a breath and clenched her teeth. The wooden ladder was mildly newer than the timber that supported the whole mine. It was dry and weak, and likely to crumble in her hand. She ignored the thought. That was what the mare wanted her to think.

"*Go away,*" a draft hissed from the shaft.

"Fuck you." Di sat on the edge of the ladder and started her descent.

It was forty feet deep if it was an inch. Her light didn't reach the bottom, but she knew it was there. It was there last time, and it would be again.

The rungs creaked in her hands and under her feet. She ignored them. Or, she tried to. In the back of her mind, she thought of the forty or so pounds less she had weighed the last time she used this ladder. It didn't matter at this point. If she fell, that was it, and that would be her fate. Worrying about it now would only feed the mare.

She heard a drip in the distance below. She heard the wind from the lower extents. It made no sense, there was nowhere for the wind to come from, but it seemed unrelenting as it moved.

Halfway down, she guessed—she couldn't tell, only feel—the moaning started. It was like a low groan at first, a distant person in pain. It was all in her head, though; it had to be. She kept moving.

One, two, a half-dozen more rungs, and she paused. She shined her light down. Blackness.

"What the?"

There was no floor, but the ladder ceased after two more rungs. There was a moment of panic as Di felt like the world had vanished underneath her. She saw herself slipping from the ladder and drifting off into an unknown realm of darkness and death. Then she saw a ripple across the obsidian. It wasn't an empty nothing; it was water. The bottom of the mine was flooded.

"Shit."

She shined the light around. She saw the mine walls, the ceiling, the path away from the ladder. The tunnels had seemed about the height of a hallway when she was a kid. She saw Wes walking. He shined his light at the ceiling, the walls, the beams, inspecting everything as he went. The mine roof was several feet above him. It stretched four feet above the water line now.

"Shit. I guess I'm getting wet." She continued down. Her shoe dipped into the water. It was cold, like freezing runoff from the mountain peaks, maybe fifty-five degrees at the warmest. She saw herself taking too long to do this and dying from hypothermia. *No.* That was what the mare wanted her to worry about.

She lowered herself deeper into the water until she reached the mine floor. Water lapped just above her belly button, and she hoped this was as deep as it was going to get.

Her light ahead, Di kept moving. Water sloshed, and the groans grew louder. She could smell the walls, the half-soaked timber, molding and slimy, waterlogged. She wondered if dry rot or rot from water would weaken them worse. If she remembered correctly, she was halfway there.

At the next junction, the mine floor descended. She could choose left, right, or straight. Her memory said to go straight. Her gut said to go right. The groans came from the left, and they were louder now. The sound reminded her of the cheesy zombie movies she'd seen over the years and their hunger for brains. But that wasn't what this was. This had to be water making the timber beams stretch and squeak. It was being amplified by reverberation against the water and hard stone walls. That had to be the cause.

"Which way?" She mumbled. Her feet were getting numb. A shiver rippled up her belly and down her arms. Splashing echoed from the left.

Di's brow wrinkled. She was sure she remembered following Wes straight through here. Jill was behind her. She asked Wes if this was far enough yet; he said *No, a little deeper*. She wished this was where he had said yes.

She took a step forward, and her gut gnawed at her. *Go right*, it said. She didn't know why. Why should she go a different way than she remembered? This wasn't the place or the time to go exploring. No, she'd listen to her memory. That had to be the right call.

She pushed on, water now chilling the bottom of her breasts. She held her arms up over the water like wings ready to flap. *Not far now*, she told herself.

There was splashing behind her. Drops of water patted the back of her head.

"Fuck?" Her heart pounded. She spun around. There was nothing there. A groan from behind her. She spun again. Nothing. Her heart was racing. "Fuck you, demon! You're not going to stop me!"

She pushed forward, forcing herself against the water. Her feet were nearly numb, only feeling the pressure of the ground beneath them.

Splashing, water on her head, the back of her neck. She ignored it. The bastard wasn't going to slow her down anymore, no matter what she felt or saw. He couldn't stop her. He wasn't real when she was awake, not unless he had a puppet to command, and she was alone here.

The moaning was louder. It was right behind her. Water moved past her leg like a current, then something brushed against her thigh. *No*, she thought, and pressed on. She was almost there. She knew it. One more junction and a right turn, and there would be... She stopped in her tracks. The mine went silent. Directly in front of her was a wall of boulders. Rocks the size of bowling balls formed a mound from the water to the ceiling.

"No!" Her voice echoed and pained her ears. How could this be? She was almost there... It was almost within her grasp.

She went to the wall and touched it. It was real. She shined her light at the broken ceiling. Boulders the size of cars leaned down, balancing against the wall of smaller stones. They rumbled above her head, and she jerked her hands away and stepped backward.

"God-dammit!" Her gut had told her. She should have gone the other way. Maybe there was a connecting path if she had.

Di spun around and faced a skull. White and grayish bone, mildew and slime, rotten teeth. There was a miner's hat on its head, rusted and strapped under the jaw, a hunk of rotting flesh pinned against the bone. A skeletal body in overalls supported it. It swayed toward her and back with the passage's tiny waves.

Di screamed. The dead thing groaned. Her eyes searched the darkened walls as if there were somewhere else to go while her brain argued, shouting, *This can't be real!* She reacted without thinking. Her fist balled. It crashed into the side of the thing's face.

The head came off, flipping upside down and floating as if its hat were a saucer-shaped boat. It crumpled forward, diving into the water toward Di.

She screamed again and rushed past the floating head through the tunnel. Bubbles rose behind her, groans popping free with each pocket of air.

"No, no, no," she repeated. She tried to move faster, but the water felt thicker the harder she fought. She pushed herself up and kicked until her other foot found the ground in a half-run, half-swim.

Groans echoed, and she refused to look back. It was more than one now, overlapping tones from multiple things. There had to be three, maybe more, by the rise in volume.

Di's heart pounded inside her chest. Why was this water so hard? She thought of the upcoming junction. Which way would she go? Left was where her intuition had told her to go. Straight would get her to the ladder and the hell out of there. She needed to go left—she needed to find another way to get the mare's stone, but her numbed feet and pounding chest disagreed. The fright that ran down her limbs said *no*, she needed to get the hell out now.

Her flashlight glimmered against the water ahead. It lapped on the wall and back into her path like a small pool of oil, waiting for victims to drench and grab and slime. And she wanted no part of it. She wanted to fly. She wanted to raise her body above this pit, smash through the rock above, and burst through the surface to safety.

But she couldn't. She had to go through that mess, and she had to go left. There was no choice, not even if she were dragged down to the depths by skeletons or drowned by slick oily water. She had to get that stone.

Splashes drenched her head from behind. She felt air whip by her back. Whatever they were back there, they were getting closer. She gripped her flashlight hard and pushed her legs even harder.

The junction came. She passed the stone corner, but her momentum nearly pushed her beyond the turn. She pressed against the wall and jerked herself left. She started down the unexplored path, and her eyes crossed her pursuers.

There were three, she was right about that, but they weren't skeletons. These were rot-covered bodies wearing the same overalls as the first. Their faces were deformed, flesh drooping as if slipping away from the bone. Their eyes glowed in the gloom, and in their hands were pickaxes.

"Fuck!" Di jumped and sprinted against the deluge. She felt water splash her flashlight and held it higher. She didn't know if it was waterproof and really didn't want to test it right now.

Moaning became growling. Gurgling throats echoed hungering calls down the tunnel. They were wet, air passing over slimy flesh and disused maws. Their voices overlapped and blended like a strange demonic choir, and Di felt them pressing on her ears and seeping into her mind.

She forced her body forward, her legs numbing from the outside in, her waist freezing, her face splashed, and her arms tightened into rigid gooseflesh.

Her thoughts repeated as she ran, *It can't be real.* The mare didn't have this power. It couldn't make things happen in the real world, it could only suggest. But she was so close now. She was so absorbed by fear, she didn't realize it. She could sense it now, though. The thickness of seeping dread. The humming vibration on the outside of her thoughts. It was near and it was pissed, and that meant something else. She remembered Wes's story about it making him see things in *The Price is Right* and a phantom horse it created in his bedroom. Maybe Marenor couldn't control things in the waking world as well as it did in dreams, but this close to the rock, it could make you see things—put visions in your head the same way it whispered. And just like in a dream, if you believed, it could kill you.

A turn lay ahead, a T junction, and she'd have to decide: left or right. Her gut said left, and this time she was going to listen.

She readied her hands. Her flesh shook, but she would make this work. She closed the small flashlight between her teeth in a snarl.

Di ran and splashed into the turn, bracing the wall as she pushed her body around the corner and then stopped. She froze, staring at the edge, waiting for them to come.

As the first one rounded, Di grabbed his pickax, then punched him in the face. His nose crumpled under her fist, popping like a tiny flesh balloon. She ripped the tool away, his hands making a soggy crunch as they went. She raised it and sank it through his hard hat and into his skull.

The second one marched around the corner, and Di ripped her pickax free. The thing sneered, and Di could see black rot inside its head. She shoved the top of the pickax forward, ramming the T into its mouth and cracking its teeth into crumbs. It swung its own at her, and she chanted inside her mind, *not real, not real, not real.*

Rusted steel passed over Di's chest. She felt wind as it seemed to return to the land of dreams, but as the tail swept by, she felt a sting, and the rusty steel gashed her skin below her collarbones. It wasn't deep, but it was a cut. It was her not believing quite well enough.

She swung again. The point of her ax dove deep into the side of the thing's head. She saw the next one coming and shoved as she ripped the weapon free. The miner's head split in two, exposing webs of black and green goo. It stretched as the halves of its head parted. They splashed and sank into the black water.

Di stepped back. She held the ax in both hands, waiting.

Not real. Not real. Not real.

Water bubbled in front of her.

It wasn't real. It was in her mind, but her chest still stung like a bitch.

The bubbles stopped.

She couldn't have killed the last one. She just pushed it. The mare may know she's onto it, but it wouldn't just quit. She stared at the water, waiting for bubbles to rise.

"Shit."

Water splashed up and onto her back. Bony hands seized her throat and yanked her backward into the black mire.

The flashlight sank, exposing a current of muck and specs of floating debris. It hit the ground, and Di could see the outline of her legs floating in front of her.

The pickax slipped from her hands as she grabbed the fingers on her neck and tore them away. She felt burning, ripping pain in her shoulder. It was biting her. With her other hand, she jabbed her fingers into its eyes. A cloud of goo burst into the water, but its jaws persisted. She screamed, releasing the hand and the last bit of air in her lungs. She seized the skull in both hands and tore at it.

She screamed inside, *I'm stronger than you!*

The head tore from its shoulders, and the miner ripped a slice of skin from her body. It dangled from its teeth.

Di convulsed. She felt water rushing into her lungs. She slammed her feet down and her body up.

She breached the surface, but half a breath of water had already made it down. Her body jerked and spasmed. The flashlight flickered from below. A brief thought crossed her mind, *I need that*, and the light was gone.

Coughing, she jerked forward and belched water. She sucked in air and coughed so hard she saw stars. She leaned on the wall.

Please don't pass out. If she did, she would drown for sure.

She coughed and gasped. The stars brightened, covering the blackened mine in waves of fireworks.

Stay awake. She fought against the pressure pounding on her brain. Her ears ached. Her lungs burned. Her head felt like it would explode at any minute, or a blood vessel would burst and leave her a stroked-out corpse.

Di imagined her niece and Virb at the mine entrance as night fell and the mare sent its next puppet after them. She saw Wes climbing down here in grief and finding her body, only to be attacked by his own set of miners.

The coughing faded. Her vision cleared of fireworks, showing instead the shapes of her imagination and the illusions imprinted on her retinas. Her head kept pounding.

After several minutes Di caught her breath. Water tapped against her waist. Her chest stung. Her ears rang and focused on every drip or long-off echo. Her eyes lied about every shape they imagined.

"I can still do this," she whispered. If she kept her wits and paid attention, she should be able to follow her path back. First, though, she needed the rock.

Di held her hand against the wall and walked forward. Its surface was bumpy, rough. She tried to orient herself based on how the other tunnel was, the one Wes had led them down. She had no frame of reference in the dark, but it seemed like if the two tunnels met, it would be ahead and on her left.

She prayed to herself. *Let it not be far.* She was ready for this to be over. She was ready to be back up in the daylight. She picked up her pace and felt the left wall with both hands, humming as she walked, blocking out the sound of unseen waves.

It took ten minutes, but she found a corner turning left. Just a few more yards, and she saw a blue light. It wasn't bright. Even in the total absence of light, she may have missed it if she weren't straining to see anything and everything.

She got closer and saw the blue glow leaking from between other rocks. There was a hole in the wall and a depression within it. She picked them up one at a time and plopped them into the water, and with each splash, the glow brightened.

Di could see the stone beneath the rest. She saw the letters and their strange writing peek through beyond the others.

"Yes!" She heard her words bounce down the tunnel and back. Her heart raced. This was it. She had found it.

Another, and another useless rock out of the way, and she had it. She held Marenor's stone in her hand. It hummed with that strange power that she hadn't felt in thirty years. Her hand felt odd, tingly, but she still wanted to grip it. It was like the thing now called her, its whispers amplified through her skin, and promises overflowed from its surface.

"No." She remembered Dad. She remembered the years of torment. The blood. There was no promise it could make to rectify the past.

She stuffed it into her pocket. It left a giant bulge in her jacket, but with layers of fabric between her and it, her thoughts were more her own.

Now she just had to find her way back.

6

Officer Stuart Harrison pulled up to 2067 Cooney Street. The mature spruces lining the road shaded the entire yard. The 50s-era bungalow looked sad to him. It wasn't that the home was dirtier or less attractive than the other homes on the street—though it was covered with grime and noticeably in need of a new roof—there was a general feeling of depression that seemed to radiate from the home.

Shaggy rose bushes waved wiry limbs in the breeze, and the cracked wooden fence swayed as broken slats dangled from their posts. It was as if the home had a sense of what had happened here in the past. The building itself had taken on the aspect of a sour old man, weary from years gone by and, from the looks of it, ready to give up.

Harrison remembered his father's notes. Most of the bodies had been in the basement corner. He said the smell was like a slaughterhouse's refuse. He wondered if that could really *kill* a house? That much evil and horror.

He stepped out of his vehicle and over the curb. He walked toward the front porch, toward the stained siding, the trim that flaked brown paint from deteriorating wood, the tarnished brass door knocker that hung like a dead limb from the broad, wooden front door.

He paused at the edge of the stairs, and all of a sudden, he didn't want to go any further. He needed to talk to Lawrence, but a wave of cold pressure seemed to want him to leave. He wanted to agree but couldn't. He needed to find out more about what had happened thirty years ago. It might have been a crazy hunch, but he had to follow it, even if every cell in his being told him to turn around and go the other way.

He looked down at the porch decking. The once-stained wood was bare and scuffed, cracked and rotting in places. An image of the basement came to him. Those rotting corpses from his father's notes. It was still here—the death—it had taken up residence and now lived full time with Lawrence. And it warned him away.

Harrison turned from the door. He looked at the driveway—no cars. There was probably no one at home. Maybe he was better off taking a look around the outside first before knocking, anyway.

He backed down the stairs and walked around the home to the right. The widows were closed, drapes drawn. He walked until the fence met the siding.

Through missing boards and cracks in the rotten wood, he gazed into the backyard. It was overgrown with weeds and long grass. Grasshoppers buzzed from one side of the scrubby ground to another. It wasn't what Harrison was looking for.

He thought about opening the gate and checking further in the back.

He didn't have a warrant, though, no cause. Instead, he turned around and walked the other way, retracing his steps, then surveying the left side of the home.

Windows were covered here as well with thick brown drapes. He neared the fence on this side and paused under the boughs of a massive spruce. He looked into the back from this side and wondered what the hell he was doing? He was sneaking around a house from a crime that happened thirty years ago with no real evidence for a case that wasn't even his problem. No matter the feelings he had, this was the type of shit that could get him reprimanded.

He muttered, "Screw this," and took a step, and the sour scent of death crossed his nose.

Harrison looked up at the curtained window and down at the basement push-out. The basement was a place of death, but the smell couldn't still be there from that long ago. He stepped up to the house, placing his hands on the ancient siding. It was gritty under his fingers.

A faint light shined through the curtained window. There must have been a lit lamp on the other side. Waving his nose and swaying his head to find the source of the smell, Harrison looked for cracks in the curtain, a way to see inside.

As he moved to the left side of the frame, he saw a quarter-inch crack between the fabric and the trim. A slice of the far wall was in view. It was painted in a maroon shade, and there was a picture on the wall. He only saw the golden frame and the shoulder of someone, a portrait though, he was sure. The scent of rot seeped through the edge of the window pane, and a nauseating clench grabbed his stomach.

He turned and crouched; maybe he could get a better view if he just—

The curtain flew wide. The dark soulless eyes of a young girl looked down at him. She smiled. It was a pale imitation, like the smile of an artificially intelligent chatbot or latex-covered android. It sent chills across his flesh, and he stepped back. He thought to grab his gun, but she held his gaze, and it was impossible. Then, he saw behind her: a putrefying woman on an antique bed. The sheets below her were yellow and green, and it was as if he could smell her even more now that her image was clear.

Bile rose in Harrison's throat, and a sharp pain rocked the rear of his skull. He felt puke rise as he dropped into the grass.

1992

1

Jim Jones roamed the halls of Custer Falls Elementary. With the kids out for recess, he finally had more than a few minutes to himself, and he wanted to use them productively.

He had crossed the Five hall and moved into the Six. Two doors down, he found Ms. Swallows' room. Her pseudonym seemed to roll off his tongue as he whispered it to himself. Through the door's narrow window, he saw her sitting at her desk. He looked her up and down, sneering at the loose, frumpy clothes she continued to wear. All this week, it'd been that crap—ever since he'd started having the dreams.

She lifted her mug above her gray sweater and sipped as she read a book. Jones couldn't see the title, but he was sure it was some trashy romance thing—women loved those. That was good. Maybe she'd be in a better mood when he saw her tonight.

He knew he shouldn't conflate the two; his logical mind demanded that this her and the one in his dreams were two different things. But as he looked at her neck, at the light purple spots where he had sucked on her skin and she had failed to hide very well with concealer, his id screamed both Swallows were one and the same.

Her lips pressed against her mug and the whisper said, "*Go.*"

Jones twisted the knob and stepped inside.

Sallow turned abruptly, her coffee spilling over the edge of her cup. She sat up straight in her seat. Her lips pressed firmly together, guarding.

He closed the door and clicked the lock. He was starting to breathe heavily as he walked toward her desk.

"Mr. Jones, can I... help you." She turned in her chair and set her mug on her desk.

"*Go*," the voice said. He crossed the space between them at a quickened pace. Her eyes went wide as he stopped beside her and lifted the hair on the side of her neck, examining the poorly covered purple blotches.

"Mr. Jones, what are you doing?" She jerked her head back and her hair with it. Fear was blossoming in her gaze.

"Don't be like that." His voice was low, insistent. "You enjoy our nights."

"What?" She began to tremble.

"You may scream, but your body says yes."

She pushed back her chair. "I don't know who's telling you about my dreams—who could know... But, you, stay away from me." Her grip pinched tightly around her armrests.

Jones grew a crooked smile. "I was just thinking... why do we have to wait until tonight."

"Get out. Now. I'll call the cops."

Jones's brow wrinkled. He looked down with disgust. He didn't want to hear what the whisper was saying now, but if he had to, he had to.

Sallow stood. The sleeve of her right arm bunched up, showing the bruised lines around her wrist. "I'm warning you."

Jones lifted his shirt and reached around to his back. Sallow pulled open the desk drawer. His arm swung around with his pistol in hand. Sallow straightened up with a shiny kitchen knife in hers.

"Put that down," Jones commanded.

"Put yours down."

They stared into the depths of each other's eyes, weapons aimed at each other's waists.

"Now." Jones nodded.

Her eyelid twitched. Every moment of each dream flashed past her, the bonds, the weapons, the beatings, the sex. Her teeth clamped down. It had been all a dream, but here he stood, just as the whispers had said he would. She was right to listen, to bring the knife. It was all going to end now, one way or another. If it was real, he was going to be dead. If it was a dream, she'd conquer the fear and beat it.

"Now." She nodded back.

His finger tightened around the trigger. She lunged forward, plunging the knife up into Jones's massive gut. She jerked left and sliced his belly open like a thick bag of sausages. His guts tumbled over his legs, and he screamed and fired. Bullets tore into her left breast, slicing lung, shattering ribs. Then her right breast, lung, ribs. Blood sprayed from her chest, then spread in a pair of swelling flowers.

She screamed and stabbed again, this time down. It split the flesh between his collarbone and his neck. She pulled it out and drove it into his arm. Under his skin, she saw thick yellow fat and red oozing muscle. As she glimpsed bone, he fired again. Her left arm sprayed blood across her desk.

She swung at the hand with the gun. Her bloody blade sliced through his wrist, catching on the bone.

"Bitch!" His gun clattered against the floor. He swayed forward and back, blood gushing from each wound. His eyes found his hanging intestines, and blood and bile bubbled up over his lips.

"Fuck you," she gasped.

He tipped back and flopped onto his ass, then to his right side. His intestines dragged along like tails on a kite.

At her feet, she spotted the gun. A genuine smile came to her face. It was one like she hadn't had in a week. It was joy. She dropped the blade and leaned over. One foot slipped in the blood beneath her, and the other followed. The left side of her head slammed into the floor with a crack, and a burst of laughter filled the room.

Sallow sat up, gun in hand. The left half of her head was a blob of matted hair and blood. Her lips and eye drooped. She giggled like a small child and pointed it at Jones's skull.

He wondered if she had ever looked this pretty before. Then, she fired.

2

The telephone in the living room trilled. A moment later, Betty Henson answered and then called upstairs, "Di! Come get this phone for your brother."

When Di made it down, Mom was in the kitchen with an Irish coffee. She hadn't committed to straight liquor yet; that wouldn't come until tomorrow, but the house's supply of both whiskey and coffee had been steadily dropping for nearly twenty-four hours.

"Yeah, Mom?" Di said. Her eyes burned as she looked at her mother, face hanging over her drink at the kitchen table. She raised a hand and pointed to the cordless on the counter. The green light was lit. "Okay."

She carried the phone upstairs, tempted but not enough to put it to her ear and ask who it was. Who could it be? Jill was on her way to her aunt's. Chris was at school.

"Here." She tossed it on the bed beside Wes and sat between him and the TV. She had decided to play Mario, a game she'd played a thousand times and required no new brain power.

Wes lifted the phone to his ear. "Hello?"

A raspy voice spoke from the other end, "Hey, you chump."

The voice's owner didn't click in Wes's head. It almost sounded like an old man.

"You forget about me already?"

Realizing who was there was like a brick to his temple. Wes shouted, "Tommy!"

Di frowned and looked back at her brother, contemplating if this was a trick.

"Finally, dude." His voice was like a man who hadn't had a drink in a year.

"Holy shit, you're awake. How?"

"I don't know. It was a bastard, but I did it."

"He's awake?" Di accepted the news. She spun and stared at the phone.

"That's awesome, man." It felt like the first good news Wes had heard in forever. "Are you getting out? Going home?"

"I don't know yet. They've had like ten doctors in here, and they called my mom. I could hear her screaming through the phone. I had to demand that they give me a minute to call you."

"Yeah? That's great news. Thanks for telling us you're awake."

"It's not just that. It's what I saw that I needed to tell you—about the mare."

"The what?"

"The thing we're up against. It's called a mare. It's some kind of old demon, a dream monster that feeds on chaotic thoughts when bad shit happens. It's somehow learned to influence people that are awake too."

"How do you even know that?"

"I saw it. I was, like, inside it—I can't explain much more than that right now. I'll call you back later once it calms down here."

"Okay. And, dude, I'm glad you're awake."

"Me too. In the meantime, don't trust anyone, awake or asleep."

3

Tommy Laskin hung up the phone and laid back against his pillow. His head was a throbbing mess, and as strange as it sounded, he really wanted to take a nap. His eyes were heavy, and every breath seemed to take more energy than he had.

I've slept enough, he told himself.

But his injured brain disagreed. He stared at the wall across from his bed and fought the pressure of his body demanding rest. Nurses buzzed around him like flies, and in the wall, he began to see a vision.

He saw the inside of the cave, not the real one, but Marenor's prison, where dozens of his schoolmates waited in limbo for their turn with him.

Jamie Madison, Cherry French, and Shelly Sullivan no longer chatted about Lonny More, Jeff Ramos, and Billy Caldwell. Now they had each other in their grips, fingers clenching shirts and shaking one another.

Lonny More, Jeff Ramos, and Billy Caldwell were shouting at each other. Lonny held a pocketknife and moved its aim from Jeff to Billy and back to Jeff. Billy bit into his lip, his fists balled and ready to throw. Jeff rose and fell on his toes, ready to pounce on whichever of his friends took the first shot.

Randy Benson was no longer screaming and trying to escape. He was sitting at the cave entrance, staring into a path he must have tried a thousand times, only to be sent back here. A hundred tiny glowing strands stretched from him into the ceiling.

"Can't stay away, can you?" a slithering voice asked.

Tommy shook his head, and the vision on the wall vanished.

4

Chris Conners was on his way back to class when an ambulance and a cop car skidded to a stop in front of the school. Mr. Swann, red-eyed and disheveled, blocked students from going inside until the officers and emergency medical technicians had passed, then he sent the kids to the gym.

Vice Principal Maynard was just inside the door. His hair was frizzed and puffy above his head, and his suit was more wrinkled than usual. He ushered in each kid from recess, saying, "Have a seat Indian-style on the floor. We hope to be through this soon." A minute later, other kids started coming in, the younger kids from the other side of the school.

"What is this?" Scott Wake said as he sat next to Chris. He was in the same shirt he'd worn for the last two days, and Chris wondered if anyone was even at his house, or if he was being completely ignored while his sister was in a coma at Memorial.

"I don't know." Chris didn't care, either. He was more interested in finding a way to take a nap and seeing if he could find that thing again. He didn't think he wanted to make the deal, but after seeing how weak Mom was this morning, after Charlotte was still missing, he was ready to have a conversation. Maybe he could put his head down in Language Arts and pretend he was listening?

A cop and two EMTs ran down the hallway past the door. They pushed a stretcher, but Chris couldn't tell who was on it.

"You see that?" Scott asked.

"Yup." He wondered if the thing could really heal his mom. It had to be possible, didn't it? Maybe if she was in his dream and he used that unicorn blood on her or something? He felt a twinge of hope for her, something he hadn't felt in a long time.

"Okay, everyone," Mr. Maynard shouted over the growing din of kids, "we're all going to wait here for your buses to come, and everyone's going home early today."

5

Jill Elden turned the corner onto 7th Avenue, barely missing Ray Trent's shadow as he ducked behind a bush. She passed the Conoco, Bended Leaf, a used bookstore, and went into Elden Insurance.

The bell dinged as she stepped inside the small office and took in the smell that she always assumed came through the wall from the bookstore: moldy old print and dust. Light followed her through the glass door, the only window in the place, and lit a thousand floating specs.

"Just a sec," Aunt Silva called from the storage room.

The bell still hummed, making Jill wonder why they even had a bell in an office this small. She imagined her six-foot-five father lying on the floor and being able to touch one wall with his foot and the opposite with his outstretched hand. There were two desks, one, her grandfather's, who almost never came into the office anymore, and one that was Silva's. Her grandfather claimed to be retired, but after fifty years of insurance customers in town, he wasn't always able to make that claim work. Some of them just wanted to talk to him rather than Silva, even if she had been there for twenty. And though he denied it, he liked still being needed.

Silva came from the storage, her blonde hair tied behind her head, reminding Jill of old pictures of models she'd seen from the forties. It brought a smile to her face, and that brought Silva's singsong Auntie welcome, "Oh, my sweet Jill!"

She pursed her lips and planted a big red lipstick stain on Jill's cheek, then immediately grabbed a tissue from the box on her desk and began wiping the red mark.

"So good to see you!" Her accent when talking with her family was faint, but there—not one of an immigrant, but one of having been brought up in her family's native tongue until she had to start school with the locals at six. "Do you not have school today?"

Jill stared at the floor and returned to her aunt. "Well..."

"It's okay," Silva sat at her desk and opened one of her drawers. "We all need time to ourselves, now and then." She reached into the drawer and withdrew a bar of Marabou, and unfolded the wrapper. A third of the chocolate bar was gone, and she broke a section off and held it out for Jill.

"Thank you." Jill seized the candy and bit a small corner. She wanted to shove the whole thing in but restrained herself. She loved Silva's imported sweets, but this wasn't just a social call, and she needed her mouth to speak, not just chew.

She took the paper from her pocket and unfolded it. The transcribed runes seemed strange on the white sheet as if they'd lost all of their importance. Here, they were just marks on a page, scratches of graphite on pulp, and so... ordinary. She felt ashamed. She wondered why she had even come all this way and wasted so much time and energy. Why had she bothered her aunt with this nonsense? There was a pressing thought that she needed to throw the paper away and run home before she made Silva angry for wasting her time too.

"Jill?" Silva looked at her niece curiously. The child had frozen, staring at the paper in her hand.

"Nothing," Jill started to move back. The weight on her head was like a flu, pressing on the sides of her temples and warning her away. She crumpled the paper and threw it at the can on the side of Silva's desk.

"Jill?"

Jill turned and put a hand on the door. She was about to open it and run, the pressure inside said she needed to run, that this would turn out horribly for everyone if she didn't. She saw her mother crying, her father red-faced, and Silva shaking her finger in anger. Then, Silva's hand rested on her shoulder.

"Jill?"

Jill's mind cleared as if a fan had blown away the fog. "What?" She put a hand on her forehead.

"You need to sit down."

Silva guided her to the chair in front of her desk, and Jill felt as if her mind was taking a shower. The confused thoughts washed away, the fear, the sense of paranoia. Was it the thing from her dreams? Had it found her here?

"Eat," Silva tapped the hand with Jill's chocolate. "It will help." She rested her hand on Jill's knee and watched.

Jill took a nibble. Sugar brought her up, and she thought, *I was so dumb.* She picked up the balled paper beside the trash can and put it on the desk. "I'm sorry. Can you read this?"

"Sorry?" Silva glanced at the paper and back to her niece. "No need for sorry, dear. Are you feeling better?"

"Yes, thank you."

Silva nodded and ran her fingers through the hair on the side of Jill's head. "Good." She went to the paper and unfolded it. Her face wrinkled as she looked over the lettering. "Where did you get this?" Her voice had grown distant.

"It was on a rock," Jill said, trying not to lie and trying not to let the crazy events of the past few days put her in a nut house.

"A rock?" Her finger traced the line of text. "This is not something I would expect to find in the USA. You need to tell me more."

"So, you can read it?"

"Yes. But I'm not sure it makes sense. Tell me what this is about."

"It's about bad dreams," Jill said. "My friend found this rock, and— ever since has been having terrible dreams. I told him you might be able to read it."

Silva nodded. "If I am reading this right—and granted, my old Norse is a bit rusty, then the rock this is written on has a mare bound to it."

"A mare?"

"An old myth—a creature that would come to people as they dreamed and give them nightmares—hence the word night-*mare*."

"I don't think it's a myth."

Silva's finger retraced the line of text. "Marenor, this one is called."

"That's his name?"

"Yes. It says he shall be bound to this earth—I think here that means the stone you're referring to. If this was real—and I'm not sure it is—more than likely someone did this as a prank—but if it were real, it would mean an old Norse shaman meant to trap this beast here for some reason."

"And what would happen if my friend broke the stone? If this was real, I mean."

"If this was real? It would free the mare—let it out of its prison. But like I said, these are all myths—scary myths at times, but myths. If I was to guess, your friend's bad dreams are from something else, and this is just a coincidence."

"So then, hypothetically, since it probably isn't real... if it was real, how would you get rid of this? Toss it in a river?"

"No. Since he found the stone, this mare is bound to him now. He would need to put it back where he found it. Even if he gave it to someone else, it wouldn't just move on. It would likely become bound to both of them."

"So, put it back... And what if that wasn't possible? If he can't go back to where he got it?"

"I don't know, dear. But like I said, it's probably a really bad prank that someone is pulling on your friend. These things, they're stories from before we could light the dark like we do today. They're collective fears given life through stories, so our ancestors could feel like they understood the world. We know there's no reason for nightmares today other than the feelings inside us, but they needed a way to explain it. Do you understand what I'm saying?"

"Yes, Auntie."

"Good." She nodded and pushed the paper away. It was an act of disgust, even if she didn't want to believe it, even if her fingers felt tingling from just being near the idea of it.

Jill stood. Silva broke another chunk of chocolate and placed it in her niece's hand.

"I'll tell him not to worry about it." Jill formed her best fake smile. "Thank you."

Silva nodded. "Okay. And come see me more often, child."

Jill walked to the door, and Silva cleared her throat, "But, Jill..."

"Yes?"

"Either way. Stay away from that stone. Even if it's fake, bad things can happen when you toy with evil things, even the idea of evil things."

"Yes, Auntie." Jill stepped outside and bit into her chocolate. She started back toward Wes's house. Ray Trent watched her go.

6

"Shit." Officer Dale Harrison stared at his cruiser's flat tire. A slit bulged from the rubber like a pair of pouting lips. "That wasn't an accident."

He went around to the driver's side, opened the door, and dropped the video cassettes on the passenger seat. He grabbed the radio and hit the mic, "Rhonda, you there?"

"Dale?" Rhonda belched back. "I've been wondering where you were— there was a shooting at the elementary school."

"Goddamn." Harrison shook his head, and thoughts of more hurt kids raced through his mind. "What happened? Is someone on it?"

"Yeah. Two teachers went at it. Luis is on it, and the staties are on the scene too."

His mind went to Stuart. "No kids hurt, I hope?"

"No, but one teacher's shot, the other's cut to hell. One dead."

"Holy..."

"Yup."

He shook his head, but his heart slowed at the thought of no kids being involved this time. And it was a job Officer Luis should be able to handle, at least with the staties' help. On the other hand, he still had kids to find.

"Rhonda, I got a pickup I need you to look up." Harrison passed on the description of the old forestry vehicle, and as he expected, there were only two registered in a fifty-mile radius around town. One was at an address near downtown, an apartment, not an easy place to take a kidnapped girl. The other was outside the city limits.

"I'm going to check on that address in the county—once I fix a flat tire. When Luis is done at the school, send him over to that apartment, just so we cover all our bases."

394

"Yes, sir. Will do."

Harrison huffed and hung up the mic, then went to the trunk for the spare.

7

When Misty Brolin woke up, it was to a skull-splitting headache, stinging lips, and her hands duct taped to the headboard of a bed. She pressed her lips together. They were cracked and tasted like blood.

Panic shot through her. What the hell was going on?

"Hello?" She yanked her arms down. The headboard rattled against the wall, but the tape didn't give. She tried bringing her head to her right hand, thinking she could bite through the tape. The covers over her chest slipped down, and she realized she was naked. Naked? She looked down and mentally checked each part of her body. Had she been touched? Raped? She felt dirty. Her head and back ached. But she didn't think she had been. She glanced at her wrists and thought, *Yet*.

She remembered the ride in her sister's van—God, Mom and Dad. Tears poured down her cheeks. She tried again for her wrist, groaned and stretched, but she couldn't reach. Her arms were too far apart to stretch that way.

"Hello!"

Her eyes went down to her nude chest. She focused on the rest of her body: pain from pine needles in her feet, bare sheets under her butt and her legs. She had bruises all over and wondered what else may be wrong that she hadn't realized.

"God damn you, Ray!"

She banged and yanked on the headboard. She pounded her legs into the bed.

"Help! Anyone?"

Tears ran into her ears and her hair. They dripped to the pillow, and she screamed.

She saw the window and the trees outside. She was in the woods. She remembered running through them. No one was going to hear her. She was going to have to figure another way out of this.

2022

1

Diana Henson followed the flooded tunnel back to the ladder, the ladder to the upper level of the mine, and the mine wall back the creeping light of day and thirty years of high school kids' broken beer bottles and crushed cans. Her eyes met the lump in her pocket. The stone was still there, and so was the gash across her chest, now bright red with irritation.

Virb barked and ran into the mine, dragging his leash.

"Virb!" Lisa shouted from the entrance.

"It's okay," Di said. "I'm here." She kneeled and wrapped her arms around Virb. He was warm, and she felt that warmth all the way inside her heart. She really had made it back. The blackness of the mine, the dead miners, and the terrifying thought that she may never get out all played back in her mind. Virb licked her face, and she couldn't help but smile.

"Aunt Di? Are you coming out?"

"Yeah." She stood, patted Virb on his side one more time, and joined Lisa in the light.

"You're wet." She passed the cheap, plastic toy from hand to hand.

"I am."

"How'd you get so wet?"

She took a deep breath. "There's a lot of water down there."

"You find what you wanted?"

"I did."

"So we can go meet Dad and Sam now?"

"Yeah. Let's get back to the car." Di could have really used a nap and a beer, but she settled for a walk in the partly sunny afternoon light. Lisa asked a question or two, but mostly they just walked, and Di was good with that.

About halfway back, they came to a boulder the height of a bench that was likely used by most hikers as a rest. Di directed Lisa to have a seat, and they both took one together. Virb laid at Di's feet.

Di glanced at the bulge in her pocket and wondered if they had done the right thing. What if they had waited until summer when they were kids and thrown it in the lake a hundred miles away? What if Jill and Tommy were wrong, and she could have just smashed it with a hammer? The idea made her chuckle—she wished she had a hammer.

"What is it?" Lisa asked. Her head cocked left. "Is it cause you're so wet?"

"No. I was just thinking about how we could stop the thing that made your bad dream last night."

"The boy that bit Sam's fingers?"

"No, the thing that made the dream happen. There's a bad guy, and he's what we need to stop."

"How do we stop him?"

"When I was young, I had the idea to smash this rock—it's his prison." Di pointed to the lump in her pocket. "But your mom said that smashing it would set him free, so we didn't do it."

"And you still want to smash it?"

"I do. I want to destroy it."

"Mom's usually right. I don't think you should."

"Yeah. Probably so." She reached and stroked Virb's back and thought about how little she knew about Lisa and Sam and their life, how she had missed just about all of it. She wondered what Wes and Jill were doing so well to make these kids think they were right about stuff. She had always assumed Mom was wrong; Dad was about sixty/forty because he always leveled with her as if she were older than she was. God, she missed him. "Tell me about you, Lisa."

"Like what?" She reached and pet Virb as well.

"I don't know. I never get to see you. What's your life like? What's Mom and Dad like? How about Sam? Are you guys friends?"

"Always. Except when we aren't—like school or when her friends are around. She really likes models. I tried them, but I'm no good. I draw instead. Um, my favorite color is pink; hers is green—I don't know why. Green is such an ugly, boy color unless it's trees or grass, then it's okay."

"And Mom and Dad? How are they?"

"Mom works a lot. She has to sell houses, but the market isn't good right now. There was a bubble, and it popped, and stuff got everywhere, so now she has to help people find the money lots of times to buy homes. She says the H-F-A helps some people, but some just can't get one no matter what. I think that's sad if they can't have a home."

Di sat back, a bit amazed she had released such a chatterbox. She was enjoying it; it even put a smile on her face as she wondered how so many words could come from the girl who had barely opened her mouth since the other day. "And your dad?"

"He's a good dad. He mostly works when we're at school or asleep and tries to do lots of stuff with us. Like if Sam won't play with me, he'll help me build things in Minecraft. And then he reads us stories and helps us make up stories. Sam's better at it than me, except when we do comics. I'm better at making comics. Dad says I'll do better at stories when I get a little bigger and get more comfortable with words, but I don't know. I just like drawing better than writing.

"There was this one time—Sam made the story, and I drew the pictures. It was the best comic because we had a good story and good pictures. It was about a dog who had a pet shop, and she delivered pets to other people in town, but then an evil monster took over the pet shop, and they had to battle."

"That sounds really fun."

"It was."

"Maybe I can see it when we get back to your house later."

"Okay. It's on my shelf next to my Dogman books."

Di stretched her legs and stood. "Well, I think we need to get going and see if your dad is back at the hotel now."

"Okay." Lisa gave Virb a final stroke, ensuring she went all the way from his head to the base of his tale. He looked at her curiously and stood as she did.

Di watched the shadows break through the trees and dance on the ground as a breeze picked up. They were on the other side now; more of the day had passed than she had realized.

"Come on." Di started back along the path.

Lisa held her toy tight and hurried to walk beside her aunt. Virb ran ahead, scanning left and right, then walked at a steady pace ten feet in front of them.

Lisa went on to share stories from some of her other comics, one with a rooster who thought he was a chicken but couldn't get any eggs to come out. One was about a girl named Layla who ran a lemonade stand but also was a superhero at night. She said Mom loved Layla but not the rooster—that was partially because he kept pooping and thinking it was an egg.

She had moved on to talking about Sam's stories when Virb stopped walking and stared into the tall brambles on the right. He looked at the base and around their sides, when a crash of leaves and branches burst from beside Di.

Hannah Gould, kitchen knife in hand, charged at Di. Di's hand went to her hip for her own, but before she could tighten her fingers around it, Gould's blade was descending.

Di stepped back and grabbed Gould's arm. Gould swung her free hand and socked Di in the gut. She punched again, trying to shake Di free.

"Bitch!" Di hit Gould in the face. Blood gushed from her nose.

Gould screamed and leaped at Di, wrapping her legs around her. They slammed to the ground, Gould on top, and Virb sprinting down the trail.

Gould pressed her blade down, her free hand on top and aiming the steel at Di's neck.

"Die," Gould shouted.

Di craned her head away and shoved at the knife, but it kept sinking. It came down into her flesh, missing the neck and slicing into nearby muscle.

Di closed her eyes and screamed. She sucked in a breath but still heard screaming. Pressure lifted from her chest. She opened her eyes and saw Virb ripping a hunk of flesh from Gould's neck. It was red and dripped over his muzzle.

Gould turned, knife in hand, swinging at Virb.

"No!" Di grabbed Gould's forearm, freezing the knife in motion. Virb lunged again, clamped down on another hunk of Gould's neck, and tore it away. Di heard a wet, ripping sound this time, as neither Gould nor her were screaming. It was followed by a gasp, and Hannah Gould went limp and thumped on top of Di.

Di groaned and rolled the other woman off. Lisa knelt on the side of the path, her hands over her eyes. With Gould off, Di began to feel the sting of the wound on her shoulder. She looked down but could barely see it. It was bleeding, but with all of Gould's blood covering it, it was hard to tell how bad.

Di stood, putting pressure on her shoulder. Virb growled at the dead principal.

"Come on," Di squeaked out and took Lisa's hand. "Let's go see your dad."

2

Officer Stuart Harrison found himself in a dim and musty place. He saw slices of light from slim slots in covered windows, mounds of old boxes, and shelves of jars and jugs. His wrists and ankles were both bound together, and when he tried to yell, only muffled tones came through taped lips.

It was the basement of the Lawrence house. He could tell that much. By the ache of his head, he knew how he got there. The first question was how to get out? And then, why did they let him live? That one was more terrifying.

The quick tapping of tiny feet above confirmed his suspicions that Lawrence was helping the girl. But why? Serial killers barely ever worked together; their egos were too big. Was this some sort of warped mentorship program? Whatever the reason—if there was one, crazy doesn't need a reason—he was pretty sure he had a finite amount of time before he became a victim.

Harrison took a closer look at the room. He spotted the corner from Dad's journal and realized the stench that he'd been breathing in. It wasn't from there—the source had to be that room he'd seen through the window—but his father's imagery returned. Bodies piled on top of each other, each missing parts, mementos taken by little Eddy.

He looked for any tools, any sharp surfaces he might be able to scoot towards and use to free himself. Nothing obvious stood out—no axes conveniently leaning blade out, no scissors or knives. But there were those jars... Maybe he could shake one from the shelves and break it? But that could also make noise. Maybe. There was a furnace humming away in another corner, a water heater, and a shelf with piles of old clothes which were likely shredded for mice bedding by their unkempt look. No, the jar might be the only way.

A larger pair of footfalls crossed the floor above. Dust rained onto Harrison's face. Muffled, low tones of an adult man, too quiet to discern.

Thumping of tiny jumping feet. The child was excited about something. They both wandered to another corner of the home.

Harrison hoped the excitement had nothing to do with him. He'd heard what the girl did when she was excited.

He moved his bound feet. They lifted and went as demanded, nothing holding them still. He leaned forward, testing his hands. They stayed put. They were attached to something behind him. He tried to lean left to see what he could have been bound to, and the door at the top of the stairs creaked open.

Harrison quietly lifted his feet and put them back where he started. He closed his eyes and stilled himself.

Clop, clop, clop. It was a man, Edward Lawrence, coming down the stairs. There was a *tink*, and Harrison saw his eyelids brighten. Feet on bare ground, closer and closer. *Thump*, dull pain in the meat of his leg, the man was kicking him.

Harrison played dead or knocked out and refused a sound or movement. He felt the man's eyes on him and braced for another kick.

It didn't come. The man made a clicking sound with his mouth, a kind of unamused deflation, and he returned up the stairs, shutting off the light and leaving.

More voices came through the ceiling, and then a door slammed. Were they leaving?

Harrison's gaze shot to the shelf of jars. His heart pumped. This was it. This was his time to get out.

They were on his right, four or five feet away. He lifted his feet and twisted his body to the right. He brought them down and made a puff of dust halfway there. He scooted his ass forward and stretched his legs again. They almost reached the bottom of the shelf. He scooted even further. His arms burned from being pulled backward. He reached with his legs and touched the shelf with the ball of his foot.

He wanted to scream, *Yes*, but he wasn't there yet.

He stretched toward the second shelf, one with a few jars that looked like they contained peaches and others that held a mixture so dark he couldn't see through it in the dim light. His foot didn't reach.

Groans unintentionally slipped through. The burn in his overstretched shoulders dug in with searing spikes. He scooted his ass forward another inch and a half. His shoulders shrieked. His toes tapped the forward-most jar.

Yes, this was it.

He tried hooking the glass with the tip of his shoe. He couldn't reach. Maybe he could knock it over, and it would roll off? He set his feet down and thought. Maybe it would work, but if it didn't, how would he get another jar? He had to risk it.

He stretched one more time and tapped the jar from the left. It wobbled and fell and rolled to the back of the shelf.

"Shit," he hissed at himself. His arms were on fire from his shoulders to his elbows. His waist burned from lifting his feet. "Shit."

He stared up at the rest of the jars, and half out of anger, half out of hope, he slammed his feet into the side of the shelf. Jars and jugs rattled from bottom to top.

His heart pounded against his chest. This was it.

He kicked again. A jar toppled over and rolled off the far side of the top. It crashed to the floor, and the sweet scent of peaches blended with the dank air and the smell of decay.

He kicked again. Another jar from the top rolled away and crashed down. A jar in the middle rolled back and got stuck between the shelf and the wall. Another from the middle rolled forward and crashed right beside his foot. Another fell from the top and slammed into his shins. Pain rocketed up his legs like lightning. He wondered if his bones could have fractured.

Harrison pulled back his feet and tried to rest for a moment. He breathed through clenched teeth and waited for the radiating pain in his shins to cease. It didn't fade much, just enough for him to think a little more clearly. He looked at the shattered glass on the floor, a thousand pea-sized crystals and two or three that he could maybe hold onto and cut with—if he could get them into his grip.

The smell of red sauce found his nose, something spicy for meatballs and spaghetti. Mixed with peaches and death, he wasn't sure if he'd be able to eat either one ever again.

He stretched one more time, setting his heels gently down into the field of broken glass and pasta sauce. He raked back everything he could. There were screeches of glass on cement. It was an awful sound. It gave him hope. *This could work*, he repeated in his head.

He glanced at the bottom of the shelf. One of the larger shards remained, others were gone. Under his heel?

He lifted his feet and set them down just beyond. He scooted his rear to the side to see what he had caught.

There they were: two large chunks, one from the side, one from the top of the jar, both sitting on a bed of glass crystals and red sauce.

He moved back further, giving his shoulder a small break and allowing him to rake his prize even closer. He did both, then scooted the rest of the way to where he had started. He pulled in the glass. His heart pounded. He was almost there. He just needed to get one of those large chunks to his fingers, and he could cut the tape that bound him.

He leaned left, almost touching his knee to the ground, and curled his legs inward. The glass followed, then *crack*. *No.* His heart shot into his throat. The chunk of glass from the top had shattered. "Shit."

How did he do that? He needed to be more careful.

His blood pumped with adrenaline, and he tried as hard as possible to slow his breath and move more precisely. He hooked his feet around the pile of glass and raked again, gentle, slow. He clenched his fists. His teeth creaked from pressing on one another. Inch by inch, he felt it move until his legs went numb.

He took his feet away and looked down. The piece of glass he needed was inches from his bound fingers. Inches.

He just needed to take a break for a minute. Let the feeling return to his hands and feet. He could curl his legs one more time and... noise upstairs.

There was a large thump, then a series of smaller ones. A large one. Smaller ones.

Panic raced through Harrison. He wasn't alone in the house. Someone was up there, and they heard him. They heard the crash, and they were coming. This was his shot, and he blew it.

"Not yet," he whispered.

He curled his legs, putting his heel just beyond the glass. It was so close to his back, it was painful just sitting like that. He never stretched, not before working out, not at all since high school, and he wasn't made for this. But he tried.

Harrison curled his heel in and felt it touch the large chunk. He pulled it closer. It wasn't close enough. He couldn't reach it with his fingers. He pulled harder and felt the edge of the glass with the tip of his finger. *Holy shit*, he was almost there.

The door at the top of the stairs creaked open. Thump on the top steps, then a pause.

Harrison squeezed hard. He had to be able to do this. His fingers flexed. His index and middle pinched the glass and pulled it in. This was it. This was his moment. He had to make it work.

Thump. Slide. Thump. Slide. Something was coming down the steps, but it sure as shit didn't sound like a person.

He cut into the tape on his wrists, hacking, slicing. Pain shot up his arm. He'd cut into himself, but he kept going.

Thump. Slide. Thump. Slide. Pause. The light came on. It was a dim bulb for a large basement, bathing the filthy space in a yellowish hue.

He wished the light were still off. He felt the tape loosen.

Thump. Slide. Thump. Slide.

Harrison turned to the stars as he cut and saw something that made him stop. The oddity.

A large man was sitting. He pulled himself forward (*slide*) and let his ass drop a single step (*thump*). He looked at Harrison with recognition and his slide and thump, sped up.

Harrison slashed like a maniac against his bonds. Warm wetness drenched his fingers. The pain in his hands throbbed. He wasn't sure anymore if he was cutting tape or skin or muscle.

The man from the steps stood on one leg and, with a crutch under one arm, began toward him. Harrison's eyes went up and down the stranger, noticing his missing foot and a shotgun in his grip.

"Please," Harrison said. At this point, he was made more of panic than reason. He stopped cutting and yanked his wrists apart as hard as his sore arms would move.

The one-legged man stepped under the incandescent bulb, and Harrison thought he recognized him. But Norris Cushing had had two feet every time he'd been to the Huckleberry Café.

Harrison's arms flung apart. He tried to stand and run, forgetting his feet were still bound together. He toppled to his right, bracing his fall on top of broken jars, sauce, and peaches. He screamed as glass shredded his palms and fingers.

Harrison rolled onto his back, curling his bleeding hands into his chest. He heard Norris Cushing take one more step closer. He didn't hear the shotgun fire.

1992

1

Jill Elden walked back toward Wes's house, her mind reeling over the idea of ancient Norse demons. If they had tales of a thing that could cause your nightmares, and it was real, what else did they know that was *lost* to the people of today? She needed to know. She decided that once this was over, she would connect with her heritage and find out. In actuality, after it was over, she would be too scared to do this, and not until college would she read a word about her ancestors.

2

A block behind Jill, stopping at one curb and then another to watch, was Ray Trent in Amanda Brolin's minivan. He still wasn't sure what he was going to do to her, but the idea of her blood on his hands was keeping his heart racing.

He watched her cross the next intersection, heading toward his dear old dad's tire shop of all places. If there was anywhere he could control what happened between the two of them, that was it.

He felt the outline of his keys in his pocket. Yes, he had the shop keys too.

Ray put the vehicle into gear and drove down 4th Avenue, looking away as he passed her. Two blocks later, he turned into the Trent Tires parking lot, opened the garage bay, and parked the minivan inside. He walked over to the front door, only feet from the sidewalk, and unlocked it. Now he just had to wait.

3

Jill wondered what Wes was going to say. Was he going to be blown away by what she'd found? By how interesting she was to have a family who knew about this stuff? Or would he think she was weird for having an aunt that could read ancient dead languages?

She crossed White Pine Road, her eyes were glued to the cars. This was where Ray Trent had dangled her into traffic like a piece of bait on a hook.

She stepped back onto the curb, back to safety, and stopped. Her blood boiled at the thought of Ray's face. How dare he do that? Was it some sort of sick joke? Did he get off on scaring girls? The idea came to mind of telling his father, and then Ray sitting in his bedroom sulking after being grounded. That would have been nice, but she wouldn't do it. She wasn't a snitch.

She saw Trent Tires up ahead. Part of her wanted to cross the street so she could walk as far away as possible from anything Trent. The other half said she shouldn't let him do that to her. He was an asshole, and she shouldn't let some asshole make her change the way she lived.

A truck rumbled by, then a station wagon. She thought about the death in her dream, the kids in comas, and the nastiness around town. Sometimes it was just better to play it safe.

She crossed 4th Avenue and walked on the far side, away from the tire shop. She refused to look as she passed, but she felt better.

4

Barton Smith watched the girl on his monitor. He had been watching her since he woke up. He cooked some eggs and made coffee. He cut a grapefruit and buried it in sugar as if that would help shrink his gut. Then, he sat and ate and watched her as if she were the newest episode of Roseanne.

She hadn't done much. She lay in the same spot, curled up under the blanket. It made Barton wonder if he should take the blanket away so he could get a better view. What she had been doing so far just wasn't working for him.

He drank the last sip of his coffee and took his dishes to the sink. He felt the soreness in his back as he leaned over and set them down on the stainless steel basin. The pain reminded him, he should have been more careful not to pull something. He'd taken all night to bury that girl and still ended up with pain in his lower back. He wouldn't make the same mistakes with this new one.

He glanced back at the screen. He definitely needed to take away that blanket. She hadn't eaten all day; maybe he'd take in some food, and when she moved to eat, he'd grab it. He still thought he could build some trust with this one if he was careful. She didn't try to escape when he grabbed the other one—maybe that meant there was a chance. Maybe she'd be more—cooperative—if he could build some trust. That could be more fun… at least initially.

Cereal, he thought. He wasn't going to cook the girl anything, but he probably had some cereal she would eat.

"*Leave*," the whisper flooded his mind.

"What?" Images of police cars and flashing lights came into his thoughts.

"*Leave*."

"Shit. Do they know? What's happening?"

"*Leave*."

He went through his actions step by step in his mind. The mall, the girls. How could someone have seen him? He gritted his teeth. This was bullshit. He finally had what he wanted, a way to get them, a place to bring them. His eyes went back to the monitor. He wasn't going to leave without her.

Barton stormed to his room to pack a bag.

5

Chris Conners pulled the key from his pocket and slid it into his front door. He gave it a clockwise turn and felt what he expected—too loose. The door was already unlocked, which meant his damn father was still home.

Lately, Dad slept it off by eleven and was ready for his afternoon shift at the feedlot on the east side of town by one. He wasn't supposed to be here now—unless he'd decided he was going to quit his job again.

It was a recurring transaction nearly every nine months as far back as Chris could remember. Dad would decide he was too good for a job at the slaughterhouse, or the feedlot, or even the corner Wesker Pump, then quit and ramble for two weeks about how a hard-working man can't get a decent job anymore. Then, two weeks later, once the booze money started to get tight, he'd return to the same job he'd quit nine or eighteen months ago.

Chris opened the door and caught a whiff of Mom's perfume, just a trace that must have been floating since she left for work. A grim picture entered his mind of Dad pulling this crap after she had died, the house with a big foreclosure notice on the door, and then them both out on the street. Dad would still find booze somewhere, even if it meant sleeping under the 9th Avenue bridge or in the park with the other bums, but what would happen to *him*? Would he be on the street too? Or taken to some foster home where he'd be a slave to another drunken asshole?

His face felt wet. He touched his cheek and realized he was crying. Why was he crying? If anything, he was more pissed at his dad than sad. He breathed in again, and her perfume rocked his knees. He wobbled to the couch and dropped into it. A flood came from his eyes that he couldn't hold back. All he could do was cover his face with his hands and let it out.

He saw Mom's funeral. He saw her lying in the casket with no hair and, instead, a ridiculous wig and hat. She had no smile, no love in her body any longer. She was a drab hunk of flesh with all of her light taken.

A shock rocked his system, ripping his hands from his face. He looked straight up with a hatred for this sadness. He couldn't let it happen. Not to his mother.

He shook his head and said to the thing, wherever it was, "I'll do it. Save my mom... Help Charlotte... and I'll do whatever."

He took a breath, followed by another. He waited, expecting some response, but nothing came. But inside, even without a word from the other, he felt better. His despair lessened. He didn't know if his answer was heard, or if it was just the act of thinking his situation through, or God forbid, his crying—something was making him feel better.

Chris stood, leaving his backpack on the couch. Dad would probably bitch about that whenever he finally showed his hungover face, but right now, Chris couldn't give a shit. He went to the kitchen and looked inside the refrigerator. He grabbed a Coke and closed the door, and on the counter, he saw something he didn't expect: a plate of his mother's cookies. He thought for a moment—she hadn't made cookies since, he couldn't remember at first. It was maybe last summer, before her prognosis.

They sat on a white plate under two layers of plastic wrap. Peanut butter and chocolate chips seemed to smile from under the transparent film, *Eat me, eat me.* His cheek was wet again.

"Look under the sink," a whisper said. The voice almost sounded like his own, that voice you hear when you're trying to work out a problem in your head. But was it really his? He found himself kneeling down and opening the cabinet door before he knew he was doing it.

Sponges, Windex, 409, rubber gloves, they were all set neatly under the sink basin, just as Mom had organized them.

"Behind the Windex."

Chris slid the glass cleaner out of the way and spotted a box of rat poison. It was strange—he didn't remember ever seeing any rats, or even mice, in the house. Before he knew what he was doing, he had picked up the box. He stood in front of the sink, a cookie in one hand and an open container of poison in the other. He shook his head and put the poison back. He picked up a knife instead.

A cold feeling ran over Chris. He carried the plate of cookies, now only half full, and went to his room to play some music.

6

Officer Dale Harrison's tire squealed as he drove through the outskirts of town on Highway 9. The land rose and fell along a forest of thick pines, cedar, and ground-hugging juniper. If it were any other day, he would have been happy to slow down and breathe in the scents and enjoy the beauty. Today, he had a nagging sensation that a girl's life may depend on how fast he could navigate the narrow roads, curves, and switchbacks on the way to Barton Smith's registered address.

Trees opened up to a wide swath of hilly pasture and a couple hundred head of black steer. A rancher waved at Harrison as he filled a giant steel tub with water. Harrison didn't even see the man.

A quarter-mile later, the road dipped, and trees returned. Harrison readied his foot as the turn for Aspen Trail came up on the left.

He braked a bit, more than he wanted, and pulled the cruiser onto

Barton's road. The tires chirped until he left the highway blacktop and skidded on Aspen Trail's dirt surface.

A rooster tail of brown dust flew from Harrison's rear as he hit the gas and soared up the hill. He passed a log home on the right, surrounded by thirty acres of trees. He saw a driveway on the left that was swallowed by pines with no sign of where it led. A post beside the next driveway held a foot-tall carved bear with a basket in his hand. In the basket was a bouquet of yellow flowers and a wooden sign reading, *Welcome*. Another eighth-mile beyond, Harrison found the sign for 6933 nailed to the front of a fence post beside a dark forested path.

Harrison hit the brakes until he was almost at a halt. He looked up the path and felt shivers run down his back. It wasn't fear. He knew fear, and though he felt some of that, fear wasn't what was riding up his spine like the zap from an electrified fence. This was more. Something else was up that driveway. The girl? Maybe—hopefully, but also, Evil. There was something up that driveway that made the old dead bum he'd found in the pond feel tame but also connected. The bloodied throat of Mr. Wimbley, the bear attack in Jason Mertz's living room—they seemed to stretch and connect to this place with invisible wires. It was like a dark current that he hadn't understood had been flowing through town, and now he was caught in its grip and getting sucked into the rapids.

He pulled his service weapon from his holster. This was odd. In the decades he'd served Custer Falls, he'd only taken it out to target practice or store safely overnight when the kids were still toddlers and got into everything. Placing it into his hand now, there was a sense of familiarity, but also a burning anxiousness.

He double-checked the chamber, one round in the pipe. The magazine, full, thirteen rounds. The safety, now off. Red is dead. He slid the pistol back into its holster and headed up Barton Smith's driveway.

Rocks and dirt crackled under the tires for a slow quarter-mile before the trees opened on a clearing about three hundred feet in diameter. In the center of the expanse of tall grasses and sage was a batten-board-sided two-story home. Its wood was stained light brown near the top, fading into gray as it neared the bottom and dark gray near the ground, where years of snowbanks had rested against the home.

Harrison's gaze went to the green pickup in the driveway that matched the vehicle he was looking for. He inspected the house, each of its windows, and finding them empty, to the woodshed, which was piled with at least two years-worth of wood.

He pulled up behind the green pickup, parking a good twenty feet back in case the man was lying on the front seat or otherwise using it for cover. He opened the door, then, thinking of what may come next, picked up the radio.

"Rhonda?"

A half-minute passed of Harrison waiting while listening for footsteps, watching the house, and checking his mirrors.

"Dale?"

"That's right. Mark me at 6933 Aspen Trail, checking out that green pickup."

"Okay. Everything alright there?"

"Just a feeling."

"Gotcha. Radio back as needed. I'll be here."

He hung up the mic and regarded the house once more. If the guy was there, he must have seen Harrison by now. So he'd either answer the door with a smile or a shotgun. Either way, that place had plenty of room to hide at least three kids, if not more. He'd have to do whatever it took to look it all over.

Harrison stepped out of the car, engine running, and shut the door. With one hand on his weapon, he walked slowly toward the front porch.

He paused at the pickup, glancing through the window. No one inside. He looked for anything that screamed a girl had been in there: a bow, a shoe, a hairpin, anything. The vehicle was immaculate. It must have been recently cleaned. But it was definitely the same model and color as the surveillance images.

He moved on toward the house, listening as he walked. Listening for footsteps, voices, screams.

At the steps to the front door, he smelled something buttery. Someone had been cooking recently. He took one more look left and right, glancing past the windows, and knocked on the door. He stepped back and waited.

Footsteps on a wooden floor. Heavy, he was big, alright. The doorknob jiggled and turned. Harrison's grip on his pistol was warm and damp, and tightening.

The door opened, and the sun slid behind the clouds. A large man stood shadowed in the entry of the home. There was a light behind him, leaving most of what Harrison could make out an outlined shadow. The shape was similar to the man in the video; he was sure of that much.

"Mr. Smith?" Harrison watched Smith's hands, one on his hip, the other on the door.

"Yessir." His gaze went to the interior of the home and then back. "But I'm pretty busy right now. Compressor on my freezer went out. If I don't see to it now, I'm going to lose all my meat. Can you come back later?"

Harrison squinted, trying to get a better look. Large hands, large shoulders, no bulges in his pockets or on his waist that he could see. But the feeling of evil still chilled. There was more here than the visible.

"I'm afraid not," Harrison said. "What I'm here about is time sensitive. Can you tell me if you were at the Custer Falls Mall this week?"

Smith looked up and pondered. "This week? No, I don't think so. See, I work at the caverns, and since the accident over there, they've had us pretty busy."

"You work at Bloodtooth?"

"Yes, sir, I work for FWP."

Harrison nodded. It was best to let Smith think he was convincing. Best to keep him docile if he was the guy. And more and more, Harrison felt sure he was the guy. The size matched the tape. The vehicle matched the tape. He felt in his gut that this guy was as bad as they get—but he couldn't match his face. He had no hard evidence yet, just coincidence. If he kept him docile, kept him talking, maybe something would shake loose.

Harrison strained to see the man's eyes and just made out the shape of Smith's face. "Accident, huh? I heard something about that, but not the cause."

"They don't know that yet. Last I heard, they said an earthquake could have set free a trapped pocket of gas. One of those hits our internal lighting system, and boom." The man smiled as he said it. It was a look Harrison had seen in the eyes of a pyromaniac teenager he'd arrested for setting fires in the national forest east of town—and then in his parents' bedroom. The look of pride.

"But nobody was hurt, right?" Harrison.

Smith's head rocked right. His shoulders drooped. "No. It was the middle of the night, so no one was there."

"Right." Harrison checked the man's hands again. Door. Hip. "So, going back to the mall. I've had a report that a pickup like yours was seen there around the time a young girl went missing the other day."

"Like I said, I wasn't at the mall. And I really have to get back to that freezer."

"Just the same, I'm sure you'd want to be helpful when it comes to finding a missing girl. So, do you mind if I take a look inside your pickup?"

"Oh. Yeah, I'd love to help, but, this freezer..." His hand moved from the door to his other hip. Both shifted along his waist.

"Oh, I understand. You can work on the freezer. I just need your permission to look inside." Harrison didn't. He was sure he had enough cause to search the thing now, with the man's nervousness, his matching body type, and the matching vehicle, but he wanted to see Smith's reaction.

"See, it's locked, and I'm not sure where those keys are. Maybe if you come back, I'll have some time to look for them later this afternoon."

The sun came from behind the clouds, lighting the interior of the home. Harrison saw an antique furniture-filled living room, a kitchen with a small television on the counter facing the other way, and in the hallway behind Smith, a large duffel bag, unzipped and filled to the brim with clothes. The evil oozing off Smith now felt palpable in the air between them. This was the guy, and if either of those girls were still alive, they were here.

"You planning a trip?" Harrison said, louder than before.

Smith glanced at his bag. He turned back with fear in his eyes.

A knocking came from somewhere to the left—something hitting wood inside the house, muffled. Harrison turned to see where the noise was coming from, and the monster was on top of him.

Harrison's back slammed into the hard rocky ground. Smith's enormous fist pounded the side of his face, and again, and stars filled his vision.

Smith stood and heaved his size thirteen boot into Harrison's side. Cracks and pops sounded from his ribs.

Harrison turned away, and the massive boot slammed into his back. Crack. Pain shot from his kidneys. He rolled further. Crack in his other side. White light as laces met the side of his face.

The world seemed to float away from Officer Dale Harrison. He had an impression that he was still shaking. That something was happening to him, but all he felt was a general vibration, like when his pickup drove over a cattle guard on the edge of a ranch, and the vehicle hummed and shook under him.

After a few moments, he stopped moving, and instead of shaking, it was someone's hands. They were following the contours of his chest and then his side. They were near where he kept his pistol while on the job.

He wondered if he was on the job now. He wanted to say no—the feeling of floating was more like sleep than work, and he wouldn't sleep at work. But what if he was? What if he was at work now?

A surge of worry tore Harrison away from the white, floating place. He was on the ground, on his back—someone was trying to take his gun.

Harrison's hand clamped down over the pistol and holster. He opened his eyes to a hazy view of a giant man suspended over him. The man pulled on his fingers. He pinched them and smacked them. Pain ripped up Harrison's hand as his ring and middle fingers were bent back. He held on.

With his other hand, Harrison felt his belt and unsnapped his knife. He slid it out as Smith—he was starting to remember where he was now and who he was fighting—pulled his other fingers free.

He felt Smith's hand on his gun, and the knife flew. It wasn't the best move he'd ever pulled, but it may have been the most important. The curved blade skated across Barton Smith's fingers, splitting skin, grazing tendons, and exposing bone. Smith jerked his hand away, and Harrison drew his weapon.

Smith turned and ran. Before Harrison could target the man through his hazy sights, Smith was around the side of the house. By the time Harrison found his feet, an engine sounded from the other side of the building.

A V8 roared, and Harrison staggered to the corner of the home. A rusty Ford Bronco tore past, clouding the yard with dust and blinding Harrison even more. And then it was gone.

The knocking returned from inside.

2022

1

As they parked at Maryville Manor, Wes Henson could already tell Sam was getting tired. And why wouldn't she be? She only got to sleep half the night, was forced into surgery and recovery, and filled with anesthetizing drugs. Now the afternoon was passing with no rest in sight. If only he could let her rest.

He remembered her as a newborn when Jill slept after giving birth. His firstborn in his arms. She was warm and still and laid in his grip with nothing to fear and no worries in the world. She breathed in tiny rhythmic breaths that nearly brought him to tears with their beauty. As she yawned in the car seat, he wondered how he was going to keep her from it.

He grabbed the handle, turned to get out, and Sam said, "Dad?"

"Yeah." He faced her, expecting one of the usual fleeting questions: "When's dinner?" "What are we doing this weekend?" "Can Judy come over and play Minecraft?"

"Do you think Mom's ever going to wake up?"

He had to sit back in his seat. The kids knew tiny bits about what was happening, and that wasn't fair. He'd always been honest, though optimistic, with them, even when he'd rather lie and not go through the tough conversations. They'd never replaced a dead hamster or fish; they'd had funerals. They'd told the truth about why Jill's aunt never visited, refusing to say she couldn't come in favor of saying the harsher fact, that she felt things in her own life were more important than coming to see their family. Now Jill might not wake up. She might die if they didn't do their job right. And Wes really just wanted to say everything was going to be okay. He was tempted more than he wanted to be. He had to settle for: "Let's talk about this inside."

Sam nodded and yawned again.

At the door to their room, Wes heard Di and Lisa inside. He sighed and shocked himself with how relieved he was. In some dark corner of his mind, one he had been refusing to accept, he didn't expect them to be there, or he expected them to be dead, killed in their sleep. A tingle came over his face as he pushed those thoughts away.

When the door opened, the smell of pizza greeted the father and eldest. Two boxes of takeout pepperoni sat on the table between Di and Lisa, and the smiles on their faces were the most joyous things Wes had seen all day.

"Pizza," Sam said in the tone of someone who hadn't just lost half of three of her fingers. She sat beside her sister, giving Lisa a one-armed half-hug along the way.

"Aaaand... Lisa raised a small box that had been hidden in the opposite chair.

"Breadsticks!" Sam held out her wounded hand, and the room stared. "Oh." She quickly hid it and held out her other one, taking a stick.

Wes settled into the empty seat between Lisa and Di, its cushion warmed by the bread box. Di passed paper plates to him and Sam, and they each took slices.

"Thank you for this," Wes said. He watched his daughters bite into their meals and have what was both the strangest meal they may have ever had and the most normal moment they'd experienced in four days. He took a bite and waited, wanting the scene to last as long as it could, wanting each of them to be able to rest their bodies and their minds, because with what was coming, they would need it.

Sam was halfway through a breadstick, Lisa was done with hers plus a slice, and Wes was chewing gratefully when Lisa asked, "So what do we have to do to save Mom?"

The food in Wes's mouth lost its taste, but he forced it down. "I guess it's time to talk about that." Both girls and Di focused on him for answers.

Over the next few minutes, Wes explained what had happened when he, Di, and Jill were younger, how the demon was after them in their dreams and trying to control the suggestible when they were awake. He talked about the kids that had fallen into comas back then, and how he thought Jill was caught in the same type of thing. And he told them about the stone: what it was, what it meant, where it had to go.

"Is that what we got today?" Lisa said.

"What?" Wes looked at her and then at Di. "You didn't." His stare hardened. "Tell me you didn't go without me—that you didn't take Lisa."

Di rose and went to the dresser. She opened the drawer and lifted an object wrapped in a hotel towel. She set it on the dresser and unfolded it, and Wes's chest grew tighter.

When the last corner of fabric lifted, unveiling the abhorrent rock, Wes felt himself pressed back into his chair the way he imagined astronauts were at liftoff. His heart pounded. He thought he should get up and examine it, but his body didn't respond. Not until Lisa stood.

She took a step toward the stone, and Wes jumped to his feet and slid in front of her. "No. Keep your distance."

She leaned to look around him. "I just wanted to see."

"Go back to your seat and see from there," Wes snapped. He could feel the stone behind him, its coldness in the center of his back. He was used to stepping between his kids and danger—that was a parent's job—but now he felt like he was holding back a great beast, a lion or tiger, on the loose.

"Okay, okay." She took another slice of pizza on her way back to her seat.

He turned to Di and spoke through his teeth, "You went and got it without me?"

She folded the towel, covering the stone.

The gears turned in Wes's head. "You took Lisa into that cave? Or you left her here alone for hours?"

"Don't freak out," Di said. "I got the thing, didn't I?"

"Which was it?" he was getting hot now. "Which way did you risk my daughter's life?"

"It wasn't like that," Di said. "She just walked me to the edge of the cave."

"And you left her there? In the woods, while you put your life at risk in that mine? You know what could have happened to her if you didn't come back up?"

"I left Virb with her. She was fine." She tried to maintain a cold expression, but cracks showed right through it.

"Fine." He nodded and turned. There was nothing he could do about it now, no matter how mad he was. He turned back and pointed. His finger could have been a gun, the way he aimed it. "If you ever put my kids in that kind of danger again—"

"I won't." The cracks had broken through. Her face was sunken as she thought about the dark, flooded mine, that crazy bitch, and what could have happened if she hadn't made it out. "I—I'm sorry."

"Really, Dad," Lisa was back on her feet. "I was safe the whole time. Up until Mrs. Gould came."

"Mrs. Gould?" Sam said. "What did she want?"

"She tried to kill Aunt Di."

"What?" Wes turned back to Di.

"She was listening to the whispers—that wasn't my fault. She could have just as easily come here."

He walked over to Di and grabbed her shoulders. He struggled for words and yanked her over and hugged her. She hugged him back, first with one hand and then two. It occurred to him how many years it had been since he had hugged his baby sister, and he held on tighter. He thought about their younger years, before the monster, before losing dad. Camping, swimming, playing Nintendo, doing magic shows for Mom and Dad. It was a part of his life that he left behind a long time ago, written off as bad reminders of what he'd lost when he lost her. But here she was now. Sober, as far as he could tell, and here. He thought about the days to come, and more than anything, he hoped not to lose her again once this was all over.

Wes glanced down and saw a wound on Di's shoulder. "What is that?" He pulled back.

"A present from their principal."

He leaned in for another look. It was red but sealed. "What..."

"Superglue. It's good for now."

Wes nodded and hugged her again. "I'm just glad you're okay."

"So, what do we do with the rock?" Sam said.

2

Edward Lawrence held a large black duffel bag as he opened the door to his home. He tossed it through the doorway onto the creak of ancient floorboards and grabbed another from just outside. He tossed that one in as well, and he and Julie Redmond came inside.

She carried her own black duffel, a smaller, kid-sized version, which she set down beside the others. As Ed shut the door, she watched the bags and thought how cool it was that she could help send all those letters.

"I'm thirsty," Julie said.

"Okay." Ed figured she would have learned by now, but apparently not. "You know where the kitchen is."

"Yeah. Do you want something?"

Ed looked at her, surprised. "Sure. Lemonade."

"You know where that is." She sneered and shook her head, laughed, and scampered into the kitchen.

"Jesus. Was I that bad?"

"Probably so," a gruff voice boomed from the living room. Norris Cushing sat on the couch, his legs up on the coffee table, centered on a square couch pillow. "Most kids are assholes."

Ed nodded. It was a symbolic gesture, one he'd seen the rest of the humans do to show a connection to a remark. He thought Norris bought it and sat in a chair across from him, the last piece of furniture his grandmother bought if he remembered correctly.

Ed examined Norris's wounds. The charred meat was gone, leaving thick, pink scars on the man's leg. It looked wet from the shine, and Ed thought it may make a weaker-stomached man queasy.

"I dealt with the guy," Norris explained. "He took the bait."

Ed nodded, and Julie walked into the room with two glasses of lemonade. She handed one to Ed and sipped the other.

"Did you eat?" Ed asked.

"Not yet." Norris rubbed the scar under his shirt, one of Ed's that was tight and scratchy. "Wasn't sure the plumbing repair was working."

"Gotta have faith, my friend. And need to keep your strength up. There's still so much to do."

"I guess so." Norris nodded.

Ed flicked on the television, where the five o'clock news had just started its opening montage of ranchers birthing cows and the mayor at his desk in the City-County building. Ed stood and headed toward the kitchen. "I've got something to throw on. Just hold tight."

"Can I help?" Julie asked.

"No, you watch. Let me know if our little shenanigans make the report."

She sipped her drink and turned to the TV.

The first story was a recap of Julie at the school, now revealing the name of the dead woman, Joanne Higgins, and showing a sketch that could have been a thousand different girls in the neighboring three counties. It seemed to take forever to get past the school thing; they talked about it being closed until next week, the superintendent spoke, then a parent's group.

Eventually, the second story came on about the death of Mr. and Mrs. Parsons. Video showed the outside of their home, yellow tape flapping in the breeze, and an EMT gurney removing a body from the house in a black bag.

Norris smirked from the couch, wondering if they had found his foot.

The third story was about a voyeur in town using a drone to spy on women through their windows, along with a phone number for tips.

When the commercial break came, Ed popped into the room. "Nothing yet?" He brought the smell of sizzling meat with him.

"Not yet," Julie said. "Except for old news about the school."

"It'll come." He returned to the kitchen.

There was a commercial for a car dealership, followed by one for the Country Kitchen. Finally, a law firm said they'd been practicing in Custer Falls for thirty-eight years and were seeking former miners with lung problems to join in class action lawsuits.

When the news returned, the camera zoomed into the female anchor, a brunette with shoulder-length hair and a hard brow. "This news is just being brought to us." The word *Alert* glowed in the corner of the screen in red letters.

"Ed," Julie shouted. "I think it's about us."

Ed walked over from the kitchen, a knife in one hand, a peeled potato in the other. He stood and watched.

"Police are warning residents to be careful with their mail today. A number of people around Custer Falls have reportedly received letters containing a mysterious white powder. Police say while it is not known what the powder is just yet, it is not anthrax, as some have suspected, and it has been sent to the state lab for analysis."

"That's it." Ed nodded.

"Officials warn that if you get any strange letters not to open them. You should set them aside and call the Custer Falls police department to come and collect them."

"How many people do you think opened them?" Julie asked.

"I don't know. Enough to call the cops."

"Why did they have to do that? Now, less people will open them."

"Remember, it's not about how many people open them or fall asleep. It's about the fear that's about to ripple through town."

She tipped her head back, considering. "He likes fear."

"He does. It's all part of it."

"He's smart."

Ed chuckled and headed back toward the kitchen. "Yes, he is."

"Again," the anchor reminded, "do not open any strange letters. Police say more on this is to come once the powder is analyzed."

3

Maggy Adams sat in the living room recliner, rocking baby Timmy in her arms. Exhaustion was weighing down her eyelids, and she wondered how much longer she could wait. Her lungs were starting to burn. The warmth in her skin had moved into a full-blown fever, and more than anything, she was ready for Clark to get home and take over with the kid.

She set him down in his rocker, and he sneezed.

"Fuck." It was bad enough that she'd caught a cold; she didn't want to pass it on to her baby as well. Such small lungs, how would he even fight it?

She sat in the chair and coughed. She needed meds.

In the kitchen cabinet, there was some. Generic NyQuil, Tylenol, antacids, and a growing collection of baby tools: a nose suction ball, a set of baby fingernail trimmers, an unopened sippy cup someone had given them that Timmy was way too young for. She didn't want to fall asleep, and she knew she was almost there, but NyQuil seemed like the only thing for a cold she had.

She poured a shot of the green fluid and tipped it back. She felt a hair better as the burn slid down her throat, then she started sweating profusely.

"Oh, God," she swayed where she stood. She looked down at the stained plastic cup and saw her fingers. They were pale, almost blue.

Maggy's heart pounded, but she felt weak, like her legs would drop her at any second. Her gaze went to Timmy. What was happening to her? What would happen to him if she passed out? His eyes were closed; it was good if he was sleeping, right? He rocked in his swing, a bead of sweat forming on his forehead.

"Clark," Maggy gasped. Her voice crackled as if she were speaking with water in her lungs. Her legs released, and she dropped to the floor with a thump and a crack. Her leg screamed with pain. A bone poked through her shin. Blood pumped over her leg and soaked into her slippers.

Maggy whimpered, and her vision went white.

1992

1

"Hello?" Officer Dale Harrison shouted into the house. He had returned to his cruiser and radioed for help, but Rhonda had no one to send just yet. Help would come eventually, but there was no way of knowing when. If Shirley Minsk or Charlotte Baker or Ronny DiMarco were the ones making that noise, he was going to have to find them himself, even with cracked ribs, broken fingers, a concussion, and whatever else may be wrong with him.

While the entrance of the house was relatively clean, Newspapers, TV Guides, People Magazines, and other periodicals littered the coffee table and kitchen counter of Barton Smith's home. It was as if he were concerned enough for visitors to guard his living room but not his personal spaces. In the bedroom, office, and closets was where Harrison would find the real depravity, later on. The black market kid porn, the magazines that would make him want to throw up, and the videos of Shirley Minsk inside that room.

There didn't seem to be any response to his calls. He had gone inside and left, and he thought he was moving in the direction of the noises he'd heard—the one that sent Smith into a frenzy—but his head was swimming. He wasn't so sure anymore.

"I'm a police officer! I'm here to help! Please let me know where you are!"

There was a muffled voice. Harrison turned, trying to find it, but he couldn't tell where it was.

"I can't find you! Tell me where you are!"

A soft, rhythmic knock began from behind and below. Was she in the floor?

The world became foggy. The bright light coming through the front door pained his eyes.

"No," he mumbled. "Basement."

He leaned against the wall as he walked. There had to be a door to the basement somewhere; he just had to find it. He found Smith's bedroom, and what was on the nightstand made him want to puke: what could only have been Shirley Minsk's underwear and a stack of Polaroids. He was forced to check the closet and refused to leaf through the smut-filled boxes—he'd leave that for the crime scene techs.

He'd checked the entire floor when he found his way back toward the kitchen. Just before the corner, there was a final door, sealed with a padlock.

Harrison pounded on the door. The noise made his head throb. "Are you down there?"

There was a sound, but he couldn't identify it. A squeak? A squeal? A cry for help?

"Stay back from the door!" He raised his pistol and aimed it at the steel plate the lock was attached to. He fired, and a wave of pain shot through his head so hard he wondered if he'd caught a ricochet. He felt around for a moment. No blood.

The padlock and its bracket still hung, but chunks of wood flowered up from the bracket's corners. Harrison stepped back, raised his foot, and slammed it into the door.

Wood cracked, and the door shattered inward. Splinters and chunks of oak tumbled down the stairs.

The basement was dark. Echoes of muffled crying reverberated from the concrete floor.

"I'm coming down!" He spotted a switch on the wall and flipped it. The light showed an unfinished, framed wall that circled the home's exterior. In the middle of the basement was a finished wall—an interior room disconnected from the walls and the ceiling—a quiet room as you might find in a recording studio.

Harrison stepped down, placing his foot on a chunk of broken door. It rolled under his weight, and his foot shot up and back.

"No!" he shouted as he tumbled forward.

He flew toward the stairs, throwing his hands up. He saw the unfinished wooden steps coming at his face and winced. For a second he debated between trying to catch himself and spinning to land on his side. Before he could choose, he crashed on his arm, left side, and hip. He slid forward and rolled twice down the remaining stairs.

He cried a garbled shout of pain, his face on the basement concrete and his foot now twisted. After a few breaths, he heard the knocking.

He wanted to lay still. Barton was gone, and help was on the way. He throbbed with the beat of his heart in too many places, and by God, he just wanted to lay still. But there was the knocking. A kid was there, not far and possibly in worse shape than himself.

Harrison cried in pain again and forced himself to his knees. *Halfway there*, he told himself. He lifted his knee, putting his pain-free foot down and hoisting himself up. He leaned on the wall and limped forward.

The limp reminded him of his football days in high school. He was just good enough to make the junior varsity team as a sophomore, just fast enough to be a running back, and in his second play, he was lucky enough to get tripped and have his ankle stepped on by his own blocker. After that break, he never played again. He couldn't stop playing now, even with no one there to help him off the field.

He rounded a corner, the knocking growing louder, and there it was: a door into the small unattached room. He drew back its deadbolt and turned the knob.

There was a sound that he didn't recognize. It was breathy and long, high. His hazy mind confused the pitch for the call of a loon at first, swaying in and out, up and down. As the door widened, though, he saw her. A girl was on the floor. She shuddered as she breathed, tears streaming from her eyes. The sound clarified into the child's cries, long and full, shaking her as they bellowed forth.

He dropped to his knees and held out his arms. "I'm here to help you."

It took her a half-second to look him over and burst across the room into his arms.

2

Jill Elden knocked on the Henson's front door. She expected Di to open it but instead heard someone yell, "Come in!" from deep within the house.

She stepped inside and heard Mrs. Henson in the kitchen. Her cup

424

clanked on something, and Jill debated if she should say hello.

"Up here," Di called from the top of the steps.

There was a glug of liquor leaving the bottle in the kitchen, and Jill ran up the stairs.

Di waited for Jill to go into Wes's room and take a seat on the end of the bed, then she shut the door behind them.

Wes was in the same place. Jill wasn't sure why she thought he might be anywhere else with that leg.

"You have to be getting really tired of sitting there," Jill said.

Wes frowned.

Di swung her hammer in front of her legs like a pendulum. "So, can I smash it?"

"No." Jill shook her head emphatically and watched Di to make sure she was listening closely. "If you smash it, you'll let it out, and things could get even worse."

"Worse?" The hammer froze in front of Di mid-swing. "That damn thing killed my dad."

"Yes, worse." She explained everything Silva had said, the mare, the spell, the prison.

"So, it has to go back," Wes said. "Like we figured. Only we can't get into that mountain."

"So, then, what do we do?" Di said.

Wes looked up and then back and forth from Jill to Di. "We put it in the cave."

"Are you going crazy, bro?" Di squinted down at him. "You just said we can't get into the cave."

"I know, I know, but listen. For the past few nights, we keep having dreams of the caverns, but each time, the thing veers us away, like it doesn't want us there."

"It does, doesn't it?"

"Every time we go in that direction, it sends us somewhere else. I think it's afraid to let us go there."

"You think we can end it *inside* the dream?" Jill asked.

"It's a dream animal, isn't it? And if we can die in dreams, why can't it?"

The room was silent as the three thought it over.

"We'd need Chris and Tommy again," Jill said. "And we'd have to stick together this time."

"Maybe we can get them over here," Wes said. "I'll call them."

"Tommy's in the hospital," Jill said. "You didn't hear. He woke up."

3

The sun was setting as Ray Trent parked in front of the old cabin. Juniper berries shined a brighter violet as the golden rays of twilight passed over them and dimmed.

He flexed his fingers around the steering wheel and replayed Jill Elden crossing the street inside his mind. How dare she? She was so close, almost in his grip. The back of his hands felt warm as he imagined the feel of her blood oozing over them.

"Bitch."

He took a breath. He was here now. The whispers had told him when he came back, he would be undisturbed. He had Misty inside, his prize. As much as he had wanted to ring that Jill bitch's neck, he had Misty now. This was better, wasn't it?

He saw how he had left her, taped to the bedrail, naked and ready. Yeah, this would be good. His thoughts shifted to his hands around her neck, squeezing. His knife inside her gut, that warm blood running over skin.

No. That wasn't why he had Misty. She was supposed to last. He didn't want to play that game with *her*. He growled and slammed his fist into the steering wheel. The car released a short blat from the horn.

"Fuck!" He realized what he had to do. It was just like rubbing one out before a date—that's what Jerry Benson in gym class had said. You were supposed to jerk off real good first, so you could go slow and enjoy it when you got the slut alone. And if he didn't want to blow it with Misty, he needed to go take care of this urge first.

Ray turned the key and backed away from the cabin.

2022

1

"Look at this." Di showed a three-dimensional rendering on her tablet's screen of the Bloodtooth cave system. Blocks in the corner offered units of scale, and cross-hatched tubes traced both the old path used for the guided tours and the cave-ins from thirty years ago.

"Where did you find that?" Wes said. He scanned the image with a discerning eye. "Look at that."

"Google. It's on the park service's web page."

"Imagine if we had that thirty years ago."

Di zoomed out of the image and scanned the text below it. "Says here, the cave system's too dangerous to allow tours, but they did open a way in—through an old mining entrance they reinforced. Apparently, they let students go in there for geological studies or something?"

"Go back to the map."

Di brought it up, and just as she had said, there was a marked spot on the schematic called *Secured Entrance*.

Wes ran his fingers over the screen, careful not to touch or drag the zoom. "That's the old entrance, and there's the path of the old tour. That's the giant cave where they killed the lights, and that—" His finger finally pressed on the screen. "That's where the hidden cave was that we found." The schematic only showed a small tube connecting two caverns that had been on the tour.

"You're sure?"

"Couldn't forget that. That's where all this shit started."

"Then that's where we have to go."

Wes's eyes crossed the room, settling on Sam and Lisa, who sat on the edge of the bed, watching television. Sponge Bob and Patrick were racing to make crabby patties as orders were backing up and customers were complaining. Their eyes were drooping, and Wes's fears were rising.

"We have to do this now," Wes said. "If they fall asleep..."

"Then let's go." Di rose from the bed and grabbed her bag.

"Girls," Wes said. "Time to leave."

2

Maggy Adams looked around and saw rocks. They hung from the ceiling and extended up from the floor. She was in a cavern she hadn't seen since childhood, and even with the weight of a dream's disconnection, she recognized where she was.

A baby's cry called to her, and her heart rate spiked. "Timmy!"

Maggy ran through the echo chamber, first right and then left, until she found the enormous central cavern. A woman sat in the middle of the floor, a baby in her arms, her baby.

"Timmy." Maggy ran to the two. Her feet dragged and slowed her. The woman looked up. She had a pleasant face and blonde hair. She was rocking him.

"Is Timmy his name?" she asked. She rocked him, and he settled.

Maggy sank to her knees, her heart slowing. "Yes." She held her arms toward him. "Please?"

"Here you go." The woman placed Timmy in his mother's arms. "I'm Jill."

"Maggy." She smiled from ear to ear as she gazed into his eyes. He was okay. He was calm. For the moment, she had completely forgotten where they were.

Jill sat back and watched. It felt like she had been alone for weeks, and she was so glad to see another human face. She didn't know if what she was seeing was an actual human or an illusion from the mare. It could even be something her own mind created to break the monotony of sitting in this cavern alone, and part of her didn't care which it was. It was just so nice to not be alone.

After a moment, Maggy looked up at Jill, then around the room. "Why... why are we here?"

Jill's smile sank. As much as she had enjoyed this moment, it had to end, didn't it? If the woman and child were an illusion, it would need to break. If she were real—that was even worse because it meant the mare had another soul to feed on when it was ready. And a baby's as well.

"Where do you think we are?" Jill asked.

"Um… it looks like Bloodtooth Caverns. I came here when I was a kid. But it's been closed for years. I don't know why I would dream this."

Jill decided she'd go with it for now. Maybe this woman was real. If she wasn't, the only way she'd find out was by digging deeper.

"You were pulled here," Jill said. "Something—I hate to say this— something wants to feed on us."

Maggy's grip on baby Timmy tightened, and she scooted back a foot from Jill. "What are you talking about?" She scanned the cave, her eyes looking for anything: other threats, validation, escape.

"I'm not going to hurt you."

"Just keep your distance." She scooted back further.

"Okay."

Maggy climbed to her feet and continued backward. "I'm going."

Jill nodded. "You can try. But it won't let you leave."

"Forgive me if I don't take your word for it." She turned and headed toward one of the cave exists.

"I'll be here."

Maggy ran into the exit tunnel just to be returned through the opposite side of the room. Her eye met Jill's and turned to hardened gems of scorn. She turned around and went back, appearing again on the opposite side of the cavern.

"I've done it a thousand times," Jill said. "But keep trying. You won't believe me until you've done it for yourself." She leaned back, propping herself up with her arms.

Maggy crossed the room and went out the other exit. This time, she came back through the same tunnel she'd left from. Her face wrinkled with worry. Her grip on her baby shook.

She walked with a wary gaze back to Jill. She guarded Timmy, holding him to her side. "What's going on here?"

"Hello?" a child's voice echoed.

"Over here," Jill called. From the other side of a massive stalagmite came one of Sam's schoolmates that Jill recognized. *Not you, too,* rang in her mind, and she feared that this may only be the start. "Hello, Janet."

1992

1

Ray Trent cruised the streets of Custer Falls, his gaze sharpened, his hunger tingling across every square inch of his flesh. He was close to his destination. He felt it. The whisper repeated in his head, telling him to stop, telling him to turn around and go back to the cabin. It told him to go enjoy Misty, enjoy his prize—and he would... but not yet.

The whisper was nearly a shout as he pulled into the parking lot of the Cozy Custer Motel. This wasn't the place, but he could find what he was looking for from here. As much as the whisper tried to tell him to leave, it hinted at the direction it *didn't* want him to go. It was right around the corner.

He parked in a spot near the end of the building between a pair of pickups. He checked inside his hoodie pocket. The knife was there, ready. Its handle was warm as he touched it as if someone had been holding it, waiting for him to grip it.

He scanned the motel, its windows and doors, and he saw no one, so he got out and walked to the building. He followed the side of the motel into the grass. He got a feeling like when he skipped school as if he was slipping away from the path he was expected to be on and could get caught at any moment. The thing was, he was already caught. The whisper knew he was breaking the rules, but still, the thrill of not listening, of being obstinately defiant, only made his fingers tingle more.

At the rear corner of the motel, Ray saw an alley, a shabby line of broken hedges, and then a row of houses. Their backs faced him, two with lights off, two with them on, one of which glowed in his mind with the radiance of unfulfilled bloodlust. That was the one.

He crossed the alley and stood within the hedge. The home's backyard was decorated with roses along the sides and a paved walk that led to a patio table and chairs. To the right was a rusted swing-set. White paint flaked from its poles, revealing solid red beneath. Ray got the feeling it was shedding its pretty facade and letting him see the decimation that was always just below.

In the window, he saw a man. It looked like a kitchen, and the man was washing his hands in the sink.

Ray muttered "He's big" without realizing the words were coming out.

The man stopped as if he had heard Ray, and Ray stepped behind the hedge. The man looked out the window for a moment, turned, and opened the refrigerator.

The back of his head was balding, and Ray could see fat rolls on the rear of his neck. He could also see massive shoulders and how the guy carried himself, like a linebacker ready to slam into a lineman.

The guy took a plate of something from the fridge and left the kitchen.

Ray crossed the hedges and hopped a small chain-link fence surrounding the backyard. He moved with a smooth, deliberate stride, putting each foot firmly on the ground and sliding the other through the night like a fated dance, doing no more than completing its predetermined steps.

He pressed himself against the kitchen window and looked inside. His heart pounded. It raced like this was his first time. The whisper screamed at him to leave and go back to Misty. This wasn't supposed to be his plan, it shouted. But he felt differently. He knew differently. This was the plan for him. He didn't believe in God or anything, but something inside told him that right now, this was exactly where the universe wanted him.

The kitchen was empty. He could see a doorway and a sliver into the next room. The television was on, *In the Heat of the Night,* maybe? One of those stupid dramas that adults loved so dearly. Its muffled voices came through the glass with a sweet smell like the dessert section of the school lunch line.

Ray stepped a few feet to the half-glass kitchen door. Through the top nine panes, he could see more of the living room and less of the television. Brown carpet covered the floor, topped with an oriental rug and a floral-printed love seat. He couldn't see the man, but it seemed like he should be in there to the left, on a floral-printed couch that matched the love seat and faced the TV.

The doorknob was cool to the touch and turned easily. It made a slight whine as it reached full rotation, but he was sure the guy couldn't hear it over the blaring noise in the other room. He pressed the door open and crept inside, closing it just enough to tap against the frame. He squeezed his knife.

Ray examined the kitchen, hoping to find another exit from the room and a way to sneak up behind this guy. There wasn't one. A small country table was to his right. A small 50s-era counter and sink were on his left. He'd have to go straight in. That was okay. He had the knife and the element of surprise.

He moved up to the doorway, feeling like some kind of cat burglar, and slowly peeked into the room. From here, he saw the couch's prints were roses, and tiny knickknacks of ceramic animals were placed on side tables and shelves around the room. It reminded him of his grandmother's house before she died. He smelled something and thought of Amanda Brolin: a mix of vomit and shit. It turned his stomach as he leaned in further.

Just a little more, he could almost see the couch. There was the coffee table. There was the couch's arm—he should have been able to see the guy's knees. Maybe he'd gone to take a piss? Ray leaned in further. The entire left half of the couch was drenched in blood.

"Wha—" His gut blazed with pain. He jerked backward, folded around the business end of an aluminum baseball bat. The bat slipped away, and he thumped to the tile floor, collapsing into the kitchen.

"He told me you were coming." The guy stormed into the kitchen, both hands ringing the bat's grip.

Ray pulled himself up. His stomach muscles didn't want to listen. They were slow and ached but gradually moved. His pants were wet. He'd pissed himself. The guy moved toward him, raising the bat and readying his swing.

"Fuck," Ray grumbled and scrambled toward the door.

"No." The guy stepped in to swing. He aimed at Ray's head but slipped on Ray's piss. His foot went left, taking the lower half of his leg with it. Ligaments ripped in his knee. He sunk and screamed as the bat crushed into Ray's back.

Ray slammed into the kitchen door, and it sealed shut, his nose and forehead crunching into the steel of its bottom half. Hot blood gushed over his face and down the door as he slid to the tile. His vision filled with stars.

"Bastard!" The guy rolled onto his back, reminding Ray of a giant turtle.

Ray's ears rang from the collision. His guts ached like his insides were on fire. His nose felt like it had been torn from his face. He watched the man rock on the floor grabbing his knee, and rage filled every other gap in Ray's consciousness. He covered his nose with one hand and gripped his knife with the other. It might not have gone as planned, but he was going to finish what he came here to do.

He crawled on his knees toward the guy.

"You son of a bitch," the guy cursed at the ceiling.

Ray pulled out the knife and moved quietly. He was just in range when the guy turned his head and looked into Ray's eyes. It was fear in there, Ray recognized it. He started to move, and Ray's knife tore forward and up. It plunged deep into the big man's side in silence. The guy opened his mouth to scream, and Ray yanked it out and shoved it back in, this time to a wet squish like a ringing sponge.

Blood flooded over Ray's hand. He yanked the knife back and stabbed again and again.

A scream bellowed from the big man, wet and gurgling. He turned toward Ray, and the shiny bat crunched into Ray's shoulder.

Ray heard the crack from his left collarbone and collapsed backward.

The bloody man rolled toward him, put his weight on his injured knee, and screamed. He slumped into a seated position and cranked the bat down on Ray's left arm. The limb crunched again and bent halfway between the shoulder and elbow.

Ray howled like he didn't know he could. He squeezed his burning waist into a sit-up and swung his knife, planting it deep in the guy's neck.

The aluminum bat clunked against Ray's head. He felt like he was sinking and watched blood spray as the guy pulled the knife free. The room fell silent as he collided with the floor.

2

To Wes Henson's surprise, Chris agreed to come this time. They sat on the four corners of the bed, Wes, Di, Jill, and Chris, each with doubtful faces, each wishing they could be anywhere but here.

Wes picked up Dad's office phone from the center of the bed. Di had run a ridiculous cord from her room to his just so they could use it for this. He dialed the hospital, then asked for Tommy's room.

"Hello?" Tommy's voice was still weak, like an elderly man with a child's tone.

"Hey. It's Wes. Hold on one sec." He pressed the speaker button, and Tommy's heavy breathing sounded across the room.

"You're awake, man," Chris called out.

"Chris? Yeah, man. Good to hear your voice."

"Yours sounds like shit. What's going on with you?"

"Tired. I've been fighting to stay awake until we talked, even though they keep telling me to rest."

Jill leaned toward the phone. "I don't blame you for not wanting to sleep."

"No shit." Tommy's end of the line went scratchy as if something was scraping across the receiver, then a muffled voice said something unintelligible. "Sorry, the nurse was bugging me again. I better make this quick, or they'll come in here and cut the cord."

"Tommy," Wes said, "you said earlier you had more to tell us. What is it?"

"Yeah, so, the thing, it's called Marenor—it's some kind of ancient demon that messes with dreams."

"A mare," Jill said, "my aunt told me it's from old Norse stories. We have some kind of stone here with a spell on it. It's imprisoned in the stone."

"That makes sense from what I saw. I somehow, like, jumped inside it in my last dream. I saw it feeding on people—their anxieties and fear. But that wasn't enough for it, and it figured out how to get inside people's heads while they were awake. That must be when it got put into that rock because it's pissed now, and it wants out."

Wes wrung his hands together. "That's kind of what we gathered. We think we need to put it back where I found it to end this, but we can't get into those caves. Someone blew up the entrances."

"Jesus."

"Yeah. So we want to try putting it back inside our dreams. It always seems to shuffle us away from there, like it doesn't want us to go there."

"I don't know if that'll work." Tommy's voice was growing dryer and harder to make out. "But I guess it's worth a shot."

Wes glanced at each person in his room and back to the phone. He sighed and clenched his fists. "And guys, I need to say something. I—I see now this is all my fault, and I'm sorry. I shouldn't have taken that thing. I don't even remember doing it, but I must have. The rock was with me when we were rescued."

Jill stretched and placed a hand on his leg. "You couldn't have known."

Chris stared down at the phone.

Di bit her lip.

"We just have to get through this," Tommy said. "And, one more thing you guys need to know: it tried to bribe me. I don't know what it wanted from me, but it was trying to get me to let it in—like, work for it or something. It said it could wake me up from my coma. I told it to fuck off, and I woke myself up, but it's probably telling other people the same shit."

"It tried me too," Jill said.

"Yeah," Chris said. "It tried to convince me too."

"I don't know why it wants us, but we have to stay strong," Tommy said. "I've seen what it can convince people to do."

"Thanks, Tommy," Wes said. There was a long silence as the weight of what they were about to do hung over the room. Wes went on, "So we're going to all go to sleep, and like before, I'll start calling everyone in."

"And then what?" Jill said.

"We fight to stay together, and we work our way to the cave. Then, we shove the goddamn rock right where it doesn't want it."

2022

1

"Don't fall asleep back there." Wes regarded Sam and Lisa in the Excursion's rearview mirror, and Lisa's head leaning on Sam's shoulder. It was bad enough they were driving to a collapsed cavern system, there were maniacs on the loose with an ancient demon in their minds, and they'd have to go midnight spelunking, but he also had to worry about his daughters being pulled into it all.

His thoughts went to Jill. He wished she were there with him. She'd been there every other step in his life, as far back as he could remember, even before he wanted to see it. And now he'd have to finish this without her.

He remembered her running from the raptors in the forest. She had been beside him when they placed the stone in the mine for what they hoped was the last time they'd ever see it. They had raised these kids together. And now it was up to him and Di to protect Sam and Lisa, and to finish this.

There were no longer any signs to the Bloodtooth Caverns exit, but knowing where it should be, they got off State Highway 11 onto a dirt road that led into the dark, overcast country.

Wes checked the mirror again. Lisa's lids slid heavily over her eyes. "Wake up, girls. Come on, almost there."

Di rotated in the passenger seat. "How about you guys lean forward and give me a couple of bounces." She moved up and down in the seat to demonstrate.

With frustrated expressions, the kids complied, unbuckling their belts, scooting forward, and bouncing up and down. It was working for the moment, but Wes had his doubts. He'd seen them pass out mid-sentence before after being up too late.

He had hoped to wait until a little later, but he grabbed the bag on the dash and passed it back. Blow Pops, chocolate bars, and cans of Red Bull clinked and clattered inside.

"Take a candy," Wes instructed. "Open one of those sodas and share it." He couldn't believe himself. He felt dirty, like he had handed them a baggy of cocaine. But was there a choice? He knew too well what could happen if they fell asleep. There was already evidence of it under Sam's bandages.

Sam popped open the Red Bull. She sipped and shouted, "Eew! This is gross."

"Just drink it. Share it with Lisa. It'll keep you awake."

The SUV shook as they crossed a cattle grate. After leaving it behind, Wes felt his chest still shaking. His heart pounded without a sip of caffeine or energy drink. It was then that a dark feeling invaded him. It called his gaze back to the mirror, to the backpack in the rear of the vehicle, to where the stone was. It was a sense of doom he hadn't felt since... since the night he had gotten rid of the thing the first time.

He watched Lisa try the Red Bull and purse her face around the can. His hands trembled on the steering wheel, and he grabbed it tight before anyone could see.

What was he walking into? What had he exposed his babies to by not solving this problem years ago? This wasn't just a drive to drop off a rock. He was going to have to crawl through tunnels, climb down rocks and walls, and who knows what else. And while he hadn't told Di yet, he would have to do it alone. She was going to argue and say she should come and help—but what about the girls? He couldn't take them in there. And someone was going to have to stay with them and keep them awake... to protect them from *his* failure.

He took a breath. It was going to be okay. He'd get them all there. He'd park everyone near the door, and he'd go in alone, and hopefully, he'd make it out alive. But at the least, he'd get that goddamn rock where it was supposed to go.

The road began to climb up the side of Bloodtooth Mountain, curving around its incline and building a steeper and steeper drop-off on the left side of the road. The Excursion roared as it ate the grade, vibrating the passengers inside. After several minutes of scaling the mountain, the road cut in, revealing the old parking lot for the main entrance.

Wooden beams crisscrossed the old cavern's opening, making a buck rail fence. The Excursion's headlights exposed a wall of boulders behind it, from the size of bowling balls to compact cars. Up above, the mountain's red fangs glared, poised to chomp.

"Jesus." Wes stopped the vehicle and stared.

"Yeah," Di said. "I saw some of the photos online. We're not getting through there."

To the left was the parking area and a small sign that read: *Secured Observation Entrance*, which stood before a path into the woods.

Wes pointed to the marker. "That looks like it."

He parked in front of the sign and gripped the wheel with both hands. He felt a weight press against him from behind. He knew what it was without looking back. That goddamn stone knew where they were, and it didn't like it.

"Are you ready?" Di said. "I'm so ready to have this over."

"Here's the thing." Wes glanced into the mirror. The kids were trying to keep their eyes open, but the fight was hard, and even the Red Bull seemed to be doing very little. "I'm going alone."

"Bullshit."

"No, listen to me." He felt a yawn fighting to get out, and he pushed it back down.

"It's bullshit."

He pointed to the backseat with his thumb. "We can't take them in there. It's too dangerous. And they need to be kept awake, so they don't get hurt."

"You want me to babysit? After all these years, I'm honored, but no."

Wes felt himself angering. He didn't want to. This was a logical choice, not one he should be angry about. It was the stone. It was draining him as it did back then. It was pulling him into its web.

"You can't take the stone," Wes said. "You don't know where it goes. I have to do that."

Di shook her head and stared out the window. She glanced back at Sam and Lisa. "Fuck."

Virb lifted his head from his seat in the third row.

"Does that mean you'll do it?"

"Yeah. I'll do it."

His eyes were heavy. He needed this conversation to end. He needed to get going. "Thank you." He put his hand on her shoulder.

"Yeah, well, don't fuck up in there, or I'll have to come in anyway and rescue you."

He smirked. "Just keep an eye out, will you." He looked around the vehicle, into the woods, and on the road they drove in on. He had the feeling there was more to this, that the mare still had plans. "I'm not sure we're alone here."

"Did you see something?" She looked around as well, a yawn spreading across her mouth.

"No. And none of that." He yawned, too, unable to control it this time.

Sam and then Lisa yawned in the back.

"No," Wes shouted. "You guys eat more candy." The words hadn't left his mouth when both the girls' eyes fell closed. "No, guys, no!"

Exhaustion fell over Wes, and he dropped into his seat. It was the goddamn mare fighting back. "We have to..." He saw Di; her eyes were shut, head against the headrest. "Goddammit." His lids closed with unrelenting force.

Part Five: Return to the Altar

Dragons and Dinosaurs, Spaceships and Astronauts

1

They stood once again outside Bloodtooth Caverns. Wes and Diana Henson looked at a wide open entrance, free of the thousands of tons of boulders that blocked the way in their waking life.

Wes studied the darkness inside the opening ahead. It pulsed, expanding and contracting like some sort of sludge, running deeply through the stone crevices and pulling back with the throbbing of his heart. He felt it watching, Marenor, its eyes hidden in the gloom. No, that wasn't right—it wasn't in the gloom, it *was* the gloom. This place, it was a manifestation of the thing itself, and they were going inside it.

He felt numbness crawl up his legs. It was like the first time he had approached the thing.

Why was he doing this? Why was he going anywhere near this thing? Then it came to him.

His waking life and his dream life overlapped for just long enough for the truth to shine through. But it wasn't one waking life. It was two. In that moment, he accepted that he was two people. He was a past self and a future one somehow joined out of time in this dreamscape. It was why everything was so familiar. Always so familiar. He had done this all before, and he had left people behind—and they were in more danger alone.

Sam, he wished her close, and she was immediately standing next to him. *Lisa*. She appeared in the lot between Wes and Di. *Jill*. She stood in front of him. *Chris*. He appeared on the left. *Tommy*. He appeared on the right.

Chris stepped ahead and looked around, pausing on Sam and then

Lisa. "Who are you?"

Di looked at Wes. Her eyes said no. He tried to figure out why or what she was worried about, and she spoke, "These are our cousins, Sam and Lisa."

The girls looked at her, confused at first, then smiled. It was like they were having a conversation that Wes couldn't hear. He tried to understand why she would say that as he looked at the others. Did she think it would be hard to explain they were his kids? Did she think they wouldn't believe it? Or was there something else going on that he wasn't seeing?

Whatever it was, Sam and Lisa seemed to understand. They waved, *Hello.*

Tommy nodded, "Okay."

"Why are they here?" Chris asked.

"The thing's been after them too," Wes said. "They want to help. What's the big deal?"

"Yeah—okay." Chris looked annoyed. He took a step toward the cavern, under the weight of its massive fangs, and stared into the open face of its stone maw. He loosened and turned back to the others. "Well, let's do it."

Tommy patted Wes on the back. "Let's put this bastard back where he belongs."

Wes considered each face of those around him. He wished they all could be somewhere else, somewhere safe. He felt the darkness ahead, a cold creeping despair that made the hairs on his arms and legs rise, and a shiver all but shouted: *some of them aren't coming back from this.*

One at a time, they stepped forward toward the cave's entrance: Chris, then Tommy, Di, Jill, and lastly, Wes and the girls.

"No matter what happens," Wes said to Sam and Lisa, "stay close. Stay together. Don't get led away by anything you see."

"Okay," Lisa said. Her gazed raced around the entrance, taking everything in.

Sam nodded. She flexed her hands, all of her digits where they belonged.

Wes knew it was a hope, wishful thinking that wouldn't prove true.

He felt his pocket as he walked. The stone was in there. He felt the bulge and the numbing pressure on his leg. He just had to get it down there.

The group stopped just inside the door. Jill squinted into the darkness, then walked deeper in.

The lights were out, or off, or completely removed. Wes couldn't tell which. He thought he had a flashlight in his hand and raised it. In the round hovering illumination, all traces of the twentieth century were gone. No railings, no lights, no plaques with diagrams of structures and what they were and what caused them. It was as if they'd gone back in time—to when, Wes wasn't sure—but it was not 1992 any longer.

"This way," Wes moved forward.

The steps that Fish Wildlife and Parks and the Forestry Department had carved into the cave floor back in the fifties were gone too. The path downward consisted of overlapping boulders, steep gravel grades, and piles of inclined rock.

Wes climbed down quickly, pausing about halfway down the first path, and stopped, realizing he was alone. He shined the light up. The rest of the group waited at the top, staring down at him.

"You guys coming?"

Yellow eyes glowed from each of them. They looked down at him with haunting gazes, and chills crept over Wes's flesh.

"Guys?"

He looked closer. The angles of their faces seemed to be changing, sharpening. Tommy, Chris, and Jill all lowered their stances, leaning forward toward him, hands swaying in front of them as if they may leap forward at any moment. Sam and Lisa crouched, aiming the tips of their fingers—their wiry-looking fingers, which stretched and scraped into the dirt.

Chills faded into fear. Wes didn't know where his friends had gone. These were not them. These were something else, and he could feel their anger tumbling down the incline toward him.

Wes backed away, the uneven slide of gravelly rock below. Chris and Tommy hunched all the way to the ground and gripped the rock in front of them. Their spines arched, and pointed bones pierced their shirts, aiming rearward. A gust of decay washed from the upper cave down and over Wes.

"What the fu—"

Chris and Tommy charged.

Wes spun and raced down the rocky hill. The flashlight's beam shook as he moved, glancing from craggy wall to crumbling ground, to an open crevice on the left half of the cave.

From Wes's visits, he remembered the left side started small and became a fifty-foot cliff—at that time guarded by a metal rail; as he ran now, it was merely a wide ledge with painful death below.

Further down the hill, the ground became mounds of rocky debris, maybe from cave-ins, maybe from mining. It was wobbly under his feet as he ran, and he wished he could slow and be careful. He lit the stones underfoot, ignoring the cave ahead.

Low growling howls echoed down the cavern's depths. First one, then two, then three and four. They made Wes think of wolves, werewolves, beasts of massive size and sharp claws. He saw the tips of bones on Tommy's back in his mind—what was he turning into? Those glowing eyes...

Footfalls sounded behind him. They moved from gravel to piled stone, and Wes felt panic rise from the depths of the old caveman part of his brain as if a sabered lion was on his tail.

He screamed and lifted his light. His heart leaped as he saw the cave wall ahead. There was supposed to be an opening there. It was supposed to bend and twist and turn left, eventually lowering and connecting with the bottom of the cliff to his left. But he didn't see that.

"No, no, where is it?"

And as if to answer him, his light found a hole in the wall. It was dark and small, not at all the human-sized path he was used to. This was an opening two feet wide by less than two feet tall. It was a size for a child or small animal, and Wes remembered he was a child, or one of him was.

He pushed his legs, feeling the heat of his pursuers behind him. He heard breathy whispers, his friends' voices but not—lower, somehow hungrier. "Come back, Wes." "You can't get away from us." "We're friends, Wes." "You'll never make it."

He ran harder and dove into the hole. There was barely room for him to move more than a crawl on his belly, his elbows, and shuffling his knees.

The smell of mud was thick inside the tunnel. A fearful thought crossed Wes's mind, mudslides and cave-ins. He ignored them, shined his light forward, and crawled as fast as his elbows and knees could push.

The tiny path echoed. "You can't get away that way." "Come back."

"No," repeated in his mind and from his lips. He prayed his feet had crossed into the tunnel's safety as something grabbed his foot. "Let go! Let go! Let go!" Wes screamed and yanked his leg. Something yanked back, and he felt himself slide backward a few inches in the dirt. He clawed at the walls, his fingers sinking into thick muddy rock.

The grip tightened, and he kicked. He slid another inch back, grabbing the walls harder and screaming.

"You're coming with us," a hissing voice said. It was high, like Jill if she were sick while filled with helium.

Wes pushed harder on the tunnel and kicked with both feet. He felt something sharp in his sole and kicked again.

Burning pain ran up Wes's leg and the pressure lifted. He pulled himself forward into the tunnel and continued flailing his legs so nothing could grab him. Forward more, kicking more.

He felt the walls shake around him. The only thing in his mind was *cave-in*. He quit kicking and crawled frantically, hands, feet, elbows, knees, inch by inch, as a rumble shook dirt from the cave roof.

A crash boomed from behind, and a gust of dirt blew past. Wes couldn't breathe. He coughed so hard he had to stop. He lifted his shirt up over his mouth, wiping away muddy spit and snot. After a moment of regaining his breath, he shined the light behind him. His passage was sealed. He shined ahead again. On and on, he saw a narrow path, no opening in sight. No widening. It was a never-ending tube of dirt and rock, and he was stuck inside it.

The walls trembled around him. His heart thumped, and all he could imagine was this being his tomb, a smothering, endless tomb.

2

Jill watched Wes descend the rocks, and as if by magic, he vanished into the darkness.

"Wes?" Jill called.

"Wes?" Di joined in.

"Where'd he go?" Chris asked.

Tommy started down the hill and stopped. "I think it took him—separated him." He turned back. "Let's stay together."

Chris nodded and stepped down into the descending gloom. Jill followed.

Sam and Lisa looked doubtfully at Di.

"He's going to be okay," she told them and took their hands. Lisa frowned. Sam firmed her lip and nodded. They all inched down the rocky incline.

"Oh, wait." Tommy reached toward the ground and picked up a stick.

Jill could have sworn it wasn't there before, but he scooped it up without a thought. He ripped into his shirt, pulling away a long strip of fabric, which he wrapped around the wood. Then, he went into his pocket, retrieved his favorite Punisher lighter, and lit the torch.

The cave around them brightened like daylight, and from within the surrounding rock walls, eyes shone at them.

Sam screamed. The rest jerked toward her and followed her eyes. Lisa screamed. Jill froze.

Outlines of beings emerged from the rock, tall, slender beings with long, snake-like fingers that waved and swayed. They came from the right and left. They dropped from the ceiling, blocking the entrance to the cavern and closing in.

"Run!" Tommy pointed down the hill.

Chris took off. Di dragged the sisters. Jill ran alongside them. Tommy waved his torch as if it might frighten the things away.

They moved in on Tommy, surrounding him. Their fingers whipped back and forth, snapping at the air, echoing down the rocky throat.

He leaned forward, stabbing one of the creatures with his flame. Embers shattered and exploded like red flowers bursting from a rock. The creatures kept coming.

Tommy planted his feet and shouted at the others, "Remember, it's a dream. Use it!" His gaze darted from one monster's eyes to the next. "Come on, you pricks."

His torch began to glow from the bottom of the stick to the top. The entire thing melted into itself and reformed into a glowing pickax. He grabbed the handle with both hands and pulled. The tool split along its shaft and, as if by mitosis, became two.

He lifted the tools above his shoulders. "I said come on!"

One rock beast darted in at him. He dropped the pickaxes down on its head, cracking the top of its skull open like an eggshell, and spraying dark, violet blood across the cave floor. Another ran in, and he wheeled to the side, smashing the ax tips into its temples and ripping its face off. Bony skull, purple brains, and violet blood crashed down, and three creatures ran at him.

Tommy crunched through another monster's head as the second reached with lengthening fingers. Their tips hardened into spikes aimed at his face.

Tommy ducked and smashed his weapon into the monster's chest as the third pounced on his back.

Deafening waves of growls and screeches pummeled the walls and radiated down the cavern. Tommy howled as the beast on his back punctured his shoulders with stone claws. Its feet clamped into his sides with pointed heels, ripping into his skin and digging for a hold.

As if by instinct, Tommy swung the pair of pickaxes backward, hooking them into the monster's ribs and flinging it forward. He gasped and gathered his breath, his back aching, burning. He counted the remaining monsters: six. He could do this.

In the corners of his eyes, he saw monsters descend. In front of him, they climbed down from the ceiling. He turned and looked behind; five, ten more, dropped down. They gathered around him like an angry mob, claws waving, amber eyes glowing, swaying back and forth, and moving steadily closer.

Their digits snapped, one after another. The sounds towered over them, fell, and swelled. They filled the cave as thick as a rising tide, and Tommy felt the noise dig into his brain.

Fuck. He held one ax forward and one back, ready to swing. "Come on motherfuckers!"

Rock creatures flooded on top of Tommy, hundreds of fingers on his body, grabbing and pulling. They dragged him as a mass and carried him to the stone wall. Stone turned into something soft and mushy, like rock-colored mud, and they squeezed into it one at a time. They pulled each other in, then, as a mob with Tommy in the center, forced themselves inside it.

He screamed, surrounded by stone.

3

Di rushed down the rocky path, one hand guiding each niece. They cried quietly as they ran. She couldn't see Chris anymore, and Jill was a dark blob a few feet ahead.

"Wait a sec." She stopped and pulled the girls together. "Hang on to each other for a minute." Their whimpers drained her. It was like something stabbing her heart and sucking her will. They didn't deserve this. They shouldn't have even been here.

She thought of Tommy making a torch out of nothing. She needed her own light now.

Remember, it's a dream. Use it!

She didn't want a torch, though. What she needed was a flashlight—no, three, the girls needed them too. She dug into her pockets. At first, there was nothing, just empty fabric.

Use it!

"They're in there," she told herself. She forced herself to believe. She felt again, this time digging deep inside until she felt something hard. She fingered the shape. It was metallic, cylindrical, yes. She pulled it out and searched with her other hand. She found another and held them both in front of her. She fumbled for the switches and found them, flipping them on.

"Hold these," she extended her hands to the girls. They were gone. Cold alarm flashed throughout her being. "Sam! Lisa!"

"What is it?" Jill came into the light.

Di spun, shining her light on every wall, across the gravelly floor, even up at the ceiling. "Sam! Lisa!"

"Where are they?" Jill asked.

"They were just here." Di spun in circles, lighting the room with a double-bladed strobe. "Where'd they go? They were just here."

Jill scanned the cave herself. She held out a hand to touch Di. "They're not here."

Di stopped and fell to her knees. Light jittered as her hands trembled. "I have to find them. I have to keep them safe."

Jill touched Di's shoulder. "It'll be okay. I'll help you." She glanced up the way they'd come and was greeted by howls, screams, and the sound of crumbling rock. "But we need to move. They aren't here, and this place isn't safe."

"We need to get to Wes. He'll know how to find them."

"Yeah. We'll find Wes." She took Di's arm and pulled.

Di rose to her feet and gave the section of cave one last survey with her light. Nothing but rock. Tears ran down her cheeks. Her face quivered. "Take this." She offered one of the lights to Jill.

Jill took it and pulled on Di's arm. "Let's go!"

Di moved, ignoring the ball of shame that had formed in her gut. They ran together down the path, over the trail of crushed and weathered rock. The side of the cave opened into a cliff as they reached the bottom.

"Where is it?" Jill said. "There's supposed to be a cave here—to go to the next section." She explored the wall with her light and found a pile of boulders. She pressed and pulled at the mammoth stones. She shined her light into the cracks where a tunnel should have been. "It's blocking the way."

Jill's light searched the rest of the wall, the side of the cave, back up the path they'd followed. "Where do we go?"

"And what happened to Chris?" Di walked to the edge of the cliff and looked over. Darkness sank in front of her to unfathomable depths. She shined her light and saw the sides of the cave descending twenty feet, and then nothing.

"I think that's the only way," Jill admitted softly.

"No way." Di shook her head, staring into the nothing at the end of her light.

Remember, it's a dream. Use it!

"It's a dream," Di muttered. "Hold on." She closed her eyes and willed. She dug into her pocket again, this time pulling out a three-pointed grappling hook and a loop of knotted rope.

4

Wes crawled and crawled. The cave was so narrow he couldn't look back, but he was sure it was getting smaller the further he went. The ceiling felt lower. The walls felt tighter. He got the idea he was in a ridiculously long funnel, and soon, it wouldn't be his hands and knees he was crawling on, it would be the tips of his fingers as he slid on his belly.

His shoulders brushed both sides at one time. The rock scraped his arms. He was sure his knees were bleeding under his pants, in his bed, maybe even as he sat parked in the Excursion outside Bloodtooth Caverns.

The thought stirred his memories: Di in the seat beside him, Sam and Lisa in the back. He flexed his grip and pushed himself on. He had to get out of there. He had to get this damn stone back in place. He had to get back to his kids.

The walls of the cave vibrated. Tremors traveled into his shoulders and up through his knees and hands. It was like the Earth was quivering. Then it stopped, and a wave of pressure slammed Wes from behind. The walls shook and flexed outward—providing momentary relief from his suppressed claustrophobia—and they slammed back in, squeezing him from every direction.

He screamed. "Stop!"

The walls relented. There was a moment when the world stilled. Wes breathed, trying to filter the dust by keeping his lips close together. And another wave of pressure raced through. Another widening of the walls.

"No, no, stop!"

It didn't stop. The walls slapped back together into his shoulders. The weight on his bones was like nothing he had ever felt. It was like he was being pressed into himself, squeezed within the hand of some giant sadist.

He groaned. His breath left his chest, and his lungs fought fruitlessly to get it back. His vision of the gray cave wall blurred, and he shifted his muscles, bones, anything he could, trying to squirm from inside the grip of this stone tube.

The cave walls loosened, and Wes slapped onto the rocky floor. He sucked in as much air as he could fit inside his lungs and blew out again. And again. A second later, he pushed himself up and forward.

He clawed at the floor and flew through the tunnel. He had to get somewhere else, away from these crushing walls.

He'd made it fifty feet when the next wave of pressure blasted past him from behind.

"No!" He screamed so loud his throat burned.

He couldn't let this happen. Not crushed inside some cave by an invisible, anonymous fiend. He had to get back to his wife, to his kids, to his sister, and his friends.

Wes forced himself to think. How could he not get crushed? Maybe if he were inside something? A shield to protect him? (like?) Like the Ninja Turtles; they had shells. But he wasn't a turtle, and he needed something harder. What was the hardest thing he knew? What could his shell be made of?

His mind went to Wolverine—his claws and bones. They were coated in an unbreakable metal. He imagined himself inside not a shell, but an egg, a round container made of adamantium, just like the shield around Wolverine's skeleton.

He prayed for it as he heard the walls rumble and the rock shift. He told himself he had to believe. He saw it in his mind, a shiny shell of an amazing metal.

From behind him came a metallic sound, something scraping, then crunching. He opened his eyes and saw his flashlight reflecting a silver inner dome back at him. He looked down and around—it was there, he was inside a metal egg.

The scraping sped up. The egg groaned. The shell vibrated under his knees, above his back, on the sides of his shoulders.

You're strong, you're strong, he repeated inside his mind. *Strongest metal in the world. He can't break you.*

The groaning stopped, the scraping sped up, and Wes felt himself shoved to the back of the egg. He was like a passenger on a rocket, hurled to the rear as if the egg had been launched into orbit.

"Shit!" His voice was like a robot, the way it echoed inside the compartment.

Scraping faded to silence, and the backward Gs slowly lifted. After a moment, there was nothing, he was floating, like in space, and the horrible realization struck Wes that he was falling. He was inside a giant egg, falling, and when he hit the ground, whether inside an impenetrable shell or not, he was going to turn into mush against its inner wall.

Cushion? Pillow? Springs? Wait... he thought of a liquid he'd seen in some movie; it had oxygen in it so you could breathe underwater. He closed his eyes and willed the egg full of that stuff. It would suck to have it inside his lungs, but he could breathe and not feel the impact.

Wes became surrounded by a gooey gel. It gushed inside his mouth and flooded down into his chest. He gagged as it crawled down his throat. His body rocked and convulsed. It reached the inside of his lungs, and he coughed it all out. His heart pounded, and he sucked it back in. His head ached as it spread to his sinuses, and he couldn't sneeze it out. He pushed against the sides of the egg—this was stupid. How did he get himself caught in all this? He breathed it out and in again. Fluid squished through his teeth and soaked his eyes. And then he found he wasn't drowning. It was working.

The egg banged. Every part of Wes slammed into the inside of the compartment, and he felt like he'd been plastered into a wall. A scraping noise like steel against sharpened steel. And everything calmed.

Had he stopped? Was the ride over? Was he in some lower cave inside the cavern complex?

Wes wished away the top of the egg. Blueish goo spilled over the edges, and bright light bathed everything.

He stood and coughed out the gunk, rubbing his eyes to see. Air reached his lungs, and surrounding Wes was a vast prehistoric prairie with brachiosauruses, stegosauruses, and ankylosauruses. In the distance were massive trees, snow-capped mountains, and one very angry volcano.

"What the hell?"

5

Sam and Lisa held each other's hands tight. They stood in a dimly lit room with metal floors, walls, and ceilings. Panels blinked with a hundred buttons on the far side of the room. Wires ran along the corners, and the air smelled of a cleaner that Mom always used in the kitchen. Their feet left the ground, and Lisa gripped tighter. On the left was a window, and outside, space and a light green alien world.

"Sam?" Lisa waved her legs, trying to put her feet back on the ground.

"It's okay," Sam said. She pulled Lisa closer. Her sister moved with the effort of dragging a balloon through the air.

"Where are we?"

"I don't know." She tried to keep her tone low. She tried not to freak out for her sister. But inside, she was screaming at the craziness of being ripped away from everyone in that cave. Her heart was racing. She just hoped to keep it together for Lisa. "But at least we aren't in that cave... right?"

Lisa studied the planet in the window. "That isn't even Earth, is it?"

"I don't think so."

"So..." She buried her face in Sam's chest. "I don't like this."

They drifted higher until Sam reached up and stopped them from bumping into the ceiling. She thought of that poor Oompa-Lumpa floating off into the sky and wondered if she could burp. Her gaze went to Lisa. "I don't either. But we're going to get through this."

Sam gave the ceiling a push, and the two of them floated back toward the floor. "I think the first thing we need to do is find out where we are."

"Aren't we in space? How do we get back?"

"We'll figure it out."

Behind them was a door with no handle. Sam only recognized it as a door from science fiction shows like *Star Trek*. It was dirty, like the rest of the room, covered in gray and black specs. The metal had tiny dents and scratches like a golf ball that had been chewed up by a pit bull.

"We go through there, I think."

Lisa uncovered her face and followed Sam's gaze. "No. Let's just stay here and wait. Someone will come. Dad or Aunt Di." She pointed to the window and the buttons. "Or over there? Maybe we can see more from that window? Or maybe there's a phone over there."

Sam wanted to scoff at the idea of a phone, but then again—what did she know? "Okay."

She held Lisa's hand and pushed off from the floor, sending them floating toward the console on the far side of the room. The air grew thicker with a metallic smell that Sam didn't recognize. It left a light burn in her nose and throat as she breathed.

Despite what it looked like from across the room, once Sam was closer, she saw the console wasn't a thousand glowing buttons, but a single screen with lots of glowing icons, like a giant tablet with a thousand apps. Its surface was scratched and dimpled like the rest of the room, but each little icon stood up just barely from the screen.

The colorful shapes had images and writing that she didn't understand, and the top right corner was cracked. Glowing green liquid leaked from the fissures and clung to the screen.

"Oh, my God," Lisa mumbled. She stared through the window.

Floating outside was a sight that froze Sam's tongue. She tried to speak, but only clicks came out.

The planet was cracked into pieces. What they had seen from the other side of the room was only the largest, a single remaining hemisphere. Its oceans poured from the surface over the edge of the crust, some looping back into its rocky insides, some spraying across space to the next chunk of stony ruin. Uncountable shards of rock and debris floated in every direction. Magma crept over the surface of devastated, partially lit cities, and fires swept across triangular forested meteors. And that was just the planet.

Immediately outside the window, floating in and out of view, was the wreckage of other crafts and their passengers. Dozens of bodies hovered in space suits. Some were missing limbs, others heads. One body drifted on what looked like a collision course for the window. Its helmet was smeared in blood. Its arms were gone, and shreds of suit, frozen muscle, and icy trails of blood followed.

"Let's go," Lisa said. "I changed my mind. Let's get out of this room."

Sam was stuck in place. She wondered who these people were. What could have caused this? Was that man going to hit the window?

Lisa pulled on her sister. She hooked her foot on the ground and pushed away from the console.

"Yeah," Sam muttered. She extended her hands to catch the approaching wall. She grabbed a handle and maneuvered them in front of the door. It didn't open. She expected it would—it would have on *Star Trek*. Then, she spotted a rectangular panel beside the door and touched it.

There wasn't a whoosh as the door moved. It opened, but with the loud sound of grinding metal and crunching gears. The smell of the hallway outside slipped through, like the metallic scent by the console. But more coppery, more like blood.

The hallway was as dim as the room. In the distance on the right, a flickering yellow light showed walls dented with what looked like gunfire. Bloody handprints drifted down and into the gloom. A chattering click repeated in bursts from down there. It was a wet sound that made Sam think of teeth and tongues slapping against each other.

She looked the other way. Mostly darkness, but a red light fell from the inside of another room a few doors down.

"Which way?" Lisa whispered.

Sam weighed the darker path on the left and the blood and the sound of organic clicking on the right. A brief moment of clarity tumbled through her thoughts. She was dreaming. This wasn't real. The world around her was all in her mind. She would wake up from this soon and see it was only a nightmare all along. That thought vanished as the flickering yellow light showed an invasion of movement.

Something flooded across the walls, covering the projectile holes, and swallowing the bloody prints. It moved like a liquid, but Sam knew that was wrong. It bulged and traveled in waves, but it wasn't wet... it was crawling. Thousands, millions, of something small and legged—they were crawling across the walls toward them. And the clicking was growing louder.

"Shit!" the word she wasn't supposed to say burst like a gunshot.

Lisa screamed.

"Back in the room!" Sam pushed them both inside and slammed the panel. The door's gears crunched. It shuddered and squealed and refused to close. She slammed it again. Nothing. "We have to go."

"No." Lisa shook her entire body as her head pleaded back and forth, *No*. "Did you see them?"

"Yes, and the door won't close. Come on!"

"No!"

"Jesus, they're going to be here any second."

Sam grabbed for Lisa's hand, and Lisa yanked it away. She pushed against the floor and sailed backward into the room.

"What are you doing?" Sam stuck her head through the door and glanced down the hall. It was too dark. She couldn't see the walls around her until she noticed the reflections. Thousands of tiny glitters in the dark each time the yellow light flickered beyond. Thousands of tiny somethings were getting closer and closer, some only feet away.

She looked back at her sister. Lisa's back was against the console. Tears streamed from her eyes. They floated into the air and drifted, small bulging drops of salty water.

Her mind raced for ideas. She wanted to leave, to take off down the hall. But she couldn't abandon Lisa. She had no weapons, and she couldn't squish a million bug-things with her hands. She thought about throwing herself into the hallway and shooting down to that red-light room. Maybe there were weapons there—a gun full of bullets that exploded into bug spray? She could come right back and save Lisa once she had a weapon, or maybe an adult who would help.

Sam grabbed the edge of the door, putting her feet against the wall. She could push with her legs and shoot down the hallway. It would be quick. It would be safe.

She took another look at Lisa. She'd say *Be right back*, and then Lisa would know she'd be okay.

Sam knew at that moment Lisa wouldn't be okay. Her hands were frozen over her mouth. Terror wrapped her face and seized her into a statue. Her skin was flushed, her eyes red and bulging with fright.

A dream. A fraction of a second of clarity returned.

Sam gripped the door, her fingers like steel, and she pushed against the wall. She groaned and pulled. The door crunched and whined, and it moved.

"Come on!" She heaved with every ounce of her muscle and her mind. "Come on!"

The door closed, inch by inch. A giant clunk, and it throttled forward a foot, and another.

It was almost there. Sam could feel the job near the end. Only another foot or so.

She heaved and felt a tickle on her hand. She looked down, and three things were crawling across the back of her wrist.

"Sam!" Lisa howled.

Sam jerked her hand away from the door and pushed with her legs. She soared across the room and brought her other hand down on her wrist. There was a clap and pain. Both of her hands burned. She looked down to see three small, navy blue bodies, crumpled and floating from her arm. On her skin was a dark purple goo, and it hurt. Not just hurt but stung like the edge of a flame.

She wiped her hands on her clothes to get the stuff off, leaving bright red skin and three small sores on both her palm and wrist. It was like its blood burned so bad it ate into her skin. And there were millions more coming.

Sam looked back at the door. A wave was crawling around it. Another crawled over the door frame. Another across the floor, and another on the ceiling. Every piece of the opening was thick with navy bugs, and her exit was now only a foot and a half wide. What had she done?

A hand touched her back, and Sam spun around. It was Lisa. She'd crossed the room completely, and those things were getting closer by the second.

"What do we do, Sam?" Lisa cried.

Sam studied the room. There had to be another way out. She didn't see one, but there had to be. She saw the window into space—obviously, that wasn't going to work. She looked over the floor, metal tiles seemingly bolted down. The walls were the same.

The bugs moved closer, halfway across the room, and the sound of clicking became louder. It resonated in Sam's ears, the pressure like going over a high mountain pass and making her want to hold her nose and blow to pop them.

She looked at the ceiling: grating, but it somehow reminded her of the ceilings at school, where tiles could be dropped and... Maybe that was the way?

Sam put her feet on the console and balanced herself between the machine and the ceiling. She pushed on the closest tile, and it lifted. Her heart rose. This was the path, she knew it. She slid the tile to the side to see what was up there, and her heart sank. There were barely a few inches, nowhere near enough space for them to fit.

"Shit!" Sam pushed herself back down to the console.

Lisa grabbed her sister. "What do we do?"

"I don't know." Sam's heart pounded. She squeezed her sister back.

The things were just feet away. They shined like waves of navy ink. They rippled as they walked, clinging to the walls. The click, click, click was like a metronome of death. She knew if they reached her in numbers, they'd swarm all over them and bite them and tear into them with thousands of tiny mouths and claws. They'd crawl inside them and eat them from the inside. They'd use whatever burning stuff was inside them and melt them away to eat them.

She shook. Every inch of her trembled.

"I love you, Lisa," Sam said. She needed to say it. She needed her little sister to know it if this was the last minute of their life.

"I love you, Sam."

Sam watched the bugs climb underneath them. They crawled up the console and moved over the edges and toward their fingers, and Sam had an idea. It might be a stupid one, but she thought it was better than just floating there and waiting to die.

"Let go," Sam said.

"What?"

"Let go! They can't get us if they can't reach us."

Lisa released the console and drifted up toward Sam. Sam grabbed her and turned her toward the gapped door.

"What are you doing?" Lisa shouted.

"We have to float. We're going to float right through."

"What?"

"You have to trust me."

Lisa whimpered. Sam turned her sister sideways, aimed, and threw her at the door like some human-shaped javelin.

Bugs filled the console. They closed in on Sam's grip as she spun herself, crouched across just a few inches of alien technology, and sent herself flying across the room.

They floated, and Sam watched the waves of bugs stop and begin rippling in the other direction. Jesus, were they that smart? They were just bugs, weren't they?

"Sam?" Lisa called out. She was drifting too high. She was nearing the ceiling and too far to the left. If she didn't do something, she was going to scrape across the roof and slam into the door.

"Lisa!" Sam reached for her sister. She couldn't get there. She was going faster than Lisa and thought she might catch up soon, but not quickly enough. Her hand grasped at empty air, inches away from Lisa's foot. Her entire body rushed with hot, angry tingles. This was all her fault. She'd thrown her sister in this direction. She was going to hit those things, and swarms would cover and devour her sister right in front of her eyes in this horrid alien place.

She stretched, a single finger in front, and an idea came. "Use one finger, Lisa. Tap the ceiling to change your direction and keep going."

"What? They'll get on me!"

"I know, but it's the only way. Tap the ceiling and fix yourself, then squish each one that touches you."

"No. I can't." She shrunk inward, cringing.

"You have to. Do it, or you'll crash, and they'll be all over you."

Lisa shuddered and cried. She reached a hesitant finger out and pulled it back.

"Do it!" Sam yelled.

She reached again. Her entire body was within a foot. Another few seconds and she'd collide.

"Be quick. Try not to scrape off more than you have to."

Lisa extended her hand and jabbed at the roof. Tens of tiny monsters swarmed her hand. She drifted down and screamed. Dozens of navy creatures floated to each side, and she mashed her hands together, crushing and crunching tiny exoskeletons.

"It burns!" she cried.

"Careful!"

Lisa was moving toward the door's opening, but it was narrow.

"Keep your body straight."

She did, and shook with tears. "It hurts so bad!"

Droplets of blood floated from her hands. They went in every direction. A few crashed into bugs on the door, and a wave of ripples swarmed them. The clicking grew louder, and the ripples moved toward the edge of the door, where Lisa was only halfway through.

"God, stay straight, Lisa!" Sam trembled as she watched.

Lisa wailed and did as she was told. She was straight as an arrow, chest, head, and out the door.

"Go for the room with the red light!" Sam was almost to the door. She wasn't high like Lisa was, but she wasn't on target. She had drifted right and was going to hit the door frame. She wasn't sure how to fix this. They covered the frame and the wall, pulsing as she neared. She worried this may be it. "Go to the red light, Lisa!"

Sam held out her hand, pointing at the wall to her right. She would tap it, just as Lisa did, and get just a hair of movement to the left, and then she'd slide right through the opening. She told herself she could do this. It may have been the last thought she would have, but she was going to believe she could do it.

She pressed into the wall just beyond the doorframe, and what seemed like a hundred bugs crawled over her finger, racing up her hand. She pushed as little as she could. She didn't want to fly off course. She flicked her hand and lost half the bugs. They floated away, their tiny legs stretching, clawing, trying to get back to her. She mushed those left behind against her side and then into her other hand, and as the burn set in, her head drifted through the open door.

She watched them reach toward her open eyes. Their tiny legs and claws extended. An image of them catching her made her entire body clench. She imagined their burning liquids eating into her face, and she wanted to scream.

Her mouth passed through the door frame. Breath rushed in and out, rapid, heavy; she saw waves in the layer of bugs as her breathing fell over them and relented.

Her shoulders went through, her arms clutched at her sides. She felt blood running from her fingers, soaking her clothes.

Her chest was through. Her stomach was through. She looked down in horror to see her waist was too close. She had pushed too hard, and she was going to hit the edge of the door before she passed.

"God, no," she muttered in a breathy tone.

She flexed her back, trying to pull her hips away. They moved, but so did her stomach and her legs. Her hips skated through, but her legs brushed against the door frame.

Sam felt herself touch and froze. This was bad. She knew it was bad but had no idea what to do.

Hundreds of bugs scurried onto Sam's legs. In her mind, she saw a thousand tiny legs touching hers, a thousand miniature claws digging into her pants and hungering to taste her.

She screamed and bent and swatted at them. Her legs hit the frame even harder, and hundreds more climbed on. She slammed her palms against her legs, squishing. She yanked herself through the door, smashing bug after bug on her body.

Her hands bled. Her legs bled. They crawled up her back, and she smacked them with her forearms. Her skin felt like she was on fire, and for a brief moment, she was glad she felt that instead of their disgusting alien feet.

Her back bled. They crawled onto her calves, her ankles, and her feet. She smashed and smashed and screamed as the burning seemed to be the only thing she could feel.

Globs of blood floated into the darkness beside the curled bodies of alien insects. Sam slammed into the far side of the hallway, and a thousand more raced onto her back.

6

Di set her foot down on the stone floor of the lower cavern. "I'm down." She stepped back from the rope, and Jill lowered herself beside her.

The floor was wet with puddles, reflecting the flashlight onto stone structures and back around the room like a rock funhouse.

"I know where we are," Jill said. She pointed back up. "There was a railing up there, and," she pointed to their right, "there was a railing there. They didn't let us walk here, but we could see it. The big room is that way."

"You think we'll run into the others there?"

"I don't know. But I think we should keep trying to get there—that's what Wes will do."

Di nodded. "Yeah. He will."

They crossed the puddles, navigated around wet stone, and entered the adjoining tunnel. A low rumble shook the cave walls around them.

"What was that?" Di stopped in her tracks. Dust fell from the ceiling.

"That noise?" Jill touched the wall. The cave vibrated beneath her hand. "You think it could be an earthquake?"

Tommy's words repeated in Di's mind: *Remember, it's a dream.* "Anything's possible here. Let's just keep moving."

Di led the way. Jill shined her light behind them as they walked. The floor hummed, and the walls trembled again, and in the distance, Di thought she saw something move in her beam.

"Something's up there." Di stopped and pointed.

"What did you see?"

"I don't know. Something shiny."

"Do you see it now? Is it still there?"

Di swept the light across the cave and saw that the tunnel was near its end. In just a dozen feet, it opened into another room. The rock ahead was bumpy and reflected light in patches of repeated patterns. It made her imagine a wall made of a dark disco ball.

"I—don't know. That wall's shiny. I guess the reflection could have..."

"It's okay, Di. Let's just keep moving." She put her hand on Di's shoulder

The hand was warm and comforting, and Di understood why Jill was always doing that to Wes. She saw how Jill had been in love with her brother even back when they were kids. She stopped and looked Jill in the eyes.

"Jill, do you *remember* this dream?"

"What do you mean, *remember*?"

"Like, you've had this dream before?"

"No. I've never had this dream before."

Di saw Jill in a hospital bed connected to tubes, and it made sense. She was in one of the mare's comas as an adult. This was only *young* Jill. She wondered what she should say—the girl should know they needed to get to Sam and Lisa. They were her kids, after all. But were they? She hadn't had them yet, so were they really *her* kids? And could that screw something up?

"Nevermind." Di walked on. "Let's keep moving."

They crossed from the tunnel into the next section of cave. The shiny wall was oddly only on one side of the room. The roof was tall and somewhat familiar, but the path wasn't.

Di walked with one hand sliding across the shiny rock. It was smooth like polished stone. "Is this tunnel supposed to be here?" Di said.

"I thought the last one was supposed to lead us to the big room with the stalactites." Jill looked up and stopped moving. "Wait." She examined the shiny wall, her eyes widening. "Out." She grabbed Di's hand and ran.

"What?" Di ran behind her. "What's wrong?"

The floor rumbled, and the shiny side of the cave slid away from them. It skated like a never-ending wall. Dust spat from beneath it and rained from above.

"What is that?" Di shouted over the shaking cave.

"Just run!" Jill guided her ahead and then right. They ducked into a tiny tunnel, and Jill pulled them both against the wall.

Di peeked through the opening and watched the sliding wall disappear, leaving two glowing amber orbs in the midst of blackness. She felt her heart banging inside her chest. She didn't remember this. What the hell was out there?

She slowly raised her flashlight until it was pointed through the opening. What she saw sent chills through her veins. Her hands shook, turning the light into a strobe. She stumbled backward, grabbing at the air, then Jill, and mumbling nonsense.

Those amber orbs glinted in the light, revealing deep black diamonds within, the eyes of something huge. The shiny wall's surface, the polished feel: scales. Below, a monstrous snout, a nose, spines flaring back, and an orange glowing light as its mouth opened.

"Run!" Di shouted.

They sprinted, turning left at a fork in the path, and were thrown from their feet by an explosive burst of pressure. Flames tore through the tunnel with a blinding light. The heat burned from feet away, and when the dragon's breath halted, the rock floor was on fire. The walls glowed red, and Di and Jill held each other, wishing for this all to be over.

The cave rocked, and booms came from the dragon. They held still. They waited.

"You think he left?" Di said.

Another blast of fire tore through the tunnel behind them.

"I think he's pissed!" Jill said. "Come on."

She ran, and another blast of heat and fire tumbled through the caves. Di screamed. Her sleeve was consumed in flames. She ran past Jill and around a corner. As Jill found her, she was shoving her arm into a puddle in the middle of the path.

Jill knelt, her mouth wide. Behind her, the caves lit up, and hot wind rushed by.

"Jesus, it hurts!" Di raised her arm from the water. Her sleeve was black, and her skin was bright red with rising blisters. She wiggled her fingers and groaned. They all worked, but they trembled as she moved.

"My God, Di." Jill reached but didn't touch.

The dragon stomped. Light flared.

Tears rolled down Di's face as she climbed to her feet. "Let's go," she muttered and stumbled forward. She clutched her burned arm, then jerked it away, crying harder and growling.

"Where does this go?" Di forced herself on.

"Away from him."

"Yeah, but is it the right direction—to where Wes is going, I mean."

Jill shook her head. "I don't know. We could ask the dragon to let us pass?"

Di shook her head as well, not even a smirk in sight. They continued on. At another junction, they turned left. At the next, they turned left again. They walked so far in the dark that Di began wondering if they were even on the same mountain.

She stopped and leaned against the wall. "I think we're lost." She blew on her arm and flinched.

Jill winced, trying to imagine what Di must be going through, then looked around. The tunnel's rough walls and worn-down floor may have looked like a path that led somewhere, but it now seemed just as likely a maze constructed by Marenor to keep them out of the way.

"Okay." Jill shrugged and sank to the ground, sitting cross-legged in the middle of the tunnel. "Ideas?"

Di slid down the wall and sat. *Remember, it's a dream. Use it!* "You know how Wes thought about you guys really hard to get you into his dream?"

"Yeah."

"What if we did the opposite? Maybe we could think really hard about going where he is?"

"You think that would work?"

"Worth a try." Di reached out with her good arm. "Give me your hand."

Jill placed her hand in Di's, and they both closed their eyes.

"Let's both think about him," Di said. "I'll try to get us there."

"Okay." Jill didn't want to say how often she was thinking about him. But now, she focused. She thought about holding his hand too. About standing beside him and looking into his handsome blue eyes. She felt warm and held onto the thought.

Di thought about playing *Street Fighter* together, about when they used to play Transformers and Barbies in her bedroom. She thought about standing beside him right now, and wished for her and Jill to be right next to him wherever he was.

7

Tommy floated in the void. He felt claw marks on his chest and back. A scrape went across his face, and his right nostril felt like it had an inch-long rip in it. But he was alive. He knew that much. Where he was, on the other hand, was another question.

He tried pushing himself like before, moving from his dream to view another's.

He thought of Chris and tried to go there. He didn't move. He thought of Wes. Nothing. He tried Jill. It was like a wall had been raised around him, and the rest of his friends were on the other side.

Maybe? he wondered and focused one last time.

Tommy heard what sounded like a loud pop inside his head, and from all around him came the sounds of kids. They argued and shouted. He opened his eyes and saw it. He was standing in the coma cave.

It was different than last time, and a feeling of bleakness consumed Tommy's thoughts. There was no playing, only fighting. The room was dim, lit in a strange red ambiance. The kids were skinnier, thin, skin hanging from their bones like pictures Tommy had seen of the Nazi concentration camps. Glowing strands stretched from them to the walls, and pulsing waves traveled from each child to the master puppeteer, wherever he was.

As if by the puppeteer's command, every eye in the cavern turned and looked at Tommy. He felt their stares inside him. They were cold, tired, and wanting. They needed to get out, to sleep a real sleep, to feed and regain themselves. He saw the idea appear in their minds that he was that cure. The mare had whispered the thought, *"Kill him, and it will all be better."*

Two kids stood behind Tommy. In front, maybe thirty or forty. On each side, another ten or so. He chose to go backward.

Both kids dropped their chins to their chests, their eyes squinting and angry. They balled their hands into fists and ran at Tommy.

Tommy sighed. He didn't want to fight these kids. They were being manipulated. He didn't want to hurt anyone, especially knowing what would happen to them in the real world.

He held his course, chest pumping, balling his own hands. He pulled them back to his sides. As he neared the two other kids, he readied himself. He watched them wind their fists back to strike, and he darted left. He ran around a boulder the size of a sports utility vehicle and kept his pace toward the back of the cave. He was almost there when he heard the screams of the others.

"Get him!"

"It's his fault!"

"Kill him!"

"Rip his heart out!"

He followed the wall left and went into the tunnel that should have been an exit. It wasn't an exit. It also wasn't the same illusion the mare had orchestrated earlier. Instead of being able to run into the tunnel and pop out on the other side of the room, there was a massive boulder sitting in the way. It reminded him of a Fred Flintstone boulder, almost perfectly round and right in the center of the opening. He wasn't getting through there.

"Fine." Tommy shook his head. "I have more up my sleeves than just that."

Headed right for him were Brice Lardon and Mira Sprint. Somehow Brice had gotten a baseball bat, and Mira had found a machete. They ran at Tommy, waving their weapons and screaming.

Tommy closed his eyes and concentrated again. He couldn't reach his friends from wherever he was before, but maybe he could find them from here.

He started with Chris. He focused on his love for Rush and his hatred for every vegetable on the planet. He saw the time at Taco Bell when they put lettuce on his tacos after he ordered them without. The cashier wanted to argue, and Tommy had to hold Chris back from fighting the guy. He reached into the ether for Chris's essence.

He felt something there, but it was faint, fuzzy, and he couldn't pin it down.

He tried again with Jill. He found her with just a thought. She was worried about Di, something about her arm. He reached out to go to her, and she vanished.

"What the hell?" he muttered and saw Brice's bat coming at his head.

Tommy held up his hand and thought: *stone*. His arm turned to granite, and as Brice's bat collided with Tommy's wrist, the wood shattered into splinters.

Mira's blade came next. She sliced through the thick, damp air screaming like a wild woman. She may have only been twelve, but her madness was full grown.

Tommy held the same granite hand in front of her blade and flinched as sparks and chips of stone sprayed across the cave.

Brice swung his fist, and Mira slashed.

"Fuck," Tommy groaned. He ducked and moved away.

Mira missed Tommy but connected with Brice's arm. She chopped into his wrist, and blood sprayed over all three. Her machete clung to the wound, and as she yanked it back, she pulled Brice along.

Angry howls grew louder. The rest of the kids were coming.

Mira jerked her blade free, and Brice collapsed and bled.

Dannie Racquet, Elsa Tuff, Pablo Roper, and Dexter Fold came up behind Mira. They carried more bats, more blades, and one spear.

Tommy stood tall, raising his bloodied hands. He shoved outward into the air, and a wave of wind shot across the cavern. Mira tumbled back. Dannie, Elsa, Pablo, and Dexter fell on top of each other. Elsa dropped on Pablo's spear, and the steel punched through one side of her bicep and out the other.

Tommy closed his eyes and breathed. He thought of Wes. He needed to get to Wes, he was the key to this whole thing, after all. He searched for his friend's thoughts across the dreamscape and yelled, "Yes!" as he found him. He felt Jill there and Di. He heard the mob of kids coming for him and wished to be gone. He imagined himself in that other place, standing right beside Wes.

8

Tiny navy bugs flooded all over Sam. She kicked away from the wall and smacked at her body everywhere she could reach. It burned. She felt now what she only imagined from the pain before. Each squish, and there was more of its blood. The blood smeared on her skin and sizzled. It burned holes in her flesh a little at a time, and each splash of its own poisonous liquid burned her deeper and deeper.

She drifted toward the red light and saw Lisa only feet away. "Go!"

Lisa floated in the middle of the hallway, her hands on her head, eyes red, and face tense. She reached for Sam.

"No, don't touch me!" Sam continued to swat and smash. Each smack burned into her hand's muscles now. She felt her insides sizzle. She felt them crawling from her feet to her neck. They were all over, and no matter how many she smashed, they seemed to never end.

Waves of navy bugs covered the hall, clicking as their tiny legs carried them in unison across the metal walls. They stretched toward Lisa and, beyond her, the red light.

"Go," Sam screamed. "They're still coming! Get away before they get you!"

Lisa refused to move. She stared with stone eyes at each and every bug on her sister. Her face trembled. She glared into the air between herself and Sam and screamed at the tiny space monsters. She howled so loud that Sam had to stop smashing and cover her ears from the pain.

Sam closed her eyes, and the burning worsened. It flashed over her from head to toe, and after a second, the screaming stopped. She opened her eyes and realized nothing was crawling on her anymore. They were gone. She looked down at the floor, the walls, and the broken door they had passed through. It was all charred black and smoking. The air smelled like burned plastic.

Sam felt a hand press gently on her back, and she spun to see Lisa. Her brain was moving slowly through the fear and the pain, but after a second, she had to ask, "Lisa? Did you?"

"Yes."

Ignoring the pain in every part of every limb, Sam wrapped her arms around her sister and squeezed. Blood soaked into Lisa's clothes, and they squeezed harder. They wept in each other's arms, and from down the hall, the clicking returned.

9

Wes walked through grasses as tall as his knees, staring at the dinosaurs ahead. They nibbled on trees and drank from the river, and he was immediately relieved that they were all herbivores.

For a brief instant, he let himself believe he was back in time in a real place, not in a made-up amalgamation of his own ideas about the great beasts. He wanted to get closer and see what their skin felt like. Was it hot or cold? What kinds of noises did they make? And then he had to admit that none of it mattered—it wasn't real. It was all a distraction to keep him away from his goal.

He glanced down and saw the bulge, the stone in his pocket. He needed to get back to the cave, to his girls. Where were the girls? He'd let the haze of dream distract him, and he'd completely forgotten what he was supposed to be doing—who he was supposed to protect. He put them in his mind, preparing to call them, and a massive boom shook the ground.

"No." He opened his eyes and looked for it. He couldn't bring them here if that sound was what he worried it was.

The herd across the grass stopped eating. They looked right toward Wes, turned, and ran.

"What did they see?" He spun and looked back.

Beyond the small patch of grassland, the trees crunched, their tops ripped apart. Roars reverberated through the ground, shaking his knees. Something was coming, something big.

Wes took the cue from the herbivores and ran the other way. Grass snapped against his shoes. The scents of fresh greenery and salty water filled his nose. It went sour as the boom of great steps grew louder.

The ground beneath Wes's feet shook faster and harder. The distinguishable beat of footsteps became an erratic rhythm of manic thunder.

The wind turned cold. It blew the stench of rotting meat across his face, and when he glanced back, what he saw informed him exactly why.

It wasn't a Tyrannosaurus as his memories of *Jurassic Park* had led him to believe. It was a group of raptors the size of t-rexes. They ran with heads low and mouths ready to snap. Their eyes were dead, and their jaws drooled.

Wes went numb with fear. As he ran, his feet rose and fell without him feeling a step. His stomach burned. He wanted to vomit and drop to the ground and bury himself. But all he could do was run.

Roars bellowed from one beast and then another. They chanted calls of hunger and rage. Wes could hear it in their voices. They wanted him dead. They wanted him ripped to meat and bone and devoured within their bellies.

Wes pushed himself harder and faster and felt every ounce of his being stressed. His body pulled and fought him to slow down, but he insisted it go onward.

He neared the riverbank. It bubbled and foamed with rapids. He debated on diving in, then heard a scream right behind him.

He spun, and Di and Jill were standing there. But how? He didn't call them. He wasn't going to do that until he somehow found safety. Now they stood transfixed on the horror that was barreling toward them. And why was Di's arm burned?

"Come on, guys!" He grabbed each of them by the shoulder, then froze as he saw what they saw—not just massive raptors, these were massive dead raptors. Their faces were scratched and torn apart. Eyes were pale. Putrescent fluids ran from their mouths and wounds. Meat hung from their limbs. One's jaw was nothing but bone. One was lacerated from shoulder to tail, exposing its muscle and allowing a thick gap of intestine to hang freely. And nonetheless, they charged.

"Come-Come on!" he repeated and jerked them from their stance. As they turned, he saw their faces, stunned and white. He looked around and saw no other way and no place to hide. He yanked them. "In the water! Downstream!"

Jill climbed down the riverbank and waded in. She was off with the water in seconds. Di looked back at the beasts.

"Go!" He took Di's hand, and they raced down to the muddy edge. Deafening roars came from too close behind them, and they jumped.

The water was like ice, and it seized them with unrelenting force. Di screamed as her arm hit the water, and she fought to keep it above the surface. Her hand slipped from Wes's, and they drifted apart downriver.

Wes swam, fighting to keep his head above the water and his eyes on his sister. He saw outcroppings of rock and submerged stones breaching above the water's surface, and he tried to swim around them. A rock or boulder or log below nailed his knee. He howled and caught a mouthful of water.

His knee was hot. He wondered how deep it might be gashed, but instead of checking on it, he coughed out water and fought toward Di.

They flew past the meadow and into a forest. The canopy grew into a solid ceiling of green, and the river slowed. Jill swam to the side and grabbed a fallen log. She waved Wes over and climbed out. He paddled that way and looked for Di—she was nowhere in sight.

"Di!" Wes called. All he heard was river. "Di!" He grabbed the log and held himself still. He scanned the water. Was she under it? Unconscious? Had she gotten out already? He looked downstream—had she passed them? He saw a primordial forest as tall as skyscrapers, but no Di. "Di!"

Jill joined in from the bank, "Di!"

Wes climbed onto shore. "I don't know where she is."

"Can you call her here?"

"Let me try." He closed his eyes and heard his heart thumping in his ears. He thought of her. He wished her there.

Di popped into existence with a splash of water against the earth. She dropped to her knees and coughed out a mouthful of river. Wes knelt beside her and smacked her on the back.

Her coughing slowed after a moment, and she wrapped her good arm around him. "Thank you." Her voice was hoarse and low.

"Anytime." Wes smirked. He took a closer look at her arm and winced, then he remembered the kids. "Hold on."

He sat back on his heels and focused on Lisa and Sam. He prayed they were safe and wished them there.

Screams belted from in front of Wes. His eyes shot open, and he leaped forward. His girls were on the ground crying. Lisa looked okay, but she trembled. Sam was covered in blood, and smoke rose from her skin.

He put an arm around each of them, scanning them from top to bottom. "What happened?"

"Bugs," Lisa said. Her breathing calmed, but still she shook and cried.

Sam trembled in his arms. Her breath hitched. He let go of Lisa and looked over Sam's wounds. She had sores across her body, some only on the surface, some so deep he could see muscle.

"My God." His hands hovered over her wounds, afraid to touch but wanting to, to somehow make it all better. Then, he wondered if she could.

"Sam?" He waited for her to look at him. After a moment, "Sam?"

She shuddered as she met his eyes. The fear, the pain, they screamed from her gaze. Wes filled with sorrow and anger, and if only he could get his hands on this mare.

He fought to steady his words. He needed to be precise. He needed her to hear him. "I think you can fix this. Remember, this is a dream world. Things are real if we make them. Right now, you're hurt, and your mind made the wounds real. You can decide to heal them. You just have to believe that."

She looked down at her quivering hand.

Wes held back his tears and his revulsion at the tendons in her fingers and palm. "You can do it."

She stared at the red mess in front of her.

"Think of it healed. Wish it that way. Believe in it."

Wes noticed Jill and Di were closer, watching. Each had worried expressions but held their tongues.

Sam's hand blurred. Red faded from view, and beautiful unbroken skin took its place.

Di's mouth dropped open. Jill glanced down and held a hand on her back.

"Good job!" Wes said. "See. Now, do the rest."

"I am," Di said. "My arm is killing me."

Sam gave a nervous chuckle and examined her hand. She inspected the skin, the joints, and every place that bled and burned and screamed at her just moments ago.

"Go on." Wes nodded.

She looked over her body and, one at a time, healed every wound. Then she changed her clothes.

"I don't know what's going to happen when we wake up." Wes glanced at Di's scarred hand—the unicorn scar. Her burned arm was better, like new, and he only wished they had known of this trick when her hand had been ripped apart. "But at least you're okay for now."

He helped both of the girls stand. Lisa had calmed and stared at her sister's healthy body with glee. Di explained how they got to this prehistoric horror and suggested they do the same to get back to the caves.

"Yeah," Wes said. "Let me see if I can bring Tommy and Chris back."

"Right here," Tommy stepped from behind some trees.

"How long have you been there?" Jill said.

"Just a minute. Didn't want to interrupt." His arm was bleeding, but not bad.

"It's just Chris then," Wes said.

"Maybe you can find him," Tommy said. "I've tried. It's like he's out there, but I just can't connect."

Wes nodded and closed his eyes. He followed the same steps. He focused on Chris, thought hard about him, and wished him there. When he opened his eyes, the same five sets of eyes were still looking at him. "Nothing."

"You think it killed him?" Jill said.

"I hope not," Tommy said, "but we probably should assume so. We have to finish this."

Wes patted the rock in his pocket. "Then let's do it."

10

Wes concentrated as hard as the dreamworld would allow, but he could not remember well enough what the area looked like where he had taken the stone. He knew he'd recognize it if he saw it, but he could not remember. It was like something was blocking him, like whenever he tried to read in his dreams, the letters would go all wonky, and words wouldn't be words, just strange combinations of scribbles. He had to assume something was in the way. Maybe the mare?

He tried to see the place where they landed after the fall, where Chris held Tommy's head and Wes's leg was shattered. It was dark and blurry, not unseeable, but not clear enough for him to believe he could go there.

He thought of the cavern above, where thick stalagmites and stalactites joined together like a forest of stone redwoods. This, he could see. It flickered under the flame of Chris's Punisher lighter, making the gray rocks look almost yellow in the tenuous light.

He held Di and Sam's hands. Di held Jill's. Sam held Lisa's. Tommy had one of Lisa's and one of Jill's, completing the circle.

Wes imagined them all moving, all transporting from the weird prehistoric land back to that cave where everything had gone so wrong. He wished for them all to be transported there as a group in their same circle.

He felt the cold draft of cavern air, the drop in temperature, and the rise in humidity. He opened his eyes to darkness and smelled the earthen scent of cave.

"Everyone here?" He dropped Di's hand and dug into his pocket for a flashlight. Others turned on before he had it, revealing five faces right where they should be. "Good. Now, no more separating. If you find yourself apart from the rest of us, immediately think of being back with the group—and get here quick."

A round of nods went through the circle.

"No shit," Tommy said.

"Everyone have a flashlight?" Wes clicked his on and held it up.

"No," Lisa said.

Wes gave her the light. "Remember, if you need something, just imagine it's in your pocket, then reach in and grab it." He pulled another from his jeans. "Anyone else?"

Sam came out of her own pocket with one and flicked it on. Everyone else seemed to have something—Tommy had another torch in hand.

"No one fall off the cliff." Tommy started walking toward that fateful edge.

Wes waited, ushering Sam and Lisa to go ahead. They held hands as they followed Tommy. Di and Jill were next, and Wes took up the rear.

He scanned around and back as they walked. The shadows danced behind the stone pillars with his gait. He knew this wasn't the end. They may have been close, but not close enough. That asshole mare had something more for them before this was done. But if he kept his eyes open and they stayed together, he was sure they should at least survive. So he watched, squinting into the gloom. He listened to the room, ignoring Sam and Lisa's whispers, Jill's tapping of her thigh, and everyone's footfalls. That was when the wind began to talk.

It was low and harmonious at first, vibrating in tune with the cave's breeze and the constant drip of water in some unknown edge of the darkness. Then there was a voice below it, though without words. There were consonants and sibilance, but they only made speech-like sounds, no real communication. And he wondered if that idea was true.

He'd heard once that speech could be hidden below music to brainwash people as they listened. And frames could be replaced in movies to implant messages into your brain. Take out a slide of John McClane and slip in one of a Russian flag, and pretty soon, everyone who watched *Die Hard* would be praising Mother Russia. So wasn't it possible the mare was speaking to him now, getting inside his head without him even knowing?

"Do you guys hear that?" Wes asked. "Those *whisper*-type sounds?"

He glanced at each person in his group: One, two, three, four, five, all there.

"I hear it," Jill said. There were four more affirmatives.

"It's got to be the mare," Wes warned. "Try not to let it in."

That was when the whispers began to make sense. They made words: *"Kill them." "Die." "They hate you." "Those aren't your friends." "They're going to kill you." "You're going to die in here."* And it went on. Repeating. Refusing to stop.

"Shut up!" Wes shouted into the cave. He covered his ears, but it didn't hush the wind at all.

"Here." Tommy stopped the group. He shined his light over the edge.

Each looked down the cliff onto the floor below. It had to be fifty feet. Wes had no idea how far the real cave was. He had seen nothing of his fall, but if it was this much and he survived, he counted himself lucky.

"Got it," Di said. She pulled another three-pronged grappling hook from her pocket with plenty of knotted rope for hand holds.

"How about a few more?" Jill said.

"Okay." Di went back into her pants, but nothing was there. "That's weird." She tried the other side.

"I think we're getting too close to count on that trick," Tommy said. He pulled a hook and rope of his own out. "It may get harder and harder to change things here as we near the mare's resting place."

"Mind if I help?" a voice came from the darkness. Each light swung over to see Chris walking up.

"Chris?" Jill ran over and hugged him. "I was worried about you."

"Yeah. Me too. I was in this awful place, and then, here I am."

"Well, thank God."

Wes and Tommy joined them and gave Chris a pat on the shoulder. Di dropped her rope over the edge and secured her hook.

"Good to see you, man," Wes said.

"Yeah, dude." Tommy nodded. "Thought we lost you there."

Chris shrugged. "So, what are we doing."

Tommy went to the edge and started lowering his rope down. "Trying to get back to the source."

"That's a long way down."

Tommy secured his hook on a nearby boulder. "Well, who's ready to climb?"

"I'll go first on mine." Di tugged on her rope. "Wait 'til I get to the bottom, and someone else can come down it."

"I'll be right behind you," Jill said.

Di held tight and started over the edge.

"Let me go first on yours?" Wes asked Tommy. "Then send Sam and Lisa?"

Tommy handed Wes the rope. "Sure." He dropped his torch down to the bottom of the cliff.

Sam stared at the cave floor below, then at Di, then Wes. "This is nuts. We're going down there?"

"You can do it," Jill said. "I already did once today. Just hold onto the knot and pinch your leg around the rope."

"We don't have a choice," Wes said. "Just think of it like gym class."

"We have a mat on the floor in gym class," Sam said.

"I'll be below you. It's going to be okay."

She shook her head no. "I guess."

Wes pulled the rope tightly to him and sat on the ledge. He checked on Di; she was already a few feet down and moving at a good pace. He placed his grip above the closest knot, wrapped his legs around the rope, and hung over the edge. Down he went.

Rocks tumbled under his feet and knees as they scraped the wall. They rained from above as the rope rubbed on the edge of the cliff. He refused to look down other than to see Di and make sure she was okay.

When he was about ten feet down, Wes called up, "Send down Sam."

"Okay," Sam's voice was shallow and quavering.

She climbed over the edge, just as Wes had, and let loose a small squeal as rocks slid past her and fell. She moved a knot down the rope, and Wes went down another knot as well.

He glanced at Di. She was almost to the bottom. Back to Sam, who was down another knot.

We might just make it down, he thought and descended a few more knots. Once Sam was twenty feet from the top, Tommy showed Lisa what to do. He waited and watched.

"Okay," Di shouted from the bottom.

Jill began down Di's rope.

11

Tommy watched Jill recede below the top of the cliff and helped Lisa onto the rope. Maybe she was a Henson cousin, but he didn't understand why she was there. This whole thing was already dangerous enough without tagalongs.

She made it past the top knot and onto the next row. Small or not, once she got the idea, she was committed.

"Almost our turn." Tommy looked back, expecting to see Chris, but he wasn't there. Shit, had he been taken again?

He searched the darkness, then along the cliff, and there was Chris. He was leaning over the edge, watching Jill. He knelt and grabbed the rope, and Tommy caught a glimmer from his hand. He had a knife.

"Chris?" Tommy straightened himself upright.

Chris glanced at Tommy, then started slicing the rope.

"Chris!" Tommy crossed the gap between them in just a few seconds, and the knife was halfway through the rope. Tommy shoved his friend. "What the hell?"

Chris slumped to the side and crawled right back to the rope, aiming his knife.

"Stop!" Tommy kicked him in the shoulder, knocking him back again. "What are you doing?"

Chris jumped to his feet and charged at Tommy, his blade in front.

"Jesus!" Tommy threw his hands up.

Chris grunted as he moved in. Tommy stepped to his side to get out of the way, but Chris turned too. The knife slid across Tommy's belly, slicing shirt and skin.

"Fuck!" Tommy jumped back even further and grabbed his stomach. Blood ran over his hands and down his pants. He saw a glimmer of muscle through the hole in his shirt. "Chris, stop!"

"What's going on?" Wes shouted from below, likely near or at the bottom by now.

Chris shook his head. "I have to." He ran at Tommy again, this time slicing wide and high.

Tommy leaned back, but Chris's blade ran across his face, cutting through cheek, lip, tongue, and cheek on the other side. He howled a wet scream, and blood gushed over his jaw.

Tommy touched his face, felt the damage, and looked at a hand that was nothing but red. His fingers shook. His hands, his arms, his body filled with fury, and he became the one charging.

Tommy grabbed Chris by the shoulders and tackled him to the ground. He sat up on Chris's chest and punched his best friend in the face over and over.

Blood poured from Tommy onto Chris. Chris's teeth shattered and ripped through his lips and cheeks.

"Bastard!" Tommy shouted, only his mouth couldn't make Bs or Ds anymore, and his voice sounded more like raw meat squishing together than words.

A sharp pain screamed from Tommy's side. He froze in mid-punch, unable to move. He looked down to see Chris's knife in his side and ripping across his gut. Blood poured, skin split, muscles widened, and intestines leaked out of the window in his belly.

He screamed, and Chris pushed him off. His entrails dangled from his body as Chris kicked him in the face and rolled him over the ledge.

12

Jill heard Tommy's scream and stopped ten feet from the ground. She looked up in time to see him roll off the edge of the cliff and soar past her.

"Tommy!"

Drops of blood tapped on her forehead and cheek.

He landed beside Di and Wes. Blood splashed on each of them as he thumped against the granite floor and his limbs shattered. He groaned.

Di screamed. Sam screamed.

"What the fuck?" Wes shouted. He took a knee beside Tommy and glared at his wounds. He reached as if to stuff Tommy's bowels back in and held back. Blood ran from everywhere and bubbled from inside Tommy's nose, mouth, and ears.

Lisa stopped and stared from halfway down the climb, and Jill felt a vibration in her rope.

"Chris? Are you up there?" She called but couldn't see anyone. "What happened to Tommy?"

The rope swayed from above.

"Chris?"

She glanced at Lisa above, felt the vibration again, and shouted, "Lisa, move! Get down!"

Lisa looked at Jill, and Jill felt the sensation of falling.

It was weightlessness but not like coming down on a trampoline or leaving the highest diving board at the Custer Falls Community Pool. This was weightlessness with an unknown timer. Weightlessness combined with impending doom.

She knew she had just looked down but had no idea how far up she had been. It had happened too fast. Was she high enough to break something? To paralyze herself? To die? She yelled as she fell, expecting only bleak, hard stone and pain.

"Jill!" Wes shouted.

She slammed into the ground, one foot, then the other, her butt, and then her back. Her first thought was, *I'm alive*. Her second was the overwhelming pain in her foot and ankle. She pushed herself up and saw her foot folded sideways.

She breathed in and out and in and out. It was so fast she began to feel lightheaded. It was nice for a moment, taking her thoughts from her mangled limb. And then it faded, and her raging ankle gripped every thought. It was pressure and twisting as if some giant had clamped her foot in a vice and was cranking and spinning her in circles.

She screamed louder than she ever had, awake or asleep.

13

Wes knelt beside Jill, his hand on her shoulder. He examined her ankle. It was distorted in a way he could only imagine from some horror movie.

"Wes!" Di shouted. "Lisa!" She pointed up to the girl.

Wes barely saw a head at the top of the cliff, but he knew it well enough to identify it as Chris. He was leaning over the rope. Wes's first thought was that he was going to climb down, but then Jill's wails jolted him into understanding.

"He's cutting the ropes," he muttered.

Wes jumped up and ran, stopping underneath Lisa. "Lisa, you need to hurry!"

She looked at Wes, at Jill, at Tommy, and back to Wes. "I don't want to be up here."

"You have to climb, sweetie. You have to climb down now, or you're going to fall."

She looked up the rope and eyed Chris and his knife. "Dad!" she called in a long, drawn-out moan.

"Dad?" Sam repeated, grasping at Wes's arm.

"Now, Lisa. Climb down, now."

She moved a few feet down and stopped.

Wes's mind spun, searching for ideas. Could he conjure up something for her to land on? It wasn't working well near the top, and he was even closer to that rock's home now, but—maybe if he tried hard, harder than ever?

He closed his eyes and thought of a thousand soft and fluffy things: a pillow, a pool, a mattress, feathers, bubbles, sheep, clouds, but as they cycled through his thoughts, he wasn't sure what to choose.

Lisa screamed. Her rope shook and twanged.

What could he do? His mind went to *Lethal Weapon*, Riggs jumping from a building and landing on that giant balloon. That had to be it.

"Dad?" Sam repeated.

Wes blocked it out. He focused on the ground below them being made of rubber. Below that, he saw air, and below that, another side. A giant balloon floor. Soft, squishy, bouncy. He wished inside his thoughts. He pictured that ground and only that ground. He squeezed his eyes closed and prayed into the ether, "Please, let it happen. Save my girl."

"What the—" Sam muttered.

Lisa screamed again, and Wes opened his eyes. She fell from the side of the cliff, rope still in hand, legs wrapped around it.

Wes moved underneath her and watched her come down, reminding himself of an outfielder after a long line drive. He held out his arms and leaned back. He was going to catch her. There was nothing else he could do. He was her father whether he was forty-two or twelve, and he had to try, even if it squashed him beneath her.

Lisa collided with his chest, and his arms curled around her. He sunk under the force of the impact, collapsing into the ground and slamming his back against the earth. The strange thing was, it didn't feel like earth. It was smooth and rubbery. It had worked!

Pain rippled through Wes's chest and arms. Sharp stabbing on his right. A broken rib, maybe?

He looked into Lisa's eyes. Tears ran down her face as she returned the stare. The rope fell from her hands, and she seized Wes and hugged him hard.

"It's okay," He hissed through his pained chest.

Sam dropped to the ground and hugged them both.

"Guys," Di said, low and slow. "Tommy..."

"What?" Wes turned. His ribs screamed.

Di was next to Tommy, her hand on his chest. "He's dead."

Tommy stared up at the blanket of blackness above. His eyes were fixed. Motionless.

"God, no," Wes forced himself up, setting Lisa gently on her feet. He crawled over and looked into Tommy's blank eyes. "Tommy." He spun and glared at the top of the cliff. "Dammit, Chris! Why?"

A rumble echoed from above, and it occurred to Wes that Chris wasn't just up there, he was almost directly above them.

"Move," Wes told Di. "Move now. Grab Jill."

He took Sam and Lisa's hands and dragged them as a boulder the size of a beach ball plummeted from above. It slammed into the rubber ground and bounced ten feet into the air. He pulled even harder. "Move!"

Di dragged Jill by her wrists as Jill screamed and tried getting up on her good foot.

A boulder slammed into Tommy, smashing his skull, spattering bone shards and red goo across the cave floor. It rolled toward Di and Jill and settled at the end of a five-foot blood trail.

Jill screamed and shook Di off. She climbed onto her good foot and hopped.

A boulder crashed and rolled at Di. She jumped, and it clipped her foot, knocking her down. Another fell onto the rubber ground and shot past Wes, Sam, and Lisa.

"Over here." Wes led his girls behind a large stalagmite. Jill and Di both limped over, and the boulders seemed to stop.

Jill slid down the rock and sat. Tears streamed down her face. She breathed fast and shallow and stared at her broken foot.

"You have to fix that," Di said.

Jill shook her head and closed her eyes. "I'll try." Her voice wavered with each syllable.

Wes glared at the cliff, watching for more boulders, his eyes resting on Tommy's headless corpse. His good friend, Tommy. How could this have happened? What could have gotten into Chris?

"I don't believe it." Wes shook his head. "How could he?"

"It promised him something," Di said. "Remember Tommy said it promised to wake him up if he listened."

"But still..."

"I know." She gave her brother a hug. "We have to keep going."

Wes, then Di, both glanced down at Jill. Her eyes were closed. Her foot was still horribly twisted to the side. Wes was amazed she was even sitting there with them. He imagined he'd be back under those boulders screaming his head off if it were him. That, or dead.

Rocks tumbled down the cliff, and Wes spun to see.

"Chris?" Di asked.

"Maybe." They could see so little through the gloom.

Rocks fell from the right side of the cliff. Then from the left.

"What is he doing?" Di asked.

More Rocks from the middle, above the carnage that had been Tommy. Six feet to the left. Six feet to the right.

"I'm not so sure that's Chris," Wes said. He checked on Jill again. They needed to get moving, but her foot was still wrecked. "Jill?"

"Leave me alone," she barked. "I'm trying."

Wes scanned into the darkness toward the place where this had all gone so terribly wrong. Deep in the distant blackness, he saw a faint glow. That was it. That was the stone's cradle, its altar, and soon, its final resting place.

He patted his pocket and felt the stone. He had to get it there. If he could get it there, it would all be over. Why else would the thing be fighting so hard to keep him away from that spot?

"I'm going ahead," Wes said. Looking at Di: "Stay with her. I'll take Sam and Lisa."

"You can't go without us," Di snapped.

"I can if I have to. It's just over there." He pointed into the shadowed world of the unseen. "I have to try to end this."

"Just wait."

Rocks flooded down the cliff wall from each side, flanking their dead friend.

"Something's coming," Wes said. "We can't stay here." He glanced at Jill's foot again. It crackled and shifted, moving halfway to where it was supposed to be. "Maybe you can jump instead of walking?"

A screech came down the side of the cliff, followed by another. It was high-pitched and painful. Other screeches—whatever was making that sound, there were more, joining from somewhere near the top. Then more still. They played like a symphony of out-of-pitch violins made from broken glass and strings of human suffering. The sounds made Wes want to gouge out his ears. It was like a chorus from Hell. And under the horrible calls, Wes heard Chris scream like he was being torn apart.

He covered his ears and looked back at Jill's foot. It crunched and cracked and shifted, almost in alignment with her leg. Maybe she would be able to do it.

Lisa screamed. Sam screamed.

Wes spun back to the cliff. Black things slithered down the rock face. They slid along the stone, gliding on slimy tentacles. One appendage moved down at a time, leaving a trail of glossy, congealed slime. Their bulbous bodies swayed, trailed by long glimmering spines. Wes got an image in his mind of a demonic squid with onyx porcupine quills.

"What the hell are those?" Di shouted.

"I—I..." Words failed him. He realized as those things descended that he was shaking. There were dozens of them dripping down the cliff like malignant sludge. One touched the cave floor, and Wes saw its luminous eyes, all six of them. One creature encircled Tommy's remains with its tentacles and started to feed on him. It squealed, and blood sprayed from the tips of its spines, drenching its horde.

"Jesus—What the fuck?" Jill said, her eyes open wide. She stared frantically at Tommy's gore and the incoming monsters.

More beasts reached the ground, and they all slithered toward Wes.

"Now," Wes said. "We have to go now. Jill—walk, hop, crawl, whatever you have to do, do it. We have to move."

Jill stood, her foot back where it should be. "I can walk. It hurts, bad, but I can walk."

"Good." He began backing into the darkness, shined his light that direction, and turned around. "Come on. Sam, Lisa, come on."

His girls lingered for only a second, watching beasts drip down the wall. Wes imagined that, in other circumstances, it could have been a somewhat relaxingly hypnotic pattern—if they weren't coming to kill you and digest you.

Jill staggered beside Sam and Lisa. Di brought up the rear, walking sideways to keep an eye on those things.

In front of Wes was a wall of darkness he only vaguely remembered. The faint blue light was all he could place, something he had hoped was a flashlight or lantern in the distance. Beyond that, his memories of the floor, the walls, and the cave ceiling were all a fog of emptiness.

He thought of that day and wished for sunlight. As he expected, nothing. The closer he moved to this place, the more the dream felt as concrete and finite as the real world. Except for the squeal of things behind them and the slipping and sloshing of their slick and slimy tentacles across the cave floor. That was not the *real world*. That was something from Hell.

"How're you doing, Di?" Wes said.

She flicked her light forward and back again. The creatures had moved from the yellow and white light of Tommy's torch into the shadows between them and the cliff. Her light crossed a mass of a few dozen bodies, and they hunched and slithered after them, gleaming like a sea of black undulating grease.

"Still behind us," Di said. "And, we may want to pick up the pace. I think they're gaining."

Wes looked at Jill. "Can you?"

She ground her teeth together. "I'll do it. Whatever."

"Okay." He walked faster into the gloom, his eyes on the blue glow ahead, and with each step, he felt it nearing.

The stone in his pocket pulsed a wave of numbness over his leg. The darkness seemed to vibrate around them, and a sound rang in his ears. It grew louder the further they went, sending chills down his arms and legs, saying: "*Go away. You aren't welcome here.*" The whispering wind joined: "*Go back, Wes. Go home, and we can work on this. Maybe we can even— bring back your father.*"

Wes trembled at the idea. Was that even possible? Dad was dead, his head smashed and sprayed all over his bedroom. There was no way.

"*I have more power than you know,*" it said. "*Go on home. Smash the rock, and we can do anything.*"

Wes saw his father over the summer on Father's Day. He'd gotten Dad a pair of pajamas, something he could lounge around in on Saturday mornings as he read the paper. They went out for Chinese food that night, and Wes was sure on that day that his father loved him, unlike so many other days. Dad had made him sit next to him and patted him on the back when they talked about the next season's Broncos and what they would do with the summer. Wes had said camping or fishing, and Dad had said both, and they said they'd do it. They hadn't been able to, though. Dad's work got in the way. But if Dad could actually come back, they could do it. They could do all the things that Wes now realized he'd end up missing out on. He felt a longing inside his chest.

"*There is a way,*" the voice insisted.

Wes's skin crawled. The numbness in his leg became a cold spot. It spread down his knee and onto his calves. It wrapped around his leg and around his rear.

The blue light ahead grew bigger. Wes could see now it was coming from a wall, and a memory struck him of his hand grasping the thing, twisting and lifting it from a cubby inside that wall. That was it, and it wasn't far anymore.

The whisper pressed images into his mind. They were hazy at first, feeling like an itch that needed to be scratched, a hint of a thought that needed to be explored. Not realizing what they were, Wes allowed it. There was Dad on the couch. It was tomorrow—he didn't know how he knew, but he did. Dad was wearing those pajamas and reading the paper. As Wes came into the room, he waved Wes over and pulled him onto the couch. A few seconds of wrestling later, and he gave Wes a hug, one of those big ones only Dad could do—strong and firm, pressure on his back, loving pressure that felt of security, honesty, and assuredness that this was what they were meant to have together.

"I could have him back?" Wes whispered.

"Of course."

"What's going on?" Di asked.

He'd slowed to half the speed, and the lead they'd built from those monsters was waning.

"Are you okay?" Di asked.

"We could have him back," Wes muttered.

"Look," Jill said. The light of Wes's flashlight fell within a few feet of the wall. The source of the blue light was visible; it was something that had been crafted. Blue crystals were fixed into the stone, jewels circling a shelf. They were like glowing sapphires, illuminating strings of markings below them.

Wes stopped walking. There was maybe twenty feet to the wall, the lights, the cubby in the altar where the stone should go, and he stopped moving.

"Wes!" Jill shouted. "Go do it."

He stared into the blue light. He saw next Christmas, his next fishing trip with Dad, on the Missouri River. He saw overnight camping and the stars that would hang from the Milky Way.

"Wes!" Jill shouted again.

Sam and Lisa pulled on his arm.

Wes kept dreaming, but something flickered at their touch.

Di stepped in front of her brother and wound back her hand. She swung with intent and slapped his face from his ear to his nose.

Wes jerked and looked at Di. He sighed and looked down. The image of Dad was gone. The feeling of his presence was gone. What remained was the empty hole in the flesh of Dad's neck, the chasm where Dad's head used to be.

"What the hell was that?" Di looked back at the things. The slippery slosh of their bodies was louder, reverberating in the blackness. "We gotta go!"

"I—Dad... yeah."

"Go!"

They moved toward the glowing blue crystals, and Wes dug into his pocket for the stone. His hand froze as he touched it. The freeze crept over his arm as he reached toward the cubby.

"No," A voice said from the darkness. A fist flew from the left, crashing into Wes's face. He tumbled backward onto the stone floor, and Ray Trent stepped in front of the ancient altar.

The mare's stone rolled out of Wes's hand. He looked up at Ray, anger burning in his chest in a way he had never experienced. They had come all this way. They had suffered through the deaths of his father, his friend, and God knows how many death-defying dreams, and now this asshole wanted to get in the way? No.

Ray squinted at Wes and surveyed the others. He paused on Jill and licked his lips.

Wes limped to his feet and started toward the mare's stone. Ray stepped before him and drew a knife from his hoodie's pocket.

"What are you doing?" Wes put his hands in front of his chest and backed up a step. "We have to stop this thing."

Wes saw his dad standing behind Ray, then Tommy. They looked at him with sad, disappointed faces. "*You can have them back,*" the whisper said. "*Or, you can die.*"

"No." Ray shook his head. "We're not going to stop it."

The screeching from behind grew louder. The things were getting nearer, almost on top of them, from the sound.

Light flashed behind Ray, and then there was Sam and Lisa. Sam shined her light on the rock, and Lisa went to pick it up.

Ray turned toward the girls, his blade rising.

Wes's thoughts overflowed with rage. Tommy and Dad vanished as he sprung forward and tackled Ray to the ground. He punched Ray in the face. Ray pulled back the knife, aiming at Wes's gut, and Wes grabbed his wrist and punched again. And punched again. And again. He was a being of fury with no thought, only movement, only wrath. Blood ran and skin tore as he kept hitting Ray over and over.

"I got it," Lisa said, reaching to lift the stone.

Wes froze. "No! Leave it!"

Lisa picked up the mare's stone. Her arm shook, but she held on.

Ray punched Wes in the face, and Jill and Di knelt on either side and held Ray's hands.

"We got this," Jill shouted.

Wes gave Ray one last blow for good measure and jumped up.

Lisa was on her way to the altar. Her eyes were blank. She moved as if she were sleepwalking, and Wes took a step toward her and stopped.

Screeches bellowed, their hunger just beyond the darkness, and then they weren't. One, then two, then twenty slimed into the flashlights' shine. Some glinted in the glow of the altar's blue crystals. They reached and pulled, reached and pulled like unrelenting, hungering octopuses from some other dimension.

Click click came from the right, beyond Sam. Wes glanced for an instant and saw what looked like a wave of spiders. They were shiny and dark but not quite black.

Sam screamed.

Groans came from the right. Into the light moved a dozen faces and two dozen hands. Bones shined through rotten skin on hands and heads. Dead eyes. Extending jaws.

"Leave him!" Wes shouted at Di and Jill, and he snatched Sam from the oncoming bugs.

Di, then Jill, released Ray and backed away toward the altar.

Ray rolled toward them, a murderous lust in his eyes, a snarl on his lips. A slimy tentacle fell on his waist and his clothes seared from beneath it. The black ooze touched his skin, and he screamed. Another tentacle wrapped around his head, and his eyes flicked from pain to terror. The thing slid over his face, and his scream muffled, then wetted, then gave way to a flood of blood that gushed down his neck and sprayed from the monster's spines. He flopped to the ground, and two others seized him, vibrated, and consumed.

Wes, Di, Jill, and Sam backed to the altar with moaning, screeching, clicking beasts inching closer.

Lisa raised the stone, held her arm below the crystals, and shook as if the thing may go flying from her grip.

Wes stood behind her and settled her wrist. "It's okay. Drop it."

The stone clattered against its rocky shelf, and the entire cave rumbled. It heaved and rested, heaved and rested. The noises around them calmed, and their lights dimmed. In his mind, Wes saw kids in a cave, vanishing, waking in hospital rooms. And the cavern disappeared.

2022

1

Wes, Di, Sam, and Lisa opened their mouths and gasped in sync. Wes took in the rest of the vehicle. Di looked back at him. Sam and Lisa looked forward, eyes blinking, questioning their surroundings.

"Is everyone okay?" Wes said.

They each examined themselves. Sam flinched as she found scars on her body where splattered bugs had been. Her eyes teared, and Wes turned in his seat, touching her shoulder.

"It's okay, sweetie."

She leaned forward and hugged him. She blinked with wide wet eyes and cried.

Wes was overcome with shame. These were more wounds she'd have to endure because of his horrendous job as a father.

Lisa stared at her sister, and Wes reached for her to join them. She leaned forward, and the three embraced as a family.

"I'm so proud of you both," Wes said, and outside, headlights shined as they came up the mountain.

"Who's that?" Di asked.

A chill ran through Wes. The night had cooled, but it wasn't just that. What was coming was evil. It radiated from halfway down the mountain.

"I don't know." His gaze went to the far back of the vehicle where his bag, his tools, and the stone waited. "But we need to change the plan." He looked at the girls, then Di. "We all go together. And we better get moving."

2

Jill took in the faces inside the cave. Close to three dozen people had shown up. She had tried speaking to most of them, but with few exceptions, they behaved like they were in their own worlds, lost in their own nightmare versions of this place. It was as if they didn't even see her. But why did she see them?

Maybe it was because she was the first? That sounded like a shit idea, but she had seen nothing to prove it wrong yet. She had already guessed that she was in a coma, maybe something like what those kids had gone through back when she was young. And most of those woke up when her and Wes and Di and... some other girls that Wes could never explain— when they had gone into the dream cave and ended it. But was there someone out there who would do that this time? She hoped Wes was. He had to.

"Fuck you, you bitch!" a man yelled near the center of the cave. He stared down at a woman, who, if Jill remembered right, showed up at the same time as him. Were they married?

The woman stared at the ground; she knew him. It had the stench of a regular occurrence and with both of them reprising their roles. Only, as she stared down, a look shined in her eyes. The submissive act struck Jill as more than just a woman looking away to placate her raving husband. And as the woman slipped a straight razor from her rear pocket and unfolded it, Jill clutched herself and held on.

"You ain't got nothing to say?" the man shouted.

She swung up. The blade's silver shine was just a glimmer. It sliced up into his groin, up and through his jeans, then belt, then shirt and belly. It stopped below his ribs, and the woman slid the blade free.

The man looked down at her with pure disbelief on his face. Not a failure to believe that he could be killed, but a refusal to accept that it was by her. That she would do something like that to him. His eyes loosened. His mouth dropped. She held the weapon to her side, and with a swing and little more than a flip of the wrist, his neck opened up, and a river of blood flowed.

Jill covered her mouth. She breathed into her hand, and for a fraction of a second, as the man dropped from his feet to his knees, she thought they shared a glance at one another. His shirt and belly spread, and his insides peeked out. Then he was gone, from the connection and from the cave. She noticed as he faded there was a hair-like golden strand drifting from his body to the cave wall in the distance.

"What the hell was that?" she wondered, and the bladed woman turned and locked eyes with her. "Shit."

The woman started across the cavern, her stare refusing to relent. She strode at Jill without a trace of the inhibition that had been there thirty seconds earlier. Her arms swayed as she walked, flinging her dead husband's blood from her blade.

Jill sat, disbelief in her own mind. Was this real? Well, not real, but really happening? Of course, it was. This was the prison of the mare. And here, it didn't have to make sense, but it could definitely slice you into bits at the hands of a pissed-off battered wife who'd finally taken enough shit.

"Easy, lady." Jill stood and put her hands forward.

The woman raised the blade, her eyes filled with anger and bloodlust, and she stopped, stiff in her pose. Her eyes rolled back into her head, and Jill thought she could hear a gagging sound from her throat. Now, there was a thin golden strand running from her back to the ceiling.

"I'll get you," a man shouted from the left. He chased after a boy who couldn't have been older than Lisa. They ran from one side of the cave to another, the boy grinning wildly.

A scream came from the right. A man held a cleaver as it sunk into another man's head. Bone cracked, and blood sprayed.

Jill drifted backward against the wall. Another shout on the other side. What was the mare doing? Did it just decide it was playtime? All of a sudden? She wedged herself between a boulder and the cave wall, hoping that, if nothing else, maybe she could stay hidden from this madness.

3

They were in Ed's work van. As they ran over ribbing and potholes on the old road, it rattled and shook like it was going to fall apart at any minute.

Julie sat in the passenger seat, a grin plastered across her face. She'd been told it was finally going to happen. They'd track down the man and his family, free their master, and she'd get to play with the little girls.

The wait had been excruciating, but she was told the plan had worked. They'd gone and gotten the stone. The mare was feeding again, thanks to their deliveries. All they had to do now was track them down and finish the job. Oh, she looked forward to the finishing.

"That's it," Cushing said from his box seat in the cargo section. He pointed through the windshield at the parking area ahead.

Julie looked back and scowled. The old man was massaging his stump. She turned to Ed, and her smile returned. It had been a long time since she'd had someone act like a dad to her. Not that she loved him or anything. She may want to snuggle with him at night after how bad Mommy was smelling now, but she hadn't decided yet if she was going to play with his insides one day or not. It would depend on how the next few days went. Still, though, she had hope. He had things to teach her about playtime, and she wanted to get better. So, time would tell.

They drove over another cattle grate, and the van vibrated Julie's insides. She stifled a laugh, and her attention went to the parked SUV on the right.

"They're here. They're here." She bounced in her seat.

"Already inside, I bet," Ed gestured to the vehicle. It looked empty from their view through the windows. He glanced at her. "We'll find them, though."

Ed parked beside the Excursion, and he and Julie got out and waited. The van's door slid open, slid shut, and Cushing found his way to the other two, swinging on his crutch.

Julie scowled again. What was the point of bringing the old man along? He could barely walk. He had a shotgun, sure, but Ed could carry that. He could use it. They didn't need the old man for that.

Ed gave the Excursion an examination and felt the hood. "Yeah, they were here not too long ago." He pointed to the sign for the side entrance. "This way."

4

Wes hooked the end of the pry bar into the gap between the door and the frame. The frame crunched as he put his weight against the bar and cranked it. There was a crack and then a thump as the door released.

The smell of dank air and cold, mildewed earth slowly billowed from inside the mountain. It was familiar in a way that made nausea rise—almost exactly as it had been in his dream twenty minutes ago and just different enough that reality's icy grip gave him chills.

"Again?" Lisa muttered.

"The same thing?" Sam said.

"Let's try not to get separated this time," Di said. She passed flashlights to the kids and ran her hand across her pistol's holster as if checking it by reflex.

Wes slid the pry bar into his backpack and hooked the pack over his shoulder. He led the way in. The girls went next. Di and Virb took up the rear.

Inside the door, a tunnel about five feet wide descended into the mountain. A string of lights hung from above, and a series of concrete steps appeared every now and then when the grade grew too steep.

Di looked around for anything she could use to block the way. She found a trash can, which she placed in front of the door. It wasn't heavy and probably wouldn't stop anyone for too long, but it was better than doing nothing.

After a few hundred feet, the cave turned right, and after another hundred, it turned left. There were moments when Wes worried that they'd somehow fallen for someone's trick and gone down a path to nowhere. Other times, he worried that the mare had gotten into their minds and was leading them in circles or toward a trap. He felt the coolness of the stone in his backpack, seeping through the fabric, making part of his back numb. He felt its drain on his mind, the way it nursed on his energy and his will. He promised himself he wouldn't fall for its visions this time, not like he'd let the idea of Dad coming back to life get to him in the dream.

A crash echoed from above, the door. Virb barked.

"The trashcan," Di whispered. "They're coming."

"Faster," Wes said.

By now, he'd had time to think about those approaching headlights. About the man and the child—it had to be them. His blood boiled as he thought of what those monsters had put Jill through. And at that moment, what he really wanted was to climb back up there and take that fucker down. But there was Sam and Lisa and the stone. Any possible revenge would have to wait until those things were dealt with and made safe.

They hurried down the path, another fifty feet or so, and all the overhead lights went out. Lisa screamed. Wes turned on a flashlight.

"Must have cut the cord up there," Wes said. His anger bubbled up.

"Let's not let it slow us down." Di flipped on hers and, again, brushed her hand over her pistol.

Wes thought he could hear the sound of a child laughing in the distance. It was her. That laugh; he'd heard it while Jill was being sliced up on the table. Virb growled, as did Wes, and they proceeded down the path a bit faster.

The lightless tunnel was an alien place. The sparkling glimmer of the walls, the lines and crevices, the shadows as rock bulged, curved, and folded in on itself. It was unlike the cave in his dream. It was like hiking into the throat of a sleeping rock beast.

They passed another corner and found a junction. A sign indicated left for Seagram's Cave, the largest room in the system, where the lights were always cut for the kiddie screams; right was to Josiah Hanging, the dog-leg-shaped room of multicolored stalactites near the old exit.

Wes paused and considered. He didn't know which was a shorter path from here, only that Seagram's cave was closer to the hidden cave. It was also the path their pursuers would assume they had taken.

"What are you doing?" Di's gaze went back and forth from Wes to the sound of approaching footsteps behind them.

If the path to Josiah Hanging was shorter, they could fool the mare's goons and wrap this up sooner. If the Seagram's route was shorter or even the same length, and they took the other one, they could end up with the exterminator and the little girl in between them and their goal.

"Will you pick already?" Di's voice was peaking with irritation.

Wes felt a flutter of panic. This single choice could determine who got to the altar first and possibly if they made it out of there. And if Jill would wake up.

He closed his eyes and thought. He'd have to go with his gut. The path left felt wrong. The path right worried him but also felt like success. It would have to be right. That was the way to the altar, danger, and getting this damn stone back, thirty years late or not.

"This way." Wes took the tunnel toward Josiah Hanging. "And don't make a sound."

They moved fast and quietly, and the cave narrowed to only a few feet wide. The ceiling lowered, and Wes felt like he was falling back into a dream. Behind them, he heard murmuring voices and shuffling feet. Ahead, he heard water dripping. Were they that close to the Josiah Hanging already?

The ground looked wetter the deeper they went. It was getting slippery under their feet, and Wes walked with his arms spread, using the walls to brace himself. The others did the same. Eventually, the moisture wasn't just on the ground. It was on the walls, creeping up as if water was running upward.

Lights shined in the distance. They must have been on a different circuit than whatever those jerks had cut. Wes assumed it was their next destination, and as they neared, the smell of rotting meat filled the dank air.

Wes stopped and pondered. He listened. He checked his hands, wet from the cave walls. He couldn't hear their pursuers anymore, and the sight from the tunnel's end, only another fifty feet, was like a bright sun-shiny day.

His heart thumped. He wanted to run ahead, get out of this darkness, out of the wet cave, but something held him back. Something didn't seem quite right.

He looked back again. Were their pursuers following but being incredibly quiet? Was there someone ahead, waiting to jump out and attack them? His mind had grown loud with thoughts, and his body weak and tired. He just wanted to lay down and take a nap, even if it had to be on wet stone.

"Wes?" Di whispered.

His legs went weak, and he slipped downward.

Di jumped and grabbed him, slowing his fall and keeping his head from smashing into the ground.

"Dad?" Sam knelt and looked into his eyes.

Lisa watched them, her face wrinkled with worry, then Virb jumped past them all and ran into the next room.

"Virb." Di hissed.

"Stop him." Wes pushed his voice through a heavy breath.

"Virb." Di jumped over Wes and ran to the end of the tunnel. She stopped in the orange light of the cave.

Wes fought through the exhaustion and sat up. It was the stone. It was stealing his energy like when he was young, but as a forty-two-year-old man, he had less to spare.

Di came back and offered her hand. "It's that damn rock, isn't it?"

"Yeah." He took her hand and stood. He saw stars as the blood rushed from his head. "I think it's preparing for something."

Di unholstered her pistol. "I'm preparing something too."

Wes braced himself on the wall. "Let's hurry. Before they beat us there."

He took a step and checked on Sam and Lisa. Their faces were grim. "We're going to do this, guys. For Mom." He held out his hand, and Sam took it. She held hers out to Lisa, who gently grasped Sam's good finger and thumb. He nodded and moved forward.

Through the end of the tunnel, Wes saw the large cave, Josiah Hanging. The room was filled with massive stalactites, some six feet or more in diameter. Underneath many were pools of water connected by tiny streams. When he was younger, there had been multicolored lights in the cave, highlighting the variety of rock colors and sediment. Now, it was all one color, a drab reenactment of a vivid memory.

He had asked what the name meant when he was a kid and was told that most rangers thought the cave was named after a man named Josiah, who had discovered the room of hanging stalactites. As he stood and swept over the cavern with half-dazed eyes, he saw something else. Across the room, near the thirty-foot ceiling, was a rock formation that looked like a man nailed to the side of the cave as if crucified. Water seeped through the rock and down his body and made him almost look like he was crying.

Di scanned the cave from one end to the other. "Virb," she hissed.

No response. No panting, nails on stone, growling, barking, or anything.

"I'm sorry, Di."

Tears welled in her eyes. "I should have left him at the hotel. He would have been safe there. That fucking thing is in his mind. I know it."

Wes touched her shoulder. "He loves you. I think he'll be back." He moved toward the main path, still worn into the cave floor and lined with railings from decades past. He guided Sam and Lisa along.

"Shit." Di slid past them and moved ahead. "It's left, right?"

"I think so."

The lights flickered. The darkness between flashes was somehow deeper than in the previous cave. It was profound and enveloping, like swimming in a pool of endless gloom. On, off, on, off—and that's how it stayed.

Wes flicked on his flashlight. His eyes went wide at what was coming. He grabbed Sam and Lisa and dragged them to the floor. "Di! Down!"

A wall of massive bats stormed overhead. Their squeal and chirp rose goose flesh over his body. He glanced up as they passed. They were the size of eagles, with six-foot wingspans and two or three-inch fangs. Their winds washed over them and then their breaths. The foul odor was that of a rotten corpse. Wes realized then, these were not real bats, not natural, anyway. These were the bats of his younger self's nightmares. These were the vampire bats of South America, Richard Matheson's cause of the end of the world, and the rise of one man as a legend. These would bite and feed on him and his girls if they even so much as smelled them.

A sharp squeal reverberated across the chamber. Wes knew it was aimed at him.

He flung his backpack aside and slid the pry bar free. He leaned back and held it above his head, and they started diving.

5

Jill gripped the rock in front of her, her fingers pressing tightly, learning the grooves as if to distract her from person after person punching, kicking, and slicing each other on the opposite side.

She wanted to stop them. She wanted to get up and slap them and tell them to knock it off, but the look in each of their eyes was something beyond insanity.

Two men beat each other bloody on the far right. They took turns knocking each other on the ground and pounding on their faces. A man on the right banged his wife's head into the rock wall, leaving blood, hair, and skin clinging to the rock face.

A few seconds later and a dozen feet away, a girl walked into view. It was Janet Steiner, who went to school with Sam and Lisa.

Janet covered her mouth, tears streaming over her cheeks. She stumbled forward, turned, and looked back with fright-filled eyes. Her mother, Alison, came into view. She raised a kitchen knife, aiming at the child.

The girl dropped her hands, and Jill could read her lips: *No, mommy, don't.*

The boulder in front of Jill became a springboard as she yanked herself forward and ran toward the child. There was no thought in her head, no plan, nothing rational, only a need to get to that girl and get her out of the way of that knife.

Alison swung the blade, and Jill grabbed for her arm. She missed Alison's wrist but was able to give Janet a shove with her hip.

The blade slid past Janet and sliced Jill's upper leg. Blood seeped onto her pants, and memories of her basement and some deranged girl came to her. The demonic smile in the child's eyes—it felt like years ago and

497

yesterday simultaneously.

Alison locked eyes with Jill. She was like a crazy person awakened from a nightmare. Red lines wrapped her wide eyes. Her teeth clenched, and a wild bestial growl leaked through them.

Jill grabbed, this time seizing the wrist. Alison yanked at her hand, and Jill held tight. The growl bellowed as Alison's mouth widened. She took the back of Jill's neck with her free hand and slammed her forehead into Jill's.

Jill screamed, and stars washed over her vision. She lost her balance and fell. Rocks scraped her hands as she clawed at the ground and slammed onto her rear. She blinked and touched her face, and remembered Alison Steiner.

The knife plunged toward her face. Jill reached again for Alison's wrist, and steel sliced through her palm and out the back. She stared at the gleaming blade, dripping with her own blood, the tip of the knife inches from her face.

Pain, sharp and agonizing, rocked her hand. She couldn't move her fingers, push, or pull. It was frozen in electrifying torture. She howled and kicked Alison in the crotch, knocking her off balance. She shoved, and Alison sunk, and Jill kicked again into the woman's chest.

Alison rolled away.

Jill scurried backward on one hand and two trembling feet.

Janet ran across the cave.

A hard surface pressed against Jill's back. She'd reached the cave wall, and Alison Steiner was rising to her feet. The woman stared Jill down like a predator, like a carnivore sizing up her dinner.

Blood poured onto Jill's chest. She looked at the knife impaling her hand, and surrealness overcame her being. She wasn't in a cave. She wasn't stabbed with a knife. The world around her detached in that instant as a mental construct, and she recognized it as only that. But she was in danger if she did nothing.

She remembered the dreams of thirty years prior, of wishing herself better and fighting for her life with Wes and Di and... two others. It rushed into her at once, the realization, those weren't Wes's cousins, those were her daughters.

Alison stepped closer. Her hands were wide, ready to attack and hold. She licked her lips.

Jill looked at her leg, her hand—she was bleeding out somewhere in the real world as she allowed Alison to play with her like this. She couldn't do that. She had to get back to Wes, to Sam, to Lisa.

It's not real, Jill thought to herself. She repeated it and made herself believe as she ripped the knife from her hand. She wished and stopped bleeding and tossed the blade aside.

Alison charged, and Jill stood. She looked the woman over; the thing had to be there. Alison's hands thrust at her shoulders. Jill grabbed her and threw her into the wall face first.

There it was. The thin golden strand stretched from Alison's back up and into the ceiling. Jill grabbed it and bent it, looping it around her hand. Then she gave it a yank and snapped it free from Alison's back.

A shallow hiss fell from the ceiling, and the strand went taught, pulling upward. Jill held firm, and it lifted her from the ground, sucking her into the cave roof.

6

Lisa screamed. Sam screamed.

Wes heaved the pry bar in a wide swing over his head and felt it thump. He swung it back the other way, and it thumped twice.

"Ow!" Sam cried.

Wes jerked around. A bat's fangs were in Sam's leg. He turned on his hands and knees and crawled. Blood ran on the cave floor, and another landed and drank from it.

"Daddy!" Sam called.

Gunshots echoed through the space. The sound was deafening.

Wes laid on top of Lisa, hiding her from the creatures. He swung down on the bat on Sam's leg and thumped into its back. It turned and stared at him. Its beady black eyes were cold and angry. Inside them, he swore it was the mare looking back at him.

The bat rose and flapped its wings, and Wes nailed it again with the pry bar, this time from the side and without fear of breaking Sam's leg. Steel crashed through its skull, and it tipped sideways, looking like it had half a head.

The one on the floor looked up, and Wes smashed it with one blow. He grabbed Sam under her shoulders and pulled her close, then swung at the beasts still overhead.

Pop, pop. Bats dropped from the air.

A sharp pain shot through Wes's leg, and he swung the bar back and down. One was next to him, its fangs deep in his calf. He swung the tool over its head, and it bit again.

"Bastard!" He aimed and crushed the thing.

Another landed beside him and lunged for Lisa. A shot rang out, and its head exploded. Squeaks and squeals, a few more swings, a few more gunshots, and the bats fled from the cave.

Di came over and knelt. She was breathing heavily and watching the bats' path.

"Dammit," Wes pressed on his wounds. He watched Sam pull up her pant leg. Two holes streamed small trickles of blood. He pointed at his bag, now a few feet away. "Di, can you hand me my pack?"

She grabbed the bag and passed it along. "Is it bad?"

"May need a few stitches when we're all done, but I'll live." He dug inside. "How about you?"

"Fine. Burned through half my ammo, though." She shook her head. "Should have known that asshole would pull something like that."

"The mare did it?" Lisa said. "I thought he could only do stuff in our dreams?"

Wes pulled out a first aid kit and sprayed disinfectant on Sam's leg, then his own. "It can't make anything real, but if it's close, like it is now—" he pointed to his backpack, "it can make you see things. The way it puts whispers in your head. They aren't real, but you see them, and if you believe them, they can hurt you."

Her face went stiff. She tried to be brave for everyone else, but fear-soaked tears poured down her cheeks.

"Sweetie." Di hugged her. "We're going to get through this. We have to stay tough."

Wes put a gauze pad on his leg and wrapped it with tape. He did the same to Sam's. "Yeah. We're going to put this thing to bed." He pushed himself to his feet and watched the stars float past his vision. He swayed forward and back and caught himself. They'd put it to sleep if the damned thing didn't kill them first.

Di helped Sam and Lisa to their feet. She looked at Sam's leg. "Can you walk?"

"I'll be okay." She nodded.

"Well, I bet they know where we are now." Di gestured at her gun.

"Doesn't change anything." Wes limped forward. His flashlight wobbled as he walked.

"I guess not." She slid the piece into her holster, and they followed behind Wes, each shining lights in different directions, searching for the next thing. She glanced down at the girls. "Keep in mind, those things may not be real, but if you believe in them just the smallest bit, they can hurt. So treat them like they are real. Okay?"

The girls nodded. They watched their father, his unsteady walk, and they held each other's hands tight.

Wes stopped at the cavern's edge, where an adjoining tunnel went up and left. It twisted like a spiral staircase made of stone.

He shined his light up and over as far as it could reach before the bend. The floor was green with mildew. It walked up the walls, making Wes wonder if it was a growth that the old maintenance crew used to keep knocked down or if it was more gross-out stuff from the mare. Once again, it didn't matter. They had to go that way.

He took the first step, a stair carved into the stone some seventy years ago or more. The fungus was slippery. He stepped up. The next was a half-boulder squeezed into place and bolted. Another half-boulder. A series of carved stairs. The further he went, the more fungus grew on the floor, the walls, and up and up. It sucked in the light, and after a dozen stone treads, the canvas of pure dark green felt like a dismal cage of slimy organic vegetation.

Despair radiated from the growth. It crawled up his legs and dragged on his heart. The mission was pointless. They were going to fail, and Jill was going to die. The kids would die down here, and he would break his legs and live in this prison for as long as it would take for him to starve or die of thirst.

"Get out of my head!" Wes screamed and stopped. His legs wouldn't move. He just couldn't.

A hand pressed on his side, and he spun as if he'd been stung. Lisa looked up at him, and sadness erupted inside. He was going to cause her death. His precious baby girl. It was all going to be on him. Tears raced down his face, and she took his hand.

Her face was as worried as ever. Forehead wrinkled, lips tense. Then she smiled. It was small, maybe even forced, but it was there. "It's going to be okay, Daddy."

Warmth rose from her touch. It spread up his arm and calmed his heart. It wasn't magic, or maybe it was. His mind still raced. He still worried that this was all about to end in tragedy. But he could move. He could take the next step.

"Thank you," he whispered.

The stairs joined a medium-sized cave that had been overgrown as severely as the stairs. The mold on the ceiling wrapped the stalactites and hung from them like Spanish moss. Wes watched as the green tips of each stone point swayed ever so slightly.

He shined his light and thought. They had spun in circles as they climbed, and with the mare's drain on his mind, it was hard. The cave sloped down to the right and up to the left. He replayed his trips to the caverns from childhood in his mind. They'd gone through a tunnel where he had to squeeze and duck into this one. They explored this room by walking downward.

"This way." He pointed his flashlight left.

The room echoed with drips and pats in the darkness. The earthy smell of dampness and the sour scent of death was heavier here. It clung to the back of Wes's nose. He wished he could avoid it, but even if he breathed through his mouth, it was still there. He wished he could scrub the stench from the inside of his nose. He wished he could get out of there. He wished he could be at home with his family, fire roaring, some stupid thing on the television, and them all laughing and cuddling together on the couch.

He shoved the thought from his mind and pulled himself back to the stink-filled room, the sticky, mucky floor, the disgusting dangling ceiling, and the creeping fog of doom overwhelming his calm. He needed to be here, in the moment, no matter the longing for this to be over.

They crossed the room, and the drips smacked into the cave floor, begging for Wes's attention. He turned and looked. Nothing. They continued on, and the sound was even louder. He ignored it until it was accompanied by a tapping. Soft, hard, soft, hard, it patted and clacked against a surface in the dark. He swept the light around again.

"What?" Di asked. She scanned the room with her light as well. "What the—" Her beam stilled in the center of the room where the fuzzy bits of green mold appeared to be swaying above the floor. Only the sway didn't return to center as she expected. It waved toward them, moved back just a little, and moved toward them again. The entire floor behind them leaned and stopped and leaned and stopped, creeping closer to them in a rhythmic dance. And as it moved, it clicked against the ground, reminding Wes of the clack of claws against stone.

"Move faster." Wes pulled on Sam's arm. She pulled Lisa.

"What is it?" Lisa said.

"I don't know, but it's not good, whatever it is."

A low hum vibrated the cave.

"Move." Wes pulled again. They rushed across the room through a series of curved green mounds and around boulders that pointed toward the path with sharp green tips.

Wes heard the tapping. He saw the wave of green moving closer in his mind and refused to look back.

"Come on, come on."

They rounded another boulder. The exit tunnel was just up ahead. Wes found himself running hand-in-hand with Sam and Lisa.

He pointed. "There it is." He felt Sam squeeze his hand.

They reached the opening, and he stopped. It was narrow, maybe a foot and a half wide, and from every surface, dark green fuzz stood and waved. It shrank the gap only a few inches, but Wes envisioned them passing between a pair of narrowly spaced blades. This stuff was bad, whatever it was. That was all he was sure of.

"Don't let it touch you." Wes's stare moved from Sam to Lisa to Di.

"What is it?" Lisa asked.

"I don't know. But we need to keep thinking, 'It's not real,' again and again. Whatever it is, we don't want anything to do with it."

She watched it wave. "Can't we go another way?"

"There's no other way, sweetie." He took a deep breath. "We can do this."

Her face said she didn't believe him.

"*It's not real.* Keep saying that."

Di stepped past the others. "Let me go first. You guide them through."

"Okay."

She turned sideways and stiffened herself upright. She slid into the gap as a dark green edge reached for her from each side of the wall.

7

Jill tumbled through space on the back of an oblong rock. She saw a mile of its surface in one direction, maybe ten in another. She saw stars roll and eons of time pass by in seconds as she soared from a sun and into the vastness of black nothingness.

Cold crept over her skin. Chills wrapped her body.

What was she doing here? She sensed a purpose, that someone else was there—but where? She gazed down the long rocky surface, looking for a clue, seeing only stone. It was hard, old, with lines of pressure and radiance of age. It had been part of a world, she somehow knew, a world that no longer was. She watched the stars drift by and understood. She was on a ship of sorts.

She stared down, smaller and smaller, into the cracks of her vessel until she was inside it. And there they were: tiny cells. The littlest of cargo she could have pictured, microscopic life clinging to the inside of the rock, unknowing where they were going or what the future had in store for them.

Jill, now the same size as it, examined the semi-transparent thing. Protein hairs waved from its outer wall as if beckoning her closer. They whipped around, looking inches long. The thing was beautiful and horrific at this scale. The hair shot toward her and wrapped around her waist.

"Stop!" she screamed, but it only tightened. Her fingers seized the hair and worked to pry it loose. It was spongy and slick and gripped her harder. "Let go!"

It pulled, dragging her toward it. Her feet slid across the bare rock and the front of the thing dented inward as if opening its mouth to swallow her whole.

She dug her nails into the slippery limb and pulled. Pus-like ooze seeped from under her nails. It was sticky and smelled like infection. It gripped her tighter, and a hissing sound came from the cell's widening crevice.

"Let go, you bitch!"

It pulled harder instead.

This is a dream, she told herself. *I can get out of this.*

She thought of a weapon, a sword, and held her arm out to grip it. Nothing happened.

What am I doing wrong? She was nearing the gaping hole. Its insides smelled worse than the pus on her fingers.

She swung and punched the blob. Her hand sunk into thick goo, returning with the same putrid smell.

"I have to get out of this. I have to get to Wes. My girls." She leaned hard away from the thing and closed her eyes. "Please, let this work."

She pictured her family. She saw Wes's face, a kind yet somewhat arrogant smile. She felt warmth inside. She saw Sam and Lisa at a table, drawing together, putting their pages in one pile to turn into a comic book, which they would come and show off to Mom and Dad later. She thought about the wonderful future awaiting them: marriage, kids of their own, long love-filled lives. And she wished with everything inside to be with them.

8

Di restricted her breath to small bursts in and out as she moved through the narrow gap in the rock. She swiveled her light down the tunnel and back, watching the green weirdness as it reached for her.

So close to her face, it was more like small strands, green strings that stretched, splitting at their tips into even smaller hand-looking threads. They shined as if they were wet, but didn't stick to one another as they brushed past, waving.

Foot after foot, Di moved deeper until the tunnel widened, and the roof lowered to just above her head.

"Come on," she called back. She shined the light so the girls could see their way.

They sent Lisa next. She followed Di's example and came right through. Next came Sam.

"I'm going forward, okay?" Di called back. "Starting to get a little cramped in here now. The ceiling's dropping."

"Go on," Wes said and started in.

Di ducked under hanging green and moved into the next section. She hadn't thought before about what might happen if the green stuff fell on her, and she tried to ignore the idea. It didn't quite work. The roof lowered as she moved, and in her head, she saw lengthening strands of green hair drooping closer and closer to her head. She glanced up and ducked lower.

The ceiling continued to come down. She walked in a squat, trying her hardest not to tip and fall on the strands reaching from the floor.

"Keep following guys. Stay low." She tried her hardest to keep her voice sounding positive for the girls and shined the light ahead. There was an upcoming turn. It was a step-down and a bend and, from what she could tell, was nearly as narrow as the beginning of this damned passage.

505

She shined the light on the girls. They followed as they had been asked. In the distance, Di saw Wes's flashlight flicker. He grunted as he slid through.

"I see a sharp turn coming up. That sound right?"

Wes whispered loudly, "Yeah. I think that's halfway, maybe?"

"Okay." She swung her light in front, dreading how narrow that turn appeared, and a puff of damp air caressed her face. It had the faint scent of skunk and stood out over the smell of decay she was starting to be able to ignore. A second later, a cough burst from her mouth. Her vision became brighter and more vibrant. She shook her head and moved forward.

Di raised her light toward the next turn. Glowing yellow eyes gleamed at her and blinked.

Di screamed and grabbed her gun.

"What?" Wes shouted. He had made it to the second section. "Are you okay?"

She trembled. Her light shook. Her heart pounded. The eyes were gone.

"Di? What's going on?" he moved faster through the tunnel, stopping behind Sam.

"I…" She gazed up and down the empty corner. Had she imagined it? Was it a trick of that bastard mare, or had whoever it was run the other way? "I thought I saw someone." She slid the pistol back into her holster.

"It's trying to mess with us," Wes said. "Remember, it's not—"

"Not real, yeah." She shook her head and took a breath. It was hard standing so she crouched over. "Here I go."

She walked the next few feet, her back starting to ache. She thought she remembered this now, crawling through here on hands and knees as a kid. She wished she could use her hands and knees right now.

She reached the corner and slowed. She held the flashlight near her shoulder, pointed into the turn, and rested her hand on the pistol's grip. She leaned into the corner and looked around the edge. It dipped, leading into a cave tall enough to stand once again. No glowing eyes. No one.

She stepped down, careful of the green edges, and stood straight up. "Oh, Jesus, that's better."

"What?" Wes asked.

He squatted so low, she almost burst into laughter as she saw him behind Sam. She took Lisa under the arms and helped her down.

"Standing again." She helped Sam down.

"Oh, I can't wait."

She moved ahead; another corner was only feet away. She peeked around it, another corner. "Looks like a zigzag?"

"Sounds about right."

She shook her head. "But we're halfway through it?"

"I think." He hopped down around the corner. "It was a long time ago, though."

"Okay." She rounded the turn and moved to the next. She lost sight of the girls but heard their feet pat behind her. She looked around the next corner, and a blast of air rushed over her face. The scent of skunk.

Di had to spit. This time she felt it in her mouth.

"Ew," Sam whined.

"Gah," Wes said.

Di wiped her nose and shined her light ahead again. The green on the next corner seemed extra wavy. It reached and widened and swung as if it were offering a high five. It was so strange, she wanted to laugh. She leaned in to see it better. She stared at the tiny splits at the edge of its strands, and a cloud of violet gas rushed over her face.

"Fuck." She stumbled backward. The skunky smell dripped from her skin. She was sticky with it. Her eyes burned, and everywhere her light shined glowed in vibrant colors. She slammed her eyes closed and rubbed them. She wanted to laugh so bad, and a yip squeaked through. "Guys?" Her voice pitched up.

"Shit," Wes stammered the word.

"I think I'm high." Another yip of laughter. She looked back and saw Lisa step around the corner. Her eyes glowed yellow, and fangs hung from her face like a rabid beast. She tilted her head and laughed in a way that chilled Di inside and out. Horns rose from her hair above the corners of her forehead, and tears rolled down Di's face.

Her heart slammed the inside of her chest. She stumbled backward, her body tingling from toes to fingertips.

"Wh—what?" Di stuttered. She pushed herself through the green and felt gusts of stinking air rise around her. Terror shook her chest. It rolled down her body in waves, over her arms, down her legs, freezing her toes as if she'd been walking barefoot in the snow.

Sam rounded the corner. Worms hung from her eyes. She cackled like a mad person. And her arms hung like snakes from her little frame.

Lisa screamed. Sam Screamed. Wes howled from around the corner.

He came through with rotting flesh hanging from his face. His eyes were white and his jaw hung wide and blood poured from between his teeth.

"Run," Wes moaned. "Get out of here."

Di pushed herself back and up and onto her feet. She pulled the gun from her waist and aimed at the monsters that had been her family. She could kill the littlest ones easily; one shot and she'd be safe. She aimed at Lisa, and the child laughed a horrific sharp sound. It was almost like a scream piercing Di's ears; it hurt so bad.

Di slammed the side of the gun into her ear. She had to stop the pain.

"Di!" the Wes-thing groaned.

He swung something, and more pain ripped through her head and her hand. A sharp bang numbed her ears. She held her hand in front her. No gun, just blood. The red vibrated in tiny points, and she screamed. The points turned into a face with fanged teeth.

"No!" She slammed her hand into the wall and ran.

9

Jill watched as if she were inside the cave wall. She saw Di aim her gun at Lisa. Their eyes were crazed, Wes, Di, and both of her babies. It was making them mad, and they were going to kill each other.

"Wes, stop her!" Jill shouted through the haze that walled their realities from one another.

Lisa cried, and Di covered her ears with the gun.

Wes leaned back and tossed his pry bar across the tunnel. It slammed into Di's gun and ripped a gash into the back of her hand. The pistol tumbled to the ground and fired, and Di stared at her hand, screaming.

Violet gas leaked from the wall all around them. They needed to move.

"Go!" she screamed. "Get out of there!"

Di took off. Lisa, Sam, and Wes followed.

Jill trailed them within the wall. It was her realm, a place where she could see but not touch.

They zigzagged around corners and found a set of stairs. Jill watched them move, watched the craze in their eyes, and wondered if they were listening to her or on a hunt. Di ran like prey. Wes and the kids ran with growling frustration in their huffs and in their strides. They wanted to catch her and kill her.

They made the top of the stairs, one, two, three, and found themselves in another large room. They had escaped the green fungus, and they stared into a vast, empty cavern.

Di shined her light in a circle. Her face was pure panic. Wes watched her, the girls by his side. He crept closer, his fists flexing. The girls held their hands forward, fingers itching to grab their aunt and do who knows what.

"Stop it!" Jill shouted.

Di, Wes, and the girls covered their ears and shook their heads. Wes kept moving, his fists ready to swing. Di turned to run, and Wes jumped on her, dragging her to the ground.

Di's face slammed into the stone floor, and blood gushed from her cheek. Wes sat on her back and punched the side of her head. The girls ran to either side and kicked Di in the ribs.

Jill could barely think as she watched her babies act like savages. Fear overcame her, not for herself, but for what would happen to them. What would they turn into? She forced herself to focus and summoned her anger instead.

"Wes! Sam! Lisa! Stop it!" Her rage shook the cave walls.

10

Wes shivered and looked up and around. He gazed at Di with new eyes. She'd been a target, something to hunt and conquer—no, this was his sister. No matter the years of estrangement, he loved her. He watched the blood on the side of her face, and shame chilled his core. He looked at his fists, fell to the side, and backed away.

"Jill?" he muttered. Did he hear Jill's voice? He must have imagined it. His eyes glowed red, but he felt the madness fading. Lisa, then Sam, dove crying into his chest and hugged him.

Di rolled over, the panic in her face subdued into fear. She looked at Wes with the same fear and violation she'd felt too many times at the men she'd been with over the years. Then she saw his eyes. There was fear there too. She sat up and scooted back.

"Are you okay?" he said. "Please, tell me you're okay?"

She spat blood and wiped her lips. She ran her hands over her head and blinked, then pushed herself onto her feet and stretched. "Not the worst beating I've had."

"Di, I..."

"Forget it." She was cold, emotionless as if part of her had been turned off.

"Please, I didn't know what was happening."

She'd heard a thousand excuses before. This one may be true, but inside, it still burned. Inside, it may have hurt the worst. "Let's keep moving. I want to get the fuck out of here."

Wes gave the girls an extra moment and hugged them harder. Fear gripped him as he realized what had just happened. He could have gone after them instead of Di. He hated himself and wanted them all to punish him. Then, he thought of how close to the end they were. Only a few more caves and they'd be there, face to face with the next thing and, shit— that asshole and the girl. Something warned Wes that this might be the last time he got to hold his girls like this. He breathed them in, and tears welled.

"Come on," Di hissed.

"Yeah." He released Sam and Lisa and looked into their eyes. "Let's go."

Wes got up and shook himself off. His joints ached. His muscles were sore. His exhaustion was coming back, the excitement ending, and he was sinking hard.

He ran his light across the room and pointed to the higher side. "That way." He glanced at Di's empty holster, then at Lisa, back at Di. "No more gun."

"Yeah. I can go back for it?"

"No." He shook his head vehemently. "Too much of a risk, and we shouldn't split up. I lost the pry bar too."

He took his pack off and dug inside it. He pulled out a can of bear spray and a folding knife. He clipped the knife onto his belt and held out the spray to Di.

She looked at it and shook her head. She patted the hunting knife on her left. "I'll make this work."

"Okay." He sealed the bag and slid it onto his back."

"You know," she said, "I'm sorry, too."

"I know."

She glanced sheepishly at Lisa. "I'm sorry."

"It's not our fault," Wes said. "Let's go."

He took Lisa by the hand and headed up the incline. Sam came after.

Di was in the back again. At the highest point of the room, they found the tunnel. Inside was where the official trail would end, and they'd cross the line into that hidden place they discovered thirty years ago. He inhaled and stepped inside.

The rail on the side of the tunnel was rust red, chipping and crumbling. The floor was wet underfoot, and Wes tried to control his feet and keep his shoes from squeaking.

He listened as he walked, held his finger to his lips, and reminded Lisa and Sam. This could be where they ran into those others. He gestured for Lisa to walk behind him, and he held the bear spray out in front.

A low growl reverberated through the cave. Wes swung his light to meet the sound and saw glowing yellow eyes at an animal's height. A wolf?

It growled louder and moved closer. Wes aimed the bear spray, waiting for it to come into the light. The eyes drew nearer, and his finger tightened on the trigger.

"Wait," Di said.

Wes glanced back.

She squatted beside him. "Virb?"

The growling ceased, and Virb bounded into the light. He panted and ran to Di. His paws were covered in blood. His lips and lower jaw dripped with it.

"What have you been doing, Virb?" she asked and stroked his neck and back. He stared in the direction he'd come from and growled. "Okay. Good boy."

11

Julie sat in the dark. It was a nice dark, a mostly quiet dark. It smelled a bit too much the way Mommy did a few days after she played with her insides, but it wasn't too bad yet.

She ran her finger lightly over the edge of her blade. She could feel the outer-most layer of skin split against the steel and stuck the finger in her mouth to touch it with her tongue.

Sharp. She held in a giggle. It was almost time.

Ed had told her to wait here. He said they'd be by any time, so just be patient.

She'd done a good job at that. It had been at least fifteen minutes, and she sat just as he'd asked. And now, it was going to pay off. She could hear them; she knew it would work. She just had to stay put until it was time, just like that old man that Ed called Norris. He'd stay in his spot until it was time, and she'd stay in hers.

She just couldn't wait, though. Her knees trembled. She ran her finger over the blade, this time slicing another line into the top layer of skin. She just wanted them to get closer. She wanted it so bad it ached inside her belly. She imagined them walking right past her, and her sneaking up from behind and slicing them good. Oh, and maybe she'd even get the eyeball she wanted, if she did it just right?

She suppressed a squeal. This was going to be amazing!

12

They passed through the tunnel, and Wes found the entrance they had discovered thirty years ago. He felt it stare at him the way only a knowing thing could. He had gone in there last time when he shouldn't have. He had taken this rock, whether intentionally or through coercion, at the cost of so many lives. It was a path that had to know what it was—a gateway to Hell.

He turned to Di, thinking of Ray Trent. "They have to be in there. If we haven't seen them yet, they have to be waiting for us at the altar."

Di looked into the passage and up the tunnel. "Probably. What are you thinking?"

"I—don't know. We're so close. I know I don't want to take them any further." He gestured at the kids. "But we can't protect them if they aren't with us. Who knows what that thing may throw at them."

"Or at us when we're in there."

"What are *you* thinking?"

Di sighed. "They have to go with us. As horrible as that sounds. It's the dream all over again."

"Okay. Then we have to split the jobs, or they could distract us, and we fail. You protect them, no matter what. I put the stone back, no matter what. You don't leave your job to help me. I don't leave mine to help you. Understood?" He knew it was bullshit as soon as he said it. If she failed, and he didn't, he'd never be able to live with himself. He couldn't go back to his life if anything happened to those girls, no matter if the rock was returned or not. So she had better do her job, or he'd abandon his, and they'd all be doomed.

"Understood."

"Good."

He led the way into the tunnel, feeling more cramped than last time, being nearly a foot taller. He crawled on hands and knees over black undulating rock. The shine from the glossy walls lit every part of him and a dozen feet further than the flashlight should have.

He reached the end of the path and looked cautiously around the next cavern. He half expected the exterminator to be standing there with an ax. There was no one, only the forest of stone columns connecting the roof to the floor.

He leaned into the passage. "Clear. As far as I can tell, anyway."

Sam came out, then Lisa, then Di. Di carried her hunting knife in one hand, her flashlight in the other. Virb trailed them all.

Wes looked at her with admiration. That was *his* sister, and she was amazing. He wished so hard that life could have gone another way—that she could have gone another way back then—that she could have had a chance at something better in life than the shit hand she'd had to deal with ever since their shit childhood.

He pushed past the pain, ache, and exhaustion and moved forward. One foot, then the next. He felt like he was swimming in concrete. Each step was like dragging his limbs through deeper and deeper muck. It didn't matter, though. He had to do it.

Their flashlights moved like strobes from side to side, checking for hidden threats. The rock columns gleamed back at them, wet and shiny from years of polish. Drips, ticks, and clicks echoed through the thick air.

Wes felt the cold numbing of his back widen across his hips, and his feet wanted to drag across the ground. The hand holding his flashlight was heavy. It wanted to drop the light and hang by his side. He shuddered and shook his limbs to wake them up.

"Dad?" Lisa whispered.

"Yeah?"

"Are you okay?"

He glanced down at her. She focused on him like he'd never seen. The general fear encapsulating her face had vanished, replaced by a firm stare with heartfelt concern.

"I'm going to be fine when this is all done," he hoped aloud.

The cave filled with the rising sound of a deep growl, then shook with a boom.

13

The cavern rumbled, and a gust of wind slammed into Di. A ball of fire from the darkness and a flash of a madman's face. Virb darted into the gloom after the source.

Pain tore into her shoulder from behind, and she screamed. Her voice was dulled from the numbness of the blast. The pain was not. It ripped and burned and moved down her back.

Wes screamed. There was a mechanical click and another scream from within the distant darkness.

Di jerked forward. Something was moving inside her. She'd been stabbed, and it was coming out.

More pain, another stab, lower this time. She dropped to her knees and spun, face to face, she stared into the eyes of a tiny girl, a brunette in this light.

The child raised her hand. She grinned with shining white teeth, and a long, bloodied knife glimmered in her grip. Di watched the blood flow down the blade and understood it was *her* blood. The girl slashed downward, cutting into Di's leg.

"Gah!" she howled. She swore she heard the child giggle before turning away and vanishing into the dark. A trail sparkled for an instant from her knife. "Fuck!"

Di dropped onto her rear, grabbing her leg. She tried to touch the pain in her back but couldn't reach it. Blood flowed over her fingers as she pressed into the leg.

14

Wes felt heat and wind, then wetness on his side. It burned. He turned to see what had happened—Lisa wasn't holding his hand—she was on the ground. He leaned toward her and screamed from the pain in his back.

"Daddy?" Sam followed him down.

A scream came from the darkness.

A scream came from Di.

The world spun around Wes. What was happening? Everything was falling into insanity around him.

Lisa laid on her back, clutching her lower leg.

"Arg!" a garbled scream from the darkness, and another boom. It lit the face of an older man and Virb's mouth around his throat.

Rocks tumbled from the ceiling. Pebbles and dust rained over Wes. He ignored it all and leaned over Lisa.

"Let me see the leg."

Tears ran down her face. She pulled back her hands. They were bloody. Her bloody fingerprints striped her leg.

He moved his flashlight over her limb as he winced in pain. A three-inch gash bled lightly from the back of her leg.

Sam groaned.

"Here," Wes said to Sam. "Put your hand here and hold."

Sam circled to Lisa's side and put her palm on the wound. "It's going to be okay."

Wes slid off his backpack and nearly screamed again. He scanned the darkness and saw Di on the ground, a blur of something disappearing into the black.

"Di? Are you okay?" He looked for the older man and saw Virb limping toward Di. He favored his rear leg. "Di!"

She climbed to her feet. She was covered in blood. She looked at Wes, at Sam and Lisa, at Virb, and dropped back to her knees.

"Di! Talk to me." The backpack had half a dozen holes in one side. He opened it and dug the first aid kit out. "How are you?"

She slumped down, sitting on her feet. She put out her hand, and Virb ducked under it, leaned against her, and sat. He rubbed his head on her chest.

"Jesus, Di. Say something!" He ripped into the first aid. It exploded over the stone floor. He picked out a gauze pad and tape.

"I'm... okay," Di said. She was crying. She stared at the girls and ran her hand over Virb's side.

"Fuck..." Wes brushed away Sam's hand and placed the pad on Lisa's leg, then wrapped tape around it. He looked into her eyes. "This should work for now. Stay put. I need to check on Di." He started to get up and grunted. His back was on fire. He touched his soaking wet side and pointed to the scattered first aid supplies. "Sam. Pick up that stuff and come with me."

Wes felt adrenaline pushing him forward. He knelt next to Di and groaned. "Fuck." From here, he could see Virb's mouth dripping with blood. It covered his jaw, his chest, and his front legs. "Looks like he gave it to whoever that was."

"Need to go make sure he's dead," Di said softly. "I think he had a shotgun."

Wes glanced again into the black. The glimpse he had seen of Virb on that man's neck looked pretty decisive. He was sure the guy was a goner, but she was right. The last thing they needed was more buckshot from the dark. "I'll go check in a sec. Did he shoot you too?"

"No. The little girl." She pointed at her leg, then at her shoulder. "Stabbed."

Wes examined the leg, ripping open her jeans around the wound. "How's he?" He pressed his shirt into her leg, soaking up the blood that blocked his view.

"I think his leg's broken."

"Not shot?"

"Don't think so."

"Good. They can fix that." He saw her eyes. Tears. It hit him how bad this hurt—not the cuts—her friend, the only one she had. "We'll get him to the vet. As soon as this is over."

He leaned over and groaned as he looked at the wound. It was long but shallow. It was bleeding but not bad.

"How about you? How bad is Lisa?"

"She was grazed on the calf. Looks about like this. I think I have a shot or two in my lower back—hurts like a son of a bitch."

Sam got down next to her dad, her hands filled with pads, medicines, and tools. Lisa sat beside them, crying and staring into the gloom.

Wes grabbed a pad and pressed it into Di's leg. He peeled off tape and secured the pad, then wobbled around to her back, cursing as he moved. Sam followed him.

He ripped open her shirt and used a pad to soak up the blood. "This one on the shoulder is deeper, but thankfully your shoulder blade stopped it from penetrating your chest." He put a series of butterflies down the wound.

"There's another one, I think. Lower."

Wes looked. "Jesus, I didn't see it under the blood." A hole was in her lower back. He couldn't tell if it was in her kidneys or liver, but it was in that general area. He cleaned and bandaged it the same as her leg, ignoring the dread boiling up inside and the fear that she wasn't going to make it out of there. "Try not to move too much." His voice shook. He hoped she didn't notice.

"Really, Wes? Now let me see you?"

He knelt next to her and pulled up his shirt. There was a hole in his side the size of a shotgun pellet, just as he suspected. She wiped it and covered it in pad and tape.

Wes got up and pointed at Di's waist. "Let me borrow that? I'm going to check on our friend."

She pulled loose her knife and handed it over. "Be careful."

"Yeah."

He clenched his teeth as he walked. Each step was like being shot all over again. He didn't know what that ball had hit, but goddamn, it hurt.

As the darkness fell away from the stranger, Wes recognized him. He was soaked in blood from neck to crotch, missing a foot, and staring blankly at the cave ceiling, but Wes knew him. Not his name, but he knew him from the café downtown. A black pump-action shotgun was by his leg, the strap over his arm.

Wes knelt and cursed. He took the shotgun and hung it from his shoulder, then searched the man for more ammo, guns, anything. He found two more shells, nothing else.

The man gasped, and Wes jumped.

The eyes still stared. Just gas escaping.

Sam screamed.

15

Di leaned forward, her head light and weary. Colored dots drifted in her sight, and a sharp pain tore into her neck. It ripped, and warm wetness flowed over her chest. She couldn't scream. She slouched forward as Sam screamed for her.

16

Julie's eyes shined. She tore the knife from the woman's neck, and a fountain of beautiful blood sprayed. The lady leaned forward, and Julie grinned delightedly.

Something moved under the woman as she collapsed. It didn't matter. Julie set her gaze on the smaller girl. She took a step around the woman—now the girl was hers.

A dog barked. It shot around the lady. It moved on three legs as if that was all it had ever known—until it tried to jump. Trying to leap with its broken limb, it floundered on the stone floor. It missed Julie's neck but found her leg.

The thing growled, blood and meat in its teeth.

Julie screamed. "Let go!" She pulled away, the flesh of her leg ripping as she moved. She remembered her knife and raised it over her head. She'd stab it. Then it would let go.

Boom.

The knife flew from Julie's hand along with most of her fingers.

She screamed and pounded on the dog. "Let go! Let go!"

The man stepped into the light. He had the shotgun. "Virb, release."

The dog did as it was told, and Julie spun. The pain. Her leg, her hand. She cried and scurried into the darkness as fast as she could.

17

"Oh, Jesus," Wes dropped to his knees beside Di. He ignored his pain and rolled her onto her back.

Her eyes were slits, fixed on nothing.

Virb lay on the ground beside her, his head on her lap.

"Di," Wes muttered. His words trembled as they flowed from his tongue. "Please, Di."

Her stare didn't move. Her chest was still.

He ran his hand over her head. How could this happen? He'd just gotten her back. After so many years without her, he'd just gotten her back, and now this?

His hands curled into fists and shook.

"You bastard!" His voice echoed, vibrating the ground beneath him.

He cried and closed her eyes. He'd have to finish this himself. She'd want him to. He had to, for his kids, for everyone else this thing would kill if he didn't do his job and fix his mistake. God—he was reminded it was all his doing and cried harder.

"Dad?" Sam said from his left.

"Dad?" Lisa said to his right.

He nodded and wiped away tears. They came right back, but he held himself up and hugged his children. His back howled at him.

"Are we leaving now?" Lisa said.

"I wish, sweetheart. We have to end this. Or even more people will die. We have to make this mean something." He shook his head. "Or she really died for nothing."

Sam walked over and picked up the girl's knife. She looked at her sister and dad. "In case she comes back."

Wes waved her closer. He handed Lisa Di's hunting knife. "If anyone tries to touch you two, you stab and stab and stab." His voice broke. He trembled all over. "Don't stop. They won't hesitate to hurt you. You hurt them first."

"Like how Mom says if someone tries to take us?" Sam said. "Hit and hit and hit until they let us go."

"Yes."

Lisa looked at the knife. "Hit them in the privates and nose and eyes."

"Yes." Wes gritted his teeth and pushed himself to his feet. He put Di's flashlight in Lisa's hand and put on his backpack. "Keep an eye out everywhere in case they come again."

Lisa swung the beam of light in every direction. There was only darkness.

He pumped the shotgun and loaded the two extra shells. "Let's go."

"Dad, the dog." Lisa pointed at Virb. He was in the same position.

"I think he wants to wait here. Let him. He did his job. We'll get him when we leave."

18

Jill hovered in the darkened recesses of some unknown place and heard the clack and crawl of tiny things. She knew they moved like soldiers, rank and file armies ready to march. But she couldn't tell what they were or even where she was.

Wes and Di and the kids had left the cave, and she had found herself stuck. She had been able to follow them over the green growth of that space, but as soon as they left—and now she was here.

She knew she wasn't awake, yet this wasn't a dream. What she was seeing was the waking world—at least for her family. But the things, the green stuff, the creatures around her, those were from another place. She had to assume her projected self—she didn't know what else to call it— was somehow able to travel with these other things from the dream world. It didn't make sense, but it was the best she could do to understand where she found herself. But these creatures around her now—why were they there?

Above and in the distance, lights moved. Two beams were at the top of a ledge, shining in all directions and down over the cliff face.

It had to be Wes and Di and the kids. She wanted to go to them like she had before, but as she tried, she was stuck. Stranded and forced to hover over these things that crawled and clicked and clacked. Things that the mare made.

"Look out!" she shouted. They had heard her before. At least they had reacted like they had. Maybe they'd hear her now? "Bugs! Bugs down here!"

She squinted and watched to see if they would acknowledge her, and she noticed there were only three. Three? Who was missing?

Panic raced through her as she tried to focus. It was too far. She knew there was a taller one and a shorter one, an adult and a kid. The third was a kid. The light passed over them every now and then. But she couldn't figure out who the adult was.

"Please let it be Wes?" She hated saying that, but she had to. "Please?"

19

After they had investigated the edge, and he was pretty sure they were alone, Wes removed his pack and took a knee. He moved the damned rock into his pocket and pulled out rope, harnesses, and carabiners. He wrapped three ropes around the rock pillar nearest the edge and tossed their ends over the cliff.

"Come here." He gestured to Lisa, holding a harness. "Step into this."

She did as asked, and he tightened it around her.

"No knotted rope?" Sam asked.

"That was a kids' dream," Wes said. "This is real. So, we use real safety equipment."

"We made it…"

"I know. And we will this time too." He held out another harness. Sam stepped inside, and he tightened it around her.

Wes put on his own harness, groaning with each movement and jolting as he yanked too hard and pushed into his wound. He ran a rope through Lisa's harness, then Sam's, and helped them over the edge.

"Just squeeze this gently, and you'll lower down the cliff." He pointed to the device. "Gently. The harder you squeeze, the faster you go. Go slow."

Sam tested it out and moved a few inches down. Lisa followed her lead and dropped a few inches as well.

"Just like that." Wes ran a rope through his harness, put his backpack and the shotgun over his shoulder, and started over the cliff. "Together." He dropped down about a foot and stopped. Remembering the dream, he took one last look around the top of the cliff, the rope, the shadows. He somewhat expected Chris Conners to walk out of the darkness with a knife and attack his rope. He didn't.

"Now you," he said to Lisa. She did, and he waited for Sam. She did, and he moved another few feet. They took turns a few more times, then were comfortable enough to go together. By the time they traveled thirty feet down and touched the ground, one may have expected them to have been trained by someone other than YouTube.

"I thought it was taller," Sam said. She started loosening her harness.

"That was a dream," Wes said. "The dream of a boy who probably thought it was a lot taller." He helped Lisa from her nylon web and then worked to free himself as the kids shined their lights on any and every object it would reach.

Wes slung the backpack over his shoulders again and aimed the shotgun forward. "Knives ready," he whispered.

They held the blades in their grips and waited.

"We don't know what else is out there, but I'm sure it's something. Be ready." He looked over his girls, terrified, guilty, loving, heartbroken. He had to get them through this. No matter what, he had to. "Are you ready?"

"Yes," Sam said.

"Yeah," Lisa said.

"Stay behind me." He took a step forward.

The damp air chilled as he moved from the wall into the cavern. The scent of death that had traveled with them from their first step into the cave became as dense as soup. It invaded his flesh as if he were the one decaying. It sank into his mind, and the whisper came: "*You're going to die down here.*"

Wes shuddered. *It didn't happen last time; it won't happen this time*, he argued inside his mind. But he knew he spoke with doubt. Part of that dream had been memory, reality and astral planes intertwined over the folds in time—but here—this wasn't a dream, wasn't a memory. There were no guarantees of where this would go. And each step made him doubt more. Would he finish this? Would he survive the cave?

"Don't listen to the voice," Wes told the girls. "No matter what it says."

They didn't answer.

"Girls?"

He stopped and looked back. They stood still, ten feet behind, Lisa's light sweeping back and forth.

"Girls?" Wes followed the light with his gaze. From the shadows, crawled things. Wes's breath hitched as he set eyes on them. He could only imagine they were from nightmares, places that didn't exist to humans and were thrust upon them by monsters like the mare. They were as large as dogs with innumerable legs. They crawled over one another and forward, gnashing at each other's appendages with mouths of black teeth and sharp tongues. And as they moved closer, he heard their hard claws clack into the floor and a hissing sound escaping their pulsating maws.

God, no, he whispered inside his own mind. He wasn't going to make it. They weren't going to make it. Those monster things were going to sink their claws into them, then their fangs, then their tongues. They would rip him and his daughters to nothing but hunks of flesh and leave only blood and viscera behind. It was the end. It was Death, real Death, with no magical means or dreamlike fixes that would heal them or let them escape. This was the end.

Wes trembled inside his core. His stomach turned and rotated inside his abdomen.

"*You will die down here,*" the whisper repeated. And that was what rocketed him forward.

Wes let the shotgun fall from his hands and hang from his back. He leaned down and grabbed one child in each arm, spun, and sprinted the other way.

Lisa screamed. Sam screamed.

Lisa shined the light behind, illuminating the monsters at his heels. He refused to look back. He stared forward. It was up there, and now, without light clouding his view, a faint blue glowed a hundred feet ahead. If he just kept running, stayed ahead of those things long enough, he could end it.

He knew he might be deluding himself. He saw nothing ahead and nothing on his sides. Where was the exterminator? What creatures laid in wait on his right and left? It didn't matter. He had to keep going.

"Dad!" Sam shouted. The rise of claw on stone, claw on chitin shell, chilled his ears and made her hard to hear. "Dad!"

He didn't want to hear it, whatever it was. "What?"

"They're getting closer!"

Shit. He tried to run harder. His shitty ankle said no. His buckshot-drilled back said no. His sheer exhaustion said no. He pushed himself faster.

"Daddy!" Lisa shrieked.

That was when the unthinkable happened. Something in the dark, a hidden inanimate thing, seized the top of his foot, and he flew forward.

The next thing was inevitable. He was going to crash into the cave floor, and only God could help him after that. The click and clack of hard, sharp, alien things were too close to avoid, at least for him.

Wes used every bit of strength in his upper body and lifted the girls as he fell. He thrust them forward and shouted, "Run!"

His chest slammed down, followed by his face. Pain ripped through his cheek and spread across his skull. It was electrifyingly sharp, and in an instant, he knew he had broken his cheekbone. But there was no time to scream. He remembered the stone in his pocket—God, had he damaged it in the fall? This all would be for nothing if so. He patted his pocket, and Lisa shrieked.

Wes looked at his girls. They stared back at him, and something plunged through his calf. He tried to call to them: *Run!* All that came out was a wail of horror.

Something else stabbed his upper leg, another in the opposite thigh. He felt the ground move beneath him. He was being dragged.

A shock rippled through Wes—he still had the stone. That piece of shit rock that was the source of all of this. He dug into his pocket. His fingers grabbed it and instantly numbed. He fought to free it from his pocket, and another beast stabbed his back. It tore through his insides, the tip driving deeper and hooking into his flesh.

"Daddy!" Lisa howled.

Wes threw the stone at his girls, and somehow unknown to him, he pulled together the strength to cry, "Run!"

20

Jill wept ethereal tears. She couldn't move her mouth to speak, but she could scream, "Run!"

The word came out of Wes's mouth, and a pair of jaws tore into the back of his neck. They ripped his head from his body. Blood gushed onto the ground, and a hundred claws dove into his abdomen, arms, and legs, rending him into nothing but chunks of flesh.

The rock stopped at Lisa's foot, but her eyes and her light rested on the blood-drenched monsters where her father had been. Her jaw hung. The knife dangled loosely in her hand.

"Pick up the rock!" Jill called. "Run!"

Lisa didn't move, but Sam saw it. She seized the stone and grabbed Lisa's arm. Her face guided a torrent of tears from cheek to chin, but she screamed at her sister, "Come on!"

21

Sam ran, and Lisa shined her light ahead. The blue crystals glowed, and they could see the end. Lisa swept the light left and right for monsters and swiped the tears from her cheeks—more followed. They drenched each girl's face, and they couldn't stop them, not for the fear, not for the job that Dad had given them. It was a deluge that Sam feared may be never-ending.

She watched the blue light swell as she came within a few dozen feet, and a glimmer of hope shined inside her. Then the form of a man stepped in front of it.

Sam felt the contents of her hands, thinking of what Dad had said: *If anyone touches you two, you stab and stab and stab.* But the knife was gone.

She had been compelled to pick up the stone. She had put the knife down when she grabbed the rock and shoved it into her pocket. Now she had Lisa's hand in her hand and nothing else. *No knife!*

She clenched her sore fingers. Pain shot up her arm. She could still follow Mom's advice: *hit and hit and hit.*

At ten feet away, she halted. Lisa's light showed a thin man, one hand forward, one behind him.

Lisa swayed, practically convulsing with wails. She saw the man and fell to her knees.

"Are you girls ready to go home now?" the man said. "Haven't you had enough of this?"

Sam said nothing. She had to get past him so she could drop the stone in the altar. She couldn't see it behind the stranger, but it had to be there, the same as in the dream.

"Just hand me the rock." He took a step toward them. "You can go home. Your mommy can meet you there, and this will all be over."

"No." Sam wanted to be strong, to show him that she wasn't afraid of him, but her voice was scratchy and weak. And she was afraid. Was he even human? He looked like it but might have been a monster in disguise.

"Give me the stone." He showed his other hand. He had a knife like Aunt Di's. He held it forward beside his open palm. "I don't want to hurt you."

Sam knew this was a lie. He did. She saw it in his face, in his eyes. He wanted to plunge that thing into her just like that girl did to Aunt Di.

"I just need the stone." He took another step.

"Give him the stone," a whisper said inside her mind.

Don't listen to the whispers, Dad had told her. She saw Dad's face, his smile, felt his hand on the side of her head as he kissed her forehead and said goodnight, and the tears rushed even harder.

"There, there." The man stepped closer. One more step, and he could grab her. "I can help you. Just hand me the stone." His knife trembled in his hand.

"Give him the stone."

She watched the knife and knew. He was eager. He was ready. He was going to stab her no matter what she did.

Sam turned to her sister. She saw the tears and wished she could take them away, wished she could take away every tear she had ever caused her. She spoke softly, "It's your turn again."

Lisa stared at her through a series of gasps. "No."

"No choice. Here we go." She turned to the man. "Okay. Let me get it."

Sam grabbed the stone inside her pocket and watched the man's face clench. His eyes were glued to the bulge inside her jacket. She lifted it out slowly, gauging his stillness and his restraint.

He took a half-step toward her, and she slammed the rock into the center of Lisa's chest. Lisa took the stone, and Sam ran forward. She punched the stranger in the nose with her good hand and dug her fingers into his cheek with her other, gouging a deep scratch in his face.

Lisa ran toward the altar.

"Arg!" the man pushed Sam off and slashed across her arm.

Sam screamed as the pain ran down her bicep.

The stranger turned and took off after Lisa.

Sam grabbed his leg and held tight. He tumbled forward, reaching for Lisa, his fingers gliding past her legs and touching nothing but air. His face slammed into the rock floor, and he roared.

Sam watched her sister with hope and pride. Lisa walked right up to the stone shelf surrounded by blue gems and placed the rock right where it belonged.

The gems pulsed and flashed and stopped. And that was it. Unlike the dream, there was no shaking of the cave, no waking with a start—it was done.

Lisa turned to her sister and spoke with a subdued voice. "Is that it?"

The man shook Sam from his leg and kicked her in the face.

She yelped, and blood streamed from her nose.

He stood and walked toward the altar. "No, you idiot. That stone is mine."

He reached to grab the mare's rock, and Sam seized his arm. She yanked, and he stumbled back.

"Goddammit!" He raised his knife high, his blade pointed at the center of her chest.

"No!" Lisa shouted. She raised Aunt Di's knife above her head and sunk it deep into the stranger's back. He dropped to his knees, and Dad's words rang in her head: *you stab and stab and stab*. And she did.

She raised and lowered, raised and lowered, again and again. Blood arced from his back, coating her hands, her chest, her face, and her legs. He flopped onto his chest, and she followed him down, stabbing again and again.

He groaned and gasped. His hands curled and released. Blood and vomit streamed from his open mouth. She kept stabbing.

"Lisa!" Sam shouted.

She didn't respond. She was covered in blood from hair to heels and stabbed the stranger's body repeatedly.

"Lisa! Stop!"

She slowed, and the knife clung to his rib.

"He's dead." Sam cried and touched her sister. She watched as tears made white lines through the blood on her sister's face. "Let's go."

Lisa stood and nearly tackled Sam with an embrace. They held each other for a long time and said nothing, only cried.

When Lisa raised her head from Sam's chest, she said, "I'm tired."

"Me too." Sam had to smile. She didn't expect her future dreams would be nice—they would surely be terrible—but they should be safe.

Part Six: After

2022

1

Sam and Lisa hesitated on their way back, but there were no more monsters. The place of their dad's death held no body, only a deep pool of blood. They moved past it and climbed the rope as if they were in gym class, first Lisa, then Sam. They stopped and said goodbye to Aunt Di, wishing they had known her better. They convinced Virb to follow them.

The rest of the caves were easy to backtrack through. The green mold was gone. The bats were gone. They saw no sign of the girl.

They went out the service door as the sun rose over the neighboring mountain and walked to Dad's Excursion. Sam used water from the stash Dad kept in the back and washed the blood off Lisa. Lisa put on new clothes from a stash Mom kept in the back and hid her bloodied ones in the bushes. Something told them they didn't want to tell a story that could lead anyone to that stone.

They helped Virb into the SUV and got inside with him. Sam found Dad's phone in the center console and prayed as she pressed the contact for *Jill*. It started ringing, and she glanced at Lisa. She was asleep, head on the door, Virb's head in her lap.

"Hello?" came from the phone.

1992

1

Wes, Di, and Jill opened their eyes to the last scene of gore they would see outside of horror movies for nearly three decades. Chris lay on the corner of the bed eviscerated, his body ripped and torn, his blood soaking into the mattress, and organs and fluids spilled onto the floor.

They screamed and called Mom and then the police. They cried. Chris had turned on them and tried to help the mare. But underneath, he was Wes and Jill's friend.

Wes tried to understand what Chris had done as he sat on the couch, watching the police and the EMTs climb and descend the stairs. Was it his mom? Her cancer? His dad? His drinking? Did the mare threaten them? When the police went to Chris's house later and discovered what had been left of his father, all of Wes's hopes fell away. The thing *had* turned Chris.

Wes tried to think that his friend had been brainwashed, that the whispers had been too strong... but the doubt remained—was Chris ever really the person he thought he was? He wouldn't admit it if he even understood it, but he would never trust anyone as blindly in the future. There would always be a wonder below any relationship to come: *is this person who I think they are?*

Di clung to no emotional connection with the body at the end of Wes's bed. He had betrayed them and tried to kill them. He was no better than the monster Wes had awakened. She didn't know it at the time, nor through the rest of her teenage years, but beyond Wes, her mind had started to emotionally disconnect from every other human on the planet. They would all prove to be like Chris; she was sure of it. The doctors at the psychiatric hospital in the spring would try to address her growing disassociation with an escalating series of drugs, not realizing that her cure wouldn't come for another few decades in the form of a dog, a pair of nieces, and reconnection with the only person in the world she could trust.

Jill called her parents soon after the police. Her mom and dad both showed up on Wes's doorstep and whisked her away immediately, rejecting the direction of the police while her mother shouted, "You can ask her questions at our house. She's not staying another minute in that murder house or with that drunk woman."

Wes didn't want her to go. He couldn't argue, though. His mother had refused to leave the downstairs to see what had happened. She moved from her bed to the kitchen, opened her whiskey, and drank until the police left. And then she returned to bed.

Wes and Di shared Di's room for the next few nights. They worked together to get his mattress out of the house along with the bedding, and to clean the carpet of blood and putrid stink. When that was as clean as they could get it, and a large brown stain still covered a sizable chunk of Wes's floor, they cut out a square from his carpet. Wes would sleep on his floor in a sleeping bag for four months before his mother decided to sell the home and move to the other side of town to help her forget. It wouldn't work.

The week following the last dream, Wes started back at school. He thought he would get strange looks and remarks from others. Instead, there was a thick cloud of disinterest in the air, not just about him but between everyone. Half of the kids, he learned, hadn't been there in a week or had been in comas. They stared at each other with wary eyes, and it hung even heavier on Wes that he was the cause of it all.

That week there were over a dozen funerals for kids Wes knew. He forced himself to go to Chris's and Tommy's, and that was all he could handle. Di refused to go to any. Jill came with him to Tommy's.

There was a quiet strength between them as they sat at the graveside ceremony. Close to twenty people came, mostly Tommy's family, none of whom spoke to Wes or Jill. They were alone in that moment, partially mourning their friend, partially staring into the autumn sky and feeling they had beaten this thing. That was when she took Wes's hand in hers, and despite him not understanding it for several years, it was the start of their life together.

2022

1

It was a week before they let Jill leave the hospital, and even then, it was at her insistence that she was going to leave on her own if they didn't discharge her. Her Aunt Silva stayed with the girls until she was released. She was the only one who they told the truth to about what had happened.

In the weeks that followed, Jill's mind went back to her coma dream again and again. They had a funeral for Wes and cried all the way through it. There was no body to bury and no proof to get a death certificate, so he would be considered missing for the next five years until she could have him declared legally dead. That would have to do.

The images of his body being torn to pieces, those things devouring him, came back to her each time someone asked about him. It was going to be a hard five years for her, for them all.

She had been told that the girls were both asleep when the police got to the caverns, and the dog, three-legged or not, was ready to fight off anyone to protect them until Lisa calmed him. To Jill, that was a dog worth keeping, and she doubted the kids would have let her do any different. Virb went to the vet, and they were able to save his leg. Now, he hopped around the house alongside Sam-I-Am, looking as pitiful as Jill with her cast and crutches.

A week later, school started with a new principal and custodian. No one could explain what Mrs. Gould did or why, and most stopped asking about it. Pretty quickly. It made as little sense as the dozens of people who'd fallen into comas, some of whom died gruesomely, unexplainably, and the others who magically awakened. Even with it being the second time this type of thing happened in thirty years, people stopped asking questions about it. It was as if some community consciousness decided they should just let it go. So they did.

Another week later, Stuart Harrison's car was found, followed by his body inside Edward Lawrence's home. There was an official funeral, even though he was off duty when it happened, and the Lawrence home was confiscated by the town to be sold at auction. Many in the same community consciousness would have rather it been demolished, but too few stood up to say so, and no one was going to pay for that. A few months later, in the middle of the night, the house somehow caught fire and burned for hours as the fire department strangely couldn't muster its men and get there with their usual swiftness. Only ashes and a charred framework of sticks remained.

By Christmas, Jill was walking with a cane and attending physical therapy twice a week. The house had dark places but also lighter ones. No one went into Wes's office except a maid that Jill hired to help out every few weeks. Even then, the woman had been told, "Just dust, nothing else."

Sam had asked for a computer for Christmas and received a Chromebook. She wanted her own place to write like her father. Lisa asked for art supplies. Together, they kept Wes alive in their minds, words, and images.

Acknowledgements

Bloodtooth was a lot of work, through countless long nights and innumerable weekends. It would not exist without the effort and kindness of many people. I thank you all and regret those I may have missed. This is just a token.

Christina Hitz — Thank you for sacrificing time together, encouraging me, and picking up all the pieces I missed through my absent-mindedness. Thank you for encouraging me and being there when I needed you.
Wolfgang and **Kaari Hitz** — Thank you for believing in me and giving me the space I needed to work, especially when you wanted to write your own words into the pages.
Melinda Parrish — Thank you for reading my work over the years, believing in me, and pushing me to put it out there.

My Editor: **Patrick C. Harrison III**, your skill and wisdom was instrumental in turning this from a bunch of pages into a book. Thank you.
My Cover Designer: **Don Noble**, your art brought this thing to life for readers. Keep strutting that massive talent.

So many supporters on social media who urged me on. Thank you, and forgive me—I'm sure I missed people: **Angel Van Atta, Corrina Morse, Jay Bower, Candace Nola, Jaime Hernandez, Luther Kross, Diana Richie, Jan Blake, Justin Boote, Stephen Cooper, Merrill David, Kelly Barker, Ivan K Conway, Shauna McGuiness, Robin Ginther-Venneri, Ronald McGillvray, Sam Phillips, Sylvester Barzey, Angel Ramon, Lyndsey Smith, Marian Elaine, Joe X Young, Stephen Landry, Lee-Ann Harp, Terry Miller, Renée Gendron, Tim Eagle, Scott Baker, Donna A Latham.**

About the Author

D.W. Hitz lives in Montana, where the inspiring scenery functions as a background character in his work. He is a lover of stories in all mediums. He enjoys writing in the genres of Horror, Supernatural/Paranormal Thriller, and Science Fiction/Fantasy.

Originally from Norfolk, VA, D.W. has degrees in Recording Arts and Web Design and Interactive Media. He has been a creative his entire life. This creativity has driven him in writing, music, and web design and development. He aspires to tell stories that thrill the heart and stimulate the imagination.

When not writing, D.W. enjoys spending time with his family, hiking, camping, and playing with the dogs.

Be sure to sign up for his newsletter today at www.DWHitz.com.

What's Next?

There's always more horror to be had from D.W. Hitz and Fedowar Press.

Check out Brady, a novella by D.W. Hitz, available now:

Brady is a mature Horror read with elements of Paranormal/Supernatural, Cosmic Horror, and graphic violence.

After Karl is forced to put down his beloved pet Brady, he unintentionally releases a beast from another dimension. If he wants to save himself and those around him, he'll have to figure out how to put the beast back and accept that none of us is ever really gone.

Also from Fedowar Press, Uncanny Valley Days by C.J. Sampera:

Rocked by grief and recurring apparitions of her dead brother, Olivia is losing her grip on reality and may have inadvertently invoked a cybernetic, serial-killing slasher demon. Or is it all in her head?

Olivia Peramo is a writer and an artist at heart, barista by trade who struggles with multiple mental health issues. All of which have only been intensified by the recent loss of both her parents and her older brother Alejandro. And to top it off, she may have just inadvertently invoked an evil entity with one passive-aggressive rage tweet.

Soon enough, the people that cross Olivia start winding up dead, and she's being made to watch each grisly murder as they unfold. Is she part of some elaborate hoax? Is this sinister force really breaking her reality and murdering innocent people? Or has Olivia completely lost it and started killing them herself? Not to mention, the ghost of her dead brother keeps popping up every time she smokes a little weed.

Or are you in the mood for 80s style slashers? Fedowar has you covered with 2 fantastic anthologies dedicated to the 80s classics. Both available now!

All available now from FedowarPress.com.

Thank you for reading.

www.FedowarPress.com

9 781956 492293